THE IMPROBABLE ADVENTURES OF SHERLOCK HOLMES

Other Anthologies by John Joseph Adams

NIGHT SHADE BOOKS PRESENTS...

THE IMPROBABLE ADVENTURES OF SHERLOCK HOLMES

TALES OF MYSTERY AND THE IMAGINATION
DETAILING THE ADVENTURES
OF THE WORLD'S MOST FAMOUS DETECTIVE,
MR. SHERLOCK HOLMES

EDITED BY JOHN JOSEPH ADAMS

WITH ASSISTANCE PROVIDED BY
THE DISTINGUISHED GENTLEMAN
MR. DAVID BARR KIRTLEY

NIGHT SHADE BOOKS
NEW YORK

CONTENTS

INTRODUCTION

by John Joseph Adams

Sherlock Holmes. The name is ubiquitous, familiar to everyone in the world whether or not they've read of his exploits. Pretty impressive for a fictional character created more than 120 years ago.

Sir Arthur Conan Doyle created Holmes in the late-nineteenth century, with the first adventure, *A Study in Scarlet*, appearing in *Beeton's Christmas Annual* in 1887. Conan Doyle's entire output of fiction featuring Holmes consists of only four novels and fifty-six stories[1]—a staggeringly small body of work considering the tremendous influence Holmes has had—but something about the detective captured the reading public's imagination like no other character of his era, and he has continued to delight and captivate readers ever since.

Holmes, the world's first (and most famous) consulting detective, was one of the first great literary action-adventure heroes whose defining qualities were his intelligence and deductive reasoning rather than bravery or brawn. Which is not to say that Holmes is a coward or a weakling; being well-versed in the art of boxing and the martial art of Bartitsu[2], he is capable of besting almost anyone in a fight—he'd just rather outwit you than beat you up.

Holmes's devotion to evidence and observation were quite revolutionary in his day, and to Conan Doyle's Victorian readers his methods must have seemed a bit like science fiction. To the modern reader, it's obvious that Holmes is employing rudimentary forensic science—a huge advantage in an age when many people still believed in fairies (as Conan Doyle did) and other supernatural phenomena.

Although Sir Arthur Conan Doyle was keenly interested in the supernatural, Holmes eschewed such ideas and believed only in what he could prove. And while Conan Doyle did place Holmes into some situations in which a supernatural explanation seemed to be a possibility, in every instance, Holmes managed to find a prosaic solution. After all, as Holmes once said: "The world is big enough for us. No ghosts need apply."[3]

Which leads us to the focus of this anthology and to another of Holmes's famous quotes: "When you have eliminated the impossible, whatever remains, *however*

---

1 Most of which appeared in the pages of *The Strand Magazine*.
2 These abilities will be highlighted in the forthcoming Guy Ritchie film, *Sherlock Holmes*, starring Robert Downey, Jr. as Holmes, due out in theaters this December.
3 In "The Adventure of the Sussex Vampire."

1

improbable, must be the truth."[4]

As a rationalist, I agree wholeheartedly with Holmes's assessment of the world. But as a science fiction and fantasy reader, I enjoy wondering *what if*. So that's the question: If Holmes investigates a crime scene and has all of his deduction techniques at his disposal, but one variable has changed—Holmes *can't* eliminate the impossible—what then?

Well, dear reader, you're about to find out. In the pages that follow you'll find twenty-eight different mystery scenarios, but when you investigate the crimes alongside Holmes you will not be able to eliminate the impossible, for in some of these stories the impossible *does* happen.

That's the idea behind this volume—to showcase the best Holmes pastiches of the last thirty years, mixing the best straight-up mystery stories with the best of those tales tinged with the fantastic[5]. Meaning that some of the cases you'll read about have prosaic solutions, while others will have a decidedly more *fantastic* resolution.

Whether you're already quite familiar with the great detective or you're just now going to be reading about him for the first time; whether you're primarily a fan of mysteries or primarily a fan of fantasy and science fiction—welcome. Holmes's world is big enough for all of us.

---

4 From *The Sign of the Four*

5 Don't let the bylines fool you into thinking you know which way—mystery or fantasy—a story will resolve; although some of the fantasy authors here do deliver fantasy tales, some of those tales are merely improbable rather than impossible, and some of the leading lights of the mystery genre may have some surprises for you as well. So, as Sherlock Holmes would surely advise, don't make too many assumptions.

A SHERLOCKIANA PRIMER

by Christopher Roden

Fog swirls thickly in the streets, its gloom penetrated from time to time by the weak gleam of a gaslight; a hansom cab grinds its steady way through the murk; there are occasional shouts from vendors and street urchins, whistles as policemen go about their business. It is the London of 1895, the London that will bring a stream of unusual characters to 221B Baker Street seeking help from the world's first and greatest consulting detective, Mr. Sherlock Holmes.

When Arthur Conan Doyle (1859–1930) first created the great detective, little did he know that he was beginning a series of stories that would still be read some 120-odd years later. But Conan Doyle was an inventive writer, and the characters that filled his stories gripped the imagination of his readers, who devoured episode after episode of the adventures of Sherlock Holmes. In many ways the characters of the Holmes stories are often more interesting than the cases themselves.

So who are the major players on the Baker Street stage? Putting Holmes himself aside (for Holmes is recognisable even to people unfamiliar with the stories themselves), Dr. John H. Watson has to be given pride of place. A veteran of the second Afghan War, Watson, who served as a Duty Surgeon, had been injured by a Jezail bullet at the battle of Maiwand, and saved from certain capture by the courage of his orderly, known to us only as Murray. Pain and illness followed and an urgent return to England became necessary. Watson naturally gravitated to London where, following an introduction by a former colleague, Stamford, he made the acquaintance of Sherlock Holmes. It did not take the two long to decide to share rooms in Baker Street. Throughout the adventures Watson is the ever faithful companion, willing to accompany Holmes at a moment's notice. He is never as smart as Holmes—indeed, his conclusions are often considerably off the mark—and Conan Doyle cleverly does not allow Watson to appear more perceptive than his readers. But without Watson there would be no Holmes stories, for Watson chronicled Holmes's adventures and made Holmes famous by publishing them for the reading public in *The Strand Magazine*.

Although Holmes knew that he could always rely on Watson's companionship and assistance, even a detective as astute as Holmes occasionally needed the wisdom and advice of others. But whose knowledge and deductive skills would

3

be sufficient to assist our genius hero? Obviously someone who shared Holmes's faculties of deduction and analysis—possibly to an even greater degree. For that person we need look no further than Holmes's older brother, Mycroft. Mycroft is an unusual character indeed, a larger-than-life figure who spends his days passing between his lodgings in Pall Mall, his office in Whitehall, and the Diogenes Club ("the queerest club in London").

It came as something of a surprise to Dr. Watson to discover that Holmes had a brother at all, and he could never have dreamed of Mycroft's influence on national affairs. ("Occasionally," Holmes told Watson, "he *is* the British Government.... His position is unique. He has made it for himself. There has never been anything like it before, nor will be again. He has the tidiest and most orderly brain, with the greatest capacity for storing facts of any man living.... The conclusions of every department are passed to him, and he is the central exchange, the clearing-house, which makes out the balance. Other men are specialists, but his specialism is omniscience.... Again and again his word has decided the national policy.")

Quite a man. It's no wonder that Holmes was able to entrust his affairs to Mycroft during the years of his "hiatus" following his presumed death at the Reichenbach Falls.

Our next major player is the long-suffering Mrs. Hudson, Holmes's landlady—a saint if ever there was one for her tolerance of Holmes's chemical experiments, the foul odours from his pipes, and his indoor pistol practice (who else, we ask, would have put up with a tenant who peppered the wall of his room with Boxer cartridges to carve out "a patriotic V. R.[1] done in bullet-pocks"?)

Smaller players, but invaluable to Holmes, are the band of a dozen or so ragged children (described as "street Arabs") known as the Baker Street Irregulars, who can go everywhere, see everything, overhear everyone, and provide vital information to the great detective.

Given the nature of Holmes's business, it is inevitable that Holmes should attract his fair share of enemies, and chief among his adversaries has to be Professor James Moriarty, the Napoleon of Crime—"the organizer of half that is evil and of nearly all that is undetected in this great city." Although Moriarty plays a major role in only one canonical story, his presence seems to pervade the canon. He is a criminal mastermind with "a brain of the first order. He sits motionless, like a spider in the centre of its web, but that web has a thousand radiations, and he knows well every quiver of each of them." As Holmes noted, Moriarty did little himself—he was the planner with numerous agents, and there was little or no reason for the authorities to suspect him of misdeeds. In what became the "Final Problem," Holmes lured Moriarty and his henchman, Colonel Sebastian Moran, to Switzerland, where a final confrontation took place above the Reichenbach Falls—a struggle which Moriarty failed to survive.

Moriarty's second-in-command, Colonel Sebastian Moran, once of Her Majesty's Indian Army, and the best heavy game shot that Britain's Eastern Empire ever

---

1 The initials of Victoria Regina, Queen of England from 1837–1901.

produced, attempted to wreak vengeance with an air rifle for Moriarty's death, in the adventure titled "The Empty House," only to be deceived by a silhouette cast by a wax bust commissioned by Holmes from the craftsman M. Oscar Meunier of Grenoble.

Other villains worthy of mention are the master blackmailer Charles Augustus Milverton ("the worst man in London"); the evil Dr. Grimesby Roylott, whose demise was brought about by the swamp adder with which he'd planned to kill his step-daughters; and the disgusting Baron Adelbert Gruner, murderer, and author of a "lust diary" which "no man, even if he had come from the gutter, could have put together."

While the Sherlockian canon is dominated by men, Holmes encounters strong women, too. Prominent among these are Kitty Winter, a victim of Baron Adelbert Gruner, who takes her revenge for mistreatment at Gruner's hand by throwing vitriol into his face. Nor should we overlook Rachel Howells ("a very good girl, but of an excitable Welsh temperament"), the jilted fiancée of the butler Brunton[2], who took her revenge by incarcerating her ex-lover in a cellar at Hurlestone Manor. Maud Bellamy[3] impressed Holmes: "[She] will always remain in my memory as a most complete and remarkable woman." But of all the women Holmes encounters during his investigations, Irene Adler, or *the* woman, as Holmes thinks of her, stands out. Irene appears in only one story[4], but her presence casts a shadow over the entire canon. In this spirited, intelligent, daring, and courageous woman, Conan Doyle created the female counterpart to Sherlock Holmes: a woman who lives by her wits, is equal to Holmes in her use of disguise, and has a splendid disregard for the mores of the time.

Inevitably, Holmes's business brings him in contact with the official police force from time to time, and during the course of the adventures we encounter a number of officers: some who are capable, and some who do little more than frustrate Holmes. We encounter the official force in the very first Holmes story, *A Study in Scarlet*, when Holmes is approached by Inspector Tobias Gregson. "Gregson is the smartest of the Scotland Yarders," Holmes tells Watson. "He and Lestrade are the pick of a bad lot." In *A Study in Scarlet*, Holmes also encounters Inspector Lestrade ("a little sallow, rat-faced, dark-eyed fellow," according to Watson), and he becomes a regular of the Holmes adventures, appearing in thirteen of the stories. Despite occasional difficulties with the official force, Holmes is always prepared to assist; but on occasion Holmes is also prepared to stretch the law for his own ends, as instanced by the wonderfully humorous episode (which shows Holmes's quiet contempt for the official force) in "The Adventure of Charles Augustus Milverton" when Lestrade visits Baker Street on the morning following Milverton's murder:

"Criminals!" exclaimed Holmes. "Plural!"

---

2 In "The Adventure of the Musgrave Ritual."

3 From "The Adventure of the Lion's Mane."

4 "A Scandal in Bohemia."

"Yes, there were two of them. They were, as nearly as possible, captured red-handed. We have their footmarks, we have their description; it's ten to one that we trace them. The first fellow was a bit too active, but the second was caught by the under-gardener, and only got away after a struggle. He was a middle-sized, strongly built man—square jaw, thick neck, moustache, a mask over his eyes."

"That's rather vague," said Sherlock Holmes. "Why, it might be a description of Watson."

"It's true," said the Inspector, with much amusement. "It might be a description of Watson."

Of the remainder of the official force, special mention need only be made of Stanley Hopkins ("for whose future Holmes had high hopes"), who appears in three of the adventures, and who seems the most likely of all to have been invited to Baker Street for a pleasant evening of conversation.

Despite the wealth of characters who appear in the Sherlockian canon, we lack information of a goodly number of others who are given no more than passing mention. We know that Holmes was involved in many more cases than are reported, because both Holmes and Watson tell us so. Who would not love to know more of the characters from the unreported cases: the Grice Patersons, who had singular adventures in the island of Uffa; Mr. & Mrs. Dundas, who separated—not through any cause of infidelity, but because Mr. Dundas was in the habit of winding up every meal by taking out his false teeth and hurling them at his wife; Merridew, of abominable memory, who is recorded in Holmes's index[5]; Ricoletti of the club-foot and his abominable wife; Mr. James Phillimore, who stepped back into his own house to get his umbrella, and was never more seen in this world. And who is not prepared to ponder what political disgrace may have ensued had the story concerning the politician, the lighthouse, and the trained cormorant been released to the public?

We should marvel at Arthur Conan Doyle's creativity and the characters he gave us. Over the years others have built upon these characters, adding more of their own in an attempt to ensure that there is always a supply of new Holmes adventures. In the pages that follow you will find characters new and old—and some "rivals" of Sherlock Holmes—making their way through the fog and the gaslight to the door of 221B Baker Street. Hark! A barrel-organ is playing at the corner of the street, the light brightens in the window of Holmes's room, and the scene is set for another adventure. The game is afoot!

---

5 Sherlock Holmes maintained an extensive series of commonplace books in which he recorded all manner of information that came to his attention. We learn from the stories that he spent several hours compiling and cross-indexing his books, but generally when we read of him referring to his "index" he seems to be referring to the commonplace books themselves.

THE DOCTOR'S CASE

by Stephen King

Stephen King's most recent book is the short fiction collection, *Just After Sunset*, which came out last fall. Other new short stories include a collaboration with his son, Joe Hill, called "Throttle," for the Richard Matheson tribute anthology *He Is Legend*, and "UR," a novella written exclusively for the Amazon Kindle. King's next novel, due in November, is *Under the Dome*, a thousand-plus-page epic he has been working on for more than twenty-five years. His other work includes dozens of classics, such as *The Stand, The Dark Tower, The Shining, 'Salem's Lot*, and many others.

Elementary, my dear Watson—or should that be, my *poor* Watson? Poor Watson, ever drawing wrong inferences, ever uninformed about some vital trivia, ever in awe of Sherlock Holmes. No matter how many cases they work on together, no matter how many times Holmes explains his methods, Watson is perpetually dumbfounded. We've all probably been acquainted with someone who seemed to effortlessly achieve brilliance while we labored in that person's shadow, putting forth every effort we could muster and achieving only mediocrity. In a very real sense Watson is us, the reader. He is both the narrator, our window into the world of Sherlock Holmes, and also the character who echoes our own unremarkable observations and ruminations. So in this story, when Watson actually beats Holmes to the punch, it's not just a victory for Watson, but for all of us, the ordinary, who must muddle through with what we were given. It's a necessary reminder that the race is not always to the swift, that even demigods may stumble, and that even the most humble among us can be struck by inspiration.

I believe there was only one occasion upon which I actually solved a crime before my slightly fabulous friend, Mr. Sherlock Holmes. I say *believe* because my memory began to grow hazy about the edges as I entered my ninth decade; now, as I approach my centennial, the whole has become downright misty. There *may* have been another occasion, but if so I do not remember it.

I doubt that I shall ever forget this particular case no matter how murky my thoughts and memories may become, and I thought I might as well set it down before God caps my pen forever. It cannot humiliate Holmes now, God knows; he is forty years in his grave. That, I think, is long enough to leave the tale untold.

7

Even Lestrade, who used Holmes upon occasion but never had any great liking for him, never broke his silence in the matter of Lord Hull—he hardly could have done so, considering the circumstances. Even if the circumstances had been different, I somehow doubt he would have. He and Holmes baited each other, and I believe that Holmes may have harboured actual hate in his heart for the policeman (although he never would have admitted to such a low emotion), but Lestrade had a queer respect for my friend.

It was a wet, dreary afternoon and the clock had just rung half past one. Holmes sat by the window, holding his violin but not playing it, looking silently out into the rain. There were times, especially once his cocaine days were behind him, when Holmes would grow moody to the point of surliness when the skies remained stubbornly gray for a week or more, and he had been doubly disappointed on this day, for the glass had been rising since late the night before and he had confidently predicted clearing skies by ten this morning at the latest. Instead, the mist which had been hanging in the air when I arose had thickened into a steady rain, and if there was anything which rendered Holmes moodier than long periods of rain, it was being wrong.

Suddenly he straightened up, tweaking a violin string with a fingernail, and smiled sardonically. "Watson! Here's a sight! The wettest bloodhound you ever saw!"

It was Lestrade, of course, seated in the back of an open wagon with water running into his close-set, fiercely inquisitive eyes. The wagon had no more than stopped before he was out, flinging the driver a coin, and striding toward 221B Baker Street. He moved so quickly that I thought he should run into our door like a battering ram.

I heard Mrs. Hudson remonstrating with him about his decidedly damp condition and the effect it might have on the rugs both downstairs and up, and then Holmes, who could make Lestrade look like a tortoise when the urge struck him, leaped across to the door and called down, "Let him up, Mrs. H.— I'll put a newspaper under his boots if he stays long, but I somehow think, yes, I really do think that..."

Then Lestrade was bounding up the stairs, leaving Mrs. Hudson to expostulate below. His colour was high, his eyes burned, and his teeth—decidedly yellowed by tobacco—were bared in a wolfish grin.

"Inspector Lestrade!" Holmes cried jovially. "What brings you out on such a—"

No further did he get. Still panting from his climb, Lestrade said, "I've heard gypsies say the devil grants wishes. Now I believe it. Come at once if you'd have a try, Holmes; the corpse is still fresh and the suspects all in a row."

"You frighten me with your ardour, Lestrade!" Holmes cried, but with a sardonic little waggle of his eyebrows.

"Don't play the shrinking violet with me, man—I've come at the run to offer you the very thing for which you in your pride have wished a hundred times or more in my own hearing: the perfect locked-room mystery!"

Holmes had started into the corner, perhaps to get the awful gold-tipped cane which he was for some reason affecting that season. Now he whirled upon our damp visitor, his eyes wide. "Lestrade! Are you serious?"

"Would I have risked wet-lung croup riding here in an open wagon if I were not?" Lestrade countered.

Then, for the only time in my hearing (despite the countless times the phrase has been attributed to him), Holmes turned to me and cried: "Quick, Watson! The game's afoot!"

On our way, Lestrade commented sourly that Holmes also had the *luck* of the devil; although Lestrade had commanded the wagon-driver to wait, we had no more than emerged from our lodgings when that exquisite rarity clip-clopped down the street: an empty hackney in what had become a driving rain. We climbed in and were off in a trice. As always, Holmes sat on the left-hand side, his eyes darting restlessly about, cataloguing everything, although there was precious little to see on *that* day... or so it seemed, at least, to the likes of me. I've no doubt every empty street corner and rain-washed shop window spoke volumes to Holmes.

Lestrade directed the driver to an address in Savile Row, and then asked Holmes if he knew Lord Hull.

"I know *of* him," Holmes said, "but have never had the good fortune of meeting him. Now I suppose I never shall. Shipping, wasn't it?"

"Shipping," Lestrade agreed, "but the good fortune was yours. Lord Hull was, by all accounts (including those of his nearest and—ahem!—dearest), a thoroughly nasty fellow, and as dotty as a puzzle-picture in a child's novelty book. He's finished practicing both nastiness and dottiness for good, however; around eleven o'clock this morning, just"—he pulled out his turnip of a pocket-watch and looked at it—"two hours and forty minutes ago, someone put a knife in his back as he sat in his study with his will on the blotter before him."

"So," Holmes said thoughtfully, lighting his pipe, "you believe the study of this unpleasant Lord Hull is the perfect locked room of my dreams, do you?" His eyes gleamed sceptically through a rising rafter of blue smoke.

"I believe," Lestrade said quietly, "that it is."

"Watson and I have dug such holes before and never struck water," Holmes remarked, and he glanced at me before returning to his ceaseless catalogue of the streets through which we passed. "Do you recall the 'Speckled Band,' Watson?"

I hardly needed to answer him. There had been a locked room in that business, true enough, but there had also been a ventilator, a poisonous snake, and a killer fiendish enough to introduce the latter into the former. It had been the work of a cruelly brilliant mind, but Holmes had seen to the bottom of the matter in almost no time at all.

"What are the facts, Inspector?" Holmes asked.

Lestrade began to lay them before us in the clipped tones of a trained policeman. Lord Albert Hull had been a tyrant in business and a despot at home. His wife had gone in fear of him, and had apparently been justified in doing so. The fact that she had borne him three sons seemed in no way to have moderated his savage approach toward their domestic affairs in general and toward her in particular. Lady Hull had been reluctant to speak of these matters, but her sons had no such reservations; their papa, they said, had missed no opportunity to dig at her, to criticize her, or to jest at her expense… all of this when they were in company. When they were alone, he virtually ignored her. Except, Lestrade added, when he felt moved to beat her, which was by no means an uncommon occurrence.

"William, the eldest, told me she always gave out the same story when she came to the breakfast table with a swollen eye or a mark on her cheek: that she had forgotten to put on her spectacles and had run into a door. 'She ran into doors once or twice a week,' William said. 'I didn't know we had that many doors in the house.'"

"Hmmm," Holmes said. "A cheery fellow! The sons never put a stop to it?"

"She wouldn't allow it," Lestrade said.

"Insanity," I returned. A man who would beat his wife is an abomination; a woman who would allow it an abomination and a perplexity.

"There was a method in her madness, though," Lestrade said. "Method and what you might call 'an informed patience.' She was, after all, twenty years younger than her lord and master. Also, Hull was a heavy drinker and a champion diner. At age seventy, five years ago, he developed gout and angina."

"Wait for the storm to end and then enjoy the sunshine," Holmes remarked.

"Yes," Lestrade said, "but it's an idea which has led many a man and woman through the devil's door, I'll be bound. Hull made sure his family knew both his worth and the provisions of his will. They were little better than slaves."

"With the will as their document of indenture," Holmes murmured.

"Exactly so, old boy. At the time of his death, Hull's worth was three hundred thousand pounds. He never asked them to take his word for this; he had his chief accountant to the house quarterly to detail the balance sheets of Hull Shipping, although he kept the purse-strings firmly in his own hands and tightly closed."

"Devilish!" I exclaimed, thinking of the cruel boys one sometimes sees in East-cheap or Piccadilly, boys who will hold out a sweet to a starving dog to see it dance… and then gobble it themselves while the hungry animal watches. I was shortly to find this comparison even more apt than I would have thought possible.

"On his death, Lady Rebecca was to receive one hundred and fifty thousand pund'. William, the eldest, was to receive fifty thousand; Jory, the middler, forty; and Stephen, the youngest, thirty."

"And the other thirty thousand?" I asked.

"Small bequests, Watson: to a cousin in Wales, an aunt in Brittany (not a cent for Lady Hull's relatives, though), five thousand in assorted bequests to the servants. Oh, and—you'll like this, Holmes—ten thousand pounds to Mrs. Hemphill's Home for Abandoned Pussies."

"You're joking!" I cried, although if Lestrade expected a similar reaction from Holmes, he was disappointed. Holmes merely re-lighted his pipe and nodded as if he had expected this… this or something like it. "With babies dying of starvation in the East End and twelve-year-old children working fifty hours a week in the mills, this fellow left ten thousand pounds to a... a boarding-hotel for *cats?*"

"Exactly so," Lestrade said pleasantly. "Furthermore, he should have left *twenty-seven times* that amount to Mrs. Hemphill's Abandoned Pussies if not for whatever happened this morning—and whoever did the business."

I could only gape at this, and try to multiply in my head. While I was coming to the conclusion that Lord Hull had intended to disinherit both wife and children in favour of a resthome for felines, Holmes was looking sourly at Lestrade and saying something which sounded to me like a total *non sequitur.* "I am going to sneeze, am I not?"

Lestrade smiled. It was a smile of transcendent sweetness. "Yes, my dear Holmes! Often and profoundly, I fear."

Holmes removed his pipe, which he had just gotten drawing to his satisfaction (I could tell by the way he settled back slightly in his seat), looked at it for a moment, and then held it out into the rain. More dumbfounded than ever, I watched him knock out the damp and smouldering tobacco.

"How many?" Holmes asked.

"Ten," Lestrade said with a fiendish grin.

"I suspected it was more than this famous locked room of yours that brought you out in the back of an open wagon on such a wet day," Holmes said sourly.

"Suspect as you like," Lestrade said gaily. "I'm afraid I must go on to the scene of the crime—duty calls, you know—but if you'd like, I could let you and the good doctor out here."

"You are the only man I ever met," Holmes said, "whose wit seems to be sharpened by foul weather. Does that perhaps say something about your character, I wonder? But never mind—that is, perhaps, a subject for another day. Tell me this, Lestrade: when did Lord Hull become sure that he was going to die?"

"*Die?*" I said. "My dear Holmes, whatever gives you the idea that the man believed—"

"It's obvious, Watson," Holmes said. "C.I.B., as I have told you at least a thousand times—character indexes behaviour. It amused him to keep them in bondage by means of his will..." He looked an aside at Lestrade. "No trust arrangements, I take it? No entailments of any sort?"

Lestrade shook his head. "None whatever."

"Extraordinary!" I said.

"Not at all, Watson; character indexes behaviour, remember. He wanted them to soldier along in the belief that all would be theirs when he did them the courtesy of dying, but he never actually intended any such thing. Such behaviour would, in fact, have run completely across the grain of his character. D'you agree, Lestrade?"

"As a matter of fact, I do," Lestrade replied.

"Then we are very well to this point, Watson, are we not? All is clear? Lord Hull realizes he is dying. He waits... makes absolutely sure that this time it's no mistake, no false alarm... and then he calls his beloved family together. When? This morning, Lestrade?"

Lestrade grunted an affirmative.

Holmes steepled his fingers beneath his chin. "He calls them together and tells them he's made a new will, one which disinherits all of them... all, that is, save for the servants, his few distant relatives, and, of course, the pussies."

I opened my mouth to speak, only to discover I was too outraged to say anything. The image which kept returning to my mind was that of those cruel boys, making the starving East End curs jump with a bit of pork or a crumb of crust from a meat pie. I must add it never occurred to me to ask whether such a will could be disputed before the bar. Today a man would have a deuce of a time slighting his closest relatives in favour of a cat-hotel, but in 1899, a man's will was a man's will, and unless many examples of insanity—not eccentricity but outright *insanity*—could be proved, a man's will, like God's, was done.

"This new will was properly witnessed?" Holmes asked.

"Indeed it was," Lestrade replied. "Yesterday Lord Hull's solicitor and one of his assistants appeared at the house and were shown into Hull's study. There they remained for about fifteen minutes. Stephen Hull says the solicitor once raised his voice in protest about something—he could not tell what—and was silenced by Hull. Jory, the middle son, was upstairs, painting, and Lady Hull was calling on a friend. But both Stephen and William Hull saw these legal fellows enter, and leave a short time later. William said that they left with their heads down, and although William spoke, asking Mr. Barnes—the solicitor—if he was well, and making some social remark about the persistence of the rain, Barnes did not reply and the assistant seemed actually to cringe. It was as if they were ashamed, William said."

Well, so much for *that* possible loophole, I thought.

"Since we are on the subject, tell me about the boys," Holmes invited.

"As you like. It goes pretty much without saying that their hatred for the pater was exceeded only by the pater's boundless contempt for them... although how he could hold Stephen in contempt is... well, never mind, I'll keep things in their proper order."

"Yes, please be so kind as to do that," Holmes said dryly.

"William is thirty-six. If his father had given him any sort of allowance, I suppose he would be a bounder. As he had little or none, he has spent his days in various gymnasiums, involved in what I believe is called 'physical culture'—he appears to be an extremely muscular fellow—and his nights in various cheap coffee-houses, for the most part. If he did happen to have a bit of money in his pockets, he was apt to take himself off to a card-parlour, where he would lose it quickly enough. Not a pleasant man, Holmes. A man who has no purpose, no skill, no hobby, and no ambition (save to outlive his father) could hardly be a pleasant man. I had the queerest idea while talking to him that I was interrogating not a man but an empty vase upon which the face of Lord Hull had been lightly stamped."

"A vase waiting to be filled up with pounds sterling," Holmes commented.

"Jory is another matter," Lestrade went on. "Lord Hull saved most of his contempt for him, calling him from his earliest childhood by such endearing pet-names as 'Fish-Face' and 'Keg-Legs' and 'Stoat-Belly.' It's not hard to understand such names, unfortunately; Jory Hull stands no more than five feet tall, if that, is bow-legged, and of a remarkably ugly countenance. He looks a bit like that poet fellow. The pouf."

"Oscar Wilde?" asked I.

Holmes turned a brief, amused glance upon me. "I think Lestrade means Algernon Swinburne," he said. "Who, I believe, is no more a pouf than you are, Watson."

"Jory Hull was born dead," Lestrade said. "After he remained blue and still for an entire minute, the doctor pronounced him so and put a napkin over his misshapen body. Lady Hull, in her one moment of heroism, sat up, removed the napkin, and dipped the baby's legs into the hot water which had been brought to be used at the birth. The baby began to squirm and squall."

Lestrade grinned and lit a cigarillo with a flourish.

"Hull claimed this immersion had caused the boy's bowed legs, and when he was in his cups, he taxed his wife with it. Told her she should have left well enough alone. Better Jory had been born dead than lived to be what he was, he sometimes said—a scuttling creature with the legs of a crab and the face of a cod."

Holmes's only reaction to this extraordinary (and to my physician's mind rather suspect) story was to comment that Lestrade had gotten a remarkably large body of information in a remarkably short period of time.

"That points up one of the aspects of the case which I thought would appeal to you, my dear Holmes," Lestrade said as we swept into Rotten Row with a splash and a swirl. "They need no coercion to speak; coercion's what it would take to shut 'em up. They've had to remain silent all too long. And then there's the fact that the new will is gone. Relief loosens tongues beyond measure, I find."

"*Gone!*" I exclaimed, but Holmes took no notice; his mind still ran upon Jory, the misshapen middle child.

"*Is* he ugly, then?" he asked Lestrade.

"Hardly handsome, but not as bad as some I've seen," Lestrade replied comfortably. "I believe his father continually heaped vituperation on his head because—"

"—because he was the only one who had no need of his father's money to make his way in the world," Holmes finished for him.

Lestrade started. "The devil! How did you know that?"

"Because Lord Hull was reduced to carping at Jory's physical faults. How it must have chafed the old devil to be faced with a potential target so well armoured in other respects! Baiting a man for his looks or his posture may be fine for schoolboys or drunken louts, but a villain like Lord Hull had no doubt become used to higher sport. I would venture the opinion that he may have been rather afraid of his bow-legged middle son. What was Jory's key to the cell door?"

"Haven't I told you? He paints," Lestrade said.

"Ah!"

Jory Hull was, as the canvases in the lower halls of Hull House later proved, a very good painter indeed. Not great; I do not mean that at all. But his renderings of his mother and brothers were faithful enough so that, years later, when I saw colour photographs for the first time, my mind flashed back to that rainy November afternoon in 1899. And the one of his father perhaps *was* a work of greatness. Certainly it startled (almost intimidated) with the malevolence that seemed to waft out of the canvas like a breath of dank graveyard air. Perhaps it *was* Algernon Swinburne that Jory resembled, but his father's likeness—at least as seen through the middle son's hand and eye—reminded me of an Oscar Wilde character: that nearly immortal *roué,* Dorian Gray.

His canvases were long, slow processes, but he was able to quick-sketch with such nimble rapidity that he might come home from Hyde Park on a Saturday afternoon with as much as twenty pounds in his pockets.

"I'll wager his father enjoyed *that,*" Holmes said. He reached automatically for his pipe, then put it back again. "The son of a Peer quick-sketching wealthy American tourists and their sweethearts like a French Bohemian."

Lestrade laughed heartily. "He *raged* over it, as you may imagine. But Jory—good for him!—wouldn't give over his selling stall in Hyde Park... not, at least, until his father agreed to an allowance of thirty-five pounds a week. He called it low blackmail."

"My heart bleeds," I said.

"As does mine, Watson," Holmes said. "The third son, Lestrade, quickly—we've almost reached the house, I believe."

As Lestrade had intimated, surely Stephen Hull had the greatest cause to hate his father. As his gout grew worse and his head more muddled, Lord Hull surrendered more and more of the company affairs to Stephen, who was only twenty-eight at the time of his father's death. The responsibilities devolved upon Stephen, and the blame also devolved upon him if his least decision proved amiss. Yet no financial gain accrued to him should he decide well and his father's affairs prosper.

Lord Hull should have looked with favour upon Stephen, as the only one of his children with an interest in and an aptitude for the business he had founded; Stephen was a perfect example of what the Bible calls "the good son." Yet instead of displaying love and gratitude, Lord Hull repaid the young man's largely successful efforts with scorn, suspicion, and jealousy. On many occasions during the last two years of his life, the old man had offered the charming opinion that Stephen "would steal the pennies from a dead man's eyes."

"The b——d!" I cried, unable to contain myself.

"Ignore the new will for a moment," Holmes said, steepling his fingers again, "and return to the old one. Even under the conditions of that marginally more generous document, Stephen Hull would have had cause for resentment. In spite of all his labours, which had not only saved the family fortune but increased it, his reward was still to have been the youngest son's share of the spoils. What, by the way, was to have been the disposition of the shipping company under the provisions of what we might call the Pussy Will?"

I looked carefully at Holmes, but, as always, it was difficult to tell if he had attempted a small *bon mot.* Even after all the years I spent with him and all the adventures we shared, Sherlock Holmes's sense of humour remains a largely undiscovered country, even to me.

"It was to be handed over to the Board of Directors, with no provision for Stephen," Lestrade said, and pitched his cigarillo out the window as the hackney swept up the curving drive of a house which looked extraordinarily ugly to me just then, as it stood amid its brown lawns in the driving rain. "Yet with the father dead and the new will nowhere to be found, Stephen Hull has what the Americans call 'leverage.' The company will have him as managing director. They should have done anyway, but now it will be on Stephen Hull's terms."

"Yes," Holmes said. "Leverage. A good word." He leaned out into the rain. "Stop short, driver!" he cried. "We've not quite done!"

"As you say, guv'nor," the driver returned, "but it's devilish wet out here."

"And you'll go with enough in your pocket to make your innards as wet and devilish as your out'ards," Holmes said. This seemed to satisfy the man, and he stopped thirty yards from the front door of the great house. I listened to the rain tip-tapping on the sides of the coach while Holmes cogitated and then said: "The old will—the one he teased them with—*that* document isn't missing, is it?"

"Absolutely not. It was on his desk, near his body."

"Four excellent suspects! Servants need not apply… or so it seems now. Finish quickly, Lestrade—the final circumstances, and the locked room."

Lestrade complied, consulting his notes from time to time. A month previous, Lord Hull had observed a small black spot on his right leg, directly behind the knee. The family doctor was called. His diagnosis was gangrene, an unusual but far from rare result of gout and poor circulation. The doctor told him the leg would have to come off, and well above the site of the infection.

Lord Hull laughed until tears streamed down his cheeks. The doctor, who had expected any reaction but this, was struck speechless. "When they stick me in my coffin, sawbones," Hull said, "it will be with both legs still attached, thank you very much."

The doctor told him that he sympathized with Lord Hull's wish to keep his leg, but that without amputation he would be dead in six months, and he would spend the last two in exquisite pain. Lord Hull asked the doctor what his chances of survival should be if he were to undergo the operation. He was still laughing, Lestrade said, as though it were the best joke he had ever heard. After some hemming and hawing, the doctor said the odds were even.

"Bunk," said I.

"Exactly what Lord Hull said," Lestrade replied, "except he used a term more often used in dosses than in drawing-rooms."

Hull told the doctor that he himself reckoned his chances at no better than one in five. "As to the pain, I don't think it will come to that," he went on, "as long as there's laudanum and a spoon to stir it with in stumping distance."

The next day, Hull finally sprang his nasty surprise—that he was thinking of changing his will. Just how he did not immediately say.

"Oh?" Holmes said, looking at Lestrade from those cool gray eyes that saw so much. "And who, pray, was surprised?"

"None of them, I should think. But you know human nature, Holmes; how people hope against hope."

"And how some plan against disaster," Holmes said dreamily.

This very morning Lord Hull had called his family into the parlour, and when all were settled, he performed an act few testators are granted, one which is usually performed by the wagging tongues of their solicitors after their own have been forever silenced. In short, he read them his new will, leaving the balance of his estate to Mrs. Hemphill's wayward pussies. In the silence which followed he rose, not without difficulty, and favoured them all with a death's-head grin. And leaning over his cane, he made the following declaration, which I find as astoundingly vile now as I did when Lestrade recounted it to us in that hackney cab: "So! All is fine, is it not? Yes, very fine! You have served me quite faithfully, woman and boys, for some forty years. Now I intend, with the clearest and most serene conscience imaginable, to cast you hence. But take heart! Things could be worse! If there was time, the pharaohs had their favourite pets—cats, for the most part—killed before they died, so the pets might be there to welcome them into the afterlife, to be kicked or petted there, at their masters' whims, forever... and forever... and forever." Then he laughed at them. He leaned over his cane and laughed from his doughy, dying face, the new will—properly signed and properly witnessed, as all of them had seen—clutched in one claw of a hand.

William rose and said, "Sir, you may be my father and the author of my existence, but you are also the lowest creature to crawl upon the face of the earth since the serpent tempted Eve in the Garden."

"Not at all!" the old monster returned, still laughing. "I know four lower. Now, if you will pardon me, I have some important papers to put away in my safe... and some worthless ones to burn in the stove."

"He still had the old will when he confronted them?" Holmes asked. He seemed more interested than startled.

"Yes."

"He could have burned it as soon as the new one was signed and witnessed," Holmes mused. "He had all the previous afternoon and evening to do so. But he didn't, did he? Why not? How say you on that question, Lestrade?"

"He hadn't had enough of teasing them even then, I suppose. He was offering them a chance—a *temptation*—he believed all would refuse."

"Perhaps he believed one of them would not refuse," Holmes said. "Hasn't that idea at least crossed your mind?" He turned his head and searched my face with the momentary beam of his brilliant—and somehow chilling—regard. "*Either* of your minds? Isn't it possible that such a black creature might hold out such a temptation, knowing that if one of his family were to succumb to it and put him out of his misery—Stephen seems most likely from what you say—that one might be caught... and swing for the crime of patricide?"

I stared at Holmes in silent horror.

"Never mind," Holmes said. "Go on, Inspector—it's time for the locked room to make its appearance, I believe."

The four of them had sat in paralyzed silence as the old man made his long, slow way up the corridor to his study. There were no sounds but the thud of his cane, the laboured rattle of his breathing, the plaintive *miaow* of a cat in the kitchen, and the steady beat of the pendulum in the parlour clock. Then they heard the squeal of hinges as Hull opened his study door and stepped inside.

"Wait!" Holmes said sharply, sitting forward. "No one actually *saw* him go in, did they?"

"I'm afraid that's not so, old chap," Lestrade returned. "Mr. Oliver Stanley, Lord Hull's valet, had heard Lord Hull's progress down the hall. He came from Hull's dressing chamber, went to the gallery railing, and called down to ask if all was well. Hull looked up—Stanley saw him as plainly as I see you right now, old fellow—and said all was absolutely tip-top. Then he rubbed the back of his head, went in, and locked the study door behind him.

"By the time his father had reached the door (the corridor is quite long and it may have taken him as much as two minutes to make his way up it unaided) Stephen had shaken off his stupor and had gone to the parlour door. He saw the exchange between his father and his father's man. Of course Lord Hull was back-to, but Stephen heard his father's voice and described the same characteristic gesture: Hull rubbing the back of his head."

"Could Stephen Hull and this Stanley fellow have spoken before the police arrived?" I asked—shrewdly, I thought.

"Of course they could," Lestrade said wearily. "They probably did. But there was no collusion."

"You feel sure of that?" Holmes asked, but he sounded uninterested.

"Yes. Stephen Hull would lie very well, I think, but Stanley would do it very badly. Accept my professional opinion or not, just as you like, Holmes."

"I accept it."

So Lord Hull passed into his study, the famous locked room, and all heard the click of the lock as he turned the key—the only key there was to that *sanctum sanctorum*. This was followed by a more unusual sound: the bolt being drawn across.

Then, silence.

The four of them—Lady Hull and her sons, so shortly to be blue-blooded paupers—looked at one another in similar silence. The cat miaowed again from the kitchen and Lady Hull said in a distracted voice that if the housekeeper wouldn't give that cat a bowl of milk, she supposed she must. She said the sound of it would drive her mad if she had to listen to it much longer. She left the parlour. Moments later, without a word among them, the three sons also left. William went to his room upstairs, Stephen wandered into the music room, and Jory went to sit upon a bench beneath the stairs where, he had told Lestrade, he had gone since earliest childhood when he was sad or had matters of deep difficulty to think over.

Less than five minutes later a shriek arose from the study. Stephen ran out of the music room, where he had been plinking out isolated notes on the piano. Jory met him at the study door. William was already halfway downstairs and saw them breaking in when Stanley, the valet, came out of Lord Hull's dressing room and went to the gallery railing for the second time. Stanley has testified to seeing Stephen Hull burst into the study; to seeing William reach the foot of the stairs and almost fall on the marble; to seeing Lady Hull come from the dining-room doorway with a pitcher of milk still in one hand. Moments later the rest of the servants had gathered.

"Lord Hull was slumped over his writing-desk with the three brothers standing by. His eyes were open, and the look in them... I believe it was surprise. Again, you are free to accept or reject my opinion just as you like, but I tell you it looked very much like surprise to me. Clutched in his hands was his will... the old one. Of the new one there was no sign. And there was a dagger in his back."

With this, Lestrade rapped for the driver to go on.

We entered the house between two constables as stone-faced as Buckingham Palace sentinels. Here to begin with was a very long hall, floored in black and white marble tiles like a chessboard. They led to an open door at the end, where two more constables were posted: the entrance to the infamous study. To the left were the stairs, to the right two doors: the parlour and the music room, I guessed.

"The family is gathered in the parlour," Lestrade said.

"Good," Holmes said pleasantly. "But perhaps Watson and I might first have a look at the scene of the crime?"

"Shall I accompany you?"

"Perhaps not," Holmes said. "Has the body been removed?"

"It was still here when I left for your lodgings, but by now it almost certainly will be gone."

"Very good."

Holmes started away. I followed. Lestrade called, "Holmes!"

Holmes turned, eyebrows raised.

"No secret panels, no secret doors. For the third time, take my word or not, as you like."

"I believe I'll wait until..." Holmes began and then his breath began to hitch. He scrambled in his pocket, found a napkin probably carried absently away from the eating-house where we had dined the previous evening, and sneezed mightily into it. I looked down and saw a large, scarred tomcat, as out of place here in this grand hall as would have been one of those urchins of whom I had been thinking earlier, twining about Holmes's legs. One of its ears was laid back against its scarred skull. The other was gone, lost in some long-ago alley battle, I supposed.

Holmes sneezed repeatedly and kicked out at the cat. It went with a reproachful backward look rather than with the angry hiss one might have expected from such an old campaigner. Holmes looked at Lestrade over the napkin with reproachful, watery eyes. Lestrade, not in the least put out of countenance, thrust his head forward and grinned like a monkey. "Ten, Holmes," he said. "*Ten*. House is full of felines. Hull loved 'em." And with that he walked off.

"How long have you suffered this affliction, old fellow?" I asked. I was a bit alarmed.

"Always," he said, and sneezed again. The word *allergy* was hardly known all those years ago, but that, of course, was his problem.

"Do you want to leave?" I asked. I had once seen a case of near asphyxiation as the result of such an aversion, this one to sheep but otherwise similar in all respects.

"He'd like that," Holmes said. I did not need him to tell me whom he meant. Holmes sneezed once more (a large red welt was appearing on his normally pale forehead) and then we passed between the constables at the study door. Holmes closed it behind him.

The room was long and relatively narrow. It was at the end of something like a wing, the main house spreading to either side from an area roughly three-quarters of the way down the hall. There were windows on two sides of the study and it was bright enough in spite of the gray, rainy day. The walls were dotted with colourful shipping charts in handsome teak frames, and among them was mounted an equally handsome set of weather instruments in a brass-bound, glass-fronted case. It contained an anemometer (Hull had the little whirling cups mounted on one of the roofpeaks, I supposed), two thermometers (one registering the outdoor temperature and the other that of the study), and a barometer much like the one which had fooled Holmes into believing the bad weather was about to break. I noticed the glass was still rising, then looked outside. The rain was falling harder than ever, rising glass or no rising glass. We believe we know a great lot, with our instruments and things, but I was old enough then to believe we don't know half as much as we think we do, and old enough now to believe we never will.

Holmes and I both turned to look at the door. The bolt was torn free, but leaning inward, as it should have been. The key was still in the study-side lock, and still turned.

Holmes's eyes, watering as they were, were everywhere at once, noting, cataloguing, storing.

"You are a little better," I said.

"Yes," he said, lowering the napkin and stuffing it indifferently back into his coat pocket. "He may have loved 'em, but he apparently didn't allow 'em in here. Not on a regular basis, anyway. What do you make of it, Watson?"

Although my eyes were slower than his, I was also looking around. The double windows were all locked with thumb-turns and small brass side-bolts. None of the panes had been broken. Most of the framed charts and the box of weather instruments were between these windows. The other two walls were filled with books. There was a small coal-stove but no fireplace; the murderer hadn't come down the chimney like Father Christmas, not unless he was narrow enough to fit through a stovepipe and clad in an asbestos suit, for the stove was still very warm.

The desk stood at one end of this long, narrow, well-lit room; the opposite end was a pleasantly bookish area, not quite a library, with two high-backed upholstered chairs and a coffee-table between them. On this table was a random stack of volumes. The floor was covered with a Turkish rug. If the murderer had come through a trap-door, I hadn't the slightest idea how he'd gotten back under that rug without disarranging it… and it was *not* disarranged, not in the slightest: the shadows of the coffee-table legs lay across it without even a hint of a ripple.

"Did you believe it, Watson?" Holmes asked, snapping me out of what was almost a hypnotic trance. Something… something about that coffee-table…

"Believe what, Holmes?"

"That all four of them simply walked out of the parlour, in four different directions, four minutes before the murder?"

"I don't know," I said faintly.

"*I* don't believe it; not for a mo—" He broke off. "Watson! Are you all right?"

"No," I said in a voice I could hardly hear myself. I collapsed into one of the library chairs. My heart was beating too fast. I couldn't seem to catch my breath. My head was pounding; my eyes seemed to have suddenly grown too large for their sockets. I could not take them from the shadows of the coffee-table legs upon the rug. "I am most… definitely not… all right."

At that moment Lestrade appeared in the study doorway. "If you've looked your fill, H—" He broke off. "What the devil's the matter with Watson?"

"I believe," said Holmes in a calm, measured voice, "that Watson has solved the case. Have you, Watson?"

I nodded my head. Not the entire case, perhaps, but most of it. I knew who; I knew how.

"Is it this way with you, Holmes?" I asked. "When you… see?"

"Yes," he said, "though I usually manage to keep my feet."

"*Watson's* solved the case?" Lestrade said impatiently. "Bah! Watson's offered a thousand solutions to a hundred cases before this, Holmes, as you very well know, and all of them wrong. It's his *bête noire*. Why, I remember just this last summer—"

"I know more about Watson than you ever shall," Holmes said, "and this time he has hit upon it. I know the look." He began to sneeze again; the cat with the missing ear had wandered into the room through the door which Lestrade had left open. It moved directly toward Holmes with an expression of what seemed to be affection on its ugly face.

"If this is how it is for you," I said, "I'll never envy you again, Holmes. My heart should burst."

"One becomes inured even to insight," Holmes said, with not the slightest trace of conceit in his voice. "Out with it, then… or shall we bring in the suspects, as in the last chapter of a detective novel?"

"No!" I cried in horror. I had seen none of them; I had no urge to. "Only I think I must *show* you how it was done. If you and Inspector Lestrade will only step out into the hall for a moment…"

The cat reached Holmes and jumped into his lap, purring like the most satisfied creature on earth.

Holmes exploded into a perfect fusillade of sneezes. The red patches on his face, which had begun to fade, burst out afresh. He pushed the cat away and stood up.

"Be quick, Watson, so we can leave this damned place," he said in a muffled voice, and left the room with his shoulders in an uncharacteristic hunch, his head down, and with not a single look back. Believe me when I say that a little of my heart went with him.

Lestrade stood leaning against the door, his wet coat steaming slightly, his lips parted in a detestable grin. "Shall I take Holmes's new admirer, Watson?"

"Leave it," I said, "and close the door when you go out."

"I'd lay a fiver you're wasting our time, old man," Lestrade said, but I saw something different in his eyes: if I'd offered to take him up on the wager, he would have found a way to squirm out of it.

"Close the door," I repeated. "I shan't be long."

He closed the door. I was alone in Hull's study... except for the cat, of course, which was now sitting in the middle of the rug, tail curled neatly about its paws, green eyes watching me.

I felt in my pockets and found my own souvenir from last night's dinner—men on their own are rather untidy people, I fear, but there was a reason for the bread other than general slovenliness. I almost always kept a crust in one pocket or the other, for it amused me to feed the pigeons that landed outside the very window where Holmes had been sitting when Lestrade drove up.

"Pussy," said I, and put the bread beneath the coffee-table—the coffee-table to which Lord Hull would have presented his back when he sat down with his two wills, the wretched old one and the even more wretched new one. "Puss-puss-puss."

The cat rose and walked languidly beneath the table to investigate the crust.

I went to the door and opened it. "Holmes! Lestrade! Quickly!"

They came in.

"Step over here," I said, and walked to the coffee-table.

Lestrade looked about and began to frown, seeing nothing; Holmes, of course, began to sneeze again. "Can't we have that wretched thing out of here?" he managed from behind the table-napkin, which was now quite soggy.

"Of course," said I. *"But where is the wretched thing, Holmes?"*

A startled expression filled his wet eyes. Lestrade whirled, walked toward Hull's writing-desk, and peered behind it. Holmes knew his reaction should not have been so violent if the cat had been on the far side of the room. He bent and looked beneath the coffee-table, saw nothing but the rug and the bottom row of the two bookcases opposite, and straightened up again. If his eyes had not been spouting like fountains, he should have seen all then; he was, after all, right on top of it. But one must also give credit where credit is due, and the illusion was devilishly good. The empty space beneath his father's coffee-table had been Jory Hull's masterpiece.

"I don't—" Holmes began, and then the cat, who found my friend much more to its liking than any stale crust of bread, strolled out from beneath the table and began once more to twine ecstatically about his ankles. Lestrade had returned, and his eyes grew so wide I thought they might actually fall out. Even having understood the trick, I myself was amazed. The scarred tomcat seemed to be materializing out of thin air; head, body, white-tipped tail last.

It rubbed against Holmes's leg, purring as Holmes sneezed.

"That's enough," I said. "You've done your job and may leave."

I picked it up, took it to the door (getting a good scratch for my pains), and tossed it unceremoniously into the hall. I shut the door behind it.

Holmes was sitting down. "My God," he said in a nasal, clogged voice. Lestrade was incapable of any speech at all. His eyes never left the table and the faded Turkish rug beneath its legs: an empty space that had somehow given birth to a cat.

"I should have seen," Holmes was muttering. "Yes... but you... how did you understand so *quickly?*" I detected the faintest hurt and pique in that voice, and forgave it at once.

"It was *those,*" I said, and pointed at the rug.

"Of course!" Holmes nearly groaned. He slapped his welted forehead. "Idiot! I'm a perfect *idiot!*"

"Nonsense," I said tartly. "With a houseful of cats—and one who has apparently picked you out for a special friend—I suspect you were seeing ten of everything."

"What about the rug?" Lestrade asked impatiently. "It's very nice, I'll grant, and probably expensive, but—"

"Not the *rug,*" I said. "The *shadows*"

"Show him, Watson," Holmes said wearily, lowering the napkin into his lap.

So I bent and picked one of them off the floor.

Lestrade sat down in the other chair, hard, like a man who has been unexpectedly punched.

"I kept looking at them, you see," I said, speaking in a tone which could not help being apologetic. This seemed all wrong. It was Holmes's job to explain the whos and hows at the end of the investigation. Yet while I saw that he now understood everything, I knew he would refuse to speak in this case. And I suppose a part of me—the part that knew I would probably never have another chance to do something like this—*wanted* to be the one to explain. And the cat was rather a nice touch, I must say. A magician could have done no better with a rabbit and a top-hat.

"I knew something was wrong, but it took a moment for it to sink in. This room is extremely bright, but today it's pouring down rain. Look around and you'll see that not a single object in this room casts a shadow... *except for these table-legs.*"

Lestrade uttered an oath.

"It's rained for nearly a week," I said, "but both Holmes's barometer and the late Lord Hull's"—I pointed to it—"said that we could expect sun today. In fact, it seemed a sure thing. So he added the shadows as a final touch."

"Who did?"

"Jory Hull," Holmes said in that same weary tone. "Who else?"

I bent down and reached my hand beneath the right end of the coffee-table. It disappeared into thin air, just as the cat had appeared. Lestrade uttered another startled oath. I tapped the back of the canvas stretched tightly between the forward legs of the coffee-table. The books and the rug bulged and rippled, and the illusion, nearly perfect as it had been, was instantly dispelled.

Jory Hull had painted the nothing under his father's coffee-table, had crouched behind the nothing as his father entered the room, locked the door, and sat at his desk with his two wills, and at last had rushed out from behind the nothing, dagger in hand.

"He was the only one who could execute such an extraordinary piece of realism," I said, this time running my hand down the face of the canvas. We could all hear the low rasping sound it made, like the purr of a very old cat. "The only one who could execute it, and the only one who could hide behind it: Jory Hull, who was no more than five feet tall, bow-legged, slump-shouldered.

"As Holmes said, the surprise of the new will was no surprise. Even if the old man had been secretive about the possibility of cutting the relatives out of the will, which he wasn't, only simpletons could have mistaken the import of the visit from the solicitor and, more important, the assistant. It takes two witnesses to make a will a valid document at Chancery. What Holmes said about some people preparing for disaster was very true. A canvas as perfect as this was not made overnight, or in a month. You may find he had it ready, should it need to be used, for as long as a year—"

"Or five," Holmes interpolated.

"I suppose. At any rate, when Hull announced that he wanted to see his family in the parlour this morning, I imagine Jory knew the time had come. After his father had gone to bed last night, he would have come down here and mounted his canvas. I suppose he may have put down the *faux* shadows at the same time, but if I had been Jory I should have tip-toed in here for another peek at the glass this morning, before the previously announced parlour gathering, just to make sure it was still rising. If the door was locked, I suppose he filched the key from his father's pocket and returned it later."

"Wasn't locked," Lestrade said laconically. "As a rule he kept the door shut to keep the cats out, but rarely locked it."

"As for the shadows, they are just strips of felt, as you now see. His eye was good, they are about where they would have been at eleven this morning... if the glass had been right."

"If he expected the sun to be shining, why did he put down shadows at all?" Lestrade grumped. "Sun puts 'em down as a matter of course, just in case you've never noticed your own, Watson."

Here I was at a loss. I looked at Holmes, who seemed grateful to have *any* part in the answer.

"Don't you see? That is the greatest irony of all! If the sun had shone as the glass suggested it would, the canvas would have *blocked* the shadows. Painted shadow-legs don't cast them, you know. He was caught by shadows on a day when there were none because he was afraid he would be caught by none on a day when his father's barometer said they would almost certainly be everywhere else in the room."

"I still don't understand how Jory got in here without Hull seeing him," Lestrade said.

"That puzzles me as well," Holmes said—dear old Holmes! I doubt that it puzzled him a bit, but that was what he said. "Watson?"

"The parlour where Lord Hull met with his wife and sons has a door which communicates with the music room, does it not?"

"Yes," Lestrade said, "and the music room has a door which communicates with Lady Hull's morning room, which is next in line as one goes toward the back of the house. But from the morning room one can only go back into the hall, Doctor Watson. If there had been *two* doors into Hull's study, I should hardly have come after Holmes on the run as I did."

He said this last in tones of faint self-justification.

"Oh, Jory went back into the hall, all right," I said, "but his father didn't see him."

"Rot!"

"I'll demonstrate," I said, and went to the writing-desk, where the dead man's cane still leaned. I picked it up and turned toward them. "The very instant Lord Hull left the parlour, Jory was up and on the run."

Lestrade shot a startled glance at Holmes; Holmes gave the inspector a cool, ironic look in return. I did not understand those looks then, nor give them much thought at all, if the whole truth be told. I did not fully understand the wider implications of the picture I was drawing for yet a while. I was too wrapped up in my own re-creation, I suppose.

"He nipped through the first connecting door, ran across the music room, and entered Lady Hull's morning room. He went to the hall door then and peeked out. If Lord Hull's gout had gotten so bad as to have brought on gangrene, he would have progressed no more than a quarter of the way down the hall, and that is optimistic. Now mark me, Inspector Lestrade, and I will show you the price a man pays for a lifetime of rich food and strong drink. If you harbour any doubts when I've done, I shall parade a dozen gout sufferers before you, and each one will show the same ambulatory symptoms I now intend to demonstrate. Please notice above all how fixed my attention is... and *where*"

With that I began to stump slowly across the room toward them, both hands clamped tightly on the ball of the cane. I would raise one foot quite high, bring it down, pause, and then draw the other leg along. Never did my eyes look up. Instead, they alternated between the cane and that forward foot.

"Yes," Holmes said quietly. "The good doctor is exactly right, Inspector Lestrade. The gout comes first; then the loss of balance; then (if the sufferer lives long enough), the characteristic stoop brought on by always looking down."

"Jory would have been very aware of how his father fixed his attention when he walked from place to place," I said. "As a result, what happened this morning was diabolically simple. When Jory reached the morning room, he peeped out the door, saw his father studying his feet and the tip of his cane—just as always—and knew he was safe. He stepped out, *right in front of his unseeing father,* and simply nipped into the study. The door, Lestrade informs us, was unlocked, and really, how great would the risk have been? They were in the hall together for no more than three seconds, and probably a little less." I paused. "That hall floor is marble, isn't it? He must have kicked off his shoes."

"He was wearing slippers," Lestrade said in a strangely calm tone of voice, and for the second time, his eyes met Holmes's.

"Ah," I said. "I see. Jory gained the study well ahead of his father and hid behind his cunning stage-flat. Then he withdrew the dagger and waited. His father reached the end of the hall. Jory heard Stanley call down to him, and heard his father call back that he was fine. Then Lord Hull entered his study for the last time... closed the door... and locked it."

They were both looking at me intently, and I understood some of the godlike power Holmes must have felt at moments like these, telling others what only he could know. And yet, I must repeat that it is a feeling I should not have wanted to have too often. I believe the urge to repeat such a feeling would have corrupted most men—men with less iron in their souls than was possessed by my friend Sherlock Holmes.

"Old Keg-Legs would have made himself as small as possible before the locking-up happened, perhaps knowing (or only suspecting) that his father would have one good look round before turning the key and shooting the bolt. He may have been gouty and going a bit soft about the edges, but that doesn't mean he was going blind."

"Stanley says his eyes were top-hole," Lestrade said. "One of the first things I asked."

"So he looked round," I said, and suddenly I could *see* it, and I suppose this was also the way it was with Holmes; this reconstruction which, while based only upon facts and deduction, seemed to be half a vision. "He saw nothing to alarm him; nothing but the study as it always was, empty save for himself. It is a remarkably open room—I see no closet door, and with the windows on both sides, there are no dark nooks and crannies even on such a day as this.

"Satisfied that he was alone, he closed the door, turned his key, and shot the bolt. Jory would have heard him stump his way across to the desk. He would have heard the heavy thump and wheeze of the chair cushion as his father landed on it—a man in whom gout is well-advanced does not sit so much as position himself over a soft spot and then drop onto it, seat-first—and then Jory would at last have risked a look out."

I glanced at Holmes.

"Go on, old man," he said warmly. "You are doing splendidly. Absolutely first rate." I saw he meant it. Thousands would have called him cold, and they would not have been wrong, precisely, but he also had a large heart. Holmes simply protected it better than most men do.

"Thank you. Jory would have seen his father put his cane aside, and place the papers—the two packets of papers—on the blotter. He did not kill his father immediately, although he could have done; that's what's so gruesomely pathetic about this business, and that's why I wouldn't go into that parlour where they are for a thousand pounds. I wouldn't go in unless you and your men dragged me."

"How do you know he didn't do it immediately?" Lestrade asked.

"The scream came several minutes after the key was turned and the bolt drawn; you said so yourself, and I assume you have enough testimony on that point not to doubt it. Yet it can only be a dozen long paces from door to desk. Even for a gouty man like Lord Hull, it would have taken half a minute, forty seconds at the outside, to cross to the chair and sit down. Add fifteen seconds for him to prop his cane where you found it, and put his wills on the blotter.

"What happened then? What happened during that last minute or two, a short time which must have seemed—to Jory Hull, at least—almost endless? I believe Lord Hull simply sat there, looking from one will to the other. Jory would have been able to tell the difference between the two easily enough; the differing colours of the parchment would have been all the clew he needed.

"He knew his father intended to throw *one* of them into the stove; I believe he waited to see which one it would be. There was, after all, a chance that the old devil was only having a cruel practical joke at his family's expense. Perhaps he would burn the new will, and put the old one back in the safe. Then he could have left the room and told his family the new will was safely put away. Do you know where it is, Lestrade? The safe?"

"Five of the books in that case swing out," Lestrade said briefly, pointing to a shelf in the library area.

"Both family and old man would have been satisfied then; the family would have known their earned inheritances were safe, and the old man would have gone to his grave believing he had perpetrated one of the cruellest practical jokes of all time... but he would have gone as God's victim or his own, and not Jory Hull's."

Yet a third time that queer look, half-amused and half-revolted, passed between Holmes and Lestrade.

"Myself, I rather think the old man was only savouring the moment, as a man may savour the prospect of an after-dinner drink in the middle of the afternoon or a sweet after a long period of abstinence. At any rate, the minute passed, and Lord Hull began to rise... but with the darker parchment in his hand, and facing the stove rather than the safe. Whatever his hopes may have been, there was no hesitation on Jory's part when the moment came. He burst from hiding, crossed the distance between the coffee-table and the desk in an instant, and plunged the knife into his father's back before he was fully up.

"I suspect the post-mortem will show the thrust clipped through the heart's right ventricle and into the lung—that would explain the quantity of blood expelled onto the desktop. It also explains why Lord Hull was able to scream before he died, and that's what did for Mr. Jory Hull."

"How so?" Lestrade asked.

"A locked room is a bad business unless you intend to pass murder off as sui-cide," I said, looking at Holmes. He smiled and nodded at this maxim of his. "The last thing Jory would have wanted was for things to look as they did... the locked room, the locked windows, the man with a knife in him where the man himself never could have put it. I think he had never foreseen his father dying with such a squawl. His plan was to stab him, burn the new will, rifle the desk, unlock one of the windows, and escape that way. He would have entered the house by another door, resumed his seat under the stairs, and then, when the body was finally discovered, it would have looked like robbery."

"Not to Hull's solicitor," Lestrade said.

"He might well have kept his silence, however," Holmes mused, and then added brightly, "I'll bet our artistic friend intended to add a few tracks, too. I have found that the better class of murderer almost always likes to throw in a few mysterious tracks leading away from the scene of the crime." He uttered a brief, humourless sound that was more bark than laugh, then looked back from the window nearest the desk to Lestrade and me. "I think we all agree it would have seemed a suspiciously convenient murder, under the circumstances, but even if the solicitor spoke up, nothing could have been *proved*."

"By screaming, Lord Hull spoiled everything," I said, "as he had been spoiling things all his life. The house was roused. Jory must have been in a total panic, frozen to the spot the way a deer is by a bright light. It was Stephen Hull who saved the day… or Jory's alibi, at least, the one which had him sitting on the bench under the stairs when his father was murdered. Stephen rushed down the hall from the music room, smashed the door open, and must have hissed at Jory to get over to the desk with him, at once, so it would look as if they had broken in togeth—"

I broke off, thunderstruck. At last I understood the glances which had been flashing between Holmes and Lestrade. I understood what they must have seen from the moment I showed them the trick hiding place: *it could not have been done alone.* The killing, yes, but the rest…

"Stephen said he and Jory met at the study door," I said slowly. "That he, Stephen, burst it in and they entered together, discovered the body together. He lied. He might have done it to protect his brother, but to lie so well when one doesn't know what has happened seems… seems…"

"*Impossible*," Holmes said, "is the word for which you are searching, Watson."

"Then Jory and Stephen went in on it together," I said. "They planned it together… and in the eyes of the law, both are guilty of their father's murder! My God!"

"Not both of them, my dear Watson," Holmes said in a tone of curious gentleness. "*All* of them."

I could only gape.

He nodded. "You have shown remarkable insight this morning, Watson; you have, in fact, burned with a deductive heat I'll wager you'll never generate again. My cap is off to you, dear fellow, as it is to any man who is able to transcend his normal nature, no matter how briefly. But in one way you have remained the same dear chap you've always been: while you understand how good people can be, you have no understanding of how black they *may* be."

I looked at him silently, almost humbly.

"Not that there was much blackness here, if half of what we've heard of Lord Hull was true," Holmes said. He rose and began to pace irritably about the study. "Who testifies that Jory was with Stephen when the door was smashed in? Jory, naturally. Stephen, naturally. But there are two other faces in this family portrait. One belongs to William, the third brother. Do you concur, Lestrade?"

"Yes," Lestrade said. "If this is the straight of the matter, William also had to be in on it. He said he was halfway down the stairs when he saw the two of them go in together, Jory a little ahead."

"How interesting!" Holmes said, eyes gleaming. "*Stephen* breaks in the door—as the younger and stronger of course he must—and so one would expect simple forward momentum would have carried him into the room first. Yet William, halfway down the stairs, saw *Jory* enter first. Why was that, Watson?"

I could only shake my head numbly.

"Ask yourself whose testimony, *and whose testimony alone,* we can trust here. The answer is the only witness who is not part of the family: Lord Hull's man, Oliver Stanley. He approached the gallery railing in time to see Stephen enter the room, and that is just as it should have been, since Stephen was alone when he broke it in. It was *William,* with a better angle from his place on the stairs, who said he saw Jory precede Stephen into the study. William said so because he had seen Stanley and knew what he *must* say. It boils down to this, Watson: we know Jory was inside this room. Since both of his brothers testify he was *outside,* there was, at the very least, collusion. But as you say, the smooth way they all pulled together suggests something far more serious."

"Conspiracy," I said.

"Yes. Do you recall my asking you, Watson, if you believed all four of them simply walked wordlessly out of that parlour in four different directions after they heard the study door locked?"

"Yes. Now I do."

"The *four* of them." He looked briefly at Lestrade, who nodded, and then back at me. "We know Jory had to have been up and off and about his business the moment the old man left the parlour in order to reach the study ahead of him, yet all four of the surviving family—including Lady Hull—say they were in the parlour when Lord Hull locked his study door. The murder of Lord Hull was very much a family affair, Watson."

I was too staggered to say anything. I looked at Lestrade and saw an expression on his face I had never seen there before nor ever did again; a kind of tired sickened gravity.

"What may they expect?" Holmes said, almost genially.

"Jory will certainly swing," Lestrade said. "Stephen will go to jail for life. William Hull may get life, but will more likely get twenty years in Wormwood Scrubs, a kind of living death."

Holmes bent and stroked the canvas stretched between the legs of the coffee-table. It made that odd hoarse purring noise.

"Lady Hull," Lestrade went on, "may expect to spend the next five years of her life in Beechwood Manor, more commonly known to the inmates as Poxy Palace... although, having met the lady, I rather suspect she will find another way out. Her husband's laudanum would be my guess."

"All because Jory Hull missed a clean strike," Holmes remarked, and sighed. "If the old man had had the common decency to die silently, all would have been well. Jory would, as Watson says, have left by the window, taking his canvas with him, of course... not to mention his trumpery shadows. Instead, he raised the house. All the servants were in, exclaiming over the dead master. The family was in confusion. How shabby their luck was, Lestrade! How close was the constable when Stanley summoned him?"

"Closer than you would believe," Lestrade said. "Hurrying up the drive to the door, as a matter of fact. He was passing on his regular rounds, and heard a scream from the house. Their luck *was* shabby."

"Holmes," I said, feeling much more comfortable in my old role, "how did you know a constable was so nearby?"

"Simplicity itself, Watson. If not, the family would have shooed the servants out long enough to hide the canvas and 'shadows.'"

"Also to unlatch at least one window, I should think," Lestrade added in a voice uncustomarily quiet.

"They *could* have taken the canvas and the shadows," I said suddenly.

Holmes turned toward me. "Yes."

Lestrade raised his eyebrows.

"It came down to a choice," I said to him. "There was time enough to burn the new will or get rid of the hugger-mugger... this would have been just Stephen and Jory, of course, in the moments after Stephen burst in the door. They—or, if you've got the temperature of the characters right, and I suppose you do, *Stephen*—decided to burn the will and hope for the best. I suppose there was just enough time to chuck it into the stove."

Lestrade turned, looked at it, then looked back. "Only a man as black as Hull would have found strength enough to scream at the end," he said.

"Only a man as black as Hull would have required a son to kill him," Holmes rejoined.

He and Lestrade looked at each other, and again something passed between them, some perfectly silent communication from which I myself was excluded.

"Have you ever done it?" Holmes asked, as if picking up on an old conversation.

Lestrade shook his head. "Once came damned close," he said. "There was a girl involved, not her fault, not really. I came close. Yet... that was only one."

"And here there are four," Holmes returned, understanding him perfectly. "Four people ill-used by a villain who should have died within six months anyway."

At last I understood what they were discussing.

Holmes turned his gray eyes on me. "What say you, Lestrade? Watson has solved this one, although he did not see all the ramifications. Shall we let Watson decide?"

"All right," Lestrade said gruffly. "Just be quick. I want to get out of this damned room."

Instead of answering, I bent down, picked up the felt shadows, rolled them into a ball, and put them in my coat pocket. I felt quite odd doing it: much as I had felt when in the grip of the fever which almost took my life in India.

"Capital fellow, Watson!" Holmes cried. "You've solved your first case, become an accessory to murder, and it's not even tea-time! And here's a souvenir for my-self—an original Jory Hull. I doubt it's signed, but one must be grateful for whatever the gods send us on rainy days." He used his penknife to loosen the artist's glue holding the canvas to the legs of the coffee-table. He made quick work of it; less than a minute later he was slipping a narrow canvas tube into the inner pocket of his voluminous greatcoat.

"This is a dirty piece of work," Lestrade said, but he crossed to one of the windows and, after a moment's hesitation, released the locks which held it and opened it half an inch or so.

"Say it's dirty work undone," Holmes said in a tone of almost hectic gaiety. "Shall we go, gentlemen?"

We crossed to the door. Lestrade opened it. One of the constables asked him if there was any progress.

On another occasion Lestrade might have shown the man the rough side of his tongue. This time he said shortly, "Looks like attempted robbery gone to something worse. I saw it at once, of course; Holmes a moment later."

"Too bad!" the other constable ventured.

"Yes," Lestrade said, "but at least the old man's scream sent the thief packing before he could steal anything. Carry on."

We left. The parlour door was open, but I kept my head down as we passed it. Holmes looked, of course; there was no way he could not have done. It was just the way he was made. As for me, I never saw any of the family. I never wanted to.

Holmes was sneezing again. His friend was twining around his legs and miaow-ing blissfully. "Let me out of here," he said, and bolted.

An hour later we were back at 221B Baker Street, in much the same positions we had occupied when Lestrade came driving up: Holmes in the window-seat, myself on the sofa.

"Well, Watson," Holmes said presently, "how do you think you'll sleep to-night?"

"Like a top," I said. "And you?"

"Likewise, I'm sure," he said. "I'm glad to be away from those damned cats, I can tell you that."

"How will Lestrade sleep, d'you think?"

Holmes looked at me and smiled. "Poorly tonight. Poorly for a week, perhaps. But then he'll be all right. Among his other talents, Lestrade has a great one for creative forgetting."

That made me laugh.

"Look, Watson!" Holmes said. "Here's a sight!" I got up and went to the window, somehow sure I would see Lestrade riding up in the wagon once more. Instead I saw the sun breaking through the clouds, bathing London in a glorious late-afternoon light.

"It came out after all," Holmes said. "Marvellous, Watson! Makes one happy to be alive!" He picked up his violin and began to play, the sun strong on his face.

I looked at his barometer and saw it was falling. That made me laugh so hard I had to sit down. When Holmes asked—in tones of mild irritation—what the matter was, I could only shake my head. I am not, in truth, sure he would have understood, anyway. It was not the way his mind worked.

THE HORROR OF THE MANY FACES

by Tim Lebbon

Tim Lebbon's latest novel is *Bar None*, a novel of "chilling suspense, apocalyptic beauty and fine ales." Other recent work includes *The Island*, and forthcoming is an original *30 Days of Night* novel, which is due out early next year, as is *Tell My Sorrows to the Stones*, a collaboration with Christopher Golden. Lebbon is a *New York Times* bestselling author, and the winner of the Stoker Award, and three British Fantasy Awards.

Our next tale is the first of three in this volume to come to us from *Shadows Over Baker Street*, a book of stories that blend the world of Sherlock Holmes with the Cthulhu Mythos of H. P. Lovecraft. Lovecraft was perhaps the most influential horror writer of the twentieth century. He was a scholar of weird fiction, having written a pioneering survey called *Supernatural Horror in Literature*, and his own groundbreaking fiction appeared mostly in the pulp magazine *Weird Tales*. For centuries horror stories had been bound up with notions of eternal damnation, and Lovecraft, a committed philosophical materialist, felt that such notions had become hokey and shopworn. Edwin Hubble's startling discovery that our galaxy was just one of billions had inspired Lovecraft to write a new kind of horror story—tales set in a vast, incomprehensible universe, where human beings were tiny and insignificant, and in danger at any moment of being snuffed out by vast, uncaring forces. Holmes says, "When you eliminate the impossible, whatever remains, however improbable, must be the truth." Lovecraft felt that the truth would drive us to insanity. Where these two worldviews collide, our next story begins.

What I saw that night defied belief, but believe it I had to because I trusted my eyes. *Seeing is believing* is certainly not an axiom that my friend would have approved of, but I was a doctor, a scientist, and for me the eyes were the most honest organs in the body.

I never believed that they could lie.

What I laid eyes upon in the murky London twilight made me the saddest man. It stripped any faith I had in the order of things, the underlying goodness of life. How can something so wrong exist in an ordered world? How, if there is a benevolent purpose behind everything, can something so insane exist?

These are the questions I asked then and still ask now, though the matter is resolved in a far different way from that which I could ever have imagined at the time.

I was on my way home from the surgery. The sun was setting into the murk of the London skyline, and the city was undergoing its usual dubious transition from light to dark. As I turned a corner into a narrow cobbled street I saw my old friend, my mentor, slaughtering a man in the gutter. He hacked and slashed with a blade that caught the red twilight, and upon seeing me he seemed to calm and perform some meticulous mutilation upon the twitching corpse.

I staggered against the wall. "Holmes!" I gasped

He looked up, and in his honest eyes there was nothing. No light, no twinkle, not a hint of the staggering intelligence that lay behind them.

Nothing except for a black, cold emptiness.

Stunned into immobility, I could only watch as Holmes butchered the corpse. He was a man of endless talents, but still I was amazed at the dexterity with which he opened the body, extracted the heart and wrapped it in his handkerchief.

No, not butchery. *Surgery.* He worked with an easy medical knowledge that appeared to surpass my own.

Holmes looked up at me where I stood frozen stiff. He smiled, a wicked grin that looked so alien on his face. Then he stood and shrugged his shoulders, moving on the spot as if settling comfortably into a set of new clothes.

"Holmes," I croaked again, but he turned and fled.

Holmes the thinker, the ponderer, the genius, ran faster than I had ever seen anyone run before. I could not even think to give chase, so shocked was I with what I had witnessed. In a matter of seconds my outlook on life had been irrevocably changed, brought to ground and savaged with a brutality I had never supposed possible. I felt as if I had been shot, hit by a train, mauled. I was winded and dizzy and ready to collapse at any moment.

But I pinched myself hard on the back of my hand, drawing blood and bringing myself around.

I closed my eyes and breathed in deeply, but when I opened them again the corpse still lay there in the gutter. Nothing had changed. However much I desired to not see this, wished it would flee my memory, I was already realising that this would never happen. This scene was etched on my mind.

One of the worst feelings in life is betrayal, the realisation that everything one held true is false, or at least fatally flawed. That look in Holmes's eyes... I would have given anything to be able to forget that.

His footsteps had vanished into the distance. The victim was surely dead, but being a doctor I had to examine him to make sure. He was a young man, handsome, slightly foreign-looking, obviously well-appointed in society because of the tasteful rings on his fingers, the tailored suit… holed now, ripped and ruptured with the vicious thrusts of Holmes's blade. And dead, of course. His chest had been opened and his heart stolen away.

Perhaps he was a dreadful criminal, a murderer in his own right whom Holmes had been tracking, chasing, pursuing for days or weeks? I spent less time with Holmes now than I had in the past, and I was not involved in every case he took on. But… murder? Not Holmes. Whatever crime this dead man may have been guilty of, nothing could justify what my friend had done to him.

I suddenly had an intense feeling of guilt, kneeling over a corpse with fresh blood on my fingertips. If anyone rounded the corner at that moment I would have trouble explaining things, I was sure, not only because of the initial impression they would gain but also the shock I was in, the *terror* I felt at what I had witnessed.

The police should have been informed. I should have found a policeman or run to the nearest station, led them to the scene of the crime. I was probably destroying valuable evidence… but then I thought of Holmes, that crazy grin, and realised that I already knew the identity of the murderer.

Instead, something made me run. Loyalty to my old friend was a small part of it, but there was fear as well. I knew even then that things were not always as they seemed. Holmes had told me that countless times before, and I kept thinking *impossible, impossible* as I replayed the scene in my mind. But I trusted my eyes, I knew what I had seen. And in my mind's eye Holmes was still grinning manically… at me.

With each impact of my feet upon the pavement, the fear grew.

Holmes was the most brilliant man I had ever known. And even in his obvious madness, I knew that he was too far beyond and above the ordinary to ever be outsmarted, outwitted or tracked down. *If his spree is to continue,* I prayed, *please God don't let him decide to visit an old friend.*

I need not have worried about informing the police of the murder. They knew already.

The day following my terrible experience I begged sick, remaining at home in bed, close to tears on occasion as I tried to find room in my life for what I had seen. My thoughts were very selfish, I admit that, because I had effectively lost my very best friend to a horrendous madness. I could never have him back. My mind wandered much that day, going back to the times we had spent together and forward to the barren desert of existence which I faced without him. I liked my surgery, enjoyed my life… but there was a terrible blandness about things without the promise of Holmes being a part of it.

I mourned, conscious all the time of the shape of my army revolver beneath my pillow.

Mixed in with this was the conviction that I should tell the police of what I had seen. But then the evening papers came and somehow, impossibly, the terrible became even worse.

There had been a further six murders in the London streets the previous night, all very similar in execution and level of violence. In each case organs had been re-moved from the bodies, though not always the same ones. The heart from one, lungs from another, and a dead lady in Wimbledon had lost her brain to the fiend.

In four cases—including the murder I had witnessed—the stolen organs had been found somewhere in the surrounding areas. Sliced, laid out on the ground in very neat order, the sections sorted perfectly by size and thickness. Sometimes masticated gobs of the tissue were found as well, as if bitten off, chewed and spat out. Tasted. *Tested*.

And there were witnesses. Not to every murder, but to enough of them to make me believe that the murderer—Holmes, I kept telling myself, Holmes—wanted to be seen. Though here lay a further mystery: each witness saw someone different. One saw a tall, fat man, heavily furred with facial hair, dressed scruffy and grim. Another described a shorter man with decent clothes, a light cloak and a sword in each hand. The third witness talked of the murderous lady he had seen… the lady with great strength, for she had stood her victim against a wall and wrenched out the unfortunate's guts.

A mystery, yes, but only for a moment. Only until my knowledge of Holmes's penchant for disguise crept in, instantly clothing my memory of him from the previous night in grubby clothes, light cloak and then a lady's dress.

"Oh dear God," I muttered. "Dear God, Holmes, what is it my old friend? The cocaine? Did the stress finally break you? The strain of having a mind that cannot rest, working with such evil and criminal matters?"

The more I dwelled upon it the worse it all became. I could not doubt what I had seen, even though all logic, all good sense forbade it. I tried reason and deduction as Holmes would have, attempting to ignore the horrors of the case to pare it down to its bare bone, setting out the facts and trying to fill in the missing pieces. But memory was disruptive; I could not help visualising my friend hunkered down over the body, hacking at first and then moving instantly into a caring, careful slicing of the dead man's chest. The blood. The strange smell in the air, like sweet honey (and a clue there, perhaps, though I could do nothing with it).

Holmes's terrible, awful smile when he saw me.

Perhaps that was the worst. The fact that he seemed to be *gloating*.

I may well have remained that way for days, my feigned sickness becoming some-thing real as my soul was torn to shreds by the truth. But on the evening of that first day following the crimes, I received a visit that spurred me to tell the truth.

Detective Inspector Jones, of Scotland Yard, came to my door looking for Holmes.

"It is a dreadful case," he said to me, "I've never seen anything like it." His face was pale with the memory of the corpses he must have been viewing that day. "Different witnesses saw different people, all across the south end of London. One man told me the murderer was his *brother*. And a woman, witness to another murder, was definitely withholding something personal to her. The murders themselves are so similar as to be almost identical in execution. The killing, then the extraction of an organ."

"It sounds terrible," I said lamely, because the truth was pressing to be spoken.

"It was," Jones nodded. Then he looked at me intently. "The papers did not say that at least three of the victims were alive when the organs were removed, and that was the method of their death."

"What times?" I asked.

"There was maybe an hour between the killings, from what we can work out. And yet different murderers in each case. And murderers who, I'm sure it will be revealed eventually, were *all* known to those bearing witness. Strange. *Strange!* Dr Watson, we've worked together before, you know of my determination. But this… this fills me with dread. I fear the sun setting tonight in case we have another slew of killings, maybe worse. How many nights of this will it take until London is in a panic? One more? Two? And I haven't a clue as to what it's all about. A sect, I suspect, made up of many members and needing these organs for some nefarious purpose of their own. But how to find them? I haven't a clue. Not a clue! And I'm sure, I'm certain, that your friend Sherlock Holmes will be fascinated with such a case."

Jones shook his head and slumped back in the armchair. He looked defeated already, I thought. I wondered what the truth would do to him. And yet I had to bear it myself, so I thought it only right to share. To *tell*. *Holmes, my old friend…* I thought fondly, and then I told Jones what I had seen.

He did not talk for several minutes. The shock on his face hid his thoughts. He stared into the fire as if seeking some alternate truth in there, but my words hung heavy, and my demeanour must have been proof enough to him that I did not lie.

"The different descriptions…" he said quietly, but I could sense that he had already worked that out.

"Disguises. Holmes is a master."

"Should I hunt Holmes? Seek him through the London he knows so well?"

"I do not see how," I said, because truly I thought ourselves totally out of control. Holmes would play whatever game he chose until its closure, and the resolution would be of his choosing. "He knows every street, every alley, shop to shop and door to door. In many cases he knows of who lives where, where they work and who they associate with. He can walk along a street and tell me stories of every house if he so chooses. He carries his card index in his brain, as well as boxed away at Baker Street. His mind… you know his mind, Mr Jones. It is *endless*."

"And you're sure, Dr Watson. Your illness has not blinded you, you haven't had hallucinations—"

"I am merely sick to the soul with what I have witnessed," I said. "I was fit and well yesterday evening."

"Then I must search him out," Jones said, but the desperation, the hopelessness in his voice told me that he had already given up. He stared into the fire some more and then stood, brushed himself down, a man of business again.

"I wish you luck," I said.

"Can you help?" Jones asked. "You know him better than anyone. You're his best friend. Have you any ideas, any reasoning as to why he would be doing these crimes, where he'll strike next?"

"None," I said. "It is madness, for sure." I wanted Jones gone then, out of my house and into the night. Here was the man who would hunt my friend, stalk him in the dark, send his men out armed and ready to shoot to kill if needs must. And whatever I had seen Holmes doing... that memory, *horrible*... I could not entertain the idea of his death.

Jones left and I jumped to my feet. He was right. I knew Holmes better than anyone, and after many years accompanying him as he had solved the most baffling of cases, I would hope that some of his intuition had rubbed off on me.

It was almost dark, red twilight kissing my window like diluted blood, and if tonight was to be like last night then my old friend was already stalking his first victim.

I would go to Baker Street. Perhaps there I would find evidence of this madness, and maybe even something that could bring hope of a cure.

The streets were very different that night.

There were fewer strollers, for a start. Many people had heard of the previous night's murders and chosen to stay at home. It was raining too, a fine mist that settled on one's clothes and soaked them instantly. Street lamps provided oases of half-light in the dark and it was these I aimed for, darting as quickly as I could between them. Even then, passing beneath the lights and seeing my shadow change direction, I felt more vulnerable than ever. I could not see beyond the lamps' meagre influence and it lit me up for anyone to see, any stranger lurking in the night, any *friend* with a knife.

I could have found my way to Baker Street in the dark. I walked quickly and surely, listening out for any hint of pursuit. I tried to see into the shadows but they retained their secrets well.

Everything felt changed. It was not only my new-found fear of the dark, but the perception that nothing, *nothing* is ever exactly as it seems. Holmes had always known that truth is in the detail, but could even he have ever guessed at the destructive parts in him, the corrupt stew of experience and knowledge and exhaustion that had led to this madness? It was a crueller London I walked through that night. Right and wrong had merged and blurred in my mind, for as sure as I was that what Holmes had done was wrong, it could never be right to hunt and kill him for it.

I had my revolver in my pocket, but I prayed with every step that I would not be forced to use it.

Shadows jumped from alleys and skirted around rooftops, but it was my imagination twisting the twilight. By the time I reached Baker Street it was fully dark, the moon a pale ghost behind London's smog.

I stood outside for a while, staring up at Holmes's window. There was no light there, of course, and no signs of habitation, but still I waited for a few minutes, safe in the refuge of memory. He would surely never attack here, not in the shadow of his long-time home. No, I feared that he had gone to ground, hidden himself away in some unknown, unknowable corner of London, or perhaps even taken his madness elsewhere in the country.

There was a sound behind me and I spun around, fumbling in my pocket for my revolver. It had been a shallow pop, as of someone opening their mouth in preparation to speak. I held my breath and aimed the revolver from my waist. There was nothing. The silence, the darkness felt loaded, brimming with secrets and something more terrible... something...

"Holmes," I said. But he would not be there, he was not foolish, not so stupid to return here when he was wanted for some of the most terrible murders—

"My friend."

I started, tried to gauge where the voice had come from. I tightened my grip on the pistol and swung it slowly left and right, ready to shoot should anything move. I was panicked, terrified beyond belief. My stomach knotted and cramped with the idea of a knife parting its skin and delving deeper.

"Is that you Holmes?"

More silence for a while, so that I began to think I was hearing things. It grew darker for a moment as if something had passed in front of the moon; I even glanced up, but there was nothing in the sky and the moon was its usual wan self.

"You feel it too!" the voice said.

"Holmes, please show yourself."

"Go to my rooms. Mrs Hudson hasn't heard of things yet, she will let you in and I will find my own way up there."

He did not sound mad. He sounded different, true, but not mad.

"Holmes, you have to know—"

"I am aware of what you saw, Watson, and you would do well to keep your revolver drawn and aimed ahead of you. Go to my rooms, back into a corner, hold your gun. For your sanity, your peace of mind, it has to remain between us for a time."

"I saw... Holmes, I saw..."

"My rooms."

And then he was gone. I did not hear him leave, caught sight of nothing moving away in the dark, but I knew that my old friend had departed. I wished for a torch to track him, but Holmes would have evaded the light. And in that thought I found my continuing belief in Holmes's abilities, his genius, his disregard for the normal levels of reasoning and measures of intelligence.

The madness he still had, but... I could not help but trust him.

From the distance, far, far away, I heard what may have been a scream. There were foxes in London, and thousands of wild dogs, and some said that wolves still roamed the forgotten byways of this sprawling city. But it had sounded like a human cry.

He could not possibly have run that far in such short a time.

Could he?

Mrs Hudson greeted me and was kind enough to ignore my preoccupation as

I climbed the stairs to Holmes's rooms.

There was another scream in the night before Holmes appeared.

I had opened the window and was standing there in the dark, looking out over London and listening to the sounds. The city was so much quieter during the night, which ironically made every sound that much louder. The barking of a dog swept across the neighbourhood, the crashing of a door echoed from walls and back again. The scream... this time it *was* human, I could have no doubt of that, and although even further away than the one I had heard earlier I could still make out its agony. It was followed seconds later by another cry, this one cut short. There was nothing else.

Go to my rooms, back into a corner, hold your gun, Holmes had said. I remained by the window. Here was escape, at least, if I needed it. I would probably break my neck in the fall, but at least I was giving myself a chance.

I've come to his rooms! I thought. Fly to a spider. Chicken to a fox's den. But even though his voice had been very different from usual—more *strained*—I could not believe that the Holmes who had spoken to me minutes before was out there now, causing those screams.

I thought briefly of Detective Inspector Jones, and hoped that he was well.

"I am sure that he is still alive," Holmes said from behind me. "He is too stupid to not be."

I spun around and brought up the revolver. Holmes was standing just inside the door. He had entered the room and closed the door behind him without me hearing. He was breathing heavily, as if he had just been running, and I stepped aside to let in the moonlight, terrified that I would see the black stain of blood on his hands and sleeves.

"How do you know I was thinking of Jones?" I asked, astounded yet again by my friend's reasoning.

"Mrs Hudson told me that he had been here looking for me. I knew then that you would be his next port of call in his search, and that you would inevitably have been forced by your high morals to relay what you have so obviously seen. You know he is out there now, hunting me down. And the scream... it sounded very much like a man, did it not?"

"Turn on the light, Holmes," I said.

I think he shook his head in the dark. "No, it will attract attention. Not that they do not know where we are... they must... fear, fear smells so sweet... to bees..."

"Holmes. Turn on the light or I will shoot you." And right then, standing in the room where my friend and I had spent years of our lives in pleasurable and business discourse, I was telling the truth. I was frightened enough to pull the trigger, because Holmes's intellect would bypass my archaic revolver, however mad he sounded. He would beat me. If he chose to—if he had lured me here to be his next victim—he would kill me.

"Very well," my friend said. "But prepare yourself Watson. It has been a somewhat eventful twenty-four hours."

The lamp flicked alight.

I gasped. He looked like a man who should be dead.

"Do not lower that revolver!" he shouted suddenly. "Keep it on me now, Watson. After what you think you saw me doing, lower your guard and you are likely to shoot me at the slightest sound or movement. That's right. Here. Aim it here." He thumped his chest and I pointed the gun that way, weak and shocked though I was.

"Holmes... you look terrible!"

"I feel worse." From Holmes that was a joke, but I could not even raise a smile. Indeed, I could barely draw a breath. Never had Holmes looked so unkempt, exhausted and bedraggled. His normally immaculate clothing was torn, muddied and wet, and his hair was sticking wildly away from his scalp. His hands were bloodied—I saw cuts there, so at least for the moment I could believe that it was his own blood—his cheek was badly scratched in several places and there was something about his eyes... wide and wild, they belied the calm his voice conveyed.

"You're mad," I said, unable to prevent the words from slipping out.

Holmes smiled, and it was far removed from that maniacal grin he had offered me as he crouched over the dying man.

"Do not jump to conclusions, Watson. Have you not learned anything in our years together?"

My hand holding the gun was starting to shake, but I kept it pointing at my friend across the room.

"I have to take you in, you know that? I will have to take you to the station. I cannot... I cannot..."

"Believe?"

I nodded. He was already playing his games, I knew. He would talk me around, offer explanations, convince me that the victims deserved to die or that he had been attacked... or that there was something far, far simpler eluding me. He would talk until he won me over, and then his attack would come.

"I cannot believe, but I must," I said, a new-found determination in my voice.

"Because you saw it? Because you *saw* me killing someone you must believe that I *did*, in fact, kill?"

"Of course."

Holmes shook his head. He frowned and for an instant he seemed distant, concentrating on something far removed from Baker Street. Then he glanced back at me, looked to the shelf above the fire and sighed.

"I will smoke my pipe, if you don't mind Watson. It will put my mind at rest. And I will explain what I know. Afterwards, if you still wish to take me in, do so. But you will thereby be condemning countless more to their deaths."

"Smoke," I said, "and tell me." *He was playing his games, playing them every second...*

Holmes lit a pipe and sat in his armchair, legs drawn up so that the pipe almost rested on his knees. He looked at the far wall, not at me where I remained standing by the window. I lowered the revolver slightly, and this time Holmes did not object.

I could see no knives, no mess on his hands other than his own smeared blood. No mess on his chin from the masticated flesh of the folks he had killed.

But that proved nothing.

"Have you ever looked into a mirror and really concentrated on the person you see there? Try it, Watson, it is an interesting exercise. After an hour of looking you see someone else. You see, eventually, what a stranger sees, not the composite picture of facial components with which you are so familiar, but individual parts of the face—the big nose, the close-together-eyes. You see yourself as a *person*. Not as *you*."

"So what are you trying to say?"

"I am saying that perception is not definite, nor is it faultless." Holmes puffed at his pipe, then drew it slowly away from his mouth. His eyes went wide and his brow furrowed. He had had some thought, and habit made me silent for a minute or two.

He glanced back up at me then, but said nothing. He looked more troubled than ever.

"I saw you killing a man, Holmes," I said. "You killed him and you laughed at me, and then you tore him open and stole his heart."

"The heart, yes," he said, looking away and disregarding me again. "The heart, the brain... parts, all part of the one... constituents of the same place..." He muttered on until his voice had all but vanished, though his lips still moved.

"Holmes!"

"It has gone quiet outside. They are coming." He said it very quietly, looked up at me from sad, terrified eyes, and I felt a cool finger run down my spine. *They're coming.* He did not mean Jones or the police, he did not mean *anyone*. No man scared Holmes as much as he was then.

"Who?" I asked. But he darted from his seat and ran at me, shoving me aside so that we stood on either side of the window.

"Listen to me, Watson. If you are my friend, if you have faith and loyalty and if you love me, you have to believe two things in the next few seconds if we are to survive: the first is that I am not a murderer; the second is that you must not trust your eyes, not for however long this may take. Instinct and faith, that is what you *can* believe in, because they cannot change that. It is too inbuilt, perhaps, too ingrained, I don't know..."

He was mumbling again, drifting in and out of coherence. And I knew that he could have killed me. He had come at me so quickly, my surprise was so complete, that I had plain forgotten the gun in my hand.

And now, the denial.

Doubt sprouted in my mind and grew rapidly as I saw the look on Holmes's face. I had seen it before, many times. It was the thrill of the chase, the excitement of discovery, the passion of experience, the knowledge that his reasoning had won out again. But underlying it all was a fear so profound that it sent me weak at the knees.

"Holmes, what are *they*?"

"You ask *What*, Watson, not *Who*. Already you're half way to believing. Quiet! Look! There, in the street!"

I looked. Running along the road, heading straight for the front door of Holmes's building, came Sherlock Holmes himself.

"I think they will come straight for me," Holmes whispered. "I am a threat."

"Holmes..." I could say little. The recent shocks had numbed me, and seemed now to be pulling me apart, hauling reality down a long, dark tunnel. I felt distanced from my surroundings even though, at that moment, I knew that I needed to be as alert and conscious of events as possible.

"Don't trust your eyes!" he hissed at me.

That man, he had been running like Holmes, the same loping stride, the same flick of the hair with each impact of foot upon pavement. The same look of determination on his face.

"Faith, Watson," Holmes said. "Faith in God if you must, but you *must* have faith in me, us, our friendship and history together. For there, I feel, will lie the answer."

There came the sound of heavy footsteps on the stairs.

"I will get them, it, the thing on the floor," Holmes said, "and you shoot it in the head. Empty your revolver, one shot may not be enough. Do not baulk, my friend. This thing here, tonight, is far bigger than just the two of us. It is London we're fighting for. Maybe more."

I could not speak. I wished Jones were there with us, someone else to make decisions and take blame. Faith, I told myself, faith in Holmes.

I had seen him kill a man.

Don't trust your eyes.

He was bloodied and dirtied from the chase, hiding from the crimes he had committed.

I am not a murderer.

And then the door burst open and Sherlock Holmes stood in the doorway lit by the lamp—tall, imposing, his clothes tattered and muddied, his face scratched, hands cut and bloodied—and I had no more time.

The room suddenly smelled of sweet honey, and turning my head slightly to look at the Holmes standing with me at the window, I caught sight of something from the corner of my eye. The Holmes in the doorway seemed to have some things buzzing about his head.

I looked straight at him and they were no more. Then he gave me the same smile I had seen as he murdered that man.

"Watson!" Holmes said, reaching across the window to grasp my arms. "Faith!"

And then the new visitor smashed the lamp with a kick, and leapt at us.

I backed away. The room was dark now, lit only by pale moonlight and the paler starlight filtering through London's constant atmosphere. I heard a grunt, a growl, the smashing of furniture and something cracking as the two Holmes tumbled into the centre of the room. I quickly became confused as to which was which.

"Away!" I heard one of them shout. "Get away! Get away!" He sounded utterly terrified. "Oh God, oh sanity, why us!"

I aimed my revolver but the shapes rolled and twisted, hands at each other's necks, eyes bulging as first one and then the other Holmes presented his face for me to shoot. I stepped forward nonetheless, still smelling that peculiar honey stench, and something stung my ankle, a tickling shape struggling inside my trousers. I slapped at it and felt the offender crushed against my leg.

Bees.

"Watson!" Holmes shouted. I pulled down the curtains to let in as much moonlight as I could. One Holmes had the other pinned to the floor, hands about his neck. "Watson, shoot it!" the uppermost Holmes commanded. His face was twisted with fear, the scratches on his cheek opened again and leaking blood. The Holmes on the floor thrashed and gurgled, choking, and as I looked down he caught my eye. Something there commanded me to watch, held my attention even as the Holmes on top exhorted me to *shoot,* shoot, *shoot it in the face!*

The vanquished Holmes calmed suddenly and brought up a hand holding a handkerchief. He wiped at the scratches on his face. They disappeared. The blood smudged a little, but with a second wipe it too had gone. The scratches were false, the blood fake.

The Holmes on top stared for a couple of seconds, and then looked back at me. A bee crawled out of his ear and up over his forehead. And then the scratches on his own cheek faded and disappeared before my eyes.

He shimmered. I saw something beneath the flesh-toned veneer, something crawling and writhing and separate, yet combined in a whole to present an image of solidness...

Bees left this whole and buzzed around the impostor's head. Holmes was still struggling on the floor, trying to prise away hands that were surely not hands.

The image pulsed and flickered in my vision, and I remembered Holmes's words: *you cannot trust your eyes... instinct and faith, that is what you can believe in...*

I stepped forward, pressed the revolver against the uppermost Holmes's head and pulled the trigger. Something splashed out across the floor and walls, but it was not blood.

Blood does not try to crawl away, take flight, buzz at the light.

My pulling the trigger—that act bridging doubt and faith—changed everything.

The thing that had been trying to kill Holmes shimmered in the moonlight. It was as if I was seeing two images being quickly flickered back and forth, so fast that my eyes almost merged them into one, surreal picture. Holmes... the thing... Holmes... the thing. And the thing, whatever it is, was monstrous.

"Again!" Holmes shouted. "Again, and again!"

I knelt so that my aim did not stray towards my friend and fired again at that horrible shape. Each impact twisted it, slowing down the alternating of images as if the bullets were blasting free truth itself. What I did not know then, but would realise later, was that the bullets were *defining* the truth. Each squeeze of the trigger dealt that thing another blow, not only physically but also in the nature of my beliefs. I *knew* it to be a false Holmes now, and that made it weak.

The sixth bullet hit only air.

It is difficult to describe what I saw in that room. I had only a few seconds to view its ambiguous self before it came apart, but even now I cannot find words to convey the very unreality of what I saw, heard and smelled. There was a honey tang on the air, but it was almost alien, like someone else's memory. The noise that briefly filled the room could have been a voice. If so it was speaking in an alien tongue, and I had no wish to understand what it was saying. A noise like that could only be mad.

All I know is that a few seconds after firing the last bullet Holmes and I were alone. I was hurriedly reloading and Holmes was already up, righting the oil lamp and giving us light. I need not have panicked so, because we were truly alone.

Save for the bees. Dead or dying, there were maybe a hundred bees spotting the fine carpet, huddled on the windowsill or crawling behind chairs or objects on the mantelpiece to die. I had been stung only once, Holmes seemed to have escaped entirely, but the bees were expiring even as we watched.

"Dear God," I gasped. I went to my knees on the floor, shaking, my shooting hand no longer able to bear the revolver's weight.

"Do you feel faint, my friend?" Holmes asked.

"Faint, no," I said. "I feel… belittled. Does that make sense, Holmes? I feel like a child who has been made aware of everything he will ever learn, all at once."

"There are indeed more things in Heaven and Earth, Watson," Holmes said. "And I believe we have just had a brush with one of them." He too had to sit, nursing his bruised throat with one hand while the other wiped his face with the handkerchief, removing any remaining make-up. He then cleaned the blood from both hands and washed away the false cuts there as well. He seemed distracted as he cleansed, his eyes distant, and more than once I wondered just where they were looking, what they were truly seeing.

"Can you tell me, Holmes?" I asked. I looked about the room, still trying to imagine where that other being had gone but knowing, in my heart of hearts, that its nature was too obscure for my meagre understanding. "Holmes? Holmes?"

But he was gone, his mind away as was its wont, searching the byways of his imagination, his intellect steering him along routes I could barely imagine as he tried to fathom the truth in what we had seen. I stood and fetched his pipe, loaded it with tobacco, lit it and placed it in his hand. He held on it but did not take a draw.

He remained like that until Jones of Scotland Yard thundered through the door.

"And you have been with him for how long?" Jones asked again.

"Hours. Maybe three."

"And the murderer? You shot him, yet where is he?"

"Yes, I shot him. It. I shot it."

I had told Jones the outline of the story three times, and his disbelief seemed to be growing with each telling. Holmes's silence was not helping his case.

Another five murders, Jones had told me. *Three witnessed, and each of the witnesses identified a close friend or family member as the murderer.*

I could only offer my own mutterings of disbelief. Even though I had an inkling now—however unreal, however unbelievable, Holmes's insistence that the improbable must follow the impossible stuck with me—I could not voice the details. The truth was too crazy.

Luckily, Holmes told it for me. He stirred and stood suddenly, staring blankly at me for a time as if he had forgotten I was there.

"Mr Holmes," Jones said. "Your friend Dr Watson here, after telling me that you were a murderer, is now protesting your innocence. His reasoning I find curious to say the least, so it would benefit me greatly if I could hear your take on the matter. There were gunshots here, and I have no body, and across London there are many more grieving folks this evening."

"And many more there will be yet," Holmes said quietly. "But not, I think, for a while." He relit his pipe and closed his eyes as he puffed. I could see that he was gathering his wits to expound his theories, but even then there was a paleness about him, a frown that did not belong on his face. It spoke of incomplete ideas, truths still hidden from his brilliant mind.

It did not comfort me one bit.

"It was fortunate for London, and perhaps for mankind itself, that I bore witness to one of the first murders. I had taken an evening stroll after spending a day performing some minor biological experiments on dead rodents, when I heard something rustling in the bushes of a front garden. It sounded larger than a dog, and when I heard what can only have been a cry I felt it prudent to investigate.

"What I saw... was impossible. I knew that it could not be. I pushed aside a heavy branch and witnessed an old man being operated on. He was dead by the time my gaze fell upon him, that was for sure, because the murderer had opened his guts and was busy extracting kidneys and liver. And the murderer, in my eyes, was the woman Irene Adler."

"No!" I gasped. "Holmes, what are you saying?"

"If you would let me continue, Doctor, all will become clear. Clearer, at least, because there are many facets to this mystery still most clouded in my mind. It *will* come, gentlemen, I am sure, but... I shall tell you. I shall talk it through, tell you, and the truth will mould itself tonight.

"And so: Adler, the woman herself, working on this old man in the garden of an up-market London house. Plainly, patently impossible and unreal. And being the logically minded person I am, and believing that *proof* defines truth rather than simply *belief*, I totally denied the truth of what I was seeing. I knew it could not be because Adler was a woman unfamiliar with, and incapable of, murder. And indeed she has not been in the country for quite some years now. My total disregard for what I was seeing meant that I was *not* viewing the truth, that something abnormal was occurring. And strange as it seemed at the time—but how clear it is now!—the woman had been heavily on my mind as I had been strolling down that street."

"Well to hear you actually admit that, Holmes, means that it is a great part of this mystery."

"Indeed," Holmes said to me, somewhat shortly. "My readiness to believe that something, shall we say, out of this world was occurring enabled me to see it. I saw the truth behind the murderer, the scene of devastation. I saw... I saw..." He trailed off, staring from the window at the ghostly night. Both Jones and I remained silent, seeing the pain Holmes was going through as he tried to continue.

"Terrible," he said at last. "Terrible."

"And what I saw," I said, trying to take up from where Holmes had left off, "was an impersonator, creating Holmes in his own image—"

"No," Holmes said. "No, it created me in *your* image, Watson. What you saw was your version of me. This *thing* delved into your mind and cloaked itself in the strongest identity it found in there: namely, me. As it is with the other murders, Mr Jones, whose witnesses no doubt saw brothers and wives and sons slaughtering complete strangers with neither rhyme, nor reason."

"But the murderer," Jones said. "Who was it? Where is he? I need a corpse, Holmes. Watson tells me that he shot the murderer, and I need a corpse."

"Don't you have enough already?" Holmes asked quietly. I saw the stare he aimed at Jones. I had never been the subject of that look, never in our friendship, but I had seen it used more than a few times. Its intent was borne of a simmering anger. Its effect, withering.

Jones faltered. He went to say something else, stammered and then backed away towards the door. "Will you come to the Yard tomorrow?" he asked. "I need help. And..."

"I will come," Holmes said. "For now, I imagine you have quite some work to do across London this evening. Five murders, you say? I guess at least that many yet to be discovered. And there must be something of a panic in the populace that needs calming."

Jones left. I turned to Holmes. And what I saw shocked me almost as much as any event from the previous twenty-four hours.

My friend was crying.

"We can never know everything," Holmes said, "but I fear that everything knows us."

We were sitting on either side of the fire. Holmes was puffing on his fourth pipe since Jones had left. The tear tracks were still unashamedly glittering on his cheeks, and my own eyes were wet in sympathy.

"What did it want?" I asked. "What motive?"

"Motive? Something so unearthly, so alien to our way of thinking and under-standing? Perhaps no motive is required. But I would suggest that examination was its prime concern. It was slaughtering and slicing and examining the victims just as casually as I have, these last few days, been poisoning and dissecting mice. The removed organs displayed that in their careful dismantling."

"But why? What reason can a thing like that have to know our make up, our build?"

Holmes stared into the fire and the flames lit up his eyes. I was glad. I could still remember the utter vacancy of the eyes I had seen on his likeness as it hunkered over the bloody body.

"Invasion," he muttered, and then he said it again. Or perhaps it was merely a sigh.

"Isn't it a major fault of our condition that, the more we wish to forget some-thing, the less likely it is that we can," I said. Holmes smiled and nodded, and I felt a childish sense of pride from saying something of which he seemed to approve.

"Outside," said Holmes, "beyond what we know or strive to know, there is a whole different place. Somewhere which, perhaps, our minds could never know. Like fitting a square block into a round hole, we were not built to understand."

"Even you?"

"Even me, my friend." He tapped his pipe out and refilled it. He looked ill. I had never seen Holmes so pale, so melancholy after a case, as if something vast had eluded him. And I think I realised what it was even then: understanding. Holmes had an idea of what had happened and it seemed to fit neatly around the event, but he did not *understand*. And that, more than anything, must have done much to depress him.

"You recall our time in Cornwall, our nightmare experience with the burning of the Devil's Foot powder?"

I nodded. "How could I forget."

"Not hallucinations," he said quietly. "I believe we were offered a drug-induced glimpse beyond. Not hallucinations, Watson. Not hallucinations at all."

We sat silently for a few minutes. As dawn started to dull the sharp edges of the darkness outside, Holmes suddenly stood and sent me away.

"I need to think on things," he said urgently. "There's much to consider. And I have to be more prepared for the next time. *Have* to be."

I left the building tired, cold and feeling smaller and more insignificant than I had ever thought possible. I walked the streets for a long time that morning. I smelled fear on the air, and one time I heard a bee buzzing from flower to flower on some honeysuckle. At that I decided to return home.

My revolver, still fully loaded, was warm where my hand grasped it in my coat pocket.

I walked along Baker Street every day for the next two weeks. Holmes was always in his rooms, I could sense that, but he never came out, nor made any attempt to contact me. Once or twice I saw his light burning and his shadow drifting to and fro inside, slightly stooped, as if something weighed heavy on his shoulders.

The only time I saw my brilliant friend in that time, I wished I had not. He was standing at the window staring out into the twilight, and although I stopped and waved he did not notice me.

He seemed to be looking intently across the rooftops as if searching for some elusive truth. And standing there watching him I felt sure that his eyes, glittering dark and so, so sad, must have been seeing nothing of this world.

THE CASE OF THE
BLOODLESS SOCK

by Anne Perry

Anne Perry is the bestselling, Edgar Award-winning author of many novels and two long-running Victorian-era mystery series; the first of these, which began with *The Cater Street Hangman*, chronicles the cases of police inspector Thomas Pitt, while the other, beginning with *The Face of a Stranger*, recounts the adventures of the amnesiac detective William Monk. Perry is also the author of a historical fiction series set during World War I (*No Graves As Yet*, et seq.), and two fantasy novels, *Tathea* and *Come Armageddon*. Her latest novels are *Buckingham Palace Gardens* and *Execution Dock*, with *A Christmas Promise* due in October.

Everyone knows Professor Moriarty as the arch-nemesis of Sherlock Holmes, but most people would probably be surprised to learn that Moriarty appeared in person in only one of Conan Doyle's Holmes stories, "The Final Problem." The author was ready to bring his Sherlock Holmes tales to a suitably dramatic conclusion, and Professor Moriarty—the Napoleon of crime, who pulls the strings of a vast criminal conspiracy—was invented to be a suitably imposing adversary, a match for the great detective, whose downfall would allow Sherlock Holmes to go out in a blaze of glory. (The character Moriarty was partially based on Adam Worth, a cultured master criminal who once stole a valuable Thomas Gainsborough painting only to discover that he liked the painting too much to sell it, which angered the men who had helped him steal it. Interestingly, Worth also—unlike Moriarty—ordered his men not to use violence in the course of their robberies.) Of course, the audience wanted more Holmes, and more Moriarty too, and so Moriarty has subsequently enjoyed a long and notorious career in books, film, and TV. Moriarty returns again in this next tale, with a characteristically diabolical scheme.

There had been no cases of any interest for some weeks, and my friend Sherlock Holmes was bored by the trivia that came his way. His temper showed it to the degree where I was happy to accept an invitation from an old friend, Robert Hunt, a widower who lived in the country, not far from the handsome city of Durham.

"By all means go, Watson," Holmes encouraged, except that that is far too joyful and heartening a word for the expression on his face that accompanied it. "Take the afternoon train," he added, scowling at the papers in front of him. "At this time of the year you will be in your village, wherever it is, before dark. Good-bye."

Thus was I dismissed. And I admit, I left without the pleasure I would have felt with a more sanguine farewell.

However the late summer journey northward from London toward the ever-widening countryside of Yorkshire, and then the climb to the dales, and the great, bare moors of County Durham, improved my spirits greatly. By the time I had taken the short, local journey to the village where Robert Hunt had his very fine house, I was smiling to myself, and fully sensitive to the peculiar beauty of that part of the world. There is nothing of the comfortable Home Counties about it, but rather a width, a great clarity of light, and rolling moorland where hill upon hill disappears into the distance, fading in subtle shades of blues and purples until the horizon melts into the sky. As I came over the high crest and looked down toward the village, it was as if I were on the roof of the world. I had almost a giddy feeling.

I had wired ahead to inform Hunt of my arrival. Imagine then, my dismay at finding no one to meet me at the deserted station, and being obliged to set out in the darkening air, chillier than I am accustomed to, being so much further north and at a considerable altitude, carrying my suitcase in my hand.

I had walked some four miles, and was worn out both from exertion and from temper, when an elderly man in a pony trap finally offered me a lift, which I accepted, and then arrived at Morton Grange tired, dusty and in far from my best humor.

I had barely set my feet upon the ground when a man I took to be a groom came running around the corner of the house, a wild hope lighting his face. "Have you found her?" he cried to me. From my bewilderment he understood immediately that I had not, and despair overtook him, the greater after his momentary surge of belief.

I was concerned for him and his obviously deep distress. "I regret I have not," I said. "Who is lost? Can I assist in your search?"

"Jenny!" he gasped. "Jenny Hunt, the master's daughter. She's only five years old! God knows where she is! She's been gone since four this afternoon, and it's near ten now. Whoever you are, sir, in pity's name, help me look—although where else there is to search I can't think."

I was appalled. How could a five-year-old child, and a girl at that, have wandered off and been gone for such a time? The light was fading rapidly and even if no harm had come to her already, soon she would be in danger from the cold, and surely terrified.

"Of course!" I said, dropping my case on the front step and starting toward him. "Where shall I begin?"

There followed one of the most dreadful hours I can remember.

My friend Robert Hunt acknowledged my presence, but was too distraught with fear for his only child to do more than thank me for my help, and then start once more to look again and again in every place we could think of. Servants had already gone to ask all the neighbors even though the closest was quarter of a mile away.

In the dark, lanterns were visible in every direction as more and more people joined in the search. We would not have given up had it taken all night. Not a man of us, nor a woman, for the female staff was all out too, even gave our comfort, our hunger or our weariness a thought.

Then at some time just after midnight there went up a great shout, and even at the distance I was, and unable to hear the words, the joy in it told me the child was found, and they believed her unhurt. I confess the overwhelming relief after such fear brought momentary tears to my eyes, and I was glad of the wind and the darkness to conceal them.

I ran toward the noise, and moments later I saw Hunt clasping in his arms a pale and frightened child who clung onto him frantically, but seemed in no way injured. A great cheer went up from all those who had turned out to search for her, and we all tramped back to the house where the cook poured out wine and spices into a great bowl, and the butler plunged a hot poker into it.

"Thanks be to God!" Hunt said, his voice shaking with emotion. "And to all of you, my dear friends." He looked around at us, shivering with cold still, hands numb, but face shining with happiness. We needed two hands each to hold the cups that were passed around, and the hot wine was like fire in our throats.

We quickly parted as relaxation took over, and the nursemaid, chattering with laughter and relief, took the child up to put her to bed.

It was not until the following morning—all of us having slept a trifle late—as Hunt and I were sitting over breakfast, that he looked at me earnestly and spoke of the mystery that still lay unaddressed.

"I am very exercised in my mind, Watson, as to how to deal with the matter for the best. Jenny is devoted to Josephine, the nursemaid. Yet how can I keep in my employ a servant who could allow a child of five to wander off and become lost? And yet if I dismiss her, Jenny will be desolated. The girl is all but a mother to her, and since her own mother died..." His voice broke for a moment and he required some effort to regain his composure. "Advise me, Watson!" he begged. "What can I do that will bring about the least harm? And yet be just... and not place Jenny in danger again?"

It was a problem that had already occurred to me, but I had not thought he would ask my counsel. I had observed for myself on the previous evening the nursemaid's care for the child, and the child's deep affection for her. Indeed after the first relief of being found, it was to her that she turned, even when her father still clung to her. It might well do her more hurt to part her from the only female companionship and care that she knew, than even the fear of being lost. She had already been bereaved once in her short life. In spite of last night's events I thought it a certain cruelty to dismiss the maid. Perhaps she would now be even more careful than any new employee would, and I was in the process of saying so, when the butler came in with a note for Hunt.

"This was just delivered, sir," he said grimly.

We had already received the post, and this had no stamp upon it, so obviously it had come by hand. Hunt tore it open, and as he read it I saw his face lose all its color and his hand shook as if he had a fever.

"What is it?" I cried, although it might well have been none of my affair.

Wordlessly he passed it across to me.

> Dear Mr. Hunt,
>
> Yesterday you lost your daughter, and last night at exactly twelve of the clock you received her back again. You may take any precautions you care to, but they will not prevent me from taking her again, any time I choose, and returning her when, and if I choose.
>
> And if it is my mind not to, then you, will never see her again.
>
> M.

I confess my own hand was shaking as I laid the piece of paper down. Suddenly everything was not the happy ending to a wretched mischance, it had become the beginning of a nightmare. Who was "M," but far more pressing than that, what did he want? He made no demand, it was simply a terrible threat, leaving us helpless to do anything about it, even to comply with his wishes, had that been possible. I looked across at my friend, and saw such fear in his face as I have only ever seen before when men faced death and had not the inner resolve prepared for it. But then a good man is always more vulnerable for those he loves than he is for himself.

Hunt rose from the table. "I must warn the servants," he said, gaining some control as he thought of action. "I have shotguns sufficient for all the outdoor staff, and we shall keep the doors locked and admit no one unknown to us. The windows have locks and I myself shall make the rounds every night to see that all is secure." He went to the door. "Excuse me, Watson, but I am sure you understand I must be about this matter with the utmost urgency."

"Of course," I agreed, rising also. My mind was racing. What would Sherlock Holmes do were he here? He would do more than defend, he would attack. He would discover all he could about the nature and identity of this creature who called himself "M." Hunt's mind was instantly concerned in doing all he could to protect the child, but I was free to apply my intelligence to the problem.

My medical experience has been with military men and the diseases and injuries of war, nevertheless I believe I may have a manner toward those who are frightened or ill which would set them at as much ease as possible. Therefore I determined to seek permission of the nursemaid, and see if I might speak with Jenny herself, and learn what she could tell me of her experience.

The maid was naturally deeply reluctant to pursue anything which might distress the child, of whom she was extraordinarily fond. I judged her to be an honest and good-hearted young woman such as anyone might choose to care for an infant who had lost her own mother. However the fact that I was a guest in the house, and above all that I was a doctor, convinced her that my intentions and my skill were both acceptable.

I found Jenny sitting at her breakfast of bread and butter cut into fingers, and a soft-boiled egg. I waited until she had finished eating before addressing her. She seemed to be little worse for her kidnap, but then of course she had no idea that the threat of that again, and worse, awaited her.

She looked at me guardedly, but without alarm, as long as her nursemaid stayed close to her.

"Good morning, Dr. Watson," she replied when I had introduced myself. I sat down on one of the small nursery chairs, so as not to tower over her. She was a beautiful child with very fair hair and wide eyes of an unusually dark blue.

"Are you all right after your adventure, yesterday night?" I asked her.

"Yes, I don't need any medicine," she said quickly. It seemed that her last taste of medicine was not one she wished to repeat.

"Good," I agreed. "Did you sleep well?"

The question did not appear to have much meaning for her. I had forgotten in the face of her solemn composure just how very young she was.

"You did not have bad dreams?" I asked.

She shook her head.

"I'm glad. Can you tell me what happened?"

"I was in the garden," she said, her eyes downcast.

"What were you doing there?" I pressed her. It was important that I learn all I could.

"Picking flowers," she whispered, then looked up at me to see how I took that. I gathered that was something she was not supposed to do.

"I see." I dismissed the subject and she looked relieved. "And someone came and spoke to you? Someone you did not know?"

She nodded.

"What did he look like? Do you remember?"

"Yes. He was old. He had no hair at the front," she indicated her brow. "His face was white. He is very big, but thin, and he talked a funny way."

"Was his hair white?" What was her idea of old?

She shook her head.

"What did you call him?" That might give some clue.

"Fessa," she replied.

"Fessa?" What an odd name.

"No!" she said impatiently. "P'fessa!" This time she emphasized the little noise at the beginning.

"Professor?" I said aghast.

She nodded. A ridiculous and horrible thought began to form in my mind. "He was thin, and pale, with a high forehead. Did he have unusual eyes?" I asked.

She shivered, suddenly the remembered fear returned to her. The nursemaid took a step closer and put her arms around the child, giving me a glare, warning me to go no further. In that moment I became convinced within myself that it was indeed Professor Moriarty that we were dealing with, and why he had kidnapped a child and returned her with a fearful warning, would in time become only too apparent.

"Where did he take you?" I asked with more urgency in my tone than I had intended.

She looked at me with anxiety. "A house," she said very quietly. "A big room."

How could I get her to describe it for me, without suggesting her answers so they would be of no value?

"Did you ride in a carriage to get there?" I began.

She looked uncertain, as if she could have said yes, and then no.

"In something else?" I guessed.

"Yes. A little kind of carriage, not like ours. It was cold."

"Did you go very far?"

"No."

I realized after I had said it that it was a foolish question. What was far in a child's mind? Holmes would chastise me for such a pointless waste of time.

"Was it warm in the room? Was there a fire?"

"No."

"Who was there, besides the Professor? Did they give you anything to eat?"

"Yes. I had teacakes with lots of butter." She smiled as she said that, apparently the memory was not unpleasant. But how could I get her to tell me something that would help find the place where she had been taken, or anything whatever which would be of use in preventing Moriarty from succeeding in his vile plan? "Did you go upstairs?" I tried.

She nodded. "Lots," she answered, looking at me solemnly. "I could see for miles and miles and miles out of the window."

"Oh?" I had no need to feign my interest. "What did you see?"

She described an entire scene for me with much vividness. I had no doubt as to at least the general area in which she had been held. It was a tall house, from the stairs she climbed, at least three stories, and situated a little to the west of the nearby village of Hampden. I thanked her profoundly, told her she was very clever, which seemed to please her, and hastened away to tell my friend Hunt of our advance in information. However I did not mention that I believed our enemy to be the infamous Moriarty.

"I have reason to think that the matter is of great gravity," I said as we sat in his study, he still ashen-faced and so beset with anxiety he was unable to keep from fidgeting first with a paper knife, then with a quill, scribbling as if he had ink in it but merely damaging the nib.

"What does he want?" he burst out in desperation. "I cannot even comply! He asks for nothing!"

"I would like your permission to go into the village and send a wire to my friend Sherlock Holmes," I replied. "I think he would involve himself in this matter willingly, and I know of no better chance in the world to detect any matter than to have his help."

His face lit with hope. "Would he? So simple a thing as a child who has been taken, and returned, with no ransom asked? It is hardly a great crime."

"It is a great crime to cause such distress," I said quite genuinely. "And the fact that he has asked no price, and yet threatened to do it again, is a mystery which I believe will intrigue him."

"Then call him, Watson, I beg you. I will have the trap sent around to the front to take you immediately. Ask him to come as soon as he may. I will reward him any and every way in my power, if there is any reward he will accept."

But I knew, of course, that the name of Moriarty would be sufficient to bring him, and so it turned out. I received a return wire within a few hours, saying that he would be there by the late train that evening, if someone would be good enough to meet him at the station. I spent the rest of the afternoon searching in the village of Hampden until I was sure that I had found the house Jenny had described, but I was careful to appear merely to be passing by on my way somewhere else, so if any watcher saw me it would cause no alarm.

In the evening I went to meet the train, and the moment it drew in and stopped amid clouds of steam, one door flew open and I saw Holmes' lean figure striding along the platform toward me. He looked a different man from the miserable figure I had left behind me in Baker Street. He reached me and said the one word, as if it were some magic incantation, his eyes alight. "Moriarty!"

I was suddenly afraid that I had miscalculated the situation, perhaps been too quick to leap to a conclusion. He so often charged me with precisely that fault. "I believe so," I said somewhat cautiously.

He gave me a quick glance. "You are uncertain. What makes you doubt, Watson? What has happened since you wired me?"

"Nothing!" I said hastily. "Nothing whatever. It is simply a deduction, not a known fact that it was he who took the child."

"Has any demand been received yet?" There was still interest in his voice, but I thought I detected a note of disappointment all the same.

"Not yet," I answered as we reached the gate to the lane where the trap was waiting. He climbed in and I drove it in silence through the winding, steep-banked roads, already shadowed in the sinking sun. I told him of my conversation with Jenny and all I had learned from it, also my location of the house, all of which he listened to without comment. I was certainly not going to apologize to him for having called him out on a matter which may not, after all, involve his archenemy. It involved the abduction of a child, which as far as I can see, is as important as any single case could be.

We were within quarter of a mile of the Grange when I saw in the dusk the gardener come running toward me, arms waving frantically. I pulled up, in case he should startle the pony and cause it to bolt. "Steady, man!" I shouted. "Whatever has happened?"

"She's gone again!" he cried while still some yards from me. He caught his breath in a sob. "She's gone!"

Instantly Holmes was all attention. He leaped out of the trap and strode to the wretched man. "I am Sherlock Holmes. Tell me precisely what has occurred. Omit no detail but tell me only what you have observed for yourself, or if someone has told you, give me their words as exactly as you can recall them."

The man made a mighty effort to regain control of himself, but his distress was palpable all the time he gasped out his story.

"The maid, Josephine, was with Jenny upstairs in the nursery. Jenny had been running around and had stubbed her toe quite badly. It was bleeding, so Josephine went to the cupboard in the dressing room where she keeps bandages and the like, and when she returned Jenny was gone. At first she was not concerned, because she had heard the hokey-pokey man outside the gates, and Jenny loves ice-cream, so she thought that she had run down for the kitchen maid to find him." He was so distraught he was gasping between his words. "But she wasn't there, and the kitchen maid said she hadn't seen her at all. We searched everywhere, upstairs and down…"

"But you did not find the child," Holmes finished for him, his own face grim.

"That's right! Please sir, in the name of heaven, if you can help us, do it! Find her for us! I know the master'll give that devil anything he wants, just so we get Jenny back again, an' not hurt."

"Where is the hokey-pokey man now?" Holmes asked.

"Percy? Why, he's right there with us, helping to look for her," the gardener replied.

"Is he local?"

"Yes. Known him most of my life. You're never thinking he would harm her? He wouldn't, but he couldn't either, because he's been here all the time."

"Then the answer lies elsewhere." Holmes climbed back into the trap. "Watson may know where she was taken the first time and we shall go there immediately. Tell your master what we have done, and continue your search in all other places. If it is indeed who we think, he will not be so obvious as to show us the place again, but we must look.

We drove with all speed to Hampden and I took Holmes to the street parallel with the one on which was the house. We searched it and found it empty. We had no time to lose in examining it closely, and only the carriage lantern with which to do it.

"She has not been here tonight," Holmes said bitterly, although we had not truly dared believe she would be. "We shall return in the morning to learn what we may."

We left to go back to the Grange to continue with any assistance we could. It was in turmoil as on the evening before, and as then, we joined the others seeking desperately for the child. Holmes questioned every one of the staff, both indoor and outdoor, and by nearly eleven o'clock we were exhausted and frantic with fear for her.

I found Holmes in the kitchen garden, having looked once again through the sheds and glass houses, holding a lantern up to see what the damp ground might tell him.

"This is a miserable business, Watson," he said, knowing my step and not bothering to raise the light to see. "There is something peculiarly vile about using a child to accomplish one's purposes. If it is in fact Moriarty, he has sunk very low indeed. But he must want something." He stared at me earnestly, the lamplight picking out the lines of his face, harsh with the anger inside him. I have never observed him show any special fondness for children, but the anguish caused to a parent had been only too clear for all to see. And Holmes despised a coward even more than he did a fool. Foolishness was more often than not an affliction of nature. Cowardice was a vice sprung from placing one's own safety before the love of truth, known as the safety and welfare of others. It is the essential selfishness, and as such he saw it as lying at the core of so much other sin.

"But he wants something, Watson. Moriarty never does anything simply because he has the power to do it. You say the child was returned last night, and this morning a note was delivered? There will be another note. He may choose to torture his victim by lengthening the process, until the poor man is so weak with the exhaustion of swinging from hope to despair and back, but sooner or later he will name his price. And you may be sure, the longer he waits, the higher the stakes he is playing for!

I tried to concentrate on what he was saying, but I was longing to take up my lantern again and renew my effort to find Jenny. After my conversation with her this morning she was no longer merely a lost child, she was a person for whom I had already grown a fondness, and I admit the thought of Moriarty using her in his plot nearly robbed me of sensible judgment. If I could have laid hands on him at that moment I might have beaten him to within an inch of his life—or closer even than that.

I walked what seemed to be miles, calling her name, stumbling over tussock and plowed field, scrambling through hedgerows and frightening birds and beasts in the little coppice of woodland. But I still returned to the house wretched and with no word of hope at all.

We were all gathered together in the kitchen, the indoor staff, the outdoor, Hunt, Holmes and myself. It was all but midnight. The cook brewed a hot, fresh pot of tea and the butler fetched the best brandy to strengthen it a little, when there was a faint sound in the passage beyond and the door swung open. As one person we turned to face it, and saw Jenny standing white-faced, one shoe off and her foot smeared with blood.

"Papa..." she started.

Hunt strode across the floor and picked her up. He held her so tightly she cried out with momentary pain, then buried her head on his shoulder and started to cry. She was not alone, every female servant in the place wept with her, and not a few of the men found a sudden need to blow their noses uncommonly fiercely, or to turn away for a moment and regain their composure.

Holmes was up before six and I found him in the hall pacing back and forth when I came down for breakfast just after half past seven. He swung around to face me. "Ah, at last," he said critically. "Go and question the child again," he commanded. "Learn anything you can, and pay particular attention to who took her and who brought her back."

"Surely you don't think one of the household staff is involved?" I dreaded the idea, and yet it had been done with such speed and efficiency I was obliged to entertain the possibility myself.

"I don't know, Watson. There is something about this that eludes me, something beyond the ordinary. It is Moriarty at his most fiendish, because it is at heart very simple."

"Simple!" I burst out. "The child has twice been taken, the second time in spite of all our attempts to safeguard her. If he has caused one of these people to betray their master in such a way, it is the work of the devil himself."

Holmes shook his head. "If so then it is co-incidental. It is very much his own work he is about. While you were asleep I buried myself learning something of Hunt's affairs. Apparently he is the main stockholder in the local mine, as well as owner of a large amount of land in the area, but he has no political aspirations or any apparent enemies. I cannot yet see why he interests Moriarty."

"Money!" I said bitterly. "Surely any man with wealth and a family, or friends he loves, can be threatened, and ultimately, by someone clever and ruthless enough, money may be extorted from him?"

"It is clumsy, Watson, and the police would pursue him for the rest of his life. Money can be traced, if the plans are carefully laid. No, such a kidnap has not the stamp of Moriarty upon it. It gives no satisfaction."

"I hope you are right," I said with little conviction. "The amount Hunt would pay to have his child safe from being taken again would be satisfaction to most thieves."

Holmes gave me a withering look, but perhaps he sensed my deep fear and anger in the matter, and instead of arguing with me, he again bade me go and question Jenny.

However I was obliged to wait until nine, and after much persuasion of the nursemaid, I found Jenny in the nursery, pale-faced but very composed for one who had had such a fearful experience not only once but twice. Perhaps she was too innocent to appreciate the danger in which she had been.

"Hello, Dr. Watson," she said, as if quite pleased to see me. "I haven't had breakfast yet. Have you?"

"No," I admitted. "I felt it more important to see how you were, after last night's adventure. How do you feel, Jenny?"

"I don't like it," she replied. "I don't want to go there again."

My heart ached that I was obliged to have her tell me of it, and I was terribly aware that a whole house full of men seemed unable to protect her. "I'm sorry. We are doing all we can to see that you never do," I told her. "But you must help me. I need to know all about it. Was it the same man again? The Professor?"

She nodded.

"And to the same place?"

"No." She shook her head. "It was a stable I think. There was a lot of straw, and a yellow horse. The straw prickled and there was nothing to do."

"How did the Professor take you from the nursery here?"

She thought for several minutes and I waited as patiently as I could.

"I don't 'member," she said at last.

"Did he carry you, or did you walk?" I tried to suggest something that might shake her memory.

"Don't 'member. I walked."

"Down the back stairs, where the servants go?" Why had no one seen her? Why had Moriarty dared such a brazen thing? Surely it had to be one of the servants in his pay? There was no other sane answer. It did not need Holmes to deduce that!

"Don't 'member," she said again.

Could she have been asleep? Could they have administered some drug to her? I looked at the face of the nursemaid and wondered if anything else lay behind her expression of love for the child.

I questioned Jenny about her return, but again to no avail. She said she did not remember, and Josephine would not allow me to press her any further. Which might have been fear I would discover something, but might equally easily have been concern that I not distress the child any more. In her place I would have forbidden it also.

I went down the stairs again expecting Holmes to be disappointed in my efforts and I felt fully deserving of his criticism. Instead he met me waving a note which had apparently just been delivered.

"This is the reason, Watson!" he said. "And in true Moriarty style. You were correct in your deduction." And he offered me the paper.

> My Dear Hunt,
>
> I see that you have called in Sherlock Holmes. How predictable Watson is! But it will avail you nothing. I can still take the child any time I choose, and you will be helpless to do anything about it.
>
> However if you should choose to sell 90% of your shares in the Morton Mine, at whatever the current market price is—I believe you will find it to be £1.3.6d more or less, then I shall trouble you no further.
>
> Moriarty.

I looked up at Holmes. "Why on earth should he wish Hunt to sell his shares?" I asked. "What good would that do Moriarty?"

"It would start a panic and plunge the value of the entire mine," Holmes replied. "Very probably of other mines in the area, in the fear that Hunt knew something damaging about his own mine which was likely to be true of all the others. Any denial he might make would only fuel speculation."

"Yes... yes, of course. And then Moriarty, or whoever he is acting for, would be able to buy them all at rock-bottom price."

"Exactly," Holmes agreed. "And not only that, but appear as a local hero as well, saving everyone's livelihood. This is the true Moriarty, Watson. This has his stamp upon it." There was a fire within him as he said it that I confess angered me. The thrill of the chase was nothing compared with the cost to Hunt, and above all to Jenny. "Now," he continued. "What have you learned from the child of how she left here?"

"Very little," I replied. "I fear she may somehow have been drugged." I repeated what little she had been able to tell me, and also a description of the stable, as far as she had been able to give one.

"We shall borrow the pony and trap and go back to the house in Hampden in daylight," he replied. "There may be something to learn from a fuller examination, and then seek the stable, although I have no doubt Moriarty has long left it now. But first I shall speak to Hunt, and persuade him to do nothing regarding the shares..."

I was appalled. "You cannot ask that of him! We have already proved that we are unable to protect Jenny. On two successive nights she has been taken from the house and returned to it, and we have never seen her go, nor seen her come back, and are helpless to prevent it happening again."

"It is not yet time to despair," Holmes said grimly. "I believe we have some hours." He pulled out his watch and looked at it. "It is only six minutes past ten. Let us give ourselves until two of the clock. That will still allow Hunt sufficient time to inform his stockbroker before close of business today, if that should be necessary, and Moriarty may be given proof of it, if the worst should befall."

"Do you see an end to it?" I asked, struggling to find some hope in the affair. It galled me bitterly to have to give in to any villain, but to Moriarty of all men. But we were too vulnerable, I had no strength to fight or to withstand any threat where the life of a child was concerned, and I know Hunt would sacrifice anything at all to save Jenny, and I said as much.

"Except his honor, Watson," Holmes replied very quickly. "It may tear at his very soul, but he will not plunge a thousand families into destitution, with their own children to feed and to care for, in order to save one, even though it is his own. But we have no time to stand here debating. Have the trap ready for us, and as soon as I have spoken with Hunt, I shall join you at the front door."

"What use is it going to Hampden, or the stable, if Moriarty has long left them?" I said miserably.

"Men leave traces of their acts, Watson," he replied, but I feared he was going only because we were desperate and had no better idea. "It might be to our advantage when we have so little time, if you were to bring a gardener or some other person who knows the area well," he continued, already striding away from me.

It was barely thirty minutes later that he returned just as the gardener drew the trap around, with me in the back ready to set out for the village. I had also questioned the gardener as to any local farms which might be vacant, and answer such slight description as Jenny had given me, or where the owner might either be unaware of such use of his stables, or be a willing accomplice.

"Did you persuade Hunt to delay action?" I asked as Holmes climbed in beside me and we set off at a brisk trot.

"Only until two," he said, tight-lipped. I know that he had had some agreement to achieve even that much time from the fact that he stepped forward in the seat and immediately engaged the gardener in conversation about every aspect of the nearby farms, their owners and any past relationship with Hunt, good or ill.

What he was told only served to make matters worse. Either the gardener, a pleasant chap of some fifty-odd years named Hodgkins, was more loyal than candid, or Hunt was generally liked in the region and had incurred a certain mild envy among one or two, but it was without malice. The death of his wife while Jenny was still an infant had brought great sympathy. Hunt was wealthy in real possessions, the house and land and the mine itself, but he had no great amount of ready money, and he lived well, but quite modestly for his station in life. He was generous to his staff, his tenants and to charity in general. Naturally he had faults, but they were such as are common to all people, a sometimes hasty tongue, a rash judgment here or there, too quick a loyalty to friends, and a certain blindness when it suited him.

Holmes grew more and more withdrawn as he listened to the catalog of praise. It told him nothing helpful, only added to the urgency that we not only find where Jenny had been taken, but far more challenging, we learn from it something of use.

We found the tall house again easily, and a few questions from neighbors elicited an excellent description of Moriarty.

We went inside and up again to the room that in the daylight answered Jenny's description in a way which startled me. It was indeed bright and airy. There was a red couch, but the grate was clean and cold, as if no fire had been lit in it recently. I saw a few crumbs on the floor, which I mentioned to Holmes as coming from the teacakes Jenny had been given.

"I do not doubt it," Holmes said with no satisfaction. "There is also a fine yellow hair on the cushion." He waved absently at the red couch while staring out of one of the many windows. "Come!" he said suddenly. "There is nothing else to be learned here. This is where he kept her, and he intended us to know it. He even left crumbs for us to find. Now why was that, do you suppose?"

"Carelessness," I replied, following him out of the door and down the stairs again, Hodgkins on his heels. "And arrogance."

"No, Watson, no! Moriarty is never careless. He has left them here for a reason. Let us find this stable. There is something… some clue, something done, or left undone, which will give me the key."

But I feared he was speaking more in hope than knowledge. He would not ever admit it, but there is a streak of kindness in him which does not always sit well with reason. Of course, I have never said so to him.

We got into the trap again and Hodgkins asked Holmes which direction he should drive. For several moments Holmes did not reply. I was about to repeat the question, for fear that he had not heard, when he sat very upright. "Which is the most obvious farm, from here?" he demanded. "That meets our requirements, that is?"

"Miller's," Hodgkins replied.

"How far?"

"Just under two miles. Shall I take you there?"

"No. Which is the second most obvious?"

Hodgkins thought for a moment or two. "I reckon the old Adams place, sir."

"Good. Then take us there, as fast as you may."

"Yes, sir!"

It proved to be some distance further than the first farm mentioned, and I admit I became anxious as the minutes passed and the time grew closer and closer to two. Holmes frequently kept me in the dark regarding his ideas, but I was very much afraid that in this instance he had no better notion of how to foil Moriarty than I did myself. Even if we found the farm, how was it going to help us? There was no reason to suppose he would be there now, or indeed ever again. I forbore from saying so perhaps out of cowardice. I did not want to hear that he had no solution, that he was as fallible and as frightened as I.

We reached the Adams' farm and the disused stable. Holmes opened the door wide to let in all the light he could, and examined the place as if he might read in the straw and dust some answers to all our needs. I thought it pointless. How could anyone find here a footprint of meaning, a child's hair, or indeed crumbs of anything? I watched him and fidgeted from one foot to the other, feeling helpless, and as if we were wasting precious moments.

"Holmes!" I burst out at last. "We..." I got no further. Triumphantly he held up a very small, grubby, white sock, such as might fit a child. He examined it quickly, and with growing amazement and delight.

"What?" I said angrily. "So it is Jenny's sock. She was here. How does that help us? He will still take her tonight, and you may be sure it will not be to this place!"

Holmes pulled his pocket watch out. "It is after one already!" he said with desperate urgency. "We have no time to lose at all. Hodgkins, take me back to the Grange as fast as the pony can go!"

It was a hectic journey. Hodgkins had more faith than I that there was some good reason for it, and he drove the animal as hard as he could short of cruelty, and I must say it gave of its best. It was a brave little creature and was lathered and blowing hard when we finally pulled in the drive at the front door and Holmes leaped out, waving the sock in his hand. "All will be well!" he shouted to Hodgkins. "Care for that excellent animal! Watson!" And he plunged into the hall, calling out for Hunt at the top of his voice.

I saw with dread that the long case clock by the foot of the stairs already said three minutes past two.

Hunt threw open his study door, his face pale, eyes wide with fear.

Holmes held up the sock. "Bloodless!" he said triumphantly. "Tell me, what time does the hokey-pokey man play?"

Hunt looked at him as if he had taken leave of his wits, and I admit the same thought had occurred to me. He stammered a blasphemy and turned on his heel, too overcome with emotion to form any answer.

Holmes strode after him, catching him by the shoulder, and Hunt swung around, his eyes blazing, his fist raised as if to strike.

"Believe me, sir, I am deadly earnest!" Holmes said grimly. "Your daughter will be perfectly safe until the ice-cream man comes..."

"The ice-cream man!" Hunt exploded. "You are mad, sir! I have known Percy Bradford all my life! He would no more..."

"With no intent," Holmes agreed, still clasping Hunt by the arm. "It is the tune he plays. Look!" He held up the small, grubby sock again. "You see, it has no blood on it! This was left where Moriarty wishes us to believe he held her last night, and that this sock somehow was left behind. But it is not so. It is no doubt her sock, but taken from the first kidnap when you were not guarding her, having no reason for concern."

"What difference does that make?" Hunt demanded, the raw edge of fear in his voice only too apparent.

"Send for the hokey-pokey man, and I will show you," Holmes replied. "Have him come to the gates as is his custom, but immediately, now in daylight, and play his tunes."

"Do it, my dear fellow!" I urged. I had seen this look of triumph in Holmes before, and now all my faith in him flooded back, although I still had no idea what he intended, or indeed what it was that he suddenly understood.

Hunt hesitated only moments, then like a man plunging into ice-cold water, he obeyed, his body clenched, his jaw so tight I was afraid he might break his teeth.

"Come!" Holmes ordered me. "I might need you, Watson. Your medical skill may be stretched to the limits." And without any explanation whatever of this extraordinary remark he started up the stairs. "Take me to the nursery!" he called over his shoulder. "Quickly, man!"

As it turned out we had some half-hour or more to wait while the ice-cream vendor was sent for and brought from his position at this hour in the village. Holmes paced the floor, every now and then going to the window and staring out until at last he saw what he wanted, and within moments we heard the happy, lilting sound of the barrel organ playing.

Holmes swiveled from the window to stare at the child. He held up one hand in command of silence, while in the same fashion forbidding me from moving.

Jenny sat perfectly still. The small woolen golliwog she had been holding fell from her fingers and, staring straight ahead of her, she rose to her feet and walked to the nursery door.

Josephine started up after her.

"No!" Holmes ordered with such fierceness that the poor girl froze.

"But..." she began in anguish as the child opened the door and walked through.

"No!" Holmes repeated. "Follow, but don't touch her. You may harm her if you do! Come…" And he set off after her himself, moving on tip-toe so that no noise should alarm her or let her know she was being followed, though indeed she seemed oblivious of everything around her.

In single file behind we pursued the child, who seemed to be walking as if in her sleep, along the corridor and up the attic stairs, narrow and winding, until she came to a stop beside a small cupboard in an angle of the combe. She opened it and crept inside, pulling a blanket over herself, and then closed the door.

Holmes turned to the maid. "When the nursery clock chimes eleven, I believe she will awaken and return to normal, confused but not physically injured. She will believe what she has been mesmerized to believe, that she was again taken by Professor Moriarty, as she was in truth the first time. No doubt he took her to at least three different places, and she will recall them in successive order, as he has told her. You will wait here so you can comfort her when she awakens and comes out, no doubt confused and frightened. Do not disturb her before that. Do you understand me?"

"Yes sir! I'll not move or speak, I swear," Josephine promised, her eyes wide with admiration and I think not a little relief.

"Good. Now we must find Hunt and assure him of Jenny's welfare. He must issue a statement denying any rumor that he might sell his holdings in the mine. In fact if he can raise the funds, a small purchase of more stock might be advantageous. We must not allow Moriarty to imagine that he has won anything, don't you agree?"

"I do!" I said vehemently. "Are you sure she will be all right, Holmes?"

"Of course, my dear Watson!" he said, allowing himself to smile at last. "She will have the most excellent medical attention possible, and a friend to assure her that she is well and strong, and that this will not occur again. Possibly eat as much ice-cream as she wishes, provided it is not accompanied by that particular tune."

"And a new pair of socks!" I agreed, wanting to laugh and cry at the same time. "You are brilliant, Holmes, quite brilliant! No resolution to a case has given me more pleasure."

"It was my good fortune she stubbed her toe," he said modestly. "And that you were wise enough to send immediately for me, of course!"

THE ADVENTURE OF THE OTHER DETECTIVE

by Bradley H. Sinor

Bradley H. Sinor's latest short story collection, *Echoes from the Darkness*, which he describes as "Urban Noir Fantasy," is just out from Arctic Wolf Publishing. He has new stories forthcoming in the anthologies *Shelter of Daylight*, *Grantville Gazette V*, and *Space Grunts* (co-written with his wife, Sue). In all, he has published more than seventy short stories in the science fiction, fantasy, horror, and mystery fields. He is also the author of more than two hundred and fifty articles appearing in magazines, newspapers, and essay anthologies.

"There but for the grace of God go I," said John Bradford, in humble acknowledgment of the role of chance and circumstance in human affairs. We can't help thinking about how things could have been different. If you hadn't gone to that party, you wouldn't have met your spouse. If you hadn't left your house at that exact moment, you wouldn't have been in that accident. It can get pretty mind-boggling to consider how many things had to happen exactly the way they did since the beginning of the universe in order for you to have been born at all. Science fiction has a long tradition of exploring the notion of alternate worlds, especially since the many-worlds interpretation of quantum mechanics suggested that any universe that can exist does exist, somewhere. If we were to shuffle through our possible lives as we shuffle the cards of a deck, we would see lovers become strangers, strangers become lovers, children vanish and other children take their place. We would see houses, apartments, cars, pets flicker by in endless permutations. We would see good men turned vile, and wicked men become heroes. There but for the grace of God go I.

The weeks following the return of Sherlock Holmes, three years after his supposed death at the hands of Professor James Moriarty, the so-called Napoleon of Crime, were busy ones for my old friend.

There was, as might be expected, a steady stream of visitors who found their way to Baker Street, everyone from the dirtiest pickpocket to a messenger who took Holmes to a private meeting at Buckingham Palace.

65

I had also returned to Baker Street.

Not twenty-four hours after Colonel Sebastian Moran had been led away in chains by Inspector Lestrade, Holmes asked if I would agree to return to Baker Street. "It would be the best medicine in the world for you, Watson," he said over one of Mrs. Hudson's excellent dinners.

As I look back on that night I must admit that I was not all that difficult to convince. My darling Mary had been gone for nearly a year. Her weak heart had taken her only three days after our fifth wedding anniversary.

The end had come so swiftly that there had been nothing that all of my medical skill could have done to save her.

Even after so many months, there were moments when I caught myself turning to ask her something, or I would look up at a sound, expecting to see her stepping around a corner.

So Holmes's invitation was a most welcome one for me.

Of cases there were many: *The Adventure of the Black Katana*, *The Quest for Pendragon's Son*, and *The Theft of Alharazad's Manuscript*, to name just a few.

By the middle of October things had returned to as much of a semblance of normality as was anything around Sherlock Holmes.

The evening of the 13th I was alone in Baker Street. Holmes was dining with his brother, Mycroft, and I did not expect his return for many hours.

I had declined the invitation to join them. I had no doubt that I would hear the details from Holmes, especially of the "favor" that he would no doubt be asked to perform by the man whom he had once described as, at times, "being the British Government."

Beside my favorite chair that evening stood a stack of medical journals, a stack that I had to admit was far too high. This past year I had sadly neglected to keep up on the literature of my profession, and it was something that I meant to correct.

The mantle clock had just tolled ten when I heard a furious pounding on the downstairs door. Moments later the familiar footsteps of Mrs. Hudson could be heard rushing to answer the summons.

The young man behind Mrs. Hudson looked vaguely familiar, in that way that so many people resemble others. He was bundled tightly against the night's chill.

"Sir, I am sorry to disturb you, but the young man says that it's an emergency," Mrs. Hudson said.

"I am afraid that Holmes has not returned, but if there is anything that I can do—"

Before I could say more, the young man cut me off with a wave.

"Sir, it wasn't Mr. Holmes that I come to fetch, but yourself. There's been an accident."

"Accident? Where?" I said, sitting bolt up.

"Three streets over," he said. "Mr. Delvechio's warehouse. It was himself Mr. Hobbs who came falling off that old balcony. I couldn't tell if he was breathing or not."

Mrs. Hudson already had my bag ready. The fog that had rolled in at sunset was heavier than I had seen it in years, enshrouding the streets like a thick blanket. A half-dozen steps from the door and Baker Street was gone from sight.

"Colder than I thought it would be," I said, pausing to pull up the collar on my coat.

"Aye, sir."

"What's your name, son?"

"Arthur, sir. Arthur Pym. I'm the new accounting clerk for Mr. Delvechio. Only been there about a half year."

It was scarcely five minutes before Pym was leading me to a side door marked DELVECHIO AND SONS, IMPORTERS.

He had to pound for several minutes before anyone came to admit us. "We got no time for—"

The door was opened by a massive man with small square-shaped glasses hanging on the end of his nose. "Oh, it's you."

"Aye, Mr. Harris. I done brought the doctor. Watson's his name."

"Don't matter what his name is. Could've saved yourself a trip. If that fall did'na kill him he'll be dead soon, after doing a header into that pile of Italian mirrors."

Not since the battlefields of Afghanistan had I seen a body covered with that much blood. Around me were hundreds, if not thousands, of shards of glass. In each one there seemed to be another me, angled and bent and torn into a million different shapes. The unfortunate Mr. Hobbs lay in the center of this display, any hope that he might still be alive ended when I found the shard of glass embedded in his jugular.

Once the police had arrived and taken statements, confirming the story of Hobbs's fall, I volunteered to remain until the body was removed. The constable said it would not be necessary, but that I should come to the local station house tomorrow to make a statement.

"Are you certain you don't want me to come with you, Doctor Watson?"

"Thank you, Arthur, but it is only a few blocks. Even in this mist I can find my way to 221B with no problem."

"You have a good night then, sir," said the constable as he opened the door.

I picked my way through the fog carefully. The occasional glow of a streetlamp gave a safe haven of scant few feet in the mist. I had to stop several times, unsure of my direction.

Standing there in the mist a feeling of nausea came crashing over me and I had to fight for each breath. My head seemed about to burst with wave after wave of pain. I had to struggle to keep from losing myself in the pain. For that instant I could have been anywhere: Delvechio's Warehouse, darkest Africa, or the cold wastes of the South Pole.

Then, just as quickly as it came, the feeling passed, leaving only a dull ache in the pit of my stomach in its wake. I pulled myself together and began to pick my way once again toward Baker Street.

When I finally reached that familiar door I felt as if I had just run ten miles with full military field pack, uphill. A good stiff shot of whiskey and my own bed were the best prescriptions I could think of right then.

I had some difficulty making my key work. It fit but did not seem to want to turn at first. Finally, by twisting it hard and pushing, the door came open. I reminded myself to mention something to Mrs. Hudson in the morning concerning it.

Under the door to our rooms I could see a light. Obviously Holmes had returned in my absence. Just inside I spied the familiar silhouette of Sherlock Holmes sitting scrunched in his chair in front of the fireplace. I was just about to say something when I heard a voice behind me.

"Say now, who might you be?"

Standing in the door to my bedroom was a figure with a revolver in his hand. When he stepped into the light I saw a face that I had not seen since I had left Afghanistan.

"Murray?" I said.

"I said, who are you? And why are you bursting into our quarters without so much as a..." His face went ashen as I stepped into the light. "God help me. It can't be! Colonel? Colonel Watson, sir? But you're dead!"

At that, my former Army aide fainted dead away. Holmes was out of his chair and across the room in an instant, kneeling beside Murray.

"If I am not mistaken, I believe that you, sir, are a doctor," he proclaimed.

"I am."

"Then I believe you have a patient." It was then that I realized the man was not Sherlock Holmes but none other than Professor James Moriarty.

One of the best restoratives available in a physician's pharmacopoeia is nothing less than good old-fashioned brandy. I've kept a small metal flask of the stuff in my case since I first took medical degree. As I expected, it brought Murray around almost immediately, gasping for breath, but awake.

I felt every bit as confused as Alice, having stumbled through the Looking Glass. If this were a dream, it was the most realistic one I had ever experienced. I felt entitled to a long swallow of brandy myself.

For that moment I had a chance to look around the room. Things were familiar, but subtly different. I recognized the familiar chemical apparatus in the corner, the violin in its case by the fireplace and the old battered coat tree near the door. Only the Persian slipper and its tobacco was missing from its accustomed place; where there should have been several rows of carefully indexed scrapbooks, I found neat matching journals, many dealing with mathematics and astronomy, bearing dates that went back some eight years, and in the far corner of the room stood a small telescope.

"Excellent work, Doctor, excellent," said Moriarty.

"Thank you," I said, looking at the man who up until a few minutes before I had been convinced lay dead at the bottom of the Reichenbach Falls in Switzerland. Only this was not exactly the man that Holmes had described. He was younger by at least ten years, if not more so, than I had expected. There was an ease and confidence about him that reminded me of Holmes.

"Would somebody mind telling me just what in the hell has happened to me?" I said finally.

"A very good question, Doctor. Watson, isn't it?" he asked as he helped Murray to his feet. My former army aide stared at me for a moment without saying a word, and then allowed me to lead him over to the couch.

"Now, Doctor, tell me how long you have lived at 221B Baker Street?" asked Moriarty, sitting down in the chair facing the yellow leather one I had taken.

"How…?"

Moriarty grinned and gestured with one finger toward my medical bag, still sitting open on the floor. "Rather revealing, I must admit," he said. There, in neat gold letters, was my name and the address, 221B Baker Street, London.

The day I had moved back into Baker Street I had retrieved my old bag from the back of the closet.

In spite of all that Holmes had told me regarding this man, I found myself warming to the fellow. I began to describe the events of the evening. Moriarty stopped me only occasionally to ask for further details, sometimes on the oddest things, the type of doorway that had fronted Delvechio's, the uniform the constable had worn, and the location of the local police station. I wanted to know why, but for the moment thought it best to keep my own counsel. Moriarty was especially interested in my impression of the fog itself.

"A most fantastic tale that you have entertained us with this evening," said Moriarty. "You have to admit it is a bit hard to accept, especially considering that Murray and I have been sharing these quarters since the spring of 1885."

His eyes were unblinking as he stared at me, waiting for my reaction.

"Professor, I am a doctor, a man of science. If I were hearing this tale from anyone but myself I would be convinced that the speaker had far too much good Scotch whiskey and had been reading one of the scientific romances of Mr. H. G. Wells. Yet as sure as I sit here, every word that I have told you is the God's own truth."

Moriarty steepled his fingers in front of his face, deep in thought. "Doctor, I believe you."

"Professor, how can you believe him?" objected Murray. "The last time I saw Colonel Watson he was dead, an Afghan spear through his chest. I supervised the burial party myself, and that was nearly ten years ago."

Dead? Me? A cold chill ran down my spine. This had to be a nightmare, but there seemed no way to escape it. I defy anyone to hear the news that he was not only dead, but a number of years buried, and not have at least some reaction.

"What would it take to convince you that this man is John H. Watson?" asked Moriarty.

Murray thought for a moment before he answered. "Look on his left forearm." I hesitated for a moment before taking off my jacket. I rolled up my sleeve and held out my arm for Moriarty to inspect.

"There should be scar there, three to four inches in length," said Murray.

"It is there," confirmed Moriarty. "How did you get it?"

I smiled, remembering well the hunting trip with my father and brother that had been the last time all three of us had been together as a family. I had brought down a boar, but not without the beast nearly ripping my arm to shreds.

Murray just shook his head. "Colonel, I don't know how you managed it, but I'm bloody glad that you did," he said finely.

"Just a minute there, Murray. That's the second time you've called me Colonel."

"Aye, sir. After all, that is your rank."

Colonel Doctor John H. Watson. That did have a nice sound to it. The only trouble was that I had never risen above the rank of Captain when I had served with the Fifth Northumberland Fusiliers and had been discharged after being wounded at the second Battle of Maiwand.

"But, Colonel, at Maiwand you weren't injured. I was."

This difference in history seemed to please Moriarty when I mentioned it.

"Unless you are one of the most convincing madmen to come along in a long time, you, sir, are telling the complete and utter truth. The facts concerning your rank only serve to help prove my theory.

"Ever since the incident of a man who walked around his carriage, out of the view of a dozen people, and utterly vanished, I have developed a theory regarding the existence of other worlds," he said.

"Like Mars and Venus?" I asked.

"I said other worlds, not other planets," he corrected. "More precisely, worlds exactly like our own, only with differences. The result of other decisions, for instance, where the American Confederate States lost their war for independence. Mathematically, it makes perfect sense.

"These worlds would on occasion touch and allow people to pass from one world to another, usually by accident, but under the right circumstances, deliberately. Tonight it seems that the fabric of space and time was stretched so thin that it allowed Dr. Watson to walk from his London to ours."

"All in the space of a few blocks," I said. Looking out the window into the fog, I knew in the pit of my stomach his theory was right. I took a long swallow out of my brandy flask and laid it on the nearby table. It was hard to fathom that everything I had known was gone, especially when I could see much of it around me.

As it had so many times before, the conversation in Baker Street was interrupted by the arrival of none other than Inspector Herbert Lestrade. The little rat-faced Scotland Yard man had been one of the first of Holmes's professional associates who had made his way to Baker Street. Naturally, he did not know me from Adam.

"Lestrade, it is always good to see you," said Moriarty, extending his hand.

"Thank you, Professor. I'm sorry if I've interrupted anything. However, my news could not wait." He paused for a moment, looking in my direction. "May I speak freely?"

"Forgive me, Inspector, I'm forgetting my manners. This is an old army friend of Murray's, Dr. John H. Watson. They served together in Afghanistan. Dr. Watson is privy to anything said here."

"Very well then," he said, sitting down in a red leather chair opposite Moriarty. "Less than an hour ago I received a telegram notifying us that Colonel Sebastian Moran has escaped from Dartmore Prison."

"Do they know just when it happened?" asked Moriarty.

"Sometime in the last three to four days. He got into a fight with some of the other prisoners. They all ended up in solitary confinement," said Lestrade.

"And current penal theory calls for prisoners so incarcerated to see and be seen by no one, except a single guard," said Moriarty.

"Even at meal times?" I asked.

"A small metal grate on the bottom of each door allows the trays to be injected and later extracted. Moran has pulled more than one hunger strike in the past. They could see a figure wrapped up in his blanket, so even though he wasn't eating, they didn't much bother with him," said Lestrade.

"How did they penetrate the ruse?"

Lestrade laughed, leaning back in the red leather chair. "One of the other prisoners, Volmer by name, suffered a stroke. He was dying, and his last request was to see Moran. Apparently they had become friends."

"Do you think that Moran will be making for sanctuary with his old comrades here in London?" asked Murray.

"Old friend, I know he will. I am also certain that Moran's employer had a hand in this; it's just his style." With that, Moriarty was out of his chair. From behind a bust of Caesar he extracted three perfectly round metal balls. He rolled them over in his hands several times and then deposited them in his vest pocket. "How much longer did Moran have left on his term in solitary confinement?"

"Three days."

"Then whatever is going to happen will happen within the next seventy-two hours." For a time Moriarty stared at the wall calendar.

"Good lord," he said.

"What is it, Professor?" asked Murray.

"If I am right, we have little time to lose."

"I'll come with you," volunteered Lestrade.

"Thank you, but no. For the moment there are things that must be done that you cannot be a part of."

"I don't like it, Professor. This is police business."

"I am aware of that. However, there is no place for you in our party this evening." Lestrade didn't say another word; his face reflected the irritation that he was feeling. Instead, he turned and walked out the door without a word.

Murray disappeared into the bedroom that had once belonged to me, emerging moments later, overcoat draped across his arm, a twin pair of Army service revolvers in his hand. "Colonel, if you would take charge of one of these," he said.

The familiar weight in my hand was another reassurance of the reality around me. It fit perfectly into my jacket pocket. "I am to accompany you then, Professor?"

"Of course, old chap. Murray and I wouldn't have it any other way."

"Professor, I am at your disposal."

In spite of the fog we were able to flag down a cab in only moments. I didn't hear the address that Moriarty gave the driver, but moments later we were shooting down the street. After a few turns I lost my way completely.

"Professor, may I ask who Colonel Moran's employer is?"

"Do you know of Moran in your London?"

"Somewhat. Ex-Indian Army, number two man in a criminal organization that stretched its tentacles into every bit of bad business through the length of London, and even England itself. Prefers to kill with a custom-made air rifle," I said.

"Air rifles, nice to know old Moran is predictable," said Murray.

"And who was the head of this criminal cabal?" asked Moriarty.

I hesitated for a moment before answering. "You, Professor."

Moriarty laughed. It was the eeriest sound that I had ever heard.

"Well, why not?" he said at last. "It sort of balances things out."

"Then who is the leader of the organization here?" I asked.

"Why, none other than Mr. Sherlock Holmes."

That announcement put a damper on conversation, at least on my part, so we rode in silence. The concept of Holmes as a criminal did not seem as shocking now as it might have a few hours before. In the back of my mind I suppose I still harbored the faint hope that this was all some strange dream that I would at any moment be roused from.

Our cab pulled to a stop in front of Number Ten Cudugin Square. A three-story private home, its windows were dark and a single gas light burned at its front door.

"On your toes, gentlemen," said Moriarty. "Our luck is with us. They are meeting tonight."

A liveried butler answered the door. The professor spoke a single word to the man. "Valhalla."

"Down the hall, sir, second door to the right."

As we walked along the hallway, I had the distinct feeling that we were being watched, which I told Moriarty.

"I would be worried if we weren't," replied the professor. "The security of those we are about to meet is of paramount importance."

Any interest I might have had in who we were going to meet vanished the moment I saw who had opened the door. The dark brunette hair fell loose around her shoulders, hazel green eyes in a familiar oval face.

It couldn't be, but it was! Mary, my own dear wife, dead these many months, but there she stood. It took all the strength I could muster to keep from grabbing her up.

"This way, gentlemen," she said.

"Easy, Colonel," said Murray, his hand on my shoulder. My former aide had always been aware of my moods, many times almost before I was.

Three men sat at the heavy oaken table that dominated the room. Two of them

I knew by sight. One was none other than Edward, Prince of Wales, and Heir Apparent to throne. Next to him was a much older man. It took me a moment or two to recognize him, considering Albert of Saxe-Coburg-Gotta, Prince Consort to Her Royal Highness Victoria, Queen of England, had died thirty-three years earlier in the world I knew. The third man was unknown to me, though he did look vaguely familiar. His thin cadaverous face suggested someone who might be found on the streets of the East End, rather than in this company. Seeing this, and most of all, Mary alive, made me pray that it was not all some nightmare.

"Professor, this is a most unexpected surprise. We haven't had the honor of your company for far too long," said Prince Albert.

"Thank you, Your Royal Highness," said Moriarty. "I believe you know Murray. This other gentleman is Dr. John H. Watson, whom I have asked to lend his aid to tonight's enterprise. I will vouch for him completely."

"That he travels in your company is proof enough of his trustworthiness," said Prince Edward, as he extracted a large cigar from his silver case. "Watson? Watson. Would you be related to the late Colonel Watson? I met him some years ago on a tour of India."

"A cousin, sir." I could hear every bit of uncertainty in my voice as I spoke. "Our parents always claimed that he and I could have passed as twins."

"Indeed. If memory serves me, you readily could have." He laughed as he lit the big cigar. "He was a good man, of whom your family can be justly proud; he was a true hero of the empire."

"Thank you."

"Now, Professor," said the Prince Consort. "What is this errand that has brought you here tonight?"

"It is a matter of gravest importance. By your own statement, even the Queen does not know just how involved you and your son are in these meetings. If it had not been for your sure hand behind the scenes, I would not care to speculate what state our country would be in now.

"However, tonight matters have reached a point where I can no longer act alone. For some years you three have known of my ongoing feud with Sherlock Holmes. More times than I care to remember, this Napoleon of Crime has managed to elude the net that I have cast for him. Tonight he made a move in a plan that will involve the escape of Jack the Ripper."

The silence that fell over the room with his words was a familiar one to me. I had known it on those occasions when it had been necessary to break the news to a patient's family that they had lost a loved one.

"You are certain of this?" said Prince Albert. At that moment he seemed twenty years older than when I had come into the room.

"Yes, and moreover, I believe that events will come to a head within the next several days. In three days' time it will be the anniversary of the first of the Ripper murders. It would suit Holmes's sense of humor to see the man walking free again on that day."

The silent man picked up his pen and began to write. A moment later the sheet was passed to Prince Edward. The younger man's cigar sat untouched in the ashtray in front of him, a gray pile of ash below it.

"You have guaranteed the silence of your companions, Professor. Very well, let both men understand that what they are about to hear may be the most dangerous secret in the entirety of the British Empire. What do you gentlemen know concerning the Ripper murders?" asked the Heir Apparent.

"Only what was in the newspapers," Murray said.

Holmes had, in fact, been called into the case, but had never confided any of the details, saying that it was a tale better left untold. I recalled the multitude of rumors that had echoed from every pub and street corner regarding the Ripper during those dark days.

"Six years ago Murray was in America handling the matter of the May Surveillance for me. Dr. Watson was also out of the country."

"Very well. As you gentlemen know, for some six months in 1888, London was frightened to its core by the series of murders committed in the Whitechapel district by the person who came to be known as Jack the Ripper.

"So far as the public knows, the Ripper was never brought to book for the crime. Some of the far more speculative journals have hinted that he may still be prowling the streets of London to this day. That has not been true for more than six years.

"Thanks to the untiring efforts of Professor Moriarty, Scotland Yard, and the late Inspector Allard, in early July of that year the Ripper was captured," said Prince Edward.

"Then why was the public never told of this?" asked Murray.

"Because of the identity of the Ripper. I still remember the night I was summoned to Scotland Yard. When I learned who the Ripper actually was I knew that it would be impossible for that knowledge to be made public," said Prince Albert, his voice shaky.

"Impossible," said his son picking up the narrative. "Because Jack the Ripper was none other than the Duke of Clarence, third in line to the throne of England; Albert Victor, my own flesh and blood, my son."

There had been rumors, of course, regarding the Queen's grandson. Like many others, I had heard them and just credited them to a frightened, overactive public's imagination.

"He was insane, of course, a mental disorder combined with syphilis. You both will understand the dilemma that we faced," said Moriarty.

"My grandson had to be cut out of the line of succession. The very idea that the heir to the throne was a murderer would have shaken the very foundations of this monarchy and our empire. So, like a mad dog, he was, in a manner of speaking, put down. With the cooperation of certain highly placed officials, we faked his death.

"For the last few years, Albert Victor, under the name Victor Wednesday, has been a patient at Druid's Hill Asylum. Not even my beloved Victoria knows the truth in this matter," said Prince Albert.

"You may rest assured, Your Royal Highness, that no one shall hear of this from either Murray or myself," I said.

"Thank you, Doctor." This was no monarch who spoke now, but a grieving grandfather.

The third man again took pen in hand. This time the paper went directly to Prince Albert.

The old man read it and nodded. "I cannot agree with you more."

"Professor, I am going to place the entire matter into your hands. You will have at your disposal all the resources of the government if you need them.

The Prince Consort scribbled a few lines on a sheet of paper, added hot wax to the bottom, and his signet ring into it. His son looked at the result, signed it and added his own signet's impression to the wax.

"This will not only gain you admittance to the asylum, but gives you full authority to act as you see fit concerning the inmate known as Victor Wednesday," said Prince Edward.

"Full authority?"

I arched an eyebrow at those words. To me that meant the power of life and death. I suspected it meant the same to Moriarty

"Full authority," the Heir Apparent repeated.

"I understand. I will attempt to exercise it with extreme discretion."

"I didn't doubt that for one minute," said the older man, quietly.

Moriarty had decided that it would be best for Murray to remain in London while the Professor and I would pay a visit to Druid's Hill. We, however, did not travel alone.

At the insistence of Prince Edward, we were accompanied by Mary Morstan.

"I think that she would be of very great help to you in this enterprise," Prince Edward had said.

I was the first to raise objection, fearing for her safety. I also found myself wondering if in this world Mary were one of the many "close friends" that Bertie was known to have in mind.

"Before you object, Doctor," she said. "Let me enlighten you to a few things. I am also a physician, fully board-certified and a graduate of Queen's College. I have been a practicing doctor for some time. My specialty these last several years has been the study of criminal insanity."

Mary had always exhibited a healthy interest in my work, but I had never considered that it had gone that far. To say I was astonished was to put the situation mildly. I had heard of women doctors, but had never encountered one before.

"What is the Prince's condition?" I asked.

"Slowly deteriorating. He has periods of lucidity, but they don't last long anymore. Like many patients suffering from syphilis, his thoughts are confused and at times make little or no sense. There are moments when he can fly into a total murderous rage at the mention of certain subjects. In the case of the Prince, it is mention of the Queen, his grandmother. Only three weeks ago he nearly killed one of the other doctors who made an offhand remark," she said.

"You understand the danger that you are placing yourself in tonight?" I asked, realizing as I did that I was speaking to the woman who had spent considerable time in the company of Jack The Ripper these past few years and lived to tell about it.

"Yes, Dr. Watson," she said. "But thank you for taking time to worry."

"If I may ask a question, Professor?" I said.

"Certainly. Given the current set of circumstances, I would imagine that you have quite a few of them."

"That rather thin gentleman back there at Cudugin Square, the one who never spoke. Who was he? He certainly seemed to have the Prince's ear."

"Indeed he does. His name is Holmes."

"Holmes? Mycroft Holmes?"

"That is exactly who he is, Watson. I take it you know him?"

"Yes. What does he do for the Prince?"

"I'm not sure, but I think that he is the head of the secret service."

"You think?"

"That's how secret it is." At least some things were the same in this world as the one I had come from.

I shook my head and turned toward Mary.

We departed Victoria Station the next morning. During the trip I found it remarkably easy to speak with Mary, she was so like the woman I had fallen in love with, and yet as different as night and day.

Druid's Hill Asylum. The name suggested a far more sinister-appearing place than the rather palatial-looking country estate we found ourselves approaching that evening. The house itself was more than three hundred years old; its basements had been built deep into solid bedrock. A fence, hidden in places by carefully placed hedges and trees, surrounded the grounds. The ornamental grating on the windows was actually reinforced iron.

"Definitely a fortress," I said.

"It will be difficult for Holmes to penetrate these grounds," Mary observed.

"Dr. Morstan, I appreciate the fact that you did not claim it impossible. Nothing is impossible," Moriarty said. "In just the journey here I have conceived of some five methods that would work. It is the sort of challenge that Holmes has always accepted in the past."

The director of Druid's Hill was a burly man with mutton-chop side whiskers named Throckmorton, Dr. R. A. Throckmorton. He seemed a self-important fellow who had found his niche and intended to protect it.

"See here, I will not have you interrupting the routine of this establishment. Barging in here in the middle of the night is the sort of thing that could destroy months and months of work with these patients. We walk a delicate balance with some of them. Dr. Morstan, I'm totally astonished that you would associate yourself with these... common adventurers."

Moriarty rose in his chair at those words, but settled back. His face was washed of emotion, his eyes two cutting gray lights starring at Dr. Throckmorton. I heard a tiny click, click, click sound, of metal hitting metal, and noticed Moriarty had the three metal balls in his hand and was rolling them back and forth.

"You have seen our authorization."

"Indeed I have. That piece of paper leads me to suspect that the dementia that afflicts Victor Wednesday may be only partially caused by the disease that he suffers from, and more from his ancestry," Throckmorton said.

"That statement borders on treason, Doctor," I said.

"It borders on the rights of a free-born Englishman to speak his mind, sir," replied Throckmorton. "A right that we all posses, republican and royalist alike."

"Dr. Throckmorton, this is not Hyde Park. You know my authority, where it comes from and the range of it. You know my personal credentials. My companions are physicians who will certainly see to the health of the patient. Will you permit me access to him?" said Moriarty.

"Yes," he said finally.

Albert Victor, Duke of Clarence, third in line for the throne of Great Britain, AKA Victor Wednesday, was awake. He was sitting on his bed staring at a small painting of a landscape hanging on the opposite wall.

The cell that they kept him in was on the lowest level of Druid's Hill, nearly thirty feet under ground. According to Mary, he was allowed out only under the most strictly controlled conditions. This section of the asylum was reserved for the most dangerous and psychotic cases. As we had made our way through the halls, I heard screams of pain and anger that cut into the very stones of the building.

"I've seen him sit for days just like that, not sleeping, just staring at it, absorbing every little nuance of it. Perhaps for him it is an escape," Mary said. "Other times he raves on every subject imaginable, making little or no sense. On rarer and rarer occasions he is coherent and seemingly aware of what he has done and what is happening to him."

We had been there an hour, and never once in that time had the Prince responded to any questions, or even so much as acknowledged our presence. He just sat on the edge of his bed and stared at the painting. I could see enough of his face to recognize the family features, echoes of those two faces that I had seen only a few hours before. He had lost weight, but no matter what name he officially bore at Druid's Hill, there was no mistaking that face.

"I wonder if he knows of the plan to free him," I asked.

"I would not put it past Holmes to have contacted him. Whether he did, it is questionable whether Victor would even remember it," said Moriarty. "At his stage of the disease, a syphilitic's memory is not reliable."

In the meantime the Prince had risen and walked across his cell to make a slight adjustment to the picture. Then he began to pace back and forth, in slow, measured steps along the length of the cell, holding himself with the dignified carriage and air that one would expect of a member of the royal family.

He stopped for a moment, looked toward us, gave a slight nod in Mary's direction and continued pacing.

"I do not expect the attack to be direct," I told Moriarty.

"Perhaps," he said.

"Sometimes a frontal assault is exactly the sort of strategy that works the best," someone said from behind us.

We turned to find Director Throckmorton standing in the door that led to the upper levels of the asylum. The voice belonged to a big bear of a man standing directly behind him, his arm around Throckmorton's neck, a pistol pressed to the doctor's temple.

"If you gentlemen and the lady would be so good as to step back against the far wall it would make things a great deal easier for the lot of us."

"Please do as he says! He's already shot two of my orderlies and who knows how many other people," pleaded the director in a whiny high-pitched voice.

"Colonel Moran, I presume?" I said.

"Indeed I am, and who might you be, sir? I know Moriarty and this girl, but you are a stranger to me."

"I am Colonel Doctor John Watson, late of the Fifth Northumberland Fusiliers. You may be more then a bit familiar with my old regiment." I elected to use the unaccustomed rank, hoping that it just might give me a tiny bit of equality in Moran's mind.

"A fine outfit. Now Colonel, if you don't get yourself up against that wall I will shoot you and then Director Throckmorton, in that order," he said.

So much for the idea of impressing him. "Oh really, Mr. Holmes," said Moriarty, shaking his head. "I do think that it would be a bit more comfortable for you if Colonel Moran would take the gun out of your ear."

For the briefest moment I wondered what kind of game he was playing. Then I saw a change come over the asylum director. Moran did indeed free him, stepping back several paces. An obviously padded jacket slipped off Throckmorton's shoulder, followed by a shirt pillow and the shock of unruly red hair and mutton-chop sideburns.

Sherlock Holmes stood stretching himself to his full height. The face was the same as that of my friend, but the lines around his eyes were harder and crueler.

"There, that is much better. The disguise was not all that difficult a thing to do, but the man has such an insufferable attitude I wonder how anyone can stand to be around him for any length of time. Tell me, Professor, when did you know it was I?"

"Not immediately. Only when I noticed that one of your sideburns was not quite glued down completely did I suspect that I was not talking to the genuine Dr. Throckmorton. Your acting was excellent. I have no doubt you would have done well treading the boards," said Moriarty.

"My thanks, Professor. Like many, I have always harbored dreams of theater. Perhaps if my life had gone down a different path. That however, is neither here nor there. Your sudden arrival has forced me to accelerate my plans."

Holmes's slim fingers reached into his vest pocket and produced a long gray key. He fitted it into the lock, swinging open the cell door with a flourish.

"Your Highness, if you would come with me."

Victor Wednesday continued to walk back and forth, ignoring Holmes's action. When he did stop, he didn't look at Sherlock Holmes, or even the open cell door, but stared at the painting.

"Is this real or but another of these endless nightmares given form?" he whispered.

"Oh, very real, Your Highness, very real. The only nightmare invoked this night will be for those who locked you away," said Holmes.

"Good," he said.

For the first time, Victor Wednesday seemed to pass away and Prince Albert Victor took his place. As he headed for the door he casually said, "It would please us greatly if you would accompany us on our journey, Dr. Morstan."

The thought of Mary in the hands of Holmes and this man who was Jack the Ripper was more than I could stand. Without a thought as to consequences, I charged at Holmes, screaming at the top of my lungs. Unfortunately, I did not get close enough to my old friend's double because a mountain stepped between us. Moran grabbed me by the lapels and slammed me hard against the cell bars.

The last thing that I recall before I blacked out was Mary calling my name.

It was at least several eternities before the darkness opened up for me. I struggled to say something, but lost the words echoing through the pounding in my head, which could very easily have been the Changing of the Guard at Buckingham Palace. I tried to rise up, but a wave of dizziness sent me rolling back onto the floor.

"Easy, Doctor. Besides having the wind knocked out of you, you slammed your head solidly into those bars. You don't appear to have a concussion, but I think you should just lie still for a moment, until your head clears," said Moriarty.

We were in the Prince's cell; that much was quickly obvious. I didn't have to ask to know that the door was securely locked.

"How long was I unconscious?"

"Ten minutes, no more."

Seemingly satisfied as to my condition, Moriarty turned away from me to examine the cell door.

"I really don't mean to belabor the obvious," I said. "But if we don't get out of here Mary may well become the sixth victim of Jack the Ripper."

"Eighth. There were two that the public never found out about. However, I think you may well be right," he said. Just then the door swung open. He turned to me and displayed a thin wire he reattached to his pocket watch chain.

"Shall we, Doctor?"

Before I could get to my feet, Moriarty crossed to the wall and reached into a trash container near a guard post. He rummaged around for a moment and then produced the army service revolver that Murray had given me the night before.

"Moran searched us both for weapons after knocking you out. While he found your gun, his ego wouldn't let him keep a common army issue weapon. I doubt he expected us to be putting it to use quite this quickly." Moriarty passed the gun to me.

The main entrance hall of Druid's Hill was almost empty. I could hear a grandfather clock chiming ten o'clock.

"They're probably making for the carriage house," said Moriarty.

I was already a dozen steps ahead of him toward the door. Unfortunately, we were not fast enough. I had barely cleared the doorway before an open carriage came ripping past the front of the house, horses at full gallop. Whoever had the reins, and it looked to be Moran, was struggling to keep control while defending himself from an attacker who seemed to be trying to push him out of the carriage. It looked like the Prince.

"We'll never catch them," yelled the professor. "Shoot, Watson, shoot!"

I fired three times.

Whatever control Moran had was lost when the animals began to charge headlong into the sharp curve of the drive. The carriage whipped sharply from one side to the other several times before tilting too far in one direction and sending its passengers and the frightened horses sprawling across the grass.

I found Mary a few feet from the wreckage. She tried to rise up on one arm to free herself from the bushes that had cushioned her fall. However, the moment she leaned any weight on her arm, her face contorted in pain.

"I can't be sure," she said. "But I think it may be broken."

It was a clean break, thankfully. Her only other injuries appeared to be cuts and bruises.

"A fair enough trade for my life," she smiled.

We found Moran sprawled on the ground unconscious. The Prince was dead; we found him beneath the overturned wagon, his neck broken. Death had been almost instantaneous.

I did not envy Moriarty the task ahead of him; informing a father and grandfather that the fiction they had invented many years before had now become fact.

"What happened in the carriage to make the Prince attack Moran?" Moriarty asked Mary.

"I can't be sure. Moran said something to the Prince just as we left the barn; he screamed bloody murder and went for Moran's throat. I'm just glad that Moran said whatever he said," Mary replied.

"Whatever the reason, it looks like Jack the Ripper probably saved your life," observed Moriarty.

That was when it occurred to me that I had seen no sign of Holmes since the carriage had overturned.

"His footprints lead off away from the asylum," said Moriarty. "There was some blood, but I lost the trail about a quarter of a mile to the east. I have no doubt that we will be hearing from Mr. Sherlock Holmes again."

"The train is late," I said, snapping the cover on my watch closed. Mary reached out, took my hand and smiled. Her left arm hung in a sling, a reminder of our encounter with the *other* Holmes.

All right, I admit that I was more than a bit nervous. Frankly, considering what had happened to me over the last few days, I would say that I had every right to be.

This wasn't Victoria Station by any means, but, rather, a country train depot. In fact, it could have been a waiting room in any depot from Liverpool to Glasgow. There were a few people lingering around the waiting area. Professor Moriarty sat with a notebook on his lap, eyes half closed, every so often jotting down a few words or numerical notations. Occasionally I heard the now familiar sounds of the small metal balls clicking together as he rolled them across his palm.

Mary and I had talked for some time, but in the last few minutes both of us had lapsed into a silence, broken only by an occasional reassuring smile.

"I believe that the train is arriving," Mary said.

The familiar sounds of a steam locomotive filled the station. From the west I could see its lights, hear the metal on metal sound of its brakes, and moments later watch the steam cloud cut across the platform as it slid to a stop.

Moriarty extracted his watch from a vest pocket. "Nine and a half minutes late; mathematically insignificant, especially considering the distance that it had to travel."

A number of people emerged from the train. Most went right to the baggage compartment, while a few lingered around, looking slightly confused. A familiar figure in frock coat and top hat, carrying a walking cane, cut his way through the crowd.

"Holmes, over here," I called out.

I must confess that until that moment I had harbored the slightest fear that all of my memories of the other world had been one long dream.

"Watson, old fellow. It is good to see you." Holmes said grasping my hand. "I have had the most remarkable journey and have seen things that even surprised me."

"They must have been a remarkable sight, then," I said.

"They were. I am sure the return journey will present even more astounding sights," he said.

I glanced at Mary. Her eyes had that remarkable wisdom that I had always looked to for strength and support.

"Holmes, where are my manners," I said "Let me introduce you to—"

"It is my pleasure, Dr. Morstan."

"I am honored, Mr. Holmes. You seem as remarkable as John has described you. Since John has explained how you both came to know my other self, I would be most interested in how you reasoned that I am a doctor."

Holmes flashed a familiar grin. "Simplicity in itself. A number of signs gave your profession away. I shall mention only two: the slight stain of silver nitrate on your uninjured hand, plus I noticed the ear piece of a stethoscope protruding from your sleeve. Since I see Watson is still carrying his in his hat, I reasoned that it most likely belonged to another doctor, you in this case," he said.

"Remarkable!" Mary laughed.

"Elementary," said Holmes. "Wouldn't you agree, Professor?"

"Indeed I would, Holmes. I note you did not fail to make use of the station's wall mirror to note my approach."

"A simple precaution, given our history. One I'm sure you would have taken had the positions been reversed."

"Indeed, you prove once again why your doppelganger has proved so elusive for these many years," chuckled Moriarty. "It is a pleasure to meet you, Mr. Sherlock Holmes,"

"The pleasure is mine, Professor Moriarty," Holmes said.

I then saw something I never in my life had expected to see: Sherlock Holmes shaking hands with Professor Moriarty.

"The note that you sent was fascinating in its implications," said Holmes.

"You had no trouble with the formulas that I suggested?"

"None. It was simply a matter of reorienting one's perceptions of the world around us to direct the train to this particular station and your world," said Holmes. "I doubt the other passengers ever noticed the difference."

"Then there should be no problem in allowing you and Watson to return, by the next train, to your world." Moriarty pulled a time table from his pocket. "Which should depart in just a bit over ten minutes, if this schedule is correct."

It was time. I squeezed Mary's hand once more before speaking. "Unfortunately, I will not be returning with Holmes."

"Indeed. And would I be wrong in assuming that at least part of your reason for remaining is Dr. Morstan?" asked Holmes. I noticed he had a very large grin on his face as he spoke.

"You would be exactly on the mark. In our world, the path for a female physician is especially difficult. Here, though not common, they are accepted more easily. As a general surgeon, I can practice anywhere. Save for a few distant cousins, I have no family left. Beyond yourself and a few other friends, none will miss me. The Professor has offered to help establish my credentials in this world," I said.

"There is then marriage in the offing?" asked Moriarty.

"Perhaps," I said.

They both knew there was, as did Mary and I. True, I had not formally proposed, but that was a matter I fully intended to correct very soon. "For now, we are definitely going into medical partnership."

"Well, Professor, it seems a good thing that I did not accept your wager," said Holmes.

"Wager?" I asked.

At that moment both Holmes and Moriarty had the same sort of twinkle in their eyes.

"Oh yes, did I forget to mention the wager that the Professor offered me? It seems that he appended a note to his missive containing the formulas for traveling here. He suggested that you might have decided to remain here, even offered to bet me ten pounds that you would.

"I did not accept that wager because, though you have been steady as a river throughout our friendship, you have at times surprised even me. From the things told me I had the feeling that this might just be one of those times." A porter appeared carrying two large carpetbags. "I also took the precaution of bringing some of your things I thought you might wish to retain in your new home."

"My thanks. Will my disappearance cause you any problems?"

"None that cannot be handled. I think with the aid of your friend, Dr. Doyle, we should be able to maintain the fiction that you are still writing your chronicles of my minor adventures."

Doyle was a good man, a decent physician and an excellent writer of historical tales. He had recommended me to the editors of the *Strand Magazine* when I had first begun to seek publication for my work. Doyle's only problem was he had an annoying habit of forgetting my name and calling me James.

"Then this is good-bye?"

"Let us simply say *Auf Wiedersehen,* Watson. I would not rule out the possibility that we will see each other again."

I watched as Holmes strode across the platform. He had only just stepped inside one of the first-class compartments when I noticed a conductor, with a worried expression on his face, approaching him.

As the train pulled away I saw Holmes nod and follow the man deep into the train.

"Do you think that there is a problem on the train, John?" Mary asked.

"Problems always seem to find their way to Holmes. Perhaps this one will not be without points of interest for him."

"Then, for Mr. Holmes, it appears that the game is once more afoot," she said.

A SCANDAL IN MONTREAL

by Edward D. Hoch

Edward D. Hoch's work has been named a winner of both the Edgar Award and the Anthony Award, and he was named a Grand Master by the Mystery Writers of America. He was known for his prodigious short story output, which, at the time of his death in 2008, numbered more than 900, many of which chronicled the adventures of Dr. Sam Hawthorne, Captain Leopold, or Nick Velvet. In addition to this story, which appeared in one of *Ellery Queen's Mystery Magazine*'s annual Sherlock Holmes tribute issues, he has also written about a dozen other Holmes stories.

Once readers fall in love with a character, they can't help wanting to know what happens to that character next. Conan Doyle twice attempted to retire Sherlock Holmes, once, dramatically, at Reichenbach Falls, and then again in a more sedate fashion, when he imagined Holmes easing into a well-deserved retirement as a beekeeper in Sussex. Readers famously rebelled against the first retirement, and many still aren't satisfied with the second. Could a man as single-minded and dynamic as Sherlock Holmes ever really retire? Surely a case must come his way every now and then. And what about Irene Adler, the woman who outwitted Holmes, the only woman he regards as his equal, *the* woman, as he calls her. Surely their paths must cross again. What happens next? We always want to know. In this next tale we see some familiar characters many years later, when they're older and their troubles are those particular to the more mature crowd—errant offspring, nostalgia, regret. It's always strange when you haven't seen someone in many years and then you meet them again. Sometimes you've both changed completely, and other times you find that you're both just the same as you've always been.

1. THE CRIME

My old companion Sherlock Holmes had been in retirement for some years when I had reason to visit him at his little Sussex villa with its breathtaking view of the English Channel. It was August of 1911 and the air was so still I could make out a familiar humming. "Are the bees enough to keep you busy?" I asked as we settled down at a little table in his garden.

"More than enough, Watson," he assured me, pouring us a little wine. "And it is peaceful here. I see you have walked from the station."

"How so, Holmes?"

"You know my methods. Your face is red from the sun, and there is dust from the road on your shoes."

"You never change," I marveled. "Are you alone here or do you see your neighbors?"

"As little as possible. They are some distance away, but I know they look out their windows each morning for signs of a German invasion. I fear they have been taking Erskine Childers too seriously."

It was eight years since publication of *The Riddle of the Sands*, but people still read it. "Do you fear war, too?"

"Not for a few years. Then we shall see what happens. But tell me what brings you here on a lovely summer's day. It has been some time since you spent a weekend with me."

"A telegram was sent to you at our old Baker Street lodgings, all the way from Canada. Mrs. Hudson couldn't find your address, so she brought it to me."

"How is she these days?"

"Infirm, but in good spirits."

"I have a housekeeper here who tends to my needs. But she is off today. If you wish to stay for dinner I can offer you only a slice of beef and bread."

"There is no need, Holmes. I came only to deliver this telegram."

"Which could have been delivered more easily by the postal service."

"It seemed important," I told him, "and I have little enough to do in my own retirement. Not even bees!"

"Well then, let us see about this urgent message."

He opened the envelope and we read it together. "Mr. Sherlock Holmes, 221B Baker Street, London. Dear Mr. Holmes, Excuse intrusion on your time, but am in urgent need of help. My son Ralph Norton gone from McGill University. Police suspect him of murder. Please come! I beg you!" It was signed simply, Irene.

"What is this, Holmes?" I asked. "Do you know the meaning of it?"

"All too well," he answered with a sigh.

"What Irene is this? Certainly not Irene Adler. She has been dead some twenty years."

"She was reported to have died, but I always doubted it. Irene was born in New Jersey, and after her marriage here to Godfrey Norton I suspected they might have fled to America to escape questions about the Bohemian affair. If this is truly from her, she would be fifty-three now, four years younger than me and not an old woman by any means. She might well have a son of university age."

"But what can you do from here, Holmes?"

"From here, nothing." He pondered the problem for several minutes, staring at her address at the bottom of the telegram. "I must respond to her at once," he decided. "This telegram was sent four days ago, on the twelfth."

"What will you tell her?"

"She begs my help, Watson. How can I refuse her?"

"You mean you would travel to Canada?" I asked in astonishment.

"I would, and I shall be immensely grateful if you are able to accompany me."

Within a week's time we were at sea, approaching the mouth of the St. Lawrence River. I wondered how Holmes ever persuaded me to accompany him on such a lengthy journey, and yet I knew the answer. I had to be present when he met Irene Adler one more time. I had to see her for myself, after all these years.

Our ship docked at one of the quays adjacent to the center of Montreal and we took a carriage to our hotel. I was surprised at the number of motor cars in the streets, and astounded at the sumptuous mansions in the city's center—the sort of homes that would be far removed from London back home. Our driver informed us that these were the homes of the city's financial and industrial magnates, an area known as the Golden Square Mile.

We checked into a small hotel across the street from the site of a new Ritz-Carlton Hotel under construction. It was on Rue Sherbrooke Ouest, close to the university, and after a telephone call to her Irene said she would join us at the hotel. I could see that Holmes was a bit fidgety at the prospect of the meeting. "I trust I will be able to help the woman with her problem," he confided. "I have never forgotten her, over all these years."

Presently the desk clerk telephoned to say that Mrs. Irene Norton was downstairs. Holmes and I went down to find her waiting in a secluded corner of the lobby, seated alone on a sofa wearing a long skirt and flowered blouse and hat. I recognized her at once from the photograph Holmes kept of her. She was still as slim and dainty as she had been on the opera stage, with a face as lovely as ever. Only a few gray hairs hinted at the passing years. "Good day, Mr. Sherlock Holmes," she said by way of greeting, almost duplicating her words when once she had followed him disguised as a boy. "And Dr. Watson. I must say, both of you have changed very little since our London days."

"You are most kind, madam," Holmes said with a little bow. "I am sorry we cannot be meeting under more pleasant circumstances."

She bid us be seated with her on the sofa. "These have been terrible weeks for me. I was at my wit's end when I telegraphed you, not even knowing if you were still available as a private consultant."

"I am retired," he told her, "but always available if you need me."

She smiled slightly. "I am honored that you should travel across an ocean for me."

"Have you lived in Montreal long?"

She nodded. "After our wedding, Godfrey felt we should leave England. Following a brief time on the Continent, he established quite a successful law practice here and we had a wonderful son, Ralph."

"I remember Godfrey as a remarkably handsome man," Holmes said.

"Sadly, he passed away three years ago. If he was with me now, perhaps I would not have summoned you across an ocean."

"But what of your son? In the telegram you said he had disappeared following a murder."

"That is so. I must tell you the entire story from the beginning. I believe it was his father's death that set Ralph off. He was never the same after that. He took to carousing at night and neglecting his schoolwork."

"What is his age?"

"He is nineteen, about to enter his second year at McGill. He met a young woman during his first year, a pretty red-haired classmate named Monica Starr. She seemed like a nice girl and I had no objection to their friendship. I thought it might get him back on track. But this summer he discovered there was a rival for her affections, a German student named Franz Faber who was entering his final year at McGill. I know the two boys had a fight, and Ralph came home a few weeks ago with a bloody nose. But it wasn't anything more than that. Ralph couldn't have—" Her voice broke then.

"What happened, Irene?" Holmes asked her softly.

"Two weeks ago, on a Thursday night, Franz Faber was stabbed to death outside a pub frequented by McGill students. It has caused a great scandal here. Things like this don't happen at McGill."

"The university was in session during August?"

"They offer some summer courses each year. Apparently Faber was taking a language course. He was a German student with only a basic knowledge of English and French. My son was seen in the pub earlier and the police came to our house to question him. He'd come home about an hour before they arrived and went to his room without speaking to me."

"Was that unusual?"

"He's been moody lately. I thought nothing of it, but when I went to his room to summon him for the police, he wasn't there. Apparently he'd gone out the back door. The next morning I discovered that Monica Starr was missing too. The police are convinced he killed Faber, but I can't believe it. He was moody, yes, just like his father, but he'd never kill anyone."

Holmes tried to calm her. "I will do whatever I can for you, Irene. You must know that. Tell me, is there any place in the city or near here where they might have gone?"

"I'm not even convinced they're together."

"I think we can assume they are, whether or not he committed the crime. Was he friendly with any of his professors or instructors at McGill?"

She considered that for a moment. "There's Professor Stephen Leacock. He's a lecturer at McGill and he's published some economics books along with collections of humorous stories. Ralph was quite friendly with him."

"What about fellow students?"

"Only Monica, so far as I know."

"I'll speak to Leacock," Holmes said. "What about you? Are you still singing?"

She gave him a wan smile. "Very little, occasionally in local productions."

"That's too bad, Irene. You have a lovely voice."

"Find him for me, Mr. Holmes," she said. "You're the only one who can help me now."

"I'll do everything possible."

We walked the short distance to the university, a series of stone buildings reached by a tree-lined carriageway from the street. A monument to James McGill, whose legacy helped found the institution ninety years earlier, stood in front of the central pavilion. Only a few students and faculty members were about, preparing for the upcoming autumn term. We asked directions to Professor Leacock's office and were directed to the political economy department in an adjoining building. Holmes led the way, moving with an intensity that surprised me.

"We have no time to lose, Watson. If the young man has indeed fled the scene it is important that we find him and convince him to return for his own good."

"Do you believe him to be guilty, Holmes?"

"It is much too soon to form an opinion."

When we located Leacock's tiny office, it was occupied by a slender young man who introduced himself as Rob Gentry. He'd been studying a map on the professor's desk and he told us, "Professor Leacock is out right now, but he should be returning shortly. There's an election coming up, you know. Please take a seat, gentlemen."

"Is he active in politics?" Holmes asked.

"Very much so, on the Conservative side. He's campaigning against our Liberal prime minister."

Almost at once a handsome broad-shouldered man with a thick moustache appeared in the doorway. "What's this? Visitors? We will need an additional chair, Rob."

"Yes sir."

"I am Professor Leacock," he said, extending his hand. I guessed him to be in his early forties, with just a hint of gray in his hair. "What can I do for you?"

"We have traveled here from London. This is my companion, Dr. Watson, and I am Mr. Holmes."

"Holmes? Holmes?" Leacock seemed astounded. "Surely not the great Mr. Sherlock Holmes!"

"The same," I replied, speaking for Holmes.

"I have published some humorous pieces about your great detective work, Mr. Holmes. At least I trust you will find them humorous."

Holmes ignored his words. "We have come on an urgent matter, Professor Leacock. Irene Norton has asked my help in finding her son, Ralph, who is suspected of murder."

Leacock seemed to pale at his words. "A terrible tragedy," he murmured.

"His mother says you were a friend of his."

"I still am. This entire business is beyond my comprehension." He shifted some papers on his desk.

"If you know his whereabouts, it would be best for the lad if we found him before the police."

"I know nothing," he insisted.

"Perhaps, but your assistant was studying a map on your desk when we entered, and now you have covered it up."

Leacock was silent for a moment, perhaps weighing his choices. Finally he said, "You are quite the detective, Mr. Holmes. Yes, I know where the boy is."

2. THE CHASE

Professor Leacock explained that he did his writing during summer vacations at a family cottage north of Lake Simcoe in the town of Orillia. It was some distance away from Montreal, actually north of Toronto. "It's on Old Brewery Bay on Lake Couchiching, but that's really an extension of Lake Simcoe."

"How do you get there?" Holmes asked.

"By train. The Canadian National Railway runs a line from Toronto through Orillia. It passes quite close to my cottage. I came back here with my family in early August as I always do, to prepare for the new term. It was just a few days before Franz Faber was killed."

"Did you know Faber?"

"Not personally. Rob here knew him."

Gentry nodded. "I used to see him in the pub on weekends. If he was between girlfriends we might have a few beers together."

Holmes looked thoughtful. "Did you see him the night he was stabbed?"

He shook his head. "I was at a picnic with some friends."

Holmes turned back to Leacock. "You said you know where young Norton is."

"He came to see me just after I returned to Montreal with my family. He wanted to get away for a few weeks, until the new term began. He wondered if I might know a place where he could go."

"And you suggested your cottage in Orillia?"

"I did."

"When was this?"

He consulted his desk calendar. "It would have been Wednesday, the ninth."

"Was he accompanied by the missing young woman, Monica Starr?"

"So far as I knew he went alone."

"And is still there now?"

"I believe so, yes. He planned to return the second week in September."

"Do you have a telephone at the cottage?"

"No. I like to spend the summers there with my wife and son, without needless interruptions."

"Then tell me how to get there by train."

"It is a full day's journey from here, well over three hundred miles."

"Watson and I are used to riding trains in England."

Leacock smiled. "I am British myself, you know. My parents migrated to Canada when I was seven and I decided to go with them."

"A wise decision," Holmes said with a smile. "Now about your cottage—"

"I don't know what is happening with Ralph, but I seem to be responsible in part, since I allowed him to use my place. If you insist on going, I will journey with you. I don't want two strangers accosting him by surprise."

I sensed something unspoken, as if he feared Irene's son was indeed capable of violence. "Very well," Holmes agreed. "Let us take the first available train."

Professor Leacock turned to his assistant. "Can you handle things here for a few days, Rob?"

"Certainly, sir."

Leacock telephoned his wife to tell her of our plans. Then he said to Holmes, "There is an early-morning train tomorrow. We can be at the cottage before nightfall."

"Very well."

"Windsor Station is several blocks south of here. Go down Rue Peel, past Dominion Square, and it will be on your right. You can't miss it. I will meet you there at eight in the morning." As we were leaving he thrust a book of his writings into my hand. "Please read this tonight, Dr. Watson, especially my little story 'Maddened by Mystery.' I trust you and Mr. Holmes will find it all in good fun."

Once outside, Holmes stared up at the sky. "An odd sort of chap, but friendly enough. Before we travel to the cottage, though, I wish to speak with the local police."

Dealing with the Sûreté du Québec proved to be both better and worse than our frequent encounters with Scotland Yard. Better, because they tended to treat Holmes with a bit more respect than some of their British counterparts, but worse because it was difficult finding the detectives investigating the murder of Franz Faber. We finally were shown to a squad room where a detective named Jean Leblond greeted Holmes with a degree of respect.

"You are certainly well known to us here," he said. "Is this your first journey to Canada, Mr. Holmes?"

"It is."

"I trust you will find our country to your liking. Now what can I help you with?"

"I have been asked to look into the murder of a McGill University student named Franz Faber. I believe he was stabbed to death outside a pub a fortnight ago."

Leblond flipped through the files on his desk. "Exactly a fortnight, on Thursday, the tenth. He lived only a few minutes after the attack."

"Were there any witnesses?" Holmes asked.

"No."

"Then why are you attempting to arrest Ralph Norton for this crime?"

"The two had fought over a woman. A police officer on patrol was the first to see Faber lying in the road. He'd been stabbed in the chest and was bleeding badly but still alive. The officer asked who stabbed him and he said Norton."

I could see that this dying statement had caught Holmes by surprise. "He's sure of that?"

The detective nodded. "He said Norton. The officer was certain. Add to that the fact that Ralph Norton fled when we came to question him and it makes a strong circumstantial case."

"Who was the woman they fought over?"

"Name is Monica Starr. She's disappeared too."

"Have you talked to her family?"

"They have a home up north, in Gaspe. She's been living on campus. They know nothing about her disappearance and claim they haven't seen her all summer. She'd remained at the university for some extra courses."

"Something of a coincidence, all these extra summer courses," Holmes mused. "Was Ralph Norton at the pub that night?"

"The bartender saw him earlier, but he wasn't there with Faber."

"Was the murder weapon recovered?"

"Not yet. We've searched the area without any luck."

When we left the Sûreté du Québec, I asked Holmes what he thought. "It seems that Ralph is the prime suspect," he answered. "We should call on Irene today, before we leave in the morning."

We called at her home, a smaller version of those mansions we'd seen on our way to the hotel. It was obvious that her husband's law practice had been profitable. Over tea Holmes explained about Leacock's cottage and told her we'd be traveling there in the morning. "You must prepare yourself, Irene. The police evidence is strong, even if not conclusive. If he's at the Leacock cottage, he might not be alone."

"That girl—"

Holmes nodded. "Monica Starr. She was here all summer with him. Something happened with the other boy, Franz Faber. They fought once and they may have fought again, outside the pub a fortnight ago. He spoke Ralph's name as he was dying."

"No!" She shook her head. "I can't believe my son would harm anyone."

"If I find him, I will have to bring him back."

She turned away, not wanting to meet his quick eyes. "He's my only child, all that I have. You must be able to help him somehow."

Holmes sighed and told her, "I will do whatever I can."

That evening, as we prepared to retire to our rooms, I took the time to read the little story Stephen Leacock had given me earlier. "Holmes!" I exclaimed before I'd finished the first few pages. "This thing of Leacock's actually makes sport of you and your methods. He refers to you as the Great Detective and describes you wearing foolish disguises as you attempt to help the prime minister and the archbishop of Canterbury!"

"Am I mentioned by name?"

"No."

"Then I view it as a compliment if readers like you immediately identify me as the Great Detective."

But that did little to calm my outrage. As I finished my reading I gasped. "At the end he has you disguised as a dog and destroyed by the dogcatchers! The man is a scoundrel and a slanderer!"

Holmes smiled just a bit. "Or a humorist."

"Do we really want to travel with such a person?"

"I am doing it for Irene and her son, not for Leacock."

And in the morning we met him at the station as planned. His teaching assistant, Rob Gentry, had come with him, which was something of a surprise. "I have some papers at the cottage," Leacock explained. "Since we'll be there at least overnight, Rob can sort through them for me and decide what I need to bring back here."

As it turned out, Gentry's presence was a good thing. It gave me someone to converse with on the long journey, and an excuse for addressing none of my remarks to the blackguard Leacock. The journey across eastern Canada was a picturesque one, and Leacock explained to Holmes why he'd chosen a summer home so far removed from Montreal. "I grew up in this area, after we came here from England. We had a place in Egypt, not far from the south shore of Lake Simcoe. A colorful country, especially in summer. The winters in Montreal are often brutal."

"It is a large country," Holmes remarked.

"Indeed it is. One can travel hundreds of miles in western Canada and see nothing but wheat fields. I believe the Lord said, 'Let there be wheat,' and Saskatchewan was born."

It was late afternoon when we left the train at Orillia and took a carriage the few short blocks to Leacock's cottage. Since there was no telephone, he'd been unable to announce our arrival in advance. A handsome young man with sandy hair and a few freckles was seated on the porch as we left the carriage. He immediately put down the Rider Haggard novel he was reading and stood up.

"Professor Leacock! What brings you here?"

"I have bad news for you, lad. Franz Faber was murdered the night before you left Montreal. The police want to question you about it."

At his words the screen door behind him opened and a lovely red-haired girl in a blue shift appeared. She had a dimple in her chin and a smile to charm any man. "Ralph was with me all the time," she told us. "He couldn't have killed anyone."

Holmes inserted himself into the conversation. "Would this be the missing Miss Starr?" he asked.

"Who are you?" Norton demanded.

"Sherlock Holmes. I am an old friend of your mother, who summoned me from England to find you."

He shook his head. "I didn't kill anyone, and I'm not going back to see the police. We're staying right here." His glance shifted to me. "Who is this man?"

"My associate, Dr. Watson," Holmes responded.

He studied me more closely. "A medical doctor?"

"Of course," I told him.

"And you know Rob, my assistant," Leacock said.

Ralph smiled slightly. "We see each other at the pub."

Leacock glanced around. "We only have three bedrooms. Is there room for us all overnight?"

"Sure," Ralph conceded. "Follow me, Mr. Holmes. We'll get everyone settled and have a bit of supper. You must be hungry after that long train ride."

Holmes and I drew a small bedroom at the rear of the cottage. When we were alone I asked, "Why was he so interested that I was a doctor?"

"You must try to be more observant, Watson. We now know why she didn't spend the summer at home with her parents. Even wearing that large shift I could detect a bit of a bulge. I believe Monica Starr to be at least six months pregnant."

3. THE CAPTURE

Seeing her seated at the dinner table later that evening, I had to agree with Holmes's diagnosis. The girl was certainly pregnant, probably entering her third trimester. It appeared that Ralph was planning to remain here with her rather than return to McGill. I wondered if Leacock and Gentry were aware of her condition. After we ate, there was still enough light for us to walk along Old Brewery Bay. It was a small arm of the lake, with Leacock's house at the innermost part. I could see that Irene's son and Monica Starr were supremely happy, even with these unexpected guests. They played catch with a red rubber ball, occasionally tossing it to Leacock or Gentry as well. At one point, Ralph ran ahead and shouted to her. "North! Catch!"

"North?" Holmes questioned after she'd caught the ball and tossed it on to Gentry.

"I'm from up north, so naturally the guys started calling me North Starr, or just North."

"Do you like it at McGill?"

"Sure, what's not to like? That's where I met Ralph. We'll be getting married soon, after we break the news to our folks."

"I wish you all the happiness you deserve," Holmes said.

Leacock had been standing close enough to overhear the conversation, and he commented to me, "Many a man in love with a dimple makes the mistake of marrying the whole girl."

"You do not approve?" I asked, addressing him for the first time since our journey began.

"It is not for me to say. Life, as we often learn too late, is in the living."

As the evening wore on, I found myself forced into further conversation with Leacock. "Did you have an opportunity to read my little piece on the Defective Detective, Dr. Watson?"

"I did, sir. It seems to me you could devote your talents to more important matters."

"Ah, but you see, I would sooner have written *Alice in Wonderland* than the whole of the *Encyclopedia Britannica*."

I had no answer for that.

Holmes and I both slept well that night. The water was still, and a big change from our Atlantic crossing. In the morning, over breakfast, the talk turned serious. It was Leacock who brought matters to a head. "You have to come back with us,

Ralph. If you don't, I must tell the police where you are."

But it was Monica who rose to his defense. "Why do you have to tell them? He's done nothing wrong."

Leacock turned appealingly toward Holmes, who said quietly, "Franz Faber named Ralph as he was dying. He told a police officer it was Norton."

"But that's impossible! I was with him all that night."

"No, you weren't, Monica," Ralph told her. "This was Thursday, the night before we left. Remember, I had to pick up some things from home. I was gone for over an hour."

"You couldn't kill anyone, Ralph," she said with a sigh. "Franz might not have seen his killer. You two'd had a fight, so your name was the one he spoke."

"He was stabbed in the chest," Holmes told her. "It's most likely he did see his killer." Then he turned back to Ralph. "What had you and Faber fought about?"

He gave a snort. "We fought over Monica. It felt like I was still a kid in high school."

"Is that true?" he asked her.

"I guess so. I went out with Franz for a while and he didn't want to give me up."

If we were to be back in Montreal that night we had to be leaving soon. Rob Gentry had gathered up the material Leacock wanted to bring back, but there was still no agreement from Ralph. "I'm not going to ride all day on the train just to tell some ignorant detective I'm innocent."

"I can stay here alone for one night," Monica told him. "Or you can come back with him," Professor Leacock suggested. "That might be best."

She shook her head. "No. I came here to get away from people—"

Holmes spoke softly. "Dr. Watson could examine you if you are concerned about your condition."

"It's not that. I just don't want to go back there."

"And neither do I," Ralph decided.

Leacock tried to reason with them. "Sooner or later the Montreal police will learn where you are, Ralph. You'll be arrested and taken back there in handcuffs. That's hardly something you'd want your mother to see."

"There's no evidence that I killed him."

"You fought, and he named you as his killer," Holmes said.

"Our fight was several days earlier. There was no reason to renew it or stab him. Monica was coming with me. I asked you about this cottage and you gave me the key a full day before Faber was killed."

"You make a good case for your innocence," Holmes agreed. "But the police want a killer and you're the only suspect they have."

It was then that Monica Starr spoke. "They have another," she said quietly. "I killed Franz Faber."

"Monica!" Ralph shouted. "Don't ever say that again! Someone might believe it."

I stared at Leacock and Gentry, seeing the disbelief in their faces. But than I glanced at Holmes and saw something quite different, something like satisfaction. "Of course she killed him. I've known it since last night. But I had to hear it from her own lips."

"How could you have known?" Ralph asked. "What happened last night?"

"You called her by a nickname, 'North.' When Franz Faber lay dying, he reverted to his native language. The officer asked who stabbed him and he didn't say Norton but *Norden,* the German word for north. He was saying you stabbed him, Monica. Do you want to tell us why you did it?"

She stared down at the floor, unable to look any of us in the eye. Finally she answered. "I love Ralph, I love him so much. My brief time with Franz was a big mistake, but when I became pregnant he threatened to tell Ralph the baby was his and not Ralph's. I couldn't let him do that. I begged him not to, but he wouldn't listen. I'd brought a knife along to threaten him, but when he saw it he just laughed. That was when I stabbed him."

"Monica—" It was almost a sob from Ralph Norton's lips.

The six of us took the long train ride back to Montreal together. Holmes telephoned Detective Leblond from a stop along the route and he was waiting for us at the station.

Holmes and I took a carriage to Irene Norton's home. He insisted on giving her the news in person. "Your son will be home soon," he told her. "He's gone to the Sûreté with Monica Starr."

"Have you solved the case?" she wanted to know. "Is my son innocent?"

"Innocent of all but a youthful love. Only time can cure him of that." He told her of Monica's confession.

"And the baby?" she asked. "Who is the father?"

"We didn't ask, but it seems Faber had reason to believe it was his. It may take Ralph some time to get over that."

She dipped her eyes, and may have shed a tear. "A scandal in Montreal. Who would have thought it? First me, all those years ago in Bohemia, and now my son."

"No one is blaming you, or your son."

She lifted her head to gaze at Holmes. "How can I ever thank you? Will you be going back now?"

He nodded. "I am retired and keep bees at my villa in Sussex. If you are ever in the vicinity, it would be my pleasure to show it to you."

"I'll keep that in mind," she said, and held out her hand to him.

THE ADVENTURE OF THE FIELD THEOREMS

by Vonda N. McIntyre

Vonda N. McIntyre is the author of the Hugo, Nebula, and Locus award-winning novel *Dreamsnake*. She is also the author of *The Moon and the Sun* (which also won the Nebula Award) and several other novels, including a *Star Wars* novel and several *Star Trek* novels. Other original novels include The Starfarers Quartet, *Barbary* (a book for younger readers), *Superluminal*, and *The Exile Waiting*. Much of her short fiction has been collected in *Fireflood and Other Stories*.

Readers have a tendency to identify authors with their characters, and this was certainly the case for Arthur Conan Doyle. He received piles of letters from readers asking for his help in solving actual crimes, to which he could only throw up his hands. Not only did Conan Doyle lack the rigorous, logical, machine-like Holmesian ability to penetrate subterfuge, but the author was also famously gullible. He repeatedly put his reputation on the line championing any hokey spiritualist who waved some ectoplasm at him. (In fact, the stage magician Houdini, who knew all the tricks of the spiritualists and who dedicated himself to unmasking them, displayed more Holmes-like behavior than the author ever did.) Perhaps the most embarrassing example of Conan Doyle's credulity was his publicizing the case of the Cottingley fairies—amazingly, the creator of Sherlock Holmes showed no skepticism when some mischievous teenage girls took photographs of themselves standing beside cardboard-cutouts of gnomes and fairies and then presented the images as real. This next tale shows us this side of Conan Doyle. Of course, in the wilds of an author's imagination, you can never be too sure what's real and what isn't.

Holmes laughed like a Bedlam escapee.

Considerably startled by his outburst, I lowered my *Times*, where I had been engrossed in an article about a new geometrical pattern discovered in the fields of Surrey. I had not yet decided whether to bring it to Holmes's attention.

"What amuses you so, Holmes?"

No interesting case had challenged Holmes of late, and I wondered, fearfully, if boredom had led him to take up, once again, the habit of cocaine.

Holmes's laughter died, and an expression of thoughtful distress replaced the levity. His eyes revealed none of the languorous excitement of the drug.

"I am amused by the delusions of our species, Watson," Holmes said. "Amusing on the surface, but, on reflection, distressing."

I waited for his explanation.

"Can you not discern the reason for my amusement, Watson—and my distress? I should think it perfectly obvious."

I considered. Should he encounter an article written particularly for its humorous content, he would pass straight over it, finding it as useless to him as the orbits of the planets. The description of some brutal crime surely would not amuse him. A trace of Moriarty would raise him to anger or plunge him into despair.

"Ah," I said, certain I had divined the truth. "You have read an account of a crime, I beg your pardon, the *resolution* of a crime, and you have seen the failings in the analysis. But," I pointed out, somewhat disturbed by my friend's indifference to the deeper ramifications, "that would indicate the arrest of an innocent victim, Holmes. Surely you should have some other reaction than laughter."

"Surely I should," Holmes said, "if that were the explanation. It is not." He shook the paper. "Here is a comment by Conan Doyle on Houdini's recent performance."

"Quite impressive it was, too," I said. "Thrilling, I would say. Did Sir Arthur find the performance compelling?"

"Conan Doyle," Holmes said with saturnine animosity, "attributes Houdini's achievements to—" Holmes sneered—"'mediumistic powers.'"

"His achievements do strain credulity," I said mildly.

"Pah!" Holmes said. "That is the *point*, Watson, the entire and complete *point*! Would you pay good money to see him *fail* to escape from a sealed coffin?"

"I suppose that I would not," I admitted.

"Were Houdini to tell you his methods, you would reply, 'But that is so simple! Anyone could achieve the same effect—using your methods!'"

As Holmes often heard the same remark after explaining his methods, I began to understand his outburst.

"I would say nothing of the sort," I said mildly. "I should say, instead, that he had brought the technique of stage magicianship to as near an exact science as it ever will be brought in this world."

Holmes recognized my comment with a brief smile, for I had often said as much to him about his practice of detection.

"But it is true, Watson," Holmes said, serious once more. "Anyone *could* achieve the same effect—were they willing to dedicate their lives to developing the methods, to studying the methods, to perfecting the methods! *Then* it is 'so simple.'"

When Holmes deigned to lead an amazed observer through his deductive reasoning, the observer's reaction was invariably the same: His methods were "perfectly obvious"; anyone, including the observer, could duplicate them with ease.

"Conan Doyle claims friendship with Houdini," Holmes said in disgust, "and yet he insults his friend. He dismisses Houdini's hard work and ingenuity. Despite Houdini's denials, Conan Doyle attributes Houdini's success to the supernatural. As if Houdini himself had very little to do with it! What a great fool, this Conan Doyle."

"Easy on," I said. "Sir Arthur is an intelligent man, a brave man. An inspired man! His imagination is every bit as exalted as that of Wells! His Professor Challenger stories compare favorably to *War of the Worlds*—!"

"I never read fiction," Holmes said. "A failing for which you berate me continually. If I did read fiction, I would not doubly waste my time with the scientific romances you find so compelling. Nor am I interested in the mad fantasies of a spiritualist." Holmes scowled through a dense cloud of pipe smoke. "The man photographs fairies in his garden."

"You are too much the materialist, Holmes," I said. "With my own eyes I saw amazing things, unbelievable things, in Afghanistan—"

"Ancient sleight of hand. Snake charming. The rope trick!" He laughed again, though without the hysterical overtones of his previous outburst. "Ah, Watson, I envy you your innocence."

I was about to object to his implications when he stayed my comment by holding up one hand.

"Mrs Hudson—"

"—with our tea," I said. "Hardly deserves the word 'deduction,' as her footsteps are plainly audible, and it is, after all, tea-time—"

"—to announce a client."

Mrs Hudson, our landlady, knocked and opened the door. "Gentleman to see you, Mr Holmes," she said. "Shall I set an extra cup?"

The figure of a man loomed behind her in the shadows.

"Thank you, Mrs Hudson," Holmes said. "That would be most kind."

Mrs Hudson placed a calling card on the tray by the doorway. Holmes rose to his feet, but did not trouble to read the card. As our visitor entered I rose as well, and made to greet him, but Holmes spoke first.

"I observe, Dr Conan Doyle," Holmes said coolly, "that you were called abruptly into the fields, and have spent the morning investigating the mystery of the damaged crops. Investigating without success, I might add. Has a new field theorem appeared?"

Conan Doyle laughed heartily, his voice booming from his powerful chest.

"So you've introduced me already, John!" he said to me. "You were looking out the window when my carriage arrived, I've no doubt." He smiled at Holmes. "Not such a clever deduction, Mr Holmes." He wrinkled his noble brow and said to me, "But how did you know I've just come to town, and how did you know of my involvement with the field theorems?"

"I'm afraid I had no idea you were our visitor, Sir Arthur," I said. "I did not even know we had a visitor until Holmes surmised your approach."

Sir Arthur chuckled. "I understand," he said. "Bad manners, revealing the tricks of the trade. Even those as simple as prior knowledge."

Holmes concealed his annoyance; I doubt anyone who knew him less well than I would have noticed it. He gazed steadily at Sir Arthur. We seldom had visitors taller than Holmes, but Sir Arthur Conan Doyle exceeds six feet by four inches. Unlike my friend Holmes, who remained slender, indeed gaunt, even during his occasional periods of slothful depression, Sir Arthur dominated the room with his hearty presence.

"How *did* you know about our visitor, Holmes?" I asked, trying to salvage the introductions.

"I heard Sir Arthur's carriage arrive," he said dismissively, "as you would have done had you been paying attention."

Though somewhat put off by his attitude, I continued. "And Sir Arthur's outing? His identity?"

"My face is hardly unknown," Sir Arthur said. "Why, my likeness was in the *Times* only last week, accompanying a review—"

"I never read the literary section of the *Times*," Holmes said. "As Watson will attest." He pointed the stem of his pipe at Sir Arthur's pants cuffs. "You are a fastidious man, Sir Arthur. You dress well, and carefully. Your shave this morning was leisurely and complete. Your moustache is freshly trimmed. Had you planned your excursion, you would surely have worn suitable clothing. Therefore, your presence was required on short notice. You have wiped the mud of the fields from your boots, but you have left a smear on the polish. You have confronted a puzzle that has distracted you from your customary appearance, which I can easily see—anyone could easily see!—is impeccable. As to the nature of the puzzle, unripe seed-heads of *Triticum aestivum* have attached themselves to your trousers cuffs. I am in no doubt that you investigated the vandalism plaguing fields in Surrey."

"Amazing," Conan Doyle whispered, his ruddy face paling. "Absolutely amazing."

I could see that Holmes was both pleased by Conan Doyle's reaction, and surprised that Sir Arthur did not laugh again and announce that his methods were simplicity itself.

Holmes finished his recitation. "That you have failed to solve the mystery is self-evident—else why come to me?"

Sir Arthur staggered. Leaping forward to support him, I helped him to a chair. I was astonished to perceive any weakness in a man of his constitution. He was quite in shock. Fortunately, Mrs Hudson chose that moment to arrive with the tea. A good hot cup, fortified with brandy from the sideboard, revived Sir Arthur considerably.

"I do apologize," he said. "I've spent the morning in the presence of strangeness beyond any I've ever before witnessed. As you divined, Mr Holmes, the experience has distracted me. To perceive your supernatural talents so soon thereafter—!"

He took a deep draught of his tea. I refilled his cup, including rather more brandy. Sir Arthur sipped his tea, and let warm, pungent steam rise around his face. His colour improved.

"'Supernatural'?" Holmes mused. "Well-honed, certainly. Extraordinary, even.

But not in the least supernatural."

Sir Arthur replied. "If John did not tell you who I am, and you did not recognize my face, then you could only have discovered my name by—reading my mind!"

"I read your name," Holmes said dryly, "from the head of your walking-stick, where it is quite clearly engraved."

Since the end of spring, the newspapers had been full of articles about mysterious damage to growing crops. Wheat stalks were crushed in great circles intersected by lines and angles, as if a cyclone had touched down to give mere humans a lesson in celestial geometry. Though the phenomena were often accompanied by strange lights in the sky, the weather was invariably fair. If the lights were lightning, it was lightning unaccompanied by thunder! No wind or rain occurred to cause any damage, much less damage in perfect geometrical form.

Many suggestions had been put forth as to the cause of the unexplained diagrams, from hailstorms to electromagnetic disturbances, but blame had not yet been fixed. The patterns were the mystery of the year; the press, in a misinterpretation of modern physics in general and the theory of Maxwell in particular, had taken to calling the devices "field theorems."

Holmes had clipped and filed the articles, and painstakingly redrawn the figures. He suspected that if the patterns were the consequence of a natural force, some common element could be derived from a comparison of the designs.

One morning, I had come into the sitting-room to find him surrounded by crumpled paper. The acrid bite of smoke thickened the air, and the Persian slipper in which Holmes kept his shag lay overturned on the mantel among the last few scattered shreds of tobacco.

"I have it, Watson!" Holmes had waved a drawing, annotated in his hand. "I believe this to be the basic pattern, from which all other field theorems are derived!"

His brother, Mycroft, speedily dismantled his proof, and took him to task for failing to complete several lemmas associated with the problem. Holmes, chagrined to have made such an elementary (to Holmes), and uncharacteristic, mistake, appeared to lose interest in the field theorems. But it was clear from his comments to Sir Arthur that they had never completely vanished from his attention.

After packing quickly, Holmes and I accompanied Sir Arthur to the station, where we boarded the train to Undershaw, his estate in Hindhead, Surrey.

"Tell me, Sir Arthur," Holmes said, as our train moved swiftly across the green and gold late-summer countryside, "how came you to be involved in this investigation?"

I wondered if Holmes were put out. The mystery had begun in early summer. Here it was nearly harvest-time before anyone called for the world's only consulting detective.

"It is my tenants who have been most troubled by the phenomena," said Sir Arthur, recovered from his earlier shock. "Fascinating as the field theorems may be, they do damage the crops. And I feel responsible for what has happened. I cannot have my tenants lose their livelihoods because of my actions."

"So you feel the vandalism is directed at you," said I. Sir Arthur had involved himself in several criminal cases, generally on the side of a suspect he felt to be innocent. His efforts differed from those of Holmes in that Holmes never ended his cases with ill-advised legal wrangles. No doubt one of Sir Arthur's less grateful supplicants was venting his rage against some imagined slight.

"Vandalism?" Sir Arthur said. "No, this is far more important, more complex, than vandalism. It's obvious that someone is trying to contact me from the other side."

"The other side?" I asked. "Of Surrey? Surely it would be easier to use the post."

Sir Arthur leaned toward me, serious and intense. "Not the other side of the country. The other side of… life and death."

Holmes barked with laughter. I sighed quietly. Intelligent and accomplished as my friend is, he occasionally overlooks proprieties. Holmes will always choose truth over politeness.

"You believe," Holmes said to Sir Arthur, "that a seance brought about these field theorems? The crushed crops are the country equivalent of ectoplasm and levitating silver trumpets?"

The scorn in Holmes's voice was plain, but Sir Arthur replied calmly. He has, of course, faced disbelief innumerable times since his conversion to spiritualism.

"Exactly so," he said, his eyes shining with hope. "Our loved ones on the other side desire to communicate with us. What better way to attract our attention than to offer us knowledge beyond our reach? Knowledge that cannot be confined within an ordinary seance cabinet? We might commune with the genius of Newton!"

"I did not realize," Holmes said, "that your family has a connection to that of Sir Isaac Newton."

"I did not intend to claim such a connection," Sir Arthur said, drawing himself stiffly upright. Holmes could make light of his spiritual beliefs, of his perceptions, but an insult to the familial dignity fell beyond the pale.

"Of course not!" I said hurriedly. "No one could imagine that you did."

I hoped that, for once, Holmes would not comment on the contradiction inherent in my statement.

Holmes gazed with hooded eyes at Sir Arthur, and held his silence.

"It's well known that entities from diverse places and times—not only relatives—communicate from the other side," I said. "How extraordinary it would be, were Isaac Newton to return, after nearly two centuries of pure thought!"

"'Extraordinary,'" Holmes muttered, "would hardly be the word for it." He fastened his gaze upon Sir Arthur. "Dr Conan Doyle," he said, "if you believe spirits are the cause of this odd phenomenon—why did you engage me to investigate?"

"Because, Mr Holmes, if *you* cannot lay the cause to any worldly agent, then the only possible explanation is a spiritual one. 'When you have eliminated the impossible, whatever remains, *however improbable*, must be the truth'! You will help me prove my case."

"I see," Holmes said. "You have engaged me to eliminate causes more impossible than the visitations of spirits. You have engaged me... to fail."

"I would not have put it so," Sir Arthur said.

The trip continued in rather strained silence. Sir Arthur fell into a restless doze. Holmes stared at the passing landscape, his long limbs taut with unspent energy. After an eternity, we reached the Hindhead station. I roused Sir Arthur, who awoke with a great gasp of breath.

"Ma'am!" he cried, then came to himself and apologized most sincerely. "I was dreaming," he said. "My dear, late mother came to me. She encourages us to proceed!"

Holmes made no reply.

Sir Arthur's carriage, drawn by a pair of fine bays, awaited us.

"The automobile can't be started, sir," the driver said. "We've sent to London for the mechanic."

"Very well, James," Sir Arthur said. He shook his head as we climbed into the carriage. "The motor was quite astonishingly reliable when first I bought it. But recently it has broken down more often than it has run."

The comment drew Holmes's attention. "When, exactly, did it begin to fail?"

"Eight weeks past," Sir Arthur said.

"At the same time the field theorems began to appear," Holmes said thoughtfully.

Sir Arthur chuckled. "Why, Mr Holmes, surely you don't believe the spirits would try to communicate by breaking my autocar!"

"No, Sir Arthur, you are quite correct. I do not believe the spirits would try to communicate by breaking your autocar."

"Merely a coincidence."

"I do not believe in coincidences."

Holmes was anxious to inspect the field theorems as soon as we arrived at Undershaw, but by then it was full dark. Sir Arthur showed the strain of a long and taxing day. He promised that we should leap out of bed before dawn and be at his tenant's field as the first rays of the morning sun touched the dewdrops of night.

And so we did; and so we were.

The descriptions and newspaper engravings of the field theorems did not do justice to the magnitude of the patterns. We stood on a hillside above the field to gain an overview of the damage. Three wide paths, perfectly circular and perfectly concentric, cut through the waving stalks of grain. A tangent, two radii, and a chord decorated the circles. I had to admit that the pattern resembled nothing so much as the proof of some otherworldly geometric proposition.

"The theorems appear only in wheat fields," Sir Arthur said. "Only in our most important crop. Never in fields of oats, nor in Indian corn."

Holmes made an inarticulate sound of acknowledgment.

We descended the hill, and Holmes entered the field.

Sir Arthur looked after him. "John," he said to me, "will your friend admit it, if he can find no natural explanation?"

"His allegiance is to the truth, Sir Arthur," I said. "He does not enjoy fail-ure—but he would fail before he would propose a solution for which there were no proof."

"Then I have nothing to worry about." He smiled a bluff English smile.

Holmes strode into the swath of flattened green wheat, quartering the scene, inspecting both upright and crushed stalks, searching the hedgerows. He muttered to himself, laughed and snarled; the sound crossed the field like a voice passing over the sea. He measured the path, the width of the stalks left standing, and the angles between the lines and curves.

The sun crept into the clear sky; the day promised heat.

"Can you feel it?" Sir Arthur said softly. "The residual power of the forces that worked here?" He stretched out his hands, as if to touch an invisible wall before him.

And indeed, I felt something, though whether it was energy spilled by unimagi-nable beings, or the Earth's quiet potential on a summer's day, I could not tell.

While Sir Arthur and I waited for Holmes to finish his search, a rough-shod man of middle years approached.

"Good morning, Robert," Conan Doyle said.

"Morning, Sir Arthur," Robert replied.

"Watson, this is one of my tenants, Robert Holder."

Robert's work clothes were shabby and sweat-stained. I thought he might have taken more care with his appearance, when he came to speak to his landlord.

To Robert Sir Arthur said, "Mr Holmes and Dr Watson have come to help us with our mystery."

"Mr Holmes?" Robert exclaimed.

He glanced out into the field, where Holmes continued to pace and stoop and murmur.

"And you're Dr Watson?" Robert's voice rose with the shock of finding himself in the presence of celebrity. "Why, it's a pleasure to meet you, sir," he said to me. "My whole family, we read your recountings in the evenings. The children learned their letters, sitting in my lap to listen to your tales."

"Er… thank you," I said, somewhat nonplussed. Though he was well-spoken for a farmer, I would not have marked him as a great reader; and, more, I consider the perils encountered by Holmes to be far too vivid for impressionable young chil-dren. However, it was not my place to correct Robert's treatment of his offspring, particularly in front of his landlord.

"Have you found the villains?" Robert asked. "The villains who have crushed my best wheat field!"

Holmes strode across the field and rejoined us, a frown furrowing his brow. He appeared not even to notice the presence of Sir Arthur's tenant.

"Useless," Holmes said. "Perfectly useless! Here, the artist stood to sketch the scene." He flung his hand toward a spot where white dust covered the scuffed ground. "And there! A photographer, with his camera and flash powder. Fully six reporters and as many policemen trampled whatever evidence might have been left." He did not pause to explain how he could tell the difference between the footprints of reporters and those of policemen. "And, no doubt, when the sightseers arrive by the next train—"

"I can easily warn them off," Sir Arthur said.

"To what purpose? The evidence is destroyed. No! I could conjecture, but conjecture is only half the task. Proof, now; that's a different story."

He glared out into the field as if it had deliberately invited careless visitors to blur the story written there.

"If only," Holmes said softly, "the scene were fresh."

He turned abruptly toward Robert. He had taken the measure of the man without appearing to observe him.

"You saw the lights," Holmes said. "Describe them to me."

"Are you Mr Holmes?"

I blushed to admit, even to myself, that the rough farmer had a better respect for common manners than did my friend.

"Of course I am. The *lights*."

"The night was calm. A bit of fog, but no rain, no storms. I heard a strange noise. Like a musical instrument, but playing no melody I ever heard. And eerie… It put the chills up my back. Made the baby cry. I went outdoors—"

"You were not frightened?"

"I was. Who would not be frightened? The Folk have fled London, but they still live in the countryside, in our hearts."

"You are a scholar and a folklorist," Holmes said without expression.

"I know the stories my family tells. Old stories. The Folk—"

"The faerie folk!" Sir Arthur said. "I've seen photographs—they *do* exist."

"The Folk," Robert said, neither agreeing nor disagreeing with Sir Arthur. "The ones who lived in this land before us."

"The lights, man!" Holmes said impatiently.

"At first I saw only a glow against the fog. Then—a ring of lights, not like candles, flickering, but steady like the gaslights of the city. All different colours. Very beautiful."

"Foxfire," Holmes said.

"No, sir. Foxfire, you see it in the marsh. Not the field. It's a soft light, not a bright one. These lights, they were bright. The circle spun, and I thought—"

He hesitated.

"Go on, man!"

"You'll think I'm mad."

"If I do, I shall keep it to myself."

Robert hesitated. "I thought I saw… a huge solid object, floating in the sky like a boat in the water."

"A flying steamship?" I said.

"An aeroplane," said Sir Arthur. "Though I would have thought we'd hear of a pilot in the area."

"More like a coracle," Robert said. "Round, and solid."

"Did you hear its motor?" Holmes asked. "A droning, perhaps, or a sound like the autocar?"

"Only the music," said Robert.

"I've never known an apparition to make a sound like a motorcar," Sir Arthur said.

"What happened then?" said Holmes. "Where did it go, what did it do?"

"It rose, and I saw above it the stars, and Mars bright and red in the midst of them." Robert hesitated, considered, continued. "Then the lights brightened even more, and it vanished in a burst of flame. I felt the fire, smelled the brimstone—At first I thought I was blinded!"

"And then?" Holmes said.

"My sight returned, and the fog closed around me."

"What have you left out?" Holmes asked sternly. "What happened afterwards?"

Robert hesitated, reluctance and distress in every line of his expression.

"The truth, man," Holmes said.

"Not afterwards. Before. *Before* the coracle disappeared. I thought I saw... a flash of light, another flash."

"From the coracle?"

"From the sky. Like a signal! White light, white, not red, from... from Mars!" He drew in a deep breath. "Then the coracle replied, and vanished."

I managed to repress my exclamation of surprise and wonder. Holmes arched one eyebrow thoughtfully. Sir Arthur stroked his mustache.

"Thank you for your help, Robert," Sir Arthur said as if Robert had said nothing out of the ordinary. "And your good observation."

"Sir Arthur," Robert said, "may I have your permission to salvage what I can from the field? The grain can't be threshed, but I could at least cut the stalks for hay."

"By no means!" Sir Arthur roared in alarm.

Robert stepped back, surprised and frightened.

"No, no," Sir Arthur said, calming himself with visible effort.

"Sir—!"

I was astonished by the tone of protest in which Robert addressed the landowner.

"It's imperative that no one enter the field!" Sir Arthur said. "The pattern mustn't be disturbed till we understand its meaning."

"Very well, Sir Arthur," Robert said reluctantly.

"And set little Robbie and his brothers to keeping the sightseers out of the patterns. They may walk around the edge, but under no circumstances may they proceed inside."

"But, Sir Arthur, this field, every year, has paid your rent. This field keeps the roof over my family's head! Sir Arthur, the crop prices have been low going on two years—"

I did not blame him for his distress, and he was fortunate that Sir Arthur is a humane and decent gentleman.

"You'll not worry about the rent," Sir Arthur said. "I relieve you of the obligation for this year."

On Robert's open face, gratitude and obligation warred.

"I cannot accept that offer, Sir Arthur," he said, "generous though it is, and grateful though I am to you for making it. You and I, we have an agreement. I cannot take charity."

Sir Arthur frowned, that his tenant would not accept such a simple solution to the difficulty.

"We'll discuss this another time," Sir Arthur said. "For the moment, keep the sightseers out of the field." His tone brooked no disagreement.

Robert touched the bill of his ragged cap in acquiescence. We returned to Sir Arthur's mansion, where his gracious wife Jean, Lady Conan Doyle, presided over a fine, if long-delayed, breakfast. After our excursion, I was famished, but Holmes merely picked at his food. This meant the mystery aroused him. As long as it kept his interest, he would hold himself free of the embrace of cocaine.

For the rest of the day, we accompanied Sir Arthur to other fields where theorems had mysteriously appeared over the past few weeks. They were all, according to Holmes, sadly trampled.

We spoke to tenants who had also seen lights in the sky, but the apparitions frightened the observers; each gave a different description, none as coherent as Robert's. I could not imagine what they had actually seen.

My mind kept returning to Robert's description. Cogent though it had been, something about it nagged at my memory. I put my unease own to the mystery of the phenomenon.

And to my wonder. Holmes's skepticism notwithstanding, it would be quite marvelous if we were visited by beings from another world, whether physical or spiritual. Naturally one would prefer friendly beings like those Sir Arthur described, over the invading forces of Mr Wells's scientific romances.

Holmes dutifully explored each damaged field, and listened to the descriptions of flashing lights in the sky. But as he was presented with nothing but old and damaged evidence, his inspections became more and more desultory as the afternoon wore on, his attention more and more distracted and impatient. He also grew more and more irritated at Sir Arthur's ruminations on spiritualism, and nothing I could do or say could divert the conversation. Like any true believer, Sir Arthur was relentless in his proselytizing.

Toward the end of the afternoon, as I began to hope for tea, we rested beneath an ancient oak near a patterned field.

"Look," Sir Arthur said, "at how the grain has been flattened without breaking. The stalks in the pattern are as green as the undisturbed growth. Don't you think it odd?"

"Quite odd," I agreed.

"Not odd at all," Holmes said.

He leapt from the carriage, snatched a handful of the crop from the edge of the field, and returned with a clump of unbroken stems still sprouting from their original earth. He held the roots in one hand and smashed the other against the stems, bending them at a right angle to their original position. Clods of dirt flew from his hand in reaction to the force of his blow.

But the stems did not break.

"*Triticum aestivum* at this stage of growth is exceedingly tough," Holmes said. "Exceedingly difficult to break."

Holmes pulled out one stem by its roots and handed it to me, then another for Sir Arthur. I tried to break my stem, and indeed it took considerable force even to put a kink in the fibrous growth. Sir Arthur bent his stem, folding it repeatedly back and forth.

"The field theorems would be more impressive," Holmes said, "if the crops *were* broken."

"But, Mr Holmes," said Sir Arthur, "the forces we are dealing with are mighty. A stem I cannot break would be like a fragile dry twig, to them. Do you not think it amazing that they can temper themselves to gentleness?"

Holmes stared at him in disbelief. "Sir Arthur! First you are impressed with a feat that appears to be difficult, then, when the action proves simple, you claim yourself impressed because it is simple! Your logic eludes me."

In Holmes's powerful hands, several stalks ripped apart.

We returned to Undershaw. We drank Earl Grey from delicate porcelain cups, surrounded by heavy, disagreeable silence. Lady Conan Doyle and I tried in vain to lighten the conversation. When Sir Arthur announced a seance to be held that very evening, Holmes's mood did not improve.

A loud knock on the door, followed by shouting, broke the tension. Sir Arthur rose to attend to the commotion.

"One of your tenants to see you, Sir Arthur," the butler said.

Robert had followed the butler from the front door; to my astonishment he crossed the threshold of the sitting room. Then he remembered his place and snatched his battered cap from his head.

"There's been another field done!" he exclaimed. "Little Robbie just discovered it, coming home to get his brothers some bread and cheese!"

Holmes leapt to his feet, his grey mood vanishing in an instant.

Sir Arthur called for his autocar and we hurried off to see the new phenomenon.

The automobile, newly repaired, motored smoothly until we turned down the final road to the new field theorem. Suddenly it died. Robert stepped down from the running board to crank it, but none of his efforts revived it.

Sir Arthur revealed a knowledge of colourful oaths in several languages.

"Bushman," Holmes muttered after a particularly exotic phrase.

I reflected that Sir Arthur must have acquired this unusual facility during his service in the Boer War.

We walked the last half-mile to the field. The afternoon's heat lingered even in the shade of the hedgerows. Birds chirped and rustled the branches.

"Well, Robert," I said, "you'll have the chance to observe Mr Holmes in action, and he can hear your story in your own words instead of mine. Holmes, Robert is a great enthusiast for your adventures."

"I am flattered," Holmes said, "though of course the credit goes entirely to you, Watson, and to your craft."

We had no more opportunity to chat, for we reached the newly patterned field. Robert's children—including Little Robbie, who was considerably taller and larger than his father—had arrived before us, despite our use of the motorcar. They stood in order of descending height on the bottom rail of the fence, exclaiming over the pattern crushed into the field.

Sir Arthur made as if to plunge into the very center of the new theorem, but Holmes clasped him by the shoulder.

"Stay back!" Holmes cried. "Robert! To the lane! Keep away the spectators!"

"Very well, Mr Holmes." Robert and his children tramped off down the path.

I marveled at the efficiency of the "bush telegraph," to give everyone such quick notice of the new field theorem.

Holmes plunged past Sir Arthur. But instead of forging into the field, he climbed the fence and balanced atop the highest rail to gaze across the waving grain. He traced with his eyes the valleys and gulches etched into the surface. Only after some minutes, and a complete circumnavigation of the field, did he venture into the field theorem itself.

Sir Arthur observed Holmes's method.

"You see, John?" Sir Arthur said. "Even your Mr Holmes acknowledges the power—the danger—present here."

"Sir Arthur," I said in the mildest tone possible, "why should danger result, if the communication is from those who loved you, in another life?"

"Why..." he said, momentarily awkward, "John, you'll understand after the seance tonight. The other side is... different."

Robert ran down the path, panting.

"I'm sorry, Mr Holmes, Sir Arthur," he said. "We kept them away as long as we could. Constable Brown ordered us to stand aside."

"More devotion to duty than to sense," Sir Arthur muttered. He sighed. "I'm sure you did your best," said he to Robert.

A group of curious people, led by Constable Brown and minimally constrained by Robert's children, approached between the hedgerows. Holmes was right: Someone, somehow, had alerted the public. Sightseers who had come to see the other field theorem now found themselves doubly fortunate.

The constable entered the field just as Holmes left it. The sightseers crowded up to the fence to view the new theorem.

Holmes rejoined Sir Arthur and myself.

"I have seen what I needed," Holmes said. "It's of no matter to me if the tourists trample the fields."

"But we must survey the theorem!" Sir Arthur said. "We still do not know its meaning!" He ordered Robert to do his best to prevent the sightseers from marring the designs.

"If we depart now," Holmes said, "before the constable realizes he is baffled by the phenomenon, we will be spared interrogation."

Dinner's being far preferable to interrogation, we took Holmes's advice. I noticed, to my amusement, that Robert's children had lined the spectators up. Some visitors even offered the boys tips, or perhaps entry fees. At least the family would not count its day an utter loss.

A photographer lowered his heavy camera from his shoulder. He set it upon its tripod and disappeared beneath the black shadow-cloth to focus the lenses. He exposed a plate, setting off a great explosion of flash powder. Smoke billowed up, bitter and sulphurous.

The journalists began to question Constable Brown, who puffed himself up with importance and replied to their questions. We hurried away, before the journalists should recognize Sir Arthur—or Holmes—and further delay us.

"If the motor starts," Sir Arthur said, "we will be in time for the seance."

For a moment I wondered if Holmes would turn *volte-face*, return to the field, and submit to questioning by Constable Brown *and* the journalists, in preference to submitting to the seance.

To our surprise, the motorcar started without hesitation. As Sir Arthur drove down the lane, Holmes puzzled over something in his hands.

"What is that, Holmes?"

"Just a bit of wood, a stake," Holmes said, putting it in his pocket. "I found it in the field."

As he was not inclined to discuss it further, we both fell silent. I wondered if we had to contend—besides the field theorems, the ghostly lights, and the seance—with wooden stakes and vampyres.

"Tell me, Sir Arthur," Holmes said over the rhythmic cough of the motor, "are any of your spirits known to live on Mars?"

"Mars?" Sir Arthur exclaimed. "Mars! I don't believe I've ever heard one mention it. But I don't believe I've ever heard one asked." He turned to Holmes, his eyes bright with anticipation. "We shall ask, this very evening! Why, that would explain Professor Schiaparelli's 'canali,' would it not?"

"Perhaps," Holmes said. "Though I fail to understand what use channels would be—to dead people."

Darkness gathered as we motored down the rough lane. Sir Arthur turned on the headlamps of the autocar, and the beams pierced the dimness, casting eerie shadows and picking out the twisted branches of trees. The wind in our face was cool and pleasant, if tinged somewhat by the scent of petrol.

The engine of the autocar died, and with it the light from the headlamps.

Sir Arthur uttered another of his exotic curses.

"I suppose it will be of no use," he said, "but would one of you gentlemen kindly try the crank?"

Holmes—knowing of my shoulder, shattered by a Jezail bullet in Afghanistan and never quite right since—leapt from the passenger seat and strode to the front of the automobile. He cranked it several times, to no avail. Without a word, he unstrapped the engine cover and opened it.

"It's too dark, Mr Holmes," Sir Arthur said. "We'll have to walk home from here."

"Perhaps not, Sir Arthur," said I. "Holmes's vision is acute." I climbed down, as well, to see if I could be of any assistance. I wished the automobile carried a kerosene lamp, though I suppose I would have had to hold it too far away from the engine, and the petrol tank, for it to be of much use.

"Can you see the difficulty, Holmes?" I asked.

His long fingers probed among the machined parts of the engine.

"Difficulty, Watson?" he said. "There is no difficulty here. Only enterprising cleverness."

The automobile rocked, and I assumed Sir Arthur was getting down to join us and try to help with the repairs.

"Cleverness?" said I. "Surely you can't mean—Ah!" Light flickered across his hawkish face, and for a moment I thought he had repaired the engine and the headlamps. Then I thought that Sir Arthur must have an innovative automobile, in which the headlamps gained their power from an independent battery rather than from the workings of the motor.

But then, I thought, they would surely not have failed at the same moment as the motor.

And finally I realized that the headlamps were dark, the engine still, and the lights on Holmes's face emanated from a separate source entirely.

I raised my eyes in the direction of the flickering lights. An eerie radiance lit the forest beyond the road. As I watched, it descended slowly beneath the tops of the trees.

"Sir Arthur!" I cried.

His silhouette moved quickly toward the mysterious lights.

Holmes and I ran after him. I felt a shiver, whether of fear or of unearthly chill, I could not have said.

Suddenly a great flash of light engulfed us, and a great shock of sound. Dazzled, I stumbled and fell, crying, "Sir Arthur!" I thought I heard one of Sir Arthur's exotic oaths, this time in the voice of Sherlock Holmes.

I came to myself, my sight flickering with brilliant black and white afterimages. When my vision cleared, I found myself staring straight up into the night. Among the constellations, Mars burned red in the darkness. I shivered in sudden dread. I sat up, groaning.

Holmes was instantly at my side.

"Stay quiet, Watson," he said. "You'll soon be right. No injuries, I fancy."

"And you, Holmes? And Sir Arthur?"

"My sight has recovered, but Sir Arthur does not answer my hallo."

"What happened, Holmes? What was that explosion?"

"It was... what Robert called a flying coracle," Holmes said. "But it has vanished, and with it Dr Conan Doyle."

"We must return to Undershaw! Call out a search party!"

"No!" Holmes exclaimed. "He has been spirited away, and we have no hope of finding the location unless I can inspect the site of his disappearance. *Before* searchers trample it."

"But Lady Conan Doyle!" I said. "She'll be frantic!"

"If we return now," Holmes said, "we can only tell her Sir Arthur is lost."

"Kidnapped!" I only wished I knew who—or what—had done the kidnapping.

"Perhaps, though I doubt he believes so."

"He could be killed—!"

"He is safe, I warrant," Holmes said.

"How can you be sure?"

"Because," Holmes said, "no one would benefit from his death." He settled into the seat of the autocar. "If we wait till dawn, we may retrieve him and return him safely to the bosom of his family. Before they have any more concern than a few hours of wondering where we have got to."

"Very well, Holmes," I said doubtfully, "but the responsibility for Sir Arthur's safety lies on your shoulders."

"I accept it," Holmes said solemnly. Suddenly, he brightened somewhat. "I fear we shall miss the seance."

I confess that I dozed, in the darkest hours of the night, cold and uncomfortable and cramped in the seat of the disabled motorcar. My last sight, before I slept, was the scarlet glow of Mars sinking beneath the tops of the trees. I dreamed of a race of beings so powerful that the canals they built could be seen from another planet.

When I woke, shivering, tiny dewdrops covered my tweeds. The silence of night gave way to the bright songs of dawn. The scent of wet grass and sulphur wafted into my nostrils. I tried to remember a particular point of my dream.

Holmes shook me.

"I'm awake, Holmes!" I said. The snatch of memory vanished without a trace. "Have you found Sir Arthur?"

"Not yet," he said. "Hold this, while I crank the motor."

He handed me a bit of metal—two strips sintered together to form one curved piece.

"What about Sir Arthur?" I asked. "What about your search?"

"My search is finished," Holmes said. "I found, overhead, a few singed tree-leaves. At my feet, a dusty spot on the ground. Marks pressed into the soil, forming the corners of a parallelogram—" He snorted. "Not even a square! Far less elegant than the field theorems. Savory food for speculation."

"But no trace of Sir Arthur?"

"Many traces, but… I think we will not find his hiding place."

I glanced up into the sky, but the stars had faded and no trace of light remained.

Holmes fell silent. He would say no more until he was ready. I feared he had failed—Holmes, failed!—and Sir Arthur lay dead in some kidnapper's lair, on or off our world.

The autocar started without hesitation. I had never driven a motorcar—it is folly to own one in the city, where a hansom is to be had for a handwave, a shout, and a few shillings. But I had observed Sir Arthur carefully. Soon we were moving down the road, and I fancy the ruts, rather than my driving, caused what jolts we felt.

"And what is this, Holmes?" I asked, giving him his bit of metal. He snatched it and pointed straight ahead. I quickly corrected the autocar's direction, for in my brief moment of inattention it had wandered toward the hedgerow.

"The bit of metal, Holmes?"

"It is," he said, "a bit of metal."

"What does it mean?" I said irritably. "Where did you find it?"

"I found it in the motor," he said, and placed it in his pocket. "And may I compliment you on your expert driving. I had no idea you numbered automobile racing among your talents."

I took his rather unsubtle hint and slowed the vehicle. Hedgerows grew close on either side; it would not be pleasant to round a turn and come upon a horse and carriage.

"I dreamed of Mars, Holmes," I said.

"Pah!" he said. "Mars!"

"Quite a wonderful dream!" I continued undaunted. "We had learned to communicate with the Martians. We could converse, with signals of light, as quickly and as easily as if we were using a telegraph. But of course that would be impossible."

"How, impossible?" Holmes asked. "Always assuming there *were* Martians with whom to converse."

"Light cannot travel so quickly between the worlds," I said.

"Light transmission is instantaneous," Holmes said in a dismissive tone.

"On the contrary," I said. "As you would know if you paid the least attention to astronomy or physics. The Michelson-Morley experiment proved light has a finite speed, and furthermore that its speed remains constant—but that is beside the point!"

"What *is* the point, pray tell?" Holmes asked. "You were, I believe, telegraphing back and forth with Martians."

"The point is that I could *not* converse instantaneously with Martians—"

"I do see a certain difficulty in stringing the wires," Holmes said drily.

"—because it would take several minutes—I would have to do the arithmetic, but at least ten—for my 'hallo!' to reach Mars, and another length of time for their 'Good day to you' to return."

"Perhaps you should use the post," Holmes said.

"And that is what troubled me about Robert's description!" I exclaimed.

"Something troubled you?" Holmes said. "You have not mentioned it before."

"I could not think what it was. But of course! He thought he saw a signal from Mars, to the coracle, at the instant after its disappearance. This is impossible, you see, Holmes, because a message would take so long to reach us. He must have been mistaken in what he saw."

Holmes rode beside me in silence for some moments, then let his breath out in a long sigh.

"As usual, Watson, you shame me," he said. "You have provided the clue to the whole mystery, and now all is clear."

"I do?" I said. "I have? It is?" I turned to him. "But what about Sir Arthur? How can the mystery be solved if we have lost Sir Arthur? Surely we cannot return to Undershaw without him!"

"Stop!" Holmes cried.

Fearing Holmes had spied a sheep in the road while my attention was otherwise occupied, I engaged the brake abruptly. The autocar lurched to a halt, and Holmes used the momentum to leap from the seat to the roadway.

Sir Arthur sat upon a stone on the verge of the track.

"Good morning, Dr Conan Doyle," Holmes said. "I trust your adventure has left you none the worse for wear?"

Sir Arthur gazed up with a beatific expression, his eyes wide and glassy.

"I have seen things, Mr Holmes," he said. "Amazing things…"

Holmes helped him to the automobile and into the passenger seat. As Sir Arthur settled himself, Holmes plucked a bit of material from Sir Arthur's shoe.

"What have you found, Holmes?" I asked.

"Nothing remarkable," replied Holmes. "A shred of dusty silk, I believe." He folded the fabric carefully, placed it into his pocket, and vaulted into the autocar.

Sir Arthur made no objection to my driving us back to Undershaw. It was as if he had visited a different world, and still lived in it in his mind. He refused to speak of it until we returned to his home, and his worried wife.

A paragon of womanhood, Lady Conan Doyle accepted Sir Arthur's assurances that he was unharmed. She led us to the morning room and settled us all in deep chairs of maroon velvet.

Sir Arthur commenced his story.

"It was amazing," Sir Arthur said. "Absolutely amazing. I saw the lights, and it was as if I were mesmerized. I felt drawn to them. I hurried through the woods. I saw the ring of illumination, just as Robert described it. Brighter than anything we can manufacture, I'd warrant—never mind that it floated in the sky! I saw the coracle. A flying vehicle, turning slowly above me, and windows—and faces! Faces peering down at me."

Holmes shifted and frowned, but said nothing.

"Then I saw a flash of light—"

"We saw it, too," said I. "We feared you'd been injured."

"Far from it!" Conan Doyle said. "Uplifted, rather! Enlightened! I swooned with the shock, and when I awoke—I was inside the coracle!"

"How did you know where you were?" Holmes demanded. "Could you see out the windows? Were you high above the ground?"

"I was in a round room, the size of the coracle, and I could feel the wafting of the winds—"

It occurred to me that the previous night had been nearly windless. But perhaps the flying coracle had risen higher and the wind aloft had freshened.

"What of the portholes?" Holmes asked.

"There were no portholes," Sir Arthur said, still speaking in a dreamy voice. "The walls were smooth black, like satin. The portholes had closed over, without leaving a trace!"

"Sir Arthur—" Holmes protested.

"Hush, Mr Holmes, please," Lady Conan Doyle said, leaning forward, her face alight with concentration. "Let my husband finish his story."

"I was not at all frightened, strangely content, and immobile," Sir Arthur said. "Then... the *people* came in and spoke to me. They looked like—like nothing on this Earth! They were very pale, and their eyes were huge and bright, shining with otherworldly intelligence. They told me—they told me, without speaking, they spoke in my mind, without moving their lips!"

"Ah," Holmes murmured, "so at least they had lips."

"Shh!" Lady Conan Doyle said, dispensing with courtesy.

"What did they tell you, Sir Arthur?" I asked.

"They wished to examine me, to determine if their people and ours are compatible, to determine if we can live together in peace."

"Live together!" I ejaculated.

"Yes. They did examine me—I cannot describe the process in polite company, except to say that it was... quite thorough. Strangely enough, I felt no fear, and very little discomfort, even when they used the needles."

"Ah, yes," Holmes murmured. "The needles."

"Who were these people?" I asked, amazed. "Where are they from?"

"They are," Sir Arthur said softly, "from Mars."

I felt dazed, not only because of my exhaustion. Lady Conan Doyle made a sound of wonder, and Holmes—Holmes growled low in his throat.

"From Mars?" he said drily. "Not from the spirit realm?"

Sir Arthur drew himself up, bristling at the implied insult.

"I'll not have it said I cannot admit I was wrong! The new evidence is overwhelming!"

Before Holmes could reply, Sir Arthur's butler appeared in the doorway.

"Sir Arthur," he said.

"Tell Robert," Holmes said without explanation, "that we have no need to examine any new field theorems. Tell him he may notify the constabulary, the journalists, and the king if he wishes."

The butler hesitated.

"And tell him," Holmes added, "that he may charge what he likes to guide them."

The butler bowed and disappeared.

"They'll trample the theorem!" Sir Arthur objected, rising from his chair. "We won't know—"

"But you already know, Sir Arthur," Holmes said. "The creators of the field theorem have spoken to you."

Sir Arthur relaxed. "That is true," he said. He smiled. "To think that I've been singled out this way—to introduce them to the world!" He leaned forward, spreading his hands in entreaty. "They're nothing like the Martians of Mr Wells," he said. "Not evil, not invaders. They wish only to be our friends. There's no need for panic."

"We're hardly in danger of panic," Holmes said. "I have done as you asked. I have solved your mystery." He nodded to me. "Thanks to my friend Dr Watson."

"There is no mystery, Mr Holmes," Sir Arthur said.

Holmes drew from his pocket the wooden stake, the metal spring, and the scrap of black silk. He placed them on the table before us. Dust drifted from the silk, emitting a burned, metallic scent and marring the polished table with a film of white.

"You are correct. There is, indeed, no mystery." He picked up the stake, and I noticed that a few green stalks remained wrapped tightly around it. "I found this in the center of the new field theorem, the one that so conveniently appeared after I expressed a desire to see one afresh. Unfortunately, its creators were unduly hurried, and could not work with their usual care. They left the center marker, to which they tied a rope, to use as a compass to form their circles."

Holmes moved his long forefinger around the stake, showing how a loop of rope had scuffed the corners of the wood, how the circular motion had pulled crop stalks into a tight coil.

"But that isn't what happened," Sir Arthur said. "The Martians explained all. They were trying to communicate with me, but the theorems are beyond our mental reach. So they risked everything to speak to me directly."

Holmes picked up the spring.

"Metal expands when it heats," he said. "This was cunningly placed so its expansion disarranged a connection in your motor. Whenever the temperature rose, the motor would stop. Naturally, you drove rapidly when you went to investigate each new field theorem. Of course your motorcar would overheat—and, consequently, misbehave—under those circumstances."

"The Martians disrupted the electrical flux of my motorcar—it's an inevitable result of the energy field that supports their coracle. It can fly through space, Mr Holmes, from Mars to Earth and back again!"

Holmes sighed, and picked up the bit of black silk.

"This is all that is left of the flying coracle," he said. "The hot-air balloon, rather. Candles at its base heated the air, kept the balloon aloft, and produced the lights."

"The lights were too bright for candles, Mr Holmes," Sir Arthur said.

Holmes continued undaunted. "Add to the balloon a handful of flash powder." He shook the bit of black silk. White dust floated from it, and a faint scent of sulphur wafted into the air. "It ignites, you are dazzled. The silk ignites! The candles, the balloon, the straw framework—all destroyed! Leaving nothing but dust... a dust of magnesium oxide." He stroked his fingertip through the powder.

"It did not burn me," Sir Arthur pointed out.

"It was not meant to burn you. It was meant to amaze you. Your abductors are neither malicious nor stupid." Holmes brushed the dust from his hands. "We were meant to imagine a craft that could fall from the sky, balance on its legs, and depart again, powered on flame, like a Chinese rocket! But it left the tracks of four legs, awkwardly spaced. I found this suspicious. Three legs, spaced regularly, would lead to more stability."

"Very inventive, Mr Holmes, but you fail to explain how the Martians transported me to their coracle, how the portholes sealed without a trace, how they spoke to me in my mind."

"Sir Arthur," Holmes said, "are you familiar with the effects of cocaine?"

"In theory, of course," said Sir Arthur. "I'm a medical doctor, after all."

"Personally familiar," Holmes said.

"I've never had occasion to use it myself, nor to prescribe it," Sir Arthur said. "So, no, I am not *personally* familiar with the effects of cocaine."

"I am," Holmes said quietly. "And you show every sign of having recently succumbed to its influence. Your eyes are glassy. Your imagination is heightened—"

"Are you saying," Sir Arthur said with disbelief, "that the Martians drugged me with cocaine?"

"There are no Martians!" Holmes said, raising his voice for the first time. "There are hoaxers, who created a clever illusion, dazzled you, drugged you, and took you to a hiding place—a raft, no doubt, that would mimic the motions of a boat floating in the air. They disguised themselves, spoke from behind masks—or behind a curtain!—taking advantage of your distracted consciousness. You saw the needle yourself, the second needle that drugged you again, so they could place you where you would be safe, and soon found!"

Sir Arthur gazed at Holmes for a long moment, then chuckled softly.

"I understand," he said softly. "I do understand."

"You understand that you have been tricked?" Holmes asked.

"I understand all. You need say no more. Some day, in the future, when you're persuaded of my complete goodwill, we'll have occasion to speak again."

Sir Arthur rose, crossed the room, and opened his desk. He drew out a sheet of paper, returned, and presented the paper to Holmes.

"This is a letter of credit," he said, "in payment for your services. It's sufficient, I hope?"

Holmes barely glanced at the paper. "More than sufficient," he said. "Most generous, I would say, from a client who believes I have been made a fool of by Martians."

"Not at all, Mr Holmes. I understand your reasoning. You are very subtle, sir, I admire you."

"Then you accept—"

"I accept your explanation as proof of my hypothesis," Sir Arthur said. "And I admire you beyond words." He smiled. "And now, we are all very tired. I must rest, and then—to work! To introduce the world to the wonders approaching us. I've taken the liberty of hiring a private train to return you to London. A token of my esteem."

Speechless, Holmes rose.

"Your luggage is in the autocar. James will drive you to the station. The autocar will not misbehave, because our visitors have gone home for the moment. But—they will return!"

Sir Arthur and Lady Conan Doyle accompanied us to the drive, so graciously that I hardly felt we were being shown the door. I climbed into the motorcar, but Sir Arthur held Holmes back for a moment, speaking to him in a low voice, shaking his hand.

Holmes joined me, nonplussed, and James drove us away. The motorcar ran flawlessly. As we passed a field that yesterday had been a smooth swath of grain, but today was marked by a field theorem more complex than any before, we saw Robert and Little Robbie directing spectators around the crushed patterns in the field. They both had taken more care with their appearance than the previous day, and wore clothes without holes or patches.

His expression hidden in the shade of his new cap, Robert turned to watch us pass.

"Holmes—" I said.

Holmes gently silenced me with a gesture. He raised one hand in farewell to the farmer. Robert saluted him. A small smile played around Holmes's lips.

As soon as we were alone in the private train car, Holmes flung himself into a luxurious leather armchair and began to laugh. He laughed so hard, and so long, that I feared he was a candidate for Bedlam.

"Holmes!" I cried. "Get hold of yourself, man!" I poured him a glass of brandy—Napoleon, I noticed in passing.

His laughter faded slowly to an occasional chuckle, and he wiped tears from his eyes.

"That's better," I said. "What is so infernally funny?"

"Human beings," Holmes said. "Human beings, Watson, are an endless source of amusement."

"I do not like leaving Sir Arthur with a misapprehension of events. Perhaps we should return—seek out the raft on which he was held captive."

"It has, no doubt, been sunk in the deepest part of the lake. We would never find it... unless we could engage the services of Mr Verne's Captain Nemo."

"I'm astonished that you've read *Twenty Thousand Leagues Under the Sea*," I said.

"I have not. But you did, and you described it to me quite fully." He sipped the brandy, and glanced at the glowing amber liquid in appreciation. "Hmm. The last good year."

I poured cognac for myself, warmed the balloon glass between my hands, and savored the sweet, intoxicating bite of its vapors. It was far too early in the day for spirits, but this one time I excused myself.

"When we return to Baker Street," said Holmes, "I might perhaps borrow your copy of *War of the Worlds*, if you would be so kind as to lend it to me."

"I will," I said, "if you promise not to rip out its pages for your files. Bertie inscribed it to me personally."

"I will guard its integrity with my life."

I snorted. The train jerked, wheels squealing against the tracks, and gathered speed.

"What about Sir Arthur?" I asked, refusing to be put off again. "He believes he's been visited by Martians!"

"Watson, old friend, Sir Arthur is a willing participant in the hoax."

"You mean—he engineered it himself? Then why engage your services?"

"An innocent, unconscious participant. He *wants* to believe. He has exchanged Occam's razor for Occam's kaleidoscope, complicating simple facts into explanations of impossible complexity. But he believes they are true, just as he believes spirits visit him, and Houdini possesses mediumistic powers, and I..." He started to chuckle again.

"I don't understand the *purpose* of this hoax!" I said, hoping to distract him before he erupted into another bout of hysteria. "Nor who perpetrated it!"

"It is a difficult question. I despaired of solving it. I wondered if Sir Arthur wished to pit his intellect against mine. If the journalists and photographers conspired to create a story. If Constable Brown wished to draw more resources to his district—and found he enjoyed the limelight!"

"Which of them was it, Holmes? Wait! It was the photographer—only he has access to flash powder!"

"And an intimate knowledge of Surrey fields? No. The flash powder is easily purchased—or purloined. It was no one you mention."

"Then who?"

"Who benefits?"

I considered. If Sir Arthur wrote of the events, he might make a tidy sum from a book and lecture tour. But Holmes had already stated that Sir Arthur was innocent. Still, what benefited Sir Arthur would benefit his whole family...

"Not Lady Conan Doyle!" I exclaimed, aghast.

"Certainly not," Holmes said.

"The butler? The driver? He would know how to sabotage the car—"

"Robert Holder, Watson!" Holmes cried. "Robert Holder! Perhaps—indeed, certainly—with help from James and the butler and other tenants in the neighborhood. But Robert was the mastermind, for all his rough appearance. A veritable Houdini of the countryside!" Holmes considered. "Indeed, he used some of my own techniques. And he almost defeated me!"

"He risked all by challenging you!"

"I was unforeseen—surely he intended Sir Arthur to conduct the investigation. When you and I arrived, Robert must have realized he would stand or fall by his boldness. He offered Sir Arthur a compelling reason to dismiss my solution—and me. Sir Arthur accepted the offering. How could he resist?"

Holmes gazed out the window of the train for a moment. Unmarred fields rippled past, like miniature green seas.

"If not for Robert's misapprehension about the velocity of light," Holmes said, "a misapprehension that I shared, I would have known *what* happened, and I would have known *how*—but I never would have been certain *who*."

"You sound curiously sympathetic, Holmes," I said with disapproval.

"Indeed I am, Watson. Robert is clearly an honourable man."

"Honourable!"

"He refused Sir Arthur's offer to relieve him of the year's rent. He has no wish to steal."

"Only to lie."

"Like Houdini. Like any entertainer, any storyteller. Shakespeare lied. You have lied yourself, my friend, in your descriptions of our adventures."

"I have disguised individuals," I said, taking offense. "I have, yes, perhaps, dissembled occasionally..." I hesitated, and then I nodded. "Very well. I have lied."

"Life is hard for people who work the land. You and I are prosperous, now, but remember what it was like when we were younger, scraping along from season to season, with never a new shirt or a pair of boots that did not let in the rain? Imagine seeing no better prospects. For the rest of your life."

I suddenly remembered father and sons, and their new clothes.

"Who can blame them for creating a diversion, a mystery to attract sightseers, people of leisure with money to spare. People," Holmes added, "with a blind eye to turn to the evidence lying plain before them?"

"What of your commitment to the truth, Holmes?" I asked with some asperity.

"I know the truth," he said. "You know it. Sir Arthur knows it, but rejects it. I have kept the solution to other mysteries confidential; it is part of my duty. How is this different?"

I suddenly understood. Holmes's sympathy was not so much directed toward the hoaxers as away from the curiosity seekers who were willing, indeed eager, to be fooled.

"Very well, Holmes," I said. "I am content, if you are."

We rode in silence for some miles, lulled by the rocking of the train, enjoying Sir Arthur's excellent cognac and the peaceful English countryside. I wondered what the world would be like if beings from another planet *did* visit us.

"Holmes," I said.

"Yes, Watson?"

"Why was Sir Arthur so willing to pay you, when he did not believe your solution? What did he say to you, just as we left?"

"He said, 'I understand why you are such an extraordinary person. Like Houdini, you have good reason to hide your abilities, your true nature. I understand why Sherlock Holmes cannot be the one to reveal the truth about our visitors. I will do it, and you may trust me to keep *your* secret.'"

"*Your* secret?"

"Yes, Watson." Holmes smiled. "Sir Arthur Conan Doyle believes I am a Martian."

THE ADVENTURE OF THE DEATH-FETCH

by Darrell Schweitzer

Darrell Schweitzer is the author of the novels *The Shattered Goddess* and *The Mask of the Sorcerer*, as well as numerous short stories, which have been collected in *Transients, Nightscapes, Refugees from an Imaginary Country*, and *Necromancies and Netherworlds*. Recent books include *The Fantastic Horizon, Ghosts of Past and Future*, and *Living with the Dead*. Well-known as an editor and critic, he co-edited the magazine *Weird Tales* for several years, and is currently editing anthologies for DAW, such as *The Secret History of Vampires* and *Cthulhu's Reign*, and an urban fantasy werewolf anthology for Pocket Books.

We all have days when the world seems too much to bear, and all we want to do is lock ourselves in our room and not come out. It's an illusion, this idea that a foot of wood and plaster can seal us off from the troubles that beset us, but it's a comforting illusion, and it resonates. Authors have spun some wonderful dramatic scenarios out of this notion of a safe room within a hostile universe. H. P. Lovecraft's "The Music of Erich Zann" is about a violinist who plays unearthly tunes to keep hostile entities from invading his apartment. China Miéville's "Details" is about a woman who has plastered over all the visible lines and angles in her apartment, because those angles are traversed by the other-dimensional terrors that assail her. The movie *Pulse* features characters who must seal up their room with red duct tape to protect themselves from malevolent spirits. There's something instantly intriguing about a person who *refuses to come out*, and also about the idea that evil could be kept at bay by something simple, such as music or duct tape. Our next tale brings us a chilling new variation on this theme.

In retrospect, the most amazing thing is that Watson confided the story to me at all. I was nobody, a nineteen-year-old college student from America visiting English relatives during Christmas break. I just happened to be in the house when the old doctor came to call. He had been a friend of my grandfather long before I was born, and was still on the closest terms with my several aunts; and of course he was *the* Doctor John Watson, who could have commanded the immediate and rapt attention of any audience he chose.

So, why did he tell me and only me? Why not, at least, my aunts? I think it was precisely because I was no one of any consequence or particular credibility and would soon be returning to school far away. He was like the servant of King Midas in the fairy tale, who can no longer bear the secret that the king has ass's ears. He has to "get it off his chest," as we Americans say. The point is not being believed, or recording the truth, but release from the sheer act of telling. The luckless courtier, fearing for his life, finally has to dig a hole in the swamp, stick his head in it, and whisper the secret. Not that it did him much good, for the wind in the rattling reeds endlessly repeated what he had said.

There being no swamp conveniently at hand for Dr. Watson, I would have to do.

The old gentleman must have been nearly eighty at the time. I remember him as stout, but not quite obese, nearly bald, with a generous white moustache. He often sat smoking by the remains of our fire long after the rest of the household had gone to bed. I imagined that he was reminiscing over a lifetime of wonderful adventures. Well, maybe.

I was up late too, that particular night, on my way into the kitchen for some tea after struggling with a wretched attempt at a novel. I chanced through the parlor. Doctor Watson stirred slightly where he sat.

"Oh, Doctor. I'm sorry. I didn't know you were still there."

He waved me to the empty chair opposite him. I sat without a further word, completely in awe of the great man.

I swallowed hard and stared at the floor for perhaps five minutes, jerking my head up once, startled, when the burnt log in the fireplace settled, throwing off sparks. I could hear occasional automobiles passing by in the street outside.

Dr. Watson's pipe had gone out and he set it aside. He folded his age-spotted hands in his lap, cleared his throat, and leaned forward.

He had my absolute attention. I knew that he was about to *tell a story*. My heart almost stopped.

"I am sure you know there were some cases of Sherlock Holmes which never worked out, and thus went unrecorded."

I lost what little composure I had and blurted, "Yes, yes, Doctor. You mention them from time to time. Like the one about the man and the umbrella —"

He raised a hand to silence me. "Not like that, boy. Some I never found the time to write up, and I inserted those allusions as reminders to myself; but others were *deliberately suppressed,* and never committed to paper at all, because Holmes expressly forbade it. One in particular —"

At least I didn't say anything as stupid as, *"Then why are you telling me?"* No, I had the good sense to sit absolutely motionless and silent, and just listen.

It was about this same season [*Watson began*] in the year 1900, a few days after Christmas if I recall correctly—I cannot be certain of such facts without my notebooks, and in any case the incident of which I speak was never entered into them—but I am certain it was a bright and brisk winter day, with new-fallen snow on the sidewalks, but no sense of festivity in the air. Instead, the city seemed to have reached a profound calm, a time to rest and tidy up and go on with one's regular business.

Holmes remarked how somehow, in defiance of all logic, it appeared that the calendar revealed patterns of criminality.

"Possibly the superstitions are true," I mused, "and lunatics really *are* driven by the moon."

"There may be scattered facts buried in the morass of superstition, Watson," said he, "if only science has the patience to ferret them out —"

We had now come, conversing as we walked, to the corner of Baker Street and Marylebone Road, having been abroad on some business or other—damn that I don't have my notes with me—when this train of thought was suddenly interrupted by an attractive, well-dressed young woman who rushed up and grasped Holmes by the arm.

"Mr. Sherlock Holmes? You *are* Mr. Sherlock Holmes, are you not?"

Holmes gently eased her hand off him. "I am indeed, Miss —"

"Oh! Thank God! My father said that no one else could possibly save him!"

To my amazement and considerable irritation, Holmes began walking briskly, leaving the poor girl to trail after us like a common beggar. I'd often had words with him in private about these lapses of the expected courtesy, but now I could only follow along, somewhat flustered. Meanwhile the young lady—whose age I would have guessed at a few years short of twenty—breathlessly related a completely disjointed tale about a mysterious curse, approaching danger, and quite a bit else I couldn't make head or tail out of.

At the doorstep of 221B, Holmes turned on her sharply.

"And now Miss—I'm afraid I did not catch your name."

"Thurston. My name is Abigail Thurston."

"Any relation to Sir Humphrey Thurston, the noted explorer of Southeast Asia?"

"He is my father, as I've already told you —"

"I am not sure you've told me much of anything—yet!" Holmes turned to go inside. Miss Thurston's features revealed a completely understandable admixture of disappointment, grief, and quite possibly—and I couldn't have blamed her—rage.

"Holmes!" I said. "Please!"

"And now Miss Abigail Thurston, as I have no other business this morning, I shall be glad to admit you." As she, then I, followed him up the stairs, he continued, "You must pardon my abrupt manner, but it has its uses."

When I had shown her to a chair and rung Mrs. Hudson for some tea, Holmes explained further, "My primary purpose has been to startle you into *sense*, Miss Thurston. A story told all in a jumble is like a brook plunging over a precipice—very pretty, but, alas, babbling. Now that the initial rush of excitement is past, perhaps now you can tell me, calmly and succinctly, why you have come to see me. I enjoin you to leave out none of the facts, however trivial they may seem to you. Describe the events *exactly,* in the order that they occurred, filling in such background as may be necessary to illuminate the entire tale."

She breathed deeply, then began in measured tones. "I am indeed the daughter of the explorer, Sir Humphrey Thurston. You are perhaps familiar with his discoveries of lost cities in the jungles of Indo-China. His books are intended for a limited, scholarly audience, but there have been numerous articles about him in the popular magazines —"

"Suffice it to say that I am familiar with your father and his admirable contributions to science. Do go on."

"My mother died when I was quite small, Mr. Holmes, and my father spent so much time abroad that he was almost a stranger to me. I was raised by relatives, under the supervision of a series of governesses. All this while Father seemed more a guardian angel than a parent, someone always looking out for my welfare, concerned and benevolent, but invisible. Oh, there were letters and gifts in the post, but he remained *outside* my actual life. Each time he came, we had to become acquainted all over again. Such is the difference in a child's life between six and eight and twelve. *I* had changed profoundly, while he was always the same, brave, mysterious, inevitably sunburnt from long years in the jungles and deserts; home for a short time to rest, write his reports, and perhaps give a few lectures before setting forth again in the quest of knowledge. So things have continued. This past month he has returned again, after an absence of three years, to discover his little girl become a *woman,* and again a stranger. He has promised to remain this time until I am married and secure in a home of my own —"

"Then it should be a happy occasion for you," said Holmes, smiling to reassure her, the corners of his mouth twitching to betray impatience. The smile vanished. "But I perceive it is not. Please get to the point then. *Why* have you come rushing to Baker Street on a winter's day when you would surely be much more comfortable in a warm house in the company of your much-travelled sire?"

She paused, looking alarmed once more, glancing to me first as if for reassurance. I could only smile and nod, wordlessly bidding her to continue.

"The first few days of his visit were indeed happy, Mr. Holmes, but very suddenly, a shadow came over him. For a week and more, he seemed distracted and brooding. Then five days ago he withdrew into his study, refusing to venture out for any reason. He is afraid, deathly afraid!"

"Of what, pray tell?"

"I cannot discern the central fear, exactly, only its broader effects. Certainly he has become morbidly afraid of his own reflection. He will not allow a mirror to be brought anywhere near him. He even shaves with his eyes closed, by touch alone, rather than risk seeing himself."

"This *is* extraordinary," I said.

"But surely," said Holmes, "this sort of mania is more in Doctor Watson's line than mine, work for a medical man of a specialized sort, not a detective."

"Oh no, Sir! My father is completely sane. I am certain of that. But I am equally certain that he is not telling me everything, perhaps in an attempt to spare me some horror—for it must be a horror that makes so bold an adventurer cringe behind a locked door with a loaded elephant gun across his knees!"

I leaned forward and spoke to her in my most soothing medical manner. "I am sure, Miss Thurston, that your father has a very good reason for acting as he does, and that, indeed, his chief object is to protect you."

"Yes," said Holmes. "I am certain it is."

"His very words were, 'Summon Sherlock Holmes, girl, or I shall not live out the week!' So here I am. Please come and see him, Mr. Holmes, *at once!"*

Holmes shot to his feet. "Watson! How foolish of us to have even removed our hats and coats. Come!" He took our guest by the hand and helped her up. "As I said, Miss Thurston, I have no other business this morning."

It was but a short cab ride to the Thurston residence, in the most fashionable part of west London. We rode in silence, crowded together, the girl in the middle, Holmes deep in thought. Unconsciously almost, Miss Thurston took my hand for reassurance. I held her firmly, but gently.

It was admittedly an intriguing problem: what, if not a sudden mania, could cause so brave a man as Sir Humphrey Thurston to be paralyzed with fear at the sight of his own reflection?

As we neared the house, the girl suddenly struggled to stand up in the still moving cab.

"Father!"

She pointed. I had only a glimpse of a tall, muscular man on the further street-corner, and noted the tan coat and top hat, white gloves, and silver-tipped stick. He turned at the sound of Miss Thurston's cry, revealing a grey-bearded face, dark eyes, and a broad, high forehead, then moved speedily away in long strides, not quite running. Abruptly, he vanished down a side street.

Holmes pounded on the ceiling of the cab for the driver to stop and we three scrambled out, I attending to Miss Thurston and the driver while Holmes set off at a furious run, only to return moments later, breathing hard, having lost all trace of Sir Humphrey.

"I don't know what explanation I can offer," said Miss Thurston. "Perhaps my father's difficulty, mania or whatever it is, has passed, and I have wasted your time."

Holmes nodded to me.

"Mental disease is not my specialty." I said, "but from what medical papers I've read, and from the talk of my colleagues, I do not think it likely that so powerful a delusion would go away so quickly. It makes no sense."

"Indeed, it does not," said Holmes. "One moment, the man behaves as if he is faced with mortal danger. The next, he is out for a stroll as if nothing had happened, but he flees the approach of his beloved daughter and vanishes with, I must confess, remarkable speed and agility."

"What do we do now, Mr. Holmes?"

"If you would admit us to his chamber. Perhaps he left some clue."

"Yes, yes. I should have thought of that. Pray forgive me —"

"Do not trouble yourself, Miss Thurston. Only lead the way."

She unlocked the door herself. Although it was a fine, large house, there were no servants in evidence. I helped her off with her coat and hung it for her in a closet off to one side. As we ascended the front stairs, she hastily explained that another of her father's inexplicable behaviors was to give leave to the entire staff until—she supposed—the crisis had passed.

"Oh, I do fear that it *is* a mania, Mr. Holmes."

I was beginning to fear as much myself, but scarcely a moment to consider the possibility when a voice thundered from above, "Abigail! Is that you?"

Miss Thurston looked to Holmes, then to me with an expression of utmost bewilderment and fright. I think she all but fainted at that moment. I made ready to catch her lest she tumble back down the stairs.

Again came the voice, from somewhere off to the left of the top of the stairs. "Abigail! If that's you, speak up girl! If it's Hawkins, you damned blackguard, I have my gun ready and am fully prepared to shoot!"

Holmes shouted in reply, "Sir Humphrey, it is Sherlock Holmes and his colleague Dr. Watson. We have been admitted by your daughter, who is here with us."

"Abigail?"

"Yes, Father, it is I. I've brought them as you asked."

Heavy footsteps crossed the floor upstairs. A door opened with a click of the lock being undone.

"Thank God, then…"

Holmes, Miss Thurston, and I were admitted into Sir Humphrey's study. I was astounded to confront the *same man* we had seen on the street. The broad shoulders, bearded face, high forehead, dark eyes, and athletic gait were unmistakable. But now he wasn't dressed for the outdoors. He wore a dressing gown and slippers. An elephant gun lay across the chair where he had obviously been sitting moments before. On the table by his right hand were a bottle and glass of brandy, a notebook, a pen and an uncapped ink jar.

"Thank God you are here, Mr. Holmes," he said. "Doubtless my daughter has told you of my distress and seeming madness. If anyone on Earth may convince me that I am *not* mad, it is you, Mr. Holmes. I can trust no one else to uncover the fiendish devices by which I have been made to see the impossible."

We all sat. Thurston offered Holmes and me glasses of brandy. Holmes waved his aside. I accepted out of politeness, but after a single sip placed it on the table beside me.

Sir Humphrey seemed about ready to speak, when Holmes interrupted.

"First, a question. Have you been, for any reason, outside of the house this morning?"

Thurston looked startled. "Certainly not. I have not been out of this *room* for five days —" He paused, as if uncertain of how to proceed.

It was Holmes's turn to be astonished, but only I, who knew him well, could detect the subtle change in his manner and expression. To the others he must have seemed, as before, calm and attentive, purely analytical.

The silence went on for a minute or two. Now that I had a chance to examine our surroundings, the room proved to be exactly what I expected, a cluttered assembly of mementoes and books, a large bronze Buddha seated on a teakwood stand, strangely demonic Asian masks hanging on the walls amid framed citations and photographs. In a place of honor behind his writing desk hung a portrait of a beautiful woman whose features resembled those of Abigail Thurston but were somewhat older. This I took to be her mother.

"Do go on, Sir Humphrey," said Holmes, "and tell us what has taken place during these five days in which you have never once left this room."

"You'll probably think I am out of my mind, Mr. Holmes. Indeed, I think so myself, whenever I am unable to convince myself that I am beguiled by some devilish trickery. For the life of me, I cannot figure out how it is *done.*"

"How what is done, Sir Humphrey?"

"Mr. Holmes, do you know what I mean when I say I have seen my *death fetch?*"

Abigail Thurston let out a cry, then covered her mouth with her hand.

Holmes seemed unperturbed. "In the superstitions of many races, a man who is about to die may encounter his spirit-likeness. The German term is *doppelganger,* meaning double-walker. Certainly such an apparition is held to be a portent of the direst sort, and to be *touched* by this figure means instantaneous death. You haven't been touched by it then, have you, Sir Humphrey?"

Thurston's face reddened. "If you mean to mock me, Mr. Holmes, then my faith in you is misplaced."

"I do not mock. Nor do I deal in phantoms. My practice stands firmly flat-footed upon the ground. No ghosts need apply. Therefore I must agree with your conclusion, even before I have examined the evidence, that you are the victim of trickery of some kind. But first, describe to me what you *think* you have seen."

"*Myself,* Mr. Holmes. My daughter has surely mentioned my sudden aversion to mirrors."

"Don't we all see ourselves in mirrors?"

"I saw myself *twice.*"

"Twice?"

"Five mornings ago, I stood before the mirror shaving, when a second image appeared in the glass, as if an *exact duplicate of myself* were looking over my shoulder. I whirled about, razor in hand, and confronted *myself* as surely as if I gazed into a second mirror, only the face of this *other* was contorted with the most venomous hatred, Mr. Holmes, the most absolute malevolence I have ever beheld. The lips were about to form an utterance which I somehow *know* would mean my immediate death.

"So I slashed frantically with my razor. I felt the blade pass through only the air, but the figure vanished, like a burst soap bubble."

"And it did not harm you in any way," said Holmes, "any more than a soap bubble—or some projected illusion of light and shadow."

"Oh no, Mr. Holmes, this was no magic-lantern show. It was a fully three-dimensional image. Each time I saw it, it was as real to my eyes as you and Dr. Watson appear now."

"You saw it, then, more than once?"

"Three times, Mr. Holmes, until I had the sense to remove all mirrors and reflective surfaces from the room. That is how it *gets in.* I am certain of that."

"And I am certain, Sir Humphrey, that *you* are certain of far more than you have told me. Unless you give me *all* of the facts, I cannot help you, however much your daughter may entreat me. Who, for instance, is the 'blackguard Hawkins' you took us for on the stairs?"

Thurston refilled his glass and took a long draught of brandy, then settled back. "Yes, you are right, of course, Mr. Holmes. I shall have to tell you and Dr. Watson everything." He turned to his daughter. "But you, my dear, perhaps should not hear what we have to say."

"Father, I think I am old enough."

"It is not a pretty story."

"My early years were wild," Sir Humphrey began. "I was no paragon of scientific respectability at twenty-one, but little more than a common criminal. I have never before admitted that I was dismissed from the Indian Army under extremely disreputable circumstances and only escaped court martial because a sympathetic officer allowed me time to flee, change my name, and disappear. The offense involved the pillage of a native temple, and the officer's sympathy had been purchased with some of the loot.

"And so, under another name, I wandered the East. I had no means by which to return to England, nor had I any desire to present myself to friends and family as a failure and a disgrace. Once in a very great while I dispatched a letter filled with fanciful, if artfully vague, tales of confidential adventures in government service.

"In the course of my travels I picked up several languages and a profound education in the ways of the world's wickedness. I fell in with the roughest possible company, and was myself more often than not on the wrong side of the law. In the gold fields of Australia there was a certain dispute and a man died of it, and once more I had to vanish. In Shanghai I worked as an agent for a wealthy mandarin, whose true activities, when they became known to the Chinese authorities, caused his head to be pickled in brine.

"But the blackest depths were in Rangoon, for there I met Wendall Hawkins. He was a vile rogue, Mr. Holmes, even among such company as I found him. Murderer, thief, pirate, and more—I am sure. He was a huge, powerful man with an enormous, dark beard, who used to jokingly boast—though I think he half believed it—that he was the reincarnation of Edward Teach, the notorious buccaneer commonly known as Blackbeard.

"Reckless as I was, my normal instinct would have been to avoid such a man as I would a live cobra, but he had something which fascinated me: an idol six inches in height, of a hideous, bat-winged dog, carven of the finest milky green jade, stylized in a manner which resembled the Chinese but wasn't. Its eyes were purest sapphires.

"Mr. Holmes, I was more than just a thieving lout in those days. Already the direction of my life's work was clear to me—though I had yet to learn its manner—for if ever I suffered from a true mania, it was the craving to penetrate the deepest secrets of the mysterious Orient. Oh, I wanted riches, yes, but more than that I hoped to come back to England famous, like some Burton or Livingstone or Speke, having brought the light of European science to the darkest and most forbidden corners of the globe.

"I knew what this idol was, even before Wendall Hawkins told me. It was an artifact of the Chan-Tzo people who inhabit the Plateau of Leng in central Asia, in that unmapped and unexplored region northwest of Tibet, where theoretically the Chinese and Russian empires adjoin, but in fact no civilized person has ever set foot—for all the ravings of Madame Blavatsky contain much nonsense about the place. The very name, Chan-Tzo, is often mistranslated as 'Corpse-Eaters,' and so occultists whisper fearfully of the hideous rites of the 'Corpse Eating Cult of Leng.' In truth necrophagia is the least of Leng's horrors. The Chan-Tzo are 'Vomiters of Souls'... but I am far ahead of myself.

"Hawkins had the idol and he had a map—which had been acquired, he darkly hinted, at the cost of several lives—written in an obscure Burmese dialect. He needed me to translate. That was why he had come to me. Otherwise he would share his treasure-hunt with as few as possible—for that was what it was to be. We would journey to Leng armed to the teeth, slaughter any natives who stood in our way, and return to civilization rich men. I tried to console my conscience with the belief that I, at least, would be travelling as much for knowledge as for wealth, and that through my efforts this find could be of scientific value.

"Hawkins and ten others had pooled funds to buy a steam launch, which we christened, to suit our leader's fancy, the *Queen Anne's Revenge*. Once we had secured sufficient ammunition and supplies, we slipped up the Irrawaddy by night and journeyed deep into the interior, beyond the reach of any colonial authorities, ultimately anchoring at Putao near the Chinese border and continuing overland.

"I don't have to tell you that the trip was a disaster. Supplies went bad or disappeared. We all had fevers. What native guides we could hire or seize at gunpoint misled us, then got away. I alone could read the damned map, but it was cryptic, even if you could make out the script. Much of the time I merely guessed and tried to find our way by the stars.

"Many times I was certain that none of us would get back alive. The first to die was the crazy American, something-or-other Jones, a lunatic who carried a bull-whip and fancied himself an archaeologist. We found Jones in his tent, bloated to half again normal size, his face eaten away by foot-long jungle leeches.

"One by one the others perished, from accidents, from disease that might have been poisoning. Gutzman, the South African, caught a dart in the neck one night.

Van Eysen, the Dutchman, tried to make off with most of our remaining food and clean water. Hawkins shot him in the back, then killed the Malay when he protested, and the Lascar on general principles. Another Englishman, Gunn, got his throat cut merely so that there would be one mouth less to feed.

"Since I alone could read the map—or pretended to—I was certain Hawkins needed me alive. In the end, there were only the two of us, ragged and emaciated wretches staggering on in a timeless delirium of pain and dread. It was nothing less than a living death.

"At last we emerged from the jungle and climbed onto the windswept tableland of central Asia. Still the journey seemed endless. I had no idea of where we were going anymore, for all I made a show of consulting the map over and over so that Hawkins would not kill me. Each night I dreamed of the black and forbidding Plateau of Leng, which was revealed to me in a series of visions, its ruins and artificial caverns of shocking antiquity, perhaps older even than mankind itself, as were the immemorial blasphemies of the Chan-Tzo.

"What Hawkins dreamed, I cannot say. His speech had ceased to be coherent, except on the point of threatening me should I waver from our purpose. I knew he was insane then, and that I would die with him, likewise insane, unless I could somehow escape his company.

"I was past thinking clearly. How fortunate, then, that my plan was simplicity itself—almost the bare truth rather than some contrived stratagem.

"I fell to the ground and refused to rise, no matter how much Hawkins screamed that he would blow my brains out with his pistol. I said I was dying, that his pistol would be a mercy. *He* would offer me no mercy. I was counting on that. Instead, he forced me to translate the map for him and make notes as best I could. There was nothing to write with by a thorn and my own blood, but I wrote, and when he was satisfied, he laughed, folded the map into his pocket, took *all* our remaining supplies, and left me to my fate on the trackless, endless plain.

"And so we parted. I hoped I had sent him to Hell, deliberately mixing up the directions so he'd end up only the Devil knew where. He, of course, assumed I would be vulture's meat before another day or two.

"But I did not die. Mad with fever and privation, my mind filled with fantastic and horrible hallucinations, I wandered for what might have been days or even weeks, until, by the kindness of providence alone, I stumbled into the camp of some nomads, who, seeing that I was a white man, bore me on camel-back into the Chinese province of Sinkiang and there turned me over to a trader, who brought me to a missionary.

"This proved to be my salvation, both physical and otherwise. I married the missionary's daughter, Abigail's mother, and largely through the influence of her family I later found a place on a much more respectable Anglo-French expedition to Angkor. That was the true beginning of my scientific career. Still the mysteries of the East haunted me, but my cravings were directed into proper channels until I achieved the renown I have today."

At this point Sir Humphrey paused. The only sound was the slow ticking of a great clock in some other room. Abigail Thurston's face was white from the shock of what she had heard. She scarcely seemed to breathe. Holmes sat very still, his chin held in his hand, staring into space.

I was the one who broke the silence.

"Surely, Sir Humphrey, there is more to the story than that. I don't see how your luckless expedition or whatever fate the rascal Hawkins must have met has anything to do with the here and now."

Thurston's reaction was explosive.

"Damn it, man! It has *everything* to do with my predicament and what may well be my inevitable fate. But... you are right. There is more to tell. After many years of roving the world, giving lectures, publishing books, after I was knighted by the Queen—after my past life seemed a bad dream from which I had finally awakened—I thought I was safe. But it was not to be. *This past fortnight I began to receive communications from the fiend Hawkins!*"

"Communications?" said Holmes. "How so?"

"There. On the desk."

Holmes reached over and opened an ornately carven, lacquered box, removing a sheaf of papers. He glanced at them briefly and gave them to me.

"What do you make of them, Watson?"

"I cannot read the writing. The paper is an Oriental rice-paper. The penmanship shows the author to be under considerable mental strain, perhaps intoxicated. Notice the frequent scratchings and blottings. Beyond that, I can make out nothing."

Sir Humphrey spoke. "The language is an archaic—some would say degenerate—form of Burmese, the script a kind of code used by criminals in the Far East. Between these two elements, I am perhaps the only *living* man who can read what is written here, for Wendall Hawkins *is not alive*, if his words are to be believed."

"Surely if he is dead," said Holmes, "your troubles are at an end."

"No, Mr. Holmes, they are not, for all of these letters were written *after* Hawkins's death—long after it. It seems that he *reached* the Plateau of Leng, which I saw only in visions. There the almost sub-human priests of the Chan-Tzo murdered him after what might have been *years* of indescribable tortures, then brought him back into a kind of half-life as an animate corpse at their command, hideously disfigured, the skin flayed from his face, his heart ripped out, the cavity in his chest filled with inextinguishable fire. He is implacable now, driven both by the will of his masters and his own rage for revenge against me, whom he blames for his unending agony. He knows all the secrets of the Chan-Tzo priests, and the conjuring of death-fetches is easily within his power."

"He says all *that* in these letters?" I asked.

"That and more, Dr. Watson, and if it is true, I am defenseless. My only hope is that Mr. Holmes and yourself can prove me to be *deluded,* the victim of a *hoax* perpetrated by the vile Hawkins who has no doubt returned, but returned, I still dare to hope, as no more than a mortal villain. If you can do this, I certainly have the means to reward you handsomely for your services."

"My services are charged on a fixed scale," said Holmes, "but let us not concern ourselves with the monetary details now. I shall indeed collar this Hawkins for you and unmask his devices—which I am sure would make the tricks of our English spirit mediums child's play in comparison—but they are devices none the less. For what else can they be?"

"Mr. Holmes, I will be forever in your debt."

"We shall watch and wait until Hawkins is forced to show his hand. But first, I think Dr. Watson should escort Miss Abigail to a safer place, my own rooms, which I shall not be needing until this affair is concluded." When Thurston's daughter made to protest, Holmes turned to her and said, "You have been a heroine, but now that the battle is actually joined, I think it best that you remove yourself from the field. Will you go with Dr. Watson?"

"Whatever you say, Mr. Holmes."

"Splendid. Now I must busy myself examining the house inside and out, to discover any way our enemy might use to gain entrance."

Thurston picked up the elephant gun and lay it across his lap, then began idly polishing the barrel with a cloth.

"I've survived five days like this. I think I shall be safe here behind the locked door for a little while longer yet. Your plan makes excellent sense, Mr. Holmes."

We left Sir Humphrey alone in the room. As Holmes and I escorted Miss Thurston down the stairs, the detective asked me, "Well, Watson, what do you think?"

"A unique case, Holmes. One worthy of your talents."

"About Sir Humphrey. What about him?"

"I judge him to be of fundamentally sound mind, but what superstitious fears he may harbor are being played upon by the murderous Hawkins, who sounds himself to be completely mad."

"Mad or not, he shall have to manifest himself in a decidedly *material* form before long, at which point he will be susceptible to capture by mundane means."

"One thing doesn't fit, Holmes. Who, or what, did we see upon our arrival here? Sir Humphrey hadn't been out of the room."

"An impostor, possibly a trained actor in league with Hawkins. I agree that all the pieces of the puzzle are not yet in place. But have patience. You know my methods."

"I am so glad that you and Dr. Watson will help Father," Miss Thurston said softly as we reached the base of the stairs. "You are sent from Heaven, both of you."

Holmes smiled indulgently. "Not from nearly so far, but we shall do what we can."

Alas, we could do but little. As we stood there at the base of the stairs and I helped Miss Thurston on with her coat, she turned and chanced to look back up the stairs. Suddenly she screamed.

"Good God!" I exclaimed.

Near the top of the stairs was a figure who appeared to be Sir Humphrey, but dressed for the outside, in coat and top hat, as we had seen him before. He *could not* have gotten past us.

"You! Stop!" Holmes was already in pursuit, bounding up the steps three at a time.

The figure moved so swiftly the eye could hardly follow, and soft-footedly. I heard only Holmes's boots pounding on the wooden stairs. Then there came a cry from within the study. Sir Humphrey shouted something in a foreign language, his tone that of abject terror, his words broken off in a gurgling scream. The elephant gun went off with a thunderous roar.

I left Miss Thurston and hurried up after Holmes. By the time I reached the study door, which was blown apart from the inside as if a cannonball had gone through it, Holmes was inside.

He rushed out again, his eyes wild, his face bloodless, and he saw Miss Abigail Thurston coming up behind me.

"For the love of God, Watson! Don't let her in!"

"Father!" she screamed. "Oh, you must let me pass!"

For all she struggled, I held her fast.

"Watson! Do not let her through no matter what happens! It is just… too horrible!"

I think that was the only time I ever saw Sherlock Holmes truly shocked, at a loss for words.

I forced Miss Thurston back down the stairs despite her vehement protests, holding onto her until the police arrived, which they did shortly, summoned by the neighbors who had heard the screams and the shot. Only after she had been conveyed away in a police wagon, accompanied by a patrolman, was I able to examine the body of Sir Humphrey Thurston, who was indeed murdered, as I had feared.

Though still seated in his chair, he had been mutilated hideously, almost beyond recognition.

His throat was cut from ear to ear. That was enough to have killed him. But the flesh had been almost entirely torn away from his face, and a strange series of symbols, like the ones I had seen in the letters, had been carved in the bare bone of his forehead. The crown of his skull had been smashed in by some blunt instrument, and—it revolted me to discover—most of his brain was gone.

The final detail was the worst, for it had been deliberately designed to mock us. The still smoking elephant gun lay across his lap, and, carefully placed so that it would be *reflected in the mirrored surface of the polished gun barrel,* was a small jade idol with emerald eyes, a stylized figure of a bat-winged dog.

"Yes, Holmes," I said, "it is entirely too horrible."

Dr Watson stopped telling the story, and I, the nineteen-year-old American college student, could only gape at him open-mouthed, like some imbecile, trying not to reach the attractively obvious conclusion that the good doctor's mind had gone soft after so many years. It was a terrible thing, just to entertain such a notion. I almost wept.

I would have remained there forever, frozen where I sat, wordless, had not Dr. Watson gone on.

"It was a case which I could not record, which Holmes *ordered* me to suppress on pain of the dissolution of our friendship. It just didn't work out."

"Wh-what do you mean, didn't work out?"

"I mean exactly that. The affair concluded too quickly and ended in abject failure. We accomplished nothing. He would have no more of the matter, the specifics, as he acidly phrased it, being left to the 'official imagination,' which, sure enough, concluded the murder to be the work of a madman or madmen, perhaps directed by a sinister Oriental cult, a new Thuggee. But even the police could not account for the powerful stench of *decay* which lingered in the explorer's study even long after the body had been removed, as if something long dead had invaded, done its worst, and departed as inexplicably as it had come.

"Enormous pressure was brought to bear to prevent any accurate reportage in the newspapers, to prevent panic. I think those instructions came from the very highest level. Sir Humphrey's obituary, ironically, listed the cause of his demise as an Asiatic fever. I signed the death certificate to that effect.

"My own conclusions were profoundly disturbing. The mystery could not be resolved. What we—even Miss Thurston—had witnessed were not merely unlikely, but *impossible*.

"'I *reject* the impossible,' said Holmes vehemently, 'as a matter of policy. Such things *cannot be* —'

"'You and I and the girl saw, Holmes. They *are*.'

"'No, Watson! No! The irrational has *no place* in detective work. We must confine ourselves to the tangible and physical, carefully building upon meticulous reason, or else the whole edifice of my life's work crumbles into dust. Against the supernatural, I am helpless, my methods of no use. My methods *have* been useful in the past, don't you think? And so they shall be in the future, but we must remain within certain bounds, and so preserve them.'"

Again I, the college boy, was left speechless.

"Holmes made me swear an oath—and I swore it—never to write up this case—and I never wrote it —"

Had he, in a sense at least, broken his oath by telling me? I dared not ask. Was there some urgency now, of which had lately become aware?

"I wanted to tell someone," was all he said. "I thought I should."

King Midas. Ass's ears. Who will believe the wind in the reeds?

I merely know that a week after I returned to school in America I received a telegram saying that Dr. Watson had died peacefully of heart failure, sitting in that very chair by the fire. A week later a parcel arrived with a note from one of my aunts, expressing some bewilderment that he had wanted me to have the contents.

It was the idol of the bat-winged dog.

THE SHOCKING AFFAIR
OF THE DUTCH
STEAMSHIP *FRIESLAND*

by Mary Robinette Kowal

Mary Robinette Kowal is the author of several short stories, including "Evil Robot Monkey," which is a current finalist for the Hugo Award. Her short fiction has appeared in *Asimov's*, *Strange Horizons*, *Cosmos*, and *Escape Pod*, and in the anthologies *Twenty Epics*, *The Solaris Book of New Science Fiction Vol. 2*, and Gardner Dozois's *The Year's Best Science Fiction*. Her first novel, *Shades of Milk and Honey*, is forthcoming from Tor Books. Kowal was also the 2008 winner of the John W. Campbell Award for Best New Writer, and when not writing she works as a professional puppeteer.

Men are notoriously reluctant to get married, and when you look at the history of weddings, who can blame them? After all, weddings are pretty dangerous places. The marriage of Claudius and Gertrude in *Hamlet* ends in what can only be termed tragedy. Good night, sweet prince. In fact, good night just about everybody. In *Monty Python and the Holy Grail*, a misinformed Sir Lancelot rampages through a wedding party, slaying many, including the best man. And these are small potatoes compared to truly disastrous affairs such as the Saint Bartholomew's Day Massacre of 1572, in which a controversial Catholic-Protestant marriage touched off a wave of violence that eventually claimed as many as thirty-thousand lives. Is it any wonder that men stay away? It's simple prudence, really. In Conan Doyle's story "The Adventure of the Norwood Builder," Watson mentions in passing the "shocking affair of the Dutch steamship *Friesland*, which so nearly cost us both our lives." Our next story imagines what this evocatively titled case might have entailed—it involves a naive young woman, a royal couple, a glassblower, and the darker side of Italian politics. And oh yes, also a wedding.

I was born Rosa Carlotta Silvana Grisanti, but in the mid-Eighties, I legally changed my name to Eve. As you have guessed in your letter, after the shocking affair of the Dutch steamship *Friesland*, my dear friends Dr. Watson and Mr. Sherlock

134

Holmes suggested that my safest course of action would be to distance myself from my family.

But I get ahead of my story; I have not Dr. Watson's gift for explaining Mr. Holmes's methods, and I fear your wish that I relay the particulars of this strange case may be met with inadequate measures.

On the twelfth of October, 1887, I was being taken by the steamship *Friesland* from our home on the Venetian isle of Murano to Africa; there to meet my betrothed, Hans Boerwinkle, a man several years my senior with whom my father had very recently made arrangements. Living as we do now, in the nineteen-twenties, it is difficult to remember what a sheltered life we girls led forty years ago, but at the time it seemed natural that my brother, Orazio Rinaldo Paride Grisanti, escorted me as chaperone. With us also was my lady's maid, Anita.

In addition to my trousseau, we had several boxes packed with the finest Murano crystal as part of my dowry. My father had blown glass without cessation after my betrothal was announced. I remember Zia Giulia asking, "What is the hurry?" At the time, I was only anxious to be an adult, which was all that marriage meant to me.

I can still recall my excitement at dinner the first evening as glittering ladies and gentlemen, in full evening dress, caught me in a dazzle of delight. Orazio and I were seated at a table with two British gentlemen and a couple from Hungary; at the captain's table sat Signore Agostino Depretis, the premier of Italy, with his new bride, Signora Michela Depretis. As I anticipated my own wedding and honeymoon, I envied the young woman and the way all eyes sought her.

But I should not dwell on my youthful fancies. The two British gentlemen, as you might have surmised, introduced themselves as Mr. Sherlock Holmes and Dr. Watson.

Mr. Holmes delighted me by having an excellent command of Italian, and asked us endless questions about glassblowing. While we bantered, Signore and Signora Comazzolo, a rival glassblower family, who also sailed on the *Friesland*, sent a bottle of expensive champagne to the bridal couple.

My brother's eyes narrowed, then laying his hand upon my arm, he said in Italian, "Would you send them a gift as well, though it means parting with a small item from your dowry?"

"Papa will send me more." I smiled at him. "I shall write a note myself."

Orazio gestured to Anita and gave her hurried instructions. In moments she returned with a small box containing a matched pair of opalescent champagne flutes ornamented by delicate tracings of crystal. I quickly penned the note that you have in your possession.

A foolish note, from a foolish girl, but—how was I to know what was to follow? Before the ink was dry, my brother snatched the note and fairly sprinted across the dining room. Bowing at the captain's table, he presented the box of flutes to Premiere Depretis and his bride. She laughed prettily, and kissed him on both cheeks to thank him.

I do not boast when I say the artistry of these flutes was without peer. My father was a brilliant glassblower; no other studio knew the secret of his opalescent glass, and of its shifting colours that bent light into translucent rainbows.

Nothing would do then but for the bridal couple to open the champagne and toast the assembly with these confections of glass. The champagne's bubbles danced as merrily as if they were celebrating with us.

Premiere Depretis said, "Ladies and gentlemen, with this lovely Murano glass I propose a toast to my fellow countrymen and to my beautiful wife. Long life and health to us all."

They drank their champagne and kissed each other with love in their eyes while we looked on, applauding wildly. Signore Comazzolo, perhaps jealous that our flutes had upstaged his champagne, called out. "How is the champagne, Premiere?"

Premiere Depretis bowed to him before burying his nose in his glass to inhale the bouquet of the champagne. "An elegant nose with nuances of honey, gingerbread, parsley and slight hints of garlic." He sipped the champagne again, savouring it. "Minerality, pears and a bright acidity. Delightful."

We applauded again, perhaps even more wildly than before. I sat, breathless with delight, darting glances at the bridal couple over each course. The first course was oysters and my brother ordered a bottle of champagne so that we could celebrate "in the same style as our Premiere and Signora Depretis."

During the second course, Signora Depretis excused herself and I looked up as she stood. Her face was pale, and she held her hand to her abdomen as if her stomach hurt. Premiere Depretis escorted her from the dining room, his own face tight.

"What is the matter, do you think?" I asked Orazio.

He shrugged. "Perhaps the oysters."

During the rest of my meal, I imagined stomach pains until, feeling nauseous, I excused myself during the fourth course.

The next day, neither Depretis came to dinner.

The third day, my lady's maid, Anita, announced that two men waited in my parlour

"Where is my brother?" I asked.

She shook her head, smiling apologetically, "I do not know, Signorina."

I hesitated to step into the parlour unchaperoned, so I motioned Anita to accompany me. You must imagine my relief to find my dinner companions, Dr. Watson and Mr. Holmes, awaiting me.

Here, I must pause to give you a word picture of Mr. Holmes. He towered above me, indeed, even among most men his lean figure loomed like a hawk. His dark shaggy brows pulled down in an expression of fixed concentration from the moment I stepped into the parlour and his eyes gleamed with a fire of excitement.

"How are you, Signorina Grisanti?" he asked in flawless Italian.

Dr. Watson hung back and watched our conversation with the eager interest of a newspaper reporter, in the scene but not part of it.

"I am well, thank you, Signore Holmes." I wondered for a moment if I might ask him for news of Premiere and Signora Depretis.

"The Depretises are dead." Mr. Holmes said, bluntly.

I gasped, both at the news and at how easily he read my thoughts. "The oysters?"

"Their nuptial toast was poisoned." Mr. Holmes gave me a long searching look. "Do you know where your brother is?"

"No." My attention was barely upon him, so horrified was I by the thought of that happy couple murdered. Assassinated.

"Well then, we shall chat with you while we wait for him, if you do not mind?"

I shook my head.

He folded himself into one of the cabin's chairs. Dr. Watson sat in a chair to the side, holding so still that in my memory he is almost invisible. Mr. Holmes leaned forward to put his elbows on his knees. "Tell me about your approaching nuptials."

I blushed and stammered but proceeded to tell him about my recent betrothal to Mr. Boerwinkle and his business arrangements with Papa. About how I was moving to Africa but Papa could not accompany me because he was busy with the upcoming elections helping with the campaign for the Left. I told him about my dress; in other words, I acted every inch the vain, silly girl that I was.

In the midst of my recitation, Mr. Holmes hesitated and then asked. "May we look at your dowry?"

"Of course." I beckoned Anita and she helped the gentlemen unpack the crates of crystal. I hovered, anxious and useless, as they lay the sparkling glass and crystal about the cabin with infinite care. Mr. Holmes stopped to admire an opalescent vase, which my father had made to serve as a centrepiece for our table.

He glanced at the matched rows of clear stemware and back at the vase. "Did you have only the flutes and the vase in this style of glass?"

"Yes." I stepped forward to admire the piece. "No other glassmaker knows how to produce the opalescence and even my father rarely makes it."

"Has he produced opalescent stemware, such as the champagne flutes, before?"

I tilted my head and thought. "Not that I know of, but I am not often in the shop."

Mr. Holmes lifted the vase to his nose and, to my bewilderment, sniffed it. "Hmm. No help there. Help me put everything back, would you, Dr. Watson?"

I was thankful that Dr. Watson looked as baffled as I felt, but he said nothing and simply helped Mr. Holmes repack everything except the vase. Mr. Holmes turned to me and said, "I am sorry for the inconvenience, Signorina Grisanti. Do let me know when your brother returns." He bowed over my hand and he and Dr. Watson took their leave.

I stared at the door after them and then picked up the vase and sniffed it. I smelled nothing.

Some hours later Orazio sauntered into the room. "Well, little Rosa, how do you like your first ocean voyage?"

"I am frightened. Dr. Watson and Signore Holmes said—"

He crossed the room in one stride and grabbed my wrists. "What did you tell them?"

"Nothing!" I twisted in his painful grasp. "I had nothing to say. I do not understand what is happening. Orazio, they said the champagne was poisoned."

He dropped my wrists and stepped back, smiling. "Did they now?"

"How can you smile when the Depretises have been murdered?"

He laughed. "Why, my dear sister, do you think we are on this boat?"

The successive shocks I received that night had hardened my nerves, or perhaps I had already begun to accept the truth. With a click, the pieces came together in my head, along with something I had not told Mr. Holmes. I knew how my father made the glass. I could not let Orazio guess at my thoughts and I forced myself to answer him as the foolish girl he thought me to be: "I'm supposed to get married."

He turned, smiling, relief written on his face. "Yes, my beautiful Rosa. That is true." He kissed me on the forehead. "I am exhausted and it is long past time that you retired for the evening."

I twisted my fingers together, faint with the awareness of what my brother had done. Had his only target been Premiere Depretis, perhaps I would not have felt as horrified, but the memory of Signora Depretis kissing my brother on his cheeks, thanking him for bringing her death, sickened me. The realization that I could, perhaps, have prevented it tore at my soul. "All the excitement has me overwrought. Do you think it would be all right if I walked on deck to cool my head?"

Orazio squeezed my hands. "I am too tired to escort you."

"Anita will serve." I smiled coquettishly, masking the anguish over what I must do. "Or did you want to dazzle the young ladies yourself?"

Laughing, my brother kissed my cheeks. "Go on, Rosa, but do not walk too late."

I called Anita and we went to the upper decks. You have asked about Mr. Holmes, so I will not trouble you with the thoughts of my long promenade. Know that the night air cooled my fevered temples and gave me the resolution I needed. Anita walked with me through the decks until we arrived at Mr. Holmes's stateroom. I blushed, thinking of how it looked for an unmarried young woman to seek a man at this hour and then in the next instant I shook my head at my foolishness. What mattered my reputation on such a night as this?

Still, the sounds of an unearthly violin haunting the night nearly undid me but I gathered my resolve and knocked on the door. It opened to a cloud of blue-smoke, swirling about like that in the chimney of my father's furnace.

"Miss Grisanti?" Dr. Watson seemed so shocked at my appearance that he forgot to speak Italian and his next sentence fell on uncomprehending ears.

Mr. Holmes tucked his violin under his arm and said in excellent Italian, "Be courteous, Dr. Watson, Signorina Grisanti doesn't have a word of English. Won't you come in?"

I shook my head. "I have come simply to tell you that my brother has returned. He knew the glass was poisoned, and it *was* the glass, Signore Holmes, not the champagne."

Mr. Holmes leaned forward on his toes. My breath caught at his eagerness, but I somehow found the air to continue speaking. "The opalescence is caused by arsenic powder blown with the glass."

"In the glass, not on the surface!" He spun happily and pointed his bow at Dr. Watson. "That explains why my tests failed to detect it."

I felt close to fainting. "But you surely suspected, else you would not have come to look at my dowry."

His bushy eyebrows arched and I blushed under his scrutiny. "Your observation is astute," he said. "Premiere and Signora Depretis's symptoms began at dinner shortly after their champagne toast. The note of garlic, which Premiere Depretis noticed in the champagne, led me to suspect arsenic. The champagne combined with arsenic would have produced arsine gas, which was consistent with the Depretis's symptoms, but there was no arsenic residue in the bottle, so I turned my attention to the flutes. Your mention of your father's involvement with politics provided a motive, but I could not deduce the method."

Dr. Watson stepped forward, asking, "You must know what this means for your father and your brother?"

"I do." I looked down and wrapped my arms about myself, feeling the hard bones of my corset and wishing they could protect me. "My father has chafed against the government since Italy annexed Venezia in 1871 and my rapid engagement to Mr. Boerwinkle must be a sham to give us reason to be here. I am certain that Orazio would have presented these flutes at another time, but took the opportunity to discredit the Comazzolo family. I know what is at stake and—" my voice faltered but I drew my head up higher. "I will not be a pawn. Their treachery is dishonourable."

From my readings of Dr. Watson's papers, I suspect this is one of the few times Mr. Holmes was ever taken aback—not at my answers, but that a young girl could have changed so, in the hours since he had interviewed me. "Signorina Grisanti, you are a noble woman. I thank you."

"I will walk on deck awhile longer." I turned to go, conscious that I had betrayed my brother and my father—but had they not betrayed my youthful ideals more? Had they not traded my hope for death? Over my shoulder, I asked, "Will you be able to complete your business before I return?"

"Yes." The smoke swirling in the room created the illusion of mist sweeping over his eyes.

I walked on deck for hours, before returning to my empty cabin. The too-tidy room betrayed signs of a struggle, which some kind soul had neatened. A folded piece of paper waited for me on the table by my lacework. I enclose it now, to complete your record of this remarkable man.

"My dear Signorina Grisanti,

"I applaud the fine intellect that brought you so swiftly to understand the intricacies of the situation. I regret that I have received a telegram indicating your betrothed, Mr. Boerwinkle, is also in league against the current Italian government. With this first step, it seems certain they intended to shift the ruling party of Italia to the Left. Your father and brother have been taken into custody for the assassination and will be duly tried."

"With these facts, it seems apparent you cannot return home, nor can you continue your voyage. Dr. Watson and I are departing the ship tomorrow and wish to offer you safe conduct."

"I await your reply,"

"Sherlock Holmes."

I wept. I wept for the truth of his words, for the loss of my home, and for the loss of my innocence. I wept till Anita came to me and held me in her arms, singing to me and comforting me for the lost child that I was.

We departed the ship the next day. On Mr. Holmes's urging, I changed my name to Eve V— and I never saw my family again. Until I received your letter, I had seen the name Grisanti only once, in a newspaper report of the arrest and execution of my brother, Orazio Rinaldo Paride Grisanti. I would not read a paper for years after— lest I see a notice of my father's trial, and know I had killed him.

Now you have my account to add to the ones Dr. Watson left of Mr. Sherlock Holmes and so, I will close by signing my old name, for the whole affair belongs to a girl much different from me.

Sincerely yours,

Rosa Carlotta Silvana Grisanti.

THE ADVENTURE OF THE MUMMY'S CURSE

by H. Paul Jeffers

H. Paul Jeffers is the author of many works of fiction and non-fiction, the most recent of which is *Taking Command*, the first biography of World War II general J. Lawton Collins. He has written many other biographies as well, including several volumes about President Teddy Roosevelt. His other non-fiction work ranges wildly from books like *Freemasons: Inside the World's Oldest Secret Society* to *With an Axe: 16 Horrific Accounts of Real-Life Axe Murderers* to *The Complete Idiot's Guide to the Great Depression*. In the realm of Sherlockiana, in addition to this story, Jeffers is the author of the novels *The Adventure of the Stalwart Companions* and *Murder Most Irregular*, as well as *The Forgotten Adventures of Sherlock Holmes*, a book of stories based on the original radio plays by Anthony Boucher and Denis Green.

"Death will slay with his wings whoever disturbs the peace of the pharaoh." This inscription was supposedly found carved on a stone tablet by British explorers Howard Carter and George Herbert when they opened the tomb of the Egyptian king Tutankhamun. It's said that when the men entered the tomb, all the lights in Cairo went out and Herbert's three-legged dog dropped dead. Herbert himself soon followed, felled by a mosquito bite. Carter's pet canary was also killed, in a freak cobra accident, and before long two dozen members of the expedition had died under mysterious circumstances, victims of the mummy's curse. Or that's the story anyway. Numerous explanations have been advanced to explain the misfortune that befell the expedition. In 1986 Dr. Caroline Stenger-Phillip proposed the intriguing notion that the explorers had been sickened by exposure to mold and bacteria that had been preserved in the hermetically sealed tomb. However, a 2002 statistical analysis in the *British Medical Journal* concluded that members of the expedition had not in fact died significantly faster than the general population. The "curse" was a media myth, albeit one that's inspired a lot of great entertainment, including our next tale.

In the three years following my introduction to Sherlock Holmes in the chemistry

141

lab of St. Bart's hospital by our mutual friend Stamford—resulting in Holmes and me sharing lodgings in Baker Street—I had grown accustomed to Holmes's investigations beginning with the arrival of a telegram or letter, our landlady announcing an unexpected caller, or the plodding footsteps of a Scotland Yard detective ascending the stairs with a grudging appeal for assistance. On one or two instances I happened to be the instrument that launched Holmes upon what he commonly called "a problem." Such was the occasion on a warm April evening in 1883. We had barely settled into our chairs in the sitting room of 221B Baker Street on the second evening following our return from the Surrey home of the villainous Dr. Grimesby Roylott when Holmes bolted from his chair and declared, "Watson, our exertions in this singular episode at Stoke Moran have earned us the reward of a superb dinner."

Half an hour later, we were seated in Simpson's-in-the Strand. As always when Holmes patronized that venerable establishment, our table in the upstairs dining room was next to a large window overlooking the busy thoroughfare. "In this passing parade of humanity," he had said in explanation on a previous occasion, "and in a city of four million inhabitants, all jostling one another, there is no telling what convergence of events or trifling happenstance might unloose a chain of events resulting in a calamity, or simply one of those incidents that seem whimsical on the surface, but are rife with dire consequences for those involved."

While Holmes alternately peered down to study the constantly changing street tableau, he picked at the roast beef that had been carved from one of the immense silver trolleys, known as "dining wagons," which had been the hallmark of Simpson's since it opened its doors in 1848. I was enjoying a steak, kidney, and mushroom pudding for which the restaurant was equally and justifiably renowned. As I glanced around the crowded, festive room, I was astonished to see a comrade from my army service striding boldly towards our table.

A burly figure in the uniform of my former regiment, the Fifth Northumberland Fusiliers, and with a shock of unruly red hair that had among his fellow officers earned him the nickname "Rusty," Major James McAndrew would have been an arresting figure anywhere, but making his way across the large dining room he was especially noticeable because of a bandage encircling his head like a laurel wreath. As he drew near our table, he flung out his powerful arms and bellowed, "By Jove, it really is you, Watson!"

"Rusty, my dear friend," said I, rising to grip his large hand. "This is a surprise. I had no idea you were in England. How good it is to see you. May I present my friend, Sherlock—"

"No introduction is required, John. It's an honour to meet you, Mr. Holmes. As a devoted reader of Watson's accounts of your investigations in *The Strand Magazine*, I assume that your keen eyes have taken my measure and your detective's mind has deduced my entire life story."

"I wouldn't go so far as to say that I know everything about your life, Major," Holmes replied as they shook hands, "but the tattoo of a ship below a cross on your left wrist and one of a mermaid on the right are evidence that you went to sea as a very young man. They are in the unmistakable style of a particular practitioner of body adornment who worked the Portsmouth docks three decades ago."

"Right you are!"

"How long it has been since you gave up seafaring for the army is impossible to state."

"Because my father had been a captain in the navy and thought I had the makings of an officer, I shipped out in 1845 at the age of thirteen, but after five years, I decided that I'd rather be in the army. Earning the rank of Major took another twenty. What else have you observed?"

"You are a man of exceptional ability, courage, loyalty, and patriotism. All of these virtues are evidenced by your lifetime of service to your country. You are also adventurous and impetuous. I deduce from these traits that you switched to the army because you craved more excitement."

"It was at the time of the Great Mutiny. My blood was boiling to punish the Mughals and Muslims for their perfidy, after all that we had done for the good of India. This is fascinating, Mr. Holmes. Please continue."

"Although the ring finger of your left hand indicates that you are not married," said Holmes, "I'm certain that a man of your dashing countenance and demeanor has not lacked opportunities to engage in affairs of the heart. You felt strongly enough about one woman called Elizabeth to have her name placed under the tattoo of the mermaid."

"That is true, sir, but I decided early on that the hard life of a sailor and later of the army on the northwest frontier of India in the aftermath of the Mutiny was not one that a gentleman should impose on the gentle sex."

"Beyond these observations, Major, I note only that you have been quite lucky in your life in that you have returned to England from the wars of the East with your body evidently intact and your spirit unbroken, undoubtedly because of a deeply religious nature that is indicated by the tattoo of the cross, and may I say, because of the strengthening of your faith by your participation in the rites and rituals of Freemasonry?"

"I see how you reached your conclusions concerning my naval and military life—it's quite simple, really. But on what basis can you state with such conviction that I am a Mason?"

"You revealed it yourself."

"Really! I don't recall—"

"I know that Watson is a Master Mason. You and he greeted one another with the unique handshake of those who have attained the third degree of Masonry, therefore you are also a Master. What I cannot state with conviction is whether you joined the fraternity before or after you entered into the army. As Watson will attest, I never guess."

"I was accepted as Entered Apprentice in a military lodge when I arrived in Bombay in 1873 and raised to Fellowcraft a year later in Calcutta. I received the apron of the Master Mason in 1879 in the lodge of the Fifth Fusiliers at the time of the Second Afghan War. I am proud to say that Watson presided over the induction ceremony as Most Worshipful Master."

Recalling that moment with pleasure and pride, I interjected, "I was honored to do so."

"When you were transferred to service with the Berkshires, I lost track of you. I later heard through the grapevine that you had been wounded and were sent home. The next thing I knew, you had become an associate and chronicler of the world's most illustrious private detective. It's wonderful to see you again, John, and to observe that you seem to have fully recovered from your wound. I must say, you look smashingly well."

"Now and then I feel a twinge in my leg to remind me of that bloody day."

"You've had quite an injury yourself, Major," Holmes observed.

Raising a hand to the bandage and gingerly touching it, McAndrew replied, "Receiving this bump was nothing as romantic as the Jezail bullet that felled John at Maiwand."

"How did your injury happen?"

"I was struck a glancing blow by a tile that had become dislodged and fell from the roof of my quarters in Pimlico Road near the Chelsea Barracks."

"You're a fortunate fellow," I said. "You could have been killed."

"Indeed so. In my case, the mummy's curse does appear to have gone amiss, but perhaps only because I was a minor member of the expedition that disturbed the old gent's bones. I am not a believer in the occult, but this incident has almost made me one."

Leaning forwards with a look of astonishment, Holmes exclaimed, "Such an extraordinary statement requires elucidation, Major."

"Yes, I suppose it does, but I'm afraid that I've kept you from enjoying your meal long enough. Another time, perhaps."

"Really, Major," said Holmes insistently, "I cannot allow you to refer to your injury as the result of a mummy's curse, then go off and leave Dr. Watson and me to simply go on eating as if nothing were more important than our next course. Draw up that chair and tell us everything from the beginning."

"I am not one of our countrymen who takes an interest in the so-called supernatural," said McAndrew as he seated himself, "but, as you observed, Mr. Holmes, I am a man of faith. You cannot be a Freemason and not believe in a Supreme Architect of the Universe."

"Quite so," said I. "It's the cornerstone of the Craft."

"Because I am a Christian," McAndrew continued, "I made my way homeward from my service in Afghanistan by way of the Holy Land. I naturally visited the biblical city of Ur and the rivers of Mesopotamia. After a few days in Baghdad, I continued to Jerusalem. I wished to see the Jewish Temple Mount, now claimed by the Mohammedans as their third most holy shrine, and to visit the Church of the Holy Sepulcher. Because I am an amateur archaeologist, I was also interested in exploring the discoveries of Edward Robinson, Charles Warren, and, of course, General Charles Gordon. As you know, he has located a skull-shaped hill and a nearby garden that he has identified as the true location of Calvary and Our Lord's burial place, rather than the tomb in the Church of the Holy Sepulcher, as the Roman Catholics believe. After my explorations of the Holy City, I journeyed to Cairo to have a look at the pyramids of the Giza Plateau and the Sphinx. During my stay at the Mena House, a very fine old hostelry in the shadow of the Great Pyramid of Cheops, I chanced to meet Basil Porter. He is a nephew of Lord Porter, under whose auspices a dig had been organised. He graciously invited me to join them. The expedition was led by Professor Felix Broadmoor of Cambridge University. Perhaps you've heard of it."

"The newspapers were full of it, and rightly so," I said emphatically. "I expect that Her Majesty will presently recognize its achievements with the appropriate honours."

"As well she should," said McAndrew. "However, Lord Porter has been subjected to a firestorm of criticism from some quarters for not consigning the expedition's finds to the nation by turning everything over to the British Museum."

"I'm certain that will eventually be sorted out," said Holmes. "Please go on with your story and the matter of the mummy's curse."

"The expedition was hoping to locate tombs from the period of the Sixth Dynasty king named Raneferef. We did not find a royal sarcophagus, but located the burial place of a minor official called Sarenput. It was a discovery of breathtaking riches. Believe me, gentlemen, nothing I had seen of the wealth of Indian maharajahs matched the treasures that we unearthed. The mummy itself was in an excellent state of preservation in a tomb that had escaped the grave robbers that through the millennia have looted so many burial chambers, perhaps because of the curse that had been carved into the door of the main chamber. It was so chilling that it is etched in my memory so indelibly that I can recite it exactly: 'The priest of Hathor will punish any of you who enters this sacred tomb or does harm to it. The gods will confront him because I am honoured by his Lord. Anyone who desecrates my tomb will drown, burn, be beaten, and be destroyed by the crocodile, hippopotamus, and lion. The scorpion and the cobra will strike him. Stones will crush the trespasser.'"

"Ah, at last," Holmes exclaimed "Now, we're getting somewhere. You have associated the stones of the curse with your unfortunate encounter with the falling tile."

"I am not a superstitious man, but my injury, occurring after some peculiar and tragic events since the conclusion of the Porter-Broadmoor expedition, has caused me to wonder if there might be something to this curse business."

"Your story becomes even more compelling," said Holmes. "What were these peculiar events, as you so colourfully put it?"

"The first was the collapse of a tunnel at the tomb site. No one was injured or killed at that time, but we had to work very rapidly to shore up the walls in order to extricate the diggers."

"The next incident?"

"One of the ships carrying several larger artefacts from the dig to England was lost in a Mediterranean storm. Again, there was no loss of life or injury, but the artefacts are now lying at a depth that leaves them unrecoverable."

"When did someone die?"

McAndrew smiled appreciatively. "I can see that Dr. Watson in his writings has not exaggerated your facility at deduction, Mr. Holmes. Several weeks ago, an expert in Egyptian hieroglyphics who translated the curse, Anthony Fulmer, was killed in a train wreck in Kent."

Recalling reading in the newspapers that several persons had died, I muttered, "A terrible accident, indeed."

"What happened next?" asked Holmes.

"Last week Felix Broadmoor was waylaid in the night by a robber on a street near his home in Cambridge. He was so badly beaten that he died without recovering. The police have attributed the incident to a gang of toughs who have been plaguing the area. As far as I know, there have been no arrests."

"How many individuals participated in the expedition?"

"Including diggers, carters, and others that we hired from the local population, there were about two hundred. Those who came out from England were Lord Porter, as financial backer; his nephew Basil; an exceptional Egyptologist from the BM named Geoffrey Desmond, who is still in Cairo; Mr. Broadmoor; and Mr. Fulmer."

"Six men," I said, "two of whom are dead and yourself injured. If one were inclined to believe in the occult, your mummy's curse would seem to have taken quite a toll."

With a sigh, McAndrew replied, "I'm certain all of this is pure coincidence, but it does provide me with a good barracks yarn. I only wish I possessed the Watson talent for spinning a riveting tale. When will I have the pleasure of reading your next story in *The Strand?*"

"You will find it especially interesting, as it involves the deadliest snake in India."

McAndrew shuddered. "The swamp adder?"

"Exactly, along with a whistle, a saucer of milk, a ventilator, and a bell pull."

"Fascinating. I'm eager to read your account of the case."

With a cautioning look at me, Holmes said, "There were aspects of the affair, involving the young woman who brought the matter to my attention, that I do not believe would serve any useful purpose if they were made public at this time. Don't you agree, Watson?"

"Quite so, Holmes."

With that, Major McAndrew repeated his concern that he was keeping Holmes and me from our dinner, voiced a hope that he and I might meet again soon to reminisce about army days, and excused himself.

"Your friend has suddenly whetted my appetite for all things Egyptian," Holmes said as the sergeant returned to his table. "This interesting encounter has provided me reason for us to call upon a remarkable man I have been wanting to meet. When we return to Baker Street you can look him up in the Index under *P.*"

A set of commonplace books, the Index was an alphabetized conglomeration of facts, snippets of data, numerous press clippings, notations by Holmes on scraps of paper, and trivia that Holmes had accumulated over a period of decades that were as astonishing in scope as his ability to recall the exact volume in which they were to be found.

"The name you seek," said Holmes, "is William Matthew Flinders Petrie."

On a biographical article torn from a two-month-old edition of the *Times*, the item noted that Petrie was the author of *Stonehenge: Plans, Description, and Theories*, published in 1880, followed recently by *The Pyramids and Temples of Gizeh*. "The son and namesake of a civil engineer and professional surveyor, and the maternal grandson of the famous navigator and explorer of the coasts of Australia, Professor Flinders Petrie is a remarkable man in his own right," declared the writer of the article. "As with many great men, he had little formal education, yet he has become a respected mathematician and highly esteemed in the emerging field of Egyptology as the father of modern archaeology."

Seated pensively in his favourite armchair and lighting a long pipe as I continued to read, Holmes said, "I do not in the least exaggerate when I state that Flinders Petrie's methodology of precisely recording and preserving data has raised the excavation of ancient sites from rooting around aimlessly in the earth with a pick and shovel to a science. You have often quoted me on the importance of trifles. Well, this fellow leaves me in the dust, so to speak. What I observe in the importance of cuffs of sleeves, thumbnails, and the great issues that hang from a boot lace, this man discerns in a shard of five-thousand-year-old Egyptian pottery. As I can reconstruct a crime and deduce the identity of a criminal from a cigar ash or an ink smudge on a sheet of stationery, Flinders Petrie divines the structure of an entire civilization."

Returning the "Index" to the shelf, I asked, "Where do we locate this paradigm?"

"Where else but the British Museum? If you have nothing to occupy you in the morning, I hope you will accompany me to Bloomsbury. Following our consultation with Flinders Petrie on the subject of mummy's curses, I shall treat you to a fine midday meal at a nearby public house, the Alpha Inn. I understand it is under new ownership, so I doubt anyone will remember me, although I spent many hours there after mornings in the Museum's Great Reading Room when I resided around the corner in Montague Place."

At eleven o'clock the next morning, as our hansom cab rattled along Marylebone Road to the Euston Road then turned down Gower Street, I allowed my mind to imagine Holmes during the time he had dwelt in Bloomsbury. Wondering what mysteries may have occupied his unique powers of observation and deduction in the years before I met him, and whether he would ever reveal them to me, I looked at him out of the corner of my eye and found a figure that had become familiar, yet always retained an air of mystery. His body was next to me, but his mind was far away. As we rode in the utter silence that I had learned to expect on such occasions, he sat to my left with his head turned slightly. He gazed through the window with a blank expression that I knew masked a brain that was alert to everything around him, but racing ahead in time in anticipation of what he expected to learn from Flinders Petrie on the subject of curses inscribed on the walls of tombs.

When the cab slowed to turn into Great Russell Street, my companion stirred, sighed, and muttered, "This was where the wine merchant Vamberry had his shop. Poor fellow. He was such a fool, wouldn't you agree, Watson?"

"How would I know? I have never heard the name."

"No, of course not. Before your time. Here we are! The good old BM."

Leaping from the hansom, he dashed through the iron gate, across the stone plaza, up the steps, and under the portico of imposing pillars so quickly that I lagged behind. As I caught up, a uniformed attendant was saying. "It's been a long time, Mr. Holmes. What game is afoot today? Blackmail? Robbery? A nice murder?"

"Perhaps, Mr. Dobbs. Perhaps," Holmes replied. "Call it the adventure of the mummy's curse. Which way to the office of Professor Flinders Petrie?"

"Up the stairs, past the Etruscan gallery, and straight ahead. Last door on the right."

"Think of it, Watson," said Holmes as we hurried up the steps and down a long corridor. "Within these magnificent walls reposes the tangible history of mankind, with its glories and tragedies catalogued and preserved, gathered from the four corners of the globe in what is the greatest gift to the world of the long reach of the British Empire!"

"Indeed?" I said, breathlessly. "What about parliamentary government?"

"Said like a true and loyal British citizen, Watson!" Stopping before a plain door with a sign that announced DEPT. OF EGYPTOLOGY, he exclaimed, "Here we are! The domain of Flinders Petrie, unquestionably."

Three swift raps on the door produced from within the room the reply, "It's open."

Entering the office, Holmes and I found a slight figure with a neatly trimmed brown beard and moustache. Wearing a white laboratory coat, he bent over a coal-black, mummified corpse. Stepping boldly across the room, Holmes said, "Professor Flinders Petrie, I presume."

Peering intently down at the mummy, the professor replied, "You arrive at an auspicious moment, gentlemen. This man is unquestionably of the Third Dynasty."

"Forgive the intrusion, Professor," said Holmes. "I am Sherlock Holmes. This is my friend and associate, Dr. John H. Watson. If our call upon you is an inconvenience, we can return at a more opportune time."

"This chap has kept his secrets for nearly four millennia, sir," replied Flinders Petrie, looking up. "A few more minutes is of no consequence, Mr. Holmes. How may I be of service?"

"You are very kind, sir. What can you tell us about the Porter-Broadmoor expedition?"

The question was greeted with a puzzled expression. "Before answering, Mr. Holmes, I must inquire as to whom you represent. Are you here on behalf of Lord Porter?"

"We represent only ourselves."

Stepping away from the mummy to a sink at the far side of the room to wash his hands, the professor said, "That is a disappointment. I was hoping that Lord Porter had sent you. If you are not his agent, why are you interested in seeing me?"

"We are here because you are universally recognised as the preeminent authority in the emerging field of Egyptology."

"Emerging is the right word. Anyone who claims to be the preeminent authority on the study of Egyptology is treading on shaky ground. We have only begun to scratch the surface of the subject, gentlemen."

Finished cleansing his hands, Flinders Petrie invited us to continue our conversation in a small, comfortable office adjacent to his laboratory that was a jumble of Egyptian artefacts. "Are you aware, Professor," said Holmes, "of a series of unfortunate events concerning the recent Porter-Broadmoor expedition that some people have attributed to a curse that was found in the tomb? I refer to the collapse of a tunnel during the excavation, the sinking of a ship carrying artefacts, and the deaths of two of the expedition members."

"Surely, Mr. Holmes, you of all people cannot lend credence to the fantastic stories that these unfortunate events were the result of a curse. Regardless of what you may have read in newspapers about promises of death and doom for members of that expedition, those incidents were coincidence, pure and simple."

"Do you doubt," asked I, "that the expedition found a curse in the mummy's tomb?"

"I would have been surprised had they not. Curses of some kind have been found in every tomb in Egypt. They are as common as quotations from the Holy Bible on the gravestones of Christians in England. For as long as history has been written there have been tales of spells and curses. Read Plato's *Republic* and you will find he noted that if anyone in his time wished to injure an enemy, for a small fee one could hire a sorcerer to bring harm to an individual through an incantation, sign, or effigy to bind the gods to serve the purpose. All of this nonsense about curses in Egyptian tombs began in the imagination of a writer of horror stories named Jane Loudon Webb. After visiting a bizarre theatrical show in Piccadilly Circus in 1821, in which several mummies were unwrapped, this woman penned a science-fiction novel entitled *The Mummy*. Set in the twenty-second century, it featured a vengeful mummy that came to life and threatened to strangle the book's hero. This fantastic tome was followed in 1828 by publication of an anonymous children's book, *The Fruits of Enterprize*, in which mummies were set ablaze to illuminate the interior of an Egyptian tomb. The understandably irate mummies went on a rampage.

"The latest of these flights of imagination was the handiwork of a quite distinguished American author. In 1868, Louisa May Alcott published a short story, 'Lost in a Pyramid, or The Mummy's Curse.' In this grotesque fantasy, an explorer used a flaming mummy to light his way into the interior chamber of a tomb, where he found a golden box containing three seeds that were taken back to America and planted. They produced flowers which his fiancée wore at her wedding. When she inhaled the perfume, she lapsed into a coma and was transformed into a living mummy. It is a pitiful comment on our age, gentlemen, that people do actually believe in all this rot.

"Now we find the shelves of our bookstores and our libraries filled with novels about monsters assembled from body parts and brought to life by mad scientists, and tales of werewolves and vampires. Even one of our country's promising new writers of stories, Arthur Conan Doyle, has dabbled in tales of the occult and supernatural, much of it apparently inspired by the American scribbler and lunatic, Mr. Edgar Allan Poe."

"You are obviously a man with strong opinions," said Holmes.

"If you seek an explanation for the unhappy events associated with the Porter-Broadmoor expedition, you would do well to look beyond the mummy's curse to the obvious explanation. It is human imagination that has discerned horror in happenstance. I refer you to a recent inventive newspaper article that appeared following the unfortunate murder of Professor Broadmoor. The item drew upon an interview in which the nephew of the financier of the expedition referred to the curse that had been found in the tomb. Suddenly, a murderous attack upon Broadmoor was in the mind of a reporter for a sensation-seeking newspaper the latest in a sequence of mysterious occurrences ominously linked to a mummy's curse. What a comment that is on the gullibility of the English people."

"You inquired as to whether Dr. Watson and I were sent to see you by Lord Porter. May I ask why you thought so?"

"I called upon him and his nephew several weeks ago in an attempt to persuade him that he bore an obligation to share his findings with the entire world by turning over the results of his expedition to the British Museum. My argument was along the line that he must choose between the transitory pleasures of personal wealth and the lasting glory of knowing that his name could forever be honoured by the naming of a wing of the Museum for him. I left his home feeling quite encouraged that he would come round to my position on the matter. A few days later, to my great delight, he sent me a letter stating that I would presently be hearing from his solicitor, the Honourable Dudley Walsingham, concerning creation of just such a permanent exhibition. When you appeared, my hope was that you were his agents. I'm afraid now that my expectation that his remarkable collection might take the form of an exhibition for the Museum is groundless. What a great loss that is, gentlemen."

Leaving Flinders Petrie to resume his examination of the mummy, Holmes asked, "Well, Watson, what do you make of our professor of Egyptology?"

"A remarkable man! I found his lecture on the subject of curses fascinating. I share his belief that the proper place for the repose of the artefacts of the Porter-Broadmoor expedition is within the British Museum. He is also spot-on about the deplorable state of the press. Its only interest seems to be in drumming up a fresh sensation in order to sell more newspapers."

"Quite so, my friend," said Holmes as we crossed Great Russell Street in the direction of the Alpha Inn on the opposite corner, "but the press can be valuable, if you know how to use it."

Although the next morning provided the kind of cold and foggy climate that invited one to remain indoors, Holmes was not present as I entered the sitting room and pulled the bell cord to signal Mrs. Hudson that I was ready for one of her bracing breakfasts. When I went to the pipe rack I kept on the mantle to choose my first briar of the day, I found a note from Holmes stating that he would return at noon.

Promptly at that hour, as I was reviewing my notes on the affair at Stoke Moran, Holmes entered the room, dropped two envelopes onto my desk, and said, "These items are for you."

Until that moment, I had accepted without comment his habit of examining the missives and parcels addressed to me and delivered by postmen, telegram delivery boys, and messengers. Not an item for me passed into my hands without first being examined and commented upon. But on this grey and depressing morning, perhaps because of my review of the horror that had recently occupied us at Stoke Moran, or as a result of the damp weather exacerbating the wound I had suffered at Maiwand, I said in exasperation, "Must you always examine my mail?"

"Why, Watson," Holmes responded in a wounded tone as he fixed me with an expression of shock and bewilderment, "I had no idea you could become upset over such a trifling matter."

I thereupon was subjected to a typical Holmesian explanation of his conduct to the effect that nothing was more instructive to a criminal investigator than handwriting, postmarks, and inks. "Have you no concept," he asked, "of all that may be detected about senders of items in the manner in which they address their correspondence? Was it written in a hurry? And what of the stationery? Volumes of information may be unearthed from a letter without opening it."

Only partly assuaged, I grumbled sarcastically, "I have no doubt that one day you will sit down and write a monograph on the subject."

Taking a pipe from his pocket, he replied, "I shall indeed. To date I have catalogued no fewer than fourteen kinds of ink used by the Royal Mail in its postmarks and very nearly one hundred watermarks of British paper manufacturers, as well as more than a score from the United States. For example, in the past year you have received eight letters of paper made in San Francisco. This has led me to deduce that a very close relative of yours is a resident of that city, and, I am sorry to observe, may recently have suffered a serious setback, probably in relation to his health." He paused to light the pipe. "Am I correct in deducing that your correspondence is regarding your brother's illness?"

"Yes, but how—"

"The writing on the first five envelopes was masculine. They were addressed to 'John Watson.' The lack of a 'Mister' or 'Dr. John H. Watson' suggests a familiarity connoting there is a family connection. The latter missives were from the same city, but written by a woman whose form of address included your title. Because a sister would write to 'John,' this indicates that she is probably your brother's wife."

"Probably? There's a word that I have never heard cross your lips."

"I am correct in stating that your brother is not well?"

"He suffers from a nervous disorder that leaves him increasingly palsied."

"When do you plan to sail to America?"

"Why do you assume that I'm contemplating such a trip?"

"Really, Watson! The second envelope you have received is a bulky one bearing the name of the Cunard Steamship Company. Its dimension can only mean it contains a schedule of Atlantic crossings."

"I have not yet made a decision."

"When you do, I shall provide whatever assistance you may require."

"Thank you. Where were you off to this morning?"

"Here and there."

With that, he settled into his chair, filled his pipe, struck a match, and lapsed into one of his long, contemplative silences that were as impenetrable as the swirling fog of Baker Street.

Gone again throughout the afternoon without explanation, he burst into the sitting room at a quarter to four, flung one of the city's sensational newspapers into my lap, and exclaimed, "Look at the Stop Press on page one."

Locating the small item, I read:

> ## LATEST VICTIM OF THE MUMMY'S CURSE?
> Our correspondent in Kent reports what appears to be another example of the curse that has befallen the recent expedition to investigate ancient tombs in Egypt. The financier of the ill-fated party, Lord Porter, was found dead early this morning in the bedroom of his estate in Kent. Although Chief Inspector William Crawford of the local constabulary stated that the elderly Lord Porter's death appears to have been of natural causes, we are reminded of the deaths of two members of the expedition, and other misfortunes that occurred since the discovery of a curse within the tomb when it was unearthed several months ago.

"Deaths of two leading participants in this expedition into the sands of Egypt may be dismissed as coincidence," said Holmes. "Three require an enquiry. There is an express train that we can catch if we hurry. I have sent a wire to Inspector Crawford asking him to rendezvous with us at the railway station at seven o'clock."

Less than a week had passed since Holmes and I had boarded another train at Waterloo Station to travel to Leatherhead, and onwards by a trap hired at the station inn to Stoke Moran. As on that occasion, it was a delightful day of fleecy clouds and bright sun, although we now passed through the spring countryside at a later hour. When the train arrived at our destination, I peered from my window at a short, rotund, middle-aged man in a brown suit and tan derby pacing the platform. Turning to Holmes, I stated, "That must be our Inspector Crawford."

"Yes," Holmes replied, looking over my shoulder. "Heavy, black shoes. One can usually spot a policeman by his choice of sturdy, comfortable footwear."

After an exchange of greetings, Holmes asked Crawford, "Has anything been disturbed in the room in which Lord Porter's body was found?"

"Except for removal of the corpse to the mortuary round nine o'clock last evening, the bedroom is just as it was," replied Crawford excitedly. "I instructed the household staff that no one was to enter the bedroom until the coroner has ascertained the cause of death."

"Excellent work, Inspector!"

Riding in a carriage driven by a uniformed constable, we arrived at the estate of Lord Porter and passed through a gateway flanked by large stone figures with human heads and the bodies of lions. At the end of a long, curving driveway bounded by tall oak trees stood an old mansion whose doorway was guarded by a pair of stone rams. Holmes's loud rap on the door was answered by the butler. As we entered a spacious foyer decorated with Egyptian artefacts, Holmes asked him, "What is your name?"

"Bradley, sir."

"How long have you been Lord Porter's butler?"

"Nearly ten years."

"Had Lord Porter seemed out of sorts lately? Was he a nervous man? Did he at any time express fear that his life was in jeopardy?"

"Not to me, sir."

"Did he ever speak to you about his recent expedition to Egypt?"

"Not about the expedition itself, sir. But lately he expressed concern about stories in the newspapers concerning allegations that he was more interested in the profits to be garnered from that adventure than in the scientific aspects and advancement of knowledge."

"Who was present in the house when Lord Porter died?"

"Only the staff, sir."

"Had there been recent visitors?"

"Lord Porter's solicitor was here on Monday."

"That would be the Honourable Dudley Walsingham?"

"Yes, sir."

"Anyone else?"

"A Major McAndrew called. He had been invited to luncheon with Lord Porter. I believe he was a member of the expedition. Last evening, Lord Porter's nephew came to dinner. Soon after they ate, Lord Porter went to bed and Mr. Basil returned to his home in London."

"I sent the nephew a telegram last evening informing him of the death," said the Inspector, "but have received no reply."

"Bradley," said Holmes, "please show us to Lord Porter's bedroom."

Located to our right at the top of a curving stairway, the bedroom was a large chamber that had the aspects of a museum.

"Please remain in the corridor, gentlemen," said Holmes brusquely, "while I have a look round the room."

What followed in the next few minutes was a scene quite familiar to me, but a matter of wonder and puzzlement to Inspector Crawford. "What is he looking for, Doctor?" he asked of me in a whisper as Holmes moved carefully through the room, examining the area around the bed, kneeling briefly to peer at the carpet, and going to the room's two large windows.

Abruptly returning to the doorway, Holmes asked the butler, "Did Lord Porter smoke?"

"Until his physician ordered him to give up tobacco two years ago, he enjoyed a pipe."

"Was he an active man?"

"Prior to the Egyptian expedition, yes."

"But not since?"

"I'm afraid the journey and the time he spent in the desert took its toll on his vitality. He spent most days either at his desk in his study or in bed."

"Thank you, Bradley. That will be all."

"Very good, sir."

"Now, Inspector," said Holmes, "take us to the mortuary."

In a small room adjacent to the office of the constabulary, the sheet-shrouded body of Lord Porter lay on a large table. Drawing back the covering, Holmes proceeded to examine the corpse from head to toe. Presently, he declared, "Interesting. Have a look, Watson. I call your attention to a slight discoloration of the skin around what seems to be a puncture just below the hairline on the right side of the back of Lord Porter's neck."

Examining a small, reddish welt, I said, "It could be an insect bite. To state exactly what it is would require examination of the tissue under a microscope."

"Inspector, " said Holmes, "I'll be interested in knowing as soon as possible to what your coroner attributes it."

"Certainly, Mr. Holmes. Is there anything else I can do?"

"Not at the moment, but you may be hearing from me quite soon." Although I was fairly bursting with curiosity as Holmes and I returned to Baker Street, I had learned that he would illuminate me when he deemed it appropriate to do so. He had said to me on several occasions that I possessed the grand gift of silence and that this had made me quite invaluable as a companion. Consequently, when he left our lodging in the morning and did not return until late in the afternoon, I was resolved to make no enquiries as to his purpose or whereabouts. It was that evening during dinner that he looked up suddenly from a platter of Mrs. Hudson's incomparable broiled trout and muttered, "These are murky waters, Watson. Whether I prove to be correct will be known only when we hear again from Inspector Crawford."

The message he awaited arrived the next afternoon. A telegram from Crawford was the briefest Holmes had ever received:

COBRA VENOM

Waving the wire as if it were a flag, Holmes said exultantly, "That is the penultimate stone in this intricate construction, Watson. All that is left is to send to

Inspector Crawford a telegram in which I shall propose a question to be put to the butler, along with my advice to Crawford that if the butler's reply is in the affirmative a charge of murder be brought against Basil Porter."

Crawford's reply arrived later that day in another brief telegram:

HE HAS GIVEN A COMPLETE CONFESSION.
DETAILS TO FOLLOW.

As I read the message, I exclaimed, "This is amazing, Holmes. You have solved this case without having met and questioned the person you suspected!"

"There was no need, Watson. I had an accumulation of facts that pointed to Basil Porter. This nefarious nephew possesses one of the most brilliant and devious minds to ever challenge my powers. You'll recall that I said after our meeting with Flinders Petrie that the press can be a valuable instrument if you know how to use it. This man seized upon the seemingly mysterious events of the tunnel collapse, the sinking of the ship, the accidental death of Anthony Fulmer, and the murder of Professor Broadmoor to plant in the mind of a newspaper reporter the idea that these events were the effects of the mummy's curse. In an attempt to lend further credibility to this explanation, he attempted to murder your old comrade in arms, Major McAndrew. Had we not encountered the Major that evening in Simpson's in the Strand, Basil Porter's crimes might have gone undetected and unpunished."

"What caused you to suspect him?"

"Among the numerous puzzling facets of this case, I found it curious that on notification of his uncle's death that Basil Porter did not rush back from London. When I found what seemed to be an insect bite in the back of Lord Porter's neck, but could have been a scratch made by a pin or a hypodermic needle, I suspected that Lord Porter had been injected with a poison. When I received confirmation that it was cobra venom, I saw no explanation that was logical, except that it had been administered by the nephew. To be certain, I had to eliminate the only other visitor to Lord Porter that day, your friend McAndrew. I had to know if the two men had been alone at any time on that day."

"That was the question you asked Crawford to pose to the butler."

"In my examination of the rug in Lord Porter's bedroom, I found not only traces of cigar ash, but evidence that someone had paced up and down in a state of extreme excitement. You know my methods. What does that tell you?"

"There had been a heated argument."

"Precisely, but concerning what? Among my excursions following our sojourn to the domain of Inspector Crawford was a call upon Lord Porter's solicitor, the Honourable Dudley Walsingham. My purpose was to inquire as to the beneficiary of Lord Porter's will. It was quite a formidable estate, even before the spectacular treasures brought back from Egypt. My enquiries directed toward knowledgeable men in the financial circles and bankers in the City resulted in evidence that Basil Porter has been on the brink of bankruptcy for quite some time."

"You therefore surmised that Basil expected to be rescued from his dilemma by killing his uncle and inheriting an estate which had been substantially increased in wealth as a result of the treasures brought back from Egypt."

"But this prospect was suddenly jeopardised," said Holmes, "when Lord Porter appeared to accede to Professor Flinders Petrie's appeal to donate the expedition's finds to the BM. It was then that Basil devised a plan for murder that he had hoped would appear to be the result of the curse found in the tomb. To lay the foundation for this fantastic proposition, he killed Professor Broadmoor and in an exceedingly clever use of the press, he called attention to the coincidental incidents of the tunnel collapse, the ship bearing expedition artefacts that sank, and the death of Fulmer in the train accident. Of course, I had no proof of any of this. Each of these occurrences could be readily explained as happenstance. The only occurrence that I was able to investigate was the curious incident of the roof tile that injured Major McAndrew. This meant a visit to his quarters in Chelsea. In examining the rooftop, I found not only that the tile had been pried loose, but footprints of the person who flung them down on McAndrew. If this attack had been done by a magically animated mummy that had been wondrously transported to Chelsea, he had taken time to be fitted for a pair of shoes. We are left with no other explanation but this extraordinary drama had to be the work of Basil Porter. At that point, I had to be certain he was the only person on that day who had the opportunity."

"But what if Major McAndrew had also been alone with Lord Porter that day?"

"Motive, Watson! What motive could McAndrew possibly have had to kill Lord Porter?"

"Well done, Holmes!"

Although Basil Porter had admitted to the murders of his uncle and Felix Broadmoor, he presented to jury and judge at his trial the fantastic explanation that his deeds were the result of a brain fever that developed into insanity, which he brazenly blamed on the mummy's curse. This astonishing device proved unavailing. Convicted of two murders, he was sentenced to death and hanged for his crimes. Meanwhile, because Lord Porter had no other heirs, the treasures of the Egyptian expedition were declared the property of the Crown and consigned by a judge of the probate court to the British Museum, there to be under the supervision of Flinders Petrie. That distinguished scholar continued his work as an archaeologist, for which he would presently be knighted and named Professor of Egyptology at University College of London in 1892. The Egyptian Research Council that he established in 1894 eventually became The British School of Archaeology and, ultimately, the Petrie Museum of Egyptian Archaeology in Malet Place.

As I was reviewing my notes on this extraordinary affair a few days after Holmes's solution to a case that I had decided to record under the title "The Mummy's Curse," I gazed across our sitting room at Holmes and interrupted his repose with a thought that had suddenly occurred to me. "You have proved that Basil Porter devised a murderous scheme to inherit vast wealth," I said, "but has it ever entered your mind that none of this has proved that all of these unfortunate events were not the result of the mummy's curse?"

Holmes leapt from his chair. "What are you saying?"

"It could be interpreted," said I, with a smile and arching eyebrows, "that Basil Porter was simply the instrument by which the mummy's curse was, in fact, fulfilled!"

"Good old Watson," said Holmes with a puff of smoke from his favorite briar. "Your romanticism is as permanent a fixture as the pyramids of Giza. And just as mysterious!"

THE THINGS THAT SHALL COME UPON THEM

by Barbara Roden

Barbara Roden, along with her husband Christopher Roden, is the proprietor of Ash-Tree Press. Together, they are also the editors of several anthologies, including *Acquainted with the Night,* which won the World Fantasy Award. Barbara is also the editor of *All Hallows,* the journal of the Ghost Story Society. Her short fiction has appeared in the anthologies *Exotic Gothic 2, The Year's Best Fantasy & Horror, By Blood We Live,* and in the Sherlock Holmes anthologies *The Mammoth Book of New Sherlock Holmes Adventures* and *Gaslight Grimoire,* the latter in which this story first appeared. Her first collection of short stories, *Northwest Passages,* will be published by Prime Books in October.

"If you eliminate the impossible," says Sherlock Holmes, in an oft-quoted remark, "then whatever remains, however improbable, must be the truth." But doesn't this bold statement perhaps presuppose a rather cavalier degree of ontological certainty? Is it really so unproblematic to sort out the possible from the impossible? Many would take issue with Holmes's unflappable rationalism, chief among them Flaxman Low, the first true psychic detective character, whose co-creator Hesketh Vernon Hesketh-Prichard was a good friend of Conan Doyle's. These two contemporaneous fictional characters go head-to-head in our next adventure, in a clash of both personality and worldview. The author writes, "The story's setting—Lufford Abbey, former home of Julian Karswell of M. R. James's classic 'Casting the Runes'—came after I watched, with our son, the film version of 'Casting the Runes', *Night of the Demon,* and found myself wondering what happened to Karswell's home after he died, in somewhat mysterious circumstances, in France. The involvement of a 'Dr. Watson' in James's story was a gift from the writing gods." The following tale, an adept blending of several different literary universes, calls to mind the common saying: "There are generally two sides to every story."

"Do you recall, Watson," said my friend Sherlock Holmes, "how I described my profession when we first took lodgings together, and you expressed curiosity as to how your fellow lodger was related to certain comments which you had read in a magazine?"

"I certainly do!" I laughed. "As I recall, you referred to yourself as the world's only consulting detective; a remark prompted by my less than effusive statements regarding the article in question. In mitigation I can only say that I did not realise, when I made those statements, that I was addressing the article's author; nor did I have the benefit of having seen your methods in action."

Holmes smiled, and bowed his head in acknowledgement of my words. "Your comments had at least the charm of honesty, Watson."

"But what prompts this recollection, Holmes?" I asked. My friend was not, as a rule, given to thoughts of the past, and I suspected that some event had given rise to his question. In answer he made a sweeping gesture which encompassed the many newspapers littering the floor of our Baker Street rooms.

"As you know, Watson, I make it a habit to familiarise myself with the contents of the many newspapers with which our metropolis is blessed; it is astonishing how even the smallest event may prove to have a bearing on some matter with which I come into professional contact. And yet it seems that every time I open a newspaper I find myself reading of yet another person who has followed where I have led."

"Imitation is, as they say, the sincerest form of flattery."

"In which case I am flattered indeed, Watson, for my imitators are numerous. When our association began there were, as I recall, no other consulting detectives, or at least none who called themselves such; yet even the most cursory glance at the papers now shows that I have, however unwittingly, been what our North American friends might call a trailblazer. Here"—and his long white arm stretched out to extricate a paper from out of the mass which surrounded him—"is an account of how Max Carrados helped Inspector Beedel of the Yard solve what the newspapers are, rather sensationally, calling 'The Holloway Flat Tragedy'; and here is a letter praising the assistance given by Dyer's Detective Agency in Lynch Court, Fleet Street. These are by no means isolated instances; and it is not only the newspapers which record the exploits of these detectives. The newsagent boasts an array of magazines in which one can read of their adventures; a turn of events for which you must assume some responsibility."

"How so?" I exclaimed.

"Your records of my doings have, I am afraid, given the public an appetite for tales of this sort, so much so that every detective worthy of the name must, it seems, have his Boswell—or Watson—to record his adventures. The doings of Mr. Martin Hewitt appear with almost monotonous regularity, and I can scarcely glance at a magazine without being informed that I will find therein breathless accounts of the cases of Paul Beck or Eugene Valmont or a certain Miss Myrl, who appears to be trying to advance the cause of women's suffrage through somewhat novel means. I understand there is a gentleman who sits in an A.B.C. teashop and solves crimes without benefit of sight, or the need of abandoning his afternoon's refreshment, while Mr. Flaxman Low purports to help those whose cases appear to be beyond the understanding of mere mortals; truly the refuge of the desperate, although from what I gather the man is not quite the charlatan he might seem." Holmes chuckled, and threw down his paper. "If this continues apace, I may find myself contemplating retirement, or at least a change of profession."

"But surely," I replied, "your reputation is such that you need have no fear of such a fate just yet! Why, every post sees applications for your assistance, and Inspector Hopkins is as assiduous a visitor as always. I do not think that Sherlock Holmes will be retiring from public view at any point in the immediate future."

"No; I may fairly claim that the demands upon my time are as frequent as they have ever been, although I confess that many of the cases which are brought to my attention could be as easily solved by a constable still wet behind the ears as by a trained professional. Yet there still remain those cases which promise something of the *outré* and which the official force would be hard-pressed to solve." Holmes rose from his chair, crossed to the table, and extracted a sheet of paper from amongst the breakfast dishes. He glanced at it for a moment, then passed it to me. "Be so good as to read this, and tell me what you make of it."

I looked at the letter, and attempted to emulate my friend's methods. "It is written on heavy paper," I began, "simply yet elegantly embossed, from which I would deduce a certain level of wealth allied with good taste. It is in a woman's hand, firm and clear, which would seem to denote that its writer is a person of determination as well as intelligence."

"And pray how do you deduce the intelligence, without having read the letter?" asked my friend.

"Why, from the fact that she has had the good sense to consult Sherlock Holmes, and not one of the pretenders to his crown."

"A touch, Watson!" laughed Holmes. "A distinct touch! But now read the lady's letter, and see what opinion you form of her and her case."

I turned my attention to the paper, and read the following:

> Lufford Abbey
> Warwickshire
> Dear Mr. Holmes,
>
> Having read of your methods and cases, I am turning to you in hopes that you will be able to bring an end to a series of disturbances which have occurred over the past two months, and which have left our local constabulary at a complete loss. What began as a series of minor annoyances has gradually become something more sinister; but as these events have not, as yet, resulted in a crime being committed, I am told that there is little the police can do.
>
> My husband is in complete agreement with me that steps must

be taken; yet I will be candid and state that he does not agree that this is a matter for Mr. Sherlock Holmes. I hasten to add that his admiration for you is as great as mine; where we differ is in our ideas as to the nature of the events. I firmly believe that a human agency is at work, whereas my husband is of the opinion that we must seek for an answer that lies beyond our five senses.

I fear that any account which I could lay before you in a letter would fail to give a true indication of what we are suffering. However, suffering we are, and I hope that you will be able to see your way to meeting with us, so that we may lay the facts before you. I have included a note of the most convenient trains, and a telegram indicating your arrival time will ensure that you are met at the station.

I thank you in advance for your consideration of this matter; merely writing this letter has taken some of the weight from my mind, and I am in hopes that your arrival and investigation will put an end to the worries with which we are beset.

Yours sincerely,
Mrs. John Fitzgerald

"Well, Watson? And what do you make of it?"

I placed the letter on the table. "The letter confirms my opinion of the lady's character and intelligence. She does not set down a jumble of facts, fancies, and theories, but rather writes in a business-like manner which yet does not conceal her anxiety. The fact that she and her husband have thought it necessary to involve the police indicates that the matter is serious, for Mrs. Fitzgerald does not, from this letter, strike me as a woman who is given to imagining things; unlike her husband, I might add."

"Yes, her husband, who believes that the solution to their problem lies beyond the evidence of our five senses." Holmes shook his head. "I have never yet met with a case which is not capable of a rational solution, however irrational it may appear at the outset, and I have no doubt that this mystery will prove the same as the others."

"You have decided to take the case, then?"

"Yes. As the lady was so thoughtful as to include a list of train times, I took the liberty of sending a telegram indicating that we would travel up on the 12.23 train. I take it that your patients can do without you for a day or so?"

"I can certainly make arrangements, Holmes, if you would like me to accompany you."

"Of course I would, Watson! A trip to the Warwickshire countryside will prove a welcome respite from a damp London spring; and I will need my chronicler with me, to record my efforts, if I am to keep pace with my colleagues." My friend was smiling as he said this; then his face became thoughtful. "Lufford Abbey," he said slowly. "That name sounds familiar; but I cannot immediately call the circumstances to mind. Ah well, we have some time before our train departs, and I shall try to lay my hands on the details."

My long association with Sherlock Holmes, coming as it did on the heels of my military career, had made me adept at packing quickly and at short notice. It was an easy matter to arrange for my patients to be seen by one of my associates, and well before the appointed time I was back in Baker Street and Holmes and I were on our way to Euston Station, where we found the platform unusually crowded. We were fortunate enough to secure a first-class compartment to ourselves, but our privacy was short-lived, for just as the barrier was closing a man hurried along the platform and, after a moment's hesitation, entered our compartment. He was middle-aged, tall, and strongly built, having about him the look of a man who has been an athlete in his youth and maintained his training in the years since. He gave us both a polite nod, then settled himself into the opposite corner of the compartment and pulled a small notebook from his pocket, in which he began to make what appeared to be notes, frequently referring to a sheaf of papers which he had placed on the seat beside him.

Holmes had shot the newcomer a penetrating glance, but, upon seeing that our companion was obviously not one to intrude his company on others, he relaxed, and was silent for a few minutes, gazing out the window as the train gathered speed and we began to leave London and its environs behind. I knew better than to intrude upon his thoughts, and eventually he settled back into his seat, put his fingers together in the familiar manner, and began to speak.

"I was not mistaken, Watson, when I said that the name of our destination was familiar to me. As you know, I am in the habit of retaining items from the newspapers which might conceivably be of interest, or have a bearing on a future case, and this habit has borne fruit on this occasion. An article in the *Times* from July of last year reported the death, in unusual circumstances, of an English traveller at Abbeville, who was struck on the head and killed instantly by a stone which fell from the tower of a church there, under which the unfortunate gentleman happened to be standing. His name was Mr. Julian Karswell, and his residence was given as Lufford Abbey in Warwickshire. It would not—"

But my friend's words were cut short by an exclamation from the third occupant of our compartment. He had laid aside his notebook and papers, and was looking from my companion to myself with a quick, inquisitive glance which avoided mere vulgar curiosity, and instead spoke of something deeper. He seemed to realise that an explanation was needed, and addressed himself to both of us in tones that were low and pleasant.

"Excuse me, gentlemen, but I could not help overhearing you speak of a Mr. Karswell and his residence, Lufford Abbey. Both names are known to me, which accounts for my surprise, particularly when I hear them from the lips of Mr. Sherlock Holmes. And you, sir"—he nodded his head towards me—"must be Dr. Watson." He noted my look of surprise, and added with a gentle smile, "I heard your friend address you by name, and it was not difficult to identify you from your likenesses in *The Strand Magazine*."

"You have the advantage of us, sir," said Holmes politely, "as well as the makings of a detective."

"My name is Flaxman Low," said our companion, "and I am, in my small way, a detective, although I do not expect that you will have heard of me."

"On the contrary," answered my friend drily, "I was speaking of you only this morning."

"Not, I fear, with any favour, to judge by your tone," replied Low. "No, Mr. Holmes, I do not take offence," he continued, forestalling my companion. "A great many people share your view, and I am accustomed to that fact. You and I are, I suspect, more alike than you think in our approach and methods. The difference lies in the fact that where I am Hamlet, you, if I may take the liberty of saying so, prefer the part of Horatio."

For a moment I feared, from the expression on my friend's face, that he would not take kindly to this remark; but after a moment his features relaxed into a smile, and he laughed.

"Perhaps that is no bad thing, Mr. Low," he remarked, "for at the end of the play Horatio is one of the few characters still in the land of the living, while the Prince of Denmark is, we presume, learning at first hand whether or not his views on the spiritual world were correct."

Flaxman Low laughed in his turn. "Well said, Mr. Holmes." Then his face turned grave. "You mentioned Lufford Abbey. May I enquire as to your interest in that house and its late owner?"

Holmes shrugged. "As to its late owner I admit of no knowledge, save for the fact of his death last year. The house, however, is our destination, hence my interest in any particulars relating to it." He gazed at Low thoughtfully. "I am not mistaken, I think, in stating that Lufford Abbey is your destination also, and that you have been summoned thence by Mr. John Fitzgerald, to look into a matter which has been troubling him."

"You are quite correct, Mr. Holmes," acknowledged Low. "Mr. Fitzgerald wrote and asked if I would be available to look into a series of events which is proving troubling to his household, and appears to be beyond the capabilities of the local police force."

"And we have received a similar letter from Mrs. Fitzgerald," said Holmes. "It appears, Mr. Low, that we shall have a practical means of comparing our methods; it will be interesting to see what results we achieve."

"Indeed." Low paused, and looked from one of us to the other. "You say that you know nothing of Julian Karswell, save for the few facts surrounding his death. Perhaps, if you will allow me, I can give further elucidation as to the character of the late owner of Lufford Abbey."

"By all means," said Holmes. "At present I am working in the dark, and any information which you can provide would be of the greatest interest."

"I am not surprised that you know little of Julian Karswell," said Low, settling back into his seat and clasping his hands behind his head, "for while I, and a few others who knew of him, felt that he had the makings of a distinguished criminal, he never committed any crimes which broke the laws of man as they currently stand."

Holmes raised his eyebrows. "Are you saying that he committed crimes which broke other laws?"

"Yes, Mr. Holmes. Karswell was interested in the occult, or the black arts—call it what you will—and he had the means to devote himself to his studies, for he was reputed to be a man of great wealth, although how he acquired this wealth was a question for much speculation. He used to joke about the many treasures of his house, although no one that I know of was ever permitted to see them. He wrote a book upon the subject of witchcraft, which was treated with contempt by most of those who bothered to read it; until, that is, it appeared that Mr. Karswell took a somewhat more practical approach to the occult than had been suspected."

"Practical?" I interjected. "In what way?"

Our companion paused before replying. When he did, his tone was grave. "Certain people who had occasion to cross Mr. Karswell suffered fates which were… curious, to say the least. A man named John Harrington, who wrote a scathing review of Karswell's book *The History of Witchcraft*, died under circumstances which were never satisfactorily explained, and another man, Edward Dunning, made what I consider to be a very narrow escape."

It was my turn to utter an exclamation, and both Holmes and Low turned to look at me. "Edward Dunning, who belongs to the ———— Association?" I asked.

"Yes," replied Low in some curiosity, while Holmes gazed at me quizzically. "Why, do you know him?"

"As a matter of fact I do," I replied. "He came to me on the recommendation of a neighbour—oh, eighteen months or so ago—and we struck up a friendship of sorts; enough that when he was seriously incommoded by illness in his household I invited him to dinner."

"When was this?" asked Low, with an eagerness which somewhat surprised me.

"Why"—I paused to think—"this was in the spring of last year; April, as I recall. His two servants were struck down by a sudden illness—food poisoning, I suspect—and the poor man seemed somewhat lost, so I invited him to dinner at my club. He seemed more pleased than the invitation itself would warrant, and was reluctant to leave; almost as if he did not want to return to his house. Indeed, he was in a rather agitated state; distracted, as if he were continually turning some problem over in his mind."

"You are very close to the truth, Doctor," said Low gravely. "The agitation which Edward Dunning displayed was occasioned by Karswell, and certain steps which that person was even then taking; steps which almost led to Dunning's death."

"Death!" exclaimed my friend. "Surely that brought Karswell within reach of the law?"

"Yes and no," replied Low after a pause. "You see, gentlemen," he continued,

"Karswell was a very clever man in some ways, and was familiar with practices which would allow him to exact revenge against someone while ensuring that he himself remained safe from prosecution; there were rumours that he was preparing another book on the subject, although nothing came of it. Unfortunately for him, he ran up against two people—Edward Dunning being one of them—who were prepared to use his own methods, and thus escape harm by throwing Karswell's own agents against him."

"Are you saying that you believe this Karswell used supernatural means to accomplish his ends?" asked Holmes in astonishment.

"That is precisely what I am saying, Mr. Holmes," replied Low gravely. "I agree with the words of St. Augustine: *Credo ut intelligam*[1]." Holmes shook his head.

"I am afraid I must side with Petrarch: *Vos vestros servate, meos mihi linquite mores*[2]. It has been my experience that no case, no matter how bizarre or otherworldly it may seem when it commences, cannot be explained by entirely natural means. Surely your own experiences, Mr. Low, will have shown you that man is capable enough of evil, without ascribing its presence to the supernatural."

"As to your last point, Mr. Holmes, we are in complete agreement. Where we differ, it seems, is in our willingness to accept that not everything we see or hear or experience can be rationalised. I enter every case I undertake with a perfectly clear mind, and no one is more pleased than I when it can be proved that something which appears to be supernatural has a completely logical explanation that would stand up in a court of law. And yet it is my belief that we are standing on the frontier of an unknown world, the rules of which we do not comprehend and can only vaguely grasp, in flashes, as our unready senses catch broken glimpses of things which obey laws we cannot understand. One day, perhaps, this other world will be understood, and mapped as fully as any known country on earth; until then we can only advance slowly, storing away pieces of the puzzle in hopes that they can be fitted together in the fullness of time."

It was an extraordinary speech to hear in the prosaic surroundings of a first-class carriage rattling through the placid English countryside; but Flaxman Low's earnest face and steady voice carried a conviction that it was impossible to ridicule. I could tell that my friend was impressed despite himself, and when he replied it was in a tone more restrained and conciliatory than would have been the case only a few minutes earlier.

"Well, Mr. Low, we must agree to disagree on certain points; but I look forward to the experience of working with you on this case. Perhaps, if you would be so good, you might tell us more of Mr. Karswell."

"But what can he have to do with this?" I interjected. "He died almost a year ago, and surely can have nothing to do with the matter in hand."

"Possibly not," said my friend, "but the fact remains that a man who appears to have died in questionable circumstances, and who himself may have been involved

---

1 I believe in order that I may understand.
2 You cling to your own ways and leave mine to me.

in the death of at least one person, has left behind him a house which is now, in turn, the scene of mysterious occurrences. This may prove to be mere coincidence, but it is not something an investigator can ignore. The more facts with which we are armed, the more likely that we shall bring Mr. and Mrs. Fitzgerald's case to a speedy—and satisfactory—conclusion."

I will not try the patience of my readers by detailing the events which Flaxman Low laid before us; Dr. James of King's College has since provided his own account of the case, which is readily available. Suffice it to say that Mr. Julian Karswell appeared to have been a deeply unpleasant person, quick to anger, sensitive to criticism both real and imagined, and with the fire of vengeance burning within him, so much so that any who crossed his path appeared to have very real cause to fear for their safety. He was, according to Low, responsible for the death of John Harrington, and very nearly killed Edward Dunning, although Holmes refused to believe that he used supernatural means to accomplish his ends; nor did he believe that Karswell's sudden death at Abbeville was anything other than the accident the French investigators deemed it to be. "For if a man will go walking about in a site where extensive repairs are being carried out, we cannot be surprised to hear that some mischance has befallen him," he said, while Flaxman Low shook his head but said nothing.

Our companion had scarcely finished narrating his story when our train began to slow, and our stop was announced. We were among only a handful of passengers who alighted, and before the train had pulled away we were approached by a coachman, who nodded his head respectfully at us.

"Mr. Holmes, Dr. Watson, and Mr. Low, is it?" he enquired. "You are all expected, gentlemen; I'll see to your baggage if you will kindly follow me."

We left the station and found a carriage awaiting us, a fine team of horses standing harnessed in front of it. Holmes ran his keen eyes over them.

"I see that we have not far to go to Lufford Abbey," he remarked, and the coachman glanced at him.

"No, sir, little more'n a mile or so. You've been here before, then?"

"No," interjected Low, before my friend could reply, "but the horses are fresh and glossy, which would indicate that they have not travelled far to get here."

Holmes's lips twitched in a slight smile. "You evidently see and observe, Mr. Low. Excellent traits in a detective."

"I have learned from a master," replied Low, giving a small bow. "Indeed, I may say that it was reading the early accounts of your cases, as penned by Dr. Watson, which first gave me the thought of applying your methods to the investigation of that frontier which we were discussing during our journey here. Indeed, one day it might come to pass that you are acknowledged as being as great a forerunner in that field as you are in the science of more ordinary detection."

Our bags had been loaded in the carriage, and we climbed in. The coachman called out to the horses and we were on our way, rumbling through the main street of a pretty village crowded with half-timbered buildings which spoke of a more peaceful way of life than existed in the bustling metropolis which we had left. The tranquillity around us contrasted so sharply with the story Flaxman Low had told us in the train, and the dark deeds hinted at in Mrs. Fitzgerald's letter, that I could not help shivering. Low, who was sitting opposite me, caught my eye and nodded.

"Yes, Doctor," he said, as if in answer to my thoughts, "it is difficult to believe that such things can exist when the evidence of our senses shows us such pleasant scenes. I hope, in all honesty, that our clients' case may prove to have an entirely logical and rational solution; but given what I know of the late owner of Lufford Abbey, I confess I fear the worst."

It seemed that we had scarcely left the village behind us when the carriage turned through a set of massive iron gates, and we found ourselves driving through beautifully maintained grounds. Bright clumps of yellow daffodils were dotted about a wide sweep of grassland, which led in turn to a thick plantation of trees on both sides of the drive. Ahead of us lay Lufford Abbey itself, an imposing building of mellow stone which seemed to glow in the warm afternoon sunlight. I did not have time to contemplate the house, however, for as soon as the carriage drew up the front door opened, and our host and hostess came out to greet us.

They were an interesting study in contrasts, Mr. and Mrs. Fitzgerald. He was tall and slender, with dark eyes set in a pale face, and an unruly shock of black hair, a lock of which he was perpetually brushing back from his forehead. His wife, while almost as tall as her husband, was more sturdily built, and her blue eyes looked out from a face which I guessed was, under normal circumstances, ruddy-complexioned and clear, as of one who spends a good deal of time in the open air. Now, however, it wore a look of anxiety, an expression shared by Mr. Fitzgerald, who stepped forward with short, nervous steps, wringing his hands together in an attitude of embarrassment.

"Mr. Low?" he enquired, looking from one of us to another, and our companion nodded his head.

"I am Flaxman Low, and these gentlemen are Mr. Holmes and Dr. Watson. We understand from your coachman that we are all expected."

"Yes, yes, of course... oh dear, this is really most awkward. I do not know how I came to make such a terrible mistake. The dates—of course, I put the wrong one in my letter to you, Mr. Low, and it was only when I spoke with my wife after that I realised what had happened. We did not intend... that is to say, we meant... such a dreadful mix-up..."

His words trailed off, and he wore a look of contrition that was almost comical. His wife stepped forward firmly and placed a hand on his arm.

"My husband is correct in saying that this is an awkward situation, gentlemen; but such events happen in the best-regulated of households, and I believe that when you hear our story you will excuse us. Matters have been somewhat"—she paused, as if in search of the correct word—"fraught here in recent days, and we were both so anxious of a solution that we proceeded independently of each other, with the result that you now see. We will, of course, understand perfectly should one of you decide that he would rather not stay."

"Explanations are unnecessary," replied Holmes, and Low nodded. "My friend and I were not previously acquainted with Mr. Low, but a fortuitous chance has ensured that we had an opportunity to discuss the matter—so far as we know it—on the way here, and I think I may safely say that we see no difficulty in combining our efforts."

"Mr. Holmes is quite correct," added Low. "While we may differ in certain of our beliefs, we are united in our determination to put an end to the difficulties which you face."

"Thank you, gentlemen," said our host, relief sweeping across his face. For a moment the look of anxiety left him, and I was able to see traces of the good humour which I suspected his countenance usually wore. "I cannot tell you how relieved we both are to hear this. Of course, we really must explain why it is that—"

"Yes, we must," interrupted Mrs. Fitzgerald, firmly but kindly. "However I do not think, John, that the front drive is the place for explanations."

"Of course; you are quite right, my dear." He turned and smiled at us. "Forgive me once more; my manners have quite escaped me. The maid will show you to your rooms, and then we will lay all the facts before you, in hopes that you will see light where we see only darkness."

Less than half-an-hour elapsed before we were assembled in a pleasantly furnished sitting-room with our host and hostess, and provided with refreshments. Both Mr. and Mrs. Fitzgerald seemed to take pleasure in the everyday ritual of pouring tea and passing cakes, and for a moment their cares and anxieties seemed to fade in the flow of casual conversation around them.

"Yes," said Mr. Fitzgerald, in answer to a question of Low's, "there was an abbey here, although nothing of it now remains apart from a few relics housed in the parish church. Most of it was destroyed in 1539, and what little was left—mainly stables and the Abbot's lodging, from what I gather—has long since vanished. Some outlying domestic buildings were the last to go; according to village gossip there was an old man who, early in the eighteenth century, could still point out the sites of some of the buildings, but this knowledge appears to have died with him. I cannot think of another similar monastic house which has disappeared so completely from the ken of man."

"You are a student of such things, then?" enquired Holmes.

"In a very modest way. Being a gentleman of leisure, I have the time and opportunity to indulge myself in that way; and have a natural inclination towards such subjects, tinged with melancholy as they are. Parts of this house were built very shortly after the abbey was dissolved, and I suspect that many of the stones from the original monastic building found their way into the construction of it, hence the house's name. Inigo Jones added to it in the seventeenth century, so we find ourselves in possession of a very interesting piece of our country's history."

"And in possession of something else, it appears," said Low. "Your letters, however, provided little by way of information on that point."

Mr. Fitzgerald's face clouded, and there was a sharp clatter as his wife placed her teacup somewhat unsteadily in its saucer. "Yes," our host replied after a moment's pause, as if summoning up strength. "The truth is, gentlemen, that I—we—found it very difficult to convey the facts of the case in a letter."

"What my husband means, I think," said Mrs. Fitzgerald, "is that the recent… events here sound, on paper, so inconsequential that they would appear laughable to someone who has not experienced them."

"I assure you, Mrs. Fitzgerald," said Low earnestly, "that none of us are inclined to laugh. I know something of the man who lived here before you, and informed Mr. Holmes and Dr. Watson of the facts surrounding him, and the manner of his death. It is not a laughing matter."

Husband and wife glanced at each other. "We are agreed," said Mrs. Fitzgerald, "that Julian Karswell—or rather something to do with him—is in some way responsible for the events which are taking place; but we do not agree as to how or why this should be. My own feeling is that there is a logical explanation behind everything, whereas my husband feels that—" Here she stopped, as if uncertain how to proceed, or unwilling to give voice to what her husband thought. Mr. Fitzgerald took up the thread.

"Elizabeth is trying to say that I feel Mr. Karswell, although dead, is still influencing the events in his former house." He gave a somewhat hollow laugh. "My father was Irish and my mother Welsh, gentlemen, so I have inherited more than my fair share of willingness to believe in what others disdain."

"Perhaps," said Holmes, with a touch of asperity, "we might hear of these events, so that we may have some idea of why, precisely, we have been invited."

"Of course, Mr. Holmes," said Mrs. Fitzgerald. "Shall I begin?"

"Please do, my dear," replied her husband. "We are in no disagreement as to the facts, and you will tell the story so much better than I."

Low and Holmes both leaned back in their chairs; Low with his hands clasped behind his head, Holmes with his fingers steepled in front of him and his eyes half-closed. I settled back into my own chair as Mrs. Fitzgerald began her tale.

"As you gentlemen know, we have not lived here very long. My family comes from Warwickshire, and I longed to return here, and when we heard that Lufford Abbey was available—well, we fairly jumped at the opportunity. It did not take us long to realise that there was considerable ill-feeling in the village towards the previous owner, about whom we knew little more than that he had died, suddenly, while on holiday in France, and that in the absence of next of kin his house and effects were being sold. We attended the sale of his possessions, as did many of the people from the immediate neighbourhood; largely, I suspect, in order to see the house for themselves, as the late owner had guarded his privacy to a quite extraordinary extent, and had not been known for his hospitality towards his neighbours. There was also, I believe, some talk of great treasures in the house, although nothing that was sold struck us as being deserving of that name.

"When Mr. Karswell's things had been disposed of we were, quite naturally, anxious to take up residence, but events conspired to make this impossible. The house, while in good repair for the most part, needed a certain amount of work done to it, particularly the rooms in which it was apparent that Mr. Karswell chiefly lived. He appeared to have kept a dog, or dogs, and they had scratched quite badly at the panelling in one of the rooms, so much so that it needed to be replaced. Some of the furnishings, too, proved difficult to dispose of; more than one person who had purchased items had a change of mind after the event, and declined to remove them, so in the end we kept one or two of the larger pieces and disposed of the rest as best we could."

"And the workmen, my dear; do not forget them."

Mrs. Fitzgerald shuddered. "How could I forget? We had no end of difficulty with the workmen we had employed to carry out the repairs. What should have been a very straightforward piece of work, according to the man who was in charge, became fraught with difficulty. Some of the men took to turning up late, or not at all, and there were delays with some of the material, and scarcely a day went by without some accident or other. Oh, they were very minor things, we were assured, but troubling nonetheless, and at one point it seemed the work would never be completed. At last we resorted to offering a larger sum than initially negotiated, and eventually all was finished and we were able to take up residence."

"One moment," said Low, at the same time that Holmes interjected with "A question, if I may." The two detectives looked at each other; then Low smiled and waved his hand towards my friend. "Please, Mr. Holmes."

"Thank you." Holmes turned to the Fitzgeralds. "The workmen who were employed: were they local men, or from further afield?"

"There were a handful of local men, Mr. Holmes," replied Mrs. Fitzgerald, "but the man in charge had to obtain most of the workforce from further away, some as far as Coventry. As I mentioned, there was some considerable ill-feeling towards the late owner of Lufford Abbey."

"Considerable indeed, if it extended even after his death," remarked Holmes. "Were you both here while this work was being carried out?"

"No; it would have been far too inconvenient. We had regular reports from the man in charge, and my husband would come by on occasion to check on the progress—or rather the lack of it."

"Thank you," said Holmes. "Mr. Low?"

"I was going to ask about the dogs," said Low, "the ones which you felt were responsible for the damage. Do you know for a fact that Karswell kept dogs?"

"No," replied Mr. Fitzgerald slowly. "Indeed, it did strike me as odd, as from what we knew of him he seemed unlikely to be a man who kept pets."

"This damage they caused; was it general, or confined to one particular place?"

"Again, it is very odd, Mr. Low. One would not expect dogs to be particular as to where they caused damage, yet it all seemed to be located in the one room, on the first floor. It is a very fine room, with views out over the park, and we understood that Karswell used it as his study."

"What sort of damage was caused?"

"Well, as my wife said, it appeared that the animals had clawed around the base of the wooden panelling in the room. Quite deep gouges they were, too, which is why the wood needed to be replaced."

"Do any of the marks remain?"

Mrs. Fitzgerald drew in her breath sharply, and Mr. Fitzgerald's already pale face seemed to go a shade whiter. It was a moment before he answered.

"When we took up residence my answer would have been no, Mr. Low; none of the marks remained. However, since then they... they have returned."

"Returned?" said Holmes sharply. "What do you mean?"

"I will come to that in a moment, Mr. Holmes," said Mrs. Fitzgerald. She paused, as if to gather her thoughts, then continued with her tale.

"As I say, we took up residence; that was in early March. At first all was well; we were busy settling in, and there were a hundred-and-one things to do and be seen to, and anything odd we put down to the fact that we were in a very old house that was still strange to us.

"Gradually, however, we became aware that things were happening which were not at all usual. It began with a sound, very faint, in the room above us..." She broke off with a shudder, and Mr. Fitzgerald looked at her with concern.

"Margaret, would you like me to continue?"

"Yes please," she said in a quiet voice, and her husband took up the tale.

"At first we both thought that it was one of the maids, cleaning; it was only later that we realised the sounds were heard at times when there should not have been anyone in the room. You will forgive us, gentlemen, for being somewhat slow to remark on this fact, but at first it seemed such a trifling matter that we gave it little thought.

"The next thing that occurred was a cold draught, which always seemed to play about the room. Now one must, I fear, expect draughts in a house as old as this, but we did not notice such a thing anywhere else; indeed, the house was, as my wife said, very sound, which made it all the more odd that it should be confined to this one room. We examined the windows and walls and around the door, and could find nothing to account for it. It began to be quite uncomfortable to be in the room, which I used, as Mr. Karswell had, as a study. I had hoped that as the spring approached the draughts would stop; but if anything they seemed to get worse.

"The sounds had continued all this time; not constant, by any means, but frequent enough to become unnerving. We told ourselves that it was some trick, perhaps related to the draughts; but one evening we heard the sounds more distinctly than before. They seemed changed, too; if we had heard them like that from the first we would not have mistaken them for the footsteps of a person. It was a dull, heavy, dragging sound, rather as if a large dog was moving with difficulty about the floor. I would go to investigate, but I never saw anything, although I found that I did not care to be alone in that room.

"Then one day one of the maids came to us, almost in tears, poor thing, because she said that she had been in the room to fill the coal scuttle and had heard what she thought was a growl, as of a large dog. She said that she had a careful look around the room, thinking that perhaps some stray animal had got in, but could see nothing untoward, and was continuing with her work when she distinctly felt something large and soft brush heavily against her, not once but twice, as if a dog had walked past her quite close and then turned back.

"Of course we went to look—it was all we could do to persuade Ellen to go back in, even though we were with her—but found nothing. We reassured the girl as best we could, and my wife took her down to the kitchen so that she could have a cup of tea, and I took one last look round; and it was then that I saw the marks on the wall."

"These are the claw marks to which your wife has alluded?" asked Holmes.

"Yes. As we explained, the panelling in that room was ripped out and completely replaced, and I remember thinking to myself what a fine job the men had done. So you can imagine my surprise and consternation when I saw marks on the woodwork. At first I thought that perhaps they had been caused by something being bumped against the wall accidentally, but when I examined them I saw that they were quite deep, and identical in every way with the marks which had been there before. I must admit, Mr. Holmes, that I was startled, to say the least, and I was glad that my wife had left the room, particularly in light of what happened next. For as I stood there, trying to make sense of it, I heard a soft, shuffling noise, such as a dog or other large animal might make, getting up and shaking itself. And then, before I could move, I felt something brush against me; something heavy, and soft."

"Did you see anything?"

"No, I did not; nor, I will say, did I stay to look about more closely. I was on the other side of the door, and had closed it, before I could think clearly once more. When I did, I locked the door, and later told the servants that we would not be using that room for a time, and that they need not bother with it unless we told them otherwise."

"The servants," said Holmes thoughtfully. "Have they been with you for some time, or did they work for Mr. Karswell?"

"None of Mr. Karswell's servants stayed on, Mr. Holmes," said Mrs. Fitzgerald; "they were dismissed immediately upon his death. From what I heard of them I would not have wished to employ any of them. A queer, secretive lot, apparently, who were disliked almost as much as their master. No, the servants here have all been with us for some time, and I trust them implicitly."

"Has anything else untoward happened?" asked Holmes. "Have either of you noticed any signs of your things having been tampered with, or has anything gone missing that you cannot account for?"

"No, Mr. Holmes," said Mrs. Fitzgerald. "The—disturbances—seem confined to that one room."

"I think, then, that we should take a look at this rather singular-sounding room," said Holmes, rising. "Will you show us the way?"

We followed the Fitzgeralds out of the room and made our way up the stairs. The spring day was drawing to a close, and the lamps were lit throughout the house. Was it my imagination, or did the hall seem a trifle darker outside the door before which our host and hostess halted? Such a thought had, I felt, occurred to Flaxman Low, for I noticed that he glanced sharply up and down the hall and then up at the light closest to us, which seemed dimmer than its fellows. Before I could remark on this, however, Mr. Fitzgerald had produced a key from his pocket, unlocked the heavy door in front of us, and pushed it open.

A sudden cold draught played around my ankles with a force which startled me, as if a tangible presence had pushed at me from within the room. I could see from the looks on the faces of my companions that they had felt what I did, and I confess that I hesitated for a moment before entering the room.

It was a large room, and I imagined that it would have been pleasant in the daylight, with its wide windows looking out over the expanse of lawn, and the panelling on the walls creating a warm, rich glow. However, in the evening dusk, with lamps the only source of illumination, and the strange tale we had been told still ringing in my ears, it presented an aspect almost of malignancy. I had a sudden feeling that we were intruding in a place which contained dark secrets, and if one of my companions had suggested we leave I would have followed willingly. However, both Holmes and Low advanced to the centre of the room and stood looking about with penetrating glances, taking in every detail. Holmes turned to Mr. Fitzgerald.

"Where are these marks of which you spoke?"

"Over here, Mr. Holmes." We followed him to one side of the room, where he knelt and pointed to a section of wall beside the fireplace, which was surmounted by a carved mantelpiece embellished with leaves and branches. We could all see plainly the deep scores running along the wood; they did, in truth, look like the claw marks of a large dog, although I would not have liked to meet the beast that made them. As Mr. Fitzgerald went to stand up, he glanced to one side of him, and uttered a soft exclamation.

"There are more!"

"Are you sure of that?" Low's voice contained a note of urgency which was not lost on Mr. Fitzgerald.

"I am positive! The last time I looked they extended no further than this panel"—he pointed—"but now you can see for yourselves that they continue further along the wall, up to the fireplace itself. I don't understand it! The room has been locked for the last week, and no one has entered it, of that I am sure. What could be doing this?"

"I have an idea, as I am sure Mr. Holmes does," said Flaxman Low quietly; "although whether or not these ideas will agree remains to be seen." He straightened up from where he had been crouching by the wall, running his hand along the marks, and looked around the room. His gaze seemed to be held by a large, ornately carved desk which stood close by. "You said that you purchased one or two pieces from the estate of Mr. Karswell. May I ask if that desk was one of those pieces?"

Mrs. Fitzgerald gazed at Low in astonishment. "Yes, it is; but how did you know?"

"Tsk, tsk," said Holmes, approaching the desk, "it is quite obvious that while the other pieces in the room were chosen by someone with an eye for symmetry and comfort, this desk was not; it does not match anything else in the room. Furthermore, it is one of two desks in the room; the other is quite obviously used extensively, to judge by the papers, pens, ink, books, and other items on its surface, whereas this one is singularly clear of any such items. Not, therefore, a piece of furniture which is in regular use, which rather suggests an afterthought of some sort, here on sufferance only."

"You are quite right," said Mr. Fitzgerald. "That was one of the items we bought from Karswell's estate, as the original purchaser unaccountably decided against buying it. At the time it seemed a reasonable enough purchase, but for some reason…" His voice trailed off.

"You found yourself unwilling to use it, and uncomfortable when you did," supplied Low.

"Precisely," said Mr. Fitzgerald gratefully. "It is, as you can see, a handsome piece, and I had some thought of making it my own desk; but for reasons that I cannot articulate I always felt uncomfortable when working at it, and it was not long before I abandoned it altogether in favour of the other desk."

Flaxman Low walked over to the carved desk and ran his hand over it. "Karswell's desk," he murmured to himself. "That is certainly intriguing."

"Yes," said Holmes crisply. "For there are few things which can tell us more about a man than his desk. Tell me, did you find anything in it?"

"That is a curious thing, Mr. Holmes. When we purchased it the desk was, as we thought, quite empty, and I made sure that nothing had been left in it; there could have been something valuable which his executors should know about. I found nothing; but a few days later, I happened to be opening one of the drawers, to place something within it, and it stuck. I pulled and pushed, and gradually worked it free, and found a small piece of paper at the back of it, which had obviously fallen out and become wedged in behind."

"Do you still have this paper?" asked Holmes eagerly, and Mr. Fitzgerald nodded towards his desk.

"I put it with my own papers; although I confess I do not know why, as it seemed without value." He moved to the other desk, where he rummaged around in one of the drawers. The rest of us stood close together, as if by common consent, and waited for him to return. When he did he was holding a small piece of yellowed paper, which he handed to my friend, who held it out so that we could all read it. There, in a neat hand, we saw the following:

Nonne haec condita sunt apud me et signata in thesauris meis.

Mea est ultio et ego retribuam in tempore ut labatur pes eorum iuxta est dies perditionis et adesse festinant tempora.

"What on earth does it mean?" I asked in some puzzlement.

"Well, I wondered that myself, Dr. Watson. My own Latin is not, I am afraid, as good as it once was, but after a little thought I realised it was from the Vulgate—Deuteronomy 32, verses 34 and 35—and translates as 'Is not this laid up in store with me, and sealed up among my treasures? To me belongeth vengeance and recompense; their foot shall slide in due time: for the day of their calamity is at hand, and the things that shall come upon them make haste.'"

Both men gave a start, and I could see that they were thinking furiously. "Treasures," said Holmes thoughtfully, while Low murmured "Vengeance and recompense." Both turned at the same moment and gazed at the section of wall where the claw marks were most visible. My friend glanced at Flaxman Low.

"I believe our thoughts are moving along the same lines, Mr. Low," he said quietly.

"Yes," replied the other, "although I suspect that our conclusions are slightly different." He turned to the Fitzgeralds, who were gazing from one man to the other with a bewildered air, and addressed our host. "Will you kindly bring an axe and a crowbar? This may prove a difficult job."

"Why, yes, of course," replied Mr. Fitzgerald. "But what is it that you are going to do?"

"I—that is to say we, for I believe Mr. Low and I have come to the same conclusion—believe that there is a concealed space hidden behind that section of wall. That is an outer wall, I take it?"

"Yes; yes, it is," said Mrs. Fitzgerald. "Do you mean… do you think that…"

"It is too early yet to say what I think," replied my friend grimly. "But I believe that the solution to this mystery lies behind that wall, and the sooner we investigate the sooner we will put an end to the events which have puzzled you both."

Mr. Fitzgerald departed to find the required implements; but in the end they proved unnecessary. While he was gone both Holmes and Low searched the fireplace, running their hands along the carvings, and within a few moments of our host's return Holmes gave a small cry of satisfaction. "Here we have it, I think," he said triumphantly, and we all heard a click which, slight as it was, seemed to echo throughout the room, so still were we all. Our gaze turned to the section of wall which we had previously examined, and I do not know which of us was the most startled to see a section of the panelling move slightly, as if it were being pushed from behind by an unseen force. Indeed, this very thought must have occurred to each of us, for we all remained motionless for some moments. It was Low, followed closely by my friend, who finally stepped towards the disturbed section of wall, and together the two men grasped the edge of the piece of panelling which, we could now see, had moved. I stepped forward with a lamp, as did Mr. Fitzgerald, while his wife stood behind us, peering anxiously over our shoulders.

The two men pulled at the wood panel, and for a moment it did not move, as if it were being held from the other side. Then, with a sound very like a sigh, the panel pulled away from the wall, leaving a rectangle of inky darkness behind it.

We all stepped back as a blast of icy air came from out the space thus revealed. After a moment we moved closer, and I held the light up in order that we could see inside.

I do not know what I expected to see, but it was not the sight which was presented to my eyes. A small table, like an altar, had been erected inside the space, which was barely wide enough to accommodate a man, and hanging above it was an inverted cross made of some dark wood, which Low dashed to the ground with an exclamation of disgust. A set of what looked like vestments was draped over one edge of the table, on the top of which was a book bound in cracked and faded black leather, and several vials of dark liquid, while the topmost of the two drawers contained pens, ink, and several thin strips of parchment. When the bottom drawer was opened Low gave an exclamation which mingled surprise with satisfaction, and withdrew a series of notebooks tied together with string, which he slit with a penknife. He glanced through the books and looked up at us.

"It is as I thought," he said quietly, and Holmes nodded.

"Yes," said my friend, "we have found what I expected to find," and he gestured to his left. Twisting our heads and looking down the narrow aperture, we saw that a set of rough stone steps was carved into the floor of the chamber, and apparently carried down between the inner and outer walls. "I have no doubt," continued my friend, "that when those stairs are examined they will prove to communicate with a hidden door on the outer wall of the house, or perhaps a tunnel which leads to some secluded spot."

We were all silent, gazing down into the black depths which seemed to swallow the light afforded by our lamps. As we stood clustered together, there came again that blast of icy air, and a faint sound, as of padding footsteps. Low immediately moved back from the opening, and motioned for us to do the same.

"I think," he said gravely, "that we would do well to close this now, and seal the room until morning. Then we can take the necessary steps to prevent any further disturbances."

By common, unspoken consent we refrained from discussing the matter that was uppermost on our minds all through supper, when servants were in and out of the dining-room. After supper Mrs. Fitzgerald retired to the sitting-room and we gentlemen were not long in following her, as we knew that she was as anxious as her husband and I to hear what the two detectives had to say. When coffee and brandy had been poured and Holmes and Low had lit their pipes, we sat back and waited for them to begin. Low motioned for my friend to go first, and Holmes addressed himself to us.

"My reading of the case began with the character of the late, and apparently unlamented, former owner of Lufford Abbey, Mr. Julian Karswell. Shorn of melodrama, what I knew of him amounted to this: that he was a man of some wealth who had a good many enemies, who chose to live in seclusion, and who died in circumstances which, though certainly out of the ordinary, could not be considered overly mysterious. Shortly after arriving I learned that his house, Lufford Abbey, was built during a time when, for various reasons, it was thought expedient by some families to have a secret room or chamber built, in order to conceal a person or persons from over-zealous eyes.

"That Karswell knew of this chamber is obvious, judging by the effects we found there; and I suspect that at least one of his servants would also have known of the existence of the room, in order to prevent a mishap should the master of the house find himself locked in and unable to emerge. In my experience, even the most secretive and close-mouthed of servants will, under the correct circumstances, divulge information of a sensitive nature, perhaps to secure esteem or reward, and I would not be surprised to find that Karswell's secret chamber was not, perhaps, the secret he thought it was amongst some of the villagers. Hence we have a man of secretive nature and some wealth, who dies suddenly, and whose household is scattered to the four winds almost immediately. That there was considerable ill-feeling towards him locally has been established, and I think it probable that some of the locals amongst the workmen who came here discovered the hidden chamber during the course of their repairs, and then found it expedient to delay work on the house, so that they might have time to examine it for more secrets.

"As to the noises of footsteps you heard, and the cold wind: all this can be explained by some person or persons—as the footsteps sounded like those of two distinct people—using the stairs and the secret chamber as a means of entering and leaving the house in order to search for something of value that they felt might be hidden; for you spoke of treasure, Mr. Low, as did you, Mrs. Fitzgerald, and these views are borne out by the passage which we found in Karswell's desk, which specifically mentions treasure. It was stated, however, that no treasures had been amongst Mr. Karswell's effects. This would suggest that his treasures were well hidden, and that someone knew—or suspected—as much, and decided to continue the search. I wager that there are more hiding spaces in this house than the one we found tonight, and that a careful search will reveal Mr. Karswell's treasure; while blocking up both entrances to the hidden chamber will eliminate the noises, and sounds, which have troubled you so much."

"But what of the feeling of something rubbing against me, Mr. Holmes?" enquired Mr. Fitzgerald. "Ellen the maid felt it too, yet neither of us saw anything."

"I suspect that the maid was imagining things, Mr. Fitzgerald; she was overwrought, as your wife stated. When you went up to the room you remembered her words, and something as simple as a draught of air became a phantom shape."

"What of the claw marks, and that odd note we found in the desk?" asked Mrs. Fitzgerald. She had brightened considerably over the past hour, as if a terrible burden had been lifted from her; but her husband, I noted, still wore a worried and drawn expression.

"Those are very easily explained. The note was, I think, meant as a taunt for any who presumed to look for Karswell's treasure, by mentioning it particularly; and I daresay that if one were to take a chisel to the panelling, one would make very similar marks to those we saw. When a person is looking for what he thinks is hidden treasure, he is not apt to be overly concerned about leaving traces of his handiwork on the walls, particularly if they are being ascribed to supernatural means which allow him to search without fear of being discovered."

Holmes sat back in his chair, and Mrs. Fitzgerald clapped her hands together softly. "Thank you, Mr. Holmes," she said quietly; "you have taken a great weight from my mind. I felt sure that there was a perfectly natural and logical explanation for these strange events, and I have no doubt but that you have hit upon the correct solution. I am sure that if we take your advice and seal up the chamber properly, there will be no further disturbances at Lufford Abbey."

"By all means seal up the chamber," said Flaxman Low, who had listened attentively to my friend's explanation, "but not before you destroy all the items found within it—as well as the desk, and any other items which belonged to Karswell—by burning them, and with as little delay as possible."

"Why do you say that, Mr. Low?" asked Mr. Fitzgerald. He, too, had listened attentively to Holmes's speech, but did not seem as convinced as did his wife.

"Because I believe that Julian Karswell was an evil man, and that anything associated with him carries that stamp of evil, and will continue to do so until it is destroyed by the purifying element of fire. Only that will put an end to your troubles." He glanced towards my friend. "Both Mr. Holmes and I agree that the cause of the disturbances in this house is Karswell; but I am prepared to grant him a much larger part than is my colleague here.

"Karswell made it his life's work to not only study and document the black arts, but to dabble in them himself. He believed, as many others have before him, that he was capable of controlling that which he unleashed; and as so many others have found, too late, he was greatly mistaken.

"We know him to have been a man both subtle and malicious, and one who desired to protect and keep secret what belonged to him. He had written a book on witchcraft, and was rumoured to have written—if not completed—a second volume. For a man such as Karswell, would this manuscript not have been a treasure beyond price? The years of work poured into it, and the price that was doubtless extracted from him for the knowledge he received, would have made him value this above all else, and I believe that he would have ensured that it was... well guarded during his absence in July of last year. That this absence was to prove permanent did not, of course, occur to him; and once set in place, the guardian appointed by Karswell would continue to do its duty, neither knowing nor caring of the death of its master."

"You speak of a guardian, Mr. Low," said our host in a low voice. "What precisely do you mean?"

Flaxman Low shrugged. "Guardians can take many shapes and forms," he replied, "depending on the skill and audacity of those who call them up. That Karswell was an adept in the field of magic is not, I think, in dispute; we have the death of one man, and the near-death of another, to attest to this. I believe that Karswell summoned a guardian that was in a shape known to him; possibly something not unlike a large dog. It was this guardian which was responsible for the claw marks on the walls, and the soft, padding sound which you heard, and the cold draught which you felt: manifestations of this sort are frequently accompanied by a chill in the atmosphere, sometimes quite severe. I also think it unlikely that the workmen discovered the chamber; there were no signs of anything within it being disturbed, and I am sure that its discovery could not have been kept a secret. The door was, as we saw, quite cleverly built, and I believe the workmen did not realise it was there."

"But why did this guardian not venture outside that one room?" asked Mr. Fitzgerald. Like his wife a few minutes earlier, he now looked considerably more relieved than he had been since we arrived; the prospect of putting an end to his troubles by following Low's advice had obviously taken a weight from his shoulders.

"Without knowing the specifics of what Karswell did to conjure it up in the first place, I cannot say. I do know, however, that very powerful constraints must be laid on these creatures, lest they turn on those who create them. It could well be that Karswell's guardian was restricted to that place, near its master's treasure." He paused, and gazed thoughtfully at his hosts. "From the manner in which the sounds it made changed, I should say that it was growing stronger as time passed, and that it is as well that we arrived when we did, before it grew even more powerful."

"And what did you make of the note, Mr. Low?" asked our host. Low smiled gently.

"I, too, took it as a taunt, although I interpreted it somewhat differently to Mr. Holmes. He seized on the word 'treasure,' whereas I was struck by the use of the word 'vengeance,' and the reference to 'the things that shall come upon them.'"

There was silence then, as we all pondered what we had just heard. Looking upon the faces of Mr. and Mrs. Fitzgerald, I could see that their troubles were, if not quite at an end, at least fading rapidly. Mr. Fitzgerald, it was clear, was prepared to believe Flaxman Low's interpretation of events, while his wife believed that Holmes had hit upon the correct solution. I caught the latter's eye as I thought this, and he must have read my thoughts, for he laughed and said, "Well, we have two solutions, and three listeners. I know that two of you have already made up your minds, so it remains for Dr. Watson to cast the deciding vote. Which shall it be, friend Watson? Tell us your verdict."

I glanced from the one detective to the other: both so alike in their methods, so sure of their case, yet so different in their explanations. I took a deep breath.

"I am glad of my Scottish heritage at this moment," I said, "for it allows me to answer, quite properly, 'Not Proven.'" And further than that I would not be drawn.

There remains little to tell of this strange case. The following morning, as soon as it was light, a proper investigation of the secret chamber was made. Nothing more was found beyond what we had already seen; and the stone steps did, as surmised, lead down through the thickness of the outer wall to a tunnel which stretched away from the house and emerged in a small outbuilding some distance away. The tunnel was in surprisingly good repair, leading Holmes to believe that his theory of treasure-seekers was correct. Low said nothing, but I noted that he spent some time scrutinising the floor of the tunnel, which was, I saw, free from any marks that would seem to indicate the recent passage of any corporeal trespasser. The entrances to both chamber and tunnel were sealed shut so as to make both impassable; but not before everything had been removed from the chamber, and everything of Karswell's taken from the study, and burned.

I have not heard that the Fitzgeralds have been troubled since that time; nor did

I ever hear of any treasures being found in the house.

One other item, perhaps, bears mentioning. Low had been invited to travel back to London with us, and we found ourselves with some time to spare in the village before our train was due to arrive. We walked, by common accord, over to the small parish church where, we recalled, some of the items salvaged from the original Abbey of Lufford had been stored, and spent a pleasant half-hour therein, admiring the church and its relics. Holmes, indicating that it was time to leave for the station, went outside, and I looked around for Flaxman Low, whom I found staring intently into a glass case which contained some of the remains of the old Abbey. As I paused by his side he turned and smiled at me.

"Ah, Dr. Watson," he said; "or should it be 'Gentleman of the Jury'? Do you still find for 'Not Proven,' or have you had any second thoughts?"

I shook my head. "I do not know," I said honestly. "I have worked with Holmes for many years, and am rather inclined to his viewpoint that there is nothing that cannot be explained logically and rationally. And yet..." I paused. "I am not, I think, more imaginative than my fellow man, nor a person inclined to foolish fancies; yet I confess to you that as we stood outside the door of that room, I would have given a good deal not to go in there; and all the while we were inside it, I felt that there was... something in the room with us, something malignant, evil." I shook my head. "I do not know," I repeated, "but I am prepared to weigh the evidence and be convinced."

Low reached out and shook my hand. "Thank you," he said quietly. Then his eyes returned to the case which he had been studying, and he pointed at an item within it. "I was reading this before you came over," he said. "It is one of the relics from the Abbey of Lufford, a tile that dates back to the fifteenth century. The original is in Middle English, and rather difficult to make out, but a translation is on the card beside it. I wonder if Karswell ever saw it; in the unlikely event that he did, he certainly paid no heed to the warning."

I gazed at the card, and read the following words from Lufford Abbey:

Think, man, thy life may not ever endure; what thou dost thyself, of that thou art sure; but what thou keepest for thy executor's care, and whether it avail thee, is but adventure.

MURDER TO MUSIC

by Anthony Burgess

Anthony Burgess is the world-renowned author of the dystopian novel *A Clock-work Orange*. His other novels include *Inside Mr. Enderby* (et seq.), *Earthly Powers*, and The Long Day Wanes trilogy. Several of his short stories, including this one, can be found in his book *The Devil's Mode*. Although most readers probably know Burgess because of his fiction, he was a prolific writer of non-fiction and criticism, and he worked on a number of screenplays and as a translator. Burgess was also a composer of music, which, as you might guess from the title, served him well in writing this tale.

The first wife of prolific author Isaac Asimov once chided him for spending so much time working, saying, "When you're on your deathbed, and you've written a hundred books, what'll you say then?" To which Asimov replied, "I'll say, 'Only a hundred!'" In point of fact, Asimov had written or edited closer to *five* hundred books by the time he died. In a world of poseurs and dilettantes, of people who chatter constantly about the art they intend to create "someday" or "when I have time," it can be inspiring to see people who are so dedicated to their work that the terms art and life become inseparable, and who keep on working right up until the end. The legendary Japanese artist Hokusai, known for masterpieces such as *Thirty-six Views of Mt. Fuji*, is said to have exclaimed on his deathbed, "If only Heaven will give me just another ten years… Just another five more years, then I could become a real painter." If you're one of those people who's moved by the idea of an artist practicing his art right up until the moment of death, you may find this next tale highly inspirational. Or maybe not, given the circumstances.

Sir Edwin Etheridge, the eminent specialist in tropical diseases, had had the kindness to invite me to share with him the examination of a patient of his in the Marylebone area. It seemed to Sir Edwin that this patient, a young man who had never set foot outside England, was suffering from an ailment known as *la-tah*—common enough in the Malay archipelago but hitherto unknown, so far as the clinical records, admittedly not very reliable, could advise, in the temperate clime of northern Europe. I was able to confirm Sir Edwin's tentative diagnosis: the young man was morbidly suggestible, imitating any action he either saw or heard described, and was, on my entrance into his bedroom, exhausting himself with the conviction that he had been metamorphosed into a bicycle. The disease is incurable but intermittent: it is of psychical rather than nervous provenance, and can best be eased by repose, solitude, opiates and tepid malt drinks. As I strolled down Marylebone Road after the consultation, it seemed to me the most natural thing in the world to turn into Baker Street to visit my old friend, lately returned, so the *Times* informed me, from some nameless assignment in Marrakesh. This, it later transpired, was the astonishing case of the Moroccan poisonous palmyra, of which the world is not yet ready to hear.

I found Holmes rather warmly clad for a London July day, in dressing gown, winter comforter and a jewelled turban which, he was to inform me, was the gift of the mufti of Fez—donated in gratitude for some service my friend was not willing to specify. He was bronzed and clearly inured to a greater heat than our own, but not, except for the turban, noticeably exoticised by his sojourn in the land of the Mohammedan. He had been trying to breathe smoke through a hubble-bubble but had given up the endeavour. "The flavour of rose water is damnably sickly, Watson," he remarked, "and the tobacco itself of a mildness further debilitated by its long transit through these ingenious but ridiculous conduits." With evident relief he drew some of his regular cut from the Turkish slipper by the fireless hearth, filled his curved pipe, lighted it with a vesta and then looked at me amiably. "You have been with Sir Edwin Etheridge," he said, "in, I should think, St John's Wood Road."

"This is astonishing, Holmes," I gasped. "How can you possibly know?"

"Easy enough," puffed my friend. "St John's Wood Road is the only London thoroughfare where deciduous redwood has been planted, and a leaf of that tree, prematurely fallen, adheres to the sole of your left boot. As for the other matter, Sir Edwin Etheridge is in the habit of sucking Baltimore mint lozenges as a kind of token prophylactic. You have been sucking one yourself. They are not on the London market, and I know of no other man who has them specially imported."

"You are quite remarkable, Holmes," I said.

"Nothing, my dear Watson. I have been perusing the *Times,* as you may have observed from its crumpled state on the floor—a womanish habit, I suppose, God bless the sex—with a view to informing myself on events of national import, in which, naturally enough, the enclosed world of Morocco takes little interest."

"Are there not French newspapers there?"

"Indeed, but they contain no news of events in the rival empire. I see we are to have a state visit from the young king of Spain."

"That would be his infant majesty Alfonso the Thirteenth," I somewhat gratuitously amplified. "I take it that his mother the regent, the fascinating Maria Christina, will be accompanying him."

"There is much sympathy for the young monarch," Holmes said, "especially here. But he has his republican and anarchist enemies. Spain is in a state of great political turbulence. It is reflected even in contemporary Spanish music." He regarded his violin, which lay waiting for its master in its open case, and resined the bow lovingly. "The petulant little fiddle tunes I heard in Morocco day and night, Watson, need to be excised from my head by something more complex and civilized. One string only, and usually one note on one string. Nothing like the excellent Sarasate." He began to play an air which he assured me was Spanish, though I heard in it something of Spain's Moorish inheritance, wailing, desolate and remote. Then with a start Holmes looked at his turnip watch, a gift from the Duke of Northumberland. "Good heavens, we'll be late. Sarasate is playing this very afternoon at St James's Hall." And he doffed his turban and robe and strode to his dressing room to habit himself more suitably for a London occasion. I kept my own counsel, as always, concerning my feelings on the subject of Sarasate and, indeed, on music in general. I lacked Holmes's artistic flair. As for Sarasate, I could not deny that he played wonderfully well for a foreign fiddler, but there was a smugness in the man's countenance as he played that I found singularly unattractive. Holmes knew nothing of my feelings and, striding in in his blue velvet jacket with trousers of a light-clothed Mediterranean cut, a white shirt of heavy silk and a black Bohemian tie carelessly knotted, he assumed in me his own anticipatory pleasure. "Come, Watson," he cried. "I have been trying in my own damnably amateurish way to make sense of Sarasate's own latest composition. Now the master himself will hand me the key. The key of D major," he added.

"Shall I leave my medical bag here?"

"No, Watson. I don't doubt that you have some gentle anaesthetic there to ease you through the more tedious phases of the recital." He smiled as he said this, but I felt abashed at his all too accurate appraisal of my attitude to the sonic art.

The hot afternoon seemed, to my fancy, to have succumbed to the drowsiness of the Middle Sea, as through Holmes's own inexplicable influence. It was difficult to find a cab and, when we arrived at St James's Hall, the recital had already begun. When we had been granted the exceptional privilege of taking our seats at the back of the hall while the performance of an item was already in progress, I was quick enough myself to prepare for a Mediterranean siesta. The great Sarasate, then at the height of his powers, was fiddling away at some abstruse mathematics of Bach, to the accompaniment on the pianoforte of a pleasant-looking young man whose complexion proclaimed him to be as Iberian as the master. He seemed nervous, though not of his capabilities on the instrument. He glanced swiftly behind him towards the curtain which shut off the platform from the wings and passages of the administrative arcana of the hall but then, as if reassured, returned wholeheartedly to his music. Meanwhile Holmes, eyes half-shut, gently tapped on his right knee the rhythm of the intolerably lengthy equation which was engaging the intellects of the musically devout, among whom I remarked the pale red-bearded young Irishman who was making his name as a critic and a polemicist. I slept.

I slept, indeed, very soundly. I was awakened not by the music but by the applause, to which Sarasate was bowing with Latin extravagance. I glanced covertly at my watch to find that a great deal of music had passed over my sleeping brain; there must have been earlier applause to which my drowsy grey cells had proved impervious. Holmes apparently had not noted my somnolence or, perhaps noting it, had been too discreet to arouse me or, now, to comment on my boorish indifference to that art he adored. "The work in question, Watson," he said, "is about to begin." And it began. It was a wild piece in which never fewer than three strings of the four were simultaneously in action, full of the rhythm of what I knew, from a brief visit to Granada, to be the *zapateado*. It ended with furious chords and a high single note that only a bat could have found euphonious. "Bravo," cried Holmes with the rest, vigorously clapping. And then the noise of what to me seemed excessive approbation was pierced by the crack of a single gunshot. There was smoke and the tang of a frying breakfast, and the young accompanist cried out. His head collapsed onto the keys of his instrument, producing a hideous jangle, and then the head, with its unseeing eyes and an open mouth from which blood relentlessly pumped in a galloping tide, raised itself and seemed to accuse the entire audience of a ghastly crime against nature. Then, astonishingly, the fingers of the right hand of the dying man picked at one note of the keyboard many times, following this with a seemingly delirious phrase of a few different notes which he repeated and would have continued to repeat if the rattle of death had not overtaken him. He slumped to the floor of the platform. The women in the audience screamed. Meanwhile the master Sarasate clutched his valuable violin to his bosom—a Stradivarius, Holmes later was to inform me—as though that had been the target of the gunshot.

Holmes was, as ever, quick to act. "Clear the hall!" he shouted. The manager appeared, trembling and deathly pale, to add a feebler shout to the same effect. Attendants somewhat roughly assisted the horrified audience to leave. The red-bearded young Irishman nodded at Holmes as he left, saying something to the effect that it was as well that the delicate fingers of the amateur should anticipate the coarse questing paws of the Metropolitan professionals, adding that it was a bad business: that young Spanish pianist had promised well. "Come, Watson," said Holmes, striding towards the platform. "He has lost much blood but he may not be quite dead." But I saw swiftly enough that he was past any help that the contents of my medical bag could possibly provide. The rear of the skull was totally shattered.

Holmes addressed Sarasate in what I took to be impeccable Castilian, dealing every courtesy and much deference. Sarasate seemed to say that the young man, whose name was Gonzáles, had served as his accompanist both in Spain and on foreign tours for a little over six months, that he knew nothing of his background though something of his ambitions as a solo artist and a composer, and that, to the master's knowledge, he had no personal enemies. Stay, though: there had been some rather unsavoury stories circulating in Barcelona about the adulterous activities of the young Gonzáles, but it was doubtful if the enraged husband, or conceivably husbands, would have pursued him to London to effect so dire and spectacular a revenge. Holmes nodded distractedly, meanwhile loosening the collar of the dead man.

"A somewhat pointless procedure," I commented. Holmes said nothing. He merely peered at the lowest segment of the nape of the corpse's neck, frowned, then wiped one hand against the other while rising from a crouch back to his feet. He asked the sweating manager if the act of assassination had by any chance been observed, either by himself or by one of his underlings, or, failing that, if any strange visitant had, to the knowledge of the management, insinuated himself into the rear area of the hall, reserved exclusively for artists and staff and protected from the rear door by a former sergeant of marines, now a member of the corps of commissionaires. A horrid thought struck the manager at once, and followed by Holmes and myself, he rushed down a corridor that led to a door which gave on to a side alley.

That door was unguarded for a very simple reason. An old man in the uniform trousers of the corps, though not, evidently because of the heat, the jacket, lay dead, the back of his grey head pierced with devilish neatness by a bullet. The assassin had then presumably effected an unimpeded transit to the curtains which separated the platform from the area of offices and dressing rooms.

"It is very much to be regretted," said the distraught manager, "that no other of the staff was present at the rear, though if one takes an excusably selfish view of the matter, it is perhaps not to be regretted. Evidently we had here a cold-blooded murderer who would stop at nothing." Holmes nodded and said:

"Poor Simpson. I knew him, Watson. He spent a life successfully avoiding death from the guns and spears of Her Imperial Majesty's enemies, only to meet it in a well-earned retirement while peacefully perusing his copy of *Sporting Life*. Perhaps," he now said to the manager, "you would be good enough to explain why the assassin had only poor Simpson to contend with. In a word, where were the other members of the staff?"

"The whole affair is very curious, Mr. Holmes," said the manager, wiping the back of his neck with a handkerchief. "I received a message just after the start of the recital, indeed shortly after your good self and your friend here had taken your seats. The message informed me that the Prince of Wales and certain friends of his were coming to the concert, though belatedly. It is, of course, well known that His Royal Highness is an admirer of Sarasate. There is a small upper box at the back of the hall normally reserved for distinguished visitors, as I think you know."

"Indeed," said Holmes. "The Maharajah of Johore was once kind enough to honour me as his guest in that exclusive retreat. But do please go on."

"Naturally, myself and my staff," the manager continued, "assembled at the entrance and remained on duty throughout the recital, assuming that the distinguished visitor might arrive only for the final items." He went on to say that, though considerably puzzled, they had remained in the vestibule until the final applause, hazarding the guess that His Royal Highness might, in the imperious but bonhomous manner that was his wont, command the Spanish fiddler to favour him with an encore in a hall filled only with the anticipatory majesty of our future King Emperor. Thus all was explained save for the essential problem of the crime itself.

"The message," Holmes demanded of the manager. "I take it that it was a written message. Might I see it?"

The manager drew from an inner pocket a sheet of notepaper headed with the princely insignia and signed with a name known to be that of His Royal Highness's private secretary. The message was clear and courteous. The date was the seventh of July. Holmes nodded indifferently at it and, when the police arrived, tucked the sheet unobtrusively into a side pocket. Inspector Stanley Hopkins had responded promptly to the summons delivered, with admirable efficiency, by one of the manager's underlings in a fast cab.

"A deplorable business, inspector," Holmes said. "Two murders, the motive for the first explained by the second, but the second as yet disclosing no motive at all. I wish you luck with your investigations."

"You will not be assisting us with the case, Mr. Holmes?" asked the intelligent young inspector. Holmes shook his head.

"I am," he said to me in the cab that took us back to Baker Street, "exhibiting my usual duplicity, Watson. This case interests me a great deal." Then he said somewhat dreamily: "Stanley Hopkins, Stanley Hopkins. The name recalls that of an old teacher of mine, Watson. It always takes me back to my youthful days at Stoneyhurst College, where I was taught Greek by a young priest of exquisite delicacy of mind. Gerard Manley Hopkins was his name." He chuckled a moment. "I was given taps from a tolly by him when I was a callow atramontarius. He was the best of the younger crows, however, always ready to pin a shouting cake with us in the haggory. Never creeping up on us in the silent oilers worn by the crab-bier jebbies."

"Your vocabulary, Holmes," I said. "It is a foreign language to me."

"The happiest days of our lives, Watson," he then said somewhat gloomily.

Over an early dinner of cold lobster and a chicken salad, helped down by an admirable white burgundy well chilled, Holmes disclosed himself as vitally concerned with pursuing this matter of the murder of a foreign national on British soil, or at least in a London concert room. He handed me the presumed royal message and asked what was my opinion of it. I examined the note with some care. "It seems perfectly in order to me," I said. "The protocol is regular, the formula, or so I take it, is the usual one. But, since the manager and his staff were duped, some irregularity in obtaining the royal notepaper must be assumed."

"Admirable, Watson. Now kindly examine the date."

"It is today's date."

"True, but the formation of the figure seven is not what one might expect."

"Ah," I said, "I see your meaning. We British do not place a bar across the number. This seven is a continental one."

"Exactly. The message has been written by a Frenchman or an Italian or, as seems much more probable, a Spaniard with access to the notepaper of His Royal Highness. The English and, as you say, the formula are impeccable. But the signatory is not British. He made a slight slip there. As for the notepaper, it would be available only to a person distinguished enough to possess access to His Royal Highness's premises and to a person unscrupulous enough to rob him of a sheet of notepaper. Something in the configuration of the letter e in this message persuades me that the signatory was Spanish. I may, naturally, be totally mistaken. But I have very little doubt that the assassin was Spanish."

"A Spanish husband, with the impetuousness of his race, exacting a very summary revenge," I said.

"I think the motive of the murder was not at all domestic. You observed my loosening the collar of the dead man and you commented with professional brusqueness on the futility of my act. You were unaware of the reason for it." Holmes, who now had his pipe alight, took a pencil and scrawled a curious symbol on the tablecloth. "Have you ever seen anything like this before, Watson?" he puffed. I frowned at the scrawl. It seemed to be a crude representation of a bird with spread wings seated on a number of upright strokes which could be taken as a nest. I shook my head. "That, Watson, is a phoenix rising from the ashes of the flames that consumed it. It is the symbol of the Catalonian separatists. They are republicans and anarchists and they detest the centralizing control of the Castilian monarchy. This symbol was tattooed on the back of the neck of the murdered man. He must have been an active member of a conspiratorial group."

"What made you think of looking for it?" I asked.

"I met, quite by chance, a Spaniard in Tangiers who inveighed in strong terms against the monarchy which had exiled him and, wiping the upper part of his body for the heat, disclosed quite frankly that he had an identical tattoo on his chest."

"You mean," I said incredulously, "that he was in undress, or, as the French put it, *en deshabille!*"

"It was an opium den in the Kasbah, Watson," Holmes said calmly. "Little attention is paid in such places to the refinements of dress. He mentioned to me that the nape of the neck was the more usual site of the declaration of faith in the Catalonian republic, but he preferred the chest, where, as he put it, he could keep an eye on the symbol and be reminded of what it signified. I had been wondering ever since the announcement of the visit to London of the young Spanish king whether there might be Catalonian assassins around. It seemed reasonable to me to look on the body of the murdered man for some indication of a political adherence."

"So," said I, "it is conceivable that this young Spaniard, dedicated to art as he seemed to be, proposed killing the harmless and innocent Alfonso the Thirteenth. The intelligence services of the Spanish monarchy have, I take it, acted promptly though illegally. All the forces of European stability should be grateful that the would-be assassin has been himself assassinated."

"And the poor old soldier who guarded the door?" Holmes riposted, his sharp eyes peering at me through the fog of his tobacco smoke. "Come, Watson, murder is always a crime." And then he began to hum, not distractedly, a snatch of tune which seemed vaguely familiar. His endless repetition of it was interrupted by the announcement that Inspector Stanley Hopkins had arrived. "I expected him, Watson," Holmes said, and when the young police officer had entered the room, he bafflingly recited:

"And I have asked to be Where no storms come,
Where the green swell is in the havens dumb, And out of the swing of the sea."

Stanley Hopkins gaped in some astonishment, as I might have myself had I not been long inured to Holmes's eccentricities of behaviour. Before Hopkins could stutter a word of bewilderment, Holmes said: "Well, inspector, I trust you have come in triumph." But there was no triumph in Hopkins's demeanour. He handed over to Holmes a sheet of paper on which there was handwriting in purple ink.

"This, Mr. Holmes, was found on the dead man's person. It is in Spanish, I think, a language with which neither I nor my colleagues are at all acquainted. I gather you know it well. I should be glad if you would assist our investigation by translating it."

Holmes read both sides of the paper keenly. "Ah, Watson," he said at length, "this either complicates or simplifies the issue, I am not as yet sure which. This seems to be a letter from the young man's father, in which he implores the son to cease meddling with republican and anarchistic affairs and concentrate on the practice of his art. He also, in the well-worn phrase, wags a will at him. No son of his disloyal to the concept of a unified Spain with a secure monarchy need expect to inherit a *patrimonio*. The father appears to be mortally sick and threatens to deliver a dying curse on his intransigent offspring. Very Spanish, I suppose. Highly dramatic. Some passages have the lilt of operatic arias. We need the Frenchman Bizet to set them to music."

"So," I said, "it is possible that the young man had announced his defection from the cause, possessed information which he proposed to make public or at least refer to a quarter which had a special interest in it, and then was brutally murdered before he could make the divulgation."

"Quite brilliant, Watson," said Holmes, and I flushed discreetly with pleasure. It was rarely that he gave voice to praise untempered by sarcasm. "And a man who has killed so remorselessly twice is all too likely to do so again. What arrangements, inspector," he asked young Hopkins, "have the authorities made for the security of our royal Spanish visitors?"

"They arrive this evening, as you doubtless know, on the last of the packets from Boulogne. At Folkestone they will be transferred immediately to a special train. They will be accommodated at the Spanish embassy. Tomorrow they travel to Windsor. The following day there will be luncheon with the prime minister. There will be a special performance of Messrs Gilbert and Sullivan's *Gondoliers*—"

"In which the Spanish nobility is mocked," said Holmes, "but no matter. You have given me the itinerary and the programme. You have not yet told me of the security arrangements."

"I was coming to that. The entire Metropolitan force will be in evidence on all occasions, and armed men out of uniform will be distributed at all points of vantage. I do not think there is anything to fear."

"I hope you are right, inspector."

"The royal party will leave the country on the fourth day by the Dover-Calais packet at one twenty-five. Again, there will be ample forces of security both on the dockside and on the boat itself. The home secretary realizes the extreme importance of the protection of a visiting monarch—especially since that regrettable incident when the Czar was viciously tripped over in the Crystal Palace."

"My own belief," Holmes said, relighting his pipe, "is that the Czar of all the Russias was intoxicated. But again, no matter." A policeman in uniform was admitted. He saluted Holmes first and then his superior. "This is open house for the Metropolitan force," Holmes remarked with good-humoured sarcasm. "Come one, come all. You are heartily welcome, sergeant. I take it you have news."

"Beg pardon, sir," the sergeant said, and to Hopkins, "We got the blighter, sir, in a manner of speaking."

"Explain yourself, sergeant. Come on, man," snapped Hopkins.

"Well, sir, there's this kind of Spanish hotel, meaning a hotel where Spaniards go when they want to be with their own sort, in the Elephant and Castle it is."

"Appropriate," Holmes interjected rapidly. "It used to be the Infanta of Castile. Goat and Compasses. God encompasses us. I apologize. Pray continue, sergeant."

"We got there and he must have known what was coming, for he got on the roof by way of the skylight, three storeys up it is, and whether he slipped or hurled himself off, his—neck was broke, sir." The printing conventions of our realm impose the employment of a dash to indicate the demotic epithet the sergeant employed. "Begging your pardon, sir."

"You're sure it's the assassin, sergeant?" asked Holmes.

"Well, sir, there was Spanish money on him and there was a knife, what they call a stiletto, and there was a revolver with two chambers let off, sir."

"A matter, inspector, of checking the bullets extracted from the two bodies with those still in the gun. I think that was your man, sergeant. My congratulations. It seems that the state visit of his infant majesty can proceed without too much foreboding on the part of the Metropolitan force. And now, inspector, I expect you have some writing to do." This was a courteous way of dismissing his two visitors. "You must be tired, Watson," he then said. "Perhaps the sergeant would be good enough to whistle a cab for you. In the street, that is. We shall meet, I trust, at the Savoy Theatre on the tenth. Immediately before curtain time. Mr. D'Oyly Carte always has two complimentary tickets waiting for me in the box office. It will be interesting to see how our Iberian visitors react to a British musical farce." He said this without levity, with a certain gloom rather. So I too was dismissed.

Holmes and I, in our evening clothes with medals on display, assisted as planned at the performance of *The Gondoliers*. My medals were orthodox enough, those of an old campaigner, but Holmes had some very strange decorations, among the least recondite of which I recognized the triple star of Siam and the crooked cross of Bolivia. We had been given excellent seats in the orchestral stalls. Sir Arthur Sullivan conducted his own work. The infant king appeared to be more interested in the electric light installations than in the action or song proceeding on stage, but his mother responded with suitable appreciation to the jokes when they had been explained to her by the Spanish ambassador. This was a musical experience more after my heart than a recital by Sarasate. I laughed heartily, nudged Holmes in the ribs at the saltier sallies and hummed the airs and choruses perhaps too boisterously, since Lady Esther Roscommon, one of my patients, as it happened, poked me from the row behind and courteously complained that I was not only loud but also out of tune. But, as I told her in the intermission, I had never laid claim to any particular musical skill. As for Holmes, his eyes were on the audience, and with opera glasses too, more than on the stage proceedings.

During the intermission, the royal party very democratically showed itself in the general bar, the young king graciously accepting a glass of British lemonade, over which, in the manner of a child unblessed by the blood, he smacked his lips. I was surprised to see that the great Sarasate, in immaculate evening garb with the orders of various foreign states, was taking a glass of champagne with none other than Sir Arthur Sullivan. I commented on the fact to Holmes, who bowed rather distantly to both, and expressed wonder that a man so eminent in the sphere of the more rarefied music should be hobnobbing with a mere entertainer, albeit one honoured by the Queen. "Music is music," Holmes explained, lighting what I took to be a Tangerine panatella. "It has many mansions. Sir Arthur has sunk, Watson, to the level he finds most profitable, and not only in terms of monetary reward, but he is known also for works of dreary piety. They are speaking Italian together." Holmes's ears were sharper than mine. "How much more impressive their reminiscences of aristocratic favour sound than in our own blunt tongue. But the second bell has sounded. What a waste of an exceptionally fine leaf." He referred to his panatella, which he doused with regret in one of the brass receptacles in the lobby. In the second half of the entertainment Holmes slept soundly. I felt I needed no more to experience the shame of an uncultivated boor when I succumbed to slumber at a more elevated musical event. As Holmes had said, somewhat blasphemously, music has many mansions.

The following morning, a hasty message from Sir Edwin Etheridge, delivered while I was at breakfast, summoned me to another consultation in the bedroom of his patient on St John's Wood Road. The young man was no longer exhibiting the symptoms of *latah;* he seemed now to be suffering from the rare Chinese disease, which I had encountered in Singapore and Hong Kong, known as *shook jong.* This is a distressing ailment, and embarrassing to describe outside of a medical journal, since its cardinal feature is the patient's fear that the capacity of generation is being removed from him by malevolent forces conjured by an overheated imagination. To combat these forces, which he believes responsible for a progressive diminution of his tangible generative asset, he attempts to obviate its shrinkage by transfixation, usually with the sharpest knife he can find. The only possible treatment was profound sedation and, in the intervals of consciousness, a light diet.

I very naturally turned onto Baker Street after the consultation, the fine weather continuing with a positively Hispanic effulgence. The great world of London seemed wholly at peace. Holmes, in dressing gown and Moorish turban, was rubbing resin onto his bow as I entered his sitting room. He was cheerful while I was not. I had been somewhat unnerved by the sight of an ailment I had thought to be confined to the Chinese, as I had been disconcerted earlier in the week by the less harmful *latah*, a property of hysterical Malays, both diseases now manifesting themselves in a young person of undoubtedly Anglo-Saxon blood. Having unburdened myself of my disquiet to Holmes, I said, perhaps wisely, "These are probably the sins visited by subject races on our imperialistic ambitions."

"They are the occluded side of progress," Holmes said, somewhat vaguely, and then, less so, "Well, Watson, the royal visit seems to have passed without mishap. The forces of Iberian dissidence have not further raised their bloody hands on our soil. And yet I am not altogether easy in my mind. Perhaps I must attribute the condition to the irrational power of music. I cannot get out of my head the spectacle of that unfortunate young man struck lifeless at the instrument he had played with so fine a touch, and then, in his death agony, striking a brief rhapsody of farewell which had little melodic sense in it." He moved his bow across the strings of his violin. "Those were the notes, Watson. I wrote them down. To write a thing down is to control it and sometimes to exorcise it." He had been playing from a scrap of paper which rested on his right knee. A sudden summer gust, a brief hot breath of July, entered by the open window and blew the scrap to the carpet. I picked it up and examined it. Holmes's bold hand was discernible in the five lines and the notes, which meant nothing to me. I was thinking more of the *shook jong*. I saw again the desperate pain of an old Chinese who had been struck down with it in Hong Kong. I had cured him by countersuggestion and he had given me in gratitude all he had to give—a bamboo flute and a little sheaf of Chinese songs.

"A little sheaf of Chinese songs I once had," I said musingly to Holmes. "They were simple but charming. I found their notation endearingly simple. Instead of the clusters of black blobs which, I confess, make less sense to me than the shop signs in Kowloon, they use merely a system of numbers. The first note of a scale is one, the second two, and so on, up to, I think, eight."

What had been intended as an inconsequent observation had an astonishing effect on Holmes. "We must hurry," he cried, rising and throwing off turban and dressing gown. "We may already be too late." And he fumbled among the reference books which stood on a shelf behind his armchair. He leafed through a Bradshaw and said: "As I remembered, at eleven fifteen. A royal coach is being added to the regular boat train to Dover. Quick, Watson—into the street while I dress. Signal a cab as if your life depended on it. The lives of others may well do so."

The great clock of the railway terminus already showed ten minutes after eleven as our cab clattered to a stop. The driver was clumsy in telling out change for my sovereign. "Keep it, keep it," I cried, following Holmes, who had not yet explained his purpose. The concourse was thronged. We were lucky enough to meet Inspector Stanley Hopkins, on duty and happy to be near the end of it, standing alertly at the barrier of Platform 12, whence the boat train was due to depart on time. The engine had already got up its head of steam. The royal party had boarded. Holmes cried with the maximum of urgency:

"They must be made to leave their carriage at once. I will explain later."

"Impossible," Hopkins said in some confusion. "I cannot give such an order."

"Then I will give it myself. Watson, wait here with the inspector. Allow no one to get through." And he hurled himself onto the platform, crying in fluent and urgent Spanish to the embassy officials and the ambassador himself the desperate necessity of the young king's leaving his compartment with all speed, along with his mother and all their entourage. It was the young Alfonso XIII, with a child's impetuousness, who responded most eagerly to the only exciting thing that had happened on his visit, jumping from the carriage gleefully, anticipating adventure but no great danger. It was only when the entire royal party had distanced itself, on Holmes's peremptory orders, sufficiently from the royal carriage that the nature of the danger in which they had stood or sat was made manifest. There was a considerable explosion, a shower of splintered wood and shattered glass, then only smoke and the echo of the noise in the confines of the great terminus. Holmes rushed to me, who stood obediently with Hopkins at the barrier.

"You let no one through, Watson, inspector?"

"None came through, Mr. Holmes," Hopkins replied, "except—"

"Except"—and I completed the phrase for him—"your revered maestro, I mean the great Sarasate."

"Sarasate?" Holmes gaped in astonishment and then direly nodded. "Sarasate. I see."

"He was with the Spanish ambassador's party," Hopkins explained. "He went in with them but left rather quickly because, as he explained to me, he had a rehearsal."

"You fool, Watson! You should have apprehended him." This was properly meant for Hopkins, to whom he now said: "He came out carrying a violin case?"

"No."

I said with heat: "Holmes, I will not be called a fool. Not, at any rate, in the presence of others."

"You fool, Watson, I say again and again, you fool! But, inspector, I take it he was carrying his violin case when he entered here with the leave-taking party?"

"Yes, now you come to mention it, he was."

"He came with it and left without it?"

"Exactly."

"You fool, Watson! In that violin case was a bomb fitted with a timing device which he placed in the royal compartment, probably under the seat. And you let him get away."

"Your idol, Holmes, your fiddling god. Now transformed suddenly into an assassin. And I will not be called a fool."

"Where did he go?" Holmes asked Hopkins, ignoring my expostulation.

"Indeed, sir," the inspector said, "where *did* he go? I do not think it much matters. Sarasate should not be difficult to find."

"For you he will be," Holmes said. "He had no rehearsal. He has no further recitals in this country. For my money he has taken a train for Harwich or Liverpool or some other port of egress to a land where your writ does not run. You can of course telegraph all the local police forces in the port areas, but from your expression I see that you have little intention of doing that."

"Exactly, Mr. Holmes. It will prove difficult to attach a charge of attempted massacre to him. A matter of supposition only."

"I suppose you are right, inspector," said Holmes after a long pause in which he looked balefully at a poster advertising Pear's Soap. "Come, Watson. I am sorry I called you a fool."

Back in Baker Street, Holmes attempted to mollify me further by opening a bottle of very old brandy, a farewell gift from another royal figure, though, as he was a Mohammedan, it may be conjectured that it was strictly against the tenets of his faith to have such a treasure in his possession, and it may be wondered why he was able to gain for his cellar a part of the Napoleonic trove claimed, on their prisoner's death, by the British authorities on St Helena.

For this remarkable cognac was certainly, as the ciphers on the label made clear, out of a bin that must have given some comfort to the imperial captive. "I must confess, Watson," said Holmes, an appreciative eye on the golden fluid in his balloon glass, one of a set presented to him by a grateful khedive, "that I was making too many assumptions, assuming, for instance, that you shared my suspicions. You knew nothing of them and yet it was yourself, all unaware, who granted me the key to the solution of the mystery. I refer to the mystery of the fingered swan song of the poor murdered man. It was a message from a man who was choking in his own blood, Watson, and hence could not speak as others do. He spoke as a musician and as a musician, moreover, who had some knowledge of an exotic system of notation. The father who wagged his will, alas, as it proved, fruitlessly, had been in diplomatic service in Hong Kong. In the letter, as I recall, something was said about an education that had given the boy some knowledge of the sempiternality of monarchical systems, from China, Russia and their own beloved Spain."

"And what did the poor boy say?" After three glasses of the superb ichor, I was already sufficiently mollified.

"First, Watson, he hammered out the note D. I have not the gift of absolute pitch, and so was able to know it for what it was only because the piece with which Sarasate concluded his recital was in the key of D major. The final chord was in my ears when the young man made his dying attack on the keyboard. Now, Watson, what we call D, and also incidentally the Germans, is called by the French, Italians and Spaniards *re*. In Italian this is the word for 'king,' close enough to the Castilian *rey*, which has the same meaning. Fool as I was, I should have seen that we were being warned about some eventuality concerning the visiting monarch. The notes that followed contained a succinct message. I puzzled about their possible meaning, but your remark this morning about the Chinese system of note-naming, note-numbering, rather, gave me the answer—only just in time, I may add. In whatever key they were played, the notes would yield the numerical figuration one-one-one-five—C-C-C-G, or D-D-D-A: the pitch is of no importance. The total message was one-one-one-five-one-one-seven. It forms a melody of no great intrinsic interest—a kind of deformed bugle call—but the meaning is clear now that we know the code: the king is in danger at eleven fifteen on the morning of the eleventh day of July. It was I who was the fool, Watson, for not perceiving the import of what could have been dying delirium but in truth was a vital communication to whoever had the wit to decipher it."

"What made you suspect Sarasate?" I asked, pouring another fingerful of the delicious liquor into my glass.

"Well, Watson, consider Sarasate's origins. His full name is Pablo Martín Melitón de Sarasate y Navascuéz and he is a son of Barcelona. A Catalonian, then, and a member of a proud family with an anti-monarchist record. I ascertained so much from judicious enquiries at the Spanish embassy. At the same time I discovered the Chinese background of the youthful Gonzáles, which, at the time, meant nothing. The republicanism of the Sarasate family should have been sufficient to cast a shadow of suspicion over him, but one always considers a great artist as somehow above the sordid intrigues of the political. There was, as I see now, something atrociously cold-blooded in the arrangement whereby the murder of his accompanist was effected only at the conclusion of his recital. Kill the man when he has fulfilled his artistic purpose—this must have been the frigid order delivered by Sarasate to the assassin. I do not doubt that the young Gonzáles had confided in Sarasate, whom, as a fellow musician and a great master, he had every apparent reason to trust. He informed him of his intention to betray the plans of the organization. We cannot be sure of the nature of his motivation—a sudden humane qualm, a shaken state of mind consequent on the receipt of his father's letter. The assassin obeyed Sarasate's order with beat-counting exactitude. My head spins to think of the master's approbation of such a murderous afterpiece to what was, you must admit, a recital of exceptional brilliance."

"The brilliance was, for me, confirmed more by the applause of others than by any judgment of my own. I take it that Sarasate was responsible for another performance less brilliant—the note from His Royal Highness's secretary and the exotic number seven."

"Evidently, Watson. At the Savoy Theatre you saw him chatting amiably with Sir Arthur Sullivan, a crony of the Prince. *Grazie a Dio,* he said among other things, that his long cycle of recitals had finished with his London performance and he could now take a well-earned rest. Any man unscrupulous enough to collaborate with that noted sneerer at the conventions Mr. William Schwenck Gilbert would be quite ready to pick up a sheet or so of the Prince's private notepaper and pass it on without enquiring into the purpose for which it was required."

"Well, Holmes," I now said, "you do not, I take it, propose to pursue Sarasate to condign punishment, to cut off his fiddle-playing career and have him apprehended as the criminal he undoubtedly is?"

"Where is my proof, Watson? As that intelligent young inspector trenchantly remarked, it is all supposition."

"And if it were not?"

Holmes sighed and picked up his violin and bow. "He is a supreme artist whom the world could ill afford to lose. Do not quote my words, Watson, to any of your church-going friends, but I am forced to the belief that art is above morality. If Sarasate, before my eyes and in this very room, strangled you to death, Watson, for your musical insensitivity, while an accomplice of his obstructed my interference with a loaded pistol, and then wrote a detailed statement of the crime, signed with the name of Pablo Martin Melitón de Sarasate y Navascuéz, I should be constrained to close my eyes to the act, destroy the statement, deposit your body in the gutter of Baker Street and remain silent while the police pursued their investigations. So much is the great artist above the moral principles that oppress lesser men. And now, Watson, pour yourself more of that noble brandy and listen to my own rendering of that piece by Sarasate. I warrant you will find it less than masterly but surely the excellence of the intention will gleam through." And so he stood, arranged his music stand, tucked his fiddle beneath his chin and began reverently to saw.

THE ADVENTURE OF THE INERTIAL ADJUSTOR

by Stephen Baxter

Stephen Baxter is a six-time nominee for the Hugo Award, and a winner of the Philip K. Dick, British SF, and John W. Campbell Memorial awards. His short work has been collected in *The Hunters of Pangaea* and *Traces*, and his latest novel, *Flood*, was released in May. Other books include the Time's Tapestry and Destiny's Children series, and the Time Odyssey series, which was co-written with Arthur C. Clarke. Baxter is also the author of the Xeelee Sequence, and several standalone novels, such as *The H-Bomb Girl*, and *The Time Ships*, an authorized sequel to H. G. Wells's *The Time Machine*.

H. G. Wells is a towering figure in the history of science fiction. His work was pivotal in defining many of the themes—time travel, space exploration, alien invasion, invisibility, genetic engineering—that would be mined by later writers. He was also a famous political activist, and his work demonstrates the power of science fiction to grapple with contemporary issues (*War of the Worlds* was an attack on European colonialism, *The Time Machine* a broadside against the British class system). Wells is also important to science fiction fans because he published the first rulebook for tabletop wargaming, which was instrumental in the development of pen & pencil role-playing games (such as *Dungeons & Dragons*) and the immensely popular computer versions that followed. Wells, who spent his later years frustrated at his inability to change the world, would no doubt be astounded to see what a vast influence his thought and writings have had, though he'd probably also be astounded to see, four hundred years after Galileo, how many people still believe that more weight causes an object to fall faster. Wells appears as a principal character in our next Sherlock Holmes case, an adventure like something right out of a scientific romance.

Our visitor was perhaps twenty-eight: a short, broad-shouldered young man, a little prone to fat, the voice high and thin, and he moved with a bright, bird-like bounce. His face, under thinning hair, was pale—perhaps he was consump-tive—and his blue eyes were striking, wide and dreaming. He could hardly have presented a greater contrast, physically and in his manner, to my friend Holmes. And yet his conversation sparked with Holmes's, as if their two minds were poles of some huge electrical battery.

This visitor had presented Holmes with a set of rather grainy photographs, taken with one of the New York Kodaks which are so popular. Holmes was inspecting these with his lens. The visitor, with some malicious glee, was challenging Holmes to deduce, from the evidence of each photograph, the elements of some unusual situation, after the manner of a parlour game. Holmes had just finished with a blurred image of some withered white flowers. I studied this for myself, and could see little untoward about the flowers, although I could not immediately place their natural order—perhaps it was the genus *Malva*—for instance, the shape of the gynoecium, clearly visible, was rather unusual. Holmes appeared rather irritated by this harmless image, and had passed on to the next, while his young visitor was grinning. "I'm not surprised he made nothing of it. The apparatus of a classic hoaxer!" he told me.

Holmes passed me the next print. "See here, Watson. What can you make of that?"

This appeared more promising—and, I observed, the visitor was somewhat more serious about it. At first glance it seemed to me an undistinguished portrait of a commonplace luncheon party—although it was set in unusual surroundings, the table and guests being all but engulfed by bulky electrical equipment, wires and cylinders and coils and cones, and in the background I could make out the fittings of a workshop: a steam lathe, metal turners, acetylene welding equipment, a sheet-metal stamp and the like. I ventured, "I observe that our visitor this evening was a guest at the lunch. I do not know these others—"

"They are the Brimicombes, of Wiltshire," said the visitor. "My hosts that day: two brothers, Ralph and Tarquin. Ralph is an old college friend of mine. The brothers work together—or did so—on mechanical and electrical inventions."

"It was a sunny day," I said. "I see a splash of light here on the tablecloth, just behind the dish containing this handsome sausage."

"Yes," said Holmes with tolerant patience, "but what of the sausage itself?"

I looked again. The sausage sat on its own plate, the centrepiece of the meal. "It is a succulent specimen. Is it German?"

Holmes sighed. "Watson, that is no sausage, German or otherwise. It is evidently a prank, of dubious taste, served on their guests by these Brimicombes."

The visitor laughed. "You have it, Mr Holmes. You should have seen our faces when that giant concoction crawled off its plate and across the tablecloth!"

"A man of your profession should recognise the beast, Watson. It is an aquatic an-nelid, of the suctorial order *Hirudinea*, employed for the extraction of blood—"

"Great Heaven," I cried, "it is a giant leech!"

"You cannot see the colour in the Kodak," said the visitor, "but you should know it was a bright red: as red as blood itself."

"But how can this be, Holmes? Is it some freak of nature?"

"Of nature—or Man's science," Holmes mused. "Consider the influences acting on that wretched leech. It is drawn towards flatness by the force of the gravity of the Earth; that much we know. And its collapse to a pancake is resisted only by its internal strength. But it is hard to believe a creature as gross as this specimen would even be able to sustain its own form. Why, then, has it evolved such a magnitude? What gives it the strength to hold itself up, to move?" He eyed his visitor sharply. "Or perhaps we should ask, *what is reducing the force which drags it down?*"

The visitor clapped his hands in delight. "You have it, sir!"

Holmes handed back the photograph. "Indeed. And perhaps you might care to set out the particulars of the case."

Confused, I asked, "Are you so sure you have a case at all, Holmes?"

"Oh, yes," he said gravely. "For did our visitor not speak of the work of these Brimicombe brothers in the past tense? Evidently something has disturbed the equilibrium of their fraternal lives; and you would not be here, sir, if that were not something serious."

"Indeed," was the reply, and now the visitor was solemn. "There could be nothing more serious, in fact: my visit here was motivated by the death of the elder brother, Ralph, in unusual circumstances—circumstances deriving from the more obscure corners of the physical sciences!"

I asked, "Is it murder?"

"The local coroner does not think so. I, however, am unsure. There are puzzling features—inconsistencies—and so I have come to you, Mr Holmes—I am a journalist and author, not a detective."

I smiled. "In fact, sir, I already know your occupation."

He seemed surprised. "Forgive me. We have not been introduced."

"No introduction is necessary, nor was any deep deduction on my part. Your portrait has been as common enough this year."

He looked flattered. "You know my work?"

"As it has been featured in the *Pall Mall Budget, The National Observer* and elsewhere. I am a great admirer of your scientific romances." I extended my hand. "It is good to meet you, Mr Wells!"

Holmes agreed to travel with Wells to the Brimicombe home, near Chippenham, and he prevailed on me to accompany him, despite my reluctance to leave London, so close was I to my bereavement. But Holmes persisted, kindly. "You know how few of my cases involve the deeper mysteries of science, Watson. Perhaps this will be a suitable candidate for your casebook! It will be quite like old times." And so it was, the very next day, that I found myself with my valise clambering aboard the 10.15 from Paddington Station. We had the carriage to ourselves, Holmes, Wells and I. Holmes wrapped himself in his grey travelling-cloak and stretched out his long legs on the cushioned seat, as Wells, in his thin, piping voice, set out the full details of the case for us.

"I have known Ralph Brimicombe since we both attended the Normal School of

Science in the '80s," he began, "and I remained in friendly contact with him until his recent death. He was a rather dream-like, remote figure—oddly impractical in the details of everyday life—to the extent that I was somewhat surprised when he married, when still a student at the Normal School. But his mind always sparked with creative energy. His subjects at the School were Astronomy, Astro-physics—all that sort of thing—along with Electricity and Magnetism. Even as a student he began to develop intriguing ideas about the coupling, as he put it, between electricity and gravity. Our theories of gravity were long due for an overhaul, he claimed. And perhaps there could even be practical applications. He was a delight to debate with!—you can imagine how I found him a soul-mate."

Holmes asked, "A coupling?"

"Gravity, as you know, is that force which imbues our bodies with weight. Ralph became convinced that the gravity of a large mass such as the Earth could be mitigated by a suitable arrangement of large currents and magnetic fluxes. Mitigated, or reduced."

"Reduced?" I said. "But if that were true, the commercial possibilities would be enormous. Think of it, Holmes. If one could reduce the weight of freight goods, for example—"

"Oh, to hang with commerce and freight!" Wells exclaimed. "Doctor Watson, Ralph Brimicombe claimed to have found a way to have removed the influence of gravity altogether. Without gravity, one could fly! He even claimed to have built a small capsule, and flown himself—alone, mind you, and without witnesses—all the way to the Moon. He showed me injuries which he said were due to an exhaustion of his food and water, an exposure to the Rays of Space, and burns from the lunar Vacuum. And he gave me a small vial, of what he claimed was Moon dust, as 'proof' of his journey. I have it about me." He patted his pockets.

Holmes raised a thin eyebrow. "And did you believe these claims?"

Wells hesitated. "Perhaps I wished to. But not entirely. Ralph was never above exaggerating his achievements, so impatient was he for acceptance and prestige.

"But I run ahead of my account. Ralph, for all his ability, could only scrape through the examinations at the Normal School, so distracted did he become by his gravitational obsession. After that, no respectable institution would take him on, and no journal would publish the revised theories and partial experimental results he claimed." Wells sighed. "Perhaps Ralph's greatest tragedy was the untimely death of his father, some months after he left the Normal School. The father had made a fortune in the Transvaal, and had retired to Chippenham, only to die of recurrent malaria. He left everything, with few tiresome legal complications, to his two sons: Ralph, and the younger Tarquin. This sudden legacy made Ralph a rich man. No longer did he need to convince peers of the value of his work. Now, he could plough a lone furrow, wherever it might take him.

"Ralph returned to Wiltshire, and devoted himself to his studies. He privately published his results which—while of great interest to students of the esoteric like myself—were roundly and rudely rejected by other scientists."

"And what of Tarquin?" Holmes asked.

"I knew Tarquin a little. I never much liked him," Wells said. "He was quite a contrast to Ralph. Full of vanity and self-regard, and not nearly so intelligent, though he has some smattering of an education, and, as I understand it, a crude grasp of his brother's accomplishments. Tarquin squandered his own inheritance in trying to follow his father's footsteps in Southern Africa, failed roundly, and came home pursued by debtors. Eventually his brother took him on as a species of senior assistant. Tarquin acquired equipment for Ralph's experiments, arranged apparatus and so forth. But even in this he proved less than competent, and Ralph was forced to demote him, effectively, to work as subordinate to Ralph's own engineer, a stolid local chap called Bryson."

I remarked, "It looked as if your lunch party took place in the midst of Ralph's apparatus."

"Yes." Wells smiled. "He was fond of such spectaculars. And I must describe the purpose of that apparatus to you, for it will be of significance to your investigation.

"I have mentioned Ralph's attempts—partially successful, he claimed—to nullify gravity. But this proved possible only over a small volume. To extend his abilities—to build greater ships which might carry teams of men across the Void of Space—Ralph pursued studies of more subtle aspects of the gravitational phenomenon, notably the Equivalence between Inertial and Gravitational Mass. You see—"

I held up my hands. "I cannot speak for Holmes, but I am already baffled, Mr Wells. I know nothing of gravity, save for its slow dragging at the lower spines and arches of my patients."

"Let me explain by analogy. Mr Holmes, can I trouble you for some coins? A sovereign and a farthing should do—there. Thank you." He held the two coins over the carriage floor. "Look here, Watson. The sovereign is considerably heavier than the farthing."

"That is clear enough."

"If I release these coins simultaneously they will fall to the floor."

"Of course."

"But which will arrive first?—the farthing, or the sovereign?"

Holmes looked amused. I felt that embarrassed frustration which sometimes comes over me when I cannot follow some elaborated chain of reasoning. And yet, the case seemed simple enough. "The sovereign," I said. "Disregarding the resistance of the air, as the heavier of the two—"

Wells released the coins. They fell side by side, and struck the carriage floor together.

"I am no expert in Gravitational Mechanics," Holmes chided me, "but I do remember my Galileo, Watson."

Wells retrieved the coins. "It is all to do with various Laws of Newton. Under gravity, all objects fall at the same rate, regardless of their mass. Think of it this way, Watson: if you were in a lift, and the cable snapped, you and the lift would fall together. You would feel as if you were floating, inside the lift car."

"Briefly," I said, "until the shaft floor was reached."

"Indeed. It was precisely this effect which Ralph strove to study. In the luncheon chamber I showed you, with an apparatus of coils and cones and loops, he managed to create a region of space in which—as Ralph showed us with a series of demonstrations and tricks—thanks to the adjustment of the gravity field with electrical energy, heavier objects did indeed fall more rapidly than the lighter! This was the 'Inertial Adjustor,' as Ralph called it. It sounds a trivial feat—and is much less spectacular than shooting a capsule at the Moon—but it is nonetheless quite remarkable. If true."

"But you doubt it," Holmes said. "In fact, you employed the word 'tricks.'"

Wells sighed. "Dear old Ralph. I do not think he lied deliberately. But his optimism and energy for his own work would sometimes cloud his critical judgement. And yet the acceptance of his theories and devices—particularly his Inertial Adjustor—were central to his life, his very mental state."

"So central, in fact, that they led to his death."

"Indeed," said Wells. "For it was in that very chamber, within the Inertial Adjustor itself, that Ralph Brimicombe died—or was killed!"

It was after three o'clock when at last we reached Chippenham. We took a trap to the Brimicombe residence, a well-appointed affair of the Regency period which had been rather allowed to run to seed.

Holmes stepped from the trap and sniffed the air. He walked to the verge of the gravel drive and inspected the lawn grass, which I noticed was discoloured here and there by small brown circles, samples of which Holmes disturbed gently with the toecap of his boot.

A young man came out to meet us: tall and blond, his eyes a vacuous grey. He greeted Wells rather contemptuously—"If it isn't Bertie Wells!"—and introduced himself as Tarquin Brimicombe. We were escorted into the house and introduced to various others of the household. Jane, the widow of Ralph, was a tall, willowy woman who was younger than I expected, and her eyes were puffy as if from habitual crying; and Jack Bryson, Ralph's trusted engineer, bald of head and square of shoulder, appeared puzzled and ill at ease.

Holmes smiled at the widow with the sudden kind warmth perceived in him only by those who know him well, and which made my own heart rise, for I sympathised all too well with this lady's loss of her spouse. "Madam," said Holmes. "My very deepest sympathies."

"Thank you."

"And how is your labrador? Is she still ill?"

She looked confused. "Convalescing, I think. But how did you know?"

He inclined his head. "The patches on the lawn are clear evidence of a canine—and a bitch at that, for it is well known that a bitch will empty her bladder in a single spot, so depositing enough material to damage the grass, whereas a dog will release small quantities of liquid to mark his territory. I have a monograph in draft on the excretory habits of other domestic and urban wildlife. And as to her breed, the golden hairs adhering to your lower skirt are evidence enough of that, Mrs Brimicombe, as well as to your affection for the animal."

"Oh! But you knew of her illness?"

Holmes smiled sadly. "If she were well, I should expect her to come bounding out with you to challenge three such rough strangers as ourselves."

Wells clucked admiringly.

Jane Brimicombe waved a hand rather vaguely. "The illness is baffling to the vets. Sheba has some difficulty standing, and her bones are oddly brittle and prone to breaking. She was involved in experiments of Ralph's, you see, and—"

"I know," said Holmes.

"You do? But how?"

But Holmes did not answer. Instead he drew me aside. "Watson, I'd be grateful if you'd take a sample of the droppings from the wretched animal. Perform some kind of assay."

"Looking for what?"

"My dear fellow, if I told you that I might prejudice your results."

"And how am I supposed to achieve it? I am no vet, Holmes, still less a chemist. And we are a long way from town."

"I am sure you will find a way." Now he turned back to Mrs Brimicombe, and with deft skill, began to draw her out on the subject of her husband's demise.

"It was early morning. I was in the kitchen. Mr Bryson had just come in, having completed an hour's work already." She avoided the eyes of the engineer Bryson, I observed, and the soubriquet "Mr Bryson" did not come naturally to her lips. "We would often eat together, though Mr Bryson was always busy and in a rush. For breakfast he would eat one fried egg and a slice of toast."

"Egg?" asked Holmes. "What egg?"

"From the small coop we keep at the back of the house," Mrs Brimicombe said.

Holmes asked, "And how was the egg that day?"

Mrs Brimicombe dropped her gaze. "Mr Bryson remarked on its fine flavour. I recall Tarquin—Mr Brimicombe—brought them in from the coop, fresh that morning."

"Really?" Holmes turned an appraising eye on the brother, Tarquin. "Sir, are you in the habit of visiting the hen-house?"

Tarquin blustered. "I should say not—I used to help Millie with the eggs as a boy—it was a fine morning—can't a fellow act on impulse once in a while?"

Wells was growing impatient. "Look here, Holmes, why are you so interested in this business of a breakfast egg? Isn't it rather trivial? And can't you see it's causing the lady distress?"

I knew my friend well enough to understand that nothing is truly trivial—there was surely some pattern to his close questioning which none of us could discern— but Mrs Brimicombe was, indeed, becoming agitated, and so Holmes dropped his interrogation of her and allowed Tarquin to lead us through to the drawing room, where he provided sherry. "I have to say I did not invite Mr Wells here," he said.

"At first I regarded his interest and his insistence on coming here as an intrusion into my family's grief. But my view has changed, as I have meditated on the recent tragic events. Now that you are here I am glad, Mr Holmes. I need your help."

"Why so?"

"Ralph's life was not lost. Mr Holmes, it was stolen. After the coroner's report, the police are not interested. I was not sure who to approach, and—"

Holmes held up his hands. "Tell me exactly what you mean."

His pale blue eyes were fixed on Holmes. "Ralph's death was no accident."

"Who was present in the Inertial Adjustor chamber at the time of the incident?"

"Only two of us. Myself and Bryson, my brother's engineer."

"Then," I said doggedly, "you are accusing Bryson—"

"—of murder. That is right, Doctor. Jack Bryson killed Ralph."

Holmes is always impatient to visit the scene of a crime, and Wells was clearly enjoying the whole affair hugely; and so we agreed to accompany Tarquin at once to the Inertial Adjustor chamber, the site of Ralph Brimicombe's death.

We had a walk of a hundred yards or so across the grounds to an out-building. By now it was late afternoon. I took deep breaths of wood-scented air, trying to clear my head after the fumes of the train. I could hear the clucking of chickens, evidently from the hen coop Mrs Brimicombe had mentioned.

I was startled when an insect no less than six inches long scuttled across my path, disturbed by my passage. At first I thought it must be a cockroach, but on closer observation, to my astonishment, it proved to be an ant. It ran with a blur of legs towards an anthill—a gigantic affair, towering over the lower trees like an eroded monument. "Good Lord, Holmes," I said. "Did you observe that? What was it, do you think, some tropical species?"

He shook his head. "Ralph Brimicombe was no collector of bugs. Given the pattern of events here I have expected some such apparition."

"You expected it? But how?"

"Surely that repulsive red leech of Wells's was enough of a clue. But in any event—all in good time, my dear friend."

We reached a laboratory, of crude but functional construction, and I ran my eyes for the first time over the gruesome details of the Inertial Adjustor itself. The main chamber was fifty feet tall; and it was dominated by the stupendous wreck of a vehicle. This latter had been a cone some fifteen feet in length and perhaps as broad, but it was without wheels, sails or runners: for its purpose, Tarquin told us in all seriousness, had been to fly, freed of gravity by Ralph's invention, into Space! To simulate to its occupant some of the stresses and impacts to be expected during a flight, the vessel had been suspended in midair, at the heart of the Inertial Adjustor itself, by a series of cables and gimbals.

Now the cables dangled uselessly. The ship, after an evident fall, had gouged a crater a few inches deep in the floor; it looked as if a great hammer had pounded into the concrete. And it was inside this capsule, this aluminium dream of flight in Space, that Ralph Brimicombe had fallen to his death.

Around the massive wreck were arrayed the elements of the Inertial Adjustor apparatus: coils and armatures, cones of paper and iron, filamented glass tubes, the poles of immense permanent magnets, great shadowy shapes which reached up and out of my vision, the whole far beyond my comprehension. There were besides some more mundane elements: drafting tables laden with dusty blueprints, lathes and vices and tools, chains for heavy lifting suspended from the ceiling.

I observed, however, that the fall of the vehicle had done a pretty damage to the equipment in that chamber, surely rendering it inoperative.

My eye was caught by a series of small glass-walled cages, beside a dissecting table. There was a series of leeches in stoppered jars, none of them as big as the specimen in Well's photograph, but all so large they were indeed unable even to sustain their characteristic tubular forms; they lay against the thick glass at the bottom of their jars, in evident distress. Among the higher animals imprisoned here there were mice, but of an unusual morphology, with remarkably long and spindly limbs. Some of the mice, indeed, had trouble supporting their own weight. I remarked on this to Holmes, but he made no comment.

Holmes, Wells and I stepped over the crater's cracked lip and walked around the wrinkled aluminium of the capsule's hull. The fall had been, I judged, no more that ten feet—a drop that seemed barely enough to injure, let alone kill a man—but it had been sufficient to compress the ship's entire structure by perhaps a third of its length.

"How terrible," Wells said. "It was in this very spot—suspended under the glittering hull of Brimicombe's Moon ship itself—that he bade us dine."

"Then perhaps you have had a lucky escape," said Holmes grimly.

"The workmen have cut the capsule open." Tarquin indicated a square rent in the wall, a shadowed interior beyond. "The body was removed after the police and the coroner studied the scene. Do you want to look in there? Then I will show you where Bryson and I were working."

"In a minute," said Holmes, and he studied the corpse of the fantastic ship with his usual bewildering keenness. He said, "What sort of man was Ralph? I see evidence of his technical abilities, but what was it like to know him—to be related, to work with him?"

"Among those he worked with, Ralph stood out." Tarquin's face was open and seemed untainted by envy. "When we were children, Ralph was always the leader. And so it remained as we entered adult life."

Wells remarked, "I never knew if you liked him."

Tarquin's eyes narrowed. "I cannot answer that, Bertie. We were brothers. I worked for him. I suppose I loved him. But we were also rivals, throughout life, as are most brothers."

Holmes asked bluntly, "Do you stand to benefit from his death?"

Tarquin Brimicombe said, "No. My father's legacy will not be transferred to me. Ralph made out his own will, leaving his assets to his wife; and there is no love lost between the two of us. You may check with the family solicitors—and with

Jane—to verify these claims. If you are looking for a murder motive, Mr Holmes, you must dig deeper. I will not resent it."

"Oh, I shall," muttered Holmes. "And Ralph Brimicombe is beyond resenting anything. Come. Let us look in the capsule."

We stepped over the shattered concrete to the entrance cut in the capsule wall. A small lamp had been set up, filling the interior with a sombre glow. I knew that the body—what was left of it—had been taken away for burial, but the craft had not been cleaned out. I dropped my eyes to the floor, expecting—what? a dramatic splash of blood?—but there were only a few irregular stains on the burst upholstery of the aviator's couch, where Ralph had been seated at the moment of his extinguishing. There was surprisingly little damage to the equipment and instrumentation, the dials and switches and levers evidently meant to control the craft; much of it had simply been crushed longways where it stood.

But there was a smell, reminiscent to me of the hospitals of my military service.

I withdrew my head. "I am not sure what I expected," I murmured. "More…carnage, I suppose."

Tarquin frowned thoughtfully; then he extended his index finger and pointed upwards.

I looked up.

It was as if a dozen bags of rust-brown paint had been hurled into the air. The upper walls and ceiling of the ship, the instruments, dials and switches that encrusted the metal, even the cabin's one small window: all were liberally coated with dried blood.

"Good Lord," said Wells, and his face blanched. "How did that get up there?"

Tarquin said, "The coroner concluded the vessel must have rolled over as it fell, thus spreading my brother's blood through its interior."

As we moved on, Wells muttered to me, "Such a size of ship, rolling over in ten feet? It hardly seems likely!"

I agreed with the young author. But Holmes would make no remark.

Tarquin took us to a gantry which crossed the chamber above the wrecked ship. We stood a few inches from a bank of cables, many of which showed necking, shearing and cracking; they had clearly snapped under extreme pressure. But one cable—a fat, orange-painted rope as thick as my arm—had a clean, gleaming termination. At my feet was a gas cutting kit, and a set of protector goggles. It seemed absurdly obvious, like a puzzle set by a child, that a load-bearing cable had been cut by this torch!

Tarquin said, "Not all the cables supported the weight of the ship. Some carried power, air for the passenger, and so forth."

Holmes said, "You say you were both working up here, on this gantry, when the accident occurred? Both you and Bryson?"

"Yes. We were doing some maintenance. We were the only people in the chamber—apart from Ralph, of course. He was inside the vessel itself, performing calculations there."

Holmes asked, "And the Inertial Adjustor was in operation at the time?"

"It was."

I pointed to the fat orange cable. "Was that the main support?"

He nodded. "Although I did not know that at the time."

"And it has been cut with this torch?"

"That is right," he said evenly. He leaned against the gantry rail, arms folded. "The flame sliced clean through, like ice under a hot tap. When the big one went the others started to stretch and snap. And soon the ship fell."

"And Bryson was using the torch? Is that what you are saying?"

"Oh, no." He looked mildly surprised at Wells's question. "I was doing the cutting. I was working it under Bryson's supervision."

I demanded, "But if you were working the torch, how can you accuse Bryson of murder?"

"Because he is responsible. Do you not see? He told me specifically to cut the orange cable. I followed his instructions, not knowing that it was supporting the capsule."

"You said you are trained to know every detail of the ship, inside and out."

"The ship itself, yes, Doctor. Not the details of this chamber, however. But Bryson knew."

Wells remarked, "But it must have taken minutes to cut through that cable. Look at its thickness! Did Bryson not see what you were doing and stop you?"

"Bryson was not here," Tarquin said coldly. "As you have heard, he was taking breakfast with my sister-in-law, as was their wont. You see, gentlemen," he went on, a controlled anger entering his voice, "I was just a tool Bryson used to achieve his ends. As innocent as that torch at your feet."

Wells stared at the torch, the ripped cables. "Tarquin, your brother knew Bryson for years. He relied on him utterly. Why would Bryson do such a thing?"

He straightened up, brushing dust from his jacket. "You must ask him that," he said.

The next step was obvious to us all: we must confront the accused.

And so we returned to the drawing room of the main house, and confronted the wretched Bryson. He stood on the carpet, his broad, strong hands dangling useless at his side, his overalls oil-stained and bulging with tools. He was, on Wells's testimony, solid, unimaginative, able—and utterly reliable. I could not avoid a sense of embarrassment as Holmes summarised to Bryson the accusation levelled against him.

Jack Bryson hung his head and ran his palm over his scalp. "So you think I killed him," he said, sounding resigned. "That is that, then. Are you going to call in the police?"

"Slow down." Holmes held his hands up. "To begin with, I do not know what possible reason you could have for wanting to harm Ralph Brimicombe."

"It was Jane," he said suddenly.

Wells frowned. "Brimicombe's wife? What about her?"

"She and I——" He hesitated. "I may as well tell you straight; you will find out anyway. I do not know if you would call it an affair. I am a good bit older than she is—but still—Ralph was so distant, you know, so wrapped up in his work. And Jane——"

"——is a woman of warmth and devotion," Holmes said gently.

Bryson said, "I knew Jane a long time. The closeness—the opportunity. Well. So there is your motive, Mr Holmes. I am the lover who slew the cuckolded husband. And my opportunity for murder is without question."

I found it painful to watch his face. There was no bitterness there, no pride: only a sour resignation.

Wells turned to Holmes. "So," he said, "the case is resolved. Are you disappointed, Holmes?"

For answer he filled and lit his pipe. "Resolved?" he said softly. "I think not."

Bryson looked confused. "Sir?"

"Do not be so fast to damn yourself, man. You are a suspect. But that does not make you a murderer: in my eyes, in the eyes of the law, or in the eyes of God."

"And will the courts accept that? I am resigned, Mr Holmes: resigned to my fate. Let it be."

To that dignified acceptance, even Holmes had nothing to say.

Holmes ordered Bryson to take us through the same grisly inspection tour as Tarquin. Soon we were walking around the wreck once more. Unlike Tarquin, Bryson had not seen this place since the day of the accident; his distress was clear as he picked his way through the remnants of the support cables. He said: "The fall took a long time, even after the main support was severed. The noise of the shearing cables went on and on, and there was not a thing I could do about it. I ran out for help, before the end. And when we heard Ralph had been killed——" Now he turned his crumpled face to Holmes's. "No matter who you call guilty in the end, Mr Holmes, I am the killer. I know that. This is my domain; Ralph Brimicombe's life was in my hands while he was in this room, and I failed——"

"Stop it, man," Holmes said sharply. "This self-destructive blame is hardly helpful. For now, we should concentrate on the facts of the case."

Holmes took Bryson to the entrance cut in the capsule. With obvious reluctance the engineer picked his way to the crude doorway. The light inside cast his trembling cheeks in sharp relief. I saw how he looked around the walls of the cabin, at the remnants of the couch on the floor. Then he stood straight and looked at Holmes, puzzled. "Has it been cleaned?"

Holmes pointed upwards.

Bryson pushed his neck through the doorway once more and looked up at the ceiling of the capsule. When he saw the human remains scattered there he gasped and stumbled back.

Holmes said gently, "Watson, would you——"

I took Bryson's arm, meaning to care for him, but he protested: "I am all right. It was just the shock."

"One question," Holmes said. "Tell me how the cable was cut."

"Tarquin was working the torch," he began. "Under my direction. The job was simple; all he had to do was snip out a faulty section of an oxygen line."

"Are you saying Ralph's death was an accident?"

"Oh, no," Bryson said firmly. "It was quite deliberate." He seemed to be challenging us to disbelieve him.

"Tell me the whole truth," said Holmes.

"I was not watching Tarquin's every move. I had given Tarquin his instructions and had left to take breakfast before progressing to another item of work."

"What exactly did you tell him to do?"

He considered, his eyes closing. "I pointed to the oxygen line, explained what it was, and showed him what he had to do. The air line is a purple-coded cable about a thumb's-width thick."

"Whereas the support cables—"

"Are all orange coded, about so thick." He made a circle with his thumbs and middle fingers. "It is hard—impossible—to confuse the two."

"Did you not see what he was doing?"

"I was at breakfast with Mrs Brimicombe when it happened. I expected to be back, however."

"Why were you not?"

He shrugged. "My breakfast egg took rather longer to cook than usual. I remember the housekeeper's apology."

Wells tutted. "Those wretched eggs again!"

"At any event," Bryson said, "I was only gone a few minutes. But by the time I returned Tarquin had sliced clean through the main support. Then the shearing began."

"So you clearly identified the gas line to Tarquin."

"I told you. I pointed to it."

"And there is no way he could have mixed it up with the support cable?"

He raised his eyebrows. "What do you think?"

I scratched my head. "Is it possible he caught the support somehow with the torch, as he was working on the gas feed?"

He laughed; it was a brief, ugly sound. "Hardly, Doctor. The support is about four feet from the air line. He had to turn round, and stretch, and keep the torch there, to do what he did. We can go up to the gantry and see if you like." He seemed to lose his confidence. "Look, Mr Holmes, I do not expect you to believe me. I know I am only an engineer, and Tarquin was Ralph's brother."

"Bryson—"

"But there is no doubt in my mind. Tarquin quite deliberately cut through that support, and ended his brother's life."

There we left our inquiries for the day.

I fulfilled Holmes's request regarding the dog Sheba. On a cursory inspection I found the poor animal's limbs to be spindly and crooked from so many breaks. I collected a sample of her urine and delivered it to the Chippenham general hospital, where an old medical school friend of mine arranged for a series of simple assays. He had the results within the hour, which I tucked into my pocket.

I rejoined my companions, who had retired to the "Little George" hostelry in Chippenham for the evening. They had been made welcome by a broad-bellied, white-aproned barman, had dined well on bread and cheese, and were enjoying the local ale (though Holmes contented himself with his pipe), and talking nine to the dozen the while.

"It is nevertheless quite a mystery," said Wells, around a mouthful of bread. "Has there even been a murder? Or could it all be simply some ghastly, misunderstood accident?"

"I think we can rule that out," said Holmes. "The fact that there are such conflicts between the accounts of the two men is enough to tell us that something is very wrong."

"One of them—presumably the murderer—is lying. But which one? Let us follow it through. Their accounts of the crucial few seconds, when the cable was cut, are ninety per cent identical; they both agree that Bryson had issued an instruction to Tarquin, who had then turned and cut through the support. The difference is that Bryson says he had quite clearly told Tarquin to cut through the air line. But Tarquin says he was instructed, just as clearly, to slice through what turned out to be the support.

"It is like a pretty problem in geometry," went on Wells. "The two versions are symmetrical, like mirror images. But which is the original and which the false copy? What about motive, then? Could Tarquin's envy of his brother—plain for all to see—have driven him to murder? But there is no financial reward for him. And then there is the engineer. Bryson was driven to his dalliance with Jane Brimicombe by the tenderness of his character. How can such tenderness chime with a capability for scheming murder? So, once again, we have symmetry. Each man has a motive—"

Holmes puffed contentedly at his pipe as Wells rattled on in this fashion. He said at last, "Speculations about the mental state of suspects are rarely so fruitful as concentration on the salient facts of the case."

I put in, "I'm sure the peculiar circumstances of the death had something to do with the nature of the Inertial Adjustor itself, though I fail to understand how."

Holmes nodded approvingly. "Good, Watson."

"But," said Wells, "we don't even know if the Adjustor ever operated, or if it was another of Ralph's vain boasts—a flight of fancy, like his trip to the Moon! I still have that vial of Moon dust about me somewhere—"

"You yourself had lunch in the chamber," Holmes said.

"I did. And Ralph performed little demonstrations of the principle. For instance: he dropped a handful of gravel, and we watched as the heaviest fragments were snatched most rapidly to Earth's bosom, contrary to Galileo's famous experiment. But I saw nothing which could not be replicated by a competent conjurer."

"And what of the mice?"

Wells frowned.

"They were rather odd, Mr Wells," I said.

"We can imagine the effect of the distorted gravity of that chamber on genera-tions of insects and animals," Holmes said. "A mouse, for instance, being small, would need the lightest of limbs to support its reduced weight."

Wells saw it. "And they would evolve in that direction, according to the principles of Darwin—of course! Succeeding generations would develop attenuated limbs. Insects like your ant, Watson, could grow to a large size. But larger animals would be dragged more strongly to the ground. A horse, for example, might need legs as thick as an elephant's to support its weight."

"You have it," said Holmes. "But I doubt if there was time, or resource, for Ralph to study more than a generation or two of the higher animals. There was only his wife's unlucky labrador to use as test subject. And when Watson opens the enve-lope in his pocket, he will find the assay of the urine samples from that animal to display excessive levels of calcium."

That startled me. I retrieved and opened the envelope, and was not surprised—I know the man!—to find the results just as Holmes had predicted.

"The calcium is from the bones of the animal," Holmes said. "Trapped by Ralph in a region in which it needed to support less weight, the bitch's musculature and bone structure must have become progressively weaker, with bone calcium being washed out in urine. The same phenomenon is observed in patients suf-fering excessive bed rest, and I saw certain indications of the syndrome in those discoloured patches of lawn."

"Then the means of his death," Wells said, "must indeed be related to Ralph Brimicombe's successful modification of gravity itself."

"Certainly," said Holmes. "And similarly related are the motive behind the crime, and the opportunity."

Wells grew excited. "You've solved it, Holmes? What a remarkable man you are!"

"For the morrow," Holmes said. "For now, let us enjoy the hospitality of the landlord, and each other's company. I too enjoyed your *Time Machine*, Wells."

He seemed flattered. "Thank you."

"Especially your depiction of the crumbling of our foolish civilisation. Although I am not convinced you had thought it through far enough. Our degradation, when it comes, will surely be more dramatic and complete."

"Oh, indeed? Then let me set you a challenge, Mr Holmes. What if I were to transport you, through time, to some remote future—as remote as the era of the great lizards—let us say, tens of millions of years. How would you deduce the former existence of mankind?"

My friend rested his legs comfortably on a stool and tamped his pipe. "A pretty question. We must remember first that everything humans construct will revert to simpler chemicals over time. One must only inspect the decay of the Egyptian pyramids to see that, and they are young compared to the geologic epochs you evoke. None of our concrete or steel or glass will last even a million years."

"But," said Wells, "perhaps some human remains might be preserved in volcanic ash, as at Pompeii and Herculaneum. These remains might have artifacts in close proximity, such as jewellery or surgical tools. And geologists of the future will surely find a layer of ash and lead and zinc to mark the presence of our once-noble civilisation—"

But Holmes did not agree—

And on they talked, H G Wells and Sherlock Holmes together, in a thickening haze of tobacco smoke and beer fumes, until my own poor head was spinning with the concepts they juggled.

The next morning, we made once more for the Brimicombe home. Holmes asked for Tarquin.

The younger Brimicombe entered the drawing room, sat comfortably and crossed his legs.

Holmes regarded him, equally at his ease. "This case has reminded me of a truism I personally find easy to forget: how little people truly understand of the world around us. You demonstrated this, Watson, with your failure to predict the correct fall of my sovereign and farthing, even though it is but an example of a process you must observe a hundred times a day. And yet it takes a man of genius—a Galileo—to be the first to perform a clear and decisive experiment in such a matter. You are no genius, Mr Brimicombe, and still less so is the engineer, Bryson. And yet you studied your brother's work; your grasp of the theory is the greater, and your understanding of the behaviour of objects inside the Inertial Adjustor is bound to be wider than poor Bryson's."

Tarquin stared at Holmes, the fingers of one hand trembling slightly.

Holmes rested his hands behind his head. "After all, it was a drop of only ten feet or so. Even Watson here could survive a fall like that—perhaps with bruises and broken bones. But it was not Ralph's fall that killed him, was it? Tarquin, what was the mass of the capsule?"

"About ten tons."

"Perhaps a hundred times Ralph's mass. And so—in the peculiar conditions of the Inertial Adjustor—*it fell to the floor a hundred times faster than Ralph.*"

And then, in a flash, I saw it all. Unlike my friendly lift cabin of Wells's analogy, the capsule would drive rapidly to the floor, engulfing Ralph. My unwelcome imagination ran away with the point: I saw the complex ceiling of the capsule smashing into Ralph's staring face, a fraction of a second before the careening metal hit his body and he burst like a balloon...

Tarquin buried his eyes in the palm of his hand. "I live with the image. Why are you telling me this?"

For answer, Holmes turned to Wells. "Mr Wells, let us test your own powers of observation. What is the single most startling aspect of the case?"

He frowned. "When we first visited the Inertial Adjustor chamber with Tarquin, I recall looking into the capsule, and scanning the floor and couch for signs of Ralph's death."

"But," Holmes said, "the evidence of Ralph's demise—bizarre, grotesque—were fixed to the ceiling, not the floor."

"Yes. Tarquin told me to look up—just as later, now I think on it, you, Mr Holmes, had to tell the engineer Bryson to raise his head, and his face twisted in horror." He studied Holmes. "So, a breaking of the symmetry at last. Tarquin knew where to look; Bryson did not. What does that tell us?"

Holmes said, "By looking down, by seeking traces of Ralph on the couch, the floor, we demonstrated we had not understood what had happened to Ralph. We had to be shown—as had Bryson! If Bryson had sought to murder Ralph he would have chosen some other method. Only someone who has studied the properties of a gravity field changed by the Inertial Adjustor would know immediately how cutting that cable would kill Ralph."

Tarquin sat very still, eyes covered. "Someone like me, you mean?"

Wells said, "Is that an admission, Tarquin?"

Tarquin lifted his face to Holmes, looking thoughtful. "You do not have any proof. And there is a counter-argument. Bryson could have stopped me, before I cut through the cable. The fact that he did not is evidence of his guilt!"

"But he was not there," Holmes said evenly. "As you arranged."

Tarquin guffawed. "He was taking breakfast with my sister-in-law! How could I arrange such a thing?"

"There is the matter of Bryson's breakfast egg, which took unusually long to cook," Holmes said.

"Your egg again, Holmes!" Wells cried.

"On that morning," said Holmes, "and that morning alone, you, Mr Brimicombe, collected fresh eggs from the coop. I checked with the housekeeper. The eggs used for breakfast here are customarily a day or more old. As you surely learned as a child fond of the hens, Tarquin, a fresh egg takes appreciably longer to cook than one that is a day or more old. A fresh egg has a volume of clear albumen solution trapped in layers of dense egg white around the yolk. These layers make the egg sit up in the frying pan. After some days the albumen layers degenerate, and the more watery egg will flatten out, and is more easily cooked."

Wells gasped. "My word, Holmes. Is there no limit to your intelligence?"

"Oh," said Brimicombe, "but this is—"

"Mr Brimicombe," Holmes said steadily, "you are not a habitual criminal. When I call in the police they will find all the proof any court in the land could require. Do you doubt that?"

Tarquin Brimicombe considered for a while, and then said: "Perhaps not." He gave Holmes a grin, like a good loser on the playing field. "Maybe I tried to be too clever; I thought I was home clear anyway, but when I knew you were coming I decided to bluff you over Bryson to be sure. I knew about his involvement with Jane; I knew he would have a motive for you to pick up—"

"And so you tried to implicate an innocent man." I could see Holmes's cool anger building.

Wells said, "So it is resolved. Tell me one thing. Tarquin. If not for your brother's money, why?"

He showed surprise. "Do you not know, Bertie? The first aviator will be the most famous man in history. I wanted to be that man, to fly Ralph's craft into the air, perhaps even to other worlds."

"But," Wells said, "Ralph claimed to have flown already all the way to the Moon and back."

Tarquin dismissed this with a gesture. "Nobody believed that. I could have been first. But my brother would never have allowed it."

"And so," said Wells bitterly, "you destroyed your brother—and his work—rather than allow him precedence."

There was a touch of pride in Tarquin's voice. "At least I can say I gave my destiny my best shot, Bertie Wells. Can you say the same?"

The formalities of Tarquin Brimicombe's arrest and charging were concluded rapidly, and the three of us, without regret, took the train for London. The journey was rather strained; Wells, having enjoyed the hunt, now seemed embittered by the unravelling of the Brimicombe affair. He said, "It is a tragedy that the equipment is so smashed up, that Ralph's note-taking was so poor, that his brother—murderer or not—is such a dullard. It will not prove possible to restore Ralph's work, I fear."

Holmes mused, "But the true tragedy here is that of a scientist who sacrificed his humanity—the love of his wife—for knowledge."

Wells grew angry. "Really. And what of you, Mr Holmes, and your dry quest for fact, fact, fact? What have you sacrificed?"

"I do not judge," Holmes said easily. "I merely observe."

"At any rate," said Wells, "it may be many years before humans truly fly to the Moon—oh. I am reminded." He dug into a coat pocket and pulled out a small, stoppered vial. It contained a quantity of grey-black dust, like charcoal. "I found it. Here is the 'Moon dust' which Ralph gave me, the last element of his hoax." He opened the bottle and shook a thimbleful of dust into the palms of Holmes and myself.

I poked at the grains. They were sharp-edged. The dust had a peculiar smell: "Like wood smoke," I opined.

"Or wet ash," Wells suggested. "Or gunpowder!"

Holmes frowned thoughtfully. "I suppose the soil of the Moon, never having been exposed to air, would react with the oxygen in our atmosphere. The iron contained therein—it would be like a slow burning—"

Wells collected the dust from us. He seemed angry and bitter. "Let us give up this foolishness. What a waste this all is. How many advances of the intellect have been betrayed by the weakness of the human heart? Oh, perhaps I might make a romance of this—but that is all that is left! Here! Have done with you!" And with an impetuous gesture he opened the carriage window and shook out the vial, scattering dust along the track. Holmes raised an elegant hand, as if to stop him, but he was too late. The dust was soon gone, and Wells discarded the bottle itself.

For the rest of the journey to Paddington, Holmes was strangely thoughtful, and said little.

MRS HUDSON'S CASE

by Laurie R. King

Laurie R. King is the bestselling author of the Mary Russell series, which began with *The Beekeeper's Apprentice*. The latest entry in the series, *The Language of Bees*, was published in April, and the next volume, currently titled *The Green Man*, is due out next year. King is the winner of the Edgar, Creasy, and Nero awards, and is slated to be the Guest of Honor at the 2010 Bouchercon World Mystery Convention. Although King writes primarily in the mystery genre, she is also the author of the post-apocalyptic novel *Califia's Daughters*, written under the pseudonym Leigh Richards.

They say it's a man's world, and that's largely true of the world of Sherlock Holmes as well. Holmes and Watson are perhaps the best known "buddy" pair in literature, and most of the characters they interact with are men—Lestrade, Moriarty, Moran. Of the more notable female characters, Irene Adler appears in only one adventure and Mrs. Hudson is very much on the periphery. This story changes all that—as you might guess from the title—placing Mrs. Hudson squarely in the center of events. Another strong female presence here is Mary Russell, a university student and protégé of Sherlock Holmes, who first appeared in the aforementioned *The Beekeeper's Apprentice*. King describes Russell as "what Sherlock Holmes would look like if Holmes, the Victorian detective, were (a) a woman, (b) of the Twentieth century, and (c) interested in theology." Russell's many talents include knife throwing, lock picking, and ancient languages. Women often exist in private solidarity with each other, sharing confidences and secrets that are kept separate from the world of men. That is certainly the case in our next adventure, which gives us a rare glimpse of Mrs. Hudson from the point of view of another woman.

As has been noted by a previous biographer, Mrs Hudson was the most long-suffering of landladies. In the years when Sherlock Holmes lived beneath her Baker Street roof, she faced with equanimity his irregular hours, his ill temper, his malodorous and occasionally dangerous chemical experiments, his (again) occasionally malodorous and even dangerous visitors, and all the other demands made on her dwelling and her person. And yet, far from rejoicing when Holmes quit London for the sea-blown expanses of the Sussex Downs, in less than three months she had turned her house over to an estate agent and followed him, to run his household as she had formerly run her own. When once I dared to ask her why, late on a celebratory evening when she had rather more drink taken than was her wont, she answered that the devil himself needed someone to look after him, and it made her fingers itch to know that Mr Holmes was not getting the care to which he was accustomed. Besides, she added under her breath, the new tenants had not been in place for a week before she knew she would go mad with boredom.

Thus, thanks to the willingness of this good woman to continue suffering in the service of genius, Holmes' life went on much as before.

Not that he was grateful, or indeed even aware of her sacrifice. He went on, as I said, much as before, feeling vexed when her tidying had removed some vital item or when her regular market-day absence meant that he had to brew his own coffee. Deep in his misogynistic soul, he was not really convinced that women had minds, rights, or lives of their own.

This may be unfair; he was certainly always more than ready to dismiss members of his own sex. However, there is no doubt that a woman, be she lady or governess, triggered in him an automatic response of polite disinterest coupled with vague impatience: it took a high degree of determination on the part of a prospective client who happened to be female to drag him into a case.

Mrs Hudson, though, was nothing if not determined. On this day in October of 1918 she had pursued him through the house and up the stairs, finally bearding him in his laboratory, where she continued to press upon him the details of her odd experience. However, her bristling Scots implacability made little headway against the carapace of English phlegm that he was turning against her. I stood in the doorway, witness to the meeting of irresistible force and immovable object.

"No, Mrs Hudson, absolutely not. I am busy." To prove it (although when I had arrived at his house twenty minutes earlier I had found him moping over the newspapers) he turned to his acid-stained workbench and reached for some beakers and a couple of long glass tubes.

"All I'm asking you to do is to rig a wee trap," she said, her accent growing with her perturbation.

Holmes snorted. "A bear trap in the kitchen, perhaps? Oh, a capital idea, Mrs Hudson."

"You're not listening to me, Mister 'Olmes. I told you, I wanted you to fix up a simple camera, so I can see who it is that's been coming in of rights and helping himself to my bits and pieces."

"Mice, Mrs Hudson. The country is full of them." He dropped a pipette into a jar and transferred a quantity of liquid into a clean beaker.

"*Mice!*" She was shocked. "In *my* kitchen? Mr Holmes, *really.*"

Holmes had gone too far, and knew it. "I do apologize, Mrs Hudson. Perhaps it was the cat?"

"And what call would a cat have for a needle and thread?" she demanded, unplacated. "Even if the beastie could work the latch on my sewing case."

"Perhaps Russell...?"

"You know full well that Mary's been away at University these four weeks."

"Oh, very well. Ask Will to change the locks on the doors." He turned his back with an optimistic attempt at finality.

"I don't want the locks changed, I want to know who it is. Things have gone missing from all the neighbours, little things mostly, but it's not nice."

I had been watching Holmes' movements at first idly, then more closely, and now I took a step into the room and caught at Mrs Hudson's sleeve. "Mrs Hudson, I'll help you with it. I'm sure I can figure out how to booby trap a camera with a flash. Come, let's go downstairs and decide where to put it."

"But I thought—"

"Come with me, Mrs Hudson."

"Mary, are you certain?"

"*Now*, Mrs Hudson." I tightened my grip on her substantial arm and hauled, just as Holmes removed his finger from the end of the pipette and allowed the substance it held to drop into the already seething mixture in the beaker. He had not been paying attention to his experiment; a cloud of noxious green gas began instantly to billow up from the mouth of the beaker. Mrs Hudson and I went with all haste down the stairs, leaving Holmes to grope his way to the shutters and fling them open, coughing and cursing furiously.

Once in her kitchen, Mrs Hudson's inborn hospitality reasserted itself, and I had to wait until she had stirred up a batch of rock cakes, questioned me about my progress and my diet up at Oxford in this, my second year there. She then put on the kettle, washed up the bowls, and swept the floor before finally settling in a chair across the soft scrubbed wood table from me.

"You were saying," I began, "that you've had a series of break-ins and small thefts."

"Some food and a bit of milk from time to time. Usually stale things, a heel of bread and a knob of dry cheese. Some wool stockings from the darning basket, two old blankets I'd intended for the church. And as I said, a couple of needles and a spool of black thread from the sewing case." She nodded at the neat piece of wooden joinery with the padded top that sat in front of her chair by the fire, and I had to agree, no cat could have worked its latch.

"Alcohol?"

"Never. And never have I missed any of the household money I keep in the tea caddy or anything of value. Mrs Prinnings down the road claims she lost a ring to the thief, but she's terribly absent-minded, she is."

"How is he getting in?"

"I think he must have a key." Seeing my expression, she hastened to explain. "There's always one on the hook at the back door, and one day last week when Will needed it, I couldn't find it. I thought he maybe borrowed it earlier and forgot to return it, that's happened before, but it could have been the thief. And I admit I'm not always good at locking up all the windows at night. Which is probably how he got in in the first place."

"So change the locks."

"The thing is, Mary, I can't help but feel it's some poor soul who is in need, and although I certainly don't want him to waltz in and out, I do want to know who it is so that I know what to do. Do you follow me?"

I did, actually. There were a handful of ex-soldiers living around the fringes of Oxford, so badly shell-shocked as to be incapable of ordinary social intercourse, who slept rough and survived by what wits were left them. Tragic figures, and one would not wish to be responsible for their starvation.

"How many people in the area have been broken into?"

"Pretty near everyone when it first started, the end of September. Since then those who have locks use them. The others seem to think it's fairies or absent-mindedness."

"Fairies?"

"The little people are a curious lot," she said. I looked closely to be sure that she was joking, but I couldn't tell.

Some invisible signal made her rise and go to the oven, and sure enough, the cakes were perfect and golden brown. We ate them with fresh butter and drank tea (Mrs Hudson carried a tray upstairs, and returned without comment but with watering eyes) and then turned our combined intellects to the problem of photographing intruders.

I returned the next morning, Saturday, with a variety of equipment. Borrowing a hammer, nails, and scraps of wood from old Will, the handyman, and a length of fine fishing twine from his grandson, by trial and error Mrs Hudson (interrupted regularly by delivery boys, shouts from upstairs, and telephone calls) and I succeeded in rigging a trip wire across the kitchen door.

During the final stages of this delicate operation, as I perched on the stepladder adjusting the camera, I was peripherally aware of Holmes' voice raised to shout down the telephone in the library. After a few minutes, silence fell, and shortly thereafter his head appeared at the level of my waist.

He didn't sneer at my efforts. He acted as if I were not there, as if he had found Mrs Hudson rolling out a pie crust rather than holding out a selection of wedges for me to use in my adjustments.

"Mrs Hudson, it appears that I shall be away for a few days. Would you sort me out some clean collars and the like?"

"*Now,* Mr Holmes?"

"Any time in the next ten minutes will be fine," he said generously, then turned and left without so much as a glance at me. I bent down to call through the doorway at his retreating back.

"I go back to Oxford tomorrow, Holmes."

"It was good of you to come by, Russell," he said, and disappeared up the stairs.

"You can leave the wedges with me, Mrs Hudson," I told her. "I'm nearly finished."

I could see her waver with the contemplation of rebellion, but we both knew full well that Holmes would leave in ten minutes, clean linen or no, and whereas I would have happily sent him on his way grubby, Mrs Hudson's professional pride was at stake. She put the wedges on the top of the stepladder and hurried off.

She and Holmes arrived simultaneously in the central room of the old cottage just as I had alighted from the ladder to examine my handiwork. I turned my gaze to Holmes, and found him dressed for Town, pulling on a pair of black leather gloves.

"A case, Holmes?"

"Merely a consultation, at this point. Scotland Yard has been reflecting on our success with the Jessica Simpson kidnapping, and in their efforts to trawl the bottom of this latest kidnapping, have decided to have me review their efforts for possible gaps. Paperwork merely, Russell," he added. "Nothing to excite you."

"This is the Oberdorfer case?" I asked. It was nearly a month since the two children, twelve-year-old Sarah and her seven-year-old brother Louis, had vanished from Hyde Park under the expensive nose of their nurse. They were orphans, the children of a cloth manufacturer with factories in three countries and his independently wealthy French wife. His brother, who had taken refuge in London during the war, had anticipated a huge demand of ransom. He was still waiting.

"Is there news?"

"There is nothing. No ransom note, no sightings, nothing. Scotland Yard is settling to the opinion that it was an outburst of anti-German sentiment that went too far, along the lines of the smashing of German shopkeepers' windows that was so common in the opening months of the war. Lestrade believes the kidnapper was a rank amateur who panicked at his own audacity and killed them, and further thinks their bodies will be found any day, no doubt by some sportsman's dog." He grimaced, tucked in the ends of his scarf, buttoned his coat against the cool autumnal day, and took the portmanteau from Mrs Hudson's hand.

"Well, good luck, Holmes," I said.

"Luck," he said austerely, "has nothing to do with it."

When he had left, Mrs Hudson and I stood looking at each other for a long minute, sobered by this reminder of what was almost certainly foul murder, and also by the revealing lack of enthusiasm and optimism in the demeanour of the man who had just driven off. Whatever he might say, our success in the Simpson case two months earlier had been guided by luck, and I had no yearning to join forces in a second kidnap case, particularly one that was patently hopeless.

I sighed, and then we turned to my trap. I explained how the camera worked, told her where to take the film to be developed and printed, and then tidied away my tools and prepared to take my own departure.

"You'll let me know if anything turns up?" I asked. "I could try to make it back down next weekend, but—"

"No, no, Mary, you mustn't interfere with your studies. I shall write and let you know."

I stepped cautiously over the taut fishing wire and paused in the doorway. "And you'll tell me if Holmes seems to need any assistance in this Oberdorfer case?"

"That I will."

I left, ruefully contemplating the irony of a man who normally avoided children like the plague (aside from those miniature adults he had scraped off the streets to form his "Irregulars" in the Baker Street days); these days he seemed to have his hands full of them.

I returned to Oxford, and my studies, and truth to tell the first I thought about Mrs Hudson's problem was more than a week later, on a Wednesday, when I realized that for the second week in a row her inevitable Tuesday letter had not come. I had not expected the first one, though she often wrote even if I had seen her the day before, but not to write after eight days was unprecedented.

I telephoned the cottage that evening. Holmes was still away, Mrs Hudson thought, interviewing the Oberdorfer uncle in Paris, and she herself sounded most peculiar. She seemed distracted, and said merely that she'd been too busy to write, apologized, and asked if there was anything in particular I was wanting?

Badly taken aback, I stammered out a question concerning our camera trap.

"Oh, yes," she said, "the camera. No, no, nothing much has come of that. Still, it was a good idea, Mary. Thank you. Well, I must be gone now, dear, take care."

The line went dead, and I slowly put up the earpiece. She hadn't even asked if I was eating well.

I was hit by a sudden absurd desire to leave immediately for Sussex. I succeeded in pushing it away, but on Saturday morning I was on the train south, and by Saturday afternoon my hand was on the kitchen door to Holmes' cottage.

A moment later my nose was nearly on the door as well, flattened against it, in fact, because the door did not open. It was locked.

This door was never locked, certainly not in the daytime when there was anyone at home, yet I could have sworn that I had heard a scurry of sound from within. When I tried to look in the window, my eyes were met by a gaily patterned tea-towel, pinned up neatly to all the edges.

"Mrs Hudson?" I called. There was no answer. Perhaps the movement had been the cat. I went around the house, tried the French doors and found them locked as well, and continued around to the front door, only to have it open as I stretched out my hand. Mrs Hudson stood in the narrow opening, her sturdy shoe planted firmly against the door's lower edge.

"Mrs Hudson, there you are! I was beginning to think you'd gone out."

"Hello there, Mary. I'm surprised to see you back down here so soon. Mr Holmes isn't back from the Continent yet, I'm sorry."

"Actually, I came to see you."

"Ah, Mary, such a pity, but I really can't have you in. I'm taking advantage of Mr Holmes' absence to turn out the house, and things are in a dreadful state. You should have checked with me first, dear."

A brief glance at her tidy, uncovered hair and her clean hand on the door made it obvious that heavy housecleaning was not her current preoccupation. Yet she did not appear afraid, as if she was being held hostage or something; she seemed merely determined. Still, I had to keep her at the door as long as I could while I searched for a clue to her odd behaviour.

Such was my intention; however, every question was met by a slight edging back into the house and an increment of closure of the door, until eventually it clicked shut before me. I heard the sound of the bolt being shot, and then Mrs Hudson's firm footsteps, retreating towards the kitchen.

I stood, away from the house, frankly astonished. I couldn't even peer in, as the sitting-room windows overlooking the kitchen had had their curtains tightly shut. I considered, and discarded, a full frontal assault, and decided that the only thing for it was stealth.

Mrs Hudson knew me well enough to expect it of me, of that I was fully aware, so I took care to stay away that evening, even ringing her from my own house several miles away to let her know that I was not outside the cottage, watching her curtains. She also knew that I had to take the Sunday night train in order to be at the Monday morning lectures, and would then begin to relax. Sunday night, therefore, was when I took up my position outside the kitchen window.

For a long time all I heard were busy kitchen sounds—a knife on a cutting board, a spoon scraping against the side of a pot, the clatter of a bowl going into the stone sink. Then without warning, at about nine o'clock Mrs Hudson spoke.

"Hello there, dear. Have a good sleep?"

"I always feel I should say 'good morning,' but it's nighttime," said a voice in response, and I was so startled I nearly knocked over a pot of herbs. The voice was that of a child, sleep-clogged but high-pitched: a child with a very faint German accent.

Enough of this, I thought. I was tempted to heave the herb pot through the window and just clamber in, but I was not sure of the condition of Mrs Hudson's heart. Instead I went silently around the house, found the door barred to my key, and ended up retrieving the long ladder from the side of the garden shed and propping it up against Holmes' window. Of course the man would have jimmy-proof latches. Finally in frustration I used a rock, and fast as Mrs Hudson was in responding to the sound of breaking glass, I still met her at the foot of the stairs, and slipped past her by feinting to the left and ducking past her on the right.

The kitchen was bare.

However, the bolt was still shot, so the owner of the German voice was here somewhere. I ignored the furious Scots woman at my back and ran my eyes over the scene: the pots of food that she would not have cooked for herself alone, the table laid for three (one of the place settings with a diminutive fork and a china mug decorated with pigs wearing toppers and tails), and two new hairbrushes lying on a towel on the side of the sink.

"Tell them to come out," I said.

She sighed deeply. "You don't know what you're doing, Mary."

"Of course I don't. How can I know anything if you keep me in the dark?"

"Oh, very well. I should have known you'd keep on until you found out. I was going to move them, but—" She paused, and raised her voice. "Sarah, Louis, come out here."

They came, not, as I had expected, from the pantry, but crawling out of the tiny cupboard in the corner. When they were standing in the room, eyeing me warily, Mrs Hudson made the introductions.

"Sarah and Louis Oberdorfer, Miss Mary Russell. Don't worry, she's a friend. A very nosy friend." She sniffed, and turned to take another place setting from the sideboard and lay it out—at the far end of the table from the three places already there.

"The Oberdorfers," I said. "How on earth did they get here? Did Holmes bring them? Don't you know that the police in two countries are looking for them?"

Twelve-year-old Sarah glowered at me. Her seven-year-old brother edged behind her fearfully. Mrs Hudson set the kettle down forcefully on the hob.

"Of course I do. And no, Mr Holmes is not aware that they are here."

"But he's actually working on the case. How could you—"

She cut me off. Chin raised, grey hair quivering, she turned on me with a porridge spoon in her hand. "Now don't you go accusing me of being a traitor, Mary Russell, not until you know what I know."

We faced off across the kitchen table, the stout, aging Scots housekeeper and the lanky Oxford undergraduate, until I realized simultaneously that whatever she was cooking smelled superb, and that perhaps I ought indeed to know what she knew. A truce was called, and we sat down at the table to break bread together.

It took a long time for the various threads of the story to trickle out, narrated by Mrs Hudson (telling how, in Holmes' absence, she could nap in the afternoons so as to sit up night after night until the door had finally been opened by the thief) and by Sarah Oberdorfer (who coolly recited how she had schemed and prepared, with map and warm clothes and enough money to get them started, and only seemed troubled at the telling of how she had been forced to take to a life of crime), with the occasional contribution by young Louis (who thought the whole thing a great lark, from the adventure of hiding among the baggage in the train from London to the thrill of wandering the Downs, unsupervised, in the moonlight). It took longer still for the entire thing to become clear in my mind. Until midnight, in fact, when the two children, who had from the beginning been sleeping days and active at night to help prevent discovery, were stretched out on the carpet in front of the fire in the next room, colouring pictures.

"Just to make sure I have this all straight," I said to Mrs Hudson, feeling rather tired, "let me go over it again. First, they say they were not kidnapped, they fled under their own power, from their uncle James Oberdorfer, because they believed he was trying to kill them in order to inherit his late brother's, their father's, property."

"You can see Sarah believes it."

I sighed. "Oh yes, I admit she does. Nobody would run away from a comfortable house, hide in a baggage car, and live in a cave for three weeks on stolen food if she didn't believe it. And yes, I admit that there seems to have been a very odd series of accidents." Mrs Hudson's own investigative machinery, though not as smooth as that of her employer, was both robust and labyrinthine: she had found through the servant sister of another landlady who had a friend who—and so forth.

There was a great deal of money involved, with factories not only here and in France, but also in Germany, where the war seemed on the verge of coming to its bloody end. These were two very wealthy orphans, with no family left but one uncle. An uncle who, according to below-the-stairs rumour collected by Mrs Hudson's network of informants, exhibited a smarmy, shallow affection to his charges. I put my head into my hands.

It all rested on Sarah. A different child I might have dismissed as being prone to imaginative stories, but those steady brown eyes of hers, daring me to disbelieve—I could see why Mrs Hudson, by no means an easy mark for a sad story, had taken them under her wing.

"And you say the footman witnessed the near-drowning?" I said without looking up.

"If he hadn't happened upon them they'd have been lost, he said. And the maid who ate some of the special pudding their uncle brought them was indeed very ill."

"But there's no proof."

"No." She wasn't making this any easier for me. We both knew that Holmes, with his attitudes towards children, and particularly girl children, would hand these two back to their uncle. Oh, he would issue the man a stern warning that he, Holmes, would in the future take a close personal interest in the safety of the Oberdorfer heirs, but after all, accidents were unpredictable things, particularly if Oberdorfer chose to return to the chaos of war-ravaged Germany. If he decided the inheritance was worth the risk, and took care that no proof was available...

No proof here either, one way or the other, and this was one case I could *not* discuss with Holmes.

"And you were planning on sending them to your cousin in Wiltshire?"

"It's a nice healthy farm near a good school, and who would question two more children orphaned by zeppelin bombs?"

"But only until Sarah is sixteen?"

"Three years and a bit. She'd be a young lady then—not legally of course, but lawyers would listen to her."

I was only eighteen myself, and could well believe that authorities who would dismiss a twelve-year-old's wild accusations would prick their ears at a self-contained sixteen-year-old. Why, even Holmes...

"All right, Mrs Hudson, you win. I'll help you get them to Wiltshire."

I was not there when Holmes returned a week later, drained and irritable at his failure to enlighten Scotland Yard. Mrs Hudson said nothing, just served him his dinner and his newspapers and went about her business. She said nothing then, and she said nothing later that evening when Holmes, who had carried his collection of papers to the basket chair in front of the fire and prepared to settle in, leapt wildly to his feet, bent over to dig among the cushions for a moment, then turned in accusation to his housekeeper with the gnawed stub of a coloured pencil in his outstretched palm.

She never did say anything, not even three years later when the young heir and his older sister (her hair piled carefully on top of her head, wearing a grown woman's hat and a dress a bit too old for her slim young frame) miraculously materialized in a solicitor's office in London, creating a stir in three countries. However, several times over the years, whenever Holmes was making some particularly irksome demand on her patience, I saw this most long-suffering of landladies take a deep breath, focus on something far away, and nod briefly, before going on her placid way with a tiny, satisfied smile on her face.

THE SINGULAR HABITS
OF WASPS

by Geoffrey A. Landis

Geoffrey A. Landis is the author of the books *Mars Crossing* and *Impact Parameter and Other Quantum Realities*. He is also the author of more than eighty short stories, which have appeared in venues such as *Analog, Asimov's,* and *The Magazine of Fantasy & Science Fiction,* and has been reprinted frequently in best-of-the-year volumes. He is the winner of the Nebula, Hugo (twice), and Locus awards for his fiction, and a Rhysling Award for SF poetry. In addition to his science fiction writing, Landis works for the NASA John Glenn Research Center, where he was part of the Mars Pathfinder rover team and the Mars Exploration Rover science team.

The character Sherlock Holmes was largely based on Dr. Joseph Bell, with whom Conan Doyle studied at medical school. Bell was renowned for making diagnoses on the basis of simple observation, and also for drawing seemingly inexplicable deductions about a patient—for example, that he had been walking earlier in a particular area of the city—based on minute details, such as the color of clay on the person's shoes. Bell was instrumental in the development of forensic science, and local law enforcement often consulted with him to help them crack tough cases, including the case of Jack the Ripper. Bell sent police a sealed envelope containing the name of the individual he believed to be responsible, and after that the murders stopped. Jack the Ripper was the world's first celebrity serial killer. He preyed on prostitutes in the Whitechapel district of London and is perhaps still the most famous of all such killers, despite having slain only a handful of victims. His fame can most likely be attributed to his evocative sobriquet and to the enduring mystery surrounding his identity and motive. Our next story presents a chilling and unexpected explanation for the Ripper's grisly crimes.

Of the many adventures in which I have participated with my friend Mr. Sherlock Holmes, none has been more singularly horrifying than the case of the Whitechapel killings, nor ever had I previously had cause to doubt the sanity of my friend. I need but close my eyes to see again the horror of that night; the awful sight of my friend, his arms red to the elbow, his knife still dripping gore, and to recall in every detail the gruesome horrors that followed.

The tale of this adventure is far too awful to allow any hint of the true course of the affair to be known. Although I dare never let this account be read by others, I have often noticed, in chronicling the adventures of my friend, that in the process of putting pen to paper a great relief occurs. A catharsis, as we call it in the medical profession. And so I hope that by putting upon paper the events of those weeks, I may ease my soul from its dread fascination with the horrid events of that night. I will write this and then secret the account away with orders that it be burned upon my death.

Genius is, as I have often remarked, closely akin to madness, so closely that at times it is hard to distinguish the one from the other, and the greatest geniuses are also often quite insane. I had for a long time known that my friend was subject to sporadic fits of blackest depression, from which he could become aroused in an instant into bursts of manic energy, in a manner not unlike the cyclic mood-swings of a madman. But the limits to his sanity I never probed.

The case began in the late springtime of 1888. All who were in London at that time will recall the perplexing afternoon of the double cannonade. Holmes and I were enjoying a cigar after lunch in our sitting room at 221B Baker Street when the hollow report of a double firing of cannon rang out from the cloudless sky, rattling the windows and causing Mrs. Hudson's china to dance upon its shelves. I rushed to the window. Holmes was in the midst of one of those profound fits of melancholia to which he is so prone, and did not rise from his chair, but did bestir himself so much as to ask what I saw. Aside from other, equally perplexed folk opening their windows to look in all directions up and down the street, I saw nothing out of the ordinary, and such I reported to him.

"Most unusual," Holmes remarked. He was still slumped almost bonelessly in his chair, but I believed I detected a bit of interest in his eye. "We shall hear more about this, I would venture to guess."

And indeed, all of London seemed to have heard the strange reports, without any source to be found, and the subject could not be avoided all that day or the next. Each newspaper ventured an opinion, and even strangers on the street talked of little else. As to conclusion, there was none, nor was the strange sound repeated. In another day the usual gossip, scandals and crimes of the city had crowded the marvel out of the papers, and the case was forgotten.

But it had, at least, the effect of breaking my friend out of his melancholia, even so far as to cause him to pay a rare visit to his brother at the Diogenes Club. Mycroft was high in the Queen's service, and there were few secrets of the Empire to which Mycroft was not privy. Holmes did not confide in me as to what result came of his inquiries of Mycroft, but he spent the remainder of the evening pacing and smoking, contemplating some mystery.

In the morning we had callers, and the mystery of the cannonade was temporarily set aside. They were two men in simple but neat clothes, both very diffident and hesitant of speech.

"I see that you have come from the south of Surrey," Holmes said calmly. "A farm near Godalming, perhaps?"

"Indeed we have, sir, from Covingham, which is a bit south of Godalming," said the elder of the visitors, "though how you could know, I'll never guess in all my born days, seeing as how I've never had the pleasure of meeting you before in my life, nor Baxter here neither."

I knew that Holmes, with his encyclopaedic knowledge, would have placed them precisely from their accents and clothing, although this elementary feat of deduction seemed to quite astound our visitors.

"And this is the first visit to London for either of you," said Holmes. "Why have you come this distance from your farm to see me?"

The two men looked at each other in astonishment. "Why, right you are again, sir! Never been to London town, nor Baxter."

"Come, come; to the point. You have traveled this distance to see me upon some matter of urgency."

"Yes, sir. It's the matter of young Gregory. A farm hand he was, sir, a strapping lad, over six feet and still lacking 'is full height. A-haying he was. A tragic accident t'was, sir, tragic."

Holmes of course noticed the use of the past tense, and his eyes brightened. "An accident, you say? Not murder?"

"Yes."

Holmes was puzzled. "Then, pray, why have you come to me?"

" 'Is body, sir. We've come about 'is body."

"What about it?"

"Why, it's gone, sir. Right vanished away."

"Ah." Holmes leaned forward in his chair, his eyes gleaming with sudden interest. "Pray, tell me all about it, and spare none of the details."

The story they told was long and involved many diversions into details of life as a hired hand at Sherringford Farm, the narration so roundabout that even Holmes's patience was tried, but the essence of the story was simple. Baxter and young Gregory had been working in the fields when Gregory had been impaled by the blade of the mechanical haying engine. "And cursed be the day that the master ever decided to buy such an infernal device," added the older man, who was the uncle and only relation of the poor Gregory. Disentangled from the machine, the young farmhand had been still alive, but very clearly dying. His abdomen had been ripped open and his viscera exposed. Baxter had laid the dying man in the shade of a hayrick, and gone to fetch help. Help had taken two hours to arrive, and when they had come, they had found the puddle of congealing blood, but no sign of Gregory. They had searched all about, but the corpse was nowhere to be found, nor was there any sign of how he had been carried away. There was no chance, Baxter insisted, that Gregory could have walked even a small distance on his own. "Not unless he dragged 'is guts after him. I've seen dying men, guv, and men what 'ave been mere wounded, and young Gregory was for it."

"This case may have some elements of interest in it," said Holmes. "Pray, leave me to cogitate upon the matter tonight. Watson, hand me the train schedule, would you? Thank you. Ah, it is as I thought. There is a 9 AM train from Waterloo." He turned to the two men. "If you would be so good as to meet me on the morrow at the platform?"

"Aye, sir, that we could."

"Then it is settled. Watson, I do believe you have a prior engagement?"

That I did, as I was making plans for my upcoming marriage, and had already made firm commitment in the morning to inspect a practice in the Paddington district with a view toward purchasing it. Much as I have enjoyed accompanying my friend upon his adventures, this was one which I should have to forego.

Holmes returned late from Surrey, and I did not see him until breakfast the next morning. As often he was when on a case, he was rather uncommunicative, and my attempts to probe the matter were met with monosyllables, except at the very last. "Most unusual," he said, as if to himself. "Most singular indeed."

"What?" I asked, eager to listen now that it appeared that Holmes was ready to break his silence.

"The tracks, Watson," he said. "The tracks. Not man, nor beast, but definitely tracks." He looked at his pocket-watch. "Well, I must be off. Time enough for cogitation when I have more facts."

"But where are you going?"

Holmes laughed. "My dear Watson, I have in my time amassed a bit of knowledge of various matters which would be considered most *recherché* to laymen. But I fear that, upon occasion, even I must consult with an expert."

"Then whom?"

"Why, I go to see Professor Huxley," he answered, and was out the door before I could ask what query he might have for the eminent biologist.

He was absent from Baker Street all afternoon. When he returned after suppertime I was anxious to ask how his interview with the esteemed professor had gone.

"Ah, Watson, even I make my occasional mistake. I should have telegraphed first. As it was, Professor Huxley had just left London, and is not to return for a week." He took out his pipe, inspected it for a moment, then set it aside and rang for Mrs. Hudson to bring in some supper. "But in this case, my journey was not in vain. I had a most delightful discussion with the professor's protégé, a Mr. Wells by name. A Cockney lad, son of a shop-keeper and no more than twenty-two, unless I miss my guess, but a most remarkable man nonetheless. Interested in a wide variety of fields, and I venture to say that in whatever field he chooses, he will outshine even his esteemed teacher. Quite an interesting conversation we had, and a most useful one."

"But what was it that you discussed?" I asked.

Holmes set aside the cold beef that Mrs. Hudson had brought, leaned back in his chair, and shut his eyes. For a while I thought that he had gone to sleep without hearing my question. At last he spoke. "Why, we discussed the planet Mars," he said, without opening his eyes. "And the singular habits of wasps."

It seemed that his researches, whatever they were, led to no distinct conclusion, for when I asked him about the case the next day, he gave no response. That day he stayed in his chambers, and through the closed door I heard only the intermittent voice of his violin speaking in its melancholy, unfathomable tongue.

I have perhaps mentioned before that my friend would habitually have more than one case on which he worked at any one time. It appeared that over the next few evenings he was about on another one, for I found him dressing to go out at a late hour.

"Another case, Holmes?" I asked.

"As you can see, Watson," he replied. He indicated his less-than-respectable outfit and the threadbare workman's jacket he was pulling on over it. "Duty calls at all hours. I shan't be more than a few hours, I expect."

"I am ready to assist."

"Not in this one, my dear friend. You may stay home tonight."

"Is there danger?"

"Danger?" He seemed surprised, as if the thought hadn't occurred to him. "Danger? Oh, perhaps a slight bit."

"You know that I would not hesitate…"

"My dear doctor," he said, and smiled. "Let me assure you that I am not worried on that score. No, it is that I go to the East End…"

The East End of London was no place for gentlemen, with slaughterhouses and tenements of the lowest order; a place for drunkards, sailors, Chinese and Indian laborers, and ruffians of all sorts. Nevertheless I was quite willing to brave much worse, if necessary, for the sake of Holmes. "Is that all?" I said. "Holmes, I do believe you underestimate me!"

"Ah, Watson…" He seemed to reflect for a moment. "No, it would not do. You are soon to be married, and have your wife-to-be to think of." He raised a hand to forestall my imminent objection. "No, not the danger, my friend. Don't worry for me on that score. I have my resources. It is… how to put it delicately? I expect that I shall meet people in places where a gentleman soon to be married would best not be seen."

"Holmes!"

"Business, my dear Watson. Business." And with that, he left.

His business there did not seem to be concluded that evening or the next. By the end of August he was visiting the East End once or twice a week. I had already become used to his odd hours and strange habits, and soon thought nothing of it. But he was so habitual about it, and so secretive, that it soon caused me to wonder whether perhaps he might be calling upon a woman. I could think of nothing that seemed less like Holmes, for in all my time with him he had never expressed a trace of romantic interest in the fairer sex. And yet, from my own medical experience, I knew that even the most steadfast of men must experience those urges common to our gender, however much he might profess to disdain romance.

Romance? Though I myself never frequented such places, as an Army man I knew quite as well as Holmes what sort of women dwelt in Whitechapel, and what profession they practiced. Indeed, he had admitted as much when he had warned me away "because I was to be married." But then, a woman of such type could well appeal to Holmes. There would be nothing of romance involved. It would be merely a business proposition for her, and a release of pressure for him. A dozen times I resolved to warn him of the dangers—the danger of disease, if nothing else—in patronizing women of that sort, and so many times my nerve failed and I said nothing.

And, if it were not what I feared, what case could it be that would take him into Whitechapel with such frequency?

One evening shortly after Holmes had left, a message boy delivered a small package addressed to him. The address proclaimed it to be from a John B. Coores and Sons, but gave no clue to its contents. This name seemed to me familiar, but, struggle as I might, I could not recall where I might have seen it before. I left it in the sitting room for Holmes, and the next morning saw that he had taken it. He made no mention of the package or of what it contained, however, and my curiosity over it remained unslaked.

But another event soon removed that curiosity from my mind. The newspaper that morning carried a report of a brutal murder on Buck's Row in Whitechapel. The body of an unidentified woman had been found on the street, and, what was even more grotesque, after her death her body had been brutally sliced open. I read the paper to Holmes as he sat drinking coffee in the morning. As far as I could tell, he had not slept the previous night, although he seemed little the worse for it. He made no comment on the article. It occurred to me that for all its gruesome features, this was the sort of commonplace murder he would have no interest in, since it seemed quite lacking in the singular points that so interested him. I made a comment to him to that effect.

"Not so, Watson," he said, without looking up. "I am quite interested to hear what the press has to say about the Nichols tragedy."

This comment startled me considerably, since the paper had given no name to the victim. I suddenly remembered that East London was exactly where Holmes was going for all these evenings, perhaps to the very place the murder had occurred.

"My God, Holmes! Did you know her?"

At this he looked up, and gave me a long, piercing stare. After a long while he looked away and gave a short laugh. "I do have my secrets, Watson. Pray, inquire no further."

But to me his laughter sounded forced.

It was a week before I saw Holmes prepare for another of his nocturnal sojourns. After napping all afternoon, Holmes was again dressing in faded and tattered clothing. This time I did not ask, but silently dressed to follow.

When he put on his ear-flapped travelling-cap, I was ready as well. I quietly walked to his side, clutching my old service revolver in the pocket of my coat. He looked at me with an expression of utmost horror and put up a hand. "My God, Watson! If you value your life and your honour, don't follow me!"

"Just tell me this, then," I said. "Are you doing something... dishonourable?"

"I am doing what I must." And he was out the door and gone in the time it took me to realize that he had in no way answered my question.

As I prepared for bed that night, wondering where Holmes had gone and what he was doing there, it suddenly occurred to me where I had seen the name John B. Coores and Sons before. I crossed the room, thrust open the cabinet where I kept medical supplies, and drew out a small wooden box. There it was. I had looked at the name a thousand times without really seeing it, neatly lettered on the side of the box: John B. Coores and Sons, Fine Surgical Instruments. But what could Holmes want with surgical tools?

And in the next evening's paper, I saw with horror that there had been another murder. The Whitechapel killer had struck again, and once more he had not contented himself with merely killing the woman. Using a surgical knife and a knowledge of anatomy, he had dissected the body and removed several organs.

That Sunday I took my beloved Mary to the theatre. My thoughts were dark, but I endeavoured to allow none of my turmoil to be communicated to her, hoping instead that her sweet presence might distract me from my dire speculations. Events plotted against me, however, for playing at the Lyceum was a most disturbing play, *The Strange Case of Dr. Jekyll and Mr. Hyde*. I watched the play with my mind awhirl, scarcely noticing the presence of my beloved at my side.

After the play I pleaded sudden ill health and fled home. Seeing my ashen face, Mary heartily agreed that I should go home to rest, and it was all I could do to dissuade her from accompanying me back to serve as nurse.

The play had been presented as fiction, but it had hit a note of purest truth. That a single man could have two personalities! Stevenson had been circumspect about naming the drug that would so polarize a man's psyche as to split his being into two parts, but with my medical knowledge I could easily fill in the name, and it was a drug I had intimate knowledge of. Yes. A man could suppress his animal instincts, could make himself into a pure reasoning machine, but the low urges would not wither away, oh no. They would still be there, lurking inside, awaiting a chance to break loose.

I had thought that either Holmes was stalking the Whitechapel killer, or else that Holmes was the killer. Now I suddenly realized that there was yet another alternative: Holmes the detective could be stalking the Whitechapel killer, completely unaware that he himself was the very criminal he sought.

It was a week before he went out again. The following day I scanned the newspapers in an agony of suspense, but there was no murder reported. Perhaps I was overwrought and imagining things? But Holmes seemed haunted by something, or perhaps hunted. There was something on his mind. When I invited him to confide in me, he looked at me for a long time and then slowly shook his head. "I dare not, Watson." He was silent for a while, and then said, "Watson, if I should suddenly die—"

At this I could take no more. "My God, Holmes, what is it? Surely you can tell me something!"

"This is important, Watson. If I should die... burn my corpse. Promise me that."

"Holmes!"

He gripped my shoulder and looked intently into my eye. "Promise me, on your honour."

"I promise."

"On your honour, Watson!"

"On my honour, I promise."

He suddenly relaxed, almost collapsing into his chair. "Thank you."

That night again he went out, and again the next. His face was drawn, as if he were desperately seeking something he had been unable to find on the previous night. Both evenings he seemed upon the brink of saying something to me, only to think better of it at the last moment, and vanish without a word into the London night.

The next evening's papers told of not one, but two murders in the East end. The Whitechapel killer—now dubbed "Jack the Ripper" by all the papers—had worked double duty. And this time a witness had given a description of the suspected killer: a tall man in a dark cutaway overcoat, wearing a felt deerstalker hat.

I confronted Holmes with the papers and my suspicions. I had hoped, more than I hope for paradise, that he would dismiss my deductions with his soft, mocking laugh, and show me some utterly commonplace alternative explanation of the facts. My hopes were in vain. He listened to my words with his eyes nearly shut, his briar pipe clenched unlit between his teeth. Finally my words ground to a stop against his stony silence. "My God, Holmes, tell me I'm wrong! Tell me that you had nothing to do with those murders, I beg of you."

"I can say nothing, my friend."

"Then give me some reason, some shred of sanity."

He was silent. Finally he said, "Do you intend to go to the police with your suspicions?"

"Do you want me to?" I asked him.

"No." His eyes closed for a moment, and then he continued, "But it doesn't matter. They would not believe you in any case." His voice was weary, but calm. His manner did not seem that of a madman, but I know that madmen can be fiendishly clever in concealing their madness from those about them. "Are you aware of how many letters and telegrams have flooded Scotland Yard in these last few weeks? The Yard is a madhouse, Watson. Landladies and madmen, people claiming to have seen the Ripper, to know the Ripper, to *be* the Ripper. They receive a thousand letters a week, Watson. Your voice would be lost in the madness." He shook his head. "They have no idea, Watson. They cannot begin to comprehend. The Whitechapel horror, they call it. If the true horror of it were known, they would flee the city; they would scream and run in terror."

Despite everything, I should have gone to the police, or at least have confided my suspicions to someone else and asked for counsel. But I knew of no one in whom to confide such an awful suspicion, least of all my Mary, who trusted Holmes nearly as a god and would hear no ill of him. And, despite all, in my heart of hearts I still believed that I must have read the evidence awry, that Holmes could not truly be a culprit of such infamy.

The next day, Holmes made no reference to our conversation. It seemed so strange that I thought to wonder if it had actually occurred, or if I had dreamed the entire thing. I determined that, without giving any outward sign of it to Holmes, I should keep my eyes sharp on him like a hawk. The next time that I saw him making preparations to leave on a nocturnal sojourn, I would follow him, whether he wanted it or no.

Holmes made several trips to Whitechapel during the daytime, and gave no objection when I asked to accompany him. It was no place for decent humans to live. The streets were littered with the filth of horses, pigs, chickens and humans, and the air clamorous with the clatter of delivery wagons and trains, the carousal of children and drunkards, and the cackling of chickens and bawling of pigs which lived side-by-side with people in the basements and doss-houses. Above us, hanging from every window, ragged wash turned dingy grey as it dried in pestilence-ridden air.

During these trips he did little other than inspect the streets and look over the blank, white-washed brick walls of warehouses and blind alleys. On occasion he would stop for a brief chat over inconsequential matters with a charwoman or a policeman he might meet walking the narrow alleyways. Contrary to his nature, he made no attempt to visit the scenes of the crimes. To me this last fact was the most damning to my suspicions. Unless he were involved in some way, surely there would have been no possibility that anything could have kept him away.

But it was all of October and a week into November before he again left upon one of his evening peregrinations. But for an accident of chance, I would have missed it entirely. I had laid out several traps for him, so as to awaken me if he tried to leave in the night, and sat wakeful in the evenings until long after I had heard him retire. One night in early November, after retiring without incident, I was unexpectedly awakened in the middle of the night by some noise. The night was foggy, and through my window I could hear only the most muffled sounds of the street, as if, from a tremendous distance, the clopping of a lone set of hooves and the call of a man hailing a hansom. For some reason I was unable to get back to sleep, and so I put on my dressing-gown and descended to the sitting room to take a finger of whisky.

Holmes was gone. His door was ajar, but the bed was empty.

I was determined to know the truth, whatever it might be, and thus in one way or another to bring this adventure to an end. I dressed hurriedly, thrust my service revolver into a pocket of my overcoat, and ran out into the night. At that hour, well after midnight, I had only the most remote hope of finding a cab anywhere near our Baker Street diggings. Sometime during the day Holmes must have surreptitiously arranged for the cab to meet him that night. As I had made no such arrangements, he had quite the head start on me. It was the better part of an hour before I made my way past Aldgate pump and entered the East End slums.

I had suspected that in the wake of the killings the streets of Whitechapel would be deserted, the public houses closed and the citizens suspicious of any strangers. But even at this late hour the streets were far from deserted. It was a busy, populous area. Wandering aimlessly on the streets, I found many open pubs, most all crowded with unemployed workmen and idle women of dubious repute. Everywhere I walked I found that I was not more than a hundred yards from a citizen's patrol or a watchful, armed constable—several of whom watched me with an intent, suspicious gaze. Even the women on the streetcorners, wearing shawls and bonnets to ward against the wet November night, stood in groups of two and three.

Holmes I could find nowhere, and it occurred to me belatedly that if he were in one of his disguises, he could be any of the people about me—one of the unemployed mechanics gambling in the front room of the Boar and Bristle, the aged clergyman hustling down Commercial Street toward some unknown destination, the sailor chatting up the serving girls at the King's Arms. Any of these could be Holmes.

Any of these could be the Ripper.

All around me there were women, in the pubs, in the doorways, walking the streets; pathetic women dressed in cheap finery, with tired smiles and the flash of a stockinged ankle for any passers-by wearing trousers—"you lonely, love?"—or with saucy greetings and friendly abuse for the other women.

I realized that the size of Whitechapel that showed on the map was deceptive. In the fog and the darkness the streets were far more narrow, the shops smaller, and the whole larger and more cluttered than I recalled from the daytime. Even if there were a hundred constables patrolling the streets it would not be enough. The blind alleys, the sparse gas lights, and the drifting banks of fog made the streets a maze in which the Ripper might kill with impunity within a few yards of a hundred or more people.

Twice I thought I caught a glimpse of Holmes, but, when I ran after him, found that I had been deceived. Every drunkard sleeping in a doorway seemed to be a fresh corpse, every anonymous stain on the cobblestones looked like blood, every wandering alley-cat seemed the shadow of a lurking killer. Several times I contemplated giving up my hopeless errand and going home, managing to keep on only by promising myself that I would stay on for just one hour more.

In the dark hour before sunrise I found him.

I had come into a pub to warm myself for a while. The barman was surly and uncommunicative, evincing a clear suspicion of my motives that, while perhaps well enough justified by recent events, nevertheless made the atmosphere inside scarcely less chill than that of the night outside. The beer was cheap and thoroughly watered. At first a few of the women had come by to pass time with me, but I found them pathetic rather than alluring, and after a bit they left me in solitude.

After an hour or so of this, I went out into the night air to clear my head of the smoke and stink. A light rain had cleared most of the fog away. I walked at random down the streets and up alleyways, paying no attention to where I headed.

After walking for some time, I was disoriented, and stopped to get my bearings. I had no idea where I was. I turned a corner and looked down into an unmarked court, hoping to descry a street sign, but had no luck. In the darkness I saw something ahead of me; a pair of legs protruding from the arch of an entranceway. I walked forward, my blood chill. It was the body of a woman laid on the cobblestones, skirts awry, half concealed in a doorway. I had seen a dozen such in the last few hours, drunkards too poor to afford a bed, but in the instant of vision a dread presentiment came to me that this one was not merely drunk and asleep. The darkness beneath her body looked darker and more liquid than any mere shadow. I knelt down, and touched her wrist to take a pulse.

Her eyes flew open. It took a moment for her to focus on me. Suddenly she shrieked and stumbled to her feet. "Lord have mercy! The Ripper!" she said in a hoarse whisper. She tripped over her petticoats in a clumsy effort to stand and run at the same time, and fell to her knees.

"My pardons, Miss," I said. "Are you all right?" Without thinking, I reached down a hand to help her up.

"Murder!" she shrieked, scrambling away on all fours like an animal. "Oh! Murder!"

"Madam, please!" I backed away into the alley behind me. It was evident that nothing I could do would calm her. She continued to yell as she clattered away, darting frightened glances back at me over her shoulder. The courtyard I was in was dark and silent, but I was afraid that her cries would wake others. I stepped backwards into a doorway, and suddenly found the door behind me yield to the pressure. It had not been latched. Off balance, I half-fell backwards into the room.

The room was thick with the cloying, coppery odor of blood. The hand I had put down to steady myself came up slick with it. By the wan light of the fire in the grate across the room I could see the bed, and the dark, twisted shape on it, and I had no need to look more closely to know what it was.

The body of the woman on the bed had been so badly mutilated that it was hardly recognizable as human. Blood was everywhere. In a daze I reached out a hand to feel for a pulse.

Her hand was already cool.

Her skirt had been removed, her petticoats cut away, and her body neatly opened from pubes to sternum by some expert dissector.

I was too late. I gave a low moan. Somewhere before me I heard a low, steady dripping. I looked up, and stared into the pale face of Sherlock Holmes.

His eyes were weary, but empty of any trace of the horror that I felt. He was standing in the room behind the body, and as my eyes adjusted to the shadow I saw that he held a dissecting knife. His arms were red to the elbows, and gore dripped in a monotonous rhythm from the knife onto the stone floor. At his feet was a worn leather shopkeeper's satchel, half open.

"There is nothing you can do for her, Doctor," said Holmes, and the calm, even voice in which he said this pierced me with chill. It was not the Holmes I knew. I was not sure if he even recognized me. He bent down to snap the satchel shut before I had more than a brief glimpse of the bloody meat within it, then wiped the scalpel on the canvas apron he wore, put it carefully back into the small wooden case, and dropped it into an outside pocket of the bag.

He tugged at his left elbow, and only then did I realize that he wore full-length gloves. He was well prepared for this venture, I thought, my mind in a state of shock. He removed the gloves, tossed them into the fire grate, and pushed at them with a poker. They smoldered for a moment and then caught fire, with the heavy charnel stink of burning blood. Beneath his apron he wore work clothes such as any tradesman might wear.

"My God, Holmes!" I stuttered. "Did you kill her?"

He sighed deeply. "I don't know. Time is short. Please follow me, Watson."

At least he recognized me. That was a good sign. I followed him out of long habit, too numb to do anything else. He closed and locked the door behind him and put the key into his pocket. He led me through a small gate, down a cluttered alley, then quickly through two narrow passageways and into a courtyard behind the slaughterhouses. The key and the apron he discarded there. I saw he had a cab waiting, the horse tethered to an unlit lamppost. There was no cabman in sight. "Take me home, Watson," he said. "You should not have come. But, since you are nevertheless here, I confess myself glad of the chance to unburden myself of the awful things that I have seen and done. Take me home, and I shall conceal nothing from you."

I drove and Holmes sat in back, meditating or sleeping, I could not tell which. We passed three constables, but I did not stop. He bade me halt at a certain mews not far from Baker Street. "The cabman will be here in half an hour," he said, as he tended expertly to the horse. "He has been paid in advance, and we need not wait."

"I believe you must think me most utterly mad, Watson," said Holmes, after he had exchanged his rough clothes for a dressing-gown, meticulously cleansed himself of dirt and spattered blood, fetched the Persian slipper in which he kept his tobacco, and settled back in his chair. "You have not loosened your grip on that service revolver of yours for the last hour. Your fingers must be cramped by now, you have been clutching it so strongly— Ah," he said, as I opened my mouth to deny this, "no use in your protesting your innocence. Your hand has not strayed from the pocket of your robe for an instant, and the distinctive weight of your pistol is quite clearly evident in it. I may be mad, my dear Watson," he said with a smile, "but I am not blind."

This was the Holmes I knew, and I relaxed. I knew I had nothing to fear from him.

His hand hesitated over his rack of pipes, selected his clay-stemmed pipe, and filled it with shag. "Indeed, Watson, at times during these last months I would not have disputed it with you myself. It would have been a relief to know myself mad, and that all I have seen and conjectured to be merely the delusions of a maniac."

He teased a coal out of the grate and lit his pipe with it. "To begin, then, with the missing corpse." He puffed the pipe until its glow matched that of the fire behind him. "Or, perhaps better," he said, "I should begin with the London cannonade." He raised a finger at my imminent objection. "I have promised to tell all, Watson, and I shall. Pray let me go about it in my own way.

"My brother Mycroft," he continued, "made a most interesting comment when I discussed the matter of the cannonade with him. He mentioned that when a highly powered cannon is fired, an observer at the front lines ahead of the artillery and distant from the firing will hear a very distinct report at the instant the shell passes. This is the crack of displaced air. This report comes considerably in advance of the actual sound of the cannon firing. If our ears were but sensitive enough to hear it, he informed me, this report would be heard as two distinct waves, one of the air compressed by the shell, and another of the air rushing inward to fill the vacuum left behind it. An aeroship which traversed faster than the velocity of sound would produce a like crack, and, if it were large enough, the two waves would be heard as distinct reports.

"My brother discussed this only as an abstract but interesting fact, but I know him well enough to understand the meaning behind his words.

"Taking this as a provisional theory, then, and judging by the fact that observers noted the timing between the two reports was briefer in the north than in the south of London, we find that the hypothetical aeroship must have been slowing down as it traveled south."

"But Holmes," I said, my mind in total consternation, "an aeroship? And one which moves faster than an artillery shell? No nation on God's Earth could make such a thing, not to mention the impossibility of keeping it secret."

"Precisely," said Holmes. He took another puff from his pipe. "This brings us to the case of the missing corpse. I had been looking for a reason to investigate south of London, and the case presented by the two farm-hands was quite fortuitous in that respect.

"You know my method, Watson. It was unfortunate that the men in the original searching party had in many places quite trampled the tracks that I needed, but in the few places where they could be clearly distinguished, the tracks told a most puzzling story. Some animals had circled the hayrick, leaving tracks like nothing I had ever seen. I could make nothing of the footprints, save that one side was dragging slightly, as if one of the animals were limping. From the depth of the impressions they must have been the size of small dogs. What was most peculiar about the set of tracks was that the animals seemed to march in precision step. The strange thought occurred to me then, that the tracks of a single animal with eight or more legs might leave exactly such impressions. The steps led to the place where the dying man had lain, and circled about. Of outgoing tracks, there were only those of the men who had tended him and those of the searchers.

"I attempted to follow the tracks backward, but could follow back no more than a mile to where they emerged from a sheep meadow and were obliterated by the hoofprints of innumerable sheep. All that I could determine from this was that the animals had been severely panicked at some time in the last few days, running over and around each other and back and forth across the field.

"I turned my attention back to the impressions made by the dying man, and the tracks of the men away from the spot. I inspected the tracks of the unusual animal further. They were extremely strange, and in some ways rather insect-like. The animal's tracks overlaid two of the other tracks, which I knew to be those of the men who had summoned me. Over these tracks, however, were those of a third man.

"I quickly determined these tracks to be those of the dying man himself. After the other two men had left, he had risen up and walked away, apparently carrying the strange animal with him."

"My God, Holmes," I interjected. The revolver lay forgotten in my pocket. "You can't be serious. Are you suggesting some sort of voodoo?"

Holmes smiled. "No, Watson, I am afraid that it was something far more serious than mere superstition.

"The man had crawled on all fours for a few feet, then stood up and walked in a staggering, unbalanced stride. After a few unsteady moments, however, he found his feet and began to walk quickly and purposefully in a straight line. Soon he came to a hard-packed road, where his traces were obliterated by the traffic and I could track his movements no further. His aim, though was quite clearly toward London, and this I took to be his goal."

Listening to his narrative I had completely forgotten the events of the previous night, the slain streetwalkers, and my suspicion of Holmes.

"At this point," Holmes continued, "I knew that I needed to consult an expert. Mr. Wells, of whom I spoke earlier, was that expert, and I could not have asked for a better source. We discussed the possibility of life on other worlds. Mr. Wells offered the opinion that, since there are millions upon millions of suns very much like our own Sun in the sky, that certainly there must be other intelligences, and other civilisations, some of which must be as far beyond ours as our English civilisation is beyond that of the African savage."

"Then you take this strange aeroship to be a vehicle from another world?" I asked. While I had heard such ideas discussed in popular lectures on astronomy, I had, heretofore, always dismissed these as purest fancy.

"A provisional hypothesis, to be confirmed or forgotten as further data became available. I went on to ask Mr. Wells whether such citizens of other worlds might be human in shape and thought. At this suggestion he was most frankly contemptuous. Such beings would have no more reason to be shaped in our form, he said, than we in that of an octopus or an ant. Likewise they might take no more notice of our civilisation and our morality than we take of the endeavors and ethics of an ant hill.

"This I had already surmised. I turned the talk to biology, and without tipping my hand, managed to steer the conversation to the unusual life-cycles of other species. One in particular he mentioned struck my attention, the life-cycle of the ichneumon, or solitary wasp."

"Really, Holmes. Wasps? I do believe that you are toying with me."

"I wish that I were, my dear doctor. Pray listen; all of this is germane to the subject at hand. The ichneumon wasp has a rather gruesome life-cycle. When the female wasp is ready to lay eggs, it finds and stings a cicada, often one much larger than itself, and then deposits its egg inside the body of the paralyzed but still living insect. This insect then serves as sustenance for the hatching larva, which forms its home within the living insect, having the instinct to avoid eating the essential organs until the very last, when it is ready to exit into the world to lay eggs of its own.

"This was enough for me to frame my provisional hypothesis. I believed that some strange being from the aeroship had not merely met the fatally injured man, but crawled inside his body and taken control of his gross physical function.

"I was struck by one fact. Of all the people that this... alien... might have met, it was a dying man who he— it— actually chose. Clearly, then, the... thing... believed itself unable to subdue an uninjured person."

"I must confess, Holmes, if I were asked to prove your sanity, this story would hardly bolster your case."

"Ah, Watson, always the practical man. Permit me." He got out of the leather chair, crossed the room to where he had put down the leather satchel, and laid it on the table in front of me.

I sat paralyzed. "I dare not, Holmes."

"Your courage has never failed you before, my friend."

With a shudder I touched the satchel, and then, steeling myself, opened it. Inside was some object covered in streaks of gore. I didn't want to look, but knew that I must.

The two eggs inside were of a translucent purplish white, large as a moderate-sized mango, and slick with a film of blood. Within each one a monstrous coiled shape could be discerned. No Earthly animal ever laid such an egg, of this I was sure. More horrible than the eggs was the other thing. I shuddered and looked away. It was something like a giant prawn, and something like some jungle millipede, with dozens of long barbed feelers and multiply-jointed appendages bristling with hooks and spines. Its head, or what passed for a head, had been nearly severed with a knife, and the wound exuded a transparent fluid rather like whale-oil, with a sharp and unpleasant odor similar to kerosene. Instead of a mouth, it had a sucking orifice rimmed with myriad tiny hooked teeth.

"This is what I removed from her body," Holmes said.

I looked up at him. "My God," I whispered. "And she was not dead?"

"You asked that question before. It is a question of definitions, Watson. All that was left alive in her body was the thing that you see. By removing it, did I kill her?"

I shuddered again, and slammed the satchel shut with my eyes averted. "No." I stood for a moment, trying to regain my composure. "But why Whitechapel?"

"What you saw was a juvenile," said Holmes. "The adult would be much larger. I would not know if it is intelligent, or what we call intelligent, but it is at least very clever. Why Whitechapel? Think, Watson. It had eggs and juveniles it must deposit into a living body. But how is it to approach a complete stranger, embrace him— or her— closely enough to? Ah, you see the picture. It was the perfect place for the thing, Watson; the only place where it could do what it needed.

"I studied the East End in minute detail, tracing the path of the mysterious stranger. Again and again I was too late, sometimes only by minutes. I removed the juveniles from the corpses out of necessity. I say corpses, Watson, for although they still walked upright they were already dead. Had I not killed them, they would have gone to cover until they were mature. I could find the one, I knew, only by concentrating on the one trail. Even then it would be a near thing. Two of them, and I were lost."

"Why didn't you go to the police?"

"And tell them what? To start a man-hunt for a thing they can only find by ripping open bodies?"

"But the letters? The ones from 'Jack the Ripper'—did you write these?"

Holmes laughed. "Why should I need to?" he said. "Fakes, forgeries, and cranks, every one. Even I am continuously amazed at how many odd people there are in London. I daresay they came from newspapers hungry to manufacture news, or from pranksters eager at a chance to make fools of Scotland Yard."

"But, what do we do?"

"We, Watson?" Holmes raised an eyebrow.

"Surely you wouldn't think that, now that I know the danger, I would let you continue alone."

"Ah, my good Watson, I would be lost without you. Well, I am hot on its trail. It cannot elude me much longer. We must find it and kill it, Watson. Before it kills again."

By the next morning the whole episode seemed a nightmare, too fantastical to credit. I wondered how I could have believed it. And yet, I had seen it— or had I? Could I have deluded myself into seeing what Holmes had wanted me to see?

No. It was real. I could not afford to doubt my own sanity, and hence I must believe in Holmes'.

In the next few days Holmes went back to his daytime reconnaissance of the East End, mapping the way buildings abutted and how doorways aligned with alleys, like a general planning his campaign, stopping for conversation with workmen and constables alike.

On the third day, my business in town kept me late into the evening. At the end of it, it was almost certain that I had purchased a practice, and at a price which I could afford, but the sealing of the deal required an obligatory toast, and then there were more papers to be inspected and signed, so that all in all, it was well past ten in the evening when I returned to Baker Street.

Of Holmes there was only a note: "I have gone to see the matter to its conclusion. It is better that you are out of it, and I shall think no less of you if you stay. But if you must follow, then look for me near the blind court at Thrawl Street." I read it and swore. He seemed determined to leave me out of this adventure, no matter how dangerous it was for him alone. I snatched my greatcoat and hat from the hall stand, fetched my revolver out from the drawer where it resided, and went out into the night.

It was the night of the great carboniferous fog. The gas-lights were pale yellow glimmers that barely pierced the roiling brown stink. The cab I hailed almost ran me down before seeing me in the street in front of him.

The fog in Whitechapel was even thicker and yellower than that of Baker Street. The cab left me off in front of the Queen's Head pub, the cabbie warning me of the danger of the neighborhood. The blind court was one which was being resurfaced by the MacAdam method, in which the street was covered with liquid tar, and a layer of gravel rolled into the tar surface. The process results in a surface which is even and far easier to repair than cobblestone. I can see the day when all of London will have such smooth, quiet streets.

Earlier Holmes had talked with some of the workmen as they rolled the gravel. Now they were long gone. The half-full cauldron of tar was still at the corner of the alley. Although the oil-pot which heated it to boiling had been removed, the cooling drum of tar still gave out quite a bit of heat.

Three unfortunate women had lit a small fire out of wood-scraps and huddled between the warm cauldron and their fire, with their hands toward the tiny fire and their backs against the cauldron for warmth. The glow of the fire gave a luminous orange cast to the surrounding fog. A tiny pile of additional wood scraps stood waiting to keep the fire going for the rest of the night.

Holmes was nowhere in sight.

The women spotted me looking at them, and whispered amongst themselves. One came up to me and attempted a smile. "Care to spend some money and buy a poor unfortunate a drink, dearie?" She tossed her head toward the end of the street where the pub was invisible in the fog, and at the same time flicked her skirt in such a way as to allow me a clear view of her bare ankle.

I averted my eyes. "I'm looking for a friend."

"I could be a friend, if you wanted me to."

"No. I don't need... that sort of comfort."

"Oh, sure you do, dearie." She giggled. "All men do. 'Sides, I h'aint even got money for me doss. Surely a fine gent like yourself has a shilling to spend on a poor lady down on 'er luck, hasn't he? Sure 'e does."

I looked at her more closely, and she preened for my inspection. She might have been a rather pretty woman, striking if not actually beautiful, if she had been given the chance. Instead I saw the lines on her face, the threadbare bonnet she wore, and the unmistakable signs of the early stages of consumption. Such a woman should be resting in bed, not out standing in the chill of a night such as this. I was about to speak to her, to invite her into the public house for the drink she requested, for no other reason than to get her out of the chill and away, perhaps, from the monster that stalked the fog-shrouded night. I could wait for Holmes as well in the pub as in the street.

As I was about to speak, I heard a man approach from the blind end of the court, although I had seen no one there previously. I started to call out, thinking it must be Holmes, but then saw that, while the man was quite as tall as Holmes, he was much bulkier, with a considerable paunch and ill-fitting clothes. As he passed, another of the women smiled at him and called a greeting. He nodded at her. As she put out her arm for him to take, he dropped his hand to the buttons of his trousers. I looked away in disgust, and as I did so the woman who had spoken to me slipped her arm around mine.

I had lost track of the third woman, and was as surprised as the others when her voice rang out from behind. "Stop, fiend!"

The voice was calm and authoritative. I looked up. The woman was holding a revolver—Holmes' hair-trigger revolver—in an unwavering grip aimed at the man's head. I looked closely at her face and saw, beneath the makeup, the thin, hawk-like nose and the unmistakable intense gaze of Sherlock Holmes.

The other man swiveled with surprising speed and sprang at Holmes. I pulled my hand loose from my lady companion and in an instant snatched my revolver free of my pocket and fired. Our two shots rang out at almost the same instant, and the man staggered and fell back. The two bullets had both hit above the left eye, and taken away the left half of the cranium.

The women screamed.

The man, with half his head missing, reached out a hand and pulled himself to his feet. He came at Holmes again.

I fired. This time my bullet removed what was left of his head. His jutting windpipe sucked at the air with a low sputtering hiss, and in the gaping neck I thought I saw purplish-white tendrils feeling about. The shot slowed him down for no more than an instant.

Holmes' shot took him in the middle of the chest. I saw the crimson spot appear and saw him rock from the impact, but it seemed to have no other effect.

We both fired together, this time lower, aiming for the horror hidden somewhere within the body. The two shots spun the headless thing around. He careened against the cauldron of tar, slipped, and fell down, knocking the cauldron over.

In an instant Holmes was upon him.

"Holmes, no!"

For a moment Holmes had the advantage. He pushed the monster forward, into the spreading pool of tar, struggling for a hold. Then the monster rose, dripping tar, and threw Holmes off his back with no more concern than a horse tossing a wayward circus monkey. The monster turned for him.

Holmes reached behind him and grabbed a brand out of the fire. As the monster grabbed him he thrust it forward, into the thing's chest.

The tar ignited with an awful whoosh. The thing clawed at its chest with both hands. Holmes grabbed the cauldron, and with one mighty heave poured the remainder of the tar onto the gaping wound where its head had once been.

Holmes drew back as the flames licked skyward. The thing reeled and staggered in a horrible parody of drunkenness. As the clothes burned away, we could see that where a man's generative organs would have been was a pulsing, wickedly barbed ovipositor with a knife-sharp end writhing blindly in the flames. As we watched it bulged and contracted, and an egg, slick and purple, oozed forth.

The monster tottered, fell over on its back, and then, slowly, the abdomen split open.

"Quickly, Watson! Here!"

Holmes shoved one of the pieces of firewood into my hands, and took another himself. We stationed ourselves at either side of the body.

The horrors which emerged were somewhat like enormous lobsters, or some vermin even more loathsome and articulated. We bludgeoned them as they emerged from the burning body, trying as we could to avoid the oily slime of them from splattering onto our clothes, trying to avoid breathing the awful stench that arose from the smoking carcass. They were tenacious in the extreme, and I think that only the disorientation of the fire and the suddenness of our attack saved our lives. In the end six of the monstrosities crawled out of the body, and six of the monstrosities we killed.

There was nothing remotely human left in the empty shell that had once been a man. Holmes pulled away his skirts and petticoat to feed the fire. The greasy blood of the monstrosities burned with a clear, hot flame, until all that remained were smoldering rags with a few pieces of unidentifiable meat and charred scraps of bone.

It seemed impossible that our shots and the sounds of our struggle had not brought a hundred citizens with constables out to see what had happened, but the narrow streets so distorted the sounds that it was impossible to tell where they had originated, and the thick blanket of fog muffled everything as well as hiding us from curious eyes.

Holmes and I left the two daughters of joy with what money we had, save for the price of a ride back to Baker Street. This we did, not with an eye toward their silence, as we knew that they would never go to the police with their story, but in the hopes—perhaps foolish—that they might have a respite from their hard trade and a warm roof over their heads during the damp and chill months of winter.

It has been two months now, and the Whitechapel killings have not resumed. Holmes is, as always, calm and unflappable, but I find myself unable to look at a wasp now without having a feeling of horror steal across me.

There are as many questions unanswered as answered. Holmes has offered the opinion that the landing was unintentional, a result of some unimaginable accident in the depths of space, and not the vanguard of some impending colonization. He bases this conclusion on the fact of the ill-preparedness and hasty improvisation of the being, relying on luck and circumstance rather than planning.

I think that the answers to most of our questions will never be known, but I believe that we have succeeded in stopping the horrors, this time. I can only hope that this was an isolated ship, blown off-course and stranded far from the expected shores in some unexpected tempest of infinite space. I look at the stars now, and shudder. What else might be out there, waiting for us?

THE AFFAIR OF THE 46TH BIRTHDAY

by Amy Myers

Amy Myers is the author of several crime novels, such as *Tom Wasp and the Murdered Stunner* and *Murder in the Mist*, and the story collection *Murder, 'Orrible Murder!* In addition to her crime fiction, she has also published several historical novels under the name Harriet Hudson. Myers's short fiction has recently appeared in *Ellery Queen Mystery Magazine, Alfred Hitchcock Mystery Magazine*, and *The Mammoth Book of Dickensian Whodunnits*. This story first appeared in the same venue as many of the original Holmes stories—*The Strand Magazine*—which is still publishing, albeit in substantially different form and after a fifty-year hiatus.

Our next story is called "The Affair of the 46th Birthday," so you're probably imagining that this is going to be a tale of celebration and joy. After all, who doesn't like birthdays? You get together with loved ones and sing songs, receive gifts, and eat cake. Well, okay, maybe it's not true that *everyone* loves birthdays. Little children do, for sure, at that age when each successive birthday means you get a little bit taller and a little bit stronger, and get taken a little more seriously. Teenagers and college students are also known to be fond of birthdays, when you can look forward to more rights and freedoms. But after that birthdays quickly lose their luster, and by the time you're forty-five, most people would probably prefer for their next birthday to remain forever on the horizon. If you're someone who's not looking forward to your next birthday, this story may help put things in perspective. They say that getting old is better than the alternative. This is a story about some highly motivated people who would very much like to see our birthday boy experience the alternative. You may be dreading your next birthday, but probably not like this.

It is only recently, with the shocking news of the assassination of the King of Italy, that my good friend Sherlock Holmes has at last permitted me to recount the full story of the late King Humbert's visit to Chartham Beeches on the occasion of his forty-sixth birthday on 14 March 1891. It is not too much to claim that without

Holmes' intervention the friendship of one of our closest allies in Europe might have been lost at a most critical time. Even now, ten years later, with the death of our own Queen so recent, who can tell what troubled waters might lie ahead?

It began, as did so many of our cases, in our old rooms at Baker Street. My wife was away, and I was enjoying a cosy breakfast with Holmes, when the door opened. Behind Mrs Hudson came two gentlemen in a high state of perturbation, the first elderly, clad in formal frock coat and top hat; the second similarly clad, but younger and with a most splendid moustache. I recognised the former immediately: it was Lord Holdhurst, the Foreign Minister in the current administration.

"Lord Holdhurst," Holmes greeted the minister. "We are honoured by your presence—and that of, if I mistake not, His Excellency the ambassador for Italy. The matter must be urgent indeed, as you have arrived together on a Saturday morning. Pray be seated."

"It is indeed His Excellency, Count Panelli," Lord Holdhurst introduced his companion.

"You must pardon us, if you please, Signor Holmes," the ambassador said in a most agitated manner, "for this early and unannounced visit, but haste is indeed essential."

Lord Holdhurst gave a questioning glance in my direction.

"You may speak freely before Dr Watson," Holmes assured him. He remained standing, a sign that his great mind was eager for employment. "How may I help you both?"

"You will no doubt have heard that King Humbert of Italy is in London," Lord Holdhurst said. "Today he celebrates his forty-sixth birthday, and is to honour me with his company at a banquet in his honour to be held at my country residence of Chartham Beeches in Surrey."

The count seemed close to tears in his agitation. "But something most terrible has occurred."

"This morning I received this, Mr Holmes." Lord Holdhurst handed my friend a letter, which Holmes quickly read, then waved it in my direction: "It is in Italian, Watson, but its message is stark. *Blood has been spilled, blood will be seen again today. Viva Sicilia.*"

"You take this seriously, Lord Holdhurst?" he asked. "It is poorly written, on paper purchased from a common store. You must receive many such threats."

"I do, but I cannot afford to ignore it. King Humbert of Savoy, now King of Italy, is always fearful that he might be assassinated. There has, as you must know, been more than one attempt in the past. You must also be aware, Mr Holmes, that not all the former Italian kingdoms relished becoming part of a united Italy. Some of their citizens are still opposed to the rule of the House of Savoy and will stop at nothing to regain what they see as their freedom. It is, however, vital for England that Italy remains united."

"Indeed." Holmes frowned. "I do not yet see a need for my services, however. Those of Scotland Yard and the local police should surely be sufficient to protect His Majesty."

"On the contrary, your presence is essential," Lord Holdhurst declared. "At tonight's banquet the emissaries of certain countries will be present."

"Come, Lord Holdhurst, if time is of the essence, I must deal in facts," Holmes said, his impatience scarcely contained. "You no doubt refer to Germany and Austro-Hungary, Italy's partners in the Triple Alliance, to which Britain is not a signatory. The Alliance guarantees mutual support in the event of instability threatened by France or by the Balkans, although not I believe by Russia."

Lord Holdhurst looked grave. "That is correct, Mr Holmes. It is not generally known, however, that there was another alliance formed shortly afterwards between ourselves and Italy alone with the object of ensuring stability in the Mediterranean. Italy was, and is, anxious to preserve good relations with England, and would not wish to support aggression against us. Our prime minister is therefore determined that this alliance should remain in force. However unless we act speedily it will be severely strained, and perhaps broken forever, a situation in which France would no doubt rejoice."

I saw Holmes' eyes flicker at this statement, engaged as he was in tasks for the French government that winter. "I believe it is Russia, not France, from which any threat would come."

Lord Holdhurst hesitated, but then spoke freely. "You are correct, Mr Holmes. Unfortunately my neighbour Count Litvov, who has close political connections with the Tsar, will be present at the banquet, which makes it imperative that nothing should mar the occasion. Count Panelli and myself, however, believe that behind this threat lies the hand of Giuseppe Rupallo, an anarchist whom we know to be currently in London."

"His Majesty," moaned the count, "is a most superstitious gentleman. He sees his birthday as being of the highest symbolic importance. If an attempt were made on his life today, it would shake his faith in England as an ally."

"King Humbert is a man of the arts, Mr Holmes," Lord Holdhurst explained. "He sees himself as the figurehead of a new Renaissance now that Italy is united. We are therefore presenting the banquet on this theme. The walls of the dining room are hung with Renaissance paintings for the occasion, Her Majesty's gift to His Majesty is an antique fifteenth-century ring and the Prime Minister's an early copy of Shakespeare's sonnets. The menu too consists of delicacies dating from the Renaissance period. Nothing must mar this important occasion. Scotland Yard's Inspector Lestrade is already present with his men, and knows where Rupallo might be found, but the man is too cunning to do the deed himself. Your presence is essential if we are to prevent this anarchist's plan from being put into effect."

"Ah yes." Holmes waved the letter impatiently. "But this threat is surely too crude, too imprecise."

"You believe it the work of a prankster?" the count asked eagerly.

"I fear not. There will most certainly be an attempt to assassinate the King. However, the most interesting fact about this letter is surely obvious."

"Its author," Count Panelli cried. "There is no doubt it is Giuseppe Rupallo."

"Not who, but *why*. Why send such a warning, when surprise must surely be of the essence? Are they searching the house?"

"They are. Most guests arrive this afternoon, but His Majesty comes at eleven o'clock for official talks. My carriage awaits, Mr Holmes." Lord Holdhurst rose to his feet. "Pray let us leave immediately for Surrey."

Although I immediately hurried to seize my revolver, my friend did not move.

"Holmes," I said anxiously, "you must surely take the case?"

I was much relieved when Holmes joined us at the door, albeit I heard a murmured: "But *which* case?"

"One, Mr Holmes," said Lord Holdhurst stiffly, "that might have serious bearing on the future of this country."

Although spring had not yet clad the trees with leaves, the gardens made the entrance to Chartham Beeches an impressive one, although my mind was distracted by the strange nature of the task set for Holmes and myself. I knew the house to be a noble and imposing one, built over a century earlier, and its mellow stone and classical proportions would make a suitably majestic setting for the banquet it was to host. As we passed the lodge, however, I could see alarm in Lord Holdhurst's expression. The gates were open, but there was no sign of the lodgekeeper, although it lacked only a few minutes to eleven o'clock.

"Where is Phelps?" he cried. "And a policeman was to be on duty." He made as if to stop the carriage, but Holmes prevented him.

"Not a moment is to be lost," he shouted. "Drive on, coachman, and pray God we are not too late."

Count Panelli was weeping with tension now, and Lord Holdhurst, whilst naturally not displaying his fear so openly, was white of face.

"One question," Holmes said quickly to him, as the carriage thundered towards the forecourt of the house. "I take it Count Litvov dwells at the large white residence I can see in the distance?"

"He does, and I could wish it were otherwise. He has not long moved to Briar Grange."

Holmes looked grave. "Nevertheless it is Rupallo whom you fear is behind this threat?"

"It is, although Litvov would rejoice were it to succeed."

"Who knows your plans for this banquet?"

"Count Panelli, naturally. My secretary, Mr Michael Anthony, who has organised the banquet itself, the gifts and decorations for this evening, and His Majesty's own secretary, Signor Carlo Mandesi, with whom Mr Anthony liaises and who conveys His Majesty's wishes over the guests."

We fell silent when the house came into sight as we turned the last bend in the drive. Already we could hear the noise of alarm, and then as our carriage came to a halt, the sight of what seemed every policeman in Surrey and Scotland Yard met our eyes. As we had all feared, they were clustered around an impressive carriage.

"His Majesty," cried the count in despair. "What has happened?"

Lord Holdhurst's face was ashen for it was obvious that something was gravely amiss. Holmes leapt down from our carriage, and I after him. I could hear his lordship behind us crying, "Impossible. This is not possible."

Holmes and I hurried to the royal carriage and the group milling around it with cries of alarm. I could see Lestrade there briefly, but all was confusion and no wonder at that. The door of the royal carriage was open and the step in place, but a terrible sight met our eyes.

A body lay half in the carriage, and half tumbling over the step. His Majesty's face was hidden from us, but the blood was not. It was still dripping to the ground, soaking his coat, and I could see it splattered over the interior. I noted that afterwards of course, for my first duty—and Lestrade did not stop me—was to see whether life remained in the body before me. As I knelt at its side, I heard Sherlock Holmes say to Lestrade:

"This is a perplexing business, is it not, Lestrade?"

"A terrible one, but quickly solved," was the reply. "It is the work of the Sicilian anarchist, Giuseppe Rupallo. My task is to return to London, where he has undoubtedly fled after his foul murder of His Majesty. The driver was his accomplice, and must have escaped as we gathered round the carriage."

I lifted the body down to the ground. As I turned it I realised with a heavy heart that there was no sign of life. Then I heard a sharp intake of breath at my side.

"Thank heaven. It is not His Majesty," Lord Holdhurst said to my astonishment. "For a moment I feared our plan had failed—"

"Plan?" Holmes picked up sharply. "What is this, Lestrade?"

"I must apologise," Lord Holdhurst said hurried, before Lestrade could answer. "It did not seem necessary to explain earlier. This is indeed the royal carriage, but this is not His Majesty. He is due to arrive in a plain carriage through another gate to the rear of the grounds."

"Then who," Holmes asked, "is this unfortunate gentleman at our feet?"

"It is His Majesty's secretary, Carlo Mandesi."

"Indeed. A plan, Lord Holdhurst, Count Panelli, that seems to have paid little regard for the safety of a mere secretary."

The count's dark eyes flashed. "It is for the honour of Italy."

"No doubt. Had you consulted me earlier, that honour could have been maintained without the waste of Signor Mandesi's life."

"His Majesty had sworn us to secrecy," Inspector Lestrade explained. "Forgive me, Mr Holmes, but Signor Mandesi was eager to play his part. We had the best advice."

"Obviously not," Holmes said grimly, "and Mr Mandesi's family would no doubt agree with me. Whoever is behind this outrage has clearly made his point. Blood has indeed been seen. However, forgive me, Lord Holdhurst, but would it not be expedient to ensure that His Majesty has indeed arrived safely in your home?"

His lordship's face paled. "But the assassination attempt has failed."

At that moment a young man came running from the house, seeking Lord Holdhurst, and with a look of relief on his face. "His Majesty has arrived, sir," he said. It was only then that he saw the terrible and bloody fate of the secretary.

"Thank you, Mr Anthony," Lord Holdhurst said. "Dreadful though this is, the danger is past for His Majesty."

"For the moment," Holmes commented drily.

"The two assassins have made their escape," Lestrade said with great confidence. "They will not return today with so many of my men here. It is clear, Mr Holmes, that the assassins must have overpowered the lodgekeeper and policeman, and waited for the carriage to draw up. One dragged the driver off his seat and took his place at the reins, the other jumped inside, performed his terrible deed and no doubt covered in blood escaped to the woodlands. It therefore remains for me to return to London to arrest Giuseppe Rupallo. You will accompany me, Mr Holmes?"

"I think not," my friend replied. "I was engaged, was I not, to ensure His Majesty's survival on his forty-sixth birthday?"

"That is true." Lord Holdhurst looked puzzled.

"That birthday is not yet over."

Lestrade laughed. "My men will ensure no one enters the house without thorough checking."

"But what of the threat from within, Lestrade?"

"My own servants are above suspicion," Lord Holdhurst said frostily. "There will be no others here save the personal valets and lady's maids of the guests who will be staying until tomorrow."

Holmes turned to me. "Watson, a task for you, I think. Might I rely on you to remove any assassins from their number?"

"Willingly, Holmes, but what shall you do?"

"Remain here. I have another task to perform. I shall think. And, Lestrade, if you would be so good, I have a question for you when you return to the Yard. A telegraph in reply would suffice."

To have his mind on other matters when His Majesty, in Holmes' own view, was still at risk, seemed extraordinary to me, but I knew better than to voice my doubts.

I have seldom spent such a frustrating afternoon. After the body of Carlo Mandesi had been removed to the police mortuary, I watched the guests arrive, and was ready to talk to their servants. A difficult task, for all my willingness to assist Holmes. What was I to say? What did my friend wish me to look for? He himself had vanished. Fortunately Mr Anthony assisted me since he could speak Italian well and many of these visiting servants would be Italian. I decided I should enquire as to Sicilian ancestry. As Giuseppe Rupallo had sent the threatening letter, I reasoned that the Sicilian connection was the more likely than the Russian, although Litvov would undoubtedly take pleasure in dissension between Italy and England.

Nevertheless I agreed with Mr Anthony that the warning had said "blood will be seen"; this had happened, and the assassins could not now return. Even with his help, however, it was a daunting task to interrogate over twenty people, and it was not until shortly before the banquet that we finished and Holmes had rejoined us. He was most complimentary about the task I had fulfilled.

"Excellent, Watson," he said after listening to my account attentively. "I now have little doubt where the root of this problem lies. Mr Anthony, show me, if you will, the banqueting room which you have designed so exquisitely."

"By all means, Mr Holmes."

He felt as I did that this was unnecessary, but nevertheless he led us to the room which was indeed fit for a king, and a Renaissance king at that. Mr Anthony proudly identified the paintings, a Lavinia Fontana portrait, a portrait of Lorenzo de' Medici, a Giotto, and a Ghirlandaio. A copy of the first printing of Shakespeare's sonnets also lay on the table of gifts, together with the ring, the gift of Her Majesty. This was a beautiful object of carved gold, with a large emerald in its centre. As for the table, it was a pleasure to regard, being lit by chandeliers of candles to supplement the low gas mantels at the sides of the room. The candles would grace the ladies' complexions, and invite an intimacy of conversation that bright lights cannot achieve.

Holmes surveyed it all with little apparent reaction. "Blood will be seen," he murmured, when I asked his opinion of the scene before us. "Pray, Mr Anthony, what time is the banquet to begin?"

"In two hours, at eight o'clock," was the secretary's reply.

"It will be dark then. The candles will be lit?"

"They will," Mr Anthony replied somewhat haughtily, "but you need not fear that darkness will permit intruders to enter."

"It might obscure their identities," I suggested.

"So it might, Watson," Holmes replied, but I did not feel he was convinced.

"Do you expect another assassin, Holmes?" Lord Holdhurst had come to join us.

"No human intruder. I am sure of that."

"Great heavens! Not human, Holmes?" I asked in horror. Did he fear some vile creature as in the case of "The Speckled Band"?

The time passed quickly, and I sensed that Lord Holdhurst wished to leave us, but Holmes would not permit it.

"Stay, Lord Holdhurst, if you wish His Majesty to survive the evening."

His eyes roved round the banqueting room, and he insisted we all four remain here at the entrance to the banqueting room.

"The answer lies here somewhere, Watson," he said privately to me. "*Somewhere.*" His gaze fell on one of the portraits. "The Medicis," he said softly. "The great Lorenzo. I begin to see. I have been a fool, Watson. A fool."

"It is a fine portrait," I said, puzzled as to his meaning.

"Ah, but it speaks of more than paint, my friend."

"Of what then?"

"Of murder. Do you not agree, Mr Anthony?"

The young man looked taken aback. "Not the Medicis, Mr Holmes. The Borgias are famed for murder."

"The Medicis too. It was not their love of the arts that kept them alive to enjoy their power."

Lord Holdhurst was impatient. "History can surely wait, Mr Holmes."

"I fear you are wrong," Holmes replied.

His lordship looked irritated. "The evening has been planned carefully with His Majesty's safety in mind."

"And with his murder," Holmes said gravely.

"But where lies the danger?" his lordship cried.

"*Here!*"

Holmes whirled round and seized the antique ring from its box. "Mr Anthony," he cried, "you chose this ring, did you not? Put it on your finger, if you please."

Reluctantly, obviously thinking he must humour Holmes, he obeyed, drawing it on slowly.

"Now, Mr Anthony, I will shake your hand." Holmes advanced to him with his own outstretched.

The young man drew back, white-faced, drawing the ring off his finger. "You shall not." He backed hastily, turned and fled along the corridor.

"Watson, tell the guards to hold him," Holmes shouted.

I obeyed instantly, and it was the work of a minute or two before Anthony was held securely by two constables. When I returned, I saw Count Panelli had joined the astonished and annoyed Lord Holdhurst.

"Kindly inform me of what my secretary stands accused, Mr Holmes," he said icily.

"That ring—Count Panelli, I really would not risk your life by examining it too closely."

It was hastily replaced in its box by the nervous count.

"The Medicis," Holmes explained, "required protection against their enemies. They needed to kill by stealth however, and the gift of a ring to an enemy whom they wished to die a particularly unpleasant death by poison was one such method. The ring slides on to the finger, but if the wearer's hand is clasped and pressure applied in one particular spot, a needle shoots out that will kill instantly. I think you will find that this is such a ring."

"My secretary betrayed me?" Lord Holdhurst sat down, looking his full age for the first time. "He wished to assassinate the King? I cannot believe this."

"Lestrade's telegraph confirmed my suspicions. Mr Anthony speaks fluent Italian, the result of his having an Italian—or as he would say a Sicilian—mother. She is the sister of Giuseppe Rupallo, but before becoming your secretary Mr Anthony worked in Paris for Count Litvov. I think you will find he is behind this whole plan, no doubt with Rupallo's full support. For once Russian interests coincided with the Italian anarchists, the latter to throw Italian unity into civil warfare, the former to cause a rift between Italy and England."

"I understand now about Anthony and Rupallo, but how can you know that Litvov was involved?" Lord Holdhurst asked.

Holmes smiled. "The ring. The stone has been replaced. It is alexandrite, the stone precious to Russia alone and the Tsar in particular, and a gem that was only discovered earlier this century. It was Litvov's arrogant signature to the crime."

"And yet it betrayed him."

"How?" I asked, bewildered.

"By day alexandrite is green. By candlelight however it appears red. *Blood* red. 'Blood will be seen again today.' The death of poor Mandesi was to make us think that the assassination attempt had failed, hence the note; but this ring—that was the symbol of blood."

"My dear Mr Holmes, how can I thank you?" Lord Holdhurst said. "Litvov would undoubtedly have revealed the cause of the King's death if this terrible plan had worked. If Her Majesty's gift were known to have been the instrument of the murder, I hesitate to think what would have happened."

"I imagine," said Holmes, "that Her Majesty would not be pleased."

"But she has no gift to present now," Count Panelli said anxiously, after adding his thanks to Lord Holdhurst's. "That will not please her either."

Holmes thought for a moment. "Might I suggest that you find a length of the purest white silk, upon it place two green leaves and between them the stone from this ring—extracted with care of course. Red, green and white, the colours of the Italian flag, symbol of a united Italy, and most disquieting for Count Litvov to see a Russian stone presented to the King as a gift. A most fitting conclusion to a most appetising banquet of a case."

THE SPECTER OF TULLYFANE ABBEY

by Peter Tremayne

Peter Tremayne is the pseudonym of Celtic scholar and historian Peter Berresford Ellis. As Tremayne, he has published many novels, including the more than two dozen in his Sister Fidelma series of seventh-century historical mysteries. Tremayne's short fiction has appeared in anthologies such as *Emerald Magic* and *Dark Detectives*, and has been collected in several volumes, most recently in *An Ensuing Evil and Others* (in which you'll find several other Holmes stories). His latest books are two Fidelma mysteries, *The Council of the Cursed* and *The Dove of Death*.

Even our closest friends are often an enigma to us, especially if we first met them as adults. It's often striking the first time you see someone you know well interacting with, for example, their parents. Suddenly so much about why that person behaves the way they do falls into place. In Conan Doyle's stories, Holmes is already a fully formed adult by the time Watson meets him, and very little of Holmes's past is ever revealed. Many readers have wondered, how does a little boy grow up to be Sherlock Holmes? What was he like as a teenager, or at university? The Disney movie *Young Sherlock Holmes* dealt with this subject, and the more engaging early sections of the film were less about solving mysteries and more about the simple pleasure of seeing a familiar character in a new light. Our next tale also deals with a younger version of Sherlock Holmes, and here we see a character who's very different from the Holmes we know—less confident in his deductions, more trusting of strangers—and yet we see in him hints of the man he will become, driven in no small part by the events that follow.

> Somewhere in the vaults of the bank of Cox and Co., at Charing Cross, there is a travel-worn and battered tin dispatch box with my name, John H. Watson MD, Late Indian Army, painted on the lid. It is filled with papers, nearly all of which are records of cases to illustrate the curious problems which Mr. Sherlock Holmes had at various times to examine.
>
> —"The Problem of Thor Bridge"

This is one of those papers. I must confess that there are few occasions on which I have seen my estimable friend, Sherlock Holmes, the famous consulting detective, in a state of some agitation. He is usually so detached that the word *calm* seems unfit to describe his general demeanor. Yet I had called upon him one evening to learn his opinion of a manuscript draft account I had made of one of his cases which I had titled "The Problem of Thor Bridge."

To my surprise, I found him seated in an attitude of tension in his armchair, his pipe unlit, his long pale fingers clutching my handwritten pages, and his brows drawn together in disapproval. "Confound it, Watson," he greeted me sharply as I came through the door. "Must you show me up to public ridicule in this fashion?"

I was, admittedly, somewhat taken aback at his uncharacteristic greeting. "I rather thought you came well out of the story," I replied defensively. "After all, you helped a remarkable woman, as you yourself observed, while, as for Mr. Gibson, I believe that he did learn an object lesson—"

He cut me short. "Tush! I do not mean the case of Grace Dunbar, which, since you refer to it, was not as glamorous as your imaginative pen elaborates on. No, Watson, no! It is here"—he waved the papers at me—"here in your cumbersome preamble. You speak of some of my unsolved cases as if they were failures. I only mentioned them to you in passing, and now you tell me, and the readers of the *Strand Magazine*, that you have noted them down and deposited the record in that odious little tin dispatch box placed in Cox's Bank."

"I did not think that you would have reason to object, Holmes," I replied with some vexation.

He waved a hand as if dismissing my feelings. "I object to the manner in which you reveal these cases! I read here, and I quote..." He peered shortsightedly at my manuscript. "'Some, and not the least interesting, were complete failures, and as such will hardly bear narrating, since no final explanation is forthcoming. A problem without a solution may interest the student, but can hardly fail to annoy the casual reader. Among these unfinished tales is that of Mr. James Phillimore, who, stepping back into his own house to get his umbrella, was never more seen in this world.' There!" He glanced up angrily.

"But, Holmes, dear fellow, that is precisely the matter as you told it to me. Where am I in error?"

"The error is making the statement itself. It is incomplete. It is not set into context. The case of James Phillimore, whose title was Colonel, incidentally, occurred when I was a young man. I had just completed my second term at Oxford. It was the first time I crossed foils, so to speak, with the man who was to cause me such grief later in my career... Professor Moriarty."

I started at this intelligence, for Holmes was always unduly reticent about his clashes with James Moriarty, that sinister figure whom Holmes seemed to hold in both contempt as a criminal and regard as an intellect.

"I did not know that, Holmes."

"Neither would you have learned further of the matter, but I find that you have squirreled away a reference to this singular event in which Moriarty achieved the better of me."

"You were bested by Moriarty?" I was now really intrigued.

"Don't sound so surprised, Watson," he admonished. "Even villains can be victorious once in a while." Then Holmes paused and added quietly, "Especially when such a villain as Moriarty enlisted the power of darkness in his nefarious design."

I began to laugh, knowing that Holmes abhorred the supernatural. I remember his outburst when we received the letter from Morrison, Morrison, and Dodd which led us into "The Adventure of the Sussex Vampire." Yet my laughter died on my lips as I caught sight of the ghastly look that crossed Holmes's features. He stared into the dancing flames of the fire as if remembering the occasion.

"I am not in jest, Watson. In this instance, Moriarty employed the forces of darkness to accomplish his evil end. Of that there can be no shadow of doubt. It is the only time that I have failed, utterly and miserably failed, to prevent a terrible tragedy whose memory will curse me to the grave."

Holmes sighed deeply and then appeared to have observed for the first time that his pipe was unlit and reached for the matches.

"Pour two glasses from that decanter of fine Hennessy on the table and sit yourself down. Having come thus far in my confession, I might as well finish the story in case that imagination of yours decides to embellish the little you do know."

"I say, Holmes——" I began to protest, but he went on, ignoring my words.

"I pray you, promise never to reveal this story until my clay has mingled with the earth from which I am sprung."

If there is a preamble to this story, it is one that I was already knowledgeable of and which I have already given some account of in the memoir I entitled "The Affray at the Kildare Street Club." Holmes was one of the Galway Holmes. Like his brother, Mycroft, he had attended Trinity College, Dublin, where he had, in the same year as his friend Oscar Wilde, won a demyship to continue his studies at Oxford. I believe the name Sherlock came from his maternal side, his mother being of another well-established Anglo-Irish family. Holmes was always reticent about this background, although the clues to his Irish origins were obvious to most discerning people. One of his frequent disguises was to assume the name of Altamont as he pretended to be an Irish-American. Altamont was his family seat near Ballysherlock.

Armed with this background knowledge, I settled back with a glass of Holmes's cognac and listened as he recounted a most singular and terrifying tale. I append it exactly as he narrated it to me.

"Having completed my first term at Oxford, I returned to Dublin to stay with my brother Mycroft at his house in Merrion Square. Yet I found myself somewhat at a loose end. There was some panic in the fiscal office of the chief secretary where Mycroft worked. This caused him to be unable to spare the time we had set aside for a fishing expedition. I was therefore persuaded to accompany Abraham Stoker, who had been at Trinity the same year as Mycroft, to the Royal to see some theatrical entertainment. Abraham, or Bram as he preferred to be called, was also a close friend of Sir William and Lady Wilde, who lived just across the square, and with whose younger son, Oscar, I was then at Oxford with.

"Bram was an ambitious man who not only worked with Mycroft at Dublin Castle but wrote theatrical criticism in his spare time and by night edited the *Dublin Halfpenny Press,* a journal which he had only just launched. He was trying to persuade me to write on famous Dublin murders for it, but as he offered no remuneration at all, I gracefully declined.

"We were in the foyer of the Royal when Bram, an amiable, booming giant with red hair, hailed someone over the heads of the throng. A thin, white-faced young man emerged to be clasped warmly by the hand. It was a youth of my own age and well known to me; Jack Phillimore was his name. He had been a fellow student at Trinity College. My heart leaped in expectation, and I searched the throng for a familiar female face which was, I will confess it, most dear to me. But Phillimore was alone. His sister Agnes, was not with him at the theater.

"In the presence of Bram, we fell to exchanging pleasantries about our alma mater. I noticed that Phillimore's heart was not in exchanging such bonhomie nor, to be honest, was mine. I was impatient for the opportunity to inquire after Phillimore's sister. Ah, let the truth be known, Watson, but only after I am not in this world.

"Love, my dear Watson. Love! I believe that you have observed that all emotions, and that one in particular, are abhorrent to my mind. This is true, and since I have become mature enough to understand, I have come to regard it as opposite to that true cold reason which I place above all things. I have never married lest I bias my judgment. Yet it was not always my intention, and this very fact is what led to my downfall, causing the tragedy which I am about to relate. Alas, Watson, if... but with an *if* we might place Paris in a bottle.

"As a youth I was deeply in love with Agnes Phillimore who was but a year older than I. When Jack Phillimore and I were in our first year at Trinity, I used to spend time at their town house by Stephen's Green. I confess, it was not the company of Phillimore that I sought then but that of Agnes.

"In my maturity I could come to admire *the* woman, as you insist I call Irene Adler, but admiration is not akin to the deep, destructive emotional power that we call love.

"It was when Bram spotted someone across the foyer that he needed to speak to that Phillimore seized the opportunity to ask abruptly what I was doing for recreation. Hearing that I was at a loose end, he suggested that I accompany him to his father's estate in Kerry for a few days. Colonel James Phillimore owned a large house and estate in that remote county. Phillimore said he was going down because it was his father's fiftieth birthday. I thought at the time that he placed a singular emphasis on that fact.

"It was then that I managed to casually ask if his sister Agnes was in Dublin or in Kerry. Phillimore, of course, like most brothers, was ignorant that his sister held any attraction for the male sex, least of all one of his friends. He was nonchalant. 'To be sure she is at Tullyfane, Holmes. Preparing for her marriage next month.'

"His glance was distracted by a man jostling through the foyer, and so he missed the effect that this intelligence had on me.

"'Married?' I gasped. 'To whom?'

"'Some professor, no less. A cove by the name of Moriarty.'

"'Moriarty?' I asked, for the name meant little to me in that context. I knew it only as a common County Kerry name. It was an Anglicizing of the Irish name Ó Muircheartaigh, meaning 'expert navigator.'

"'He is our neighbor, he is quite besotted with my sister, and it seems that it is arranged that they will marry next month. A rum cove, is the professor. Good education and holds a chair of mathematics at Queen's University in Belfast.'

"'Professor James Moriarty,' I muttered savagely. Phillimore's news of Agnes's intentions had shattered all my illusions.

"'Do you know him?' Phillimore asked, observing my displeasure. 'He's all right, isn't he? I mean... he's not a bounder, eh?'

"'I have seen him once only and that from a distance in the Kildare Street Club,' I confessed. I had nothing against Moriarty at that time. 'My brother Mycroft pointed him out to me. I did not meet him. Yet I have heard of his reputation. His *Dynamics of an Asteroid* ascended to such rarefied heights of pure mathematics that no man in the scientific press was capable of criticizing it.'

"Phillimore chuckled.

"'That is beyond me. Thank God I am merely a student of theology. But it sounds as though you are an admirer.'

"I admire intellect, Phillimore,' I replied simply. Moriarty, as I recalled, must have been all of ten years older than Agnes. What is ten years at our age? But to me, a callow youth, I felt the age difference that existed between Agnes and James Moriarty was obscene. I explain this simply because my attitude has a bearing on my future disposition.

"'So come down with me to Tullyfane Abbey,' pressed Phillimore, oblivious to the emotional turmoil that he had created in me.

"I was about to coldly decline the invitation when Phillimore, observing my negative expression, was suddenly very serious. He leaned close to me and said softly: 'You see, Holmes, old fellow, we are having increasing problems with the family ghost, and as I recall, you have a canny way of solving bizarre problems.'

"I knew enough of his character to realize that jesting was beyond his capacity.

"'The family ghost?'

"'A damned infernal specter that is driving my father quite out of his wits. Not to mention Agnes.'

"'Your father and sister are afraid of a specter?'

"'Agnes is scared at the deterioration in my father's demeanor. Seriously, Holmes, I really don't know what to do. My sister's letters speak of such a bizarre set of circumstances that I am inclined to think that she is hallucinating or that my father has been driven mad already.'

"My inclination was to avoid opening old wounds now by meeting Agnes again. I could spend the rest of my vacation in Marsh's Library, where they have an excellent collection of medieval cryptogram manuscripts. I hesitated—hesitated and was lost. I had to admit that I was intrigued to hear more of the matter in spite of my emotional distress, for any mystery sends the adrenaline coursing in my body.

"The very next morning I accompanied Jack Phillimore to Kingsbridge Railway Station and boarded the train to Killarney. En route he explained some of the problems.

"Tullyfane Abbey was supposed to be cursed. It was situated on the extremity of the Iveragh Peninsula in a wild and deserted spot. Tullyfane Abbey was, of course, never an abbey. It was a dignified Georgian country house. The Anglo-Irish gentry in the eighteenth century had a taste for the grandiose and called their houses *abbeys* or *castles* even when they were unassuming dwellings inhabited only by families of modest fortune.

"Phillimore told me that the firstborn of every generation of the lords of Tullyfane were to meet with terrible deaths on the attainment of their fiftieth birthdays even down to the seventh generation. It seems that first lord of Tullyfane had hanged a young boy for sheep stealing. The boy turned out to be innocent, and his mother, a widow who had doted on the lad as insurance for comfort in her old age, had duly uttered the curse. Whereupon, each lord of Tullyfane, for the last six generations, had met an untimely end.

"Phillimore assured me that the first lord of Tullyfane had not even been a direct ancestor of his, but that his great-grandfather had purchased Tullyfane Abbey when the owner, concerned at the imminent prospect of departing this life on his fiftieth birthday, decided to sell and depart for healthier climes in England. This sleight of hand of ownership had not prevented Jack's great-grandfather, General Phillimore, from falling off his horse and breaking his neck on his fiftieth birthday. Jack's grandfather, a redoubtable judge, was shot on his fiftieth birthday. The local inspector of the Royal Irish Constabulary had assumed that his untimely demise could be ascribed more to his profession than to the paranormal. Judges and policemen often experienced sudden terminations to their careers in a country where they were considered part of the colonial occupation by ordinary folk.

"'I presume your father, Colonel James Phillimore, is now approaching his fiftieth birthday and hence his alarm?' I asked Phillimore as the train rolled through the Tipperary countryside toward the Kerry border.

"Phillimore nodded slowly.

"'My sister has, in her letters, written that she has heard the specter crying at night. She reports that my father has even witnessed the apparition, the form of a young boy, crying on the turret of the abbey.'

"I raised my eyebrows unintentionally.

"'Seen as well as heard?' I demanded. 'And by two witnesses? Well, I can assure you that there is nothing in this world that exists unless it is due to some scientifically explainable reason.'

"'Nothing in this world,' muttered Phillimore. 'But what of the next?'

"'If your family believes in this curse, why remain at Tullyfane?' I demanded. 'Would it not be better to quit the house and estate if you are so sure that the curse is potent?'

"'My father is stubborn, Holmes. He will not quit the place, for he has sunk every penny he has into it apart from our town house in Dublin. If it were me, I would sell it to Moriarty and leave the accursed spot.'

"'Sell it to Moriarty? Why him, particularly?'

"'He offered to buy Father out in order to help resolve the situation.'

"'Rather magnanimous of him,' I observed. 'Presumably he has no fear of the curse?'

"'He reckons that the curse would only be directed at Anglo-Irish families like us, while he, being a pure Milesian, a Gael of the Gaels, so to speak, would be immune to the curse.'

"Colonel Phillimore had sent a calèche to Killarney Station to bring Phillimore and me to Tullyfane Abbey. The old colonel was clearly not in the best of spirits when he greeted us in the library. I noticed his hand shook a little as he raised it to greet me.

"'Friend of Jack's, eh? Yes, I remember you. One of the Galway Holmeses. Mycroft Holmes is your brother? Works for Lord Hartington, eh? Chief Secretary, eh?'

"He had an irritating manner of putting *eh* after each telegraphic phrase as a punctuation.

"It was then that Agnes Phillimore came in to welcome us. God, Watson, I was young and ardent in those days. Even now, as I look back with a more critical eye and colder blood, I acknowledge that she was rare and wonderful in her beauty. She held out her hand to me with a smile, but I saw at once that it lacked the warmth and friendship that I thought it had once held for me alone. Her speech was reserved, and she greeted me as a distant friend. Perhaps she had grown into a woman while I held to her image with boyish passion? It was impossible for me to acknowledge this at that time, but the passion was all on my side. Ah, immature youth, what else is there to say?

"We dined in somber mode that evening. Somber for me because I was wrestling with life's cruel realities; somber for the Phillimores because of the curse that hung over the house. We were just finishing the dessert when Agnes suddenly froze, her fork halfway to her mouth. Then Colonel Phillimore dropped his spoon with a crash on his plate and gave a piteous moan.

"In the silence that followed I heard it plainly. It was the sound of a sobbing child. It seemed to echo all around the room. Even Jack Phillimore looked distracted.

"I pushed back my chair and stood up, trying to pinpoint the direction from which the sounds came.

"'What lies directly beneath this dining room?' I demanded of the colonel. He was white in the face, too far gone with shock to answer me.

"I turned to Jack Phillimore. He replied with some nervousness.

"'The cellars, Holmes.'

"'Come, then,' I cried, grabbing a candelabra from the table and striding swiftly to the door.

"As I reached the door, Agnes stamped her foot twice on the floor as if agitated.

"'Really, Mr. Holmes,' she cried, 'you cannot do battle with an ethereal being!'

"I paused in the doorway to smile briefly at her.

"'I doubt that I shall find an ethereal being, Miss Phillimore.'

"Jack Phillimore led the way to the cellar, and we searched it thoroughly, finding nothing.

"'What did you expect to find?' demanded Phillimore, seeing my disappointment as we returned to the dining room.

"'A small boy, corporeal in form and not a spirit,' I replied firmly.

"'Would that it were so.' Agnes greeted our return without disguising her look of satisfaction that I could produce no physical entity in explanation. 'Do you not think that I have caused this house to be searched time and time again? My father is on the verge of madness. I do believe that he has come to the end of his composure. I fear for what he might do to himself.'

"'And the day after tomorrow is his fiftieth birthday,' added Phillimore soberly.

"We were standing in the entrance to the dining room when Malone, the aging butler, answered a summons to the front door by the jangle of the bell.

"'It's a Professor Moriarty,' he intoned.

"Moriarty was tall and thin, with a forehead domed in a white curve and deeply set eyes. His face protruded forward and had a curious habit of slowly oscillating from side to side in what, in the harsh judgment of my youth, I felt to be a curiously reptilian fashion. I suppose, looking back, he was handsome in a way and somewhat distinguished. He had been young for his professorship, and there was no doubting the sharpness of his mind and intellect.

"Agnes greeted him with warmth while Phillimore was indifferent. As for myself, I felt I had to suppress my ill humor. He had come to join us for coffee and brandy and made sympathetic overtures to the colonel over his apparent state of ill health.

"'My offer still stands, dear sir,' he said. 'Best be rid of the abbey and the curse in one fell swoop. Not, of course, that you would lose it entirely, for when Agnes and I are married, you will always be a welcome guest here.'

"Colonel Phillimore actually growled. A soft rumbling sound in the back of his throat, like an animal at bay and goaded into response.

"'I intend to see this through. I refuse to be chased out of my home by a specter when Akbar Khan and his screaming Afghans could not budge me from the fort at Peiwar Pass. No, sir. Here I intend to stay and see my fiftieth birthday through.'

"'I think you should at least consider James's offer, Father,' Agnes rebuked him. 'This whole business is affecting your nerves. Better get rid of the place and move to Dublin.'

"'Nonsense!' snapped her father. 'I shall see it through. I will hear no more.'

"We went to bed early that night, and I confess, I spent some time analyzing my feelings for Agnes before dropping into a dozing slumber.

"The crying woke me. I hauled on a dressing gown and hastened to the window through which a full white moon sent its soft light. The cry was like a banshee's wail. It seemed to be coming from above me. I hastened from the room and in the corridor outside I came across Jack Phillimore, similarly attired in a dressing gown. His face looked ghastly.

"'Tell me that I am not dreaming, Holmes,' he cried.

"'Not unless we share a dream,' I replied tersely. 'Do you have a revolver?'

"He looked startled.

"'What do you hope to achieve with a revolver?' he demanded.

"'I think it might be efficacious in dealing with ghosts, ghouls, and apparitions.' I smiled thinly.

"Phillimore shook his head.

"'The guns are locked below in the gun room. My father has the key.'

"'Ah well,' I replied in resignation, 'we can probably proceed without them. This crying is emanating from above. What's up there?'

"'The turret room. That's where Father said he saw the apparition before.'

"'Lead me to the turret room, then.'

"Spurred on by the urgency of my tone, Phillimore turned to lead the way. We flew up the stairs of a circular tower and emerged onto a flat roof. At the far end of the building rose a similar, though larger, tower or, more accurately, a round turret. Encircling it, ten feet above the roof level there ran a small balcony.

"'My God!' cried Phillimore, halting so abruptly that I cannoned in to him.

"It took me a moment to recover before I saw what had caused his distress. On this balcony there stood the figure of a small boy. He was clearly lit in the bright moonlight and yet, yet I will tell you no lie, Watson, his entire body and clothes glowed with a strange luminescence. The boy it was who was letting out the eerie, wailing sounds.

"'Do you see it, Holmes?' cried Phillimore.

"'I see the young rascal, whoever he is!' I yelled, running toward the tower over the flat roof.

"Then the apparition was gone. How or where, I did not observe.

"I reached the base of the tower and looked for a way to scramble up to the balcony. There was only one way of egress from the roof. A small door in the tower which seemed clearly barred on the inside.

"'Come, Phillimore, the child is escaping!' I cried in frustration.

"'Escaping, eh?' It was the colonel who emerged out of the darkness behind us. His face was ashen. He was clad only in his pajamas.

"'Specters don't need to escape, eh! No, sir! Now that you have seen it, too, I can say I am not mad. At least, not mad, eh?'

"'How do I get into the turret?' I demanded, ignoring the colonel's ranting.

"'Boarded up for years, Holmes,' Phillimore explained, moving to support his frail father for fear the old man might topple over. 'There's no way anyone could have entered or left it.'

"'Someone did,' I affirmed. 'That was no specter. I think this has been arranged. I think you should call in the police.'

"The colonel refused to speak further of the matter and retired to bed. I spent most of the night checking the approaches to the turret room and was forced to admit that all means of entrance and exit seemed perfectly secured. But I was sure that when I started to run across the roof toward the tower, the boy had bobbed away with such a startled expression that no self-respecting ghost in the middle of haunting would have assumed.

"The next morning, over breakfast, I was forceful in my exhortations to the colonel that he should put the matter forthwith in the hands of the local police. I told him that I had no doubts that some bizarre game was afoot. The colonel had recovered some of his equilibrium and listened attentively to my arguments.

"Surprisingly, the opposition came from Agnes. She was still in favor of her father departing the house and putting an end to the curse.

"We were just finishing breakfast when Malone announced the arrival of Professor Moriarty.

"Agnes went to join him in the library while we three finished our meal, by the end of which, Colonel Phillimore had made up his mind to follow my advice. It was decided that we accompany Colonel Phillimore directly after breakfast to discuss the matter with the local Inspector of the Royal Irish Constabulary. Agnes and Moriarty joined us, and having heard the story from Agnes, Moriarty actually said that it was the best course of action, although Agnes still had her doubts. In fact, Moriarty offered to accompany us. Agnes excused herself a little ungraciously, I thought, because she had arranged to make an inventory of the wines in the cellar.

"So the colonel, Phillimore, Moriarty, and I agreed to walk the two miles into the town. It must be observed that a few miles' walk was nothing for those who lived in the country in those days. Now, in London, everyone is forever hailing hansom carriages even if they merely desire to journey to the end of the street.

"We left the house and began to stroll down the path. We had barely gone twenty yards when the colonel, casting an eye at the sky, excused himself and said he needed his umbrella and would be but a moment. He turned, hurried back to his front door, and entered. That was when he disappeared from this world forever.

"The three of us waited patiently for a few moments. Moriarty then said that if we continued to stroll at an easy pace, the colonel would catch us up. Yet when we reached the gates of the estate, I began to grow concerned that there was still no sign of the colonel. I caused our party to wait at the gates. Ten minutes passed, and then I felt I should return to find out what had delayed the colonel.

"The umbrella was still in the hall stand. There was no sign of the colonel. I rang the bell for old Malone and he swore that as far as he was aware the colonel had left with us and had not returned. There was no budging him on that point. Grumbling more than a little, he set off to the colonel's room; I went to the study. Soon the entire house was being searched as Jack Phillimore and Moriarty arrived back to discover the cause of the delay.

"It was then that Agnes emerged from the cellars, looking a little disheveled, an inventory in her hand. When she heard that her father had simply vanished, she grew distraught and Malone had to fetch the brandy.

"In the wine cellar, she told me, she had heard and seen nothing. Moriarty volunteered to search the cellar just to make the examination of the house complete. I told Phillimore to look after his sister and accompanied Moriarty. While I disliked the man, there was no doubt that Moriarty could hardly have engineered the colonel's disappearance as he had left the house with us and remained with us outside the house. Naturally, our search of the cellars proved futile. They were large, and one could probably have hidden a whole army in them if one so desired. But the entrance from the hall led to the area used for wine storage, and no one could have descended into the cellar without passing this area and thus being seen by Agnes. No answer to Colonel James Phillimore's disappearance presented itself to me.

"I spent a week at Tullyfane attempting to form some conclusion. The local RIC eventually gave up the search. I had to return to Oxford, and it became obvious to me that neither Agnes nor Moriarty required my company further. After that, I had but one letter from Jack Phillimore, and this several months later and postmarked at Marseille.

"Apparently, at the end of two weeks, a suicide note was found in the colonel's desk stating that he could not stand the strange hauntings in Tullyfane Abbey. Rather than await the terrible death on his fiftieth birthday, he proposed to put an end to it himself. There was attached a new will, giving the estate to Agnes in acknowledgment of her forthcoming marriage and the house in Stephen's Green to Jack. Phillimore wrote that although the will was bizarre, and there was no proof of his father's death, he nevertheless had refused to contest it. I heard later that this was against the advice of Phillimore's solicitor. But it seemed that Jack Phillimore wanted no part of the curse or the estate. He wished his sister joy of it and then took himself to Africa as a missionary where, two years later, I heard that he had been killed in some native uprising in British East Africa. It was not even on his fiftieth birthday. So much for curses.

"And Agnes Phillimore? She married James Moriarty and the property passed to him. She was dead within six months. She drowned in a boating accident when Moriarty was taking her to Beginish, just off the Kerry coast, to show her the columnar basaltic formations similar to those of the Giant's Causeway. Moriarty was the only survivor of the tragedy.

"He sold Tullyfane Abbey and its estate to an American and moved to London to become a gentleman of leisure, although his money was soon squandered due to his dissipated lifestyle. He resorted to more overt illegal activities to replenish his wealth. I have not called him the 'Napoleon of crime' without cause.

"As for Tullyfane, the American tried to run the estate, but fell foul of the Land Wars of a few years ago when the Land Leaguers forced radical changes in the way the great estates in Ireland were run. That was when a new word was added to the language—boycott—when the Land Leaguers ostracized Charles Boycott, the estate agent of Lord Erne at Lough Mask. The American pulled out of Tullyfane Abbey, which fell into ruin and became derelict.

"Without being able to find out what happened when James Phillimore stepped back beyond his front door to retrieve his umbrella, I was unable to bring the blame to where, I believed with every fiber in my body, it lay; namely, to James Moriarty. I believe that it was Moriarty who planned the whole dastardly scheme of obtaining the estate which he presumed would set him up for life. He was not in love with poor Agnes. He saw her as the quick means of becoming rich and, not content to wait for her marriage portion, I believe he forged the suicide note and will and then found an ingenious way to dispatch the colonel, having failed to drive him insane by playing on the curse. Once he had secured the estate, poor Agnes became dispensable.

"How he worked the curse, I was not sure until a singular event was reported to me some years later.

"It was in London, only a few years ago, that I happened to encounter Bram Stoker's younger brother, George. Like most of the Stoker brothers, with the exception of Bram, George had gone into medicine and was a Licentiate of the Royal College of Surgeons in Dublin. George had just married a lady from County Kerry, actually the sister of the McGillycuddy of the Reeks, one of the old Gaelic nobility.

"It was George who supplied me with an important piece of the jigsaw. He was actually informed of the occurrence by none other than his brother-in-law, Dennis McGillycuddy, who had been a witness to the event.

"About a year after the occurrences at Tullyfane Abbey, the body of a young boy was found in an old mine working in the Reeks. I should explain that the Reeks are the mountains on the Iveragh Peninsula which are the highest peaks in Ireland and, of course, Tullyfane stands in their shadows. The boy's body had not badly decomposed, because it had lain in the ice-cold temperatures of the small lochs one gets in the area. It so happened that a well-known Dublin medical man, Dr. John MacDonnell, the first person to perform an operation under anesthetic in Ireland, was staying in Killarney. He agreed to perform the autopsy because the local coroner had noticed a peculiar aspect to the body; he observed that in the dark the corpse of the boy was glowing.

"MacDonnell found that the entire body of the boy had been coated in a waxy yellow substance; indeed, it was the cause of death, for it had so clogged the pores of his skin that the unfortunate child had simply been asphyxiated. Upon analysis, it was discerned that the substance was a form of natural phosphorus, found in the caves in the area. I immediately realized the significance of this.

"The child, so I presumed, was one of the hapless and miserable wretches doomed to wander the byways of Ireland, perhaps orphaned during the failure of the potato crops in 1871, which had spread starvation and typhus among the peasants. Moriarty had forced or persuaded him to act the part of the wailing child whom we had observed. This child was our specter, appearing now and then at Moriarty's command to scream and cry in certain places. The phosphorus would have emitted the ethereal glow.

"Having served his purpose, Moriarty, knowing well the properties of the waxy substance with which he had coated the child's body, left the child to suffocate and dumped the body in the mountains."

I waited for some time after Holmes had finished the story, and then I ventured to ask the question to which he had, so far, provided no answer. As I did so, I made the following preamble.

"Accepting that Moriarty had accomplished a fiendish scheme to enrich himself and that it was only in retrospect you realized how he managed to use the child to impersonate a specter—"

Holmes breathed out sharply as he interrupted. "It is a failure of my deductive capabilities that I have no wish to advertise, Watson."

"Yet there is one thing—just how did Moriarty manage to spirit away the body of James Phillimore after he stepped back inside the door of the house to retrieve his umbrella? By your own statement, Moriarty, Jack Phillimore, and yourself were all together, waiting for the colonel, outside his house. The family retainer, old Malone, swore the colonel did not reenter the house. How was it done? Was Malone in the pay of Moriarty?"

"It was a thought that crossed my mind. The RIC likewise questioned old Malone very closely and came to the conclusion that he was part of no plot. In fact, Malone could not say one way or another if the colonel had returned, as he was in the kitchen with two housemaids as witnesses at the time."

"And Agnes?..."

"Agnes was in the cellar. She saw nothing. When all is said and done, there is no logical answer. James Phillimore vanished the moment he stepped back over the threshold. I have thought about every conceivable explanation for the last twenty years and have come to no suitable explanation except one...."

"Which is?"

"The powers of darkness were exalted that day, and Moriarty had made a pact with the devil, selling his soul for his ambition."

I stared at Holmes for a moment. I had never seen him admit to any explanation of events that was not in keeping with scientific logic. Was he correct that the answer lay with the supernatural, or was he merely covering up for the fact of his own lack of knowledge or, even more horrific to my susceptibilities, did the truth lie in some part of my old friend's mind which he refused to admit even to himself?

Pinned to John H. Watson's manuscript was a small yellowing cutting from the *Kerry Evening News;* alas the date had not been noted.

"During the recent building of an RIC Barracks on the ruins of Tullyfane Abbey, a well-preserved male skeleton was discovered. Sub-Inspector Dalton told our reporter that it could not be estimated how long the skeleton had lain there. The precise location was in a bricked-up area of the former cellars of the abbey.

"Doctor Simms-Taafe said that he adduced, from the condition of the skeleton, that it had belonged to a man in midlife who had met his demise within the last twenty or thirty years. The back of the skull had been smashed in due to a severe blow, which might account for the death.

"Sub-Inspector Dalton opined that the death might well be linked with the disappearance of Colonel Phillimore, then the owner of Tullyfane Abbey, some thirty years ago. As the next owner, Professor James Moriarty was reported to have met his death in Switzerland, the last owner having been an American who returned to his homeland, and the Phillimores being no longer domiciled in the country, the RIC are placing the matter in their file of unsolved suspicious deaths."

A few lines were scrawled on the cutting in Dr. Watson's hand, which ran, "I think it was obvious that Colonel Phillimore was murdered as soon as he reentered the house. I have come to believe that the truth did lie in a dark recess of my old friend's mind which he refused to admit was the grotesque and terrible truth of the affair. Patricide, even at the instigation of a lover with whom one is besotted, is the most hideous crime of all. Could it be that Holmes had come to regard the young woman herself as representing the powers of darkness?" The last sentence was heavily underscored.

THE VALE OF THE WHITE HORSE

by Sharyn McCrumb

Sharyn McCrumb is the author of the Appalachian Ballad series, which includes the *New York Times* bestsellers *She Walks These Hills*, *The Hangman's Beautiful Daughter*, and *The Ballad of Frankie Silver*. Her novel *The Rosewood Casket* is currently in production for a feature film adaptation, and forthcoming novels include *The Devil Amongst the Lawyers*, and a book co-authored with NASCAR driver Adam Edwards called *Faster Pastor*. McCrumb has been honored with the Library of Virginia Award and her book, *St. Dale*, received the Book of the Year Award from the Appalachian Writers Association. In 2008, she was also presented with the Virginia Women of History Award.

The Uffington White Horse is a giant prehistoric chalk carving cut into the bedrock of a hillside in southern England. McCrumb says that she is fascinated by British folklore and prehistoric landmarks, and when she visited Wiltshire and saw the Horse, she knew that she wanted to incorporate it into a story someday. "The Vale of the White Horse" is the result.

This story is one of those rare ones in which we get to see the great detective Sherlock Holmes from the point of view of someone other than Watson. Of this character, the author explains, "Grisel Rountree is the English counterpart of a favorite character from my Ballad novels, the Appalachian wise woman Nora Bonesteel." She adds that the story is inspired in part by "my resentment of the urban know-it-alls who think that country people are less intelligent or sophisticated than city dwellers. I enjoyed making Grisel Rountree every bit as astute and eccentric as Holmes."

Grisel Rountree was the first to see that something was strange about the white chalk horse.

As she stood on the summit of the high down, in the ruins of the hill fort that overlooked the dry chalk valley, she squinted at the white shape on the hillside below, wondering for a moment or two what was altered. Carved into the steep slope

267

across the valley, the primitive outline of a white horse shone in the sunshine of a June morning. Although Grisel Rountree had lived in the valley all seven decades of her life, she never tired of the sight of the ancient symbol, large as a hayfield, shining like polished ivory in the long grass of early summer.

The white horse had been old two thousand years ago when the Romans arrived in Britain, and the people in the valley had long ago forgotten the reason for its existence, but there were stories about its magic. Some said that King Arthur had fought his last battle on that hill, and others claimed that the horse was the symbol for the nearby Wayland Smithy, the local name for a stone chamber where folk said that a pagan god had been condemned to shoe the horses of mortals for all eternity.

Whatever the truth of its origins, the village took a quiet pride in its proximity to the great horse. Every year when the weather broke, folk would make an excursion up the slope to clean the chalk form of the great beast, and to pull any encroaching weeds that threatened to blur the symmetry of its outline. They made a day of it, taking picnic lunches and bottles of ale, and the children played tag in the long grass while their elders worked. When Grisel was a young girl, her father had told her that the chalk figure was a dragon whose imprint had been burned into the hill where it had been killed by St. George himself. When she became old enough to go to the village dances, the laughing young men had insisted that the white beast was a unicorn, and that if a virgin should let herself be kissed within the eye of the chalk figure, the unicorn would come to life and gallop away. It was a great jest to invite the unmarried lasses up to the hill "to make the unicorn run," though of course it never did.

Nowadays everyone simply said the creature was a horse, though they did allow that whoever drew it hadn't made much of a job of it. It was too stretched and skinny to look like a proper horse, but given its enormous size, perhaps the marvel was that the figure looked like anything at all.

The hill fort provided the best view of the great white horse. Anyone standing beside the chalk ramparts of the ancient ruins could look down across the valley and see the entire figure of the horse sprawled out below like the scribble of some infant giant. Grisel Rountree did not believe in giants, but she did believe in tansy leaves, which was why she was up at the hill fort so early that morning. A few leaves of tansy put in each shoe prevented the wearer from coming down with ague. Although she seldom had the ague Grisel Rountree considered it prudent to stock up on the remedy as a precaution anyhow. Besides, half the village came to her at one time or another to cure their aches and pains, and it was just as well to be ready with a good supply before winter set in.

She had got up at first light, fed the hens and did the morning chores around her cottage, and then set off with a clean feed sack to gather herbs for her remedies and potions. She had been up at the ruins when the clouds broke, and a shaft of sunlight seemed to shine right down on the chalk horse. She had stopped looking for plants then, and when she stood up to admire the sight, she noticed it.

The eye of the great white horse was red.

"Now, there's a thing," she said to herself.

She shaded her eyes from the sun and squinted to get a clearer image of the patch of red, but she still couldn't make it out. The eye did not appear to have been painted. It was more like something red had been put more or less in the space where the horse's eye ought to be, but at this distance, she couldn't quite make out what it was. She picked up the basket of herbs and made her way down the slope. No use hurrying—it would take her at least half an hour to cross the valley and climb the hill to the eye of the white horse. Besides, since whatever-it-was in the eye was not moving, it would probably be there whenever she reached it.

"It'll be goings-on, I'll warrant," she muttered to herself, picturing a courting couple fallen asleep in their trysting place. Grisel Rountree did not hold with "goings-on," certainly not in broad daylight at the top of a great hill before God and everybody. She tried to think of who in the village might be up to such shenanigans these days, but no likely couple came to mind. They were all either past the point of outdoor courting or still working up to it.

Out of ideas, she plodded on. "Knowing is better than guessing," she muttered, resolving to ignore the twinge of rheumatism that bedeviled her joints with every step she took. The walk would do her good, she thought, and if it didn't, there was always some willow tea back in the cottage waiting to be brewed.

Half an hour later, the old woman had crossed the valley and reached the summit where the chalk horse lay. Now that she was nearer she could see that the splash of red she had spotted from afar was a bit of cloth, but it wasn't lying flat against the ground like a proper cape or blanket should. She felt a shiver of cold along her backbone, knowing what she was to find.

In the eye of the white horse, Grisel knelt beside the scarlet cloak spread open on the ground. She wore a look of grim determination, but she would not be shocked. She had been midwife to the village these forty years, and she laid out the dead as well, so she'd seen the worse, taken all round. She lifted the edge of the blanket and found herself staring into the sightless eyes of a stranger. A moment's examination told her that the man was a gentleman—the cut of his blood-stained clothes would have told her that, but besides his wardrobe, the man had the smooth hands and the well-kept look of one who has been waited on all his life. She noted this without any resentment of the differences in their stations: such things just were.

The man was alive, but only just.

"Can you tell me who did this to you?" she said, knowing that this was all the help he could be given, and that if there were time for only one question, it should be that. The rest could be found out later, one way or another.

The man's eyes seemed to focus on her for a moment, and in a calm, wondering voice he said clearly, "Not a maiden..."

And then he died. Grisel Rountree did not stay to examine him further, because the short blade sticking out of the dead man's stomach told her that this was not a matter for the layer out of the dead but for the village constable.

"Rest in peace, my lad," said the old woman, laying the blanket back into place.

"I'll bring back someone directly to fetch you down."

"Missus Rountree!" Young Tom Cowper stood under the apple tree beside the old woman's cottage, gasping for breath from his run from the village, but too big with news to wait for composure. "They're bringing a gentleman down from London on account of the murder!"

Grisel Rountree swirled the wooden paddle around the sides of the steaming black kettle, fishing a bit of bed sheet out of the froth and examining it for dirt. Not clean yet. "From London?" she grunted. "I shouldn't wonder. Our PC Waller is out of his depth, and so I told him when I took him up to the white horse."

"Yes'm," said Tom, mindful of the sixpence he had been given to deliver the message. "The London gentleman—he's staying at the White Horse, him and a friend—at the Inn, I mean."

Grisel snorted. "I didn't suppose you meant the white horse on the hill, lad."

"No. Well, he's asking to see you, missus. On account of you finding the body. They say I'm to take you to the village."

The old woman stopped stirring the wash pot and fixed the boy with a baleful eye. "Oh, I'm to come to the village, am I? Look here, Tom Cowper, you go back to the inn and tell the gentleman that anybody can tell him the way to my cottage, and if he wants a word with me, here I'll be."

"But missus..."

"Go!"

For a moment Tom gaped at the tall, white-haired figure, pointing imperiously at him. People roundabouts said she were a witch, and of course he didn't hold with such foolishness, but there was a limit to what sixpence would buy a gentleman in the way of his services as a messenger. Choosing the better part of valor, he turned and ran.

"Who is this London fellow?" Grisel called after the boy.

Without breaking stride Tom called back to her, "Mis-terr Sher-lock Holmes!"

Grisel Rountree finished her washing, swept the cottage again, and set to work making a batch of scones in case the gentleman from London should arrive at tea time, which, if he had any sense, he would, because anybody hereabouts could tell him that Grisel Rountree's baking was far better than the alternately scorched and floury efforts of the cook at the village inn.

The old woman was not surprised that London had taken an interest in the case, considering that the dead man had turned out to be from London himself, and a society doctor to boot. James Dacre, his name was, and he was one of the Hampshire Dacres, and the brother of the young baronet over at Ramsmeade. The wonder of it was that the doctor should be visiting here, for he had never done so before, though they saw his brother the baronet often enough.

A few months back, the young baronet had been a guest of the local hunt, and during the course of the visit he had met Miss Evelyn Ambry, the daughter of the local squire and the beauty of the county. She was a tall, spirited young woman, much more beautiful than her sisters and by far the best rider. People said she was as fearless as she was flawless, but among the villagers there was a hint of reserve in their voices when they spoke of her. There was a local tradition about the Ambrys, people didn't speak of it in these enlightened times, but they never quite forgot it either. Miss Evelyn was one of the Ambry changelings, right enough. There was one along in nearly every generation.

By all accounts Miss Evelyn Ambry had made a conquest of the noble guest, and the baronet's visits to the district became so frequent that people began to talk of a match being made between the pair of them. Some folk said they would been betrothed already if Miss Evelyn's aunt had not suddenly taken ill and died two weeks back, so that Miss Evelyn had to observe mourning for the next several months. And now there was more mourning to keep them apart—his lordship's own brother.

Grisel Rountree was sorry about the young man's untimely death, but it's an ill wind that blows nobody good, she told herself, and if the doctor's passing kept his brother from wedding the Ambry changeling, it might be a blessing after all. Whenever a silly woman sighed at the prospect of a wedding between Miss Evelyn and the baronet, Grisel always held her peace on the subject, but she'd not be drinking the health of the handsome couple if the wedding day ever came. It boded ill for the bridegroom, she thought. It always had done when a besotted suitor wed an Ambry changeling, and so Grisel had been expecting a tragedy in the offing—but not this particular tragedy. The baronet's younger brother dying in the eye of the white horse. She didn't know what it meant, and that worried her. And his last words—"Not a maiden"—put her in mind of the village lads' old jest about the unicorn, but how could a gentleman doctor from London know about that? It was a puzzle, right enough, and she could not see the sense of it yet, but one thing she did know for certain: death comes in threes.

She was just dusting the top of the oak cupboard for the second time when she heard voices in the garden.

"Do let me handle this, Holmes," came the voice of a London gentleman. "You may frighten the poor old creature out of her wits with your abrupt ways."

"Nonsense!" said a sharper voice. "I am the soul of tact, always!"

She had flung open the cottage door before they could knock. "Good afternoon, good sirs," she said, addressing her remarks to the tall, saturnine gentleman in the cape and the deerstalker hat. Just from the look of him, you could tell that he was the one in charge.

The short, sandy-haired fellow with the bushy mustache and kind eyes gave her a reassuring smile. "It's Mistress Rountree, is it not? I am Dr. John Watson. Allow me to introduce my companion, Mr. Sherlock Holmes, the eminent detective from London. We are indeed hoping for a word with you. May we come in?"

She nodded and stepped aside to let them pass. "You're wanting to talk about young Dacre's death," she said. "It was me that found him. But you needn't be afraid of upsetting me, young man. I may not have seen the horrors you did with the army in Afghanistan, but I'll warrant I've seen my share in forty years of birthing and burying folk in these parts."

The sandy-haired man took a step backward and stared at her. "But how did you know that I had been in Afghanistan?"

"Really, Watson!" said his companion. "Will you never cease to be amazed by parlor tricks? Shall I tell you how the good lady ferreted out your secret? I did it myself at our first meeting, you may recall."

"Yes, yes," said Watson with a nervous laugh. "I remember. I was a bit startled, because the innkeeper said that Mistress Rountree had a bit of reputation hereabouts as a witch. I thought this might be a sample of it."

"I expect it is," said Holmes. "People are always spinning tales to explain that which they do not understand. No doubt they'll be coming out with some outlandish nonsense about the body of Mr. Dacre being found in the eye of the white horse. I believe you found him, madam?"

Grisel Rountree motioned for them to sit down. "I've laid the tea on, and there are scones on the table. You can be getting on with that while I'm telling you." In a few words she gave the visitors a concise account of her actions on the morning of James Dacre's murder.

"You'll be in the employ of his lordship the baronet," she said, giving Holmes an appraising look.

He nodded. "Indeed, that gentleman is most anxious to discover the circumstances surrounding his brother's murder. And you tell me that Dr. Dacre was in fact alive when you found him?"

"Only just, sir. He had been stabbed in the stomach, and he had bled like a stuck pig. Must have lain there a good hour or more, judging by all the blood on the grass thereabouts."

"And you saw no one? There are very few trees on those downs. Did you scan the distance for a retreating figure?"

She nodded. "Even before I knew what had happened, I looked. I was on the opposite hill, mind, when I first noticed the red on the horse's eye, so I could see for miles, and there were nothing moving, not so much as a cow, sir, much less a man."

"No. You'd have told the constable if it had been otherwise. And the poor man's final words to you were—"

"Just like I told you. He opened his eyes and said clear as day, Not a maiden. Then he laid back and died."

"Not a maiden. He was not addressing you, I take it?"

"He were not," snapped the old woman. "And he would have been wrong if he had been."

"Did the phrase convey anything to you at the time?"

"Only the old tale about the white horse. The village lads used to say that if anyone were to kiss a proper maiden standing upon the chalk horse, the beast would get up and walk away. So perhaps he had been kissing a lady? But that's not what I thought. The poor man was stabbed with a woman's weapon—a seam ripper, it were, from a lady's sewing kit—and I think he was saying that the one who used it was not a woman, despite the look of it."

Holmes nodded. "Let's leave that for a bit. I find it curious that the doctor was walking on the downs at such an odd hour. In fact, why was he here at all? The family estate, Ramsmeade, is some distance from here."

"The doctor's brother is engaged to squire's daughter hereabouts," said the old woman.

"So I am told. I believe the Dacres had come to attend a funeral at the Hall."

"T'were the squire's younger sister. Christabel, her name was. Fanciful name for a flighty sort of woman, if you ask me. Ill for a long while, she was, and her not thirty-five yet, even. Young Dacre were a doctor, you know. So when the squire's sister took sick, the family asked Dr. Dacre to do what he could for the poor lady, on account of the family connection, you see. The doctor's brother affianced to the niece of the sick woman."

"Ah! Mr. Dacre often visited here to treat his patient then?"

"Not he. He has a fine clinic up in London. She went up there to be looked after. Out of her head with worry, she was, poor lamb. Even came here once to see if I had any kind of a tonic that might set her to rights. Now, Mistress Rountree, she says to me, I've got such a pain in my tummy that I don't care if I live or die, only I must make it stop. Is there anything you can give me for it? But I told her there were nought I could do for her, excepting to pray. There never has been for such as she. An Ambry changeling, she was. Know it to look at her, though I kept still about that. So up she went to London, and died upon the operating table up at the Dacre clinic."

"It was not, by any chance, a childbirth?" said Watson.

Grisel Rountree gave him a scornful look. "Childbirth? Not she! I told you: an Ambry changeling she was. Not that I believe all the tales that are bandied here-abouts, but call it what you will, there is a mark on that family."

"Now that is interesting," said Holmes. He had left off eating scones now, and was pacing the length of the cottage while he listened. "What do people say about the Ambrys? A family curse."

"Not a curse. That could be lifted, maybe. This is in the blood and there's no getting away from it. The Ambrys are an old family. They've been living at the Hall since the time of the Crusades, that I do know. Churchyard will tell you that much. But folk in these parts say that one of the Ambry lords, a long time back, married one of the fair folk…" She hesitated, choosing her words carefully. "One of the lords and ladies…"

"He married into the nobility, you mean?" asked Watson.

"Stranger than that, I think," said Holmes still pacing. "I think Mistress Roun-tree is using the countryman's polite—and wary—circumlocution to tell us that an Ambry ancestor took a bride from among the Shining Folk. In short, a fairy wife."

The old woman nodded. "Just so. They do say that she stayed for all of twenty years and twenty days with her mortal husband, and she bore him children, but then she slipped away in the night and went back to her own people. She was never seen again, but her bloodline carries on in the Ambrys to this day. Their union was blessed with five children—or blessed with four, perhaps. The fifth one took after the mother. And ever since that time there has been in nearly every generation that one daughter who takes after the fairy side of the family—a changeling."

"Fascinating," said Holmes.

"But hardly germane to an ordinary stabbing death," said Watson.

"One never knows, Watson. Let us hear a bit more. By what signs do you know that an Ambry boy or girl is the family changeling?"

"It's always a girl," said the old woman. "The prettiest one of the bunch, for one thing. Tall and slender, with beautiful dark hair and what some might call an elf face—big eyes and sharp cheek bones—not your chocolate box pretty girl, but a beauty all the same."

"A lovely girl in every generation?" Dr. Watson laughed. "That sounds like the sort of curse any family would envy."

"But that's not the whole of it," said Grisel. "That's only the good part."

"I suppose they were high-tempered ladies," Watson said, smiling. "The pretty ones often are, I find. Still, I hardly think that fairy stories would deter a modern gentleman."

"There is a good deal of sense wrapped in country fables," said Holmes. "He might do well to heed them. However, I don't quite see its connection to the death of the good doctor. Was the Ambry family angry that Miss Christabel Ambry had died in the doctor's care?"

"No. She were in a bad way, and they knew there was little hope for her. They didn't suppose anybody could have done any more than what he did."

"I wonder what was the matter with her?" mused Watson.

"That is your province, Watson," said Holmes. "You might call in at the clinic and ask. I shall pursue my present line of inquiry. We know that Dacre arrived here on the Friday. The funeral then was on Saturday, and he was found dying within the white horse in the early hours of Sunday morning. He had been stabbed with a silver seam ripper from a sewing kit, but his last words—presumably on the subject of his murderer—were not a maiden."

"Is there a tailor in these parts?"

"Watson, I hardly think that James Dacre would be taking an evening stroll across the downs with the village tailor."

Nor do I," said Grisel Rountree. "Anyhow, we don't have one. So you do think the person up on the hill was a lady after all?"

"We must not theorize ahead of the facts," said Holmes. "This seems to be a country of riddles, and the meaning of the doctor's words is still not clear."

A few days later Sir Henry Dacre, Bart. received his distinguished London visitors in his oak-paneled study at Ramsmeade. He was an amiable young man with watery blue eyes and a diffident smile. At his side was a dark-haired woman, whose imperious nature made her seem more the aristocrat than he. She was nearly as tall as Sir Henry, and her sharp features and glowing white skin were accentuated by the black of her mourning clothes.

"Good morning, Mr. Holmes, Dr. Watson," Sir Henry said. "May I present my fiancée, Miss Evelyn Ambry. My dear, these are the gentlemen I told you about. They are looking into the circumstances surrounding the death of poor James."

She inclined her head regally towards them. "Do sit down, gentlemen. We are so anxious to hear of your progress."

Dr. Watson raised his eyebrows, glancing first at Holmes and then at their host. "The matters we have to discuss are somewhat delicate for a lady's ears," he said. "Perhaps Miss Ambry would prefer not to be present."

Evelyn Ambry gave him a cool stare. "If the matter concerns my family, I shall insist on being present."

Sir Henry gave them a tentative smile. "There you have it, gentlemen. She will have her way. If Miss Ambry wishes to be present, I'm sure she has every right to do so."

With a curt nod Sherlock Holmes settled himself in an armchair near the fire. "As you wish," he said. "I have never been squeamish about medical matters myself. By all means let us proceed. As to the physical facts concerning the death of your late brother, we have done little more than confirm what was already known: that he died in the early hours of June 12 as the result of a stab wound inflicted in his upper abdomen. The weapon was a seam ripper, but it was not of the professional grade used by tailors. Rather it seemed more appropriate to the sewing kit of a woman."

"I have not the patience for sewing," said Miss Ambry. "Such an idle past-time. Grouse shooting is rather more in my line."

"Yet the instrument was of silver, which seems to preclude the villagers from ownership. Does anyone in your household possess such an item?"

She shrugged. "Not to my knowledge. Did you ask the household staff?"

"Yes. They could not be certain either way. Leaving that aside, we know that the doctor came to the village to attend the funeral of his patient, Miss Christabel Ambry, that he stayed at the inn, and after seven in the evening, when he had a pint in the residents' lounge, he was not seen until the next morning, when his body was found in the vale of the White Horse. This much we knew. So we turned our attention to London."

Sir Henry nodded. "You think some enemy may have followed my brother down from London and quarreled with him?"

"I thought it most unlikely," Holmes replied. "In the event we were able to discover no enemies."

"No, indeed," said Watson. "Dr. Dacre was highly esteemed in the medical profession. His colleagues liked him, and his patients are quite distressed that he has been taken from them."

"He was the clever one of the family," said Sir Henry. "But a dear fellow all the same."

"Are you quite sure that James had no enemies?" asked Evelyn Ambry. "Surely you did not interview every one of his patients? What about the relatives of the deceased ones?"

"Indeed we have not yet spoken with you," said Holmes. "I believe you would be included in the latter category. Had your family any resentment toward Dr. Dacre as a physician?"

"Certainly not!" Her cheeks reddened and she pursed her lips in annoyance. "Christabel was very ill. We had long feared the worst. I never go to doctors myself, but I thought James was an exceptional physician. He was tireless on Christabel's behalf. He fought even after we all had given up hope."

"Had the doctor ever mentioned any unhappy patients?" asked Watson, addressing Sir Henry.

"Never," said Sir Henry. "He seemed quite content in his relations with mankind, taken all round."

"Which brings us to womankind," murmured Holmes. "I am thinking of the doctor's final words: Not a maiden. Had your brother any romantic attachments, Sir Henry?"

"Yes. James was engaged to an American heiress. She was in New York at the time of his death, and as she was unable to return for the funeral, she has remained in America with her family. She is quite distraught. They were devoted to one another."

"I see. So there is no question then of a dalliance with a village maiden?" He glanced at Miss Ambry to see if the question called for an apology, but she had managed a taut smile.

"James was not at all that sort of man," she said. "Anyone can tell you that. He lived for his work, and he was quite happy to allocate the rest of his attention to Anne. She is a charming girl."

Dr. Watson cleared his throat. "I have been examining the medical records of Dr. Dacre's patients. They all seem straightforward enough. He specialized in cancer—a sad duty most of the time. I did wonder about your aunt, though, Miss Ambry. The records on her case were missing. There was only an empty folder with her name on it, and a scribbled note: "No hope! Orchids?"

"Do you know what Christabel Ambry died of?"

"Cancer, of course," said Evelyn. "We knew that. I'm afraid we did not press for details. Christabel seemed not to want inquiry on the subject."

"In that case, why did Dacre destroy the records?" said Watson. "He seems to have discussed the case with no one. And what of the notation on the folder?"

"Orchids? Well, perhaps he was thinking of sending flowers for the funeral," Sir Henry suggested.

"Orchids would be most unsuitable, Henry," said his fiancée.

"Well, I suppose they would be. At any rate I know he sent a wreath, but I'm dashed if I know what it was. White flowers, I think. I confess it is all Greek to me, gentlemen."

Sherlock Holmes stared. "I wonder if..." He stood up and began pacing before the hearth. After a few more moments of muttering, during which he ignored their questions, Holmes held up his hand for silence. "Well, we must know. Watson, again your medical skills will be called upon. Let us go and see the squire. I fear that we must discover a buried secret."

"I will not give you a love potion, Millie Hopgood, and that's final," said Grisel Rountree to the rabbit of a girl in her cottage door. "That young man of yours is a Wilberforce, and everybody knows the Wilberforces are mortally shy. He's the undertaker's boy, and he don't know how to talk to live people, I reckon."

"Yes, but—"

"All he wants is a bit of plain speaking from you, and if you won't make up your mind to that, all the potions in the world won't help you."

"Oh, I couldn't, I'm sure, Missus Rountree!" gasped the girl. "But as you'll be seeing him up to the Hall today, I was thinking you might have a word with him yourself."

"Me going to the Hall? First I've heard of it."

The girl pulled an envelope out of her apron pocket, holding it out to the old woman so that she could see the wax seal crest of the Ambrys sealing the flap. "I'm just bringing it now. The two gentlemen from London are back, and they'd like a word with you."

"Well? And what has your young Wilberforce to do with it?"

"Please, missus, they're going into the vault—after Miss Christabel."

"I am coming then," said the old woman. "See you tell Miss Evelyn that I am coming straight away."

Grisel Rountree found Sherlock Holmes walking in the grounds of Old Hall within site of the Ambry family vault. It was a warm June afternoon, but she felt a chill on seeing him pacing the lawn, oblivious to the riot of colors in the flower beds or the beauty of the ancient oaks. As single-minded as Death, he was. And as inevitable.

"So you've gone and dug up Miss Christabel, then?" she said. "Well, I don't suppose dug up is the right term, as she were in a vault."

He nodded. "It all seemed to come down to that. Dr. Watson is in the scullery there, performing an autopsy, but I think we both know what he will find."

"The lady died of cancer," said Grisel Rountree, looking away.

"Christabel Ambry died of cancer, yes," said Holmes.

"Ah," said the old woman. "So you do know something about it."

"I fancy I do, yes." He turned in response to a shout from the door of the scullery. "Here he is now. Shall we hear his report or will you speak now?"

"Does Miss Evelyn know what you are doing?"

"She has gone out with a shooting party," said Holmes. "We are quite alone, except for the undertaker's boy."

"Wilberforce," she said with a dismissive sigh. "He hasn't the sense to grasp what to gossip about, so that's safe. Let the doctor tell you what he makes of it."

Watson reached them then, rolling down his sleeves, his forearms still damp from washing up after the procedure. "Well, it's done, Holmes," he said. "Shall I tell you in private?"

Holmes shook his head. "Miss Rountree here is a midwife and local herbalist. I rather fancy that makes her a colleague of yours. In any case, she has always known what you have just been at pains to discover. Do tell us, Watson. Of what did Christabel Ambry die?"

Watson reddened. "Cancer, right enough," he said gruffly. "Testicular cancer."

"You must have been surprised."

"I've heard of such cases," said Watson. "They are mercifully rare. It is a defect in the development of the foetus before birth, apparently. When I opened up the abdomen, I found that the deceased had the…er…the reproductive organs of a male. The testes, which had become cancerous, were inside the abdomen, and there was no womb. The deceased's vagina, only a few inches long, ended at nothing. I must conclude that the patient was—technically—male."

"An Ambry changeling," said Holmes.

"But how did you know, Holmes?"

"It was only a guess, but I knew, you see, that *orchis* is the Greek word for testis, and I was still thinking about the changeling story. It was an old country attempt to describe a real occurrence, is it not so, madam?"

Grisel Rountree nodded. "We midwives never knew what their insides were like, of course, but the thing about the Ambry changelings is that they were barren. Always. Oh, they might marry, right enough, especially to an outsider who didn't know the story about the Ambrys, but there was never a child born to one of them. Some of them were good wives, and some were bad, and more than a few died young, like Christabel Ambry, rest her soul—but there was never an Ambry changeling that bore a child. That could be curse enough to a landed family with the property entailed, don't you reckon?"

"Indeed," said Holmes." And the doctor knew of this?"

"He did not," said Grisel Rountree. "None of us were like to tell him—no business of his, anyhow. And when Miss Christabel came to see me, she said she might be going up to London to the clinic. 'But I'll not be airing the family linen for Dr. Dacre, Grisel,' she says to me. 'Not with Evelyn engaged to his brother.' Miss Christabel put off going to a doctor for the longest time, afraid he'd find out too much as it was."

"And Miss Evelyn stated that she never consults physicians."

Watson gasped. "Holmes! You don't suppose that Evelyn Ambry is…is…well, a man?"

"I suppose so, in the strictest sense of the definition, but the salient thing here, Watson, is that Evelyn Ambry cannot bear children. Since she is engaged to the possessor of an entailed estate, that is surely a matter of concern. I fear that when Dr. James Dacre discovered the truth of the matter, he conveyed his concerns to Evelyn Ambry—probably at the funeral. They arranged to meet that night to discuss the matter…"

"Why did he not tell his brother straight away?"

"Out of some concern for the feelings of both parties, I should think," said Holmes. "Far better to allow the lady—let us call her a lady still; it is too confusing to do otherwise—to allow the lady to end it on some pretext."

Grisel Rountree nodded. "He mistook his...person," she said. "Miss Evelyn was not one to give up anything without a fight. I'll warrant she took that weapon with her in case the worse came to the worst."

"Not a maiden," murmured Watson. "Well, that is true enough, I fear. But the scandal will be ruinous! Not just the murder, but the cause... Poor Sir Henry! What happens now?"

From the downs above the Old Hall the sound of a single shot rang out, echoing in the clear summer air.

"It has already happened," said Grisel Rountree, turning to go. "It's best if I see to the laying out myself."

"Now there's a thing," said Sherlock Holmes.

THE ADVENTURE OF THE DORSET STREET LODGER

by Michael Moorcock

Michael Moorcock is best known for his genre-redefining swords-and-sorcery series featuring the albino anti-hero Elric of Melniboné. Books featuring Elric include *Stormbringer*, *The Bane of the Black Sword*, and *The Weird of the White Wolf*, among many others. Other prominent works include the Eternal Champion series, the Warrior of Mars series, the Jerry Cornelius series, and the Hawkmoon series. Moorcock is a winner of numerous awards, including several career awards, such as being named a SFWA Grand Master and being inducted into the SF Hall of Fame, as well as being honored with the World Fantasy and Stoker life-time achievement awards.

Say you've just learned that a wealthy relative you didn't even know existed recently passed away and has left to you, his or her only living descendant, a stately property. In fact, this doesn't happen very often, but you wouldn't know it judging from literature, particularly Victorian literature, where it sometimes seems as if eighty percent of the population is blessed with wealthy, generous, childless, and heretofore unknown relatives. Or maybe blessed isn't exactly the word, because properties that come to us in this manner seem to always be mixed up with business such as ghosts or witchcraft or ancient feuds. And how is it that so many people are so ignorant of their own familial relations to begin with? Perhaps back in Victorian times families were so huge that it was easier to misplace a few relatives here and there. Our next tale is another in which a man is contacted by a wealthy relative he never knew existed. In this case though, our contactee is a wealthy man himself, and isn't looking for any free houses to come his way simply by dint of a few fortuitous chromosomes. No, there are no haunted houses here, but plenty of trouble nonetheless.

It was one of those singularly hot Septembers, when the whole of London seemed to wilt from over-exposure to the sun, like some vast Arctic sea-beast foundering upon a tropical beach and doomed to die of unnatural exposure. Where Rome or even Paris might have shimmered and lazed, London merely gasped.

Our windows wide open to the noisy staleness of the air and our blinds drawn against the glaring light, we lay in a kind of torpor, Holmes stretched upon the sofa while I dozed in my easy chair and recalled my years in India, when such heat had been normal and our accommodation rather better equipped to cope with it. I had been looking forward to some fly fishing in the Yorkshire Dales but meanwhile, a patient of mine began to experience a difficult and potentially dangerous confinement so I could not in conscience go far from London. However, we had both planned to be elsewhere at this time and had confused the estimable Mrs. Hudson, who had expected Holmes himself to be gone.

Languidly, Holmes dropped to the floor the note he had been reading. There was a hint of irritation in his voice when he spoke.

"It seems, Watson, that we are about to be evicted from our quarters. I had hoped this would not happen while you were staying."

My friend's fondness for the dramatic statement was familiar to me, so I hardly blinked when I asked: "Evicted, Holmes?" I understood that his rent was, as usual, paid in advance for the year.

"Temporarily only, Watson. You will recall that we had both intended to be absent from London at about this time, until circumstances dictated otherwise. On that initial understanding, Mrs. Hudson commissioned Messrs Peach, Peach, Peach and Praisegod to refurbish and decorate 221B. This is our notice. They begin work next week and would be obliged if we would vacate the premises since minor structural work is involved. We are to be homeless for a fortnight, old friend. We must find new accommodations, Watson, but they must not be too far from here. You have your delicate patient and I have my work. I must have access to my files and my microscope."

I am not a man to take readily to change. I had already suffered several setbacks to my plans and the news, combined with the heat, shortened my temper a little. "Every criminal in London will be trying to take advantage of the situation," I said. "What if a Peach or Praisegod were in the pay of some new Moriarty?"

"Faithful Watson! That Reichenbach affair made a deep impression. It is the one deception for which I feel thorough remorse. Rest assured, dear friend. Moriarty is no more and there is never likely to be another criminal mind like his. I agree, however, that we should be able to keep an eye on things here. There are no hotels in the area fit for human habitation. And no friends or relatives nearby to put us up." It was almost touching to see that master of deduction fall into deep thought and begin to cogitate our domestic problem with the same attention he would give to one of his most difficult cases. It was this power of concentration, devoted to any matter in hand, which had first impressed me with his unique talents. At last he snapped his fingers, grinning like a Barbary ape, his deep-set eyes blazing with intelligence and self-mockery... "I have it, Watson. We shall, of course, ask Mrs. Hudson if she has a neighbour who rents rooms!"

"An excellent idea, Holmes!" I was amused by my friend's almost innocent pleasure in discovering, if not a solution to our dilemma, the best person to provide a solution for us!

Recovered from my poor temper, I rose to my feet and pulled the bellrope.

Within moments our housekeeper, Mrs. Hudson, was at the door and standing before us.

"I must say I am very sorry for the misunderstanding, sir," she said to me. "But patients is patients, I suppose, and your Scottish trout will have to wait a bit until you have a chance to catch them. But as for you, Mr. Holmes, it seems to me that hassassination or no hassassination, you could still do with a nice seaside holiday. My sister in Hove would look after you as thoroughly as if you were here in London."

"I do not doubt it, Mrs. Hudson. However, the assassination of one's host is inclined to cast a pall over the notion of vacations and while Prince Ulrich was no more than an acquaintance and the circumstances of his death all too clear, I feel obliged to give the matter a certain amount of consideration. It is useful to me to have my various analytical instruments to hand. Which brings us to a problem I am incapable of solving—if not Hove, Mrs. Hudson, where? Watson and I need bed and board and it must be close by."

Clearly the good woman disapproved of Holmes's unhealthy habits but despaired of converting him to her cause.

She frowned to express her lack of satisfaction with his reply and then spoke a little reluctantly. "There's my sister-in-law's over in Dorset Street, sir. Number 2, sir. I will admit that her cookery is a little too Frenchified for my taste, but it's a nice, clean, comfortable house with a pretty garden at the back and she has already made the offer."

"And she is a discreet woman, is she Mrs. Hudson, like yourself?"

"As a church, sir. My late husband used to say of his sister that she could hold a secret better than the Pope's confessor."

"Very well, Mrs. Hudson. It is settled! We shall decant for Dorset Street next Friday, enabling your workman to come in on Monday. I will arrange for certain papers and effects to be moved over and the rest shall be secure, I am sure, beneath a good covering. Well, Watson, what do you say? You shall have your vacation, but it will be a little closer to home that you planned and with rather poorer fishing!"

My friend was in such positive spirits that it was impossible for me to retain my mood and indeed events began to move so rapidly from that point on, that any minor inconvenience was soon forgotten.

Our removal to Number 2, Dorset Street, went as smoothly as could be expected and we were soon in residence. Holmes's untidiness, such a natural part of the man, soon gave the impression that our new chambers had been occupied by him for at least a century. Our private rooms had views of a garden which might have been transported from Sussex and our front parlour looked out onto the street, where, at the corner, it was possible to observe customers coming and going from the opulent pawn-brokers, often on their way to the Wheatsheaf Tavern, whose "well-aired beds" we had rejected in favour of Mrs. Ackroyd's somewhat luxurious appointments. A further pleasing aspect of the house was the blooming wisteria vine, of some age, which crept up the front of the building and further added to the countrified aspect. I suspect some of our comforts were not standard to all her lodgers. The good lady, of solid Lancashire stock, was clearly delighted at what she called "the honour" of looking after us and we both agreed we had never experienced better attention. She had pleasant, broad features and a practical, no nonsense manner to her which suited us both. While I would never have said so to either woman, her cooking was rather a pleasant change from Mrs. Hudson's good, plain fare.

And so we settled in. Because my patient was experiencing a difficult progress towards motherhood, it was important that I could be easily reached, but I chose to spend the rest of my time as if I really were enjoying a vacation. Indeed, Holmes himself shared something of my determination, and we had several pleasant evenings together, visiting the theatres and music halls for which London is justly famed. While I had developed an interest in the modern problem plays of Ibsen and Pinero, Holmes still favoured the atmosphere of the Empire and the Hippodrome, while Gilbert and Sullivan at the Savoy was his idea of perfection. Many a night I have sat beside him, often in the box which he preferred, glancing at his rapt features and wondering how an intellect so high could take such pleasure in low comedy and Cockney character-songs.

The sunny atmosphere of 2 Dorset Street actually seemed to lift my friend's spirits and give him a slightly boyish air which made me remark one day that he must have discovered the "waters of life," he was so rejuvenated. He looked at me a little oddly when I said this and told me to remind him to mention the discoveries he had made in Tibet, where he had spent much time after "dying" during his struggle with Professor Moriarty. He agreed, however, that this change was doing him good. He was able to continue his researches when he felt like it, but did not feel obliged to remain at home. He even insisted that we visit the kinema together, but the heat of the building in which it was housed, coupled with the natural odours emanating from our fellow customers, drove us into the fresh air before the show was over. Holmes showed little real interest in the invention. He was inclined to recognize progress only where it touched directly upon his own profession. He told me that he believed the kinema had no relevance to criminology, unless it could be used in the reconstruction of an offence and thus help lead to the capture of a perpetrator.

We were returning in the early evening to our temporary lodgings, having watched the kinema show at Madame Tussaud's in Marylebone Road, when Holmes became suddenly alert, pointing his stick ahead of him and saying in that urgent murmur I knew so well, "What do you make of this fellow, Watson? The one with the brand new top hat, the red whiskers and a borrowed morning coat who recently arrived from the United States but has just returned from the northwestern suburbs where he made an assignation he might now be regretting?"

I chuckled at this. "Come off it, Holmes!" I declared. "I can see a chap in a topper lugging a heavy bag, but how you could say he was from the United States and so on, I have no idea. I believe you're making it up, old man."

"Certainly not, my dear Watson! Surely you have noticed that the morning coat is actually beginning to part on the back seam and is therefore too small for the wearer. The most likely explanation is that he borrowed a coat for the purpose of making a particular visit. The hat is obviously purchased recently for the same reason while the man's boots have the 'gaucho' heel characteristic of the South Western United States, a style found only in that region and adapted, of course, from a Spanish riding boot. I have made a study of human heels, Watson, as well as of human souls!"

We kept an even distance behind the subject of our discussion. The traffic along Baker Street was at its heaviest, full of noisy carriages, snorting horses, yelling drivers and all of London's varied humanity pressing its way homeward, desperate to find some means of cooling its collective body. Our "quarry" had periodically to stop and put down his bag, occasionally changing hands before continuing.

"But why do you say he arrived recently? And has been visiting north-west London?" I asked.

"That, Watson, is elementary. If you think for a moment, it will come clear to you that our friend is wealthy enough to afford the best in hats and Gladstone bags, yet wears a morning coat too small for him. It suggests he came with little luggage, or perhaps his luggage was stolen, and had no time to visit a tailor. Or he went to one of the ready-made places and took *the* nearest fit. Thus, the new bag, also, which he no doubt bought to carry *the* object he has just acquired. That he did not realize how heavy it was is clear and I am sure if he were not staying nearby, he would have hired a cab for himself. He could well be regretting his acquisition. Perhaps it was something very costly, but not exactly what he was expecting to get... He certainly did not realize how awkward it would be to carry, especially in this weather. That suggests to me that he believed he could walk from Baker Street Underground Railway station, which in turn suggests he has been visiting north-west London, which is the chiefly served from Baker Street."

It was rarely that I questioned my friend's judgments, but privately I found this one too fanciful. I was a little surprised, therefore, when I saw the top-hatted gentleman turn left into Dorset Street and disappear. Holmes immediately increased his pace. "Quickly, Watson! I believe I know where he's going."

Rounding the corner, we were just in time to see the American arrive at the door of Number 2 Dorset Street, and put a latch-key to the lock!

"Well, Watson," said Holmes in some triumph. "Shall we attempt to verify my analysis?" Whereupon he strode up to our fellow lodger, raised his hat and offered to help him with the bag.

The man reacted rather dramatically, falling backwards against the railings and almost knocking his own hat over his eyes. He glared at Holmes, panting, and then with a wordless growl, pushed on into the front hall, lugging the heavy Gladstone behind him and slamming the door in my friend's face. Holmes lifted his eyebrows in an expression of baffled amusement. "No doubt the efforts with the bag have put the gentleman in poor temper, Watson!"

Once within, we were in time to see the man, hat still precariously on his head, heaving his bag up the stairs. The thing had come undone and I caught a glimpse of silver, the gleam of gold, the representation, I thought, of a tiny human hand. When he recognized us he stopped in some confusion, then murmured in a dramatic tone:

"Be warned, gentleman. I possess a revolver and I know how to use it."

Holmes accepted this news gravely and informed the man that while he understood an exchange of pistol fire to be something in the nature of an introductory courtesy in Texas, in England it was still considered unnecessary to support one's cause by letting off guns in the house. This I found a little like hypocrisy from one given to target practice in the parlour!

However, our fellow lodger looked suitably embarrassed and began to recover himself. "Forgive me, gentlemen," he said. "I am a stranger here and I must admit I'm rather confused as to who my friends and enemies are. I have been warned to be careful. How did you get in?"

"With a key, as you did, my dear sir. Doctor Watson and myself are guests here for a few weeks."

"Doctor Watson!" The man's voice established him immediately as an American. The drawling brogue identified him as a South Westerner and I trusted Holmes's ear enough to believe that he must be Texan.

"I am he." I was mystified by his evident enthusiasm but illuminated when he turned his attention to my companion.

"Then you must be Mr. Sherlock Holmes! Oh, my good sir, forgive me my bad manners! I am a great admirer, gentlemen. I have followed all your cases. You are, in part, the reason I took rooms near Baker Street. Unfortunately, when I called at your house yesterday, I found it occupied by contractors who could not tell me where you were. Time being short, I was forced to act on my own account. And I fear I have not been too successful! I had no idea that you were lodging in this very building!"

"Our landlady," said Holmes dryly, "is renowned for her discretion. I doubt if her pet cat has heard our names in this house."

The American was about thirty-five years old, his skin turned dark by the sun, with a shock of red hair, a full red moustache and a heavy jaw. If it were not for his intelligent green eyes and delicate hands, I might have mistaken him for an Irish prize fighter. "I'm James Macklesworth, sir, of Galveston, Texas. I'm in the import/export business over there. We ship upriver all the way to Austin, our State Capital, and have a good reputation for honest trading. My grandfather fought to establish our Republic and was the first to take a steam-boat up the Colorado to trade with Port Sabatini and the river-towns." In the manner of Americans, he offered us a resume of his background, life and times, even as we shook hands. It is a custom necessary in those wild and still largely unsettled regions of the United States.

Holmes was cordial, as if scenting a mystery to his taste, and invited the Texan to join us in an hour, when, over a whiskey and soda, we could discuss his business in comfort.

Mr. Macklesworth accepted with alacrity and promised that he would bring with him the contents of his bag and a full explanation of his recent behaviour.

Before James Macklesworth arrived, I asked Holmes if he had any impression of the man. I saw him as an honest enough fellow, perhaps a business man who had got in too deep and wanted Sherlock Holmes to help him out. If that were all he required of my friend, I was certain Holmes would refuse the case. On the other hand, there was every chance that this was an unusual affair.

Holmes said that he found the man interesting and, he believed, honest. But he could not be sure, as yet, if he were the dupe of some clever villain or acting out of character. "For my guess is there is definitely a crime involved here, Watson, and I would guess a pretty devilish one. You have no doubt heard of the Fellini Perseus."

"Who has not? It is said to be Fellini's finest work—cast of solid silver and chased with gold. It represents Perseus with the head of Medusa, which itself is made of sapphires, emeralds, rubies and pearls."

"Your memory as always is excellent, Watson. For many years it was the prize in the collection of Sir Geoffrey Macklesworth, son of the famous Iron Master said to be the richest man in England. Sir Geoffrey, I gather, died one of the poorest. He was fond of art but did not understand money. This made him, I understand, prey to many kinds of social vampires! In his younger years he was involved with the aesthetic movement, a friend of Whistler's and Wilde's. In fact Wilde was, for a while, a good friend to him, attempting to dissuade him from some of his more spectacular blue and white excesses!"

"Macklesworth!" I exclaimed.

"Exactly, Watson." Holmes paused to light his pipe, staring down into the street where the daily business of London continued its familiar and unspectacular round. "The thing was stolen about ten years ago. A daring robbery which I, at the time, ascribed to Moriarty. There was every indication it had been spirited from the country and sold abroad. Yet I recognized it—or else a very fine copy—in that bag James Macklesworth was carrying up the stairs. He would have read of the affair, I'm sure, especially considering his name. Therefore he must have known the Fellini statue was stolen. Yet clearly he went somewhere today and returned here with it. Why? He's no thief, Watson, I'd stake my life on it."

"Let us hope he intends to illuminate us," I said as a knock came at our door.

Mr. James Macklesworth was a changed man. Bathed and dressed in his own clothes, he appeared far more confident and at ease. His suit was of a kind favoured in his part of the world, with a distinctly Spanish cut to it, and he wore a flowing tie beneath the wings of a wide-collared soft shirt, a dark red waistcoat and pointed oxblood boots. He looked every inch the romantic frontiersman.

He began by apologizing for his costume. He had not realized, he said, until he arrived in London yesterday, that his dress was unusual and remarkable in England. We both assured him that his sartorial appearance was in no way offensive to us. Indeed, we found it attractive.

"But it marks me pretty well for who I am, is that not so, gentlemen?"

We agreed that in Oxford Street there would not be a great many people dressed in his fashion.

"That's why I bought the English clothes," he said. "I wanted to fit in and not be noticed. The top hat was too big and the morning coat was too small. The trousers were the only thing the right size. The bag was the largest of its shape I could find."

"So, suitably attired, as you thought, you took the Metropolitan Railway this morning to—?"

"To Willesden, Mr. Holmes. Hey! How did you know that? Have you been following me all day?"

"Certainly not, Mr. Macklesworth. And in Willesden you took possession of the Fellini Perseus did you not?"

"You know everything ahead of me telling it, Mr. Holmes! I need speak no more. Your reputation is thoroughly deserved, sir. If I were not a rational man, I would believe you possessed of psychic powers!"

"Simple deductions, Mr. Macklesworth. One develops a skill, you know. But it might take a longer acquaintance for me to deduce how you came to cross some six thousand miles of land and sea to arrive in London, go straight to Willesden and come away with one of the finest pieces of Renaissance silver the world has ever seen. All in a day, too."

"I can assure you, Mr. Holmes, that such adventuring is not familiar to me. Until a few months ago I was the owner of a successful shipping and wholesaling business. My wife died several years ago and I never remarried. My children are all grown now and married, living far from Texas. I was a little lonely, I suppose, but reasonably content. That all changed, as you have guessed, when the Fellini Perseus came into my life."

"You received word of it in Texas, Mr. Macklesworth?"

"Well, sir, it's an odd thing. Embarrassing, too. But I guess I'm going to have to be square with you and come out with it. The gentleman from whom the Perseus was stolen was a cousin of mine. We'd corresponded a little. In the course of that correspondence he revealed a secret which has now become a burden to me. I was his only living male relative, you see, and he had family business to do. There was another cousin, he thought in New Orleans, but he had yet to be found. Well, gentlemen, the long and the short of it was that I swore on my honour to carry out Sir Geoffrey's instructions in the event of something happening to him or to the Fellini Perseus. His instructions led me to take a train for New York and from New York the *Arcadia* for London. I arrived yesterday afternoon."

"So you came all this way, Mr. Macklesworth, on a matter of honour?" I was somewhat impressed.

"You could say so, sir. We set high store by family loyalty in my part of the world. Sir Geoffrey's estate, as you know, went to pay his debts. But that part of my trip has to do with a private matter. My reason for seeking you out was connected with it. I believe Sir Geoffrey was murdered, Mr. Holmes. Someone was blackmailing him and he spoke of 'financial commitments.' His letters increasingly showed his anxiety and were often rather rambling accounts of his fears that there should be nothing left for his heirs. I told him he had no direct heirs and he might as well reconcile himself to that. He did not seem to take in what I said. He begged me to help him. And he begged me to be discreet. I promised. One of the last letters I had from him told me that if I ever heard news of his death, I must immediately sail for England and upon arriving take a good sized bag to 18 Dahlia Gardens, Willesden Green, North West London, and supply proof of my identity, whereupon I would take responsibility for the object most precious to the Macklesworths. Whereupon I must return to Galveston with all possible speed. Moreover I must swear to keep the object identified with the family name forever.

"This I swore and only a couple of months later I read in the Galveston paper the news of the robbery. Not long after, there followed an account of poor Sir Geoffrey's suicide. There was nothing else I could do, Mr. Holmes, but follow his instructions, as I had sworn I would. However I became convinced that Sir Geoffrey had scarcely been in his right mind at the end. I suspected he feared nothing less than murder. He spoke of people who would go to any lengths to possess the Fellini Silver. He did not care that the rest of his estate was mortgaged to the hilt or that he would die, effectively, a pauper. The Silver was of overweening importance. That is why I suspect the robbery and his murder are connected."

"But the verdict was suicide," I said. "A note was found. The coroner was satisfied."

"The note was covered in blood was it not?" Holmes murmured from where he sat lounging back in his chair, his finger tips together upon his chin.

"I gather that was the case, Mr. Holmes. But since no foul play was suspected, no investigation was made."

"I see. Pray continue, Mr. Macklesworth."

"Well, gentlemen, I've little to add. All I have is a nagging suspicion that something is wrong. I do not wish to be party to a crime, nor to hold back information of use to the police, but I am honour-bound to fulfil my pledge to my cousin. I came to you not necessarily to ask you to solve a crime, but to put my mind at rest if no crime were committed."

"A crime has already been committed, if Sir Geoffrey announced a burglary that did not happen. But it is not much of one, I'd agree. What did you want of us in particular, Mr. Macklesworth?"

"I was hoping you or Dr Watson might accompany me to the address—for a variety of obvious reasons. I am a law-abiding man, Mr. Holmes and wish to remain so. There again, considerations of honour…"

"Quite so," interrupted Holmes. "Now, Mr. Macklesworth, tell us what you found at 18 Dahlia Gardens, Willesden!"

"Well, it was a rather dingy house of a kind I'm completely unfamiliar with. All crowded along a little road about a quarter of a mile from the station. Not at all what I'd expected. Number 18 was dingier than the rest—a poor sort of a place altogether, with peeling paint, an overgrown yard, bulging garbage cans and all the kind of thing you expect to see in East Side New York, not in a suburb of London.

"All this notwithstanding, I found the dirty knocker and hammered upon the door until it was opened by a surprisingly attractive woman of what I should describe as the octoroon persuasion. A large woman, too, with long but surprisingly well-manicured hands. Indeed, she was impeccable in her appearance, in distinct contrast to her surroundings. She was expecting me. Her name was Mrs. Gallibasta. I knew the name at once. Sir Geoffrey had often spoken of her, in terms of considerable affection and trust. She had been, she told me, Sir Geoffrey's housekeeper. He had enjoined her, before he died, to perform this last loyal deed for him. She handed me a note he had written to that effect. Here it is, Mr. Holmes."

He reached across and gave it to my friend who studied it carefully. "You recognize the writing, of course?"

The American was in no doubt. "It is in the flowing, slightly erratic, masculine hand I recognize. As you can see, the note says that I must accept the family heirloom from Mrs. Gallibasta and, in all secrecy, transport it to America, where it must remain in my charge until such time as the other 'missing' Macklesworth cousin was found. If he had male heirs, it must be passed on to one of them at my discretion. If no male heir can be found, it should be passed on to one of my daughters—I have no living sons—on condition that they add the Macklesworth name to their own. I understand, Mr. Holmes, that to some extent I am betraying my trust. But I know so little of English society and customs. I have a strong sense of family and did not know I was related to such an illustrious line until Sir Geoffrey wrote and told me. Although we only corresponded, I feel obliged to carry out his last wishes. However, I am not so foolish as to believe I know exactly what I am doing and require guidance. I want to assure myself that no foul play has been involved and I know that, of all the men in England, you will not betray my secret."

"I am flattered by your presumption, Mr. Macklesworth. Pray, could you tell me the date of the last letter you received from Sir Geoffrey?"

"It was undated, but I remember the post mark. It was the fifteenth day of June of this year."

"I see. And the date of Sir Geoffrey's death?"

"The thirteenth. I supposed him to have posted the letter before his death but it was not collected until afterward."

"A reasonable assumption. And you are very familiar, you say, with Sir Geoffrey's hand-writing."

"We corresponded for several years, Mr. Holmes. The hand is identical. No forger, no matter how clever, could manage those idiosyncrasies, those unpredictable lapses into barely readable words. But usually his hand was a fine, bold, idiosyncratic one. It was not a forgery, Mr. Holmes. And neither was the note he left with his housekeeper."

"But you never met Sir Geoffrey?"

"Sadly, no. He spoke sometimes of coming out to ranch in Texas, but I believe other concerns took up his attention.

"Indeed, I knew him slightly some years ago, when we belonged to the same club. An artistic type, fond of Japanese prints and Scottish furniture. An affable, absent-minded fellow, rather retiring. Of a markedly gentle disposition. Too good for this world, as we used to say."

"When would that have been, Mr. Holmes?" Our visitor leaned forward, showing considerable curiosity.

"Oh, about twenty years ago, when I was just starting in practice. I was able to provide some evidence in a case concerning a young friend of his who had got himself into trouble. He was gracious enough to believe I had been able to turn a good man back to a better path. I recall that he frequently showed genuine concern for the fate of his fellow creatures. He remained a confirmed bachelor, I understand. I was sorry to hear of the robbery. And then the poor man killed himself. I was a little surprised, but no foul play was suspected and I was involved in some rather difficult problems at the time. A kindly sort of old-fashioned gentleman. The patron of many a destitute young artist. It was art, I gather, which largely reduced his fortune."

"He did not speak much of art to me, Mr. Holmes. I fear he had changed considerably over the intervening years. The man I knew became increasingly nervous and given to what seemed somewhat irrational anxieties. It was to quell these anxieties that I agreed to carry out his request. I was, after all, the last of the Macklesworth and obliged to accept certain responsibilities. I was honoured, Mr. Holmes, by the responsibility, but disturbed by what was asked of me."

"You are clearly a man of profound common sense, Mr. Macklesworth, as well as a man of honour. I sympathize entirely with your predicament. You were right to come to us and we shall do all we can to help!"

The relief of the American's face was considerable. "Thank you, Mr. Holmes. Thank you, Doctor Watson. I feel I can now act with some coherence."

"Sir Geoffrey had already mentioned his housekeeper, I take it?"

"He had sir, in nothing less than glowing terms. She had come to him about five years ago and had worked hard to try to put his affairs in order. If it were not for her, he said, he would have faced the bankruptcy court earlier. Indeed, he spoke so warmly of her that I will admit to the passing thought that—well, sir, that they were..."

"I take your meaning, Mr. Macklesworth. It might also explain why your cousin never married. No doubt the class differences were insurmountable, if what we suspect were the case."

"I have no wish to impugn the name of my relative, Mr. Holmes."

"But we must look realistically at the problem, I think." Holmes gestured with his long hand. "I wonder if we might be permitted to see the statue you picked up today?"

"Certainly, sir. I fear the newspaper in which it was wrapped has come loose here and there—"

"Which is how I recognized the Fellini workmanship," said Holmes, his face becoming almost rapturous as the extraordinary figure was revealed. He reached to run his fingers over musculature which might have been living flesh in miniature, it was so perfect. The silver itself was vibrant with some inner energy and the gold chasing, the precious stones, all served to give the most wonderful impression of Perseus, a bloody sword in one hand, his shield on his arm, holding up the snake-crowned head which glared at us through sapphire eyes and threatened to turn us to stone!

"It is obvious why Sir Geoffrey, whose taste was so refined, would have wished this to remain in the family," I said. "Now I understand why he became so obsessed towards the end. Yet I would have thought he might have willed it to a museum—or made a bequest—rather than go to such elaborate lengths to preserve it. It's something which the public deserves to see."

"I agree with you completely, sir. That is why I intend to have a special display room built for it in Galveston. But until that time, I was warned by both Sir Geoffrey and by Mrs. Gallibasta, that news of its existence would bring immense problems—not so much from the police as from the other thieves who covet what is, perhaps, the world's finest single example of Florentine Renaissance silver. It must be worth thousands!

"I intend to insure it for a million dollars, when I get home," volunteered the Texan.

"Perhaps you would entrust the sculpture with us for the night and until tomorrow evening?" Holmes asked our visitor.

"Well, sir, as you know I am supposed to take the *Arcadia* back to New York. She sails tomorrow evening from Tilbury. She's one of the few steamers of her class leaving from London. If I delay, I shall have to go back via Liverpool."

"But you are prepared to do so, if necessary?"

"I cannot leave without the Silver, Mr. Holmes. Therefore, while it remains in your possession, I shall have to stay." John Macklesworth offered us a brief smile and the suggestion of a wink. "Besides, I have to say that the mystery of my cousin's death is of rather more concern than the mystery of his last wishes."

"Excellent, Mr. Macklesworth. I see we are of like mind. It will be a pleasure to put whatever talents I possess at your disposal. Sir Geoffrey resided, as I recall, in Oxfordshire."

"About ten miles from Oxford itself, he said. Near a pleasant little market town called Witney. The house is known as Cogges Old Manor and it was once the centre of a good-sized estate, including a working farm. But the land was sold and now only the house and grounds remain. They, too, of course, are up for sale by my cousin's creditors. Mrs. Gallibasta said that she did not believe it would be long before someone bought the place. The nearest hamlet is High Cogges. The nearest railway station is at South Leigh, about a mile distant. I know the place as if it were my own, Mr. Holmes, Sir Geoffrey's descriptions were so vivid."

"Indeed! Did you, by the by, contact him originally?"

"No, sir! Sir Geoffrey had an interest in heraldry and lineage. In attempting to trace the descendants of Sir Robert Macklesworth, our mutual great-grandfather, he came across my name and wrote to me. Until that time I had no idea I was so closely related to the English aristocracy! For a while Sir Geoffrey spoke of my inheriting the title—but I am a convinced republican. We don't go much for titles and such in Texas—not unless they are earned!"

"You told him you were not interested in inheriting the title?"

"I had no wish to inherit anything, sir." John Macklesworth rose to leave. "I merely enjoyed the correspondence. I became concerned when his letters grew increasingly more anxious and rambling and he began to speak of suicide."

"Yet still you suspect murder?"

"I do, sir. Put it down to an instinct for the truth—or an overwrought imagination. It is up to you!"

"I suspect it is the former, Mr. Macklesworth. I shall see you here again tomorrow evening. Until then, goodnight."

We shook hands.

"Goodnight, gentlemen. I shall sleep easy tonight, for the first time in months." And with that our Texan visitor departed.

"What do you make of it, Watson?" Holmes asked, as he reached for his long-stemmed clay pipe and filled it with tobacco from the slipper he had brought with him. "Do you think our Mr. Macklesworth is 'the real article' as his compatriots would say?"

"I was very favourably impressed, Holmes. But I do believe he has been duped into involving himself in an adventure which, if he obeyed his own honest instincts, he would never have considered. I do not believe that Sir Geoffrey was everything he claimed to be. Perhaps he was when you knew him, Holmes, but since then he has clearly degenerated. He keeps an octoroon mistress, gets heavily into debt and then plans to steal his own treasure in order to preserve it from creditors. He involves our decent Texan friend, conjuring up family ties and knowing how important such things are to Southerners. Then, I surmise, he conspires with his housekeeper to fake his own death."

"And gives his treasure up to his cousin? Why would he do that, Watson?"

"He's using Macklesworth to transport it to America, where he plans to sell it."

"Because he doesn't want to be identified with it, or caught with it. Whereas Mr. Macklesworth is so manifestly innocent he is the perfect one to carry the Silver to Galveston. Well, Watson, it's not a bad theory and I suspect much of it is relevant."

"But you know something else?"

"Just a feeling, really. I believe that Sir Geoffrey is dead. I read the coroner's report. He blew his brains out, Watson. That was why there was so much blood on the suicide note. If he planned a crime, he did not live to complete it.'"

"So the housekeeper decided to continue with the plan?"

"There's only one flaw there, Watson. Sir Geoffrey appears to have anticipated his own suicide and left instructions with her. Mr. Macklesworth identified the handwriting. I read the note myself. Mr. Macklesworth has corresponded with Sir Geoffrey for years. He confirmed that the note was clearly Sir Geoffrey's."

"So the housekeeper is also innocent. We must look for a third party."

"We must take an expedition into the countryside, Watson." Holmes was already consulting his Bradshaw's. "There's a train from Paddington in the morning which will involve a change at Oxford and will get us to South Leigh before lunch. Can your patient resist the lure of motherhood for another day or so, Watson?"

"Happily there's every indication that she is determined to enjoy an elephantine confinement."

"Good, then tomorrow we shall please Mrs. Hudson by sampling the fresh air and simple fare of the English countryside."

And with that my friend, who was in high spirits at the prospect of setting that fine mind to something worthy of it, sat back in his chair, took a deep draft of his pipe, and closed his eyes.

We could not have picked a better day for our expedition. While still warm, the air had a balmy quality to it and even before we had reached Oxford we could smell the delicious richness of an early English autumn. Everywhere the corn had been harvested and the hedgerows were full of colour. Thatch and slate slid past our window which looked out to what was best in an England whose people had built to the natural roll of the land and planted with an instinctive eye for beauty as well as practicality. This was what I had missed in Afghanistan and what Holmes had missed in Tibet, when he had learned so many things at the feet of the High Lama himself. Nothing ever compensated, in my opinion, for the wealth and variety of the typical English country landscape.

In no time we were at South Leigh station and able to hire a pony-cart with which to drive ourselves up the road to High Cogges. We made our way through winding lanes, between tall hedges, enjoying the sultry tranquillity of a day whose silence was broken only by the sound of bird-song and the occasional lowing of a cow.

We drove through the hamlet, which was served by a Norman church and a grocer's shop which also acted as the local post office. High Cogges itself was reached by a rough lane, little more than a farm track leading past some pictur-esque farm cottages with thatched roofs, which seemed to have been there since the beginning of time and were thickly covered with roses and honeysuckle, a rather vulgar modern house whose owner had made a number of hideous addi-tions in the popular taste of the day, a farmhouse and outbuildings of the warm, local stone which seemed to have grown from out of the landscape as naturally as the spinney and orchard behind it, and then we had arrived at the locked gates of Cogges Old Manor which bore an air of neglect. It seemed to me that it had been many years since the place had been properly cared for.

True to form, my friend began exploring and had soon discovered a gap in a wall through which we could squeeze in order to explore the grounds. These were little more than a good-sized lawn, some shrubberies and dilapidated greenhouses, an abandoned stables, various other sheds, and a workshop which was in surprisingly neat order. This, Holmes told me, was where Sir Geoffrey had died. It had been thoroughly cleaned. He had placed his gun in a vice and shot himself through the mouth. At the inquest, his housekeeper, who had clearly been devoted to him, had spoken of his money worries, his fears that he had dishonoured the family name. The scrawled note had been soaked in blood and only partially legible, but it was clearly his.

"There was no hint of foul play, you see, Watson. Everyone knew that Sir Geoffrey led the Bohemian life until he settled here. He had squandered the family fortune, largely on artists and their work. No doubt some of his many modern canvasses would become valuable, at least to someone, but at present the artists he had patronized had yet to realize any material value. I have the impression that half the denizens of the Cafe Royal depended on the Macklesworth millions until they finally dried up. I also believe that Sir Geoffrey was either distracted in his last years, or depressed. Possibly both. I think we must make an effort to interview Mrs. Gallibasta. First, however, let's visit the post office—the source of all wisdom in these little communities."

The post office-general store was a converted thatched cottage, with a white picket fence and a display of early September flowers which would not have been out of place in a painting. Within the cool shade of the shop, full of every possible item a local person might require, from books to boiled sweets, we were greeted by the proprietress whose name over her doorway we had already noted.

Mrs. Beck was a plump, pink woman in plain prints and a starched pinafore, with humorous eyes and a slight pursing of the mouth which suggested a conflict between a natural warmth and a slightly censorious temperament. Indeed, this is exactly what we discovered. She had known both Sir Geoffrey and Mrs. Gallibasta. She had been on good terms with a number of the servants, she said, although one by one they had left and had not been replaced.

"There was talk, gentlemen, that the poor gentlemen was next to destitute and couldn't afford new servants. But he was never behind with the wages and those who worked for him were loyal enough. Especially his housekeeper. She had an odd, distant sort of air, but there's no question she looked after him well and since his prospects were already known, she didn't seem to be hanging around waiting for his money."

"Yet you were not fond of the woman?" murmured Holmes, his eyes studying an advertisement for toffee.

"I will admit that I found her a little strange, sir. She was a foreign woman, Spanish I think. It wasn't her gypsy looks that bothered me, but I never could get on with her. She was always very polite and pleasant in her conversation. I saw her almost every day, too—though never in church. She'd come in here to pick up whatever small necessities they needed. She always paid cash and never asked for credit. Though I had no love for her, it seemed that she was supporting Sir Geoffrey, not the other way around. Some said she had a temper to her and that once she had taken a rake to an under-footman, but I saw no evidence of it. She'd spend a few minutes chatting with me, sometimes purchase a newspaper, collect whatever mail there was and walk back up the lane to the manor. Rain or shine, sir, she'd be here. A big, healthy woman she was. She'd joke about what a handful it all was, him and the estate, but she didn't seem to mind. I only knew one odd thing about her. When she was sick, no matter how sick she became, she always refused a doctor. She had a blind terror of the medical profession, sir. The very suggestion of calling Doctor Shapiro would send her into screaming insistence that she needed no 'sawbones.' Otherwise, she was what Sir Geoffrey needed, him being so gentle and strange and with his head in the clouds. He was like that since a boy."

"But given to irrational fears and notions, I gather?"

"Not so far as I ever observed, sir. He never seemed to change. She was the funny one. Though he stayed at the house for the past several years and I only saw him occasionally. But when I did he was his usual sunny self."

"That's most interesting, Mrs. Beck. I am grateful to you. I think I will have a quarter-pound of your best bullseyes, if you please. Oh, I forgot to ask. Do you remember Sir Geoffrey receiving any letters from America?"

"Oh, yes, sir. Frequently. He looked forward to them, she said. I remember the envelope and the stamps. It was almost his only regular correspondent."

"And Sir Geoffrey sent his replies from here?"

"I wouldn't know that, sir. The mail's collected from a pillar-box near the station. You'll see it, if you're going back that way."

"Mrs. Gallibasta, I believe, has left the neighbourhood."

"Not two weeks since, sir. My son carried her boxes to the station for her. She took all her things. He mentioned how heavy her luggage was. He said if he hadn't attended Sir Geoffrey's service at St James's himself he'd have thought she had him in her trunk. If you'll pardon the levity, sir."

"I am greatly obliged to you, Mrs. Beck." The detective lifted his hat and bowed. I recognized Holmes's brisk, excited mood. He was on a trail now and had scented some form of quarry. As we left, he murmured: "I must go round to 221B as soon as we get back and look in my early files."

As I drove the dog-cart back to the station, Holmes scarcely spoke a further word. He was lost in thought all the way back to London. I was used to my friend's moods and habits and was content to let that brilliant mind exercise itself while I gave myself up to the world's concerns in the morning's *Telegraph*.

Mr. Macklesworth joined us for tea that afternoon. Mrs. Ackroyd had outdone herself with smoked salmon and cucumber sandwiches, small savouries, scones and cakes. The tea was my favourite Darjeeling, whose delicate flavour is best appreciated at that time in the afternoon, and even Holmes remarked that we might be guests at Sinclair's or the Grosvenor.

Our ritual was overseen by the splendid Fellini Silver which, perhaps to catch the best of the light, Holmes had placed in our sitting-room window, looking out to the street. It was as if we ate our tea in the presence of an angel. Mr. Macklesworth balanced his plate on his knee wearing an expression of delight. "I have heard of this ceremony, gentlemen, but never expected to be taking part in a High Tea with Mr. Sherlock Holmes and Doctor Watson!"

"Indeed, you are doing no such thing, sir," Holmes said gently. "It is a common misconception, I gather, among our American cousins that High- and Afternoon-tea are the same thing. They are very different meals, taken at quite different times. High Tea was in my day only eaten at certain seats of learning, and was a hot, early supper. The same kind of supper, served in a nursery, has of late been known as High Tea. Afternoon-tea, which consists of a conventional cold sandwich selection, sometimes with scones, clotted cream and strawberry jam, is eaten by adults, generally at four o'clock. High Tea, by and large, is eaten by children at six o'clock. The sausage was always very evident at such meals when I was young." Holmes appeared to shudder subtly.

"I stand corrected and instructed, sir," said the Texan jovially, and waved a delicate sandwich by way of emphasis. Whereupon all three of us broke into laughter—Holmes at his own pedantry and Mr. Macklesworth almost by way of relief from the weighty matters on his mind.

"Did you discover any clues to the mystery in High Cogges?" our guest wished to know.

"Oh, indeed, Mr. Macklesworth," said Holmes, "I have one or two things to verify, but think the case is solved." He chuckled again, this time at the expression of delighted astonishment on the American's face.

"Solved, Mr. Holmes?"

"Solved, Mr. Macklesworth, but not proven. Doctor Watson, as usual, contributed greatly to my deductions. It was you, Watson, who suggested the motive for involving this gentleman in what, I believe, was a frightful and utterly cold-blooded crime."

"So I was right, Mr. Holmes! Sir Geoffrey was murdered!"

"Murdered or driven to self-murder, Mr. Macklesworth, it is scarcely material."

"You know the culprit, sir?

"I believe I do. Pray, Mr. Macklesworth," now Holmes pulled a piece of yellowed paper from an inner pocket, "would you look at this? I took it from my files on the way here and apologize for its somewhat dusty condition."

Frowning slightly, the Texan accepted the folded paper and then scratched his head in some puzzlement, reading aloud. "My dear Holmes, Thank you so much for your generous assistance in the recent business concerning my young painter friend... Needless to say, I remain permanently in your debt. Yours very sincerely..." He looked up in some confusion. "The notepaper is unfamiliar to me, Mr. Holmes. Doubtless the Athenaeum is one of your clubs. But the signature is false."

"I had an idea you might determine that, sir," said Holmes, taking the paper from our guest. Far from being discommoded by the information, he seemed satisfied by it. I wondered how far back the roots of this crime were to be found. "Now, before I explain further, I feel a need to demonstrate something. I wonder if you would be good enough to write a note to Mrs. Gallibasta in Willesden. I would like you to tell her that you have changed your mind about returning to the United States and have decided to live in England for a time. Meanwhile, you intend to place the Fellini Silver in a bank vault until you go back to the United States, whereupon you are considering taking legal advice as to what to do with the statue."

"If I did that, Mr. Holmes, I would not be honouring my vow to my cousin. And I would be telling a lie to a lady."

"Believe me, Mr. Macklesworth, if I assure you, with all emphasis, that you will not be breaking a promise to your cousin and you will not be telling a lie to a lady. Indeed, you will be doing Sir Geoffrey Macklesworth and, I hope, both our great nations, an important service if you follow my instructions."

"Very well, Mr. Holmes," said Macklesworth, firming his jaw and adopting a serious expression, "if that's your word, I'm ready to go along with whatever you ask."

"Good man, Macklesworth!" Sherlock Holmes's lips were drawn back a little from his teeth, rather like a wolf which sees its prey finally become vulnerable. "By the by, have you ever heard in your country of a creature known as 'Little Peter' or sometimes 'French Pete'?"

"Certainly I have. He was a popular subject in the sensational press and remains so to this day. He operated out of New Orleans about a decade ago. Jean 'Petit Pierre' Fromental. An entertainer of some sort. He was part Arcadian and, some said, part Cree. A powerful, handsome man. He was famous for a series of particularly vicious murders of well-known dignitaries in the private rooms of those establishments for which Picayune is famous. A woman accomplice was also involved. She was said to have lured the men to their deaths. Fromental was captured eventually but the woman was never arrested. Some believe it was she who helped him escape when he did. As I remember, Mr. Holmes, Fromental was never caught. Was there not some evidence that he, in turn, had been murdered by a woman? Do you think Fromental and Sir Geoffrey were both victims of the same murderess?"

"In a sense, Mr. Macklesworth. As I said, I am reluctant to give you my whole theory until I have put some of it to the test. But none of this is the work of a woman, that I can assure you. Will you do as I say?"

"Count on me, Mr. Holmes. I will compose the telegram now."

When Mr. Macklesworth had left our rooms, I turned to Holmes, hoping for a little further illumination, but he was nursing his solution to him as if it were a favourite child. The expression on his face was extremely irritating to me. "Come, Holmes, this won't do! You say I helped solve the problem, yet you'll give me no hint as to the solution. Mrs. Gallibasta is not the murderess, yet you say a murder is most likely involved. My theory—that Sir Geoffrey had the Silver spirited away and then killed himself so that he would not be committing a crime, as he would if he had been bankrupted—seems to confirm this. His handwriting has identified him as the author of letters claiming Mr. Macklesworth as a relative—Macklesworth had nothing to do with that—and then suddenly you speak of some Louisiana desperado known as 'Little Pierre,' who seems to be your main suspect until Mr. Macklesworth revealed that he was dead."

"I agree with you, Watson, that it seems very confusing. I hope for illumination tonight. Do you have your revolver with you, old friend?"

"I am not in the habit of carrying a gun about, Holmes."

At this, Sherlock Holmes crossed the room and produced a large shoe-box which he had also brought from 221B that afternoon. From it he produced two modern Webley revolvers and a box of ammunition. "We may need these to defend our lives, Watson. We are dealing with a master criminal intelligence. An intelligence both patient and calculating, who has planned this crime over many years and now believes there is some chance of being thwarted."

"You think Mrs. Gallibasta is in league with him and will warn him when the telegram arrives?"

"Let us just say, Watson, that we must expect a visitor tonight. That is why the Fellini Silver stands in our window, to be recognized by anyone who is familiar with it."

I told my friend that at my age and station I was losing patience for this kind of charade, but reluctantly I agreed to position myself where he instructed and, taking a firm grip on my revolver, settled down for the night.

The night was almost as sultry as the day and I was beginning to wish that I had availed myself of lighter clothing and a glass of water when I heard a strange, scraping noise from somewhere in the street and risked a glance down from where I stood behind the curtain. I was astonished to see a figure, careless of any observer, yet fully visible in the yellow light of the lamps, climbing rapidly up the wisteria vine!

Within seconds the man—for man it was, and a gigantic individual, at that—had slipped a knife from his belt and was opening the catch on the window in which the Fellini Silver still sat. It was all I could do to hold my position. I feared the fellow would grasp the statue and take it out with him. But then common sense told me that, unless he planned to lower it from the window, he must come in and attempt to leave by the stairs.

The audacious burglar remained careless of onlookers, as if his goal so filled his mind that he was oblivious to all other considerations. I caught a glimpse of his features in the lamp-light. He had thick, wavy hair tied back in a bandanna, a couple of days' stubble on his chin and dark, almost negroid skin I guessed at once that he was a relative of Mrs. Gallibasta.

Then he had snapped back the catch of the window and I heard his breath hissing from his lips as he raised the sash and slipped inside.

The next moment Holmes emerged from his hiding place and levelled the revolver at the man who turned with the blazing eyes of a trapped beast, knife in hand, seeking escape.

"There is a loaded revolver levelled at your head, man," said Holmes evenly, "and you would be wise to drop that knife and give yourself up!"

With a wordless snarl, the intruder flung himself towards the Silver, placing it between himself and our guns. "Shoot if you dare!" he cried. "You will be destroying more than my unworthy life! You will be destroying everything you have conspired to preserve! I underestimated you, Macklesworth. I thought you were an easy dupe—dazzled by the notion of being related to a knight of the realm, with whom you had an intimate correspondence! I worked for years to discover everything I could about you. You seemed perfect. You were willing to do anything, so long as it was described as a matter of family honour. Oh, how I planned! How I held myself in check! How patient I was. How noble in all my deeds! All so that I would one day own not merely that fool Geoffrey's money, but also his most prized treasure! I had his love—but I wanted everything else besides!"

It was then I realized suddenly what Holmes had been telling me. I almost gasped aloud as I understood the truth of the situation!

At that moment I saw a flash of silver and heard the sickening sound of steel entering flesh. Holmes fell back, his pistol dropping from his hand and with a cry of rage I discharged my own revolver, careless of Fellini or his art, in my belief that my friend was once again to be taken from me—this time before my eyes.

I saw Jean-Pierre Fromental, alias Linda Gallibasta, fall backwards, arms raised, and crash through the window by which he had entered. With a terrible cry he staggered, flailed at the air, then fell into an appalling silence.

At that moment, the door burst open and in came John Macklesworth, closely followed by our old friend Inspector Lestrade, Mrs. Beck and one or two other tenants of 2 Dorset Street.

"It's all right, Watson," I heard Holmes say, a little faintly. "Only a flesh wound. It was foolish of me not to think he could throw a Bowie-knife! Get down there, Lestrade, and see what you can do. I'd hoped to take him alive. It could be the only way we'll be able to locate the money he has been stealing from his benefactor over all these years. Good night to you, Mr. Macklesworth. I had hoped to convince you of my solution, but I had not expected to suffer quite so much injury in the performance." His smile was faint and his eyes were flooded with pain.

Luckily, I was able to reach my friend before he collapsed upon my arm and allowed me to lead him to a chair, where I took a look at the wound. The knife had stuck in his shoulder and, as Holmes knew, had done no permanent damage, but I did not envy him the discomfort he was suffering.

Poor Macklesworth was completely stunned. His entire notion of things had been turned topsy-turvy and he was having difficulty taking everything in. After dressing Holmes's wound, I told Macklesworth to sit down while I fetched everyone a brandy. Both the American and myself were bursting to learn everything Holmes had deduced, but contained ourselves until my friend would be in better health. Now that the initial shock was over, however, he was in high spirits and greatly amused by our expressions.

"Your explanation was ingenious, Watson, and touched on the truth, but I fear it was not the answer. If you will kindly look in my inside jacket pocket, you will find two pieces of paper there. Would you be good enough to draw them out so that we might all see them?"

I did as my friend instructed. One piece contained the last letter Sir Geoffrey had written to John Macklesworth and, ostensibly, left with Mrs. Gallibasta. The other, far older, contained the letter John Macklesworth had read out earlier that day. Although there was a slight similarity to the handwriting, they were clearly by different authors.

"You said this was the forgery," said Holmes, holding up the letter in his left hand, "but unfortunately it was not. It is probably the only example of Sir Geoffrey's handwriting you have ever seen, Mr. Macklesworth."

"You mean he dictated everything to his—to that devil?"

"I doubt, Mr. Macklesworth, that your namesake had ever heard of your existence."

"He could not write to a man he had never heard of, Mr. Holmes!"

"Your correspondence, my dear sir, was not with Sir Geoffrey at all, but with the man who lies on the pavement down there. His name, as Doctor Watson has already deduced, is Jean-Pierre Fromental. No doubt he fled to England after the Picayune murders and got in with the Bohemian crowd surrounding Lord Alfred Douglas and others, eventually finding exactly the kind of dupe he was looking for. It is possible he kept his persona of Linda Gallibasta all along. Certainly that would explain why he became so terrified at the thought of being examined by a doctor—you'll recall the postmistresses words. It is hard to know if he was permanently dressing as a woman—that, after all, is how he had lured his Louisiana victims to their deaths—and whether Sir Geoffrey knew much about him, but clearly he made himself invaluable to his employer and was able, bit by bit, to salt away the remains of the Macklesworth fortune. But what he really craved, was the Fellini Silver, and that was when he determined the course of action which led to his calculating deception of you, Mr. Macklesworth. He needed a namesake living not far from New Orleans. As an added insurance he invented another cousin. By the simple device of writing to you on Sir Geoffrey's stationery he built up an entire series of lies, each of which had the appearance of verifying the other. Because, as Linda Gallibasta, he always collected the mail, Sir Geoffrey was never once aware of the deception."

It was John Macklesworth's turn to sit down suddenly as realization dawned. "Good heavens, Mr. Holmes. Now I understand!"

"Fromental wanted the Fellini Silver. He became obsessed with the notion of owning it. But he knew that if he stole it there was little chance of his ever getting it out of the country. He needed a dupe. That dupe was you, Mr. Macklesworth. I regret that you are probably not a cousin of the murdered man. Neither did Sir Geoffrey fear for his Silver. He appears quite reconciled to his poverty and had long since assured that the Fellini Silver would remain in trust for his family or the public forever. In respect of the Silver he was sheltered from all debt by a special covenant with Parliament. There was never a danger of the piece going to his creditors. There was, of course, no way, in those circumstances, that Fromental could get the Silver for himself. He had to engineer first a burglary—and then a murder, which looked like a consequence of that burglary. The suicide note was a forgery, but hard to decipher. His plan was to use your honesty and decency, Mr. Macklesworth, to carry the Silver through to America. Then he planned to obtain it from you by any means he found necessary."

Macklesworth shuddered. "I am very glad I found you, Mr. Holmes. If I had not, by coincidence, chosen rooms in Dorset Street, I would even now be conspiring to further that villain's ends!"

"As, it seems, did Sir Geoffrey. For years he trusted Fromental. He appears to have doted on him, indeed. He was blind to the fact that his estate was being stripped of its remaining assets. He put everything down to his own bad judgment and thanked Fromental for helping him! Fromental had no difficulty, of course, in murdering Sir Geoffrey when the time came. It must have been hideously simple. That suicide note was the only forgery, as such, in the case, gentlemen. Unless, of course, you count the murderer himself."

Once again, the world had been made a safer and saner place by the astonishing deductive powers of my friend Sherlock Holmes.

POSTSCRIPT

And that was the end of the Dorset Street affair. The Fellini Silver was taken by the Victoria and Albert Museum who, for some years, kept it in the special "Macklesworth" Wing before it was transferred, by agreement, to the Sir John Soane Museum. There the Macklesworth name lives on. John Macklesworth returned to America a poorer and wiser man. Fromental died in hospital, without revealing the whereabouts of his stolen fortune, but happily a bank book was found at Willesden and the money was distributed amongst Sir Geoffrey's creditors, so that the house did not have to be sold. It is now in the possession of a genuine Macklesworth cousin. Life soon settled back to normal and it was with some regret that we eventually left Dorset Street to take up residence again at 221B. I have occasion, even today, to pass that pleasant house and recall with a certain nostalgia the few days when it had been the focus of an extraordinary adventure.

THE ADVENTURE OF THE LOST WORLD

by Dominic Green

Dominic Green is the author of several short stories, more than a dozen of which have appeared in the British SF magazine *Interzone*. His work has also appeared in the anthologies *Decalog 5* and *The Year's Best Science Fiction*. In 2006, his story, "The Clockwork Atom Bomb," was a finalist for the Hugo Award. This story first appeared in the online *BBCi Cult Sherlock Holmes Magazine,* along with four other original Holmes tales.

When Sherlock Holmes and Professor Moriarty toppled to their deaths from Reichenbach Falls, the reading public was outraged. People loved Sherlock Holmes, and just didn't want to accept that he was dead. People have had much the same feeling about dinosaurs, ever since the first dinosaur fossils were widely exhibited in the early nineteenth century. Dinosaurs were just so great, so awe-inspiring, so fun, that people didn't want to believe that the dinosaurs were all dead, and novelists fed this hunger. Maybe there were dinosaurs in South America. Maybe at the North Pole. Arthur Conan Doyle, author of Sherlock Holmes, wrote one of the best-known of these dinosaur romps, called *The Lost World*. As exploration foreclosed these possibilities, dino-loving authors resorted to increasingly desperate ploys. Maybe there were dinosaurs *inside the Earth.* Maybe you could *clone* dinosaurs from dino blood found in amber-encrusted mosquitoes. Sadly, the Earth has turned out to be depressingly un-hollow, and there's not much chance of genetic material hanging around for sixty-five million years. This next tale takes us back to a simpler, happier time, when one could more easily imagine gigantic, blood-crazed lizards haunting the forests of the night.

It was in the autumn of 1918, when my medical practice was burgeoning on account of casualties from the recent war, when my friend Sherlock Holmes called upon me in the most unexpected circumstances. Loyal readers of the *Strand Magazine* will, no doubt, already be indoctrinated in such exploits of Holmes as the intrigue surrounding the Ruritanian Abdication Crisis. However, at that time Holmes had failed to uncover anything incomprehensible to the human mind for several weeks, and I was beginning to fear for his health.

I was conducting surgery on an elderly Major of Rifles who had lost a leg in the Egyptian campaign, and whom I was treating for scrofula of the stump, when I all of a sudden heard the ghostly, unexpected voice of my friend Holmes.

"I apologize for this peculiar method of gaining entry to your consulting rooms, Watson, but I must beg your company right away."

I looked up, behind me, and all about the room, but could see nowhere my one-time room-mate and companion. I stared at the laudanum bottle I had been about to hand over to my patient.

"The Major was otherwise disposed today, Watson," said the Major. "I have taken the liberty of taking his place. The streets are not safe for me to walk in my customary attire at present."

"But the leg, Holmes," I stammered. "How did you do the leg?"

"Ah, Watson," said Holmes in a voice of immensely pleased conceit, "you have been making the assumption all the time that I had two legs to begin with."

"But Holmes," I protested. "I have seen you run, and jump!"

"Have you, Watson? Have you really?"

"Are you, at present, engaged upon an investigation?"

"An investigation more brutal and savage, perhaps, than any other I have previously been involved in. I consider it normal to see a man's life taken from him by another for the pursuit of criminal gain, Watson; but it is rare indeed for him to be eaten afterwards."

Even I, who have been in Afghanistan, was appalled. "Surely not."

"Just so, Watson. In the past seven days, on Hampstead Heath, there have been seven attacks upon street musicians, each the player of a trombone of some description, and each attacked, if those who heard the attacks are to be believed, whilst executing the closing bars of Gustav Holst's Thaxted. In each case, the victim appears to have been attacked from above, the flesh crushed and cut, the bones splintered, the capital extremity entirely missing in many cases. Each victim's body was also notable for the stench of corruption which hung about it, like gas gangrene."

"Accidental death has been ruled out, then? A recurrent trombone malfunction of some order—"

"—has already been checked for. The instruments were produced by different manufacturers, all of the very highest reputation and with large portfolios of quite living, healthy customers. However, I do not trust the unmedical minds of London's Metropolitan Police, Watson. I require your keen anatomical brain. A fresh body has been discovered on the Heath this very hour. I enjoin you to take the new-fangled subterranean railway to Hampstead. I will be waiting outside the station, though of course you will not know me."

The London fog was thick as wool pulled over the eyes when I stepped out of the station at the pleasant rustic hamlet of Hampstead. Streetlamps were already being lit, each surrounded by a saintly halo in the murk. I bought a paper from a decrepit scion of the lower classes and sat down on a bench to wait for my tardy associate.

"Watson!" hissed a voice through the gloom.

"Egad," I replied. "Where are you, Holmes?"

"I have just sold you a copy of the *London Evening Standard*. LATEST NEWS, GUVNOR! Though I had thought you might have remarked on my trombone."

I remarked on his trombone. "Good lord, Holmes! You have a trombone. Are you mad?"

"Not in the least. This is quite a singular trombone. It was discovered, twenty feet up in the branches of a tree, but otherwise almost entirely unharmed, a hundred yards from the body of the penultimate victim. It plays beautifully." He essayed a bar of Thaxted.

"An improvement on your violin, at any rate. And now, where is the last man to be murdered?"

Holmes led me with the accuracy of a homing pigeon through a white haze out of which trees drifted like gigantic submarine fauna. Finally, he came upon a spot where two policemen sat playing cards over the sad, torn body of one of our city's street musicians.

"Evening, Mr. 'Olmes," they chorused.

"Good evening, officers. Now, Watson, your medical training will almost certainly draw your attention to the body's non-possession of a head. What I wish to know is, what removed that head so swiftly and so irrevocably?"

I examined the poor corpse as thoroughly as I could. "I have seen something similar to this at only one point in my career," I said. "An Indian mugger, not a man but a crocodile, which caused a commotion in our billet in Peshawar. One night, one of our subalterns, answering the call of nature by the waterside, was seized about a part of his anatomy I dread to name by the scaly abomination. Sixteen rifle bullets were needed to kill it, by which time the unfortunate officer was long dead. The brutes have jaws capable of cracking a man's ribcage like an egg."

"Interesting. And what do you suppose did this?"

"Something, I would hazard a guess," I said, "with bigger jaws."

Holmes was striding out across the frozen grass, tapping his heel with his cane impatiently. "So, what do you suppose has bigger jaws than a crocodile?"

"I have no idea. An extraordinarily large lion escaped from a zoo, perhaps."

"Come here, Watson."

I walked closer. Holmes was standing over something, an impression in the turf.

"There. What do you imagine that is?"

I looked. Then, I stared.

"It's a footprint, Watson," said Holmes. "It is the footprint of a gigantic ten-thousand-pound theropod from Hell."

Ten minutes later I was staring at Holmes as though he were the starkest mad-man.

"A megalosaurus?"

"The very same. You know my maxim—when you have eliminated the impossible, whatever remains, however improbable, must be, etcetera, etcetera."

I began to feel somewhat light-headed. "Holmes, the megalosaurus has been extinct for nearly two hundred million years."

"Not so, Watson." At this point Holmes fished out a stack of books and papers he had been concealing in his trombone case and began flicking frantically through a periodical. "I considered all the animals that currently exist in the world and are capable of killing a man, and eliminated them one by one from my inquiries. The leopard lacked the sheer height to attack from above unless concealed in a tree, and I could find no claw marks in the bark of any tree hereabouts. The elephant, meanwhile, whilst possessing sufficient elevation, would gore or trample in preference to biting. Finally, I concluded that the attacker was an animal unrecognized by conventional zoology.

"Therefore I switched from zoology to palaeontology. The characteristic dual puncture wounds of a sabre-toothed tiger attack were not present, nor were the sixfold blunt contusions that would indicate a charging uintatherium. I went through ten heavy tomes at the British Museum before I alighted on my culprit. A megalosaurus had performed this crime, Watson—a huge Jurassic beast moving on powerful three-clawed feet and with a mouth like a cavern of stalactites. I know what you will say, Watson—nowhere on Earth does a megalosaurus currently exist. But there are reports from the Belgian Congo of creatures that resemble a stegosaurus more than a stegosaurus's maiden aunt, and in addition, there are the remarkable accounts which I now commend to you." He had now found the pages he had been looking for, and set to reading aloud enthusiastically.

"Proceedings of the London Zoological Institute, June 13th, 1917: an address to be delivered by Professor Challenger to a general assembly of all members, regarding extraordinary discoveries recently made in a high tributary of the Amazon..."

"That was all poppycock. Totally discredited. The expedition brought back no evidence of the existence of living dinosauria in the Amazon whatsoever."

"You must remember, Watson, that the generally accepted public account of the expedition is that of Mr. Edward Malone of the *Daily Gazette*," admonished Holmes. "But I have recently been across the Channel to purchase Professor Challenger's own version of events and it makes most enlightening reading. As you know, the Professor's account was savaged by Her Majesty's censors, only a few select copies making their way here across the Channel after having had to be published in France."

He switched to a different volume, this one hardbound and bearing a lurid cover engraving of a lady in night attire being improbably menaced by a tumescent Mesozoic reptile.

"September 13th, 1916. Violently, bestially drunk on that fermented mash of giant spiders the natives call ghula-ghula. Still see huge green dinosaurs everywhere. Am having to gradually force myself to face the horrid truth that they might actually be real. After tea, with Roxton, Malone and Summerlee out of the camp, disported myself with two of the hallucinatory Stone Age women hereabouts, enjoying to the full their supple and surprisingly real-seeming honey-coloured bodies—"

"That is quite enough, Holmes," I snapped. "The ravings of a man in an arachnolysin-induced delirium are hardly proof of the continued existence of dinosaurs."

"Agreed, Watson. But if we read on! If we but read on! December 1, 1916. Our return to England has been safely negotiated without either my confederates or Customs & Excise suspecting I had more in my baggage than declared. The egg is ovoid—as is only to be expected—about the size of a large coconut, porous skinned, and a bright saffron yellow in colour. I have been incubating it by stealing into the cargo hold and covering it with rotting kitchen waste, and in addition, whenever possible, sit on the egg personally. When questioned why I was sitting in rotting kitchen waste in the cargo hold by the ship's purser, I simply replied that I was incubating an egg which, when it hatched out, would develop into a twenty-foot-long man-eating lizard, whereupon he simply grinned, tapped his cap in a friendly way, and left me to my own devices.

"February 2, 1917. My hatchling has arrived. Have been feeding it turkey giblets, which it consumes with gusto. Have named it Gladys, after Malone's carnivorous reptilian fiancée. Gladys very attracted to bright objects and movement. Already appear to have lost the cat, a huge fluffy useless article good only for destroying valuable furnishings. Wife distraught. Am beginning to like Gladys already.

"April 10. Gladys over six feet long now. Intend to take her in to one of that confounded bore Walton's lectures on the malleability of germ plasm. I will say nothing and announce nothing—just take her in on the end of a long piece of string, and sit at the back, and stare. Then let that pieheaded buffoon deny the existence of living palaeozoons.

"Green, the children's music teacher, has packed his things and left. Complained about having to deliver lessons in the same room as Gladys; claims music drives her into a bestial fury. Good riddance, for his music drives me into just such a fury, as he practises nothing but Holst's Jupiter at every hour of the day and night.

"To the point, Holmes."

"September 23. Have negotiated a regular meat supply for Gladys from a Mr. Glass, a heavily bearded importer of fine Irish beef. Have surveyed Mr. Glass's warehouse and suspect his beef was formerly in the habit of whinnying, but his prices are cheap. Two of his associates delivered the first consignment to our drawing room, where Gladys is currently residing. The impertinent lackeys passed doubt on the ability of the window bars to prevent Gladys from escaping. Was only too ready to demonstrate to them how the windows could only be opened on the outside.

"September 25. Donned diver's helmet and steel gauntlets and took half horse carcass in to Gladys as a treat. Disaster! Window open, drawing room empty, three-toed clawprints disappearing over the lawn into the distance."

Holmes snapped the book shut.

"Are you seriously suggesting that a palaeozoic carnivore is stalking Hampstead Heath?"

"I have been checking public records, Watson. There have been over fifteen cases of unexplained decapitations and disappearing animals on and around the Heath in the last twelve months. The police no doubt failed to connect them with this investigation due to the fact that none of them involved trombones."

"So a prehistoric monster is responsible for these killings?"

"Not entirely, Watson. There are still facets of the affair that elude me. For example, in all six cases, listeners reported that the trombonist's solo was accompanied by a lone fiddle part which joined the refrain just before the notes suddenly, tragically choked off. No, my friend—I am thinking that the mind behind these enormities evolved quite recently."

Several days later, the eternal fog still covered the city. I was treating a case of phossie-jaw in a middle-aged match worker. My signature was still wet on the prescription for morphia when the worker suddenly spoke up—quite impossible in a patient whose jaw had entirely dissolved into a sort of calcareous mush—taking me momentarily aback.

"Good morning, Watson."

This time, however, I regained control with a steely resolve. I did not even look up.

"Good day, Holmes. I hope you realize you have just wasted fifteen minutes' valuable consulting time."

"I do apologize, dear fellow. The streets remain dangerous, and I had to see you. It was the excitement of finishing a case that has been puzzling me for some time."

"The Hampstead trombonist decapitations?"

"The very same. I have found what I believe to be an answer, Watson, in forensic palaeontology." Holmes fidgeted in his chair nervously. "Don't you want to know how I feigned a jaw entirely dissolved by phosphor poisoning?"

"I most certainly do not."

"Very well. It is a case, Watson, that will go down in the annals of all cases in which a dinosaur was used as a murder weapon. For there is a human being behind these deeds, Watson, make no mistake of it." Out of a carpet bag on the floor he drew another volume of bound periodicals. "These are the observations of a Mr. Barnum Brown, who has recently discovered a colossal ornithopod in the fastnesses of Alberta which he names Corythosaurus Casuarius. This creature, a member of the hadrosauridae or duck-billed dinosaurs, possesses a singular crest on its skull—a hollow, air-filled bony structure which some palaeontologists have wrongly supposed to have been used for breathing while the animal snorkelled like a scaly submarine. There is, however, a slight drawback to this theory in that the crest possesses no exterior nostril—"

"The murders, Holmes."

"Ah, yes. There is, you see, Watson, a school of thought who believe the crest formed a sort of resonating chamber with which the beast would be capable of making distinct musical notes—not unlike, one would imagine, a trombone."

"Holmes, I cannot see any conceivable reason why a house-sized prehistoric creature would wish to make a noise like a trombone."

"These creatures were not the sharpest of sorts, Watson. Some of them needed secondary brains in their abdominal regions to remain capable of coordinating their movements. It is also true that large creatures do not necessarily have acute senses; the rhinoceros is notoriously short-sighted, and relies on its sharper sense of hearing to detect approaching hunters.

"Consider, then, a herd of such creatures. Like African herbivores, they might not all be members of the same species. Multiple species of African antelope often gather at the same water-hole to drink. However, our antelope weigh five tons and are only marginally cleverer than the pond scum they are lapping up. It is quite possible that they might elect to mate with the wrong species if they are not pro-vided with some constant audible cue. Some species of hadrosaur might therefore have made noises like trombones, as if to say, Here I am! I am a trombone-crested hadrosaur, and other trombone-crested hadrosaurs may profitably choose to mate with me. But the noises they made would not be of interest solely to their mates. They might also have interested their predators."

"Good God, Holmes," I cried. "Are you telling me those poor wretches died simply because their instruments made sounds resembling that creature's natural prey?"

"I not only believe it," said Holmes, "I intend to prove it, by the most direct means possible."

He drew out the trombone from his bag, along with a copy of the sheet music for Thaxted.

"You will not need your pistol, Watson. It would be entirely useless against the creature. Shooting it accurately in the brain would be as hard as hitting a bull from a hundred yards, and I imagine even four-five-five ball would simply bounce off its scaly hide."

We were walking through a wilderness of winter-deadened trees, in a fog in which an entire herd of hadrosauridae could have stood shoulder to shoulder unobserved. A bandstand loomed out of the murk. Posters announced a forth-coming event involving royalty.

"There do not seem to be any dinosaurs in the vicinity, Holmes. I feel sure that such large animals would advertise their presence."

"A predator," said Holmes, "never advertises its presence." And he raised the trombone to his lips, and blew out the final bar of Thaxted. A tear rose to my eye at the thought of the country all of whose ways are gentleness, all of whose paths are peace.

Then the hairs at the back of my neck stood on end as I heard a distant, clumsy crashing from far away in the fog, as if a drunken coachman were attempting to drive an omnibus through heavy brush.

"The hunter's afoot," said Holmes. "And it is we who are the game." He motioned to me to follow as he stole away.

"Confound it, Holmes! I hadn't expected your damnable theory to actually be correct!"

"My theories, Watson, are always correct." With that, he plunged into a nearby drain or ha-ha and squelched ponderously along it, not appearing in any hurry to get to the other side. "Into the water, Watson. In this fog the beast will hunt by scent."

I have no shame in relating that I piled into the water more smartly than I have ever piled into water before, particularly since I heard, at a somewhat lesser distance now, the immense crackling whisper of something dreadfully, fearfully heavy walking across the carpet of fallen leaves on the Heath towards our former position. Walking slowly, and appearing to deviate to left and right, like a questing hound. I believe I actually heard breath, escaping like a head of steam from a ship's boiler.

"Do not make a sound, Watson, for your life depends on it."

Holmes claims that he still saw nothing at that point—I would have been able to see nothing even had the beast been standing right next to me, for I had my eyes tight shut. But at that point, we heard another sound, deep and sonorous, singing out through the fog—the sound of the low notes of a violin. It is difficult to convey how I knew purely from the sounds I heard through the mist that a Mesozoic lizard was cocking its head on one side, but somehow I knew this was what was happening, as if a bird on a branch had heard another bird whistle, or a dog heard its owner call.

We heard it plunge away through the fog.

"As I suspected," said Holmes. "There are two hadrosaur species."

We sat in the pleasant surroundings of the Jack Straw's Castle inn near the flagstaff on the northern perimeter of the Heath. Warm beer was a welcome antidote to the cold.

"I cannot understand, Holmes, how the fact that there were two species of hadrosauriwhatsit can possibly be significant."

"Quite simple, I imagine. The first species, whose calls sound like those of a trombonist executing the final bars of Thaxted, are our megalosaurus's preferred prey. The second species, meanwhile, whose call is more violinlike, are a related animal which moves with the herds of the first. But our carnivore will not attack this second species."

"It will not?"

"I will stake my life on it. These animals are not prey. Their flesh is shunned by our megalosaurus, which will nevertheless follow them in much the same way a lion will follow an animal it is incapable of bringing down, such as a rhinoceros, in the hope of finding other herbivores it can bring down. Nevertheless, Watson, whoever is controlling this creature is playing fiddle with the Devil. And he is about to walk through that door, right about—now."

The doors opened to admit a shabby-looking street musician, similar in appearance to the poor devil I had examined only a day earlier.

"Mr. Green, I believe," said Holmes. "Formerly music teacher to the family of Professor Challenger of Enmore Park. No, don't trouble yourself to pull out that revolver. You will find that almost every person in this hostelry right now is an armed member of Her Majesty's Metropolitan Police."

Eerily, as if Holmes were some macabre puppeteer, every single one of the establishment's customers turned round and raised their hats to the newcomer.

"You will perhaps be mystified as to how I know your name. You are, of course, an adherent of the Fenian cause and a proponent of Home Rule for Ireland. The merits or demerits of that question I leave to politicians. I involve myself only at the point when people believe their political causes justify murder. Your principal mistake was in presenting yourself, in disguise, to your former employer as a meat wholesaler of the name of Glass. 'Glas,' as Watson doubtless does not know but I certainly do, is the Gaelic for Green, a childish conceit which led to your downfall. You noticed several months ago whilst tutoring Professor Challenger's children that the notes of the trombone appeared to induce a blind killing rage in the juvenile megalosaurus chained up at the other end of the drawing room. The notes of the violin, meanwhile, served only to attract its attention and cause it to follow the violinist round the room. It was after learning these facts that you formulated your plan.

You planned to remove the beast from confinement using two of your Fenian confederates, and train it to attack human beings. The small number of bites inflicted on his serving staff had convinced Challenger that the creature did not seek out human beings as prey; it needed to be taught to do so. And you, Mr. Green, have been teaching it to kill for the last twelve months. And why have you been doing so? Why, in only one week's time, His Majesty King George is due to attend an open air concert at the Parliament Hill bandstand on the Heath, where the final piece on the programme will be Mr. Spring-Rice's inspired lyrics to Thaxted by Gustav Holst. In fact, it is only the final note of that tune that sets off the beast, am I right?" Holmes began whistling the final few bars of Thaxted.

The musician's face palled.

"For pity's sake," he exclaimed, in a pronounced Dublin brogue, "you do not know what you're doing. If you value your life, if you value all our lives, stop!"

And Holmes did stop, drawing out that long penultimate note, and laughed. "Indeed," he chuckled. "How could it be otherwise? We have Professor Challenger's word that you practised Holst's Jupiter in the beast's presence without ill effect. Jupiter, of course, would have been safe to practise, for in Jupiter, which is otherwise identical to Thaxted, the final note never resolves. Were you, perhaps, hoping that the beast would wreak such havoc among the crowd that His Majesty would be trampled?"

The scarlet-haired Fenian shook his head. "You do me an injustice, sir. If you had only troubled to look further into the cast of the orchestra, you would have discovered I was to play the principal trombone. I intended to place myself directly before the monarch of your despicable island, blowing my horn for all I was worth. The beast would surely have taken the ermine-laden buffoon after it had finished with me."

Holmes nodded. "I see you are a man of courage, if a misguided one. I am offering you an honourable way out."

He extended a hand, proffering the trombone. The Irishman nodded sadly and accepted it. Holmes picked up the untouched pint of ale he had been nursing since we arrived, and held it up as well.

"A last drink for a condemned man."

Green accepted the pint, and drained it with gusto. Then, he turned round to the assembled police officers and cried:

"Fianna Fail!"

—before striding out through the inn doors into the white murk. We saw no more of him; but heard, droning in from without, the clear, calm notes of that timeless patriotic hymn which, I became more acutely aware than ever before, apply to any country, any King, and more especially to that great country we all hope to become citizens of upon our end.

Then, suddenly, there was a great thundering crash, and a hideous roaring, and the notes of the trombone ceased as the instrument itself was flung out of the fog, bent double, towards the window where we sat.

"Gods, what a beast! It will take a troop of soldiers with an artillery piece to kill it!"

"I think not," said Holmes. "That pint of ale contained enough strychnine to kill ten elephants. Now, I believe there is time for me to consume another less dangerous pint before we repair to the bandstand, where I believe the local brass ensemble is currently setting up to practise. I fancy I could stand to hear that tune again."

And he clicked his fingers for the barman to bring him another beer.

THE ADVENTURE OF THE ANTIQUARIAN'S NIECE

by Barbara Hambly

Barbara Hambly is the bestselling author of dozens of books, including the James Asher vampire series, *Those Who Hunt the Night* and *Traveling with the Dead*. She has written many other novels as well, such as the popular *Dragonsbane* and its sequels, as well as media tie-in projects for *Star Trek* and *Star Wars*. Her Benjamin January series may be of interest to Holmes fans, being as it is both mystery and historical (set in 1830s New Orleans). Hambly has also written other novels of historical fiction, such as *Patriot Hearts*, and has a Masters degree in Medieval History.

H. P. Lovecraft went to great pains to make his fantastic otherworldly creations appear authentic. One of his techniques was to write his fiction in an extremely detailed faux-documentary format, incorporating, for example, realistic-sounding newspaper clippings that corroborated elements of his narrators' tales. Another technique was to reuse certain names from story to story, and to encourage other writers to make use of those names as well. Lovecraft felt that made-up names would resonate with more authority if the reader had heard those names somewhere before. The best known of his creations are the evil octopus-headed god Cthulhu and the book of black magic, the *Necronomicon*. A similar accursed tome is the *Book of Eibon*, invented by Lovecraft's friend Clark Ashton Smith and used by Lovecraft in several of his own stories. Lovecraft also made multiple references to Yog-Sothoth and Shub-Niggurath, malevolent gods, and to shoggoths, large protoplasmic servants. Many of these creations are now ubiquitous in popular culture and are familiar even if you've never heard of Lovecraft. Our next story continues the tradition of using these familiar elements to connect the tale to a larger body of fantastic literature.

In my career as the chronicler of the cases of Mr. Sherlock Holmes, I have attempted (his assertions to the contrary) to present both his successes and his failures. In most instances his keen mind and logical deductive facility led him to the solutions of seemingly insoluble puzzles. Upon some occasions, such as the strange behavior of Mrs. Effie Munro, his conclusions were astray due to unknown and unforeseen facts; on others, such as the puzzle of the dancing men or the horrifying contents of the letter received by Mr. John Openshaw, his correct assessment of the situation came too late to save the life of his client.

In a small percentage of his cases, it was simply not possible to determine the correctness or incorrectness of his reasoning because no conclusion was ever reached. Such a case was that of Mr. Burnwell Colby and his fiancée, and the abominable inhabitants of Depewatch Priory. Holmes long kept the singular memento of his investigation in a red cardboard box in his room, and if I have not written of these events before, it is because of the fearful shadow which they left upon my heart. I only now write of them in the light of the new findings of Mr. Freud concerning the strange workings of the human mind.

Burnwell Colby came to the lodgings that I shared with Holmes in Baker Street in the summer of 1894. It was one of those sticky London afternoons that make one long for the luxury of the seashore or the Scottish moors. Confirmed Londoner that Holmes was, I am sure he was no more aware of the heat than a fish is of water: whatever conditions prevailed in the city, he preferred to be surrounded by the noise and hurry, the curious street-scenes and odd contretemps engendered by the close proximity of over a million fellow-creatures than by any amount of fresh air. As for myself, the expenses incurred by my dear wife's final illness prevented me from even thinking of quitting the metropolis—and the depression of spirits that had overtaken me from the same source sometimes prevented me from thinking at all. While Holmes never by word or look referred to my bereavement, he was an astonishingly restful companion in those days, treating me as he always had instead of offering a sympathy which I would have found unendurable.

He was, as I recall, preparing to concoct some appalling chemical mess at the parlor table when Mrs. Hudson's knock sounded at the door. "A Mr. Burnwell Colby to see you, sir."

"What, at this season of the year?" Holmes thumbed the card she handed him, angled it to the window's glaring light. "Heavy stock, one-and-six the hundred, printed in America in a typeface of a restraint generally only found in the most petrified of diplomatic circles but smelling of...." He broke off, and glanced at Mrs. Hudson with eyes suddenly sharp with wary interest. "Yes," he said. "Yes, I shall see this gentleman. Watson, if you would remain I would much appreciate an outsider's unbiased view of our guest."

For I had folded together the newspaper which for the past hour I had stared at, unseeing, preparatory to making a retreat to my bedroom. To tell the truth I welcomed the invitation to remain, and helped Holmes in his rapid disposal of alembic and pipettes into his own chamber. As I reached down for the card, still lying on the much-scarred rosewood, Holmes twitched it from my fingers and slipped it into an envelope, which he set in an obscure corner of the bookcase. "Let us not drip premature surmise into the distilled waters of your observation," he said with a smile. "I am curious to read what would be writ upon a *tabula rasa*."

"Behold me unbesmirched," I replied, throwing up my hands, and settled back onto the settee as the door opened to admit one of the most robust specimens of American manhood that it has ever been my privilege to encounter. Six feet tall, broad of shoulder and chest, he had dark eyes luminous with intelligence under a noble brow in a rather long face, and by his well-cut, if rather American, brown suit and gloves of fawn kid, he clearly added material wealth to the blessings of kindly nature. He held out his hand to Holmes and introduced himself, and Holmes inclined his head.

"And this is my partner and amanuensis, Dr. Watson," said Holmes, and Mr. Colby turned unhesitatingly to shake my hand. "Anything that may be said to me, may be said in his presence as well."

"Of course," said Colby, in his deep, pleasing voice, "of course. I have no secrets—that's what gravels me." And he shook his head with a ghost of a chuckle. "The Colbys are one of the wealthiest families in New England: we've traded with China for fifty years and with India for twice that, and our railroad interests now will better those profits a thousand percent. I've been educated at Harvard and Oxford, and if I may say so without tooting my own horn, I'm reasonably good to look on and I don't eat with my knife or sleep in my boots. So what would there be about me, Mr. Holmes, that would cause a respectable girl's guardians to reject my suit out of hand and forbid me to exchange a word with her?"

"Oh, I could name a dozen commonplace possibilities," replied Holmes, gesturing him to a chair. "And a score more if we wished to peruse a catalogue of the *outré*. Perhaps you could tell me, Mr. Colby, the name of this unfortunate young lady and the circumstances under which you were so rudely ejected from her parents' favor?"

"Guardians," corrected our visitor. "Her uncle is the Honorable Carstairs Delapore, and her grandfather, Gaius, Viscount Delapore of Depewatch Priory in Shropshire. It's a crumbling, moldering, Gothic old pile, sinking into decay. My family's money could easily rescue it—as I've said to Mr. Delapore, any number of times, and he agrees with me."

"A curious thing to do, for a man rejecting your suit."

Colby's breath gusted again in exasperated laughter. "Isn't it? It isn't as if I were a stranger off the street, Mr. Holmes. I've been Mr. Delapore's pupil for a year, have lived in his household on week-ends, eaten at his table. When I first came to study with him I could have sworn he approved of my love for Judith."

"And what, precisely, would you say is the nature of Mr. Delapore's teaching?" Holmes leaned back in the basket-chair, fingertips pressed lightly together, closely watching the young American's face.

"I guess you'd say he's... an antiquarian." Colby's voice was hesitant, as if picking his words. "One of the most remarkable students of ancient folklore and legend in the world. Indeed, it was in the hopes of studying with him that I came to Oxford. I am—I guess you might call me the intellectual black sheep of the Colby family." He chuckled again. "My father left the firm to my brothers and myself, but on the whole I've been content to let them run it as they wished. The making of money… the constant clamor of stocks and rail-shares and directors… From the time I was a small boy I sensed there were deeper matters than that in the world, forgotten shadows lurking behind the gaslights' artificial glare."

Holmes said nothing to this, but his eyelids lowered, as if he were listening for something behind the words. Colby, hands clasped, seemed almost to have forgotten his presence, or mine, or the reality of the stuffy summer heat. He went on, "I had corresponded with Carstairs Delapore on… on the subject of some of the more obscure Lammas-tide customs of the Welsh borderlands. As I'd hoped, he agreed to guide my studies, both at Oxford and, later, among the books of his private collection—marvelous volumes that clarified ancient folkloric rites and put them into contexts of philosophy, history, the very fabric of time itself! Depewatch Priory…."

He seemed to come to himself with a start, glanced at Holmes, then at me, and went on in a more constrained voice, "It was at Depewatch Priory that I first met Mr. Delapore's niece, Judith. She is eighteen, the daughter of Mr. Delapore's brother Fynch, a spirit of light and innocence in that… in that dreary old pile. She had just returned from finishing-school in Switzerland, though plans for her come-out into London society had run aground on the family's poverty. Any other girl I know would have been pouting and in tears at being robbed of her season on the town. Not she! She bore it bravely and sweetly, though it was clear that she faced a lifetime of stagnation in a tiny mountain town, looking after a decrepit house and a… a difficult old man."

From his jacket pocket Colby withdrew an embossed cardboard photograph-case, opening it to show the image of a most beautiful young lady. Thin and rather fragile-looking, she wore her soft curls in a chignon. Her eyes seemed light, blue or hazel so far as I could tell from the photograph, her hair a medium shade—perhaps red, but more likely light brown—and her complexion pale to ghostliness. Her expression was one of grave innocence, trusting and unself-conscious.

"Old Viscount Delapore is a grim old autocrat who rules his son, his niece, and every soul in the village of Watchgate as if it were 1394 instead of 1894. He owns all of the land thereabouts—the family has, I gather, from time immemorial—and so violent is his temper that the villagers dare not cross him. From the first moment Judith declared her love for me, I offered to take her away from the place—to take her clean out of the country, if need be, though I hardly think he would come after her, as she seems to fear."

"Does she fear her grandfather?" Holmes turned the photograph thoughtfully over in his hands, examining the back as well as the front most minutely.

Colby nodded, his face clouding with anger. "She claims she's free to come and go, that there's no influence being brought to bear upon her. But there is, Mr. Holmes, there is! When she speaks of Viscount Gaius she glances over her shoulder, as if she imagines he could hear her wherever she is. And the look in her lovely eyes…! She fears him, Mr. Holmes. He has some evil and unwholesome hold upon the girl. He's not her legal guardian—that's Mr. Carstairs Delapore. But the old man's influence extends to his son as well. When I received this—" He drew from the same pocket as the photograph a single sheet of folded paper, which he passed across to Holmes, "I begged him to countermand his father's order, to at least let me present my case. But this card…" He handed a large, stiff note to Holmes, "was all I got back."

The letter was dated August 16, four days ago.

"My best beloved,

"My heart is torn from my breast by this most terrible news. My grandfather has forbidden me to see you again, forbidden even that your name be mentioned in this house. He will give no reason for this beyond that it is his will that I remain here with him, as his servant—I fear, as his slave! I have written to my father but fear he will do nothing. I am in despair! Do nothing, but wait and be ready.

"Thine only,
Judith."

The delicate pink paper, scented with patchouli and with the faint smoke of the oil-lamp by which it must have been written, was blotted with tears.

Her father's card said merely:

"Remove her from your thoughts. There is nothing which can be done."

Burnwell Colby smote the palm of one hand with the fist of the other, and his strong jaw jutted forward. "My grandfather didn't let the mandarins of Hong Kong chase him away, and my father refused to be stopped by Sioux Indians or winter snows in the Rockies," he declared. "Nor shall this stop me. Will you find out for me, Mr. Holmes, what vile hold Lord Gaius has upon his granddaughter and his son, that I may free the gentlest girl that ever lived from the clutches of an evil old man who seeks to make a drudge of her forever?"

"And is this all," asked Holmes, raising his eyelids to meet the American's earnest gaze, "that you have to tell me about Carstairs Delapore and his father? Or about these 'lurking shadows' that are Delapore's study?"

The young man frowned, as if the question took him momentarily aback. "Oh, the squeamish may speak of decadence," he said after a moment, not off-handedly, but as if carefully considering his words. "And some of the practices which Delapore has uncovered are fairly ugly by modern standards. Certainly they'd make my old pater blink, and my poor hidebound brothers." He chuckled, as if at the recollection of a schoolboy prank. "But at bottom it's all only legends, you know, and bogies in the dark."

"Indeed," said Holmes, rising, and held out his hand to the young suitor. "I shall learn of this what I can, Mr. Colby. Where might I reach you?"

"The Excelsior Hotel in Brighton." The young man fished from his vest-pocket a card to write the address upon—he seemed to carry everything loose in his pockets, jumbled together like cabbages in a barrow. "I always stay there," he explained as he scribbled. "It was how Miss Delapore knew where to reach me. How you can abide to remain in town in weather like this beats me!" And he departed, apparently unaware that not everyone's grandfather rammed opium down Chinese throats in order to pay the Excelsior's summer-holiday prices.

"So what do you think of our American Romeo?" inquired Holmes, as the rattle of Colby's cab departed down Baker Street. "What sort of man does he appear to be?"

"A wealthy one," I said, still stung by that careless remark about those who remained in town. "One not used to hearing the word 'No.' But earnest and good of heart, I would say. Certainly he takes a balanced view of these 'decadent' studies—to which the Delapores can scarcely object, if they share them."

"True enough." Holmes set letter and note upon the table, and went to the bookcase to draw out his copy of the *Court Gazette*, which was so interleaved with snipped-out society columns, newspaper clippings, and notes in Holmes' neat, strong handwriting as to bulge to almost double its original size. "But what are the nature of these folkloric 'practices' which are 'fairly ugly by modern standards'? Ugliness by the standards of a world which has invented the Maxim gun can scarcely be termed bogies in the dark.

"Carstairs Delapore," he read, opening the book upon his long arm. "Questioned concerning his whereabouts on the night of the 27th August, 1890, when the owner of a public house in Whitechapel reported her ten-year-old son Thomas missing; a man of Delapore's description—he is evidently of fairly unforgettable appearance—seen speaking with the boy that evening. Thomas never found. I thought I recognized the name. Delapore was also questioned in 1873 by the Manchester police—he was in that city, for no discernable reason, when two little mill-girls went missing... I must say I'm astonished that anyone reported their disappearance. Mudlarks and street-urchins vanish every day from the streets of London and no one inquires after them anymore than one inquires the whereabouts of butterflies once they flitter over the garden fence. A man need not even be very clever, to kidnap children in London." He shut the book, his eyes narrowing as he turned his gaze to the endless wasteland of brick that lay beyond the window. "Merely careful to pick the dirtiest and hungriest, and those without parents or homes."

"That's a serious conclusion to jump to," I said, startled and repelled.

"It is," Holmes replied. "Which is why I jump to nothing. But Gaius, Viscount Delapore, was mentioned three times in the early reports of the Metropolitan police—between 1833 and 1850—in connection with precisely such investigations, at the same time that he was publishing a series of monographs on 'Demonic Ritual Survivals along the Welsh Borders' for the discredited Eye of Dawn Society. And in 1863 an American reporter disappeared while investigating rumors of a pagan cult in western Shropshire, not five miles from Watchgate village, which lies below the hill upon which Depewatch Priory stands."

"But even so," I said, "even if the Delapores are involved in some kind of theosophistic studies—or white slaving for that matter—would they not seek rather to get an outsider like Delapore's niece out of the house, rather than keeping her there as a potential source of trouble? And how would the old man use a pack of occult rubbish to dominate his granddaughter and his son against their will?"

"How indeed?" Holmes went to the bookcase again, and took down the envelope in which he had bestowed Burnwell Colby's card. "I, too, found our American visitor—despite his patent desire to disown association with his hidebound and boring family—an ingenuous and harmless young man. Which makes this all the more curious."

He held out the envelope to me, and I took it out and examined it as he had. The stock, as he had said, was expensive and the typeface rigidly correct, although the card itself bore slight traces of having been carried about loose in Mr. Colby's pockets with pens, notes, and photographs of his beloved Judith. Only when I brought it close to examine the small dents and scratches on its surface was I conscious of the smell that seemed to imbue the thick, soft paper, a nauseating mix of frankincense, charred hair, and....

I looked up at Holmes, my eyes wide. I had been a soldier in India, and a physician for most of my life. I knew the smell.

"Blood," I said.

The note Holmes sent that afternoon received an answer within hours, and after we had finished our supper he invited me to accompany him to the home of a friend on the Embankment near the Temple: "A curious customer who may fill in for you some hitherto unsuspected colors in the palette of London life," he said. Mr. Carnaki was a thin young man of medium height and attenuated build, whose large gray eyes regarded one from behind thick spectacle lenses with an expression it is hard to define: as if he were always watching for something that others do not see. His tall, narrow house was filled with books, even lining the walls of the hallways on both sides so that a broad-built man would have been obliged to sidle through crab-wise, and through the darkened doorways I glimpsed the flicker of gas-light across what appeared to be complex chemical and electrical apparatus. He listened to Holmes' account of Burnwell Colby's visit without comment, his chin resting on one long, spidery hand, then rose from his chair and climbed a pair of steps to an upper shelf of one of the many bookcases that walled the small study at the back of the house to which he'd led us.

"Depewatch Priory," he read aloud, "stands on a cliff above the village of Watchgate in the wild hill country on the borders of Wales, where in 1215 King John confirmed the appointment of an Augustinian prior over an existing 'hooly howse' of religion said to date back to foundation by Joseph of Arimathea. It appears from its inception to have been the center of a cycle of legends and whispers: indeed, the King's original intent was apparently to have the place pulled down and salt strewed on its foundations. One Philip of Mundberg petitioned Edward IV, describing the monks there engaged in 'comerce wyth daemons yt did issue forth from Hell, and make knowne theyr wants by means of certain dremes,' but he apparently never reached the King himself and the investigation was dropped. There were repeated accusations of heresy involving the transmigration of the souls of certain priors, rumors which apparently transferred themselves to the Grimsley family to whom

Henry VIII presented the priory in 1540, and surfaced in the 1780s in connection with the Delapores, who succeeded them through marriage.

"William Punt…" He tapped the black leathern covers of the volume as he set it on the table beside Holmes, "in his *Catalogue of Secret Abominations* described the place in 1793 as being a 'goodly manor of gray stone' built upon the foundations of the Plantagenet cloister, but says that the original core of the establishment is the ruin of a tower, probably Roman in origin. Punt speaks of stairs leading down to a sub-crypt, where the priors used to sleep upon a crude altar after appalling rites. When Lord Rupert Grimsley was murdered by his wife and daughters in 1687, they apparently boiled his body and buried his bones in the sub-crypt, reserving his skull, which they placed in a niche at the foot of the main stair in the manor-house itself, 'that evil dare not pass.'"

I could not repress a chuckle. "As protective totems go, it didn't do Lord Rupert much good, did it?"

"I daresay not," returned Holmes with a smile. "Yet my reading of the 1840 Amsterdam edition of Punt's *Catalogue* leads me to infer that the local population didn't regard Rupert Grimsley's murder as particularly evil; the villagers impeded the Metropolitan police in the pursuit of their duties to such effect that the three murderesses got completely away."

"Good heavens, yes." Carnaki turned, and drew out another volume, more innocuous than the sinister-looking tome of abominations: this one was simply a History of West Country Families, as heavily interleaved with clippings and notes as was Holmes' *Gazette*. "Rupert Grimsley was feared as a sorcerer from Shrewsbury to the Estuary; he is widely reputed to have worked the roads as a highwayman, carrying off, not valuables, but travelers who were never seen again. Demons were said to come and go at his command, and at least two lunatics from that section of the Welsh border—one in the early part of the eighteenth century and one as recently as 1842—swore that old Lord Rupert dwelled in the bodies of all the successive Lords of Depewatch."

"You mean that he was being constantly reincarnated?" I admit this surfacing of this Thibetan belief in the prosaic hill-country of Wales startled me considerably.

Carnaki shook his head. "That the spirit—the consciousness—of Rupert Grimsley passed from body to body, battening like a parasite upon that of the heir and driving out the younger man's soul, as the human portion of each Lord of Depewatch died."

The young antiquarian looked so serious as he said this that again I was hard-put to suffocate a laugh; Carnaki's expression did not alter, but his eyes flicked from my face to Holmes'. "I suppose," said the young man after a moment, "that this had something to do with the fact that each of the gentlemen in question were rumored to be involved with mysterious disappearances among the coal-miners of the district: Viscount Gerald Delapore, who is reputed to have undergone so terrifying a change in personality at his accession to the title that his wife left him and fled to America… and the young Gaius Delapore himself."

"Indeed?" Holmes leaned forward eagerly in his chair, his hand still resting on the *Catalogue*, which he had been examining with the delighted reverence of a true lover of ancient volumes. He had hardly taken his eyes from the many tomes that stacked every table and most of the corners of Carnaki's little study, some of them the musty calf or morocco of Georgian bookbinders, others the heavier, more archaic black-letter incunabula of the early days of printing, with not a few older still, hand-written in Latin upon parchment or vellum and illuminated with spidery marginalia that even at a distance disturbed me by their anomalous *bizarrité*. "And what, precisely, is the evil that is ascribed by legend to Depewatch Priory, and for what purpose did Rupert Grimsley and his successors seek out those who had no power, and whom society would not miss?"

Carnaki set aside his History and seated himself on the oak bookcase steps, his long, thin arms resting on his knees. He glanced again at me, not as if I had offended him with my earlier laughter but as if gauging how to phrase things so that I would understand them; then his eyes returned to Holmes.

"You have heard, I think, of the six thousand steps, that are hinted at—never directly—in the remote legends of both the old Cymric tribes that preceded the Celts, and of the American Indian? Of the pit that lies deep at the heart of the world, and of the entities that are said to dwell in the abysses beyond it?"

"I have heard of these things," said Holmes quietly. "There was a case in Arkham, Massachusetts, in 1869...."

"The Whateley case, yes." Carnaki's long, sensitive mouth twitched with remembered distaste, and his glance turned to me. "These legends—remembered only through two cults of quite shockingly degenerate Indian tribes, one in Maine and the other, curiously, in northeastern Arizona, where they are shunned by the surrounding Navajo and Hopi—speak of things, entities, sentient yet not wholly material, that have occupied the lightless chasms of space and time since the days before humankind's furthest ancestors first stood upright. These elder beings fear the light of the sun, yet with the coming of darkness would creep forth from certain places in the world to prey upon human bodies and human dreams, through the centuries making surprising and dreadful bargains with individuals of mankind in return for most hideous payment."

"And this is what Gaius Delapore and his son believe they have in their basement?" My eyebrows shot up. "It should make it easy enough for us to assist young Mr. Colby in freeing his fiancée from the influence of two obvious lunatics."

Holmes said softly, "So it should."

We remained at Carnaki's until nearly midnight, while Holmes and the young antiquarian—for so I assumed Carnaki to be—spoke of the appalling folkloric and theosophical speculations that evidently fuelled Viscount Delapore's madness: hideous tales of creatures beyond human imaginings or human dreams, monstrous legends of dim survivals from impossibly ancient aeons, and of those deluded madmen whose twisted minds accepted such absurdities for truth. Holmes was right in his assertion that the visit would supply the palette of my knowledge of

London with hitherto unsuspected hues. What surprised me was Holmes' knowledge of such things, for on the whole he was a man of practical bent, never giving his attention to a subject unless it was with some end in view.

Yet when Carnaki spoke of the abomination of abominations, of the terrible amorphous shuggoths and the Watcher of the Gate, Holmes nodded, as one does who hears familiar names. The shocking rites engaged in by the covens of ancient believers, whether American Indians or decayed cults to be found in the fastnesses of Greenland or Thibet, did not surprise him, and it was he, not our host, who spoke of the insane legend of the shapeless god who plays the pipe in the dark heart of chaos, and who sends forth the dreams that drive men mad.

"I did not know that you made a study of such absurdities, Holmes," I said, when we stood once more on the fog-shrouded Embankment, listening for the approaching clip of a cab-horse's hooves. "I would hardly have said theosophy was your line."

"My line is anything that will—or has—provided a motive for men's crimes, Watson." He lifted his hand and whistled for the Jehu, an eerie sound in the muffled stillness. His face in the glare of the gaslight seemed pale and set. "Whether a man bows down to God or Mammon or to Cthulhu in his dark house at R'lyeh is no affair of mine... Until he sheds one drop of blood not his own in his deity's name. Then God have mercy upon him, for I shall not."

All of these events took place on Monday, the 20th of August. The following day Holmes was engaged with turning over the pages of his scrapbooks of clippings regarding unsolved crimes, seeming, it appeared to me, to concentrate on disappearances during the later part of the summer in years back almost to the beginning of the century. On Wednesday Mrs. Hudson sent up the familiar elegantly restrained calling-card of the American folklorist, the man himself following hard upon her heels and almost thrusting her out of the way as he entered our parlor.

"Well, Holmes, it's all settled and done with," he declared, in a loud voice very unlike his own. "Thank you for your patience with old Delapore's damned rodomontade, but I've seen the old man myself—he came down to town yesterday, damn his impudence—and made him see reason."

"Have you?" asked Holmes politely, gesturing to the chair in which he had first sat.

Colby waved him impatiently away. "Simplest thing in nature, really. Feed a cur and he'll shut up barking. And here's for you." And he drew from his pocket a small leather bag which he tossed carelessly onto the table. It struck with the heavy, metallic ring of golden coin. "Thank you again."

"And I thank you." Holmes bowed, but he watched Colby's face as he spoke, and I could see his own face had turned very pale. "Surely you are too generous."

"S'blood, man, what's a few guineas to me? I can tear up little Judi's poor letter, now we're to be wed all right and tight...." He winked lewdly at Holmes, and held out his hand. "And her old Dad's damned impudent note as well, if you would."

Holmes looked around him vaguely, and picked up various of his scrapbooks from the table to look beneath them: "Didn't you tuck it behind the clock?" I asked.

"Did I?" Holmes went immediately to the mantle—cluttered as always with newspapers, books, and unanswered correspondence—and after a brief search shook his head. "I shall find it, never fear," he said, his brow furrowing. "And return it, if you would be so kind as to give me your direction once more."

Colby hesitated, then snatched the nearest piece of paper from the table—a bill from Holmes' tailor, I believe it was—and scribbled an address upon it. "I'm off to Watchgate this afternoon," he said. "This will find me."

"Thank you," said Holmes, and I noticed that he neither touched the paper, nor came within arm's reach of the man who stood before him. "I shall have it in the post before nightfall. I can't think what can have become of it. It has been a pleasure to make your acquaintance, Mr. Colby. My felicitations on the happy outcome of your suit."

When Colby was gone Holmes stood for a time beside the table, looking after him a little blankly, his hands knotted into fists where they rested among the scrapbooks. He whispered, "Damn him," as if he had forgotten my presence in the room. "My God, I had not believed it...."

Then, turning sharply, he went to the mantelpiece and immediately withdrew from behind the clock the note which Carstairs Delapore had sent to Colby. This he tucked into an envelope and sealed. As he copied the direction he asked in a stiff, expressionless tone, "What did you make of our guest, Watson?"

"That success has made him bumptious," I replied, for I had liked Colby less in his elevated and energized mood than I had when he was merely unthinking about his own and other peoples' money. "Holmes, what is it? What's wrong?"

"Did you happen to notice which hand he wrote out his direction with?"

I thought for a moment, picturing the man scribbling, then said, "His left."

"Yet when he wrote the address of the Hotel Excelsior the day before yesterday," said Holmes, "he did so with his right hand."

"So he did." I came to his side and picked up the tailor's bill, and compared the writing on it with that of the Excelsior address, which lay on the table among the scrapbooks and clippings. "That would account for the hand being so very different."

Holmes said, "Indeed." But he spoke looking out the window into Baker Street, and the harsh glare of the morning sunlight gave his eyes a steely cast, faraway and cold, as if he saw from a distance some terrible event taking place. "I am going to Shropshire, Watson," he said after a moment. "I'm leaving tonight, on the last train; I should be back—"

"Then you find Viscount Gaius' sudden capitulation as sinister as I do," I said.

He looked at me with blank surprise, as if that construction of young Colby's information had been the farthest thing from his mind. Then he laughed, a single sharp mirthless breath, and said, "Yes. Yes, I find it... sinister."

"Do you think young Colby is walking into some peril, returning to Depewatch Priory?"

"I think my client is in peril, yes," said Holmes quietly. "And if I cannot save him, then the least that I can do is avenge."

Holmes at first refused to hear of me accompanying him to the borders of Wales, sending instead a note to Carnaki with instructions to be ready to depart by the eight o'clock train. But when Billy the messenger-boy returned with the information that Carnaki was away from home and would not return until the following day, he assented, sending a second communication to the young antiquarian requesting that he meet us in the village of High Clum, a few miles from Watchgate, the following day.

It puzzled me that Holmes should have chosen the late train, if he feared for Colby's life should the young man return to fetch his fiancée from the hands of the two monomaniacs at Depewatch Priory. Still more did it puzzle me that, upon our arrival at midnight in the market town of High Clum, Holmes took rooms for us at the Cross of Gold, as if he were deliberately putting distance between us and the man he spoke of—when he could be induced to speak at all—as if he were already dead.

In the morning, instead of attempting to communicate with Colby, Holmes hired a pony trap and a boy to drive us to the wooded ridge that divided High Clum from the vale in which the village of Watchgate stood. "Queer folk there," the lad said, as the sturdy cob leaned into its collars on the slope. "It's only a matter of four mile, but it's like as if they lived in another land. You never do hear of one of their lads come courtin' in Clum, and the folk there's so odd now none of ours'n will go there. They come for the market, once a week. Sometimes you'll see Mr. Carstairs drive to town, all bent and withered up like a tree hit by lightnin', starin' about him with those pale eyes: yellow hazel, like all the Delapore; rotten apples my mum calls 'em. And old Gaius with him sometimes, treatin' him like as if he was a dog, the way he treats everyone."

The boy drew his horse to a halt, and pointed out across the valley with his whip: "That'll be the Priory, sir."

After all that had been spoken of monstrous survivals and ancient cults, I had half-expected to see some blackened Gothic pile thrusting flamboyant spires above the level of the trees. But in fact, as Carnaki had read in William Punt's book, Depewatch Priory appeared, from across the valley, to be simply a 'goodly manor of gray stone,' its walls rather overgrown with ivy and several windows broken and boarded shut. I frowned, remembering the casual way in which Colby had thrown his sack of guineas onto Holmes' table: Feed a cur and he'll shut up barking....

Yet old Gaius had originally turned down Colby's offer to help him bring the Priory back into proper repair.

Behind the low roof-line of the original house I could see what had to be the Roman tower Carnaki had spoken of—beyond doubt the original "watch" of both priory and village names. It had clearly been kept in intermittent repair up until the early part of this century, an astonishing survival. Beneath it, I recalled, Carnaki had said the sub-crypt lay: the center of that decadent cult that dated to pre-Roman times. I found myself wondering if old Gaius descended the stairs to sleep on the ancient altar, as the notorious Lord Rupert Grimsley had been said to sleep, and if so, what dreams had come to him there.

After London's stuffy heat the thick-wooded foothills were deliciously cool. The breezes brought the scent of water from the heights, and the sharp nip of rain. Perhaps this contrast was what brought upon me what happened later that day, and that horrible night—I know not. For surely, after I returned to the Cross of Gold, I must have come down ill, and lain delirious. There is no other explanation—I pray there is no other explanation—for the ghastly dreams, worse than any delirium I experienced while sick with fever in India, that dragged me through abysses of horror while I slept and have for years shadowed not only my sleep, but upon occasion my waking as well.

I remember that Holmes took the trap to the station to meet Carnaki. I remember, too, sitting by the window of our pleasant sitting-room, cleaning my pistol, for I feared that, if Holmes had in fact found some proof that the evil Viscount had kidnapped beggar-children for some ancient and unspeakable rite, there might be trouble when we confronted the old autocrat with it. I certainly felt no preliminary shiver, no premonitory dizziness of fever, when I rose to answer the knock at the parlor door.

The man who stood framed there could be no one but Carstairs Delapore. "Withered all up like a tree hit by lightnin," the stable-lad had said: had his back been straight he still would not have been as tall as I, and he looked up at me sideways, twisting his head upon a skinny neck like a bird's.

His eyes were a light hazel, almost golden, as the boy had said.

They are my last memory of the waking world that afternoon.

I dreamed of lying in darkness. I ached all over, my neck and spine pinched and stiff, and from somewhere near me I heard a thin, harsh sobbing, like an old man in terror or pain. I called out: "Who is it? What is wrong?" and my voice sounded hoarse in my own ears, like the rusty caw of a crow, as alien as my body felt when I tried to move.

"My God," sobbed the old man's voice, "my God, the pit of six thousand stairs! It is Lammas-tide, the night of sacrifice—dear God, dear God save me! Iä! Shub-Niggurath! It waits for us, waits for us, the Goat With Ten Thousand Young!"

I crawled across an uneven floor, wet and slimy, and the smells around me were the scents of deep earth, dripping rock, and far off the terrible fetors of still worse things: corruption, charred flesh, and the sickeningly familiar scent of incense. My hands touched my companion in this darkness and he pulled away: "No, never! Fiends, that you used poor Judith as bait, to bring me to you! The Hooded Thing in the darkness taught you how, as it taught others before you—showed you the passages in the *Book of Eibon*—told you how to take the bodies of others, how to leave their minds trapped in your old and dying body… the body that you then sacrificed to them! A new body, a strong body, a man's body, healthy and fit…."

"Hush," I whispered, "hush, you are raving! Who are you, where is this?" Again I touched his hands, and felt the stick-like bones and flaccid, silky flesh of a very old man. At the same moment those frail hands fumbled at my face, my shoulders in the dark, and he cried out:

"Get away from me! You weren't good enough for him, twisted and crippled and weak! And your daughter only a woman, without the power of a man! It was all a trap, wasn't it? A trap to lure me, thinking it was *she* who sent for me to set her free...." His thin voice rose to a shriek and he thrust me from him with feeble hysteria. "And now you will send me down to the pit, down to the pit of the shuggoths!" As his sobs changed to thin, giggling laughter I heard a stirring, far away in the darkness; a soughing, as if of the movement of things infinitely huge, and soft.

I staggered to my feet, my legs responding queerly; I reeled and limped like a drunken man. I followed the wall in darkness, feeling it to be in places ancient stones set without mortar, and in others the naked rock of the hill itself. There was a door, desiccated wood strapped with iron that grated, rusty and harsh, under my hands. I stumbled back into the darkness, and struck against something—a stone table, pitted with ancient carvings—and beside it found the only means of egress, a square opening in the floor, in which a flight of worn, shallow steps led downwards.

Gropingly I descended, hands outstretched on either side to feel the wet rock of the wall that sometimes narrowed to the straightest of seams: terrified of what might lie below me, yet I feared to be in the power of the madmen I knew to be above. I was dizzy, panting, my mind prey to a thousand illusions, the most terrifying of which was that of the sounds that I seemed to hear, not above me, but below.

In time the darkness glowed with thin smears of blue phosphor, illuminating the abyss below me. Far down I could descry a chamber, a sort of high-roofed cave where the niter dripped from the walls and showed up a crumbling stone altar, ruinously ancient and stained black with horrible corruption. There was an obscene aberration to the entire geometry of the chamber, as if the angles of floor and walls should not have met in the fashion they appeared to; as if I viewed an optical illusion, a trick of darkness and shadow. From the innermost angle of that chamber darkness issued, like a thicker flow of night, blackness that seemed one moment to congeal into discrete forms which the next proved to be only inchoate stirrings. Yet there was something there, something the fear of which kept me from moving on, from making a sound—from breathing, even, lest the gasp of my breath bring upon me some unimaginably nightmarish fate.

My fellow captive's high, hysterical giggling on the stair above me drove me into a niche in the wet rock. He was coming down—and he was not alone. Pressed into the narrow darkness I only heard the sounds of bodies passing on the stair. A moment later others followed them, while I crouched, praying to all the gods ever worshipped by fearful man to be spared the notice of anything that walked that eldritch abyss. At the same moment sounds rose from below, a rhythmless wailing or chittering that nevertheless seemed to hold the form of music, underlain by a thick lapping or surging sound, as if of thick, unspeakably vile liquid rising among stones.

Looking around the sheltering coign of rock, I saw by the growing purplish hell-glare below me the tall figure of Burnwell Colby, standing beside the altar, an unfleshed skull held upraised in his hands. Darkness ringed him, but it seemed almost as if the skull itself gave light, a pulsing and horrible radiation that showed me—almost—the shapes of which the utter blackness was comprised. I bit my hand to keep from crying out, and wondered that the pain of it did not wake me; an old man lay on the altar, and by his sobbing giggles I knew him to be he who had been shut into the stone crypt above with me. Colby's deep voice rang out above the strident piping: "*Ygnaiih... ygnaiih... thflthkh'ngha....*"

And the things in the darkness—horrible half-seen suggestions of squamous, eyeless heads, of tentacles glistening and of small round mouths opening and closing with an appalling glint of teeth—answered with a thick and greedy wail.

"*H'ehye n'grkdl'lh, h'ehye...* in the name of Yog-Sothoth I call, I command...."

Something—I know not what nor do I dare to think—raised itself behind the altar, something shapeless that glowed and yet seemed to swallow all light, hooded in utter darkness. The old man on the altar began to scream, a high thin steady shriek of absolute terror, and Colby shouted, "I command you... I command...!" Then it seemed to me that he gasped, and swallowed, as if his breath stopped within his lungs, before he held up the skull again and cried, "*N'grkdl'lh y'bthnk*, Shub-Niggurath! In the name of the Goat With Ten Thousand Young I command!"

Then the darkness swallowed the altar, and where a moment before I could see the old man writhing there I could see only churning darkness, while a hideous fetor of blood and death rolled up from the pit, nearly making me faint. "Before the Five Hundred," cried Colby... then he staggered suddenly, nearly dropping the skull he held. "Before the Five Hundred...."

He gasped, as if struggling to speak. The thing upon the altar lifted its hooded head, and in the sudden silence the dreadful lapping sound of the deeper darkness seemed to fill the unholy place, and the far-off answering echo of the now-silenced pipes.

Then with a cry Colby fell to his knees, the skull slipping from his hands. He choked, grasping for it, and from the darkness of the stair behind him another form darted forward, small and slim, and stooped to snatch up the talisman skull of the terrible ancestor who had ruled this place.

"*Ygnaiih, ygnaiih* Yog-Sothoth!" cried a woman's voice, high and powerful, filling the hideous chamber, and the darkness that had surged forward toward her seemed for a moment to close in as it had closed around the old man on the altar, then to fall back. By the queer, actinic luminosity of the skull I could see the woman's face, and recognized her as Judith Delapore, niece and granddaughter of the madmen who ruled Depewatch. Yet how different from the sweet countenance painted on Colby's miniature! Like the ivory mask of a goddess, cold and lined with concentration, she bent her eyes on the heaving swirl of nightmare that surrounded her, not even glancing at her lover, who lay gasping, twisting in convulsions at her feet. In a high, hard voice she repeated the dreadful words of the incantations, and neither flinched nor wavered as the dreadful things flittered and crawled and bounced in the darkness.

Only when the hideous rite was ended, and the unspeakable congregation had trickled away through the blasphemous angle of the inner walls, did the young woman lower the skull she held. She stood in her black gown, outlined in the gleam of the niter on the walls, staring into the abyss from which those dreadful unhuman things had come, barely seeming to notice me as I stumbled and staggered down the last of the stairs.

Of the old man's body that had lain upon the altar nothing whatsoever remained. A thick layer of slime covered the stone and ran down onto the floor, which was perhaps half an inch deep in a brownish liquid that glistened in the feeble blue gleam of the niter. Having seen Burnwell Colby engulfed by that wriggling darkness I staggered to where he had lain with some confused idea of helping him, but as I dropped to my knees I saw that only a lumpy mass of half-dissolved flesh and bones remained. The bones themselves had the appearance of being charred, almost melted. I looked up in horror at the woman with the skull and her eyes met mine, clear golden hazel, like other eyes I could not quite recall. Her eyes widened and filled with anger and hate:

"You," she whispered. "So you did not take him after all?"

I only shook my head, her words making no sense to me in my shaken state, and she went on, "As you have seen, Uncle, it is I, now, and not Grandfather —Grandfather who has not existed for over fifty years—who rules now here." And to my horror she held out her hand toward that hideously anomalous angle of the walls where the darkness lay waiting. "*Y'bfnk—ng'haiie....*"

I cried out. At the same instant light blazed up on the stairway that led to the upper and innocent realms of the ignorant world: blue-white incandescence, like lightning, and the crackle of ozone filled the reeking air.

"My dear Miss Delapore," said Holmes, "if you will pardon my interruption, I fear you are laboring under a misapprehension." He came down the last of the stair, bearing in one hand a metal rod, from which a flickering corona of electricity seemed to sparkle, flowing back to a similar rod held up by Carnaki, who followed him down the stair. Carnaki wore a sort of pack or rucksack upon his back, of the kind one sees porters in Constantinople carrying; a dozen wires joined it to the rod in his hand, and lightnings leaped from that rod to Holmes', seeming to surround the two men in a deadly nimbus of light. The cold glare blanched all color from his face, so that his eyebrows stood out nearly black, like a man who has received a mortal blow and bleeds within.

Looking down at me he asked, as if we shared a cup of tea at Baker Street, "What was your wife's favorite flower?"

Miss Delapore, startled, opened her mouth to speak, but I cried in a convulsion of grief: "How can you ask that, Holmes? How can you speak of my Mary in this place, after what we have seen? Her life was all goodness, all joy, and it was for *nothing*, do you understand? If this—this blasphemy—this monstrous abyss underlies all of our world, how can any good, any joy exist in safety? It is a mockery—love, care, tenderness… it means nothing, and we are all fools for believing in any of it.…"

"Watson!" thundered Holmes, and again Miss Delapore turned her eyes to him in astonishment.

"Watson?" she whispered.

His gaze held mine, and he asked again: "What was Mrs. Watson's favorite flower?"

"Lily of the valley," I said, and buried my face in my hands. Even as I did so I saw—such was the horror and strangeness of my dream—that they were the hands of an elderly man, thin and twisted with arthritis, and the wedding-band that I had never ceased to wear with my Mary's death was gone. "But none of it matters now, nor ever will again, knowing what I now know of the true nature of this world."

Through my weeping I heard Carnacki say softly, "We'll have to switch off the electrical field. I don't think we can get him up the stairs."

"You will be safe," said Miss Delapore's voice. "I command Them now—as did my grandfather, or the thing that for so many years passed itself off as my grandfather. I knew his goal—its goal—was to take over Burnwell's body, as it had taken over my grandfather's fifty years ago. He despised my uncle, as he despised my father, and as he despised me as a woman, thinking us all too weak to withstand the power raised by the Rite of the *Book of Eibon*. Why else did he bring me home from school, save to lure that poor American to his fate?"

"With a letter blotted with tears," said Holmes drily. "Even in the margins, and the blank upper portion by the address. Hardly the places where a girl's tears would fall while writing, but it's difficult to keep drops from spattering there when they're dipped from a bedroom pitcher with the fingers."

"Had I not written that letter," she replied, "it would be I, not Grandfather, who was given to the Hooded One tonight. At least by luring Burnwell to me I was able to give him poison—brown spider-mushroom, that does not take effect for many days. Grandfather would have had him, one way or another—he does not give up easily."

"And was it you who sent for him, to meet your grandfather in Brighton?"

"No. But I knew it would come. When Grandfather—when Lord Rupert's vampire spirit—entered poor Burnwell's body, that body was already dying, though none knew it but I. I knew Uncle Carstairs had mastered the technique too, of crossing from body to body—I assume it is you who were his target, and not your friend."

"Even so," said Holmes, and his voice was quiet and bitterly cold. "He underestimated me—and both underestimated you, it seems."

And there was the smallest touch of defiance in her voice as she replied, "Men do. Yourself included, it seems."

The snapping hiss of the electricity ceased. I opened my eyes to see them kneeling around me, in the horror of that nighted cavern: Holmes and Carnacki, holding their electrical rods to either of my hands, and Miss Delapore looking into my eyes. Somehow despite the darkness I could see her clearly, could see into her golden eyes, as one can in dreams. What she said to me I do not remember, lost as it was in the shock and cold when Carnaki touched the switch....

I opened my eyes to summer morning. My head ached; when I brought my hand up to touch it, I saw that my wrists were bruised and chafed, as if I had been bound. "You were off your head for much of the night," said Holmes, sitting beside the bed. "We feared you would do yourself an injury—indeed, you gave us great cause for concern."

I looked around me at the simple wall-paper and white curtains of my bedroom at the Cross of Gold in High Clum. I stammered, "I don't remember what happened...."

"Fever," said Carnaki, coming into the room with a slender young lady whom I instantly recognized from the miniature Burnwell Colby had showed us as Miss Judith Delapore. "I have never seen so rapid a rise of temperature in so short a time; you must have taken quite a severe chill."

I shook my head, wondering what it was about Miss Delapore's haggard calm, about her golden-hazel eyes, that filled me with such uneasy horror. "I remember nothing," I said. "Dreams.... Your uncle came here, I believe," I added, after Holmes had introduced the young lady. "At least... I believe it was your uncle...." Why was I so certain that the wizened, twisted little man who had come to my room—whom I believed had come to my room—yesterday had been Carstairs Delapore? I could recall nothing of what he had said. Only his eyes....

"It was my uncle," said Miss Delapore, and as I looked at her again I realized that she wore mourning. "You remember nothing of why he came here yesterday? For before he could mention the visit to anyone at the Priory...." And here she glanced across at Holmes; "He fell down the stairs there, and died at the bottom."

I expressed my horrified condolences, while trying to suppress an inexplicable sense of deepest relief that I somehow associated with dreams I had had while delirious. After inclining her head in thanks, Miss Delapore turned to Holmes, and held out to him a box of stout red cardboard, tied up with string. "As I promised," she said.

I lay back, overcome again by a terrible exhaustion—as much of the spirit, it seemed, as of the body. While Carnaki prepared a sedative draught for me Holmes walked Miss Delapore out to our mutual parlor, and I heard the outer door open.

"I have heard much of your deductive abilities, Mr. Holmes," said the young woman's voice, barely heard through the half-open bedroom door. "How did you know that my uncle, who must have come here to take you as my grandfather took Burnwell, had seized upon your friend instead?"

"There was no deduction necessary, Miss Delapore," said Holmes. "I know Watson—and I know what I have heard of your uncle. Would Carstairs Delapore have come down into danger, to see what he could do for an injured man?"

"Do not think ill of my family, Mr. Holmes," said Miss Delapore, after a time of silence. "The way which leads down the six thousand stairs cannot be sealed. It must always have a guardian. That is the nature of such things. And it is always easier to find a venal successor who is willing to trade to Them the things They want—the blood They crave—in exchange for gifts and services, than to find one willing to serve a lonely guardianship solely that the world above may remain safe. They feared Lord Rupert—if the thing that all knew as Lord Rupert was in fact not some older spirit still. His bones, buried in the sub-crypt, shall, I hope, prove a barrier that They are unwilling to cross. Now that the skull, which was the talisman that commanded Their favors, is gone, perhaps there will be less temptation among those who study in the house."

"There is always temptation, Miss Delapore," said Holmes.

"Get thee behind me, Mr. Holmes," replied the woman's voice, with a touch of silvery amusement far beyond her years. "I saw what that temptation did to my uncle, in his desperate craving to snatch the rule of the things from my grandfather. I saw what my grandfather became. These are things I shall remember, when the time comes to seek a disciple of my own."

I was drowsing already from Carnaki's draught when Holmes returned to the bedroom. "Did you speak to Colby?" I asked, struggling to keep my eyes open as he went to the table and picked up the red cardboard box. "Is he all right?" For my dreams as to his fate had been foul, terrible, and equivocal. "Warn him... prevent the old Viscount from doing harm?"

Holmes hesitated for a long time, looking down at me with a concern that I did not quite understand in his eyes. "I did," he replied at length. "To such effect that Viscount Gaius has disappeared from the district—for good, one hopes. But as for Burnwell, he too has... departed. I fear that Miss Delapore is destined to lead a rather difficult and lonely life."

He glanced across at Carnaki, who was packing up what appeared to be an electrical battery and an array of steel rods and wires into a rucksack, the purpose of which I could not imagine. Their eyes met. Then Carnaki nodded, very slightly, as if approving what Holmes had said.

"Because of what was revealed," I asked, stifling a terrible yawn, "about this... this blackmail that was being practiced? The young hound, to desert a young lady like that." My eyelids slipped closed. I fought them open again, seized by sudden panic, by the terror that I might slide into sleep and find myself again in that dreadful abyss, watching the horrible things that fluttered and crept from those angles of darkness that should not have been there. "Did you learn... anything of these studies they practiced?"

"Indeed we did," said Carnaki. And then, a little airily, "There was nothing in them, though."

"What did Miss Delapore bring you, then?"

"Merely a memento of the case," said Holmes. "As for young Mr. Colby, do not be too hard on him, Watson. He did the best he could, as do we all. I am not sure that he would have been entirely happy with Miss Delapore in any event. She was… much the stronger of the two."

Holmes never did elucidate for me the means by which he bridged the gap be-tween his supposition that Viscount Delapore was engaged in kidnapping children for the purposes of some vile cult centered in Depewatch Priory, and evidence sufficient to make that evil man flee the country. If he and Carnaki found such evidence at the Priory—which I assume was the reason he had asked the young antiquarian to accompany us to Shropshire—he did not speak to me of it. Indeed, he showed a great reluctance to refer to the case at all.

For this I was grateful. The effects of the fever I had caught were slow to leave me, and even as much as three years later I found myself prey to the sense that I had learned—and mercifully forgotten—something that would utterly destroy all my sense of what the world is and should be; that would make either life or sanity impossible, if it should turn out to be true.

Only once did Holmes mention the affair, some years later, during a conversa-tion on Freud's theories of insanity, when he spoke in passing of the old Viscount Delapore's conviction—evidently held by others in what is now termed a *folie à deux*—that the old man had in fact been the reincarnated or astrally transposed spirit of Lord Rupert Grimsley, once Lord of Depewatch Priory. And then he spoke circumspectly, watching me, as if he feared to wake my old dreams again and cause me many sleepless nights.

I can only be sorry that the case ended without firm conclusion, for it did, as Holmes promised me that night on the Embankment, show me unsuspected colors in the spectrum of human mentality and human existence. Yet this was not an unmixed blessing. For though I know that my fever-dream was no more than that—a fantastic hallucination brought on by illness and by Carnaki's own curious monomania about otherworld cults and ancient writings—sometimes in the shadowland between sleep and waking I think of that terrible blue-lit abyss that lies beneath an old Priory on the borders of Wales, and imagine that I hear the eerie piping of chaos rising up out of blasphemous angles of night. And in my dreams I see again the enigmatic Miss Delapore, standing before the chittering congregation of nightmares, holding aloft in her hands the skull of Lord Rupert Grimsley: the skull that now reposes in a corner of Holmes' room, wrapped in its red cardboard box.

DYNAMICS OF
A HANGING

by Tony Pi

Tony Pi has a Ph.D. in Linguistics and currently works as an administrator at the Cinema Studies Institute at the University of Toronto. At the time of this writing, he is a finalist for the John W. Campbell Award for best new writer. His work has appeared in (or is forthcoming from) *Abyss & Apex, On Spec, Intergalactic Medicine Show,* and the anthologies *Ages of Wonder, Cinema Spec,* and *Writers of the Future XXIII.* He is currently working on a novel manuscript about the shapeshifters who first appeared in his story "Metamorphoses in Amber," which was a finalist for the Prix Aurora Award.

Most people know Lewis Carroll (the pen name of Charles Lutwidge Dodgson) as the author of *Alice's Adventures in Wonderland.* Dodgson became good friends with the family of one of his academic colleagues, the Liddells, and would often take their children along with him when he went rowing on the nearby rivers. During these expeditions he would make up fanciful tales to entertain the children, and one of the girls, Alice, was so enchanted that she begged Dodgson to write it all down. The enthusiastic reception for the manuscript by fantasy author George MacDonald and his children convinced Dodgson to pursue publication. Dodgson's private life has been the subject of intense speculation, especially regarding his relationship with the Liddells. (Dodgson's family apparently destroyed several pages of his diary, presumably to protect his reputation.) We know that he was tormented by feelings of guilt and shame, which apparently restrained him from following his father into the priesthood. It's all very mysterious. One thing that's beyond any doubt though is that Dodgson demonstrated brilliance in many different fields. Notably, he held a lectureship in mathematics, and wrote books on logic. It's those abilities that he puts to good use in our next adventure.

It was in the fall of 1891 that I received a telegram from the Reverend Charles Dodgson, inviting me to his residence in Guildford, Surrey. It was not for a medical consultation, but of vital importance to the present trial of the Moriarty gang: the mystery of Professor Moriarty's cipher.

Reverend Dodgson was both an author of children's books and a mathematician. My wife was fond of the Alice books under his *nom-de-plume*, Lewis Carroll, while Holmes once recommended me to read his *Game of Logic* to hone my analytical reasoning. It surprised me that Dodgson knew of the coded notebooks, as their existence had been suppressed. It was not five months ago that my friend Sherlock Holmes perished at Reichenbach Falls in his final confrontation with James Moriarty. Even in death, Holmes struck a fatal blow against Moriarty's criminal confederates, leaving documents that thoroughly incriminated them. Inspector Patterson invited me to examine the materials recovered from one of Moriarty's secret lairs: vials of opiates among blueprints and handwritten musical scores; purloined paintings beside burned account books; and most intriguing, notebooks written in Moriarty's hand, the oldest of which had a page torn out.

Moriarty's notebooks contained mathematical formulae interspersed with code. Mycroft Holmes speculated it was a Vigenère cipher, but even he couldn't solve it. "Alas, both the Kasiski and Kerckhoffs methods failed," said Mycroft. "If only we knew what the coded messages were about. Are they musings on mathematics, or something more sinister? Find the key, Watson, and we'll glimpse Moriarty's mind."

I was intrigued by Dodgson's message. Did he know the key, when even Mycroft Holmes failed? I immediately dispatched a telegram accepting his invitation.

Thus I found myself in Guildford, sipping tea with Charles Dodgson in his parlour. The Reverend, a thin man with uneven blue eyes and sloped shoulders, tilted his left ear towards me as we talked.

"My condolences, Doctor Watson, on the untimely passing of Mr. Holmes," said he. "I fear I must bear some of the burden for his demise."

"Oh? Did you know him?" I asked.

"I knew of Holmes at Oxford, though we never met. It was James Moriarty I knew, through our years at Christ Church debating mathematics and logic. Is there a volume from Moriarty's effects, with a single coded page torn out?"

"Indeed!" I exclaimed. "How did you know?"

"Because I have that page." Dodgson retrieved a copy of *Through the Looking Glass* from his collection. Tucked within was the coded page he spoke of, folded and yellowed with age. "Tenniel's Jabberwock illustration always reminds me of Moriarty, hypnotic and serpentine."

"How did you get this?"

"That, Doctor, is a twisted tale," said he. "It began with the Order of Copernicus, and ended with the tragic murder of a young prodigy named Arthur Doyle."

The Order of Copernicus is a fellowship of scholars, physicians, mathematicians and philosophers. The Copernicans often invite new members to enrich their symposia with fresh ideas and voices. Moriarty first introduced me to the Order years ago, after he completed his dissertation on the Binomial Theorem. I found their debates enthralling, and participated whenever I could.

In early summer, 1879, Moriarty and I were invited to Aston by a fellow

Copernican, Doctor Reginald Hoare. Reginald introduced us to his young lodger, Arthur Doyle, a medical student who was working as a dispensing assistant taking house calls on Reginald's behalf. I found him an engaging conversationalist and a sharp observer.

"What do you plan to do with your future, Arthur?" I asked.

"Surgery, sir," said Arthur. "I'm very much inspired by Doctor Bell at the Edinburgh University. But I'd also like to become a writer like you, actually, and have written some stories for Reginald's children. Edgar Allan Poe's another inspiration, and I'm attempting a mystery now."

"Poe! Now there was a true Copernican. I heard he was a great cryptographer," I said.

Moriarty disagreed. "He indulged in substitution codes, barely worth the effort to solve, unlike Vigenère ciphers."

Arthur asked what a Vigenère cipher was.

"It's based on the Caesar cipher, which shifted letters by a chosen number of positions, looping back to the beginning of the alphabet if necessary," I explained. "Shift the word JABBERWOCKY four positions to the right, you'd have NEFFIVSGOC. To solve the coded message, apply the shift in reverse.

"The Vigenère cipher uses a keyword where each letter in the alphabet represented a different shift. For example, if ALICE were my keyword, that would mean shifts of 0, 11, 8, 2, and 5. The keyword is repeated as needed, and so JABBERWOCKY becomes JLJDIRHWEOY."

Moriarty nodded. "There are mathematical ways to solve a Vigenère code. Kasiski's method determines the length of the keyword by measuring distances between repeating combinations, then uses frequency analysis to break the code. Kerckhoffs' method focuses on solving the keyword itself."

"Moriarty, didn't you have a notebook at Christ Church where you jotted down your formulae?" I asked. "You used a cipher on the annotations. Was that Vigenère?"

Moriarty smiled. "It was, to ensure that the musings and errors of my youth were for my eyes alone. But I'm confident that my code cannot be broken by either the Kerckhoffs or Kasiski solutions. They assume the keyword would be short, and repeated. But if the keyword's significantly long, like a piece of text, then a coded message would be virtually unbreakable."

"Respectfully, Professor, the keyword may be impervious to analysis, but the codemaker is not," said Arthur. "At medical school, Professor Bell taught us to observe the person as well as the disease in our diagnoses. By analyzing the man's habits, experiences and indulgences, one can deduce the choice of text he uses for his code."

"You presume to unriddle my cipher by mere observation?" asked Moriarty.

"If I had the chance to get to know you better, Professor, I daresay I could figure out your code," said Arthur.

"I know a challenge when I hear one! Reginald, indulge me by releasing Arthur from his obligations on weekends. My university's not far, and I will pay for travel and lodging. He may observe me in my element, while I in turn will mentor him and provide him with a sample of cipher to unriddle. If he succeeds by summer's end, I will pay his tuition."

Moriarty had obviously taken a liking to Arthur Doyle, perhaps eager to guide a young man into his genius.

Reginald heartily agreed. "If he doesn't fall behind his duties here, why not?"

Arthur smiled. "It will be a pleasure learning from you, Professor."

"Before I forget, gentlemen, Samuel Haughton left these for you on his last visit," Reginald said, giving us each a copy of a treatise titled *On Hanging*. Reverend Haughton was a doctor and fellow Copernican from Dublin who dabbled in mathematics. "Haughton claims the mathematics of hanging can be useful in medicine. Humane versus inhumane hangings: depending on the criminal's weight and the length of drop, it could mean the difference between a quick death from snapping his spinal cord, to a long death from strangulation."

We argued awhile over the need for executions, with Moriarty maintaining ambivalence. When the topic somehow drifted onto the three-body problem in astronomy, which I had little interest in, Arthur and I excused ourselves so I could see his story manuscripts.

Arthur's room was modest, and his desk cluttered with papers on medicine, scraps of writing, and sheet music. Among his medical books were works by Burton, Dickens, Leibniz, and of course, Poe. He moved a violin case off a chair so I could sit and read his stories. I found them well-written and engaging, and encouraged Arthur to continue writing.

Arthur retrieved a book bound in red Moroccan leather, gilt in silver: a copy of *Alice's Adventures in Wonderland*. "Would you mind signing this, Reverend, for Herr Gleiwitz? I see him on my rounds, and feel sorry for the man. He's down on his luck, raising his children on what little income he receives from giving German lessons. Perhaps your book will give his family some joy."

I gladly signed the copy.

Arthur wrote to me at Oxford thereafter, telling me of his tutelage under Moriarty. At first, his letters were ebullient, saying that the Professor's cunning rivaled that of Doctor Bell's. Whereas Bell emphasized observation, Moriarty taught him anticipation. *Predicting behaviour was as crucial as establishing history*, he wrote, explaining Moriarty's philosophy. *The world was a chessboard and men were as predictable as game pieces.*

But Arthur's later letters were sombre, hinting at a rift between himself and Moriarty. Did Moriarty's enthusiasm for his student turn to envy? Or did Arthur discover Moriarty's dark dealings? In any event, it spelled death for him.

In late summer, both Moriarty and I accepted an invitation from a fellow Copernican in London. On our third night there, upon our return from the symphony, we learned by telegram that tragedy had struck: Arthur Doyle was found dead, hanged.

"Arthur had been concerned about matters in Aston, but refused to say more," said Moriarty, stunned by the news. "I ought to have foreseen disaster."

I consoled him. "How could you have known?"

"We owe it to the boy to investigate his death, Charles," he insisted.

And so Moriarty and I returned to Aston, bearing our condolences to Reginald.

Reginald recounted the details of Arthur's death. "Arthur had returned from house calls and retired to his room that evening as usual. The following morning, we were shocked to hear Arthur had been found in the bell tower at St. Mary's, the church down the street. Inspector Ives took me there to identify Arthur's body."

"Cause of death?" asked Moriarty.

"All the signs pointed towards asphyxiation. Inspector Ives believes it was suicide," said Reginald.

"Arthur would hardly take his own life," said Moriarty. "Reginald, come with us and describe what you saw?"

Reluctantly, the good doctor accompanied us to St. Mary's. The bell tower was several stories tall, with a ladder up to a trapdoor that led into the belfry. The bell's rope dangled through a large opening in the belfry floor.

"The noose was tied to the bell's gudgeon," explained Reginald. "He was dangling six feet off the ground when we found him. He couldn't have kicked away a support, or we'd have discovered one. He must have jumped from the bell chamber."

"He could have pushed off the ladder," observed Moriarty. "But the momentum might have swung his body into the wall opposite. Any bruising on his arms or legs?"

"No," said Reginald.

"A dying man's instinct is to claw at the noose, even if he intended to die. Did you find any scratch marks around his neck?" continued Moriarty.

"No."

"But his hands weren't bound?"

"Correct."

"Then the evidence points towards a sudden drop from above," said Moriarty. "Except that's impossible."

"Why?" asked Reginald, perplexed.

"Mathematics," I explained, remembering Haughton's treatise on hanging. "Given his weight, a rope that exceeded twelve feet would make the force of the drop so great that the noose wouldn't simply snap his neck, it would cut clean through."

Moriarty nodded. "Given the marks on his neck, where was the noose's knot placed, Reginald?"

"Corner of his left jaw."

"A knot placed there would throw the head back upon falling, resulting in a fracture or dislocation of the neck. He would have died of a snapped neck, not strangulated," Moriarty concluded. "We're faced with contradictory facts. Arthur couldn't have jumped from that height without decapitation, but neither could he have hung himself in a manner consistent with asphyxiation."

"A vorpal paradox indeed," I agreed.

"That leaves but one conclusion: that Arthur Doyle was dead before someone strung him up," said Moriarty.

"Perhaps he was strangled in his sleep? Marks from a garrote would have been hidden by the bruising of the noose," I suggested.

"Perhaps. His room may yield more clues," said Moriarty.

In Arthur's room, Moriarty moved a familiar red, leather-bound book gilt in gold off the desk, and rifled through the young man's papers.

"Here's a draft of a paper he was writing for the British Medical Journal," said Moriarty. "*The Uses of Gelseminum As A Poison*, by Arthur Conan Doyle. Arthur had been experimenting on himself with gelseminum, also known as jessamine, in the interest of medical research. We have our poison, gentlemen."

"Poisoned! I thought his death was consistent with respiratory failure," I said.

"Do you know what gelseminum does, Reginald?" asked Moriarty.

"It's efficacious against spasmodic disorders, like epilepsy and hysteria, inhibiting nerve control and respitory functions," replied Reginald. "A large enough dose would paralyze a man, even arrest his breathing and stop his heart! I naturally assumed it was strangulation by hanging, and never considered poison. You *are* as brilliant as Arthur said, Moriarty!"

Moriarty cracked a thin smile. "It takes only observation to tell truth from lie."

"But who would kill him, and why?" I asked.

"I suspect if Reginald inventories his medicinal store, he'll discover narcotics missing," said Moriarty, with utter confidence. "Suppose Arthur was blackmailed into stealing the drugs. He might have threatened to go to the police, forcing his blackmailers to eliminate him quietly with an overdose of gelseminum, of which Arthur had in sufficient quantity to kill. To conceal their crime, they hoisted up his body in the bell tower to suggest suicide."

Reginald paled. "Arthur, embroiled in such dreadful business?"

"Appearances can be deceiving," said Moriarty. "Let us check the dispensary." They left, but I stayed behind to say a prayer for the lad.

Moriarty's analysis seemed plausible, but I didn't believe it of Arthur. I observed two peculiarities. Arthur's violin case was missing, and the book on the desk was a copy of *Through the Looking Glass*, not *Alice's Adventures in Wonderland*. I had chosen the different gilt decorations for each myself. I flipped open the cover and found a forgery of my signature, but not a good one: my name was misspelled. It read: *C.L. Dodgson (alias Lewis Carlool)*.

Why would Arthur go to the trouble of forging my signature, but spell it wrong? I came to the conclusion that Arthur left that clue for me alone. No one else would know I hadn't signed *Looking Glass*.

Reginald checked his inventory and discovered that drugs were indeed missing. Further forensic examination of Arthur's body confirmed he died of gelseminum poisoning, and the police started a search for Arthur's killers. Moriarty returned to his college, but I stayed behind in Acton to investigate the lead of the forged autograph. I made some quiet inquiries and found Herr Gleiwitz, who welcomed me into his home.

"Mr. Doyle had been kind to us, God rest his soul," said Herr Gleiwitz. "Once, when I couldn't pay for the medicine, he gave me his watch and said I should sell it. I tried to give it back, but he wouldn't have it. Several days ago, he gave my eldest a violin and made the boy promise to learn how to play." He brought the instrument for my examination.

I could find no hidden compartments in the violin case, but I discovered a folded piece of paper inside the violin through its F-holes. It took several frustrating tries to get it out intact. It was a torn page written in code in Moriarty's hand, and it must have been worth killing for. For the first time, I suspected that James Moriarty murdered Arthur Doyle in cold blood.

I was certain that Arthur had done what he promised: he had deduced Moriarty's key by observation alone. But the younger Moriarty was proud, and would have taken great risks to protect his secrets. And so he orchestrated Arthur's murder, with the perfect alibi—he was in London with me. He then hid his own involvement by playing detective to his own crime. What better way to throw the police off his scent?

I asked Herr Gleiwitz never to speak of my visit, and returned to Oxford. I worked in frenzy to solve the code, but to no avail. Finally, I decided to visit Moriarty, to observe him as Arthur had, look into his eyes, and hope to find a soul.

I called on Moriarty in late September, bringing pages for my next book, *Curiosa Mathematica, Part Two*, as pretext. Soon we were discussing math problems over tea in his den.

Moriarty's taste in books was eclectic: art, algebra, music, astronomy. There were so many texts that could be his Vigenère key, it would have taken months just to check the coded page against the first few pages of each book!

Moriarty remained the confident and controlled gentleman he always was. But when I mentioned that he never did express his views on capital punishment, a sneer crept onto his face. "Death is the only punishment." He smirked, then turned the topic to eighteenth-century painters. It was enough to convince me that he hid the heart of a villain.

Yet I had no evidence. If I went to the police with only an unsolved page of code, I too would have been marked for death. I resolved to engineer Moriarty's fall in secret. So I wrote anonymous letters to key figures in his university town, hinting at shady dealings. The vile rumours spread, and soon Moriarty resigned his chair, retiring to London to become an army coach.

I thought the loss of the professorship would have taught him a lesson, but I was wrong. Instead, he built a veneer of self-effacement after his resignation, and became supremely cautious. I wonder what hand I had in his perfection as a criminal mastermind?

Reverend Dodgson stopped there, and I poured him another cup of tea. "Why didn't Arthur tell someone? Or write a letter detailing what he discovered?" I asked.

"Moriarty would have silenced anyone who knew. Written declarations might have been found and destroyed. I suspect the forgery of my name was the only clue left intact," said Dodgson.

"And still unsolved, I gather," I said.

"You have it, Doctor Watson," agreed Dodgson. "I was hoping we could solve the key together."

I was about to suggest enlisting Mycroft's aid, but young Arthur Doyle had meant the message for Dodgson, so it must draw upon the Reverend's personal knowledge. Perhaps all he needed were my insights into the problem, as wrong as they might be, to help him arrive at the right answer.

"The misspelled name, *Carlool*. Was that the key word?" I asked.

"No. It has to be a long text, as Moriarty said, to foil simple decoding."

"Could the code be based on *Wonderland* or *Looking Glass*?"

"Doubtful. Moriarty used the notebook while he was writing his dissertation, which was years before I wrote those books."

What would Holmes say? He'd ask me how I'd send a message to a mathematician. With numbers, I'd reply.

And there was the answer. "The point of departure from your *nom-de-plume* comes after *Car*. It isn't *lool*, but one-thousand and one!" I cried triumphantly.

Dodgson's eyes widened. "I never thought of that."

"Moriarty used Burton's *The Book of the Thousand Nights and a Night* as his key, then," I said, remembering Dodgson's list of Arthur's books.

"But that was published in 1885, years after Arthur's death. He would only know of Burton's travel writings," argued Dodgson.

I thought about it further. "Poe write a story called *The Thousand-and-Second Tale of Scheherazade*? Not an exact match to one-thousand and one, and I'm certain it was published in 1845. Didn't Arthur have a copy of Poe on his shelves?"

"Books? Wait, Arthur read Leibniz!" said Dodgson excitedly. "Gottfried Leibniz invented the binary number system. In binary, *one-zero-zero-one* is the number nine. Also, one-thousand-and-one is the product of three consecutive prime numbers: seven, eleven, and thirteen. They would be consecutive odd numbers but for the conspicuous absence of the number nine. Arthur hid that number twice in plain sight!"

"But how would *nine* be the key?" I asked.

We wrestled over the new question. My thoughts kept drifting back to Holmes. What would he consider next? He'd be fascinated by that violin, of course—

"The violin!" I cried. "It's no accident that the note was hidden in it; it's the missing clue. Moriarty loved music, didn't he?"

"He did," said Dodgson.

"If he wanted to remember a passage as a key, the lyrics of a song might be easiest to remember," I suggested. "And there's one symphony set to lyrics."

"Beethoven's Ninth, *Ode to Joy*!" he exclaimed. "Friedrich von Schiller's poem set to music, in the original German. That's why Moriarty was confident that a Kerckhoffs statistical analysis of his key would fail. Letter frequencies differ from language to language."

We immediately set about deciphering the page using *Ode to Joy* as the key. It took many tries to determine how the key aligned to the code, but we barely noticed the passage of time. At last, Dodgson finished deciphering the entire page.

"What does it say?" I asked, breathless.

"It alludes to Moriarty's triumphant murder of his mentor, someone who was as devilish as he was." Dodgson handed me the coded page and its solution. "Alas, the name does not appear on this page, but the rest of the notebook should reveal who made Moriarty what he was, how he died, and why."

"And perhaps other crimes, other accomplices," I added. Now that we had the right key, we would learn at last about Moriarty and the trials that shaped him. "I'll let Mycroft Holmes know. Thank you, Reverend."

"No, thank you for restoring a man's good name, Doctor Watson. Holmes would be proud," said Dodgson. "At long last, we've put Arthur Doyle's ghost to rest."

MERRIDEW OF
ABOMINABLE MEMORY

by Chris Roberson

Chris Roberson's latest novels are *Three Unbroken, Dawn of War II, End of the Century,* and *Book of Secrets,* the first in his Nekropolis series. His short stories have appeared in several anthologies, such as *The Many Faces of Van Helsing, FutureShocks,* and *Sideways in Crime,* and in a variety of magazines, including *Asimov's* and *Interzone.* He is a winner of the Sidewise Award for best works of alternate history, and his novel *The Dragon's Nine Sons* was a finalist for this year's award. In addition to being a writer, Roberson (along with his wife, Allison) is the publisher of indie press MonkeyBrain Books.

William Faulkner wrote, "The past isn't dead. It isn't even past." The past is always with us, the only guide we have for judging how we should act in the present and in the future. And yet our understanding of even our own pasts is gravely limited by our memory. Many people would likely be shocked to be confronted with just how unreliable their memory can be. Eyewitness testimony is often hopelessly confused, and many innocent people have gone to prison on the basis of false memories of childhood abuse. On the other hand there are people with staggeringly precise memories, who can recite pi to thousands of decimal places, or remember what they were doing on any day for the past several decades. Often such exceptional memory comes at the price of some other cognitive impairment. Sherlock Holmes, upon his return from the dead in "The Adventure of the Empty House," remarks on various criminals of his acquaintance whose names begin with M. "Moriarty himself is enough to make any letter illustrious," says Holmes, "and here is Morgan the poisoner, and Merridew of abominable memory." What follows is the story of this Merridew—a tale you won't soon forget.

The old man reclined on a chaise-longue, warmed by the rays of the rising sun which slanted through the windows on the eastern wall. In the garden below, he could see the other patients and convalescents already at work tending the greenery with varying degrees of attention. The gardens of the Holloway Sanatorium were the responsibility of the patients, at least those tasks which didn't involve sharp implements, and the nurses and wardens saw to it that the grounds were immaculate. Not that the patients ever complained, of course. Tending a hedge or planting a row of flowers was serene and contemplative compared to the stresses which had lead most of the patients to take refuge here, dirty fingernails and suntanned necks notwithstanding.

No one had asked John Watson to help tend the garden, but then, he could hardly blame them. Entering the middle years of his eighth decade of life, his days of useful manual labor were far behind him, even if he wasn't plagued by ancient injuries in leg and shoulder. But it was not infirmities of the body that had led John here to Virginia Water in Surry; rather, it was a certain infirmity of the mind.

John's problem was memory, or memories to be precise. The dogged persistence of some, the fleeting loss of others. Increasingly in recent months and years, he had found it difficult to recall the present moment, having trouble remembering where he was, and what was going on around him. At the same time, though, recollections of events long past were so strong, so vivid, that they seemed to overwhelm him. Even at the best of times, when he felt in complete control of his faculties, he still found that the memories of a day forty years past were more vivid than his recollections of the week previous.

John had been content to look upon these bouts of forgetfulness as little more than occasional lapses, and no cause for concern. When visiting London that spring, though, he had managed to get so befuddled in a fugue that he'd wandered round to Baker Street, fully expecting his old friend to be in at the rooms they once shared. The present tenant, a detective himself as it happened, was charitable enough about the episode, but it was clear that Blake had little desire to be bothered again by a confused old greybearded pensioner.

After the episode in London, John had begun to suspect that there was no other explanation for it than that he was suffering from the onset of dementia, and that the lapses he suffered would become increasingly less occasional in the days to come. In the hopes of finding treatment, keeping the condition from worsening if improvement were out of the question, he checked himself into Holloway for evaluation.

Warmed by the morning sun, John found himself recalling the weeks spent in Peshawar after the Battle of Maiwand, near mindless in a haze of enteric fever, something about the commingling of warmth and mental confusion bringing those days to mind.

His reverie was interrupted by the arrival of an orderly, sent to fetch John for his morning appointment with the staff physician, the young Doctor Rhys.

As the orderly led him through the halls of Holloway, they passed other convalescents not equal to the task of tending the emerald gardens outside. There were some few hundred patients in the facility, all of them being treated for mental distress of one sort or another, whether brought on by domestic or business troubles, by worry or overwork. Not a few of them had addled their own senses with spirits, which brought to John's mind his elder brother Henry, Jr., who had died of drink three decades past.

There were others, though, who had seen their senses addled through no fault of their own. Some of the patients were young men, not yet out of their third decade, who seemed never to have recovered from the things they did and saw in the trenches of the Great War. Their eyes had a haunted look, as they stared unseeing into the middle distance.

John well remembered being that young. If he closed his eyes, he could recall the sounds and smells of the Battle of Maiwand as though it had occurred yesterday. As he walked along beside the orderly, he reached up and tenderly probed his left shoulder, the sensation of the Jezail bullet striking suddenly prominent in his thoughts.

Finally, they reached Doctor Rhys's study, and found the young man waiting there for them. Once John was safely ensconced in a well-upholstered chair, the orderly retreated, closing the door behind him.

"And now, Mr. Watson, how does the day find you, hmm?"

"Doctor," John said, his voice sounding strained and ancient in his own ears. He cleared his throat, setting off a coughing jag.

"Yes?" Rhys replied, eyebrow raised.

"*Doctor* Watson."

Rhys nodded vigorously, wearing an apologetic expression. "Quite right, my apologies. How are you today, then, *Dr*. Watson?"

John essayed a shrug. "No better than yesterday, one supposes, and little worse."

Rhys had a little notebook open on his knee, and jotted down a note. "The staff informs me that you have not availed yourself of many of our facilities, in the course of your stay."

It was a statement, though John knew it for a question. "No," he answered, shaking his head.

In the sanatorium, there was more than enough to occupy one's day. Those seeking exercise could use the cricket pitch, badminton court, and swimming pool, while those of a less strenuous bent could retire to the snooker room and social club. In his days at Holloway, though, John had been content to do little but sit in an eastern-facing room in the mornings, in a western-facing room in the afternoons, sitting always in the sunlight. It was as though he were a flower seeking out as many of the sun's rays as possible in the brief time remaining to him. The less charitably minded might even accuse him of seeking out the light through some fear of shadows, since by night the electric lights in his room were never extinguished, and when he slept it was in a red-lidded darkness, never black.

"Tell me, Dr. Watson," Rhys continued, glancing up from his notes, "have you given any further thought to our discussion yesterday?"

John sighed. Rhys was an earnest young man, who had studied with Freud in Vienna, and who was fervent in his belief that science and medicine could cure all ills. When John first arrived in Holloway weeks before, he had taken this passion as encouraging, but as the days wore on and his condition failed to improve, his own aging enthusiasms had begun to wane.

Had Watson ever been so young, so convinced of the unassailable power of knowledge? He remembered working in the surgery at St. Bartholomew's, scarcely past his twentieth birthday, his degree from the University of London still years in his future. The smell of the surgery filled his nostrils, and he squinted against the glare of gaslights reflecting off polished tiles, the sound of bone saws rasping in his ears.

"Dr. Watson?"

John blinked, to find Rhys's hand on his knee, a concerned look on his face.

"I'm sorry," John managed. "My mind... drifted."

Rhys nodded sympathetically. "Memory is a pernicious thing, Dr. Watson. But it is still a wonder and a blessing. After our meeting yesterday I consulted my library, and found some interesting notes on the subject. Are you familiar with Pliny's *Naturalis historia*?"

John dipped his head in an abbreviated nod. "Though my Latin was hardly equal to the task in my days at Wellington."

Rhys flipped back a few pages in his moleskin-bound notebook. "Pliny cites several historical cases of prodigious memory. He mentions the Persian king Cyrus, who could recall the name of each soldier in his army, and Mithridates Eupator, who administered his empire's laws in twenty-two languages, and Metrodorus, who could faithfully repeat anything he had heard only once."

John managed a wan smile. "It is a fascinating list, doctor, but I'm afraid that my problem involves the *loss* of memory, not its retention."

Rhys raised a finger. "Ah, but I suspect that the two are simply different facets of the same facility. I would argue, Dr. Watson, that nothing is ever actually forgotten, in the conventional sense. It is either hidden away, or never remembered at all."

"Now I am afraid you have lost me."

"Freud teaches that repression is the act of expelling painful thoughts and memories from our conscious awareness by hiding them in the subconscious. If you were having difficulty recalling your distant past, I might consider repression a culprit. But your problem is of a different nature, in that your past memories are pristine and acute, but your present recollections are transient and thin."

John chuckled, somewhat humorlessly. "I remember well enough that I described my own condition to you in virtually the same terms upon my arrival."

Rhys raised his hands in a gesture of apology. "Forgive me, I tend to forget your own medical credentials, and have a bad habit of extemporizing. But tell me, doctor, what do you know of Freud's theories concerning the reasons dreams are often forgotten on waking?"

John shook his head. "More than the man on the Clapham omnibus, I suppose, but considerably less than you, I hazard to guess."

"Freud contends that we are wont soon to forget a large number of sensations and perceptions from dreams because they are too feeble, without any substantial emotional weight. The weak images of dreams are driven from our thoughts by the stronger images of our waking lives."

"I remember my dreams no better or worse than the next man."

"But it seems to me, based on our conversations here, that the images of your past *are* stronger and more vivid than those of your present circumstances. The celebrated cases in which you took part, the adventures you shared. How could the drab, gray days of your present existence compare?"

John rubbed at his lower lip with a dry, wrinkled fingertip, his expression thoughtful. "So you think it is *not* dementia which addles my thoughts, but that I forget my present because my past is so vivid in my mind?"

Rhys made a dismissive gesture. "Dementia is merely a name applied to maladies poorly understood. The categories of mental distress understood in the last century—mania, hysteria, melancholia, *dementia*—are merely overly convenient categories into which large numbers of unrelated conditions might be dumped. More a symptom than a cause." He closed his notebook and leaned forward, regarding John closely. "I think, Dr. Watson, that you forget because you are too good at remembering."

Rhys fell silent, waiting for a response.

John was thoughtful. He closed his eyes, his thoughts following a chain of association, memory leading to memory, from this drab and grey present to his more vivid, more adventure-filled past.

"Dr. Watson?" Rhys touched his knee. "Are you drifting again?"

John smiled somewhat sadly, and shook his head, eyes still closed. Opening them, he met Rhys's gaze. "No, doctor. Merely remembering. Recalling one of those 'celebrated cases' you mention, though perhaps not as celebrated as many others. It involved a man who could not forget, and who once experienced a memory so vivid that no other things could be recalled ever after."

We have spoken about my old friend Sherlock Holmes, *John Watson began.* It has been some years since I last saw him, and at this late date I have trouble remembering just when. I saw little of Holmes after he retired to Sussex, only the occasional weekend visit. But as hazy as those last visits are in my mind, if I close my eyes I can see as vividly as this morning's sunlight those days when Victoria still sat upon the throne, and when Holmes and I still shared rooms at No. 221B Baker Street.

The case I'm speaking of came to us in the spring of 1889, some weeks before I met the woman who was to become the second Mrs. Watson, god rest her, when Holmes and I were once again living together in Baker Street. The papers each day were filled with stories regarding the Dockside Dismemberer. He is scarcely remembered today, overshadowed by other killers who live larger in the popular imagination, but at the time the Dismemberer was the name on everyone's lips.

At first, it had been thought that the Ripper might again be prowling the streets. Holmes and I, of course, knew full well what had become of *him.* But like the Ripper before him, the Dismemberer seemed to become more vicious, more brutal, with each new killing. By the time Inspector Lestrade reluctantly engaged Holmes's services in the pursuit of the Dismemberer, there had been three victims found, each more brutally savaged than the last. On the morning in which the man of prodigious memory came into our lives, the papers carried news of yet another, the Dismemberer's fourth victim.

By that time, we had been on the case for nearly a fortnight, but were no nearer a resolution than we'd been at the beginning. The news of still another victim put Holmes in a foul mood, and I had cause to worry after his mood. Holmes was never melancholic except when he had no industry to occupy his thoughts, but to pursue such a gruesome killer for so many days without any measurable success had worn on my friend's good spirits.

"Blast it!" Holmes was folded in his favorite chair, his knees tucked up to his chest, his arms wrapped tightly around his legs. "And I assume this latest is no more identifiable than the last?"

I consulted the news article again, and shook my head. "There is to be an inquest this morning, but as yet there is no indication that the authorities have any inkling who the victim might be. Only that he was male, like the others."

Holmes glowered. "And doubtless savaged, as well, features ruined." He shook his head, angrily. "The first bodies attributed to this so-called 'Dismemberer' had been killed and mutilated, with the apparent intention of hiding their identities. These more recent victims, though, appear to have been killed by someone who took a positive delight in the act itself."

I nodded. We'd had opportunity to examine the previous three victims, or rather to examine what remained of them, and Holmes's assessment was my own. Even the Ripper had only approached such degradations in his final, and most gruesome killing.

I turned the pages of the paper, searching out some bit of news which might raise my friend's spirits, or distract him for the moment if nothing else. It was on the sixth page that I found what I was seeking.

"Ah, here is an interesting morsel, Holmes," I said as casually as I was able. "It is an obituary notice of an Argentinean who, if the story is to be believed, was rather remarkable. Ireneo Funes, dead at the age of twenty-one, is said to have had a memory of such singular character that he could recall anything to which it was exposed. Witnesses are quoted as saying that Funes could recall each day of his life in such detail that the recollection itself took an entire day simply to process."

Holmes still glowered, but there was a lightening to his eyes that suggested my gambit had met with some small success. "Have I ever told you about Merridew, Watson?" I allowed that he hadn't. "He was a stage performer I once saw, while traveling in America as a younger man. A mentalist performing under the name 'Merridew the Memorialist,' he appeared to have total recall. I myself saw him read two pages at a time, one with each eye, and then a quarter of an hour later recite with perfect accuracy texts he had glimpsed for only a moment."

Had I but known of Pliny's list of prodigious memories, Doctor Rhys, I might have suggested this Merridew for inclusion in the rolls. As it was, Holmes and I mused about the vagaries of memory for a brief moment before our discussion was interrupted by the arrival of a guest.

Our housekeeper Mrs. Hudson ushered the man into our sitting room. Holmes recognized him at a glance, but it wasn't until our visitor introduced himself as one Mr. Dupry that I knew him. A baronet and scion of a vast family fortune, Dupry was one of the wealthiest men in London, and in fact in the whole of the British Empire.

"Mr. Holmes," Dupry said, dispensing with any pleasantries. "I want to engage your services to investigate a theft."

Holmes leaned forward in his chair, his interest piqued. "What is it that's been stolen, Mr. Dupry?"

"Nothing," Dupry answered. "Not yet, at any rate. I'm looking to you to make sure that remains the case."

Holmes uncrossed his legs, his hands on the armrests of his chair. "I'll admit that you have me intrigued. Please continue."

Dupry went on to relate how a number of his peers and business associates—Tomlinson, Elton, Coville, Parsons, and Underhill—had in recent months been the victims of bank fraud. Someone had gained access to privileged financial information and used it against their interests. The amounts stolen from Tomlinson and Elton had been so relatively small as to remain unnoticed for some time, while the funds taken from Coville and Parsons were more substantial, but poor Underhill had been rendered all but destitute. After seeing so many of his contemporaries fall victim to the machinations of parties unknown, Dupry felt certain it was only a matter of time before he himself became a target, and thus his interest in securing the services of Sherlock Holmes.

Suffice it to say, Holmes took the case.

I explained to Dupry that we were still engaged in the matter of the Dockside Dismemberer, and so would have to continue to address matters relating to that investigation while beginning to look into his own concerns. We had the inquest of the fourth victim to attend that morning, after which we would meet Dupry at his home to survey the grounds and make a preliminary assessment.

At the inquest we were met by Inspector Lestrade, who seemed even more foul-tempered than Holmes at the lack of progress so far accomplished. Of substantive findings relating to this fourth victim, there were scarcely any. The body had been recovered from the Thames near Temple Stairs, in a state of early decomposition. Aside from a tattoo on the victim's upper arm, depicting an anchor ringed by a rope of intertwining vines, there were no distinguishing marks. It was the opinion of New Scotland Yard that the killer was not the so-called "Torso Murderer," who had been depositing body parts around the greater London area for the better part of two years, given the markedly different nature of the wounds and the condition of the remains, and the suggestion in the popular press that it was Jack the Ripper walking abroad once more was not even merited with a response.

Following the inquest, Holmes and I accompanied Lestrade to the chamber in New Scotland Yard in which the remains had been laid. In all my years, both as a medical man and as a seeker after criminals, I have seldom seen so gruesome a sight. The condition of the wounds suggested that the victim had been alive for some time before expiring from them. The oldest of the wounds had begun partially to heal over, while the newest were ragged an unhealed. The police surgeon and I agreed that the killer may well have taken a period of days inflicting cuts, severing digits, and slicing off appendages, one by one, before finally delivering a killing blow.

Insult was added to injury by the innumerable tiny incisions all over the body, which could be nothing but the bites of fish who had attempted to make a meal of the remains as it drifted in the Thames.

I had seldom seen so gruesome a sight. Little did I realize then that it would pale in comparison to what came after.

With our business at New Scotland Yard completed, Holmes having made a careful study of the victim's tattoo for future reference, the two of us traveled across town to Kensington, to the home of Dupry.

"Have you come about the position?" asked the servant who answered the door.

"What can you tell us about it?" Holmes said, carefully phrasing his response neither to confirm or deny.

The poor man seemed haggard. He explained that the under-butler had run off in the night, and that the house steward was now in the process of interviewing candidates. The servant at the door was normally occupied in the livery, and so was unaccustomed to dealing with visitors, a task which normally fell to the under-butler. When we revealed that we were not, in fact, applicants for the position, the servant apologized profusely, and ushered us into Dupry's study.

"A damn nuisance," Dupry blustered, when Holmes mentioned the missing under-butler. "He seemed a stout enough fellow, and here he's disappeared without warning. If I can't hire a trustworthy man for twenty pounds a year, where *am* I to find good help, I ask you?"

"I'm afraid I have no idea, Mr. Dupry," Holmes answered as solicitously as he was able. "Now, with your permission, may we examine your home? In particular, can you show me where you keep materials of a, shall we say, sensitive nature?"

For the next three quarters of an hour, Dupry showed us around his home, paying particular attention to his study, and to the wall safe there. When it was opened, though, revealed to contain neatly bound stacks of pound notes, bullion, and other valuables, Dupry held up a single piece of paper as the most valuable item in his possession.

"This, gentleman," he said, careful to keep the document's face away from our view, "is the key to my fortune. You see, the vast majority of my liquid holdings are held in an account in Geneva."

I was confused, but Holmes nodded in understanding. "You see, Watson," he explained, "Swiss bankers are obliged by law to keep a numerical register of their clientele and their transactions, but are prohibited from divulging this information to anyone but the client concerned. You and I might need our balance books to access our account at Child & Co., but one would only need the appropriate register numbers to access a Swiss account, as not even the bank clerks themselves are made aware of the identities of the clients they serve."

"Quite right," Dupry said, appearing impressed. He returned the document to the wall safe, careful to keep the printed side from our line of sight, and then closed the door, spinning the combination to lock it. Even with his precaution, though, I managed to glimpse the paper's front for the briefest second, though I couldn't begin to call to mind the words and numbers I'd seen in that instant. "And if that information were to fall into the wrong hands, I would be ruined. I suspect that my colleagues who have seen their fortunes plundered allowed information regarding their own Swiss accounts to be learned, and that the thief took advantage of the anonymity of the Swiss system." He turned and fixed Holmes with a stare. "I keep my information safely under lock and key, Mr. Holmes. I am hiring *you* to ensure that it remains there."

After we had completed an initial investigation of Dupry's home and its locks, bars, and other security features, Holmes suggested that we visit some of the men whom Dupry indicated had fallen victim to the thief before.

First on our agenda was Underhill. The younger son of a well-established family, Underhill lived in a large Cubitt-designed home in Pimlico. If the state of the residence when Holmes and I arrived was any indication, though, it was clear that Underhill would not be in residence for much longer. The man answered the door himself, dressed only in shirt sleeves, harried almost to the point of tears. After we explained who we were, and our connection to his associate Dupry, Underhill admitted us, and explained that he was now all but destitute. He had been forced to let the majority of his household staff go, having lost the funds with which to pay them. It had been difficult to keep them even before, though, having lost two men from the staff in as many months before his fortune was even lost.

From there, we visited the homes of Coville, Elton, and Parsons who, if they were not as badly off as Underhill, seemed hardly much better. All three, too, mentioned having lost members of their domestic staffs in recent months.

When we called at the home of Tomlinson, we found him not in, having left the city to visit the continent. We were instead welcomed by his house steward, a man named Phipps.

"What is it I can do for you, gentlemen?" Phipps asked, with more urgency than seemed necessary. Standing in close proximity, I detected a strangely familiar but confusing scent wafting from him, which it took me a moment to recognize as an exceptionally strong cleaning agent, such as those used to clean tiles in large houses. Given the size of the staff apparently on hand in the Tomlinson home, it seemed odd that the house steward, the head of the staff, would lower himself to cleaning kitchen tiles.

Holmes explained that we had been engaged by Dupry, and that in connection with that engagement were investigating the rash of bank fraud whose victims had included Phipps's employer, Mr. Tomlinson.

For the briefest instant, I fancied that panic flitted across the steward's face, but as quickly as it had come it had passed, and he treated us to a friendly, open smile. "I'm happy to help in any way I can, of course." Still, I couldn't help but notice the sunken quality of his cheeks, the sallow coloration of his skin. He was clean scrubbed, for all that he smelled like bleach and lye, but I could not escape the impression that he was less than entirely healthy.

"Tell me, Phipps, have any members of your staff gone unaccountably missing in the recent past?"

The house steward continued smiling, but shook his head. "No, sir," he said, his voice even and level, "not a one." He paused, and then chuckled. "I took a brief vacation myself, this past winter, to visit family abroad, but returned to my post just as expected, so can hardly be considered 'missing.'"

As the day ended, we returned to Baker Street, to find Inspector Lestrade waiting for us.

"We've identified the tattoo," Lestrade said, without preamble, "and the man."

Holmes nodded. "So you have found a man who sailed the Atlantic Ocean as a deckhand onboard a ship of Her Majesty's Navy, I take it?"

Lestrade's eyes widened, and as I smiled he began to glare at Holmes. "Blast it, Holmes, how did you know that?"

"Simple observation, my dear fellow," Holmes answered. "Now, who was our late seaman, and who was it identified him?"

Lestrade grumbled, but answered. "His name was Denham. Until a few weeks ago, he was employed as a footman in the Parsons household."

Holmes and I exchanged a glance. "Parsons?"

Lestrade nodded. "I spoke to the house steward myself. Seems Denham just stopped showing up to work some weeks back. Stranger still, his replacement, an American chap, went missing a short time after."

"Was this before or after Parsons discovered a portion of his fortune had been stolen?"

Lestrade raised an eyebrow. "Now how did you know about *that?*"

Holmes explained in cursory detail our other ongoing investigation, and in particular the fact that we had earlier questioned Parsons himself.

"Well, the steward *did* mention the theft, at that, and said that for a brief time he'd suspected the two missing men of playing a part. But Parsons had felt sure that there was no way that a retired sailor or an addled American could possibly have been responsible, and had instead blamed the whole mess on a conspiracy of the Swiss."

That certainly was in line with what Parsons had told us earlier that day.

"Why addled?" Holmes asked. "Why did Parsons regard the American as addled?"

Lestrade lifted his shoulders in a shrug. "Something about him becoming easily distracted. The American had come highly recommended, but seemed a poor hand at his duties, always staring at a patch of sunlight on the wall, or counting the number of trefoils on a rug, or some such, and his conversation rambled all over the place." Lestrade chuckled. "Of course, it seems to me the steward had little room to talk, given how long he banged on about the whole matter. Seemed hungry for conversation, I suppose."

I failed to see the significance of any of this, save that several of the men on Dupry's list had lost members of their domestic staffs before their fortunes were ransacked, and that one of the missing servants had apparently fallen victim to the Dockside Dismemberer. But Holmes appeared to divine a much subtler truth for it all.

"Come along, Watson," Holmes said, slipping back into his great coat and making for the door. "You'd better come, too, inspector. Unless I'm mistaken, we have only a short time left to prevent another fortune being stolen, and perhaps even another murder from being committed."

It was late afternoon, the sun still lingering in the western sky, when we reached Dupry's house. The unfortunate stable-hand had evidently been sent back to his duties, as Dupry's butler answered the door.

"Can I help you gentlemen?"

"Where is Mr. Dupry?" Holmes asked, abandoning all courtesies.

"Interviewing a prospective applicant for the under-butler position, sir." The butler sniffed, haughtily. "I am confident that by this interview's conclusion the position will be filled."

"Why does everyone take me for a domestic?" Holmes fairly snarled. "Tell me quickly, man! This applicant? He comes to you well recommended, seemingly perfectly suited for the task and able to start immediately?"

The butler was a little taken aback. "W-why, yes," he stammered. "We had the most glowing report of his services from the house steward at the Tomlinson estate…"

"Take me to Dupry right away," Holmes interrupted, shouldering his way into the door. The butler, a portrait of confusion, merely bowed in response and hurried to do as he'd been bid. Lestrade and I followed close behind, neither of us any more aware of what Holmes was about than the other.

We came upon Dupry in his office, interviewing a man of middle years. The interviewee was speaking as we entered unceremoniously, and I detected a distinct accent to his speech, Canadian or possibly American.

"What's the meaning of this?" Dupry blustered.

Before the butler could answer, the interviewee in the chair turned, and when his eyes lit on Holmes it was with visible recognition.

After only a moment's pause, Holmes's own face lit up, and he snapped his fingers in sudden realization. "Merridew!" he said.

I recalled the name of the mentalist Holmes had reported seeing in America, years before.

"The Hippodrome Theatre, Baltimore, January 5th, 1880," the man said in a strangely sing-song voice. Then, the syllables running together like one elongated word, he recited, "What art thou that usurp'st this time of night, Together with that fair and warlike form, In which the majesty of buried Denmark, Did sometimes march? By heaven I charge thee speak!"

"It is some years since I trod the boards," Holmes said, not unkindly. "You have gotten yourself mixed up in some messy business, I fear, Merridew."

The American lowered his eyes, looking somewhat shamed. "Horatio, thou art e'en as just a man, As e'er my conversation cop'd withal."

"What is this, Holmes?" Lestrade demanded, pushing forward. "What the devil is he talking about?"

"Memories, inspector," Holmes explained. "This is a man who trucks in memories."

"See here," Dupry said, slamming his hand down upon his desk, "I demand an explanation."

Holmes clasped his hands behind his back. "A moment, Mr. Dupry, and a full accounting will be presented." He turned to the American in the chair. "You didn't hatch this one yourself, Merridew. You haven't the stomach for the darker work this scheme requires. So who was it?"

Merridew, surprisingly, did not even attempt to dissemble. He calmly and patiently explained that he had come to England some months before with an eye towards performing his mentalist act on the English stage, but that he had fallen in with another passenger on the ship, a man who gave his name only as Stuart. When Merridew had demonstrated his ability for total recall, Stuart had hit upon a scheme. It appeared that he had recently come into a considerable amount of money, having gotten hold of confidential financial information belonging to his employer. The sum Stuart had embezzled was scarcely large enough to be noticed by his wealthy employer, but was a small fortune to him. And now he was hungry for more. Stuart could not take much more from his employer without tipping his hand, though, and so he would need to gain similarly sensitive information from other wealthy men.

Stuart identified their targets by looking over his employer's business transactions to locate those with the largest fortunes invested in the appropriate ways. Once the target was chosen, Stuart would select a member of their household staff, and eliminate them. With a position vacant, Stuart would equip Merridew with a flawless resume and sterling recommendations, put in perfect position to be hired as the missing man's replacement. Then Merridew would simply wait for the chance to get even the barest glimpse of the target's financial documents. Only an instant was needed, and then he would be able to recall all of the information in perfect detail.

"And this man Stuart," Holmes said, "which doubtless was merely an alias? Where did you meet with him?"

Merridew gave an address in the East End, and said that he'd been instructed by Stuart to meet him there at the conclusion of each assignment.

Holmes turned to me and Lestrade and smiled. "Gentlemen? Anyone fancy a trip to the East End?"

We hired a growler in the street outside Dupry's home, and the four of us rode east, Holmes and Merridew on one side of the carriage, Lestrade and I on the other. There was a strange, almost childlike quality to Merridew. He seemed lost in a world of his own, and would answer truthfully any question put directly to him, unless he had some prepared answer already provided. It appeared that was how this "Stuart" had been able to work Merridew's skills to his advantage, training him to act and speak just enough like a household domestic that he could pass a few days in the wealthy households, just long enough to catch a fleeting glimpse of a piece of paper such as the one Dupry had shown us. And with eyes that could read an entire page of text in a single glance, it was a task of complete ease to recall only a string of digits and a few words. And with that information, this Stuart would have complete access to the target's Swiss account.

As we rode west, away from the setting sun, Holmes played the alienist, asking Merridew questions about the man in pursuit of whom we rode. It was hard for me not to feel sorry for this idiot savant, who seemed little more than a dupe in this business. But as Merridew described the man with whom he worked, I was reminded that four men lay mutilated and dead at this Stuart's hands, and that in a just world some of the blame for that carnage had to be laid at Merridew's feet as well. His hands may not have been red with their blood, and he claimed never to have seen the men whom he was positioned to replace, alive or dead, but he was still implicated in their deaths.

Urged by Holmes's questioning, Merridew explained that Stuart appeared to have grown unsettled in recent weeks. Stuart had arranged a set of signals by which he and Merridew could communicate, without ever coming face to face unless necessary. There was a north-facing window on the top floor of the building in which they met, visible from the street, at which hung two drapes, one red and one black. If the window was curtained in black, Merridew was to mount the stairs and enter, where he would find Stuart waiting for him. If the red curtain was instead drawn, Merridew was to stay away, and not to approach under any circumstances.

"Red curtain," Merridew said as we stepped down from the growler to the street. "Stay away."

"Come along, Merridew," Holmes said, taking the American by the elbow and steering him towards the door. "The signal suggests that your Mr. Stuart is in, and he is a man that my friends and I would very much like to meet."

When we reached the top of the stairs, in the deeply shadowed gloom of the ill-lit interior, I caught a strong smell of bleach and lye, overlying something stronger, ranker, more unsettling. Through the flimsy wooden door at the landing, I could hear faint moaning, somewhere between the cry of a child and the mewling of a drowning cat.

"Red curtain, stay away," Merridew repeated, looking visibly shaken.

"You've been here before," I said, feeling the irresistible urge to cheer him, if possible. "What is there to be afraid of?"

Merridew shook his head, and fixed me with a pathetic gaze. "When I came before, it had always been cleaned. Now, I think, it is still dirty."

"Enough of this nonsense." Lestrade pushed ahead of us, and pounded on the door. "Open up in the name of Her Majesty!" He pounded again, louder. "It'll only go harder on you if you resist."

The moaning on the door's far side took on a different quality, and I could hear the sound of scuttling, feet pounding against wooden boards, as if somewhere were trying to flee. But the room occupied the entire floor of the narrow building, and the only out would be through the window.

"He's trying to scarper," Lestrade said.

"Not today, I think," Holmes said. Stepping back, he carefully studied the door in the dim light. "There, I think." He pointed to a spot midway up, near the jamb. Then, after taking a deep breath, he lashed out with his foot, kicking the door at the point he evidently felt the weakest. He'd been right, as it happened, for the thin door flew inwards, shattering into three pieces.

The stairway and landing had been darkened, a gloaming scarcely lighter than a moonless night, but in the room beyond candles burned in their dozens, in their hundreds. Their flickering light cast shadows that vied across the walls and floor, shifting archipelagoes of light and darkness. The room itself might once have been suitable for a human dwelling, but had been transformed into an abattoir. Bits of viscera hung like garlands from the rafters, and blood and offal painted the walls and floor. A pair of severed limbs had been transformed into grotesque marionettes, strung up on bits of intestine tied with ligaments, a kind of macabre Punch and Judy awaiting some inhuman audience.

It took an instant for me to recognize the figure that lay stretched on the floor as being that of a human being at all, so little was left of him, the rest having been spun out and excised to decorate the room. And a further instant to recognize as human the figure crouched by the now-open window, his arms and face covered with blood as red as the curtain he'd torn out of his way. In one hand, the man held a knife, in the other what appeared to be some severed piece of human anatomy. The blood-covered man regarded us with crazed eyes, lips curled in a snarl baring red-stained teeth, his cheeks sunken.

"Don't do it, Phipps," Holmes shouted, taking a single step forward, and only then did I recognize the steward of the Tomlinson household.

There must have been some confusion when Merridew and the man first met, and the American's strange recall had fixed on a term he'd misunderstood. Phipps had simply never corrected him when Merridew assumed his *name* was Stuart, not his *profession* that of steward.

Phipps snarled like an animal. "Money is power, blood is power, both are mine." He threw one leg over the window's sash. "You cannot stop me, nothing can."

I don't know whether Phipps truly believed in that moment that he could not be hurt, or even that he might be able to fly. When he struck the cobblestones below a heartbeat later, though, he quickly learned that neither notion was true.

While Lestrade rushed to the window, already too late to do anything about Phipps, Holmes and I turned our attention to the man on the floor. He was alive, but only barely, and would doubtless perish before any help could arrive, or before he could be transported anywhere else.

"Dupry's under-butler," Holmes said, his hand over his nose and mouth to block the worst of the smell.

"Poor fellow." I held a handkerchief over my own nose, but still the fetid stench of the place threatened to overwhelm me.

Lestrade stepped over from the window, his expression screwed up in distaste. "The man 'removed' so that Merridew could take his place, I take it."

"The most recent of five," Holmes corrected. "Most recent and final victim of the so-called Dismemberer."

It was only then that I thought to see where Merridew had got to. I turned, and saw him standing there in the doorway, just as he had been when Holmes had kicked the door down. The American idiot savant had not moved, but had stood stock still with his eyes wide open and fixed on the scene before him, his mouth hanging slightly open, slack-jawed.

"Merridew?" I said, stepping towards him.

But it was clear that Merridew would not be answering, not then, not ever. He could not look away from the horrible carnage that his erstwhile partner in crime had wrought, and for which he in some sense at least had been responsible. Eyes that could recall entire books in a single glance, that could find untold levels of detail in the patterns of shadows' falling or the curve of a cloud, took in every detail of the grisly scene. And having seen it, Merridew would never see anything, ever again. He would live, but his mind would be so occupied by that macabre sight in all its untold detail that his mind would refuse to allow any other sensations or impressions to enter. He would live forever in that moment, in the horrible realization of the horrors he had, however inadvertently, helped to accomplish.

I remember that day as if it were yesterday, and yet I know that I can not recall even a scintilla of the detail that Merridew retained. But even that tiniest amount, even that small iota of recollection, is enough to haunt me to the end of my days.

Doctor Rhys regarded John Watson, his eyes wide with sympathetic horror.

"I can't help but think of all those young men," John continued, waving towards the door and indicating the whole of Holloway Sanatorium beyond, "those tending the garden, or around the snooker table, or else just lounging in the corridors. So young, with so much life ahead of them, and yet their minds are fixed on the horrors of the trenches, their attentions forever fixed on the Great War."

John leaned forward, meeting the doctor's gaze.

"If it were up to me, doctor," John went on, "you would spend less time studying how it is that we remember, and marveling over the prodigious memories of the past, and instead devote your attentions to discovering how it is that we *forget*."

John closed his eyes, and eased back in his chair.

"Memory is no wonder, Dr. Rhys, nor is it a blessing."

John pressed his lips together tightly, trying to forget that awful day, and the smells that lingered beneath the scent of bleach and lye.

"Memory is a *curse*."

COMMONPLACES

by Naomi Novik

Naomi Novik is the bestselling author of the Temeraire series, which consists of *His Majesty's Dragon, Throne of Jade, Black Powder War, Empire of Ivory,* and *Victory of Eagles*. The series as a whole has been optioned for film by *Lord of the Rings* director Peter Jackson. The first volume of the series, *His Majesty's Dragon*, was a finalist for the Hugo Award, and Novik also won the John W. Campbell Award for Best New Writer, and the Locus and Compton Crook awards for best first novel. Her short fiction has appeared in the anthology *Fast Ships, Black Sails*, and is forthcoming in the anthologies *The Naked City* and *Zombies vs. Unicorns*.

In 2009 a young millionaire named Marcus Schrenker leapt from his single-engine plane and parachuted to the ground, leaving his auto-piloted aircraft to crash just fifty yards from a residential neighborhood in Florida. Schrenker, who apparently intended for the plane to fly into the ocean and be lost forever, was attempting to fake his own death in order to escape from a mounting pile of personal, financial, and criminal problems. Many of us were astounded by Schrenker's reckless disregard for others, but we also had to grudgingly admit that his plan had a certain panache, however badly he ended up botching things. Of course, when it comes to faking your own death with panache, nobody beats Sherlock Holmes, who spent several years traveling the globe after his apparent death at Reichenbach Falls, and who managed to keep the fact that he was still alive a secret even from his good friend Dr. Watson. But many readers have wondered, why couldn't Holmes have found some secret way to set the good doctor's mind at ease? Our next tale, in which we get an old acquaintance's view of Holmes during the Great Hiatus, suggests an answer to this mystery.

> "My life is spent in one long effort to escape from the commonplaces of existence."
> —Sherlock Holmes, "The Red-Headed League"

The newspaper in Lisbon came at eight and went to Godfrey first, before he should leave for his office. "My wife is that treasure who does not require entertainment at the breakfast table," he liked to say of her to his friends; it would have been a little more accurate to say, Irene did not require the sort of entertainment she was

356

likely to get out of Godfrey at the breakfast table, which did not very well meet the name.

She would have liked to take a section of the paper, but while Godfrey naturally obliged any such request, he would interrupt her in asking for pages back, that he might finish those items begun earlier. It was easier in the end to be patient, to let Godfrey keep the pages in neat order until he was done, while she spent her own breakfast sitting quietly in contemplation of her day and the small square of garden their cottage boasted. Her mornings when he had gone did not lack leisure.

"Sherlock Holmes is dead," he told her, before the maid had brought out the eggs, "at Reichenbach Falls."

She made absent expressions of dismay and shock, and when he had gone to his office, she read the story over three times: a bare paragraph describing the famous detective lost, a criminal mastermind claiming a final victim, his old companion left behind to give the report.

It was not much, and reading it over again did not make it grow longer. She already could have told the story over verbatim—years of practice from studying librettos—but even so she did not like to leave the paper on the table to be swept away; instead she carried it into the bedroom and put it into her bureau, and went outside to tend the roses. In twenty minutes she came back inside and read it once more, and then went out to the front stoop.

The street boys knew her, courtesy of a ball returned after a broken window without more than a calm request they should aim away from her house in future. They were happy to take a few pennies to fan out into the town for news for her. An hour brought her a slightly worn copy of *The Strand* with Dr. Watson's voice thick as old treacle on the page, full of studied melodrama and real grief.

At breakfast the next morning, she read it over and over again, while across the table Godfrey placidly read a fresh newspaper, full of different news.

There was no reason it ought to have cut up her peace. She had not seen the man in two years and then had known him not at all: that he had once invaded her house in guise to rob her was not much foundation for affection, except what one might feel, she supposed, for a satisfying opponent one has bested. The story—of course she had read it—the story had been very flattering, but she had enough of admirers to discount the value of another, even one who put her photograph above emeralds. And in any case, now he was dead.

The magazine went into the drawer with the newspaper, however.

Her mornings were of a settled round these days: what little management the little house needed, a trifle of work in the garden, a handful of calls received and returned. If her marriage had not made her wholly respectable, it had made her sufficiently so to permit her neighbors to excuse an acquaintance which so satisfyingly allowed them to partake of just the least bit of notoriety, indirectly; to mention in whispers, at assemblies and balls, yes, that is her, the famous—

Irene tried not to think in such a way of them, those kind and stupid ladies who came visiting. Ordinarily she did not. She could not begrudge anyone a little excitement at so little expense to her, and they *were* kind: when she had been ill, last year—so wretchedly inadequate a word for that hollowed-out experience, tears standing in her eyes because she would not, would not let them run, not in front of the businesslike doctor speaking to Godfrey over her head, telling him prosaically they must be cautious, warning against another attempt too soon, while he washed his hands of the blood—

They had been really kind then, beyond polite expressions of sympathy: food appearing in those first few days when she could think not at all, and clean linen; Mrs. Lydgate and Mrs. Darrow coming by in the mornings with embroidery, sitting in perfect silence for hours while the window-squares of sun tracked a pathway across the sitting room. They had asked her to sing, a week later on, and when she had stopped halfway through *Una voce poco fa*, drooping over the pianoforte, they had taken up without a word a conversation about their unreliable maidservants, until she had mastered herself.

So she could not despise them anymore, because the kindness was real, as all the crowned glories had proven not to be; she knew better now, or thought she knew, how to value the treasures of the world against one another. But that week she found herself freshly impatient; she did not attend to the conversation in Mrs. Wessex's drawing room, until someone said to her, a little cautiously, "But you knew him, my dear, didn't you?"

"No," she said, "no more than the hare knows the hound."

"Well, it's a pity," Mrs. Ballou said, in her comfortably stolid way, without ever looking up from her knitting. "I'm sure I don't know what he was about, though, letting that dreadful man throw him off a mountain instead of calling the police, like a sensible man."

"Oh," Irene said, "yes," and taking her leave very abruptly went outside and stood in the street, half-angry and half-amused with herself, to be so schooled by a fat old dowager. Of course he was not dead.

She was not sure what to feel for a moment, but her sense of humor won out in the end, and she laughed on the doorstep and went home to throw the papers into the dustbin at last. There was an end of it, she told herself; it was the inherent absurdity of the story which had gnawed at her.

John Watson believed his own story, she was sure. He was, she thought, very much like Godfrey: the sort of man who would think it—not *romantic*, but rather quite ordinary *pro patria mori*, even if there were convenient alternatives to be had for the cost of a little reasoning. The sort of man who would trust in what a friend told him, unquestioningly, because to doubt would be faintly disloyal. Easy to fool such a man, and more than a little cruel to do so.

"Is something distressing you, my dear?" Godfrey asked, and she realized she was drumming her fingertips upon the writing table, while her correspondence went unanswered.

"I am only out of sorts," she said. "This wretched heat!" This was not very just: it was only the beginning of June.

Two days later she took a train to Paris: alone, but for her maid. "If you would not mind waiting a week, I could tie up my affairs tolerably well," Godfrey said.

"You are very good, but in a week, I dare say the fit will have passed, and I will not want to go anywhere," Irene said. "Besides, I know you could not leave things in a state such as would leave you with an easy mind. No, I will fly away to Paris and repair my plumage, see some disreputable old friends and my very respectable singing-master, and come back just as soon as you have begun to miss me properly."

"Then you should have to turn around as soon as you had set foot out of the door," he said, gallantly.

She could be cruel too; perhaps that was what interested her.

In Paris, she left her maid behind in the hotel and went hunting. The whole enterprise was a shot at a venture, of course, but she thought either here or Vienna, and Paris was closer to Geneva. Irene spent the days sitting outside small cafés, legs crossed in neatly pressed trousers with her hair pinned back sharply under a top hat, sipping coffee and watching all the world as it passed before her table, noisy and vivid; watched women in elegant dresses going stately by like something from another life. Her nose was not yet used to the stench of the hansom cabs after so long in the quiet countryside; she felt herself set apart from it all, an observer by the side of the river.

When the lamplighters came around, she left a handful of coins and slipped away: to the Opéra, to the Symphony, where she bribed the ushers to let her in after the first act. Standing in the high tiers and off to the side, she studied the faces of the orchestras through a glass while below her Faust was carried away by demons, or Tchaikovsky's sixth tripped and glittered off the bows. Afterwards she went backstage with a bouquet of roses, instant camouflage against inquiry, and walked among the musicians to fish for accents.

On the fourth night she went to the Opéra-Comique, and the third violinist was a man with a narrow face, cheeks sallow and nose hawklike, who studied his music with more fierce concentration than a professional ought to have required.

She did not write to Godfrey that night: she spent it practicing beside the open window of her room, breathing in the warm, humid air of Paris, heads on the street turning up in the circle of gaslight below to look up as they went by. Behind her, the maid unpacked the dresses from the traveling trunk and pressed them with a heated iron. In the morning, through an acquaintance, Irene presented herself to the director as Madame Richards from America, and sang just well enough to be placed in the chorus and considered a possible understudy for Rosette in *Manon*.

In her first rehearsals the next morning, she watched the violinist's shoulders. He did not turn from the music at all, but when she sang, one of fifteen voices, his head tilted a little, searching.

She did not speak to him: he deserved, she thought, as much chance to escape as he had given her. But he was waiting for her when she came out of the stage door that evening, standing lean and straight beyond the waiting gaggle of boys who had brought flowers for the chorus girls. He was just out of the circle of lamplight, the brim of his top hat casting his face into shadow. She paused on the stairs, ignoring the handful of small bouquets offered to her consequence by those who, lacking some other object of affections, were considering whether to settle themselves upon her.

She smiled down at them and said in her full voice, undisguised, "Gentlemen, you are in my way." They let her through, not without a few looks after her, some a little surprised. But they were all boys, and the lovely young Mademoiselle Parnaud was directly behind her, so there were no eyes following by the time Irene reached him. She studied his face, curiously, as she had not had the opportunity to do before: he had handsome eyes, large and clear and grey, and his mouth was narrow but expressive.

"I have been insufficiently cautious, I find," he said, and offered her his arm. It was well-muscled, if lean. They walked away together towards the Rue de Richelieu.

"I hope you do not have much cause for concern," she said. "If your nemesis indeed ended at the bottom of the Falls?"

"Yes," he said. "After I shot him, of course."

They had dinner in another of the small anonymous cafés, sitting on the sidewalk with the noise of conversation and carriages around them. "Some of his lieutenants have escaped the net," he said, waving an impatient hand, long-fingered and pale, "but they are not of his caliber. They are all watching Watson, in any case."

"I suppose," she said thoughtfully, "that you will find that an excellent excuse to give him."

He looked at her sharply.

"It is not always easy to be adored," she said.

"No," he said. Then his mouth twisted a little, in wry amusement. "The only thing worse, of course—"

She nodded, and looked down into her coffee cup.

Her prince had taught her that lesson, with his jewels and his exclamations of surprise. He had never imagined she would take his engagement so badly. He had thought she was a woman of the world. He had thought she understood—and so indeed she *had* understood, after the fact: she had been loved only as a flower, set upon the mantel in a vase, inevitably to be discarded with the cloudy water.

Even in that first moment of harsh pain, she had not regretted *him* in his person, not even on the rawest level—his broad shoulders, his strong mouth. All her anger was to have been so cheaply held, so easily cast off. She might have dismissed it as his weakness, not hers; but she had chosen him, after all.

She had taught *him* to regret *her*, though, and then she had forgiven herself the mistake: she had been only a girl then, not yet twenty, and after all she had learned quickly. Only to be adored was, in the end, nothing; to be adored by someone worthy, everything.

And oh, Godfrey was worthy, and she loved him, even if something wild and errant in her still fought and struggled against the necessary sacrifice of liberty and always would; but she could not have him without it.

"How did you learn?" she asked, abruptly. "What taught *you*—?"

"He married," Holmes said.

No need to ask who he meant, of course. "I encouraged it," he added. "I wished that he were not necessary to me, and so I convinced myself he was not; that I would do better for solitude." He smiled, that wry look again. "I have had more than enough leisure since to contemplate the irony of having successfully deceived myself, who could scarcely be led astray by the most dedicated attempts of all the criminals in London."

She did not ask him, of course, but there was a weary regret in his face that made her quite certain the two of them had never been lovers. He had thought of it, and rejected it, likely in defense of that same independence. Watson would have crossed that Rubicon for him, but he would never have left, afterwards. A line from the story recalled itself to her: *He never spoke of the softer passions, save with a gibe and a sneer*—some bitterness there, in Watson's words; he knew he had been refused, whether consciously or not. The marriage, Irene thought, had been some part revenge, and one startlingly complete, to have driven the man across the table into flight.

Irene had never before had the least cause to be grateful to that injustice which had made the sacrifice of her own virtue her own easiest road to independence, but at least she had never been tempted, afterwards, to think herself above such needs. "Will you go back?" she asked.

"Not while she lives," he said.

His room would have been untidy, but for the lack of possessions; no letters, no photographs, only a scattering of sheets of music on the windowsill and the dresser, and pieces of rosin for his bow left on the writing desk.

He was inexpert enough to confirm her suspicions, and taken aback by his own responses: a strange wrenched look on his face afterwards. She laughed at him softly, a greater kindness than pity, because he shook off the expression and came back into her almost fiercely.

Reputation had given her a dozen lovers, but in truth he was only the third to pass her bedroom door, and so very different from the others: thin and restless, and once he grew a little more sure of his ground, wholly without hesitation. It was splendid to feel she did not need to comfort or reassure, or indeed make any pretense whatsoever; she could interest herself only in her own pleasure, and in the freshness of the experience. She liked the hard planes of him, and the skillfulness of his hands, and his intensity: something almost of a fever running beneath his skin, which left a flush beneath the sharp-edged cheekbones.

In the morning she rose early and wrote Godfrey a letter from the writing desk, while Holmes slept on in the wreckage of the bed behind her, pale light through the window on his skin and the tangled white sheets; it was raining.

Paris is wet and beautiful in the spring as always, she wrote, *and I am glad that I came, but my darling, what is best is to know I have you to come home to, when I like the city have been watered at my roots. I feel myself again as I have not since last year. I am ready to be incautious again.*

THE ADVENTURE OF THE PIRATES OF DEVIL'S CAPE

by Rob Rogers

Rob Rogers is the author of the novel *Devil's Cape*, a superhero thriller set in Louisiana. Rob lives in Richardson, Texas, where he is working on a sequel. This story, which is original to this volume, takes place in the same milieu as *Devil's Cape*, but is set in the Victorian era, taking Holmes and Watson from the familiarity of London to the dark and dangerous city of Devil's Cape, which Holmes describes as "a city that swallows law."

Pirates have always been popular, whether it's in novels—*Treasure Island* by Robert Louis Stevenson and *On Stranger Tides* by Tim Powers—or in video games—*Sid Meier's Pirates!* and Ron Gilbert's *The Secret of Monkey Island*. But pirate popularity soared to new heights with the release of Disney's film *Pirates of the Caribbean*, featuring a memorable performance by Johnny Depp as spacey rock-star pirate Jack Sparrow. Suddenly it seemed like pirates were everywhere… even in Somalia. Yes, real-life pirates are suddenly a major concern again, prompting *Daily Show* correspondent John Oliver to quip, "Apparently Barack Obama won't just be fighting the challenges of the twenty-first century, but also of the eighteenth." Pirates now even have their own holiday, September 19th, International Talk Like a Pirate Day. But what's been missing in all the hoopla over pirates is, of course, Sherlock Holmes. We aim to rectify that with our next story, a tale of adventure that takes our heroes far from their usual haunts in Baker Street and off into the strange, pirate-haunted bayous of Louisiana. So grab a talking parrot and pour yourself some grog. This one's a treasure.

A substantial fog had settled over Northumberland Dock, and the thick, moist air, coupled with the odors of industry and the Tyne River, stifled our breathing. Or perhaps, if I might indulge in melodrama, we were smelling doom nearby.

The navy sailors guarding the Dutch steamship *Friesland* called out softly to one another across the dock, their voices echoing and distorted by the nearby water.

But no sound at all came from the *Friesland*.

Of the four of us approaching the ship, only my old friend Mr. Sherlock Holmes seemed undaunted by the atmosphere. I reached for my handkerchief often to mop my brow. Poor Inspector Lestrade cleared his throat every few minutes. And the navy man, Lieutenant-Commander Sebastian Powell wheezed noticeably.

"I am still curious," said Lestrade, clearing his throat once more, his narrow, sallow face constricted in annoyance, "as to why you insisted that Mr. Holmes and Dr. Watson accompany us. The events as you described them seemed quite straightforward." Lestrade himself had been called in only to consult, as the critical events had certainly occurred outside his jurisdiction. This placed him on equal footing with Holmes, a situation that left him discomfited.

Without slowing his pace, Lieutenant-Commander Powell removed his cap, brushed his salt-and-pepper hair back from his face with thick fingers, and then returned the cap smartly to his head. He was a muscular walrus of a man, perhaps fifty-five years of age, with piercing cobalt eyes. "There are certain factors, inspector, that make me question the obvious conclusion," he said. "Not the least of which the fact that the obvious conclusion could lead to war."

Holmes had characteristically taken the lead in our walk through the fog, but he stopped now in front of the *Friesland*. "Lieutenant-Commander, it is a logical fallacy to reject a conclusion simply because it is unsavory," he said. "However, I applaud your caution in this matter." His eyes flashed with anticipation. "I was struck by one element of your tale, an element that perhaps might elude others." His gaze encompassed Inspector Lestrade, who flushed and twitched his ratlike nose in annoyance.

I forced a chuckle and mopped my brow again. "Well, it eluded me, Holmes," I said. "Perhaps we should proceed aboard, though I am reluctant to see with my own eyes the sad scene that Lieutenant-Commander Powell described."

And with that, we proceeded aboard the *Friesland* and embarked on one of the more remarkable adventures of Mr. Sherlock Holmes's long career.

The *Friesland* was an iron steamship of the relatively new "three island" design, with a casing in the center, a monkey forecastle, and a short poop deck forming three "islands" above the main deck. She bore two masts with limited sail, and Powell estimated her weight at over two thousand tons. She bore the flag of Koehler House, one of perhaps a dozen such ships. As we boarded her, I took note of two large holes in her hull, above the waterline, as well as the jagged stump of the front mast. Still, the ship seemed quiet and secure against the dock, the water lapping gently against it. The *Friesland* did not look like a ghost ship.

"Early last week, the *Friesland* traveled from London to Stavanger, Norway. She left Stavanger five days ago and set course for Newfoundland. Yesterday evening, a Royal Navy patrol discovered her adrift thirteen miles off the coast of Scotland, near Aberdeen," Powell said, leading the way to the deck. He was repeating facts he had shared with us earlier in the day in our parlor at 221B Baker Street, per- haps to distract himself from the sights he would soon reencounter. "In addition to several tons of a fish oil product processed in Stavanger, the cargo included an exhibit that the Rijksmuseum in Amsterdam intends to share with the Roscoe Clay Hall of Culture in Vanguard City. The collection features paintings by Vermeer and Rembrandt. As far as we have been able to determine, the cargo is still intact." He stopped and turned to face us as we stepped onto the deck. "The Navy ship discovered no living souls on board." He shook his head. "Many of the crew are missing, quite likely thrown overboard. Two American passengers, John and Harold Smith, are missing as well. We found the bodies of ten crewmembers throughout the ship, most shot dead, a few stabbed. And we found three other bodies in the ship's corridors, all dressed in Royal Danish Navy uniforms. Our Navy brought the *Friesland* here so we could learn the truth before informing the Dutch and Danish governments of the gruesome discovery."

"The ship's course would have taken it near Iceland?" Holmes asked. He was peering past Powell's shoulder, toward the body of a crewman, arms splayed out, laying face down on the deck.

Powell nodded.

Holmes walked purposefully toward the body.

Lestrade coughed. "The Danish government has been strident in recent years about steamships fishing near Icelandic waters," the inspector said, "and the appropriate distance for fishing boats to keep from Iceland has been in dispute. Danish gun ships have chased off British fisherman, for example. The newspapers call it the Cod War."

Holmes, kneeling by the body, chuckled and stood back up. "The only fish of concern here isn't cod," he said. "It's herring. The red variety." He addressed Powell. "I'll need to see the bodies of the alleged Danish sailors," he said. "But I doubt seriously that next week's newspapers will be reporting war between the Netherlands and Denmark."

The carnage aboard the *Friesland* was grim indeed. The Dutch sailors had not died cleanly. Most were shot several times, and many bore gruesome knife wounds. One had been decapitated, the poor soul's head staring balefully from one end of a corridor while his body rested at the opposite side. And wherever we walked, we saw blood, much more blood than the bodies we encountered could account for. "I'm not sure I've seen its like since the Battle of Maiwand," I said quietly.

Holmes investigated in turn each of the three men in the uniforms of the Royal Danish Navy. We came to the final such body in the entryway to the cabin assigned to the Americans John and Harold Smith. "Aha!" Holmes said as he examined the fallen man.

"What is it, Holmes?" asked Lestrade. "Will you illuminate the rest of us? Or are we simply supposed to stand here admiringly?"

Holmes stood gracefully. "I am but observing, Lestrade, confirming suspicions I've had since Lieutenant-Commander Powell first informed us of the bizarre attack on this vessel."

"And what are these suspicions, Holmes?" Lestrade sounded more curious than querulous now.

"There is no shame in overlooking some of these facts, Lestrade, although that oversight could indeed have led to war between Denmark and the Netherlands. Some of these details could only have been discovered by the most trained eyes." When Lestrade's face reddened, Holmes's eyes gleamed with that peculiar satisfaction they showed when he was able to goad our old sparring partner. "Perhaps I do you a disservice. I presume that you noted that it would be strongly out of character for the Danish Royal Navy to attack in such a way. Even if we hypothesize that the *Friesland* entered into what the Danish government contends are Icelandic waters, and again hypothesize that the ship was mistaken to be on a fishing expedition, the aggression displayed here is disproportionate to the imagined offense."

Lestrade's back straightened. "I had drawn the same conclusion myself," he said.

Holmes nodded. "And of course you determined that the uniforms were counterfeit?"

Lestrade did not slump at hearing this, but it was clear the information was news to him.

Holmes nodded. "The fabric has the right appearance, in the main. But it is neither strong enough nor well-tailored enough to hold up against the rigors of combat. The costumes of these unfortunate boarders display torn stitching, frayed edges, and mud stains that could hardly have been picked up aboard this ship. Other details, such as the misalignment of the buttons, are close enough to fool only casual observers."

"Well done, Mr. Holmes," Lieutenant-Commander Powell said.

Holmes inclined his head politely. "This next observation is persuasive rather than conclusive." He strode down the passageway. "Come with me, gentlemen," he said. "We will return to the cabin presently, for it has grave import, but I'd like to draw your attention to one factor first."

Holmes led us to the body of an unfortunate young ship's officer, barely more than a boy, blond hair curled in ringlets over his ears. His left hand was split down the middle from warding off a knife, and he'd been shot in the forehead and the left eye. Blood had pooled around his head and his mouth was half open in surprise and fear.

"Dear God," I said softly.

"Eh?" said Holmes. "Oh, yes, quite. Very regrettable. You are always the one with the heart, Dr. Watson. It adds to your value as a friend, but perhaps detracts from your value as an investigator." He drew out his magnifying lens and held it over the young man's forehead, beckoning us all closer. "Look here," he said, tapping the edge of the lens. "This wound is indicative of what I've observed among the other bodies," he said. "A large-caliber handgun, poorly maintained. Not the sidearm of a military man."

"Pirates!" Powell spat.

Holmes nodded. "Quite skillful and cunning ones, to have accomplished what they did."

"But piracy has nearly died out, particularly in this part of the world," Powell said.

"I suspect that the mind behind this attack venerates the tactics of the pirates of a bygone age."

"But Holmes," I said, alarmed, "so close to the shores of the British Navy? And why disguise themselves? Who could benefit from such deception? With the cargo intact, they didn't even get what they came for."

"Ah, Watson, I often underestimate your ability to go to the thrust of the matter. Who benefits, indeed? Cui bono?" His long legs carried him around us rapidly, his footfalls echoing through the halls. "I believe the cabin we just vacated might answer your excellent question."

Holmes stopped beside the body of the pirate lying in the entryway to the Americans' cabin, forbearing us from going farther. The room beyond was narrow and spare, containing only a single wide stool, two cots pressed close together, a dressing table, a Persian rug, and a mirror. "Lieutenant-Commander, you reported that two Americans named John and Harold Smith purchased passage on this ship, and were sharing this cabin, correct? And as there are no living witnesses, you learned this from an entry in the ship's register."

"Yes," Powell said. He reached inside his coat and pulled out a folded piece of paper taken from the ship's log. "They signed in here."

Holmes grunted and I prepared myself to endure a long harangue about preservation of evidence and the countless small clues that had undoubtedly been obliterated when the page was torn and folded and placed into Powell's pocket. But Holmes merely spread the paper gingerly in his long fingers and smiled in triumph. "Marvelous," he said.

I examined the signatures that had captured Holmes's interest. Given my long association with him, I hoped I could glean some significant detail from the paper, but I surrendered with a sigh. "I can see that one is left-handed and the other right," I said, "but can conclude nothing of consequence from that. John Smith is frequently a pseudonym. Is that it, Holmes? They lied about their identities? They were in league with the pirates?"

"They did indeed lie," Holmes said. "But in league with the pirates? Tut, tut, Watson. Let me first direct you to our pirate here." He turned back the edge of the man's right sleeve. A small cloth bag was tied snug to the wrist by a leather strap. Holmes carefully detached it and held it out.

"What a horrible smell," gasped Lestrade. "What is that rubbish?"

"By my account," Holmes said, "the bag contains chervil, unguent, nail clippings, and a chicken bone. That dirt you see is almost certainly from a grave. This is a voodoo talisman called *gris-gris*."

"Voodoo!" said Lestrade. "But that's practiced in Africa, isn't it? This man is hardly African, Holmes."

"No," Holmes agreed. "But let me now redirect your attention. Note the distinctive mud stains on the knees."

We crouched to examine the dead man's pants, indeed stained with mud in mottled shades of red, brown, and black.

"The pattern of the stain suggests he knelt in several very different forms of soil simultaneously: red clay found in Georgia and Tennessee, river silt, and bog peat. And with my lens I identified two insect legs trapped in the fabric, certainly from a boll weevil. This confluence doesn't occur naturally in so concentrated an area."

"A greenhouse?" I mused.

"Perhaps," Holmes said dismissively. "But I am reminded of an American named John Bullocq, sometimes called the dirt magnate. In the 1850s, he made his fortune carting dirt from around the Southern states to Devil's Cape, Louisiana, where the average elevation was barely above sea level. He used the dirt to create hills that the wealthier citizens of the city could build their homes upon. They competed in their extravagant purchases of his dirt, each hoping to have his own mansion look down upon the others. Bullocq's enterprise made the soil of Devil's Cape quite uniquely varied."

Powell's face reddened. "Devil's Cape has voodoo," he said, "and pirates."

Devil's Cape had in fact been founded by pirates. The masked pirate St. Diable, scourge of the Caribbean and the Gulf of Mexico, and occasionally the waters of South America, Africa, and even Europe, had built a fortress in Louisiana to house his loot, his men, and his slaves. The fortress had ultimately grown to a city that rivaled its nearby sister, New Orleans, in size. Once years earlier at 221B Baker Street, Holmes had declared it the most corrupt and dangerous city on the face of the planet. "It is a city that swallows law, Watson," he had said. "That embraces corruption on such a grand scale as to make it almost a separate nation unto itself."

Lestrade's nose wrinkled. "So that is your conclusion, Holmes? The *Friesland* was attacked by pirates from Devil's Cape?"

Holmes nodded. "St. Diable, the city's founder, is long dead. But a succession of crime lords has followed, ruling the city from behind the scenes. The most recent, O Jacaré, or 'the Alligator,' adopted St. Diable's style of piracy wholesale. After the demise of my long-time adversary Professor Moriarty, I had occasion to review some of his correspondence. Moriarty and Jacaré had developed a friendship and wrote each other about such diverse topics as Calvinism, forgery, fencing, the ancient game of Go, and how best to dispose of me. Jacaré is cunning and ruthless, certainly capable of orchestrating this massacre if the motivation was strong enough, and I believe it was."

Lestrade snorted. "The attack ended many lives, but his pirates didn't even get what they came for."

"Didn't they?" Holmes smiled thinly. "The Jacaré sobriquet is misleading. For while he is certainly as fierce as an alligator, he is much less single-minded. He has a labyrinthine brain. I shouldn't be surprised if he had several goals in this single attack." He held up a finger. "The first was the subterfuge with the uniforms. Had we not pierced this veil, it could have led to a war between Denmark and the Netherlands, and quite possibly other nations in the region."

Powell frowned. "But a naval war is a grave danger for pirates. Patrols increase. More warships head to sea." He shook his head.

"Yet the war creates predictable patterns," Holmes said. "The escalation you describe is regionalized. Other areas become more vulnerable. By creating conflict here, O Jacaré could create opportunity elsewhere." He held up a second finger. "Your inventory confirmed that none of the works of art had gone astray. That was the element of your tale that originally struck me as most intriguing. But consider forgeries. If the pirates indeed stole several paintings, but left reasonable facsimiles in their place, it might take years before the truth came out. I predict further investigation will verify this." He held up a third finger. "The key to the third and final motive, however, lies in the cabin before us."

I stared past him. "You said the Americans were not in league with the pirates, Holmes," I said. "So they were his targets? Who were they?"

Holmes smiled slyly, a magician about to commence with the most astounding stage of his illusion. "You should know, Watson. After all, you have beheld them with your own eyes."

"What!"

"Examine the room, Watson. Point out the remarkable details."

I was about to retort that I saw nothing remarkable about the room at all, but stopped myself. I would never outpace Holmes, but if I applied my own powers of observation carefully, I could at least keep from being left behind. I pursed my lips. "The chair," I said. "The cots would not be comfortable for sitting, yet there is only a single chair."

"Go on."

I stared at the cots, then blushed. "The men's cots are pushed closely together," I said.

"And what do you conclude from that, Watson?"

"Well, I say, Holmes!" I blushed further. "I think that should be quite clear without speaking it aloud. It's hardly unheard of, after all, even in London."

"Why, Watson! How cosmopolitan of you!" Holmes chuckled. "Though somewhat off the mark. Did you notice the shoeprints in the rug? And the depression the chair makes in it?"

With Holmes stepping aside, I walked into the room, careful to avoid the rug. "The depression is quite deep," I said. "Whoever sat in it must have been heavy. The footprints are deep as well," I added, "though the shoes are not particularly large—perhaps my own size." I blinked. "And there's only the one pair."

"Excellent!" Holmes said. "Now, Inspector Lestrade. Would you please examine the chest wound of the pirate in the doorway?"

Lestrade crouched and looked as carefully as he could without touching the body. Long experienced with Holmes's oddities, he even sniffed the dead man's chest. Finally he stood. "Clean shot to the heart. No gunpowder on the shirt, so the shot came from several feet away at least."

Holmes looked at me. "Watson?"

Had I not known from Holmes's expression that Lestrade had missed something, I would have drawn the same conclusion as the inspector. As it was, I continued staring at the fatal wound for close to a minute before drawing back in surprise.

I took Holmes's excellent magnifying lens and looked more closely. "Good God," I said.

"What is it?" Lestrade demanded.

"The injury is nearly circular, but not quite," I said. "This man wasn't shot a single time. He was shot four times, all in the same spot, all at more or less the same moment."

"How is that possible?" he asked.

"Watson," Holmes said. "Surely you remember now where you saw these men? That circular we noted at Piccadilly Circus this Saturday past, some twenty feet south of the haberdashery?"

"Holmes! The Siamese twins?"

"Janus and Harvey Holingbroke. The circular proclaimed them the greatest sensation and greatest marksmen of the Wild West."

I looked at the fallen pirate. "Four shots aimed in perfect synchronization," I said. I turned to Holmes. "I read about them in one of my medical journals the next day, as a matter of fact," I said. "They are called parapagus twins. Their upper torsos are separate, but they share the same body below that point." I nodded back at the room. "That explains the single chair, the cots, the deep depressions from their shared weight."

"And the signatures," he said. "The 'J' in John Smith was quite bold and confident, while the rest of the name was more hesitant. And the 'Har' in Harold Smith was similar."

"For Janus and Harvey," I said, understanding. "Each hesitated when he began to depart from his own name." I looked at Powell. "The brothers made a fortune mining for gold in California and retired to Devil's Cape."

Powell glowered. "Devil's Cape," he said, shaking his head. "You are familiar with the story of Lady Danger?" he asked.

If Holmes was surprised at the sudden turn in the conversation, he didn't show it. "She was a privateer," Holmes said. "A masked heroine who served the English court and often crossed blades with St. Diable. She disappeared near Devil's Cape more than a century ago. Her real name was Lady Penelope Powell." He raised his eyebrows. "Ah," he said.

Powell nodded. "My great, great aunt," he said.

"I read a biography of her as a boy," I said gently. "It suggested that she and St. Diable were in love."

Powell spat upon the floor. "The man was scum," he said. "Some of the stories make him out to be a glamorous rogue, but a masked pirate is still a damned murderer. He undoubtedly killed Great Aunt Penny. They say that she loved him. But how could you love someone you worked against? An adversary? It makes no sense to me. Hogwash."

I couldn't help but glance at Holmes. He knew something of the attraction an adversary could have, his own experience with "the woman," as he called her, the mysterious Irene Adler.

But he merely nodded at Powell and walked down the passageway to the exit.

"O Jacaré arranged all of this to murder these twins?" Lestrade asked.

"Murder would have been simpler," Holmes said. "Though I'm sure that the assault on the ship appealed to Jacaré's pirate instincts, his goal was clearly to kidnap the brothers while they were traveling incognito, ensuring that no one knew that he has them in his power, or indeed that they are still alive."

"But what does he want them for, Holmes?"

"When Dr. Watson and I get to Devil's Cape," Holmes said, "we shall ask him."

I had assumed that the long summer boat journey, particularly the sweltering leg that took us through the Caribbean Sea and into the Gulf of Mexico, had prepared me for the heat of Devil's Cape, but I was wrong. It was a tangible, constant presence, like walking through water.

Holmes and I emerged from the steamship that had carried us there—not that different, really, than the *Friesland*—squinting into the sun, having left our trunks behind with instructions for them to be transported to a nearby inn where I had arranged rooms. The docks were a swarm of faces and voices. A crew of black men was singing a chantey while unloading our ship. Three Chinamen hawked cool beverages and roasted nuts, arguing about prices and stirring cinnamon-coated pecans over small pails of hot coals. Masses of people milled back and forth, shoving and swearing. I heard traces of French and Portuguese and Hindi. I stared openmouthed, taking it in.

"Not so fast," Holmes said, darting out an arm and catching a street urchin by the ear. The lad, blond-haired and tan as leather, winced as Holmes took hold of his elbow and forced a wallet out of his hand. My own wallet, I recognized. "Tut, tut," Holmes said, handing my wallet back to me, and I wasn't certain if he was scolding the boy or me. He gave the boy a quick kick in the rump and sent him scurrying off.

I nodded my thanks. "Not unlike one of the Baker Street Irregulars," I said. "Where to, Holmes?"

He pointed at a black hansom drawing up, pulled by an Appaloosa horse. "I believe our transport has arrived," he said.

The driver stepped from the cab and swaggered to us. He was smartly dressed in a tailored suit, the jacket open in front, a diamond gleaming from a ring on his pinkie. He had tanned skin, a handlebar moustache, and a confident smile. A golden police badge shaped like a sail was pinned to his jacket. "Holmes and Watson, right?" he asked in what I'd later come to identify as a Cajun accent. "I hope you not been standing here too long, you." He shook Holmes's hand, then mine, his grip forceful enough to grind my knuckles together. "My boss, he ask me to show you around town real nice and send you back where you belong, see," he said. "Now, my cousin, he ask me to help you any way I can." He grinned, showing an infectious smile and a chipped tooth. "I'll leave you to guess which one I'll listen to best. You got some boys bringing your things to your rooms?"

I nodded.

"That's good," he said. "We can start right quick, then, though I fear your entire trip's been a waste." He patted the hansom. "Hop in, gentlemen," he said. We climbed inside, and he climbed above us, taking the reins. Then his head popped up in front of us, upside down, as he looked through the front of the cab. "Aw, hell," he said. "I forgot to introduce myself." He smiled again. "I'm Deputy Chief Jackson Lestrade. Welcome to Devil's Cape."

As the hansom rolled away from our ship, we passed several older sailing vessels permanently lashed to the dock. They were brightly painted and adorned with pirate flags and cannons.

"Part of our history," Deputy Chief Lestrade said with a chuckle. "One or two of them even sailed under St. Diable's flag. That one there"—he leaned down and pointed at one decorated in garish pinks and purples, a rather undressed figurehead on the prow—"is Madame Beth's Bordello. Finest in all of Louisiana. Would you care to stop?"

We demurred, and his chuckle bubbled into a guffaw. A scandalously dressed woman waved a feather boa from the deck of the ship and called out, "Come here, Jackie," but Lestrade pressed on.

He led us out of the wharfs up a blustery road he identified as Cap de Creus Street. The wind did little to cut the heat. As we made our way through Devil's Cape's notoriously curving, crooked streets, we passed bars, a single ornate church decorated with mismatched gargoyles, and shops selling voodoo curses, hardware, and firearms. One pharmacy quite frankly advertised its selection of cocaine, heroin, and opium. Taking it in, Holmes's eyes took on a particular focus.

"Did you know to expect this Lestrade, Holmes?" I asked.

Holmes blinked slowly, then turned his attention to me, his lips twitching in sardonic acknowledgment of my distraction. "A cousin to our own ally," he said. "The inspector mentioned him before we left. He cabled ahead as a courtesy."

"Quite fortuitous," I said.

Holmes frowned. He lowered his voice to a faint whisper I could barely hear over the clopping of the Appaloosa's hooves. "I have made unkind assessments about the intellect of our own Inspector Lestrade in the past, but he is at heart an honest man. Do not assume the same of his cousin. If you expect that this Lestrade is a viper—or, to respect the fauna of our location, a copperhead—poised to strike at the earliest opportunity, you would not be far from the mark."

I glanced nervously upward, as though to see this Lestrade through the roof of the cab, but of course Holmes would never be overheard unless he intended it.

"His clothing, that ring. These are not the marks of an honest policeman," he said. "I may be doing him a disservice, but it is wisest to show him only whatever trust he earns. He is likely in the employ of O Jacaré or someone like him." He leaned out of the cab, slapping the roof smartly to draw Lestrade's attention. "I presume by our course that you intend to take us to your home for dinner?" he asked.

Lestrade yanked the reins, jerking us to a stop at the edge of the street, and I noted for the first time the rough scars along the horse's back. The man vaulted down beside us, eyes wide in astonishment.

"I have but studied a map and used some elementary deduction," my companion explained. "The Holingbroke brothers' estate is to the northeast, near the Chien Jaune River. The police headquarters is in Government Center, also north of here. We passed our inn several minutes ago and also half a dozen serviceable taverns and restaurants. Since we turned off of Cap de Creus Street, you have headed almost exclusively eastward, away from any other logical destination."

Lestrade flashed that chipped tooth again. "You really are all they say." My eyes were drawn to the ring Holmes had mentioned, and the cut of his clothing. "My wife, she'll treat you to an étouffée make you sit up and take notice," he said. He was broader and more handsome than our own Lestrade, more confident and charming. But his eyes were hard, and a chill swept through me despite the heat.

Lestrade's home was long and narrow, one and a half stories raised nearly six feet above the ground on brick piers. "Keeps us safe in floods," he told us. "And the air underneath cools us." The house had a gabled roof and curved, ornate brass decorations. It was the largest and finest along his street, and did nothing to disprove Holmes's theory.

Madame Lestrade was a stout, handsome woman, her accent so thick I could scarcely recognize that we spoke the same tongue. She greeted us warmly and then retired to the kitchen, where we could hear her instructing her two menservants in hushed, urgent tones.

"My cousin cabled me," Lestrade said, "that you think O Jacaré rustled up an attack on a European ship? All to kidnap Janus and Harvey Holingbroke?" He clucked his tongue dismissively.

"I'll admit that it seems rather elaborate," Holmes said. "Yet the facts support it." He described the evidence in detail. By the time he was finished, the servants had dished up the promised étouffée. It was a dish of shrimp, peppers, onions, rice, and spices so flavorful and fiery that I feared poison, yet Holmes dug into it with relish.

"Even saying that someone from our city did this," Lestrade said. "Why suspect O Jacaré?"

Holmes arched an eyebrow. "Oh, come now, Lestrade," he said. "Jacaré is the current heir apparent to St. Diable. Every strand of crime committed in and from this city leads into a web, with Jacaré the spider at its center. It could be no one else."

"But why?"

Holmes took another spoonful of étouffée, then dabbed at his lips with his napkin. "I was hoping, deputy chief, that you could tell me. Do they hold some sort of power over him?"

"Janus and Harvey? Nah. They could shoot him, I suppose. They're real good at that. But they'd have to find him first, and he's a slippery one."

"You know the Holingbrokes, then?"

"Oh, sure. They're real popular, them, despite being a couple of freaks."

"Popular enough that he might prefer it not be known that he engineered an attack on them?"

Lestrade shrugged. "Maybe," he said. "They're charming, and near rich as Rockefeller."

"The gold?"

"Sure. They found a mountain of it out in California a while back."

"And their fortune is kept in a bank?"

Lestrade shifted uncomfortably. He looked toward the kitchen and snapped, "Them sausages coming out anytime soon?" He pushed his plate away. "Nah," he said. "Every once in a while, they show up with a new gold bar. Got their stash hidden away somewhere good."

Holmes smiled with satisfaction. "Motive enough," he said.

"You don't understand. O Jacaré, he doesn't need money, not that bad. He got more than he can spend."

"I understand him better than you might think," Holmes said. "It is not the gold he seeks, but the satisfaction of the mystery solved."

It was late when Lestrade pulled the hansom up to our inn. The heat hadn't subsided, and I looked forward to a bath and sleep.

"You still want to search for O Jacaré tomorrow," Lestrade said, "come down to the station and I'll help you as I can. Like as not, though, if he has them, they'll be dead."

Holmes stepped out of the cab. "We followed quickly on the heels of whatever ship Jacaré sent to Europe," he said. "They only need to hold out against his scrutiny for a short time. And I have set things in motion." He turned to me. "What time is it, Watson?"

I consulted my watch. "A quarter past ten o'clock."

"Ah, then. They shall be free by midnight."

Lestrade gaped. "You know where they are, then?"

Holmes smiled. "An assistant of mine does," he said. "He shall take care of the details on our behalf." He bowed slightly. "Good night, deputy chief."

Lestrade looked shaken as he climbed back into his carriage and snapped the reins.

"Holmes!" I said, watching Lestrade depart. "Who is this assistant you're referring to?"

Holmes walked briskly down the street. "Why, Lestrade himself, of course," he said. "He clearly knows where the brothers are being held and is now rushing to verify they are still secure. Hurry, Watson! The game is afoot!"

Holmes, it transpired, had arranged for a carriage of our own to be kept waiting just around the corner from our inn. It was a nondescript brown vehicle similar to many we'd passed on the streets earlier in the day. "Climb in and slump down, Watson," Holmes said, unhitching our horse from its post and patting the creature affectionately on the withers. "It's vital Lestrade not recognize us." He slipped on a porkpie hat and hunched his shoulders, and had I not seen the transformation or been sitting right beside him, I would have never suspected that the man beside me was my old friend. He clucked his tongue and sent our horse down the road, and when he shouted at some roustabouts to clear out of our way, his accent sounded as Cajun as a native's. Our horse was a dusky mare with a placid demeanor, padded shoes, and swift legs, and though the Appaloosa and its hansom cab had slipped out of sight, Holmes had some instinct for where he was going and we spotted them again within just a few minutes.

"I thought for a while he might poison us," I said.

Holmes smiled. "Not prepared for the Cajun spices, Watson? Remind me to tell you of the spices a friend of mine from Tibet uses to accent his yak butter and blood sausages." He slowed our mare to keep more distance from Lestrade. The traffic of Devil's Cape was not as congested at night as during the day, but it was rougher and rowdier, and we were hardly conspicuous. "But I know enough of Jacaré to dispose of poison as a concern. He is much more visceral than that—remember the poor sailors aboard the *Friesland*. And he knows of me from Moriarty and your own florid accounts of our adventures. A creature of his ego could not allow me to die within his own city without looking me in the eye first. No, his initial plan was to use Lestrade to put us off the scent. Failing that, he wants to encounter me face to face."

"And you him."

Holmes stared at a group of rowdies passing around bottles of whiskey and rum. "Just so," he said. "Since Reichenbach Falls, Watson, and the demise of that malignant brain who so long plagued us, I have been eager for a challenge worthy of our efforts. O Jacaré lacks Moriarty's subtlety, yet, government aside, he rules this city. Deputy Chief Lestrade is hardly his only puppet, just the most convenient one for this task because our long familiarity with his cousin might have made us set caution aside. If the mayor and chief of police don't kiss Jacaré's ring, then they at least lower their heads in his presence and allow him free rein."

We passed by closely packed homes and taverns, twisting and turning through the city's maze of streets. Holmes occasionally took a path that branched away from Lestrade's, to keep him from recognizing our approach, but could not do so with as much confidence as he might have in the streets of London. We lost sight of him for nearly five minutes and I saw creases of tension in Holmes's face, sweat along his brow. Should we lose track of Lestrade now, I realized, the brothers Holingbroke would never live to see the dawn. When eventually we spotted him again, we both sighed in relief, and Holmes pressed our calm mare forward. Any exhaustion I'd felt earlier in the night was gone. The thrill of the hunt exhilarated us both.

Lestrade eventually pulled away from the city, heading east toward a mass of marshlands and swamp that Holmes identified as Bayou Tarango. Of necessity, we dropped even farther behind him, but the route was clearer here, with fewer twists and forks. The ground grew muddy and we passed among huge trees swathed in Spanish moss. Insects hummed and chirped constantly and water bubbled in the bog. Mosquitoes and gnats swarmed around us. The swamp smelled of earth and decay, and strange lights flickered in the distance.

Lestrade turned in our direction for a moment, then pressed on.

"One way or another, Holmes, he will soon realize that he is being followed," I said.

Holmes grunted and swatted a mosquito that had landed on his jaw, and in the moonlight I saw a drop of blood roll down his face. "Be prepared for danger, Watson," he said.

I nodded.

He slowed as Lestrade approached a fork in the road, allowing the hansom to gain some more distance from us. For his part, Lestrade seemed to be gathering speed, anxious to reach his destination. He selected the wider path and disappeared beyond a cluster of trees, cattails, and reeds.

Our carriage rolled forward and then Holmes brought us to a shuddering stop. Lestrade's hansom stood at the side of the road, empty.

We moved quickly, climbing out of the carriage, spreading out, peering around in hopes of spotting him.

Lestrade had selected the spot for his ambush well indeed. It was very dark, the moonlight shrouded by branches and hanging moss. Holmes turned his attention to the ground, making out footprints despite the dim light. He spun on his heel, deducing where Lestrade was hidden, but he was too late. Lestrade stepped from behind a tree where he had hidden, nearly knee-deep in swamp muck, and pointed a pistol at Holmes's chest.

"Nice hat," Lestrade said sarcastically.

Holmes doffed the porkpie hat and sent it spinning into the swamp. "It served its purpose," he said.

"We can drop them games," Lestrade said. "You tricked me good, but I tricked you, too."

"Perhaps."

"Led you the wrong way, didn't I? Got you trapped, don't I?"

"You didn't note our presence until a few minutes ago," Holmes said, "just before you made that last turn. Should we go back to that last fork, I surmise we will find what we seek."

Lestrade flinched. But his pistol did not waver. He stepped closer to Holmes. "You're real smart," he said. "But smart don't matter when you're dead." He took another step. "What's the matter? Got nothing else clever to say?" Another step. "You're smiling," he said. "Why in heaven is that?"

"I'm smiling, Lestrade," Holmes said, "because you're holding the pistol on the wrong man."

While Holmes had engaged the deputy chief's attention, I had carefully drawn my old service revolver. At this cue, I aimed carefully and fired. Lestrade collapsed as though thunderstruck, and Holmes quickly stepped forward and put the policeman's weapon into his own pocket.

"The shoulder, Watson?"

"Villain or not, he is still a police officer and the cousin of a trusted ally," I said, hurrying to tend to Lestrade's injury. It was no glancing wound. He would live, but he had already slipped into unconsciousness and would not wake soon. "Look, Holmes," I said. I held up a small *gris-gris* I had discovered on a leather band beneath Lestrade's shirt.

"A symbol of fealty to Jacaré, perhaps," Holmes said. "Leave him in his cab. Your gunshot might have been noted and there is little time to lose."

If we had followed Lestrade with caution, then we now moved with reckless urgency. One carriage wheel left the ground as we spun onto the fork that Lestrade had led us away from.

"Open the chest there," Holmes said, nodding at a small wooden chest at our feet.

I did so and discovered two gun belts, each with two holstered pistols. "Good God, Holmes," I said. "Are my own weapon and Lestrade's not enough?"

Holmes steered the carriage around a deep puddle in our path. "Peacemakers," he said. "I believe those are the types of weapons the Holingbrokes favor. Should Jacaré have accomplices close to hand, we might need their assistance."

We traveled a few minutes more before Holmes pulled our carriage over again. I had spotted nothing to differentiate this stretch of road from any other, but Holmes gestured for me to leave our conveyance behind. "I smell smoke," he said. "And there is light ahead. Let us proceed on foot."

I slung the gun belts over my shoulder and followed him. What we were on could hardly be called a road anymore. The ground was muddy and split by grasses. I nearly lost my shoes at one spot. Bats swooped and dove amongst the trees around us, feasting on insects.

After several minutes we heard shouts, coarse laughter, and screams of pain. We emerged from a cluster of cypress trees into a clearing, the moonlight suddenly bright. Perhaps a dozen men were gathered near a ramshackle house beside the waters of the swamp, jostling each other as they paced along a wooden deck and a long pier, a bonfire blazing beside them near the shoreline. They looked like pirates from a century or more earlier, with wide-brimmed hats and vests over loose-fitting shirts. They brandished swords, too, though their guns were modern enough.

It was obvious which man was O Jacaré. No matter what else held their attention, the others stepped from his path with expressions of deference and fear. Jacaré wore a sweeping, rakish hat with a bandana tied beneath. A single gem, perhaps an opal, gleamed in the center of a patch over his left eye. He had a full black beard that stretched down to his belly, a jade-green jacket, and alligator boots. The sword that hung from his waist glittered with gold and gems.

But more striking even than the figure of Jacaré was the sight that held the pirates' attention. A huge, dead bald cypress tree at the water's edge was being used as a sort of gallows, a rope slung over one heavy branch and held in the massive hands of a huge pirate, bald and shirtless, nearly seven feet tall. At the other end of the rope, just barely above the water, dangled the twisted form of the Holingbroke brothers, struggling against their bonds and howling in pain and fear as the giant shook them.

As Holmes and I crept closer, I was shocked by the sight of the brothers. They were shirtless, their backs bloody from the lashes of a whip. I had seen an illustration of them before, and read of their condition in my medical journal, but my mind had trouble reconciling the sight of them, two upper bodies, nearly identical, sharing a single waist and single pair of legs.

Then I saw something that shocked me even more.

Something enormous frothed the water beneath them, some tremendous beast hidden in the muck. The pirate dangled the brothers lower until one's head splashed into the water, and then the beast reared up, trying to take his head in its enormous pale jaws. The pirate yanked them back upward and the creature missed by inches, crashing back into the water with a frustrated hiss and splashing the pier with a white, scaled tail.

I turned toward Holmes in astonishment, but he was using the distraction to run toward the bonfire at an oblique angle, keeping it between him and the pirates. I followed his example.

"Holmes, that creature—"

"An albino alligator," he said. "Quite large. Jacaré wrote about it to Professor Moriarty. It lives nearby and he lures it close from time to time for games such as these." He peered past the flames. "Twelve men," he said. "And should the large one drop his rope, it will doom the Holingbrokes. Suggestions?"

I looked at the situation again, recalling my military experience, recalling Afghanistan. It was hopeless on the face of it. Two against twelve, the leader a ruthless criminal overlord. I turned to Holmes. "Yes," I said. "I have a plan."

A heavy hand fell on my shoulder. I spun around and found myself face to face with O Jacaré, a smile cutting through the mass of his huge black beard. "I hope it's a mighty fine plan, Dr. Watson. Cause if I were in your shoes, I'd be sweating, I tell you true."

Jacaré and his pirates led us to the dock where the Holingbroke brothers still swayed upside down from the rope, their faces resolute. I'd managed to shift the gun belts away from view under my coat, though that seemed little enough advantage for the moment.

"Heard a lot about you, Mr. Holmes," the pirate said. "Impressive, you tracking me from so far away."

"Elementary," said Holmes.

"You tricked Lestrade into leading you here, right? He dead?"

"Merely incapacitated."

"Like I say, impressive. He ain't dumb. Little less impressive, though, you getting caught."

I cleared my throat. "Holmes lacks your legion of followers," I said.

Jacaré turned to me. "This your plan, doc? Get my dander up so I have my men back off and challenge Holmes to a fair fight?"

"I wouldn't recommend it," I said. "A fair fight didn't work out well for

Professor Moriarty."

Jacaré leaned back and for a moment I was certain he was going to draw his sword and strike me down. Instead, he laughed, a tremendous braying laugh that echoed across the swamp and set the albino alligator back to churning the waters. "I'm not much for fair," he said. "But I like entertaining. Twelve on two, where's the sport in that? We'll make it two on two." He nodded at the huge bald man. "Darcé," he said. "Tie off that rope. You can kill Dr. Watson while I murder Mr. Sherlock Holmes."

Darcé's fingers flew as he tied the rope to the pier using some complicated sailor's knot. As he strode toward me, I saw that he was even more gigantic than I had first estimated. His muscles bulged as he stepped toward me. He smiled a gap-toothed grin. "You scared?" he asked.

I forced myself to stand straight, raising my fists in preparation. "Are you?" I challenged.

Out of the corner of my eye, I saw Jacaré squaring off against Holmes. The pirate had drawn his gleaming sword, but my friend was unarmed and I feared for him.

Letting Holmes's plight draw my attention was a mistake. I didn't even see Darcé raise his heavy arm for the first blow. I was slammed backward, careening off the dock to the mud. My chest ached. He charged after me, standing over me and leaning over to punch me in the face. When I rolled to the left, avoiding the blow, he straightened up and kicked me in the ribs. I rolled away, gasping in pain, and this time grabbed at his ankle as he tried to kick me again. It was like trying to uproot a tree, but I rolled into it with all my weight and he toppled beside me to the ground. He growled and snorted and pulled himself to his knees. I punched him in the jaw, but I had little leverage and he seemed barely to notice.

The pirates were cheering on Darcé and Jacaré, alternately laughing and jeering. I could neither see nor hear Holmes, but took some slight comfort in the fact that his fight evidently had not ended yet.

Darcé butted me in the face with his head. The blow split the skin over my right eyebrow and blood flowed into my eye. I swayed, stunned, while the giant climbed to his feet, and could do little but groan in protest as his iron hands lifted me up above his head. Then he took three long steps toward the bonfire and prepared to throw me into the flames. Fearing for my life, I wrenched around, throwing my arm over his neck, and we fell to the mud together. The fall took the wind out of me, and my old war wound from the Jezail bullet throbbed. But Darcé's face was in the mud and that gave me a brief moment of opportunity. I struck the back of his neck with great force twice, stunning him, then struggled to my feet. I plucked a heavy branch from the bonfire, wincing in further pain at the heat, and swung the fiery end of it at the pirate's bald head. His skin hissed as the torch struck him, and I shuddered at the horror of it, but I raised the branch once more and hit him again and he lay still.

The pirates stared at me in stunned disbelief. With Darcé vanquished and Jacaré engaged with Holmes, they were unsure what to do with me. I knew, however, that

that advantage could not last long.

I looked at Holmes. He stood on the end of the pier, holding off Jacaré with a board he had pulled from the deck. His jacket had been sliced open just over the left elbow and blood streaked his arm. My first instinct was to draw my revolver and shoot the pirate lord, but I stopped myself. If I missed, I could hit Holmes. And the other pirates' indecision would soon evaporate if I began shooting at their master.

Jacaré swung his cutlass at Holmes, who stepped to one side, precariously close to the edge of the pier, and blocked the blow with his board, which shattered into splinters.

"Skillful," Jacaré said admiringly. "You learn kung fu?"

"Baritsu," Holmes answered shortly, eyes watching the pirate carefully.

Making up my mind, I pulled Darcé's sword from his belt. "Holmes!" I shouted, rushing forward and sliding the weapon to him along the pier.

Holmes crouched and grabbed the sword by the hilt just as it was about to tilt into the swamp. "My thanks, Watson," he said. Then he raised the blade to Jacaré. "*En garde*," he said.

The huge, pale alligator splashed the water again and I was drawn once more to the Holingbrokes' danger. I rushed to the rope that held them and began pulling it, trying to figure out how best to get them down.

The brothers watched me groggily, nearly unconscious from the beating and the strain of being held upside down.

I made little progress. Slippery from the mud, my hands kept losing purchase. I pulled off my coat and wrapped it around the rope. The pirates moved closer, drawing blades and guns, still not quite sure whether to murder me now or later.

Holmes and Jacaré continued their duel, the blows from their swords ringing out like bells. "What the hell are you waiting for?" Jacaré called out to his men. "Kill the doctor."

I sighed, certain I would never see England again.

"Those belts!" cried out a raspy voice.

"Throw us them belts!" said another. I looked in surprise to see the Holingbroke brothers, all four arms outstretched, reaching for the gun belts I still had slung over my shoulder.

With no time to think, and the pirates closing in, I did what the twins asked.

I had occasionally indulged myself in the past by reading stories of Western gunslingers in the penny dreadfuls, always assuming that their feats were greatly exaggerated. The circular Holmes and I had seen in Piccadilly Circus had described the Holingbroke brothers as the greatest marksmen of the Wild West, and again I assumed hyperbole. But I have rarely seen anything move so fast as those Siamese twins. Even beaten, exhausted, and hung upside down, they snatched the belts out of the air and drew the Peacemakers in less time than it would take me to blink. All four pistols rang out repeatedly, like thunder rolling across the swamp. I turned around, wiping blood from my face, and saw to my eternal amazement that all the pirates around me had been shot dead.

"I got six, you got four," said one of the brothers.

"I got five," the other said.

"No, we both shot that last one, but I shot him first. You want credit for shooting a corpse now?"

"I shot him first."

"Nope. It's six to four, me," the first brother said. "Don't take it too hard, I think you got whipped more than me, too."

"I think you got hit in the head harder," the second brother said. "Affects your counting." He turned to me. "Hey, doc! You mind helping us down?"

I looked at Holmes, still locked in combat with Jacaré. They'd moved from the pier to the deck, and his back was up against the ramshackle building. He'd been wounded again, a gash along one cheek, but I could see him smiling in the firelight, and he shook his head at me when I began to raise my revolver toward his opponent.

Without the pirates surrounding me, helping the Holingbroke brothers down presented little challenge, and soon they were sitting in the mud, rubbing at the wounds the ropes had burned into their legs and watching the duel.

"It's over," Holmes said to Jacaré, blocking another blow. Holmes was clearly not as skilled in swordplay as his opponent, and made few attacks of his own, but he managed to ward off the worst of Jacaré's assaults, and continually maneuvered himself over to the pirate's left side, using his opponent's eyepatch as an advantage.

"Maybe so," the pirate said. "Maybe I should have killed you straight out, but it seemed like a waste."

"Surrender," Holmes said.

"Nah," Jacaré answered. "T'ain't my way." He raised his sword for another blow.

"You have a very interesting accent," Holmes said. "It took me a while to place it. Your method of hiding your secrets is a bold one."

For whatever reason, this last comment rattled Jacaré, who bellowed and charged at Holmes with all his speed.

Holmes dropped his sword, bent down, and kicked Jacaré at the side of the knee. The pirate howled in agony, fell, and splashed into the water.

Alarmed, Holmes rushed forward, holding an arm out to his opponent.

Jacaré splashed to the surface.

"Quickly, man," Holmes said.

But Jacaré, his face calm, ignored Holmes's offer of help. There was a tremendous splash beside him, and then the massive pale jaws of the alligator flashed in the moonlight. Jacaré screamed once in pain and then the beast pulled him under the water, its body rolling over and over. The bog bubbled and churned as the creature shook and began to consume its prey.

Weeks later, safely ensconced once more at 221B Baker Street, our wounds mostly healed, I broached the topic of the pirates of Devil's Cape over tea.

We had departed the city nearly as quickly as we had arrived. The death of O Jacaré had left a void in the city as large as that of a fallen king, and by morning, when news of his death had spread, there was rioting in the streets.

Before leaving, we made certain that the Holingbrokes were safe, and confirmed Holmes's suspicions, first that they had been traveling aboard the *Friesland* incognito because some of Jacaré's men had accosted them on their European tour, and second that Jacaré had been fascinated, even obsessed, with the mystery of where they hid their gold. "I believe our traveling days are done for a while," Janus Holingbroke told us. "Best to settle down here for a spell."

Somewhat to my relief, Deputy Chief Lestrade survived the shot to his shoulder. Holmes prepared documentation of his crimes and forwarded them to the office of Governor Murphy J. Foster of the state of Louisiana, but we never received a response. Our own Inspector Lestrade was appalled and consternated to learn of his cousin's crimes, not the least because of the opportunity it gave Holmes to jibe him about his relative.

"Holmes," I said, topping off my cup and taking a sip of Mrs. Hudson's excellent brew. "I do wish you would settle that last detail for me."

"Last detail, Watson?" he answered breezily, feigning confusion.

"Your comment about Jacaré's accent," I said, "and why it flustered him so."

"He was alone and defeated. Even had he managed to strike me down, you and the other two sharpshooters would have killed him in turn."

I waved off the implied compliment. "Defeated or not," I persisted, "your words conquered him as surely as the blow to his leg. What did you deduce from his accent?"

Holmes sighed. "With mysterious deaths and Siamese twins and a giant alligator, this adventure was extraordinary enough," he said. "I am reluctant to add another level of mystery to the tale."

"Oh, come now, Holmes!"

He drank from his own cup and stared at the latest addition to our parlor, a small painting of Lady Danger we had received from Lieutenant-Commander Powell, who was grateful for our defeating the pirates and returning the seven paintings that they had stolen from the Rijksmuseum exhibit. "Sometimes, Watson, a conclusion, no matter how sound, can defy belief." He tapped the cup. "O Jacaré seemed to revere the old pirate St. Diable in many ways: his tactics, his accoutrements, his mental discipline. There were some cosmetic differences, of course, such as the beard and the eyepatch, but in many ways, Jacaré seemed like a continuation of St. Diable himself."

"A disciple," I said. "He studied St. Diable and emulated him."

"Perhaps," Holmes said. "That is certainly the most likely explanation. But as you know, I have a rather disciplined ear for language and accents. As we dueled, as he spoke to me, I found myself struggling not just to preserve my life, but to place his accent. And I realized that if I considered not just different locales, but different times, and the evolution of language over time, I might finally have a solution."

"Holmes!" I cried. "You're saying that Jacaré *was* St. Diable? That's preposterous!

He'd have to be nearly three centuries old."

"And now you know why I was reluctant to discuss the subject. The mechanics of such a thing—how it could be possible—elude me entirely. But answer this for me, Watson: If my solution was as preposterous as you say, then why did my comment shake him so badly?"

I stared into space, lost in thought, my hand trembling as I sipped my tea. Try as I might, I could not answer Holmes's question.

THE ADVENTURE OF
THE GREEN SKULL

by Mark Valentine

Mark Valentine is the author of the novels *In Violet Veils*, *Masques and Citadels*, and, with John Howard, *The Rite of Trebizond*, which are about an "aesthetical occult detective" and are collectively known as the Tales of The Connoisseur. He is the editor of the psychic sleuth anthology *The Black Veil* and *The Werewolf Pack*. He also edits *Wormwood*, a journal of fantasy, supernatural and decadent literature, and writes regularly for *Book & Magazine Collector* about neglected authors.

A revenant is a visible ghost or animated corpse that returns to terrorize the living, often in retribution for some wrong visited on that person in life. Wrongs done create ghosts, and many wrongs were committed against the workers of London in the early days of industrialization. Many of these deprivations were chronicled by the author Charles Dickens, who was so traumatized by the time he spent working in a dangerous, squalorous blacking factory that for the rest of his life he wore gloves and washed his hands constantly. The Sadler Committee once interviewed a young man named Matthew Crabtree, who testified that he had started work in a factory at the age of eight, commonly worked sixteen-hour days, and was beaten severely for the slightest infraction. He also testified that in all his years in the factory, not an hour had passed that you couldn't hear one of the child workers wailing. Many people don't realize that the thick, impenetrable London fogs that we associate with Sherlock Holmes were a result of terrible air pollution. The Victorian Age was romantic, but it was also a dark time, when business interests were totally unrestrained.

I have mentioned before the three massive manuscript volumes that contain my notes on our cases for the year 1894. Circumstances now allow me to reveal the details of one of these, as weird and tragic a case as any we encountered. It was, I see, the beginning of November, and Holmes was on capital form, pleased to be back at the hub of matters in London after his long incognito wanderings in the East and elsewhere. There had been a high wind wailing outside our rooms and throughout the city, and Holmes was just beginning to become restless for some new matter to whet his keen mind upon. As was his habit, therefore, he was scouring the pages of the *Times* at breakfast, seeking evidence of anything untoward. Today his researches had an especial edge, for he had received word that Inspector Lestrade would call later, if convenient.

"Read that, Watson," he said, passing the paper to me, and pointing to a brief paragraph.

"'Mr Josiah Walvis, 51, an overseer at the Bow-side match-works, met an untimely end on Saturday evening when he fell from a high wall abutting the East India Wharf, and cracked his skull. The cause of his sad accident has not been ascertained. It is understood Mr Walvis had been entertaining friends at the Lamb & Flag public house before making his way home. Interviewed, his associates say the deceased was of his normal disposition upon departing, and was not excessively inebriated. It is considered possible Mr Walvis was contemplating a shorter route to his home but missed his footing. Two witnesses, a watchman and a street boy, aver that they saw the victim pursued some moments beforehand, but this cannot be better corroborated. The proprietor of the Bow match-works reports that Mr Walvis was a diligent and just employee who—well, etc, etc'"

"There is the barest hint of promise in that, Watson: the pursuer, you know. But it is otherwise a drab affair. Yet it is all there is. Inventive evil appears to have quite vanished from London."

Holmes sighed, and began to gather up the dottles for his morning pipe.

The visit of our colleague from Scotland Yard did not at first obviate his gloom. For it seemed Lestrade had indeed nothing better to offer.

"It's the Walvis business, Mr Holmes."

"Oh, indeed? But that happened two days ago, Lestrade. The gales will have rushed all the evidence to the four corners. There is no point in coming to me now."

"Well, it seems a straightforward case that is hardly worth your while. But one of the constables, a keen lad, saw something he didn't quite like."

"Indeed?"

"Yes. Of course, an accident is quite the likeliest explanation. There was no robbery, and no other marks on the body but those caused by the fall. Yet, here is the thing. In the deceased's left hand, between the two middle fingers, protruding outwards, was a spent match."

"Ah. That is singular." I saw my friend's eyes gleam.

"Quite so. A drowning man may clutch at a straw, but—I say to myself—a falling man does not. He splays his fingers, so..."

"Therefore, the match was placed there after the fall," I interjected.

"Exactly, Doctor," returned Lestrade. "Now I am inclined to regard it as merely a macabre little joke on the part of the friends who found him. They all worked at the match factory, you know. They were pretty far gone in drink. So they put it there as if to say 'you, Walvis, have struck your last match.' I questioned them pretty fiercely about that, but they deny it. Half didn't notice it at all, the others say it must have blown there..."

"You have preserved the match, Lestrade?" Holmes demanded.

"I have, Mr Holmes, and—knowing your ways—have brought it with me." Lestrade produced a twist of paper from his waistcoat pocket and handed it over.

Holmes inspected the exhibit carefully between thumb and forefinger, then handed it back.

"It tells us little. It is a Lyphant & Bray match—the people who have the Bow works. So it could well have come from his colleagues. Or from almost anybody. It is a very popular brand. Yet, someone who has handled it may be an actor."

We both looked suitably astonished, and Holmes favoured us with an explanation. "It is very simple. I have studied the shape, size and composition of over forty types of lucifer or match—the matter complements my researches upon tobacco ash, you know. A combination of a certain ash and a certain match may help to mark a man. But not in this case. No ash, and a very common brand."

"The theatrical connection?" I urged.

Holmes shrugged. "Oh, merely that someone has left a small smudge of grease-paint upon the stick. Not you or your constable, I assume, Lestrade?"

"Indeed not."

"Well, it does not get us very far. But what about this evidence of a pursuer, Inspector?"

Our visitor's face settled into a satisfied smirk.

"The witnesses are not very sound. An aged watchman, half deaf and almost wholly foolish. A street arab, with a lively imagination."

"And what do they say?"

"Well, Mr Holmes, I don't give it much credit. Indeed, I am trying what I can to suppress their little yarn. It doesn't take much to spread unreasoning terror abroad."

There was a brittle silence, Lestrade savouring the matter that had really brought him to us, Holmes quiveringly alert.

"They say they saw Walvis chased down the street by a phantom. It wore a hooded cloak, but they caught a glimpse of its face—if you can call it that. It looked more like, they said, it looked more like—a green skull."

Sherlock Holmes rose from his chair and rubbed his hands together. "Come now," he said. "This sounds promising."

The case may have caught my friend's imagination, because of its peculiarities, but for some days he made little progress. The scene, as he had anticipated, had been quite wiped clean by the wind and rain of the intervening days, and all the witnesses he interviewed stuck resolutely to the stories they had given the police, even the two who had seen the spectral pursuer. Lyphant & Bray would give nothing but a sound character to Walvis, conceding only that by some he might be regarded as somewhat stern in his duties. There was little more for Holmes to do, and he was succumbing again to his blue devils when, barely a week later, Mrs Hudson ushered in a new client. He was an angular, brisk young man, pale and peremptory in manner.

"Sit down, Mr Reynolds. This is my friend and associate, Dr Watson. What is your business with us?"

"I have read of you, Mr Holmes, from Dr Watson's accounts. I have observed that you see importance in matters others overlook."

"You are very kind. And you think you have a similar matter?"

"I do. My employer, Mr Thomas Mostyn, died last night."

"I see. The cause?"

"Heart failure."

Holmes looked crestfallen.

"It is certain?"

"Yes. His medical man has treated him for years. He has long had indifferent health. I could see this for myself too."

"Then why—"

"That was the cause of his death, Mr Holmes. I am concerned about the occasion of it."

"There is something here that does not satisfy you?"

"A number of matters."

Holmes tapped his fingers upon the arm of his chair. "Pray proceed."

"Mr Mostyn's face in death was distorted most disturbingly. It was a grimacing mask, exhibiting naked fear."

I interrupted. "Rictus, Mr Reynolds. It can give the most distressing effects."

Our client turned to me. "I understand. But there is rather more. Though in his nightgown and dressing-gown, as if prepared for bed, Mr Mostyn met his end in his study. Some matter had taken him there. And in death he was clutching between his middle fingers, pointing outwards—"

"A match."

Mr Reynolds' face was a picture of astonishment. "Great heavens, yes. How did you know?"

Holmes smiled. "No matter. It was used?"

"Yes."

"Well, perhaps he was about to enjoy a cigar before retiring. It is not uncommon."

"Certainly not, Mr Holmes. My employer disapproved of smoking. It was the only matter of disagreement between us. If I wished to smoke, I must do so clandestinely."

"I see. He does not sound very companionable. Well, Mr Reynolds, let us have more of your story. You are his private secretary?"

"I am. I deal—I dealt—with nearly all his business and personal correspondence. He has many financial interests. I have been with him some seven years, since I successfully answered an advertisement he had placed upon his return from Guiana. He was reticent about his wealth, but that he had made a very great deal in the Americas was evident enough to me from his investments."

"And had made enemies, no doubt?"

"I never heard of any. Indeed, all of his affairs appeared to me almost entirely untroubled, until—well, that is, until the particular incident that brings me to you. On Tuesday last week, I opened Mr Mostyn's correspondence as usual, and there was nothing out of the ordinary run of things, but one: an envelope that contained no letter, only a handful of matches. I could not imagine what the sender's purpose was, although sometimes the advertisement men do try the most foolish tricks to engage attention. I threw it in the basket. When I took in the rest of the day's post and went through it with my employer, we dealt with it all well enough, until—at the end—I mentioned the matches, light-heartedly. Quite a remarkable change came over his face. I had never seen him so agitated, except perhaps once when he felt he had been browbeaten by a hothead of a lawyer into some settlement he did not like—the one matter, as it happens, where he did not confide in me."

"I see. The envelope arrived—what, eight days ago? Go on, Mr Reynolds. This may all be more germane than you know."

"In his agitation, Mr Mostyn asked me exactly how many matches there were. I am afraid I laughed and said I did not know. He became vehement and told me to go and count them at once. I could scarcely believe the order, but I did as he bid."

"And?"

"There were nine or ten."

"Nine or ten? Mr Reynolds!"

"Ten, then. It seemed of no moment."

"Do you have them?"

"Well, yes I do. But only because I found them in my employer's desk drawer, next to his appointments diary. I cannot imagine why he kept them."

Our visitor handed them over and Holmes subjected them to scrutiny, separating three from the others.

Mr Reynolds regarded Holmes's actions quizzically, then resumed. "A little later that day, Mr Mostyn gave me a most unusual instruction. He said that business compelled him to go abroad again, it might be for some time. I was to realise as much as I could, and as quickly as I could, of his investments, so that within one week—he was most insistent upon that—within one week, he should be ready to leave."

"He had never done such a thing before?"

"No. I was very much surprised. From what I knew of his business affairs, there was nothing of any consequence to call his attention overseas. But by requiring me to turn his holdings to cash so quickly, he forfeited a great deal of their value. I could not imagine what would impel him to that."

"Is there anything more, Mr Reynolds?"

Our visitor hesitated.

"No."

"Think back very carefully, sir. Over this recent period, has there been any matter whatever at all out of the ordinary?"

"Oh, only foolish talk from the boot-boy. He reads too much sensational literature."

"Indeed? I find it has much to commend it. And what was his prattle? Spring-Heeled Jack? The Wild Boys of the Sewers?"

"Ha, very nearly so, Mr Holmes. He said he saw some figure skulking around the garden at night. He has an attic room that commands a view. He should have been asleep, but no doubt was reading his rubbish. He said he saw Death with a lantern. The maid, superstitious soul, says it had come for Mr Mostyn. I had to speak severely to both of them... Of course, there may have been an interloper, but scarcely in that form. Now, Mr Holmes, what is your advice?"

"I should like to visit the scene without delay, Mr Reynolds. And I am concerned for you, sir. You have had an unpleasant experience. Now there is no necessity for subterfuge, help yourself to one of these—a Macedonian—you will find it quite soothing—while we get ready. Now, where are my matches? You have some with you? Good. good. We shall not be long."

Despite the tragedy that had taken place in No 4, Pavia Court, Mostyn's address, I relished our visit, for it was a pleasure to see Holmes prowling throughout the house and its modest grounds in his customary keen-eyed search for any clue that might bring substance to the shadows that had gathered here. I saw him crawling carefully around the garden at the rear, and its narrow entrance gate, examining the sash upon the study window that overlooked it on the ground floor, and walking up and down the small, blind street, itself off a very minor thoroughfare, that comprised the Court, in all these places picking up and examining any piece of unregarded flotsam. I heard of him also in the pantry in animated conversation with Victor, the boot-boy, comparing the merits of various thrilling pamphlets: and in the study, questioning Reynolds closely about his employer's business holdings.

For my part, I sought out Mostyn's doctor, Hawkins, on the pretext that I was a medical advisor to his insurance people. Although, as a matter of form, the district police had been called, they had relied upon his assurance that a heart failure was responsible for the death. He conceded he had quite expected—and indeed hoped, since Mostyn paid well—that his patient would have survived some years longer, but it was still quite within the bounds of medical science that the condition had taken him earlier. Might—I suggested—some additional anxiety in his affairs, even some shock or other, have contributed? Dr Hawkins was affable: yes, of course, it very well might.

It was clear to me that Holmes had some definite line of enquiry in his sights, though I could not tell what. The next day, he was missing from our rooms for much of the time, and would say only that he had paid a call upon one of the new independent lucifer-makers. I was, therefore, a little taken aback when, shortly after our visit to Mostyn's home, the boot-boy Victor presented himself, somewhat wind-ruffled but evidently bursting with news.

"I did 'sactly as you said, Mr Holmes. I took a place in the bun shop opposite this inventor cove's place, Raffles, and watched and watched. I had to eat getting on for a dozen stickies before your mark came out, corst a terrible lot they did—" (a clink) "well, thank you very much sir, anyways after you'd been to see him and he'd shut up shop that day, it was hours and hours after, he looks about him and sets off smartish. But I'm on his track like you told me…"

"You see, Watson, nobody ever pays attention to small boys loitering or getting up to mischief. It's what they do. A perfect disguise: behaving naturally. Well, where did (ahem) the inventor Raffles go?"

"He went out Chelsea way, where all the artists and anarchists are, sir, they're always up to plots in The Black Paper, 'sfact."

"So they are, Victor. And who are they are in league with, eh?"

"That's what I was going to find out. He heads for a door in a yard off Blyth Street, and he's looking all around him, see: furtive, that's what they call it. But he doesn't see me. And he knocks and there's a wait and like a judas in the door opens, but I can't see much. And then—then the door opens just a crack, and he talks very excited like, and he gets let in. And he stays there not long, twenty minutes maybe."

"See anything when the door opened?"

"You bet. Woundy—beg pardon sir—scary."

"You're sure, Victor?"

"Blood honour, sir."

"That's good enough for me."

I looked from one to the other. "Well?"

Holmes raised an eyebrow.

"He saw Death, Watson. Isn't that right? The thing that came to Mr Mostyn's garden?"

The youth nodded solemnly.

Holmes wasted no time. After swift directions from the boy, amply rewarded, we hailed a cab to the hidden, curious quarter he had indicated. In the neighbourhood, my friend enlisted another ragamuffin helper, a blind match-seller. A sovereign and a swift rehearsal of her role ensued. God knows she was battered enough looking, but she made her condition look even more distressing and knocked weakly and repeatedly at the door, imploring help. At the first the face behind the shutter ushered her away, but she swayed and cried and pleaded. The figure within went away a while, and then the door opened very slowly. We then abandoned all subtlety and flung ourselves at the crack. The child ran off, there was a harsh shout and a scurrying, and we burst in.

We were confronted by—a thing at bay. In one corner of the bare, meanly furnished room, there stood glowering at us a figure wrapped around in cloaks from which emerged a hairless, shrunken, bony head, where such meagre flesh as there was had a vile, livid hue.

"I do not know who or what you are," Sherlock Holmes said, "but your business is at an end. I have evidence that will connect you with two deaths."

The creature's eyes were filled with hatred, and cast wildly about for escape. Then they seemed to dim, and the skull sank down, before it looked up at us again.

"You have no evidence that would convince a court. Yet perhaps it is time to let things rest. And I believe you will not speak so harshly when you have heard my story."

I gasped, and I could sense that even the icy Holmes was taken aback. For the voice was that of a gentlewoman, clear and well-modulated. She beckoned us to two rough chairs. We made introductions and looked at her enquiringly.

"My name is of no consequence. I was born in the colony of Guiana, where my mother succumbed young to the foul waters. My father and a native nursemaid looked after me in my infancy, but he was taken too by some disease of the unhealthy conditions there. We had no close kin, but there was a distant cousin who had been once in the colony and had come to know my father before returning to England. I found that I—and my father's wealth—were entrusted to this person, and I was shipped to a land I had never known as home. The next part of my story will hardly surprise you. This cousin and guardian, so called, claimed my father's business affairs were in disorder and it was all he could do to settle his debts, penurying himself in the process. I must be put to work. I was sent to the Lyphant & Bray match factory, and housed nearby in squalid lodgings. From then onwards—I was twelve, mark you—my life was one of unremitting drudgery and callousness, in the most terrible conditions. I saw my guardian infrequently and then, I am sure, he came only to ensure I was secure. The fact that I had been educated and prepared for a gentler place made matters worse. The taskmaster—Walvis—took a hatred of me. I believe he was in league with my guardian, for I saw them confer together when he came. My natural rebelliousness against the conditions meant this creature was able to taunt, scold, fine and beat me. There was not the slightest opportunity I might escape—I was kept under close watch and had no money anyway."

"It is pitiable, Madam," I conceded.

"It is the life of many of your fellow creatures. It would be mine still, had I not taken the one opportunity that came my way. You will recall of course the great match-girls' protest some five or six years ago? I am proud to confess I was one of the agitators. After much hardship, the proprietors permitted a tour of inspection of the factory by some eminent sympathisers—it was all well-managed, of course. But some of the more astute of them realised this, and deliberately looked for an opportunity to become detached from the party and learn the untutored truth. I told my story hurriedly to Mr Shardlow, the Radical, and he was much affected and promised to see me have justice. I know now that he confronted my guardian and wrung from him some settlement on my behalf—Mr Shardlow is a lawyer and a strong orator, of course. Since this release, I have done what I can for those left behind. The terrible yellow phosphorous that Lyphant & Bray use must be abolished: there are safer alternatives. That was my campaign. But it will be too late for me."

"You have phossy-jaw, Madam? It is a bad business."

"Exactly, Dr. Watson. You may see the symptoms."

I turned to Holmes. "It affects those over-exposed to the noxious chemicals used in the match trade. It brings a green pallor, a sinking of the cheek bones, complete loss of hair, a shrinking of the flesh. It is incurable. But forgive me, madam—yours is an exceptionally severe case. "

"It is well advanced, Doctor. But also, since I cannot disguise its ravages, I decided to accentuate them, to render my appearance still more ghastly. For I had determined to confront my persecutors face to face with what they had done. With the cunning of theatrical make-up, I thought I could strike terror in their hearts and jolt them into some realisation of their evil. My craft was good. It worked somewhat better than I expected. Poor Walvis fled from me in mad panic and plunged to his doom. While—"

She hesitated.

"Mostyn," supplied Holmes.

"Yes, I see you know everything. Mostyn was already full of fear from the little message I sent him."

"The spent matches," I put in.

"Yes, Doctor. You were my accomplice in those, of course."

"I—why, I..."

"I read with great relish your account of the Five Orange Pips sent as a sinister warning. And so has half London, I should think. It gave me an idea."

"So I see," remarked Holmes, drily.

"Mostyn was an implacable opponent of the match reforms, and as a chief investor in Lyphant & Bray, was an obstacle to my plans. I had to chase him away. My guardian, I reasoned, would have heard of the strange death of his accomplice, the overseer Walvis. He will not be quite sure if it were the accident it seemed. He will hardly miss the significance of a packet of dead matches delivered to him. And a man less vilely cunning than he would reason that seven matches equals seven days. It was a fair warning. His face when I slid open the sash of his study and advanced upon him was dreadful to behold: yet not, you can see, so dreadful as what he had done to me."

There was a silence.

"And now, gentlemen, what do you intend? You hardly have any case, you know. And it is all one to me. I cannot live much longer: but I would not harm my cause."

Sherlock Holmes stared piercingly at her.

"There must be no more apparitions."

"There will be none."

"Then this matter is concluded. I am my own law, and you are not, as I judge, in default of it."

That the case had shaken Holmes I could tell from the brooding silence he observed on our way back to Baker Street in a cab. But once in our rooms again, and after he had played over Swettenham's sweetly melancholy violin sonata, he became somewhat restored.

"I shall be able to use this case in due course as an exemplar for my monograph on lucifers, matches, and spills," he observed. "Here are the ones left on the dead men and sent in the envelope—all Lyphant & Bray—see the squared-off stalks and yellow residue at the head. Here are three that Reynolds cast in the waste basket after having several secret cigarettes—they are identical to the one he left here after smoking one of my Macedonians. They are from the Phoebus Match Co, a rounded stem and a more friable head. They led Mostyn to think he had ten days before Nemesis would strike: in fact, he had only a week.

"And here are those I found in Pavia Court. One at the top of the street, by the sign: struck to check it was the right street; one by the gate; one in the garden, for the dark lantern. These were my treasures. They are a very uncommon match indeed—Raphael's Hygienic. An experimental type, to see if some less deadly form of phosphor can be used in match manufacture, one that will do no harm to the poor creatures in the match manufactories. The lady of the skull, Watson, used Lyphant & Bray, the instruments of her oppression as a calling card on those she wished to harm, but in her everyday use she naturally patronised, and indeed part-funded, the safer design. I merely had to make known that I had connected the apparition to the Raphael workshop, and I felt sure the young inventor there would hurry to let her know and warn her off. In the morning, Watson, I shall visit to reassure him: and, after all we have heard, to place our order for matches always with him."

THE HUMAN MYSTERY

by Tanith Lee

Tanith Lee, a two-time winner of the World Fantasy Award, is the author of more than 100 books. These include The Piratica series, The Wolf Tower/Claidi Journals, and the Blood Opera series. Other novels include *The Birthgrave* (a finalist for the Nebula Award), and *Death's Master* (winner of the British Fantasy Award). Her Flat Earth series is now being brought back into print, with two new volumes in the series on the way. Lee also has several new short stories forthcoming in various magazines and anthologies. Her most recent book is a new story collection, *Tempting the Gods*.

If you were to ask readers what makes Sherlock Holmes such an intriguing character, many people would probably answer that it's what he *knows*—his encyclopedic knowledge of mud stains, handwriting, postmarks, poisons, etc. Holmes's intellect is certainly captivating, and often we can only gape in awe, as Watson does, at the great detective's recall of some obscure fact. Who doesn't fantasize about having a mind so well honed? But when you think about it, what really makes Holmes so fascinating is not just what he knows, but also what he *doesn't* know. A character who always knows everything would be a bit dull and predictable. Holmes is such a genius that it sometimes seems that he knows everything, but we often forget that Holmes is able to recall so much information relating to detective work because he has purposely remained ignorant about so much else. In "A Study in Scarlet," Holmes claims not to know that the Earth orbits the sun, because that fact does not directly relate to solving crimes. Fascinating. Our next adventure, which involves a lady, a house, and a curse, takes Holmes deep into one of those territories about which he still has much to learn.

1

Although I have written so often of the genius of Mr. Sherlock Holmes, a reader may have noticed, it was not always to Holmes's satisfaction. With that in mind, I suspect the reader may also have wondered if, on occasion, certain exploits were never committed to paper. This I confess to be true.

The causes are various. In some instances the investigation had been of so delicate a nature that, sworn to secrecy myself, as was Holmes, I could not break my vow. Elsewhere Holmes had perhaps acted alone, and never fully enlightened me, due mostly, I believe, to a certain boredom he often exhibited, when a case was just then complete. Other adventures proved ultimately dull, and dullness I have never readily associated with Sherlock Holmes.

Otherwise a small body of events remain, rogues of their kind.

They would not please the more devoted reader, as indeed at the time they had not pleased Holmes, or myself. I do not mean to imply here any failure, anything dishonourable or paltry on the part of Holmes. Although he has his faults, that glowing brain of his, when once electrically charged, transcends them. In this, or in any age, I daresay, he would be a great man. Nevertheless, certain rare happenings have bruised his spirit, and in such a way that I, his chronicler, have let them lie.

A year has gone by, however. An insignificant item in the newspaper brings me to my pen. No other may ever read what it writes. It seems to me, even so, that what was a distasteful, sad curiosity, has become a tragedy.

Holmes, although he will, almost undoubtedly, have seen the item, has not alluded to it. I well remember his sometime comment that more recent work pushes from his memory the ventures of the past. It is therefore possible he has forgotten the case of the Caston Gall.

One winter afternoon, a few days before Christmas, Holmes and I returned to our rooms from some business near Trafalgar Square. The water in the fountain had been frozen, and I had great sympathy with it. The Baker Street fire was blazing, and the lamps soon lit, for the afternoon was already spent and very dark, with a light snow now falling.

Holmes regarded the snow from the window a moment, then turning, held out to me a letter. "I wonder if the weather will deter our visitor?"

"Which visitor is that?"

"This arrived earlier. I saved it to show you on our return."

> Dear Mr. Holmes,
>
> I should like to call upon you this afternoon at three o'clock.
>
> Hopefully, this will be of no inconvenience to you. Should it prove otherwise, I will return at some more favourable hour.

I looked up. "How unusual, Holmes. A client who fails to assume you are always in residence, awaiting them!"

"Indeed. I also was struck by that."

The letter continued:

> I am divided in my mind whether or not to ask your opinion. The matter at hand seems strange and foreboding to me, but I am acutely conscious your time is often filled, and perhaps I am fanciful. Finally I have decided to set the facts before you, that you may be the judge. Please believe me, Mr. Holmes, if you can assure me I have no cause for fear, I shall depart at once with a light heart.

"Good heavens!" I exclaimed.

Holmes stood by the window. "She sets great store by my opinion, it seems. She will allow me to decide her fate merely on hearsay."

"She? Ah yes, a lady." The signature read "Eleanor Caston." It was a strong, educated hand, and the paper of good quality.

"What do you make of it, Watson?" Holmes asked, as was his wont.

I told him my views on the paper, and added, "I think she is quite young, although not a girl."

"Ah, do you say so. And why?"

"The writing is formed, but there is none of the stiffness in it which tends to come with age. Nor does she seem querulous. She has all the courteous thought of someone used to getting her own way. Conversely, she knows of and trusts you. Wisdom, but with a bold spirit. A young woman."

"Watson, I stand in awe."

"I suppose," I added, not quite liking his tone, "an elderly lady will now enter the room."

"Probably not. Mrs. Hudson caught sight of her earlier. But do go on."

"I can think of nothing else. Except I have used this writing paper myself. It is good but hardly extravagant."

"Two other things are apparent," said Holmes, leaning to the letter. "She wears a ring slightly too large for her, on her right hand. It has slipped and caught in the ink, here and here, do you see? And she does not, as most of her sex do, favour scent."

I sniffed the paper. "No, it seems not."

"For that reason, I think, Watson, you at first deduced the letter had been penned by a man. A faint floweriness is often present in these cases. Besides, her writing is well-formed but a trifle masculine."

Below, I heard the bell ring. "And here she is."

Presently Eleanor Caston was admitted to the room.

She was slim, and quite tall, her movements extremely graceful. She wore a tawny costume, trimmed with marten fur, and a hat of the same material. Her complexion was white and clear, and she had fine eyes of a dark grey. Her hair was decidedly the crowning glory, luxuriant, elegantly dressed, and of a colour not unlike polished mahogany. I was surprised to note, when she had taken off her gloves, that contrary to Holmes's statement, she wore no rings.

Although her appearance was quite captivating, she was not, I thought, a woman one would especially notice. But I had not been in her company more than five minutes, before I realized hers was a face that seemed constantly changeable. She would, in a few moments, pass from a certain prettiness to an ordinariness to vivid flashes of beauty. It was quite bewitching.

"Thank you, Mr. Holmes, Doctor Watson, for allowing me this interview today. Your time is a precious commodity."

Holmes had sat down facing her. "Time is precious to all of us, Miss Caston. You seem to have some fear for yours."

Until that moment she had not looked directly at him. Now she did so, and she paled. Lowering her eyes, she said, rather haltingly, "You must forgive me. This is, as you suspect, perhaps a matter of life or death to me."

Without taking his eyes from her, Holmes signalled to me. I rose at once and poured for her a glass of water. She thanked me, sipped it, and set it aside.

She said, "I have followed many of your cases, Mr. Holmes, in the literature of Doctor Watson."

"Literature—ah, yes," Holmes remarked.

"The curiosity of it is, therefore, that I seem almost to be acquainted with you. Which enables me to speak freely."

"Then by all means, Miss Caston, speak."

"Until this summer, I have lived an uneventful life. My work has been in the libraries of others, interesting enough, if not highly remunerative. Then I was suddenly informed I had come into a house and an amount of money which, to me, represents a fortune. The idea I need no longer labour for others, but might indulge in study, books and music on my own account, was a boon beyond price. You see, a very distant relative, a sort of aunt I had never known I had, died last Christmas, and left all her property to me, as her only relation. You will note, I am not in mourning. As I say, I did not know her, and I dislike hypocrisy. I soon removed to the large house near Chislehurst, with its grounds and view of fields and woodland. Perhaps you can envisage my happiness."

She paused. Holmes said, "And then?"

"Autumn came, and with it a change. The servants, who until then had been efficient and cheerful, altered. My maid, Lucy, left my service. She was in tears and said she had liked her position very well, but then gave some pretext of a sick mother."

"And how could you be sure it was a pretext, Miss Caston?"

"I could not, Mr. Holmes, and so I had to let her go. But it had been my understanding that she, as I, was without family or any close friends."

At this instant she raised her head fiercely, and her eyes burned, and I saw she was indeed a very beautiful woman, and conceivably a courageous one. Despite her self-possession, it was obvious to me that Holmes made her shy and uneasy. She turned more often to me in speech. This phenomenon was not quite uncommon, I must admit. She had admitted after all to reading my histories, and so might have some awareness of Holmes's opinion of women.

"Presently," she went on, "I had recourse to my aunt's papers. I should have explained, a box of them had been left for me, with instructions from my aunt to read them. That is, the instruction was not directed solely at me, but at any woman bearing the Caston name, and living alone in the house. Until then I had put the task off. I thought I should be bored."

"But you were not," said Holmes.

"At first I found only legal documents. But then I came to these. I have them here." She produced and held out to him two sheets of paper. He read the first. Then, having got up and handed both papers to me, Holmes walked about the room. Reaching the window, he stayed to look out into the soft flurry of the falling snow and the darkness of impending night. "And she had died at Christmas?"

"Yes, Mr. Holmes, she had. So had they all."

The first paper was a letter from Miss Caston's aunt. It bore out my earlier amateur theory, for the writing was crotchety and crabbed. The aunt was a woman in her late sixties, it seemed, her hand tired by much writing.

> To any female of the Caston family, living in this house a single life, unwed, or lacking the presence of a father or a brother: Be aware now that there is a curse put on the solitary spinsters of our line.
>
> You may live well in this house at any time of year save the five days which forerun and culminate in Christmas Eve. If you would know more, you must read the following page, which I have copied from Derwent's *Legends of Ancient Houses*. You will find the very book in the library here. Take heed of it, and all will be well. It is a dogged curse, and easy to outwit, if inconvenient. Should you disregard my warning, at Christmas, you will die here.

I turned to the second paper. Holmes all this while stood silent, his back to us both. The young woman kept silent too, her eyes fixed on him now as if she had pinned them there, with her hopes.

"Watson," said Holmes, "kindly read Derwent's commentary aloud to me."

I did so.

> In the year 1407, the knight Hugh de Castone is said to have left his bane on the old manor-farm at Crowby, near Chislehurst.
>
> A notorious woman-hater, Sir Hugh decreed that if any Castone woman lived on the property without husband, father or brother to command her obedience, she would die there a sudden death at Yuletide. It must be noted that this was the season at which de Castone's own wife and sister had conspired to poison him, failed, and been mercilessly hanged by his own hands. However, the curse is heard of no more until the late seventeenth century, when Mistress Hannah Castone, her husband three months dead, held a modest festival in the house. She accordingly died from choking on the bone of a fowl, on Christmas Eve. One curiosity which was noted at the time, and which caused perplexity, was that a white fox had been spotted in the neighbourhood, which after Mistress Castone's burial, vanished. A white fox it seems, had been the blazon of Sir Hugh de Castone, as depicted on his coat of arms.

I stopped here and glanced at Miss Caston. She had turned from us both and was gazing in the fire. She appeared calm as marble, but it occurred to me that might be a brave woman's mask for agitation.

"Watson, why have you stopped?" came from the window.

I went on.

> Again the curse fell dormant. It may be that only married ladies thereafter dwelled at the farm, sisters with brothers or daughters with their fathers. However, in 1794, during the great and awful Revolution in France, a French descendant of the Castons took refuge in the house, a woman whose husband had been lost to the guillotine. Three nights before the eve of Christmas, charmed, as she said, by glimpsing a white fox running along the terrace, the lady stepped out, missed her footing on the icy stair, and falling, broke her neck. There has in this century been only one violent death of a Caston woman at the house in Crowby. Maria Caston, following the death of her father the previous year, set up her home there. But on the evening preceding Christmas Eve, she was shot and killed, supposedly by an unwanted lover, although the man was never apprehended. It is generally said that this curse, which is popularly called the Caston Gall, is abridged by midnight on Christmas Eve, since the holiness of Christmas Day itself defeats it.

I put down the paper, and Holmes sprang round from the window.

"Tell me, Miss Caston," he said, "are you very superstitious?"

"No, Mr. Holmes. Not at all. I have never credited anything which could not be proved. Left to myself, I would say all this was nonsense."

"However?"

"The lady I call my aunt died on Christmas Eve, about eleven o'clock at night. She had had to break her own custom. Normally she would leave the house ten days before Christmas, staying with friends in London, and returning three days after St. Stevens. But this year she fell ill on the very day she was to leave. She was too unwell to travel, and remained so. I heard all this, you understand, from the servants, when once I had read the papers in the box, and questioned my staff firmly."

"How did she die?"

"She was asleep in her bed, and rallying, the doctor believed. The maid slipped out for a moment, and coming back found my aunt had risen as if much frightened, and was now lying by the fireplace. Her face was congested and full of horror. She was rigid, they told me, as a stone."

"The cause?"

"It was determined as a seizure of the heart."

"Could it not have been?"

"Of course her heart may have been the culprit."

Holmes glanced at me. His face was haughty and remote but his eyes had in them that dry mercurial glitter I connect with his interest.

"Mr. Holmes," said Eleanor Caston, standing up as if to confront him, "when I had questioned my servants, I put the story away with the papers. I engaged a new maid to replace Lucy. I went on with my improved life. But the months passed, and late in November, Lucy wrote to me. It was she who found my aunt lying dead, and now the girl told me she herself had also that day seen a white fox in the fields. It would be, of course, an albino, and our local hunt, I know, would think it unsporting to destroy such a creature. No, no. You must not think for a moment any of this daunted me."

"What has?"

"Three days ago, another letter came."

"From your maid?"

"Possibly. I can hardly say."

On the table near the fire she now let fall a thin, pinkish paper. Holmes bent over it. He read aloud, slowly, "'Go you out and live, or stay to die.'" He added, "Watson, come and look at this."

The paper was cheap, of a type that might be found in a thousand stationers who catered to the poor. Upon it every word had been pasted. These words were not cut from a book or newspaper, however. Each seemed to have been taken from a specimen of handwriting, and no two were alike. I remarked on this.

"Yes, Watson. Even the paper on which each word is written is of a different sort. The inks are different. Even the implement used to cut them out, unless I am much mistaken, is different." He raised the letter, and held it close to his face, and next against the light of a lamp. "A scissors here, for example, and there a small knife. And see, this edge—a larger, blunter blade. And there, the trace of a water-mark. And this one is very old. Observe the grain, and how the ink has faded, a wonder it withstood the paste—Hallo, this word is oddly spelled."

I peered more closely and saw that what had been read as 'out' was in fact 'our.' "Some error," said Holmes, "or else they could not find the proper word and substituted this. Miss Caston, I trust you have kept the envelope."

"Here it is."

"What a pity! The postmark is smudged and unreadable—from light snow or rain, perhaps."

"There had been sleet."

"But a cheap envelope, to coincide with the note-paper. The writing on the envelope is unfamiliar to you, or you would have drawn some conclusion from it. No doubt it is disguised. It looks malformed." He tossed the envelope down and rounded on her like an uncoiling snake.

"Mr. Holmes—I assure you, I was no more than mildly upset by this. People can be meddlesome and malicious."

"Do you think that you have enemies, Miss Caston?"

"None I could name. But then, I have been struck by fortune. It is sometimes possible to form a strong passion concerning another, only by reading of them say, in a newspaper. I gained my good luck suddenly, and without any merit on my part. Someone may be envious of me, without ever having met me."

"I see your studies include the human mystery, Miss Caston."

Her colour rose. One was not always certain with Holmes, if he complimented or scorned. She said, rather low, "Other things have occurred since this letter."

"Please list them."

She had gained all his attention, and now she did not falter.

"After the sleet, there was snow in our part of the country, for some days. In this snow, letters were written, under the terrace yesterday. An E, an N and an R and a V. No footsteps showed near them. This morning, I found, on coming into my study, the number five written large, and in red, on the wall. I sleep in an adjoining room and had heard nothing. Conversely, the servants say the house is full of rustlings and scratchings."

"And the white fox? Shall I assume it has been seen?"

"Oh, not by me, Mr. Holmes. But by my cook, yes, and my footman, a sensible lad. He has seen it twice, I gather, in the last week. I do not say any of this must be uncanny. But it comes very near to me."

"Indeed it seems to."

"I might leave, but why should I? I have gone long years with little or nothing, without a decent home, and now I have things I value. It would appal me to live as did my aunt, in flight each Christmas, and at length dying in such distress. Meanwhile, the day after tomorrow will be Christmas Eve."

2

After Miss Caston had departed, Holmes sat a while in meditation. It seemed our visitor wished to collect some rare books, as now and then she did, from Lightlaws in Great Orme Street. We were to meet her at Charing Cross station and board the Kentish train together at six o'clock.

"Well, Watson," said Holmes at length, "let me have your thoughts."

"It appears but too simple. Someone has taken against her luck, as she guesses. They have discovered the Caston legend and are attempting to frighten her away."

"Someone. But who is that someone?"

"As she speculated, it might be anyone."

"Come, Watson. It might, but probably things are not so vague. This would seem a most definite grudge."

"Some person then who reckons the inheritance should be theirs?"

"Perhaps."

"It has an eerie cast, nonetheless. The letters in the snow: ENRV. That has a mediaeval sound which fits Sir Hugh. The number five on the study wall. The fox."

"Pray do not omit the rustlings and scratchings."

I left him to cogitate.

Below, Mrs. Hudson was in some disarray. "Is Mr. Holmes not to be here for the festive meal?"

"I fear he may not be. Nor I. We are bound for Kent."

"And I had bought a goose!"

Outside the night was raw, and smoky with the London air. The snow had settled only somewhat, but more was promised by the look of the sky.

On the platform, Miss Caston awaited us, her parcel of books in her arm.

Holmes did not converse with us during the journey. He brooded, and might have been alone in the carriage. I was glad enough to talk to Miss Caston, who now seemed, despite the circumstances, serene and not unhappy. She spoke intelligently and amusingly, and I thought her occasional informed references to the classics might have interested Holmes, had he listened. Not once did she try to break in upon his thoughts, and yet I sensed she derived much of her resolution from his presence. I found her altogether quite charming.

Her carriage was in readiness at Chislehurst station. The drive to Crowby was a slow one, for here the snow had long settled and begun to freeze, making the lanes treacherous. How unlike the nights of London, the country night through which we moved. The atmosphere was sharp and glassy clear, and the stars blazed cold and white.

Presently we passed through an open gateway, decorated with an ancient crest. Beyond, a short drive ran between bare lime trees, to the house. It was evident the manor-farm had lost, over the years, the greater part of its grounds, although ample gardens remained, and a small area of grazing. Old, powerful oaks, their bareness outlined in white, skirted the building. This too had lost much of its original character to a later restoration, and festoons of ivy. Lights burned in tall windows at the front.

Miss Caston's small staff had done well. Fires and lamps were lit. Upstairs, Holmes and I were conducted to adjacent rooms, supplied with every comfort. The modern wallpaper and gas lighting in the corridors did not dispel the feeling of antiquity, for hilly floors and low ceilings inclined one to remember the fifteenth century.

We descended to the dining room. Here seemed to be the heart of the house. It was a broad, high chamber with beams of carved oak, russet walls, and curtains of heavy plush. Here and there hung something from another age, a Saxon double-axe, swords, and several dim paintings in gilded frames. A fire roared on the great hearth.

"Watson, leave your worship of the fire, and come out on to the terrace."

Somewhat reluctantly I followed Holmes, who now flung open the terrace doors and stalked forth into the winter night.

We were at the back of the house. Defined by snow, the gardens spread away to fields and pasture, darkly blotted by woods.

"Not there, Watson. Look down. Do you see?"

Under the steps leading from the terrace—those very steps on which the French Madame Caston had met her death—the snow lay thick and scarcely disturbed. The light of the room fell full there, upon four deeply incised letters: ENRV.

As I gazed, Holmes was off down the stair, kneeling by the letters and examining them closely.

"The snow has frozen hard and locked them in," I said. But other marks caught my eye. "Look, there are footsteps!"

"A woman's shoe. They will be Miss Caston's," said Holmes. "She too, it seems, did as I do now."

"Of course. But that was brave of her."

"She is a forthright woman, Watson. And highly acute, I believe."

Other than the scatter of woman's steps, the letters themselves, nothing was to be seen.

"They might have dropped from the sky."

Holmes stood up. "Despite her valour, it was a pity she walked about here. Some clue may have been defaced." He looked out over the gardens, with their shrubs and small trees, towards the wider landscape. "Watson, your silent shivering disturbs me. Go back indoors."

Affronted, I returned to the dining room, and found Miss Caston there, in a wine-red gown.

"They will serve dinner directly," she said. "Does Mr. Holmes join us, or shall something be kept hot for him?"

"You must excuse Holmes, Miss Caston. The problem always comes first. He is a creature of the mind."

"I know it, Doctor. Your excellent stories have described him exactly. He is the High Priest of logic and all pure, rational things. But also," she added, smiling, "dangerous, partly unhuman, a leopard, with the brain almost of a god."

I was taken aback. Yet, in the extreme colourfulness of what she had said, I did seem to make out Sherlock Holmes, both as I had portrayed him, and as I had seen him to be. A being unique.

However, at that moment Holmes returned into the room and Miss Caston moved away, casting at him only one sidelong glance.

The dinner was excellent, ably served by one of Miss Caston's two maids, and less well by the footman, Vine, a surly boy of eighteen or so. Miss Caston had told us she had dispensed with all the servants but these, a gardener and the cook.

I noticed Holmes observed the maid and the boy carefully. When they had left the room, he expressed the wish to interview each of the servants in turn. Miss Caston assured him all, save the gardener, who it seemed had gone elsewhere for Christmas, should make themselves available. The lady then left us, graciously, to our cigars.

"She is a fine and a most attractive woman," I said.

"Ah, Watson," said Holmes. He shook his head, half smiling.

"At least grant her this, she has, from what she has said, known a life less than perfect, yet she has a breeding far beyond her former station. Her talk betrays intellect and many accomplishments. But she is also womanly. She deserves her good fortune. It suits her."

"Perhaps. But our mysterious grudge-bearer does not agree with you." Then he held up his hand for silence.

From a nearby room, the crystal notes of a piano had begun to issue. It seemed very much in keeping with the lady that she should play so modestly apart, yet so beautifully, and with such delicate expression. The piece seemed transcribed from the works of Purcell, or Handel, perhaps, at his most melancholy.

"Yes," I said, "indeed, she plays delightfully."

"Watson," Holmes hissed at me. "Not the piano. Listen!"

Then I heard another sound, a dry sharp scratching, like claws. It came, I thought, from the far side of the large room, but then, startling me, it seemed to rise up into the air itself. After that there was a sort of soft quick rushing, like a fall of snow, but inside the house. We waited. All was quiet. Even the piano had fallen still.

"What can it have been, Holmes?"

He got up, and crossed to the fireplace. He began to walk about there, now and then tapping absently on the marble mantle, and the wall.

"The chimney?" I asked. "A bird, perhaps."

"Well, it has stopped."

I too went to the fireplace. On the hearth's marble lintel, upheld by two pillars, was the escutcheon I had glimpsed at the gate.

"There it is, Holmes, on the shield. De Castone's fox!"

3

To my mind, Holmes had seemed almost leisurely so far in his examination. He had not, for example, gone upstairs at once to view the study wall. Now however, he took his seat by the fire of the side parlour, and one by one, the remaining servants entered.

First came the cook, a Mrs. Castle. She was a large woman, neat and tidy, with a sad face which, I hazarded, had once been merry.

"Now, Mrs. Castle. We must thank you for your splendid dinner."

"Oh, Mr. Holmes," she said, "I am so glad that it was enjoyed. I seldom have a chance to cook for more than Miss Caston, who has only a little appetite."

"Perhaps the former Miss Caston ate more heartily."

"Indeed, sir, she did. She was a stout lady who took an interest in her food."

"But I think you have other reasons to be uneasy."

"I have seen it!"

"You refer—?"

"The white fox. Last week, before the snow fell, I saw it, shining like a ghost under the moon. I know the story of wicked old Sir Hugh. It was often told in these parts. I grew up in Chislehurst Village. The fox was said to be a legend, but my brother saw just such a white fox, when he was a boy."

"Did he indeed."

"Then there are those letters cut in the snow. And the number upstairs, and all of us asleep—a five, done in red, high upon the wall. The five days before Christmas, when the lady is in peril. A horrible thing, Mr. Holmes, if a woman may not live at her own property alone, but she must go in fear of her life."

"After the death of your former employer, you take these signs seriously."

"The first Miss Caston had never had a day's indisposition until last Christmas. She always went away just before that time. But last year her carriage stood ready on the drive every day, and every day the poor old lady would want to go down, but she was much too ill. Her poor hands and feet were swollen, and she was so dizzy she could scarce stand. Then, she was struck down, just as she had always dreaded."

"And the fox?" Holmes asked her.

The cook blinked. She said, "Yes, that was strange."

"So you did not yourself see it, on that former tragic occasion?"

"No, sir. No one did."

"But surely, Mrs. Castle, the present Miss Caston's former maid, Lucy, saw the white fox in the fields at the time of the elder lady's death?"

"Perhaps she did, sir. For it would have been about," Mrs. Castle replied ominously.

"Well, I must not keep you any longer, Mrs. Castle."

"No, sir. I need to see to my kitchen. Some cold cuts of meat have been stolen from the larder, just as happened before."

"Cold meat, you say?"

"I think someone has been in. Someone other than should have been, sir. Twice I found the door to the yard unlocked."

When she had left us, Holmes did not pause. He called in the footman, Vine. The boy appeared nervous and awkward as he had during dinner. From his mumblings, we learned that he had seen the white fox, yesterday, but no other alien thing.

"However, food has been stolen from the kitchen, has it not?"

"So cook says," the boy answered sullenly.

"A gypsy, perhaps, or a vagrant."

"I saw no one. And in the snow, they would leave their footprints."

"Well done. Yes, one would think so."

"I saw the letters dug out there," blurted the boy, "and Miss Caston standing over them, with her hand to her mouth. Look here, she says to me, who has written this?"

"And who had?"

The boy stared hard at Holmes. "You are a famous gentleman, sir. And I am nothing. Do you suspect me?"

"Should I?"

Vine cried out, "I never did anything I should not have! Not I. I wish I never had stayed here. I should have left when Lucy did. Miss Caston was a hard mistress."

I frowned, but Holmes said, amiably, "Lucy. She was obliged to care for her ailing mother, I believe."

Vine looked flustered, but he said, "The mistress never mourned her aunt, the old woman. Mistress likes only her books and piano, and her thoughts. I asked her leave to go home for the Christmas afternoon. We live only a mile or so distant, at Crowby. I should have been back by nightfall. And she says to me, Oh no, Vine. I will have you here."

"It was your place to be here," I said, "at such a time. You were then the only man in the house."

Holmes dismissed the boy.

I would have said more, but Holmes forestalled me. Instead we saw the maid, Reynolds, who had waited at dinner. She had nothing to tell us except that she had heard recent noises in the house, but took them for mice. She had been here in old Miss Caston's time, and believed the old woman died of a bad heart, aggravated by superstitious fear. Reynolds undertook to inform Holmes of this without hesitation. She also presented me with a full, if untrained, medical diagnosis, adding, "As a doctor, you will follow me, I am sure, sir."

Lastly Nettie Prince came in, the successor to Lucy, and now Miss Caston's personal maid. She had been at the house only a few months.

Nettie was decorous and at ease, treating Holmes, I thought, to his surprise, as some kind of elevated policeman.

"Is your mistress fair to you?" Holmes asked her at once.

"Yes, sir. Perfectly fair."

"You have no cause for complaint."

"None, sir. In my last employment the mistress had a temper. But Miss Caston stays cool."

"You are not fond of her, then?"

Nettie Prince raised her eyes. "I do not ask to love her, sir. Only to please her as best I can. She is appreciative of what I do, in her own way."

"Do you believe the tales of a curse on the Caston women?"

"I have heard stranger things."

"Have you."

"Miss Caston is not afraid of it, sir. I think besides she would be the match for any man, thief or murderer—even a ghost. Old Sir Hugh de Castone himself would have had to be wary of her."

"Why do you say that?"

"She talks very little of her past, but she made her way in the world with only her wits. She will not suffer a fool. And she knows a great deal."

"Yet she has sent for me."

"Yes, sir." Nettie Prince looked down. "She spoke of you, sir, and I understand you are a very important and clever gentleman."

"And yet."

Nettie said, "I am amazed, sir, at her, wanting you in. From all I know of Miss Caston, I would say she would sit up with a pistol or a dagger in her lap, and face anything out—alone!"

"Well, Watson," said Holmes, when we were once more by ourselves in the parlour.

"That last girl, Nettie Prince, seems to have the right of it. An admirable woman, Miss Caston, brave as a lioness."

"But also cold and selfish. Unsympathetic to and intolerant of her inferiors. Does anything else strike you?"

"An oddity in names, Holmes."

Holmes glanced my way. "Pray enlighten me."

"The letters in the snow, ENRV. And here we have a Nettie, a Reynolds and a Vine."

"The E?"

"Perhaps for Eleanor Caston herself."

"I see. And perhaps it strikes you too, Watson, the similarity between the names Castle and Caston? Or between Caston and Watson, each of which is almost an anagram of the other, with only the C and the W being different. Just as, for example, both your name and that of our own paragon, Mrs. Hudson, end in S.O.N."

"Holmes!"

"No, Watson, my dear fellow, you are being too complex. Think."

I thought, and shook my head.

"ENR," said Holmes, "I believe to be an abbreviation of the one name, Eleanor, where the E begins, the N centres, and the R finishes."

"But the V, Holmes."

"Not a V, Watson, a Roman five. A warning of the five dangerous days, or that Miss Caston will be the fifth victim of the Gall. Just as the number five is written in her study, where I should now like to inspect it."

Miss Caston had not gone to bed. This was not to be wondered at, yet she asked us nothing when she appeared in the upper corridor, where now the gas burned low.

"The room is here," she said, and opened a door. "A moment, while I light a lamp."

When she moved forward and struck the match, her elegant figure was outlined on the light. As she raised the lamp, a bright blue flash on the forefinger of her right hand showed a ring. It was a square cut gem, which I took at first for a pale sapphire.

"There, Mr. Holmes, Doctor. Do you see?"

The number was written in red, and quite large, above the height of a man, on the old plaster of the wall which, in most other areas, was hidden by shelves of books.

"Quite so." Holmes went forward, looked about, and took hold of a librarian's steps, kept no doubt so that Miss Caston could reach the higher book shelves. Standing up on the steps, Holmes craned close, and inspected the number. "Would you bring the lamp nearer. Thank you. Why, Miss Caston, what an exquisite ring."

"Yes, it is. It was my aunt's and too big for me, but in London today it was made to fit. A blue topaz. I am often fascinated, Mr. Holmes, by those things which are reckoned to be one thing, but are, in reality, another."

"Where are you, Watson?" asked Holmes. I duly approached. "Look at this number." I obeyed. The five was very carefully drawn, I thought, despite its size, yet in some places the edges had run, giving it a thorny, bloody look. Holmes said no more, however, and descended from the steps.

"Is it paint, Holmes?"

"Ink, I believe."

Miss Caston assented. She pointed to a bottle standing on her desk, among the books and papers there. "My own ink. And the instrument too—this paper knife."

"Yes. The stain is still on it. And here is another stain, on the blotting paper, where it was laid down."

Holmes crossed the room, and pulled aside one of the velvet curtains. Outside the night had again given way to snow. Opening the window, he leaned forth into the fluttering darkness. "The ivy is torn somewhat on the wall." He leaned out yet further. Snow fell past him, and dappled the floor. "But, curiously, not further down." He now craned upwards and the lamplight caught his face, hard as ivory, the eyes gleaming. "It is possible the intruder came down from the roof rather than up from the garden below. The bough of a tree almost touches the leads just there. But it is very thin."

"The man must be an acrobat," I exclaimed.

Holmes drew back into the room. He said, "Or admirably bold."

Miss Caston seemed pale. She stared at the window until the curtain was closed again. The room was very silent, so that the ticking of a clock on the mantle seemed loud.

Holmes spoke abruptly. "And now to bed. Tomorrow, Miss Caston, there will be much to do."

Her face to me seemed suddenly desolate. As Holmes walked from the room, I said to her, "Rest as well as you can, Miss Caston. You are in the best of hands."

"I know it, Doctor. Tomorrow, then."

4

The next morning, directly after breakfast, Holmes dispatched me to investigate the hamlet of Crowby. I had not seen Miss Caston; it seemed she was a late riser. Holmes, abroad unusually early, meanwhile wished to look at the bedchamber of the deceased elder Miss Caston. He later reported this was ornate but ordinary, equipped with swagged curtains and a bell-rope by the fire.

As I set out, not, I admit, in the best of humours, I noted that the sinister letters and the Roman number five had been obliterated from the ground below the terrace by a night's snow.

Elsewhere the heavy fall had settled, but not frozen, and in fact I had a pleasing and bracing walk. Among the beech coppices I spied pheasant, and on the holly, red berries gleamed.

Crowby was a sleepy spot, comprising two or three scattered clusters of houses, some quite fine, a lane or two, and an old ruin of a tower, where birds were nesting. There was neither a church nor an inn, the only public facility being a stone trough for the convenience of horses.

Vine's people lived in a small place nearby, but since Holmes had not suggested I look for it, or accost them, I went round the lanes and returned.

My spirits were quite high from the refreshing air, by the time I came back among the fields. Keeping to the footpath, I looked all about. It was a peaceful winter scene, with nothing abnormal or alarming in it.

When I came in sight of the house, I had the same impression. The building looked gracious, set in the white of the snow, the chimneys smoking splendidly.

Indoors, I found Vine, Reynolds and Nettie engaged in decorating the dining room with fresh-cut holly, while a tree stood ready to be dressed.

Holmes and Miss Caston were in the side parlour and I hesitated a moment before entering. A fire blazed on the parlour hearth, and a coffee pot steamed on the table. Holmes was speaking of a former case, affably and at some length. The lady sat rapt, now and then asking a sensible question.

Seeing me, however, Holmes got up and led me in.

"I have been regaling Miss Caston with an old history of ours, Watson. It turns out she has never read your account of it, though nothing else seems to have escaped her."

We passed an enjoyable couple of hours before luncheon. I thought I had seldom seen Holmes so unlike himself in company, so relaxed and amenable. Miss Caston cast a powerful spell, if even he was subject to it. But presently, when he and I were alone, he changed his face at once, like a mask.

"Watson, I believe this interesting house is no less than a rat-trap, and we are all the rats in it."

"For God's sake, Holmes, what do you mean?"

"A plot is afoot," he said, "we must on no account show full knowledge of."

"Then she is in great danger?" I asked.

He glanced at me and said, coldly, "Oh, yes, my dear Watson. I do believe she is. We are dealing with high villainy here. Be on guard. Be ready. For now, I can tell you nothing else. Except that I have looked at the elder Miss Caston's papers myself, and made an obvious discovery."

"Which is?"

"The warning or threatening letter which was sent my client had all its words cut from various correspondence kept here. I have traced every word, save one. No doubt I would find that if I persisted. They were part of bills and letters, one of which was written in the early seventeenth century. Our enemy effaced them without a care. One other incidental. The footman, Vine, resents the dismissal of his sweetheart, Lucy, who was Miss Caston's former maid."

"His sweetheart?"

"Yes, Watson. You will remember how Vine spoke of his employer, saying that she was a hard mistress."

"But surely that was because she would not let him go off for Christmas."

"That too, no doubt. But when he mentioned her hardness, it was in the past tense, and in the same breath as Lucy's dismissal. He declared he 'should have left when Lucy did.'"

"She was not dismissed, Holmes. She went of her own accord."

"No. During our morning's friendly conversation, I put it to Miss Caston that she had perhaps sent Lucy away due to some misconduct with Vine. Our client did not attempt to deceive me on this. She said at once there had been trouble of that sort."

"That then furnishes Vine and Lucy with a strong reason for malice."

"Perhaps it does."

"Did she say why she had not told you this before?"

"Miss Caston said she herself did not think either Lucy or Vine had the wit for a game of this sort. Besides, she had not wanted to blacken the girl's character. Indeed, I understand she gave Lucy an excellent reference. Miss Caston expressed to me the opinion that Lucy had only been foolish and too ardent in love. She would be perfectly useful in another household."

"This is all very like her. She is a generous and intelligent woman."

Reynolds alone attended to us at lunch. The hall was by now nicely decked with boughs of holly. Miss Caston announced she would dress the tree herself in the afternoon. This she did, assisted by myself. Holmes moodily went off about his investigations.

My conversation with her was light. I felt I should do my part and try to cheer her, and she seemed glad to put dark thoughts aside. By the time tea was served, the tree had been hung with small gold and silver baubles, and the candles were in place. Miss Caston lit them just before dinner. It was a pretty sight.

That night too, Mrs. Castle had excelled. We dined royally on pheasant, with two or three ancient and dusty bottles to add zest.

Later, when Miss Caston made to leave us, Holmes asked her to remain.

"Then, I will, Mr. Holmes, but please do smoke. I have no objection to cigars. I like their smell. I think many women are of my mind, and sorry to be excluded."

The servants had withdrawn, Vine too, having noisily seen to the fire. The candles on the tree glittered. Nothing seemed further from this old, comfortable, festive room than our task.

"Miss Caston," said Holmes, regarding her keenly through the blue smoke, "the time has come when we must talk most gravely."

She took up her glass, and sipped the wine, through which the firelight shone in a crimson dart. "You find me attentive, Mr. Holmes."

"Then I will say at once what I think you know. The author of these quaint events is probably in this house."

She looked at him. "You say that I know this?"

"Were you not suspicious of it?"

"You are not intending to say that after all I believe Sir Hugh de Castone haunts me?"

"Hardly, Miss Caston."

"Then whom must I suspect? My poor servants? The affair with Lucy was nothing. She was too passionate and not clever enough. Vine was a dunce. They were better parted."

"Aside from your servants, some other may be at work here."

Just at that moment the most astonishing and unearthly screech burst through the chamber. It was loud and close and seemed to rock the very table. Holmes started violently and I sprang to my feet. Miss Caston gave a cry and the glass almost dropped from her hand. The shriek then came again, yet louder and more terribly. The hair rose on my head. I looked wildly about, and even as I did so, a scratching and scrabbling, incorporeal yet insistent, rushed as it seemed through thin air itself, ascending until high above our heads in the beamed ceiling, where it ended.

I stood transfixed, until I heard Holmes's rare dry laughter.

"Well, Watson, and have you never heard such a noise?"

Miss Caston in her turn also suddenly began laughing, although she seemed quite shaken.

"A fox, Watson. It was a fox."

"But in God's name, Holmes—it seemed to go up through the air—"

"Through the wall, no doubt, and up into the roof."

I sat and poured myself another glass of brandy. Holmes, as almost always, was quite right. A fox has an uncanny, ghastly cry, well known to country dwellers. "But then the creature exists?"

"Why not?" said Holmes. "White foxes sometimes occur hereabouts, so we have learnt from Mrs. Castle, and from Derwent's book. Besides, in this case, someone has made sure a white fox is present. Before we left London, I made an inquiry of Messrs Samps and Brown, the eccentric furriers in Kempton Street, who deal in such rarities. They advised me that a live albino fox had been purchased through them, a few months ago."

"By whom?" I asked.

"By a man who was clearly the agent of another, a curious gentleman, very much muffled up and, alas, so far untraceable." Holmes looked directly at Miss Caston. "I think you can never have read all the papers which your aunt left you. Or you would be aware of three secret passages which run through this house. None is very wide or high, but they were intended to conceal men at times of religious or political unrest, and are not impassable."

"Mr. Holmes, I have said, I never bothered much with the papers. Do you mean that someone is hiding—in my very walls?"

"Certainly the white fox has made its earth there. No doubt encouraged to do so by a trail of meat stolen from the larder."

"What is this persecutor's aim?" she demanded fiercely. "To frighten me away?"

"Rather more than that, I think," said Holmes, laconically.

"And there is a man involved?"

"It would seem so, Miss Caston, would you not say?"

She rose and moved slowly to the hearth. There she stood in graceful profile, gazing at the shield above the fireplace.

"Am I," she said at last, "surrounded by enemies?"

"No, Miss Caston," I replied. "We are here."

"What should I do?"

Holmes said, "Perhaps you should think very clearly, Miss Caston, delve into the library of your mind, and see what can be found there."

"Then I will." She faced him. She was not beseeching, more proud. "But you mean to save me, Mr. Holmes?"

He showed no expression. His eyes had turned black as two jets in the lamplight. "I will save whomever I can, Miss Caston, that deserves it. But never rate me too highly. I am not infallible."

She averted her head suddenly, as if at a light blow. "But you are one of the greatest men living."

So saying, and without bidding us good night, she gathered her skirts and left the room. Holmes got up, and walked to the fire, into which he cast the butt of his cigar.

"Watson, did you bring your revolver?"

"Of course I did."

"That is just as well."

"Tomorrow is Christmas Eve," I said, "according to the story, the last day of the Gall."

"Hmm." He knocked lightly on the wall, producing a hollow note. "One of the passages runs behind this wall, Watson, and up into the attics, I am sure. The other two I have not yet been able to locate, since the plans are old and hardly to be deciphered. Just like the postmark on the letter sent to Miss Caston. Did you notice, by the by, Watson, that although the envelope had been wetted and so conveniently smudged, no moisture penetrated to the letter itself?"

I too tossed my cigar butt into the flames.

"Fires have the look of Hell, do you think, Watson? Is Hell cheerful after all, for the malign ones cast down there?"

"You seem depressed. And you spoke to her as if the case might be beyond you."

"Did I, old man? Well, there must be one or two matches I lose. I am not, as I said, infallible."

Leaving me amazed, he vacated the room, and soon after I followed him. In my well-appointed bedchamber, I fell into a restless sleep, and woke with first light, uneasy and perplexed.

5

I now acknowledged that Holmes was keeping back from me several elements of the puzzle he was grappling with. This was not the first occasion when he had done so, nor would it be the last. Though I felt the exclusion sharply, I knew he would have reasons for it, which seemed wise to him, at least.

However, I checked my revolver before breakfast. Going downstairs, I found I would eat my toast and drink my coffee alone. Miss Caston, as yesterday, was above, and Holmes had gone off, Vine grudgingly told me, on his own errands.

I amused myself as I could, examining the old swords, and finding a distinct lack of newspapers, tried the books in the library. They proved too heavy for my present scope of concentration.

About noon, Holmes returned, shaking the snow off his coat and hat. A blizzard was blowing up, the white flakes whirling, hiding the lawns, trees and fields beyond the windows. We went into the dining room.

"Read this," said Holmes, thrusting a telegram into my hands. I read it. It came from the firm of Samps and Brown, Furriers to the Discerning. A white fox had been purchased through their auspices on 15th October, and delivered to the care of a Mr. Smith.

"But Holmes, this was the very information you relayed last night."

"Just so. It was the information I expected to get today. But the telegram was kept for me at Chislehurst Village."

"Then why—"

"I gambled for once on its being a fact. I dearly wanted to see how Miss Caston would take it."

"It frightened her, Holmes, I have no doubt. What else?"

"Oh, did it frighten her? She kept a cool head."

"She is brave and self-possessed."

"She is a schemer."

He shocked me. I took a moment to find words. "Why on earth do you say so?"

"Watson, I despair of you. A lady's charms can disarm you utterly. And she well knows that, I think."

"She speaks more highly of you," I angrily asserted.

"I am sure that she does, which is also a way of disarming you, my dear fellow. Sit down, and listen to me. No, not there, this chair, I suggest, away from the fire."

I obeyed him. "You believe someone listens in the secret passage behind the wall there?"

"I think it possible. But this is a peculiar business and certainly its heroine has got me into a mode of distrust."

We sat down, and Holmes began to talk: "Miss Caston came to us, Watson, well-versed in all your tales of my work, inaccurate and embellished as they are. She brought with her the legend of the Caston Gall, which legend seems to be real enough, in as much as it exists in Derwent and elsewhere. Four Caston women, widows or spinsters, have apparently died here on one of the five days before Christmas. But the causes of Miss Caston's recent alarm—the writing in the snow, the number on the wall, the warning letter, the white fox—all these things have been achieved, I now suppose, by the lady herself."

"You will tell me how."

"I will. She had easy access to the letters and documents of her aunt, and herself cut out the words, using different implements, and pasting them on a sheet of cheap paper which may be come on almost anywhere. She was impatient, it is true, and used the word 'our' where 'out' eluded her. In her impatience, too, she hired some low person of no imagination to procure the fox and bring it here—Mr. Smith, indeed. Then she herself took cold meat from the larder to lure the animal to a tenancy inside the passageway, where it has since been heard scratching and running about. The door of the kitchen was found—not forced, nor tampered with, I have checked—but unlocked, twice. And if unlocked from the outside, why not from the inside? Again, her impatience perhaps, led her to this casualness. She would have done better to have left some sign of more criminal work, but then again, she may have hoped it would be put down to the carelessness of her staff. The letters in the snow she scratched there herself, then stood over them exclaiming. Hence her footsteps mark the snow, but no others. The abbreviation of her name and the use of the Roman five are not uningenious, I will admit—she has been somewhat heavy-handed elsewhere. In the study, she herself wrote the number five upon the wall. Standing on the librarian's steps, I had to lean down some way, the exact distance needed for a woman of her height, on those same steps, to form the number. You noticed the five, though drawn carefully, was also three times abruptly smeared, particularly on the lower curve. This was where her blue topaz ring, which at that time did not properly fit her, slipped down and pulled the ink, just as it had on her note to me. The ivy she herself disarranged from the window, with an almost insolent lack of conviction."

"Holmes, it seems to me that this once you assume a great deal too much—"

"At Baker Street I watched her in the window as she looked at me. My back was turned to her, and in her obvious unease, she forgot I might see her lamplit reflection on the night outside. Her face, Watson, was as predatory as that of any hawk. I fancied then she was not to be trusted. And there is too much that fits my notion."

"When the fox screamed, I thought she would faint."

"It is a frightful cry, and she had not anticipated it. That one moment was quite genuine."

"Vine," I said, "and Lucy."

"I have not decided on their role in this, save that the boy is obviously disgruntled and the girl maybe was not sensible. As for the letter Lucy is said to have written to Miss Caston, that first warning which so unfortunately was thrown away, being thought at the time of no importance—it never existed. Why should Lucy, dismissed from her employment and her lover, desire to warn the inventor of her loss?"

"Perhaps Lucy meant to frighten her."

"An interesting deduction, Watson, on which I congratulate you. However, you must look at the other side of the coin. If the inventor of Lucy's loss received a sinister warning from her, would she too not conclude it was an attempt to frighten?"

"Very well. But the deaths, Holmes. I too have read Derwent. The elder Miss Caston undeniably died here. The other three women certainly seem to have done."

"There is such a thing as coincidence, Watson. Mistress Hannah Castone choked on a chicken bone. The French lady slipped on the icy stair. Maria Caston was shot by a spurned and vengeful suitor. The aunt was apoplectic and terrified out of her wits by having to remain in the house at Christmas. You as a doctor will easily see the possibility of death in such a situation."

"She had left her bed and lay by the fireplace."

"In her agony, and finding herself alone, she struggled to reach the bell-rope and so summon help."

"And the bell-rope is by the fire."

"Phenomenal, Watson."

"By God, Holmes, for once I wish you might be in error."

"I seldom am in error. Think of our subject, Watson. She has come from a miserable life, which has toughened her almost into steel, to a great fortune. Now she thinks she may have anything she wants, and do as she wishes. She flies in the face of convention, as exemplified in her refusal to wear mourning for the old lady. She prefers, now she can afford better, an inferior writing-paper she likes—a little thing, but how stubborn, how wilful. And she has got us here by dint of her wiles and her lies."

"Then in God's name why?"

"Of that I have no definite idea. But she is in the grip of someone, we may be sure of it. Some powerful man who bears me a grudge. He has a honed and evil cast of mind, and works her strings like a master of marionettes. Certain women, and often the more strong among their sex, are made slaves by the man who can subdue them. And now, old chap, I shall be delighted to see you later."

I was so downcast and irascible after our talk, I went up to my room, where I wrote out the facts of the case up to that point. These notes have assisted me now, in putting the story together at last.

When I went down to lunch, I found Holmes once more absent, and Miss Caston also. She sent me her compliments by Nettie, who said her mistress was suffering from a cruel headache to which she was prone. Naturally I asked if I could be of any help. I was rather relieved, things standing as now they did, when Nettie thanked me and declined.

Vine waited on me at lunch, in a slapdash manner. Afterwards I played Patience in the side parlour, and was soundly beaten, as it were, nothing coming out. Beyond the long windows which ran to the floor, as they did in the dining room, the snow swirled on with a leaden feverishness.

Finally I went upstairs again to dress for dinner. I had on me, I remember, that sensation I experienced in my army days when an action was delayed. Some great battle was imminent, but the facts of it obscured. I could only curb my fretfulness and wait, trusting to my commander, Sherlock Holmes.

Outside, night had thickened, and the snow still fell. Dressed, I kept my revolver by me. Tonight was the fifth night of the Caston curse, and despite Holmes's words, perhaps because of them, I still feared not only for my friend, but for Eleanor Caston.

As I went down the corridor, for some reason I paused to look out again, through a window there. Before me on the pale ground I saw something run glimmering, like a phantom. Despite what we had learned, I drew back, startled. It was the Caston fox, pure white, its eyes flashing green in the light of the windows.

"Yes, sir. The beast exists."

I turned, and there stood the footman, Vine. He was clad, not in his uniform, but in a decent farmer's best, and looked in it both older and more sober.

"The fox is not a myth," I said.

"No, sir."

"Why are you dressed in that way?"

"I am going home. I have given her my notice. I have no mind to stay longer. I will take up my life on the land, as I was meant to. There is a living to be made there, without bowing and scraping. And when I have enough put by, I shall bring Lucy home, and marry her."

From a bad-tempered boy he had become a man, I saw. My instinct was to respect him, but I said, "And what of your mistress, Miss Caston?"

"She may do as she pleases. There was love, but nothing improper between Lucy and me. That was her excuse. Miss Caston threw Lucy out on account of her reading—and I will say it now, on account of you, sir, and Mr. Holmes."

Dumbfounded, I asked what he meant.

"Why, sir, when Miss Caston came here, she would rather have read the coal-scuttle than anything of yours."

"Indeed."

"Any popular story was beneath her. She likes the Greek philosophers and all such. But when she had her headaches, Lucy read to her, and one day it was a tale of yours, sir, concerning Mr. Holmes. And after that, Lucy read others, since Miss Caston asked for them."

My vanity was touched, I confess. But there was more to this than my vanity.

"She made a regular study of Mr. Holmes, through your tales, Doctor. And then, this last September, she said Lucy must go, as her conduct with me was unseemly, which it never was. Even so, she gave my girl a fine reference, and Lucy has work now in a house better than this one."

I was searching in my mind for what to say, when the lad gave me a nod, and walked away. There was a travelling bag in his hand.

"But the weather, the snow," I said.

"This is a cold house," said he. "Snow is nothing to that." And he was gone.

Downstairs, I found Holmes, as I had hoped to. He stood by the dining room hearth, drinking a whisky and soda.

"Well, Watson, some insight has come your way."

"How do you know?"

"Merely look in a mirror. Something has fired you up."

We drew back from the hearth, mindful of a listener in the secret place behind it, and I told him what Vine had said.

"Ah, yes," said Holmes. "She has studied me. This confirms what I suspected. I think you see it too, do you not?"

"It is very strange."

"But the man who is her master, despite all my efforts, with which I will not tax you, he eludes me. What is his purpose? His name? It is a long way round to come at me."

Just then, Eleanor Caston entered the room. She wore a gown the dark colour of the green holly, which displayed her milk-white shoulders. Her burnished hair was worn partly loose. Seldom have I seen so fetching a woman.

Our dinner was an oddity. Only Reynolds waited on us, but efficiently. No one spoke of the affair at hand, as if it did not exist and we were simply there to celebrate the season.

Then Miss Caston said, "At midnight, all this will be over. I shall be safe, then, surely. I do believe your presence, Mr. Holmes, has driven the danger off. I will be forever in your debt."

Holmes had talked during the meal with wit and energy. When he set himself to charm, which was not often, there was none better. Now he lit a cigarette, and said, "The danger is not at all far off, Miss Caston. Notice the clock. It lacks only half an hour to midnight. Now we approach the summit, and the peril is more close than it has ever been."

She stared at him, very pale, her bright eyes wide.

"What then?" she asked.

"Watson," said Holmes, "be so kind, old man, as to excuse us. Miss Caston and I will retire into the parlour there. It is necessary I speak to her alone. Will you remain here, in the outer room, and stay alert?"

I was at once full of apprehension. Nevertheless I rose without argument, as they left the table. Eleanor Caston seemed to me in those moments almost like a woman gliding in a trance. She and Holmes moved into the parlour, and the door was shut. I took my stance by the fireplace of the dining room.

How slowly those minutes ticked by. Never before, or since, I think, have I observed both hands of a clock moving. Through a gap in the curtains, snow and black night blew violently about together. A log settled, and I started. There was no other sound. Yet then I heard Miss Caston laugh. She had a pretty laugh, musical as her piano. There after, the silence came again.

I began to pace about. Holmes had given me no indication whether I should listen at the door, or what I should do. Now and then I touched the revolver in my pocket.

At last, the hands of the clock closed upon midnight. At this hour, the curse of the Gall, real or imagined, was said to end.

Taking up my glass, I drained it. The next second I heard Miss Caston give a wild shrill cry, followed by a bang, and a crash like that of a breaking vase.

I ran to the parlour door and flung it open. I met a scene that checked me.

The long doors stood wide on the terrace and the night and in at them blew the wild snow, flurrying down upon the carpet. Only Eleanor Caston was in the room. She lay across the sofa, her hair streaming, her face as white as porcelain, still as a waxwork.

I crossed to her, my feet crunching on glass that had scattered from a broken pane of the windows. I thought to find her dead, but as I reached her, she stirred and opened her eyes.

"Miss Caston—what has happened? Are you hurt?"

"Yes," she said, "wounded mortally."

There was no mark on her, however, and now she gave me an awful smile. "He is out there."

"Who is? Where is Holmes?"

She sank back again and shut her eyes. "On the terrace. Or in the garden. Gone."

I went at once to the windows, taking out the revolver as I did so. Even through the movement of the snow, I saw Holmes at once, at the far end of the terrace, lit up by the lighted windows of the house. He was quite alone. I called to him, and at my voice he turned, glancing at me, shaking his head, and holding up one hand to bar me from the night. He too appeared unharmed and his order to remain where I was seemed very clear.

Going back into the dining room I fetched a glass of brandy. Miss Caston had sat up, and took it from me on my return.

"How chivalrous you always are, Doctor."

Her pulse was strong, although not steady. I hesitated to increase her distress but the circumstances brooked no delay. "Miss Caston, what has gone on here?"

"Oh, I have gambled and lost. Shall I tell you? Pray sit down. Close the window if you wish. He will not return this way."

Unwillingly I did as she said, and noted Holmes had now vanished, presumably into the icy garden below.

"Well then, Miss Caston."

She smiled again that sorry smile, and began to speak.

"All my life I have had nothing, but then my luck changed. It was as if Fate took me by the hand, and anything I had ever wanted might at last be mine. I have always been alone. I had no parents, no friends. I do not care for people much, they are generally so stupid. And then, Lucy, my maid read me your stories, Doctor, of the wonderful Mr. Holmes. Oh, I was not struck by your great literary ability. My intimates have been Dante and Sophocles, Milton, Aristotle and Erasmus. I am sure you do not aspire to compete with them. But Holmes, of course—ah, there. His genius shines through your pages like a great white light from an obscure lantern. At first I thought you had invented this marvellous being, this man of so many parts: chemist, athlete, actor, detective, deceiver—the most effulgent mind this century has known. So ignorant I was. But little Lucy told me that Sherlock Holmes was quite real. She even knew of his address, 221B Baker Street, London."

Miss Caston gazed into her thoughts and I watched her, prepared at any moment for a relapse, for she was so blanched, and she trembled visibly.

"From your stories, I have learned that Holmes is attracted by anything which engages his full interest. That he honours a mind which can duel with his own. And here you have it all, Doctor. I had before me in the legend of this house, the precise means to offer him just such a plot as many of your tales describe—the Caston Gall, which of course is a farrago of anecdote, coincidence and superstition. I had had nothing, but now I had been given so much, why should I not try for everything?"

"You are saying you thought that Holmes—"

"I am saying I wanted the esteem and friendship of Mr. Sherlock Holmes, that especial friendship and esteem which any woman hopes for, from the man she has come to reverence above all others."

"In God's name, Miss Caston! Holmes!"

"Oh, you have written often enough of his coldness, his arrogance, and his dislike of my sex. But then, what are women as a rule but silly witless creatures, geese done up in ribbons. I have a mind. I sought to show him. I knew he would solve my riddle in the end, and so he did. I thought he would laugh and shake my hand."

"He believed you in the toils of some villain, a man ruthless and powerful."

"As if no woman could ever connive for herself. He told me what he thought. I convinced him of the truth, and that I worked only for myself, but never to harm him. I wanted simply to render him some sport."

"Miss Caston," I said, aghast, "you will have angered him beyond reason."

Her form drooped. She shut her eyes once more. "Yes, you are quite right. I have enraged him. Never have I seen such pitiless fury in a face. It was as if he struck me with a lash of steel. I was mistaken, and have lost everything."

Agitated as I was, I tried to make her sip the brandy but she only held it listlessly in one hand, and stood up, leaning by the fireplace.

"I sent Lucy away because she began, I thought, to suspect my passion. There has been nothing but ill-will round me since then. You see, I am becoming as superstitious as the rest. I should like to beg you to intercede for me—but I know it to be useless."

"I will attempt to explain to him, when he is calmer, that you meant no annoyance. That you mistakenly thought to amuse him."

As I faltered, she rounded on me, her eyes flaming. "You think you are worthy of him, Watson? The only friend he will tolerate. What I would have offered him! My knowledge, such as it is, my ability to work, which is marvellous. All my funds. My love, which I have never given any other. In return I would have asked little. Not marriage, not one touch of his hand. I would have lain down and let him walk upon me if it would have given him ease."

She raised her glass suddenly and threw it on the hearth. It broke in sparkling pieces.

"There is my heart," said she. "Good night, Doctor." And with no more than that, she went from the room.

I never saw her again. In the morning when we left that benighted house, she sent down no word. Her carriage took us to Chislehurst, from where we made a difficult Christmas journey back to London. Holmes's mood was beyond me, and I kept silent as we travelled. He was like one frozen, but to my relief his health seemed sound. On our return, I left him alone as much as I could. Nor did I quiz him on what he did, or what means he used to allay his bitterness and inevitable rage. It was plain to me the episode had been infinitely horrible to him. He was so finely attuned. Another would not have felt it so. She had outraged his very spirit.

Worse, she had trespassed.

Not until the coming of a new year did he refer to the matter, and then only once. "The Caston woman, Watson. I am grateful to you for your tact."

"It was unfortunate."

"You suppose her deranged and vulgar, and that I am affronted at having been duped."

"No, Holmes. I should never put it in that way. And she was but too plausible."

"There are serpents among the apples, Watson," was all he said. And turning from me, he struck out two or three discordant notes on his violin, then put it from him and strode into the other room.

We have not discussed it since, the case of the Caston Gall.

A year later, this morning, which is once more the day of Christmas Eve, I noted a small item in the paper. A Miss Eleanor Rose Caston died yesterday, at her house near Chislehurst. It is so far understood she had accidentally taken too much of an opiate prescribed to her for debilitating headaches. She passed in her sleep, and left no family nor any heirs. She was twenty-six years of age.

Whether Holmes, who takes an interest in all notices of death, has seen this sad little obituary, I do not know. He has said nothing. For myself, I feel a deep regret for her. If we were all to be punished for our foolishness, as I believe Hamlet says, who should 'scape whipping? Although crime is often solvable, there can be no greater mystery than that of the human heart.

This story is respectfully dedicated to the memory of the late, unique Jeremy Brett, a fine actor, and a definitive Sherlock Holmes.

—Tanith Lee

A STUDY IN EMERALD

by Neil Gaiman

Neil Gaiman's most recent novel, *The Graveyard Book*, won the prestigious New-bery Medal, given to great works of children's literature. Other books include *American Gods, Coraline*, and *Anansi Boys*, among many others. In addition to his novel-writing, Gaiman is also the writer of the popular *Sandman* comic book series, and has done work in television and film. His novels *Coraline* and *Stardust* were recently made into feature films.

A central character in Lovecraft's fictional world is the evil extraterrestrial god Cthulhu, described most fully in the story "The Call of Cthulhu." Cthulhu, octopus-headed and dragon-winged, was imprisoned on Earth long ago in the underwater city R'lyeh, where he exists in a state of undeath, transmitting his otherworldly dreams to certain psychically sensitive individuals, some of whom have sworn to serve him when the stars are right and Cthulhu rises to conquer the world. In Lovecraft's fiction, such a cataclysmic event always lies in our future, but this next story presents an alternate reality in which such monsters have dominated humanity for centuries. This version of England saw not a Norman conquest but a Lovecraftian one, and these strange creatures have established themselves as monarchs around the globe. Conan Doyle's first Sherlock Holmes adventure was called *A Study in Scarlet*, in reference to a bloody murder. The title "A Study in Emerald" also refers to a bloody murder, albeit one involving an entirely different sort of victim and an entirely different sort of blood. This is a world darker and stranger than our own, and this is a case that will pose quite a challenge to a certain detective and his loyal sidekick.

1. THE NEW FRIEND

Fresh *From Their Stupendous European Tour, where they performed before several of the* **CROWNED HEADS OF EUROPE,** *garnering their* plaudits *and* praise *with* magnificent dramatic performances, *combining both* **COMEDY** *and* **TRAGEDY,** *the* Strand Players *wish to make it known that they shall be appearing at the* Royal Court Theatre, Drury Lane, *for a* **LIMITED ENGAGEMENT** *in April,* *at which they will present* "My Look-Alike Brother Tom!" "The

421

*Littlest Violet-Seller" and "The Great Old Ones Come," (this last
an Historical Epic of Pageantry and Delight); each an entire play in
one act! Tickets are available now from the Box Office.*

It is the immensity, I believe. The hugeness of things below. The darkness of dreams.

But I am wool-gathering. Forgive me. I am not a literary man.

I had been in need of lodgings. That was how I met him. I wanted someone to share the cost of rooms with me. We were introduced by a mutual acquaintance, in the chemical laboratories of St. Bart's. "You have been in Afghanistan, I perceive"; that was what he said to me, and my mouth fell open and my eyes opened very wide.

"Astonishing," I said.

"Not really," said the stranger in the white lab coat who was to become my friend. "From the way you hold your arm, I see you have been wounded, and in a particular way. You have a deep tan. You also have a military bearing, and there are few enough places in the Empire that a military man can be both tanned and, given the nature of the injury to your shoulder and the traditions of the Afghan cave folk, tortured."

Put like that, of course, it was absurdly simple. But then, it always was. I had been tanned nut brown. And I had indeed, as he had observed, been tortured.

The gods and men of Afghanistan were savages, unwilling to be ruled from Whitehall or from Berlin or even from Moscow, and unprepared to see reason. I had been sent into those hills, attached to the —th Regiment. As long as the fighting remained in the hills and mountains, we fought on an equal footing. When the skirmishes descended into the caves and the darkness, then we found ourselves, as it were, out of our depth and in over our heads.

I shall not forget the mirrored surface of the underground lake, nor the thing that emerged from the lake, its eyes opening and closing, and the singing whispers that accompanied it as it rose, wreathing their way about it like the buzzing of flies bigger than worlds.

That I survived was a miracle, but survive I did, and I returned to England with my nerves in shreds and tatters. The place that leechlike mouth had touched me was tattooed forever, frog white, into the skin of my now-withered shoulder. I had once been a crack shot. Now I had nothing, save a fear of the world-beneath-the-world akin to panic, which meant that I would gladly pay sixpence of my army pension for a hansom cab rather than a penny to travel underground.

Still, the fogs and darknesses of London comforted me, took me in. I had lost my first lodgings because I screamed in the night. I had been in Afghanistan; I was there no longer.

"I scream in the night," I told him.

"I have been told that I snore," he said. "Also I keep irregular hours, and I often use the mantelpiece for target practice. I will need the sitting room to meet clients. I am selfish, private, and easily bored. Will this be a problem?"

I smiled and shook my head and extended my hand. We shook on it.

The rooms he had found for us, in Baker Street, were more than adequate for two bachelors. I bore in mind all my friend had said about his desire for privacy, and I forbore from asking what it was he did for a living. Still, there was much to pique my curiosity. Visitors would arrive at all hours, and when they did I would leave the sitting room and repair to my bedroom, pondering what they could have in common with my friend: the pale woman with one eye bone white, the small man who looked like a commercial traveller, the portly dandy in his velvet jacket, and the rest. Some were frequent visitors; many others came only once, spoke to him, and left, looking troubled or looking satisfied.

He was a mystery to me.

We were partaking of one of our landlady's magnificent breakfasts one morning when my friend rang the bell to summon that good lady. "There will be a gentleman joining us, in about four minutes," he said. "We will need another place at table."

"Very good," she said, "I'll put more sausages under the grill."

My friend returned to perusing his morning paper. I waited for an explanation with growing impatience. Finally, I could stand it no longer. "I don't understand. How could you know that in four minutes we would be receiving a visitor? There was no telegram, no message of any kind."

He smiled thinly. "You did not hear the clatter of a brougham several minutes ago? It slowed as it passed us—obviously as the driver identified our door—then it sped up and went past, up into the Marylebone Road. There is a crush of carriages and taxicabs letting off passengers at the railway station and at the waxworks, and it is in that crush that anyone wishing to alight without being observed will go. The walk from there to here is but four minutes…"

He glanced at his pocket watch, and as he did so I heard a tread on the stairs outside.

"Come in, Lestrade," he called. "The door is ajar, and your sausages are just coming out from under the grill."

A man I took to be Lestrade opened the door, then closed it carefully behind him. "I should not," he said. "But truth to tell, I have not had a chance to break my fast this morning. And I could certainly do justice to a few of those sausages." He was the small man I had observed on several occasions previously, whose demeanour was that of a traveller in rubber novelties or patent nostrums.

My friend waited until our landlady had left the room before he said, "Obviously, I take it this is a matter of national importance."

"My stars," said Lestrade, and he paled. "Surely the word cannot be out already. Tell me it is not." He began to pile his plate high with sausages, kipper fillets, kedgeree, and toast, but his hands shook a little.

"Of course not," said my friend. "I know the squeak of your brougham wheels, though, after all this time: an oscillating G-sharp above high C. And if Inspector Lestrade of Scotland Yard cannot publically be seen to come into the parlour of London's only consulting detective, yet comes anyway, and without having had his breakfast, then I know that this is not a routine case. Ergo, it involves those above us and is a matter of national importance."

Lestrade dabbed egg yolk from his chin with his napkin. I stared at him. He did not look like my idea of a police inspector, but then, my friend looked little enough like my idea of a consulting detective—whatever that might be.

"Perhaps we should discuss the matter privately," Lestrade said, glancing at me.

My friend began to smile impishly, and his head moved on his shoulders as it did when he was enjoying a private joke. "Nonsense," he said. "Two heads are better than one. And what is said to one of us is said to us both."

"If I am intruding—" I said gruffly, but he motioned me to silence.

Lestrade shrugged. "It's all the same to me," he said, after a moment. "If you solve the case, then I have my job. If you don't, then I have no job. You use your methods, that's what I say. It can't make things any worse."

"If there's one thing that a study of history has taught us, it is that things can always get worse," said my friend. "When do we go to Shoreditch?"

Lestrade dropped his fork. "This is too bad!" he exclaimed. "Here you are, making sport of me, when you know all about the matter! You should be ashamed—"

"No one has told me anything of the matter. When a police inspector walks into my room with fresh splashes of mud of that peculiar yellow hue on his boots and trouser legs, I can surely be forgiven for presuming that he has recently walked past the diggings at Hobbs Lane in Shoreditch, which is the only place in London that particular mustard-coloured clay seems to be found."

Inspector Lestrade looked embarrassed. "Now you put it like that," he said, "it seems so obvious."

My friend pushed his plate away from him. "Of course it does," he said, slightly testily.

We rode to the East End in a cab. Inspector Lestrade had walked up to the Marylebone Road to find his brougham, and left us alone.

"So you are truly a consulting detective?" I said.

"The only one in London, or perhaps the world," said my friend. "I do not take cases. Instead, I consult. Others bring me their insoluble problems, they describe them, and, sometimes, I solve them."

"Then those people who come to you..."

"Are, in the main, police officers, or are detectives themselves, yes."

It was a fine morning, but we were now jolting about the edges of the Rookery of St. Giles, that warren of thieves and cutthroats which sits on London like a cancer on the face of a pretty flower seller, and the only light to enter the cab was dim and faint.

"Are you sure that you wish me along with you?"

In reply, my friend stared at me without blinking. "I have a feeling," he said. "I have a feeling that we were meant to be together. That we have fought the good fight, side by side, in the past or in the future, I do not know. I am a rational man, but I have learned the value of a good companion, and from the moment I clapped eyes on you, I knew I trusted you as well as I do myself. Yes. I want you with me."

I blushed, or said something meaningless. For the first time since Afghanistan, I felt that I had worth in the world.

2. THE ROOM

Victor's "Vitae"! An electrical fluid! Do your limbs and nether regions lack life? Do you look back on the days of your youth with envy? Are the pleasures of the flesh now buried and forgot? Victor's "Vitae" will bring life where life has long been lost: even the oldest warhorse can be a proud stallion once more! Bringing Life to the Dead: from an old family recipe and the best of modern science. To receive signed attestations of the efficacy of Victor's "Vitae" write to the V. von F. Company. 1b Cheap Street. London.

It was a cheap rooming house in Shoreditch. There was a policeman at the front door. Lestrade greeted him by name and made to usher us in, but my friend squatted on the doorstep and pulled a magnifying glass from his coat pocket. He examined the mud on the wrought-iron boot scraper, prodding at it with his forefinger. Only when he was satisfied would he let us go inside.

We walked upstairs. The room in which the crime had been committed was obvious: it was flanked by two burly constables.

Lestrade nodded to the men, and they stood aside. We walked in.

I am not, as I said, a writer by profession, and I hesitate to describe that place, knowing that my words cannot do it justice. Still, I have begun this narrative, and I fear I must continue. A murder had been committed in that little bedsit. The body, what was left of it, was still there on the floor. I saw it, but at first, somehow, I did not see it. What I saw instead was what had sprayed and gushed from the throat and chest of the victim: in colour it ranged from bile green to grass green. It had soaked into the threadbare carpet and spattered the wallpaper. I imagined it for one moment the work of some hellish artist who had decided to create a study in emerald.

After what seemed like a hundred years I looked down at the body, opened like a rabbit on a butcher's slab, and tried to make sense of what I saw. I removed my hat, and my friend did the same.

He knelt and inspected the body, examining the cuts and gashes. Then he pulled out his magnifying glass and walked over to the wall, investigating the gouts of drying ichor.

"We've already done that," said Inspector Lestrade.

"Indeed?" said my friend. "What did you make of this, then? I do believe it is a word."

Lestrade walked to the place my friend was standing and looked up. There was a word, written in capitals, in green blood, on the faded yellow wallpaper, some little way above Lestrade's head. "*Rache...?*" said Lestrade, spelling it out. "Obviously he was going to write *Rachel,* but he was interrupted. So—we must look for a woman..."

My friend said nothing. He walked back to the corpse, and picked up its hands, one after the other. The fingertips were clean of ichor. "I think we have established that the word was not written by His Royal Highness."

"What the devil makes you say—"

"My dear Lestrade. Please give me some credit for having a brain. The corpse is obviously not that of a man—the colour of his blood, the number of limbs, the eyes, the position of the face—all these things bespeak the blood royal. While I cannot say *which* royal line, I would hazard that he is an heir, perhaps—no, second to the throne—in one of the German principalities."

"That is amazing." Lestrade hesitated, then he said, "This is Prince Franz Drago of Bohemia. He was here in Albion as a guest of Her Majesty Victoria. Here for a holiday and a change of air..."

"For the theatres, the whores, and the gaming tables, you mean."

"If you say so." Lestrade looked put out. "Anyway, you've given us a fine lead with this Rachel woman. Although I don't doubt we would have found her on our own."

"Doubtless," said my friend.

He inspected the room further, commenting acidly several times that the police had obscured footprints with their boots and moved things that might have been of use to anyone attempting to reconstruct the events of the previous night. Still, he seemed interested in a small patch of mud he found behind the door.

Beside the fireplace he found what appeared to be some ash or dirt.

"Did you see this?" he asked Lestrade.

"Her Majesty's police," replied Lestrade, "tend not to be excited by ash in a fireplace. It's where ash tends to be found." And he chuckled at that.

My friend took a pinch of the ash and rubbed it between his fingers, then sniffed the remains. Finally, he scooped up what was left of the material and tipped it into a glass vial, which he stoppered and placed in an inner pocket of his coat.

He stood up. "And the body?"

Lestrade said, "The palace will send their own people."

My friend nodded at me, and together we walked to the door. My friend sighed. "Inspector. Your quest for Miss Rachel may prove fruitless. Among other things, *Rache* is a German word. It means 'revenge.' Check your dictionary. There are other meanings."

We reached the bottom of the stair and walked out onto the street.

"You have never seen royalty before this morning, have you?" he asked. I shook my head. "Well, the sight can be unnerving, if you're unprepared. Why my good fellow—you are trembling!"

"Forgive me. I shall be fine in moments."

"Would it do you good to walk?" he asked, and I assented, certain that if I did not walk I would begin to scream.

"West, then," said my friend, pointing to the dark tower of the palace. And we commenced to walk.

"So," said my friend, after some time. "You have never had any personal encounters with any of the crowned heads of Europe?"

"No," I said.

"I believe I can confidently state that you shall," he told me. "And not with a corpse this time. Very soon."

"My dear fellow, whatever makes you believe—?"

In reply he pointed to a carriage, black-painted, that had pulled up fifty yards ahead of us. A man in a black top hat and a greatcoat stood by the door, holding it open, waiting silently. A coat of arms familiar to every child in Albion was painted in gold upon the carriage door.

"There are invitations one does not refuse," said my friend. He doffed his own hat to the footman, and I do believe that he was smiling as he climbed into the boxlike space and relaxed back into the soft leathery cushions.

When I attempted to speak with him during the journey to the palace, he placed his finger over his lips. Then he closed his eyes and seemed sunk deep in thought. I, for my part, tried to remember what I knew of German royalty, but apart from the Queen's consort, Prince Albert, being German, I knew little enough.

I put a hand in my pocket, pulled out a handful of coins—brown and silver, black and copper green. I stared at the portrait of our Queen stamped on each of them, and felt both patriotic pride and stark dread. I told myself I had once been a military man, and a stranger to fear, and I could remember a time when this had been the plain truth. For a moment I remembered a time when I had been a crack shot—even, I liked to think, something of a marksman—but now my right hand shook as if it were palsied, and the coins jingled and chinked, and I felt only regret.

3. THE PALACE

At Long Last Dr. Henry Jekyll is proud to announce the general release of the world-renowned "Jekyll's Powders" for popular consumption. No longer the province of the privileged few. Release the Inner You! For Inner and Outer Cleanliness! **TOO MANY PEOPLE,** *both men and women, suffer from* **CONSTIPATION OF THE SOUL!** *Relief is immediate and cheap—with Jekyll's powders! (Available in Vanilla and Original Mentholatum Formulations.)*

The Queen's consort, Prince Albert, was a big man, with an impressive handlebar mustache and a receding hairline, and he was undeniably and entirely human. He met us in the corridor, nodded to my friend and to me, did not ask us for our names or offer to shake hands.

"The Queen is most upset," he said. He had an accent. He pronounced his Ss as

Zs: Mozt. Upzet. "Franz was one of her favourites. She has many nephews. But he made her laugh so. You will find the ones who did this to him."

"I will do my best," said my friend.

"I have read your monographs," said Prince Albert. "It was I who told them that you should be consulted. I hope I did right."

"As do I," said my friend.

And then the great door was opened, and we were ushered into the darkness and the presence of the Queen.

She was called Victoria because she had beaten us in battle seven hundred years before, and she was called Gloriana because she was glorious, and she was called the Queen because the human mouth was not shaped to say her true name. She was huge— huger than I had imagined possible—and she squatted in the shadows staring down at us without moving.

Thizsz muzzst be zsolved. The words came from the shadows.

"Indeed, ma'am," said my friend.

A limb squirmed and pointed at me. *Zstepp forward.*

I wanted to walk. My legs would not move.

My friend came to my rescue then. He took me by the elbow and walked me toward Her Majesty.

Isz not to be afraid. Isz to be worthy. Isz to be a companion. That was what she said to me. Her voice was a very sweet contralto, with a distant buzz. Then the limb uncoiled and extended, and she touched my shoulder. There was a moment, but only a moment, of pain deeper and more profound than anything I have ever experienced, and then it was replaced by a pervasive sense of well-being. I could feel the muscles in my shoulder relax, and for the first time since Afghanistan, I was free from pain.

Then my friend walked forward. Victoria spoke to him, yet I could not hear her words; I wondered if they went, somehow, directly from her mind to his, if this was the Queen's counsel I had read about in the histories. He replied aloud.

"Certainly, ma'am. I can tell you that there were two other men with your nephew in that room in Shoreditch, that night—the footprints, although obscured, were unmistakable." And then, "Yes. I understand… I believe so… yes."

He was quiet when we left and said nothing to me as we rode back to Baker Street.

It was dark already. I wondered how long we had spent in the palace.

Upon our return to Baker Street, in the looking glass of my room, I observed that the frog-white skin across my shoulder had taken on a pinkish tinge. I hoped that I was not imagining it, that it was not merely the moonlight through the window.

4. THE PERFORMANCE

LIVER COMPLAINTS?! BILIOUS ATTACKS?! NEU-RASTHENIC DISTURBANCES?! QUINSY?! ARTHRITIS?!

These are just a handful of the complaints for which a professional EXSANGUINATION *can be the remedy. In our offices we have sheaves of* TESTIMONIALS *which can be inspected by the public at any time. Do not put your health in the hands of amateurs!! We have been doing this for a very long time:* V. TEPES—PROFESSIONAL EXSANGUINATOR. *(Remember! It is pronounced* Tzsep-pesh!) *Romania, Paris, London, Whitby.* You've tried the rest—NOW TRY THE BEST!!

That my friend was a master of disguise should have come as no surprise to me, yet surprise me it did. Over the next ten days a strange assortment of characters came in through our door on Baker Street—an elderly Chinese man, a young roué, a fat, red-haired woman of whose former profession there could be little doubt, and a venerable old buffer, his foot swollen and bandaged from gout. Each of them would walk into my friend's room, and with a speed that would have done justice to a music-hall "quick-change artist," my friend would walk out.

He would not talk about what he had been doing on these occasions, preferring to relax and stare off into space, occasionally making notations on any scrap of paper to hand—notations I found, frankly, incomprehensible. He seemed entirely preoccupied, so much so that I found myself worrying about his well-being. And then, late one afternoon, he came home dressed in his own clothes, with an easy grin upon his face, and he asked if I was interested in the theatre.

"As much as the next man," I told him.

"Then fetch your opera glasses," he told me. "We are off to Drury Lane."

I had expected a light opera, or something of the kind, but instead I found myself in what must have been the worst theatre in Drury Lane, for all that it had named itself after the royal court—and to be honest, it was barely in Drury Lane at all, being situated at the Shaftesbury Avenue end of the road, where the avenue approaches the Rookery of St. Giles. On my friend's advice I concealed my wallet, and following his example, I carried a stout stick.

Once we were seated in the stalls (I had bought a threepenny orange from one of the lovely young women who sold them to the members of the audience, and I sucked it as we waited), my friend said quietly, "You should only count yourself lucky that you did not need to accompany me to the gambling dens or the brothels. Or the madhouses—another place that Prince Franz delighted in visiting, as I have learned. But there was nowhere he went to more than once. Nowhere but—"

The orchestra struck up, and the curtain was raised. My friend was silent.

It was a fine-enough show in its way: three one-act plays were performed. Comic songs were sung between the acts. The leading man was tall, languid, and had a fine singing voice; the leading lady was elegant, and her voice carried through all the theatre; the comedian had a fine touch for patter songs.

The first play was a broad comedy of mistaken identities: the leading man played a pair of identical twins who had never met, but had managed, by a set of comical misadventures, each to find himself engaged to be married to the same young

430 • NEIL GAIMAN

lady—who, amusingly, thought herself engaged to only one man. Doors swung open and closed as the actor changed from identity to identity.

The second play was a heartbreaking tale of an orphan girl who starved in the snow selling hothouse violets—her grandmother recognised her at the last, and swore that she was the babe stolen ten years back by bandits, but it was too late, and the frozen little angel breathed her last. I must confess I found myself wiping my eyes with my linen handkerchief more than once.

The performance finished with a rousing historical narrative: the entire company played the men and women of a village on the shore of the ocean, seven hundred years before our modern times. They saw shapes rising from the sea, in the distance. The hero joyously proclaimed to the villagers that these were the Old Ones, whose coming was foretold, returning to us from R'lyeh, and from dim Carcosa, and from the plains of Leng, where they had slept, or waited, or passed out the time of their death. The comedian opined that the other villagers had all been eating too many pies and drinking too much ale, and they were imagining the shapes. A portly gentleman playing a priest of the Roman god tells the villagers that the shapes in the sea are monsters and demons, and must be destroyed.

At the climax, the hero beat the priest to death with his own crucifix, and prepared to welcome Them as They come. The heroine sang a haunting aria, whilst in an astonishing display of magic-lantern trickery, it seemed as if we saw Their shadows cross the sky at the back of the stage: the Queen of Albion herself, and the Black One of Egypt (in shape almost like a man), followed by the Ancient Goat, Parent to a Thousand, Emperor of all China, and the Czar Unanswerable, and He Who Presides over the New World, and the White Lady of the Antarctic Fastness, and the others. And as each shadow crossed the stage, or appeared to, from out of every throat in the gallery came, unbidden, a mighty "Huzzah!" until the air itself seemed to vibrate. The moon rose in the painted sky, and then, at its height, in one final moment of theatrical magic, it turned from a pallid yellow, as it was in the old tales, to the comforting crimson of the moon that shines down upon us all today.

The members of the cast took their bows and their curtain calls to cheers and laughter, and the curtain fell for the last time, and the show was done.

"There," said my friend. "What did you think?"

"Jolly, jolly good," I told him, my hands sore from applauding.

"Stout fellow," he said with a smile. "Let us go backstage."

We walked outside and into an alley beside the theatre, to the stage door, where a thin woman with a wen on her cheek knitted busily. My friend showed her a visiting card and she directed us into the building and up some steps to a small communal dressing room.

Oil lamps and candles guttered in front of smeared looking glasses, and men and women were taking off their makeup and costumes with no regard to the proprieties of gender. I averted my eyes. My friend seemed unperturbed. "Might I talk to Mr. Vernet?" he asked loudly.

A young woman who had played the heroine's best friend in the first play, and the saucy innkeeper's daughter in the last, pointed us to the end of the room. "Sherry! Sherry Vernet!" she called.

The man who stood up in response was lean; less conventionally handsome than he had seemed from the other side of the footlights. He peered at us quizzically. "I do not believe I have had the pleasure...?"

"My name is Henry Camberley," said my friend, drawling his speech somewhat. "You may have heard of me."

"I must confess that I have not had that privilege," said Vernet.

My friend presented the actor with an engraved card. The man looked at it with unfeigned interest. "A theatrical promoter? From the New World? My, my. And this is...?" He looked at me.

"This is a friend of mine, Mr. Sebastian. He is not of the profession."

I muttered something about having enjoyed the performance enormously, and shook hands with the actor.

My friend said, "Have you ever visited the New World?"

"I have not yet had that honour," admitted Vernet, "although it has always been my dearest wish."

"Well, my good man," said my friend, with the easy informality of a New Worlder, "maybe you'll get your wish. That last play. I've never seen anything like it. Did you write it?"

"Alas, no. The playwright is a good friend of mine. Although I devised the mechanism of the magic-lantern shadow show. You'll not see finer on the stage today."

"Would you give me the playwright's name? Perhaps I should speak to him directly, this friend of yours."

Vernet shook his head. "That will not be possible, I am afraid. He is a professional man, and does not wish his connection with the stage publically to be known."

"I see." My friend pulled a pipe from his pocket and put it in his mouth. Then he patted his pockets. "I am sorry," he began. "I have forgotten to bring my tobacco pouch."

"I smoke a strong black shag," said the actor, "but if you have no objection—"

"None!" said my friend heartily. "Why, I smoke a strong shag myself," and he filled his pipe with the actor's tobacco, and the two men puffed away while my friend described a vision he had for a play that could tour the cities of the New World, from Manhattan Island all the way to the farthest tip of the continent in the distant south. The first act would be the last play we had seen. The rest of the play might tell of the dominion of the Old Ones over humanity and its gods, perhaps imagining what might have happened if people had had no royal families to look up to—a world of barbarism and darkness. "But your mysterious professional man would be the play's author, and what occurs would be his alone to decide. Our drama would be his. But I can guarantee you audiences beyond your imaginings, and a significant share of the takings at the door. Let us say fifty percent?"

"This is most exciting," said Vernet. "I hope it will not turn out to have been a pipe dream!"

"No, sir, it shall not!" said my friend, puffing on his own pipe, chuckling at the man's joke. "Come to my rooms in Baker Street tomorrow morning, after breakfast time, say at ten, in company with your author friend, and I shall have the contracts drawn up and waiting."

With that, the actor clambered up onto his chair and clapped his hands for silence. "Ladies and gentlemen of the company, I have an announcement to make," he said, his resonant voice filling the room. "This gentleman is Henry Camberley, the theatrical promoter, and he is proposing to take us across the Atlantic Ocean, and on to fame and fortune."

There were several cheers, and the comedian said, "Well, it'll make a change from herrings and pickled cabbage," and the company laughed. It was to the smiles of all of them that we walked out of the theatre and onto the fog-wreathed streets.

"My dear fellow," I said. "Whatever was—"

"Not another word," said my friend. "There are many ears in the city."

And not another word was spoken until we had hailed a cab and clambered inside and were rattling up the Charing Cross Road.

And even then, before he said anything, my friend took his pipe from his mouth and emptied the half-smoked contents of the bowl into a small tin. He pressed the lid onto the tin and placed it into his pocket.

"There," he said. "That's the Tall Man found, or I'm a Dutchman. Now, we just have to hope that the cupidity and the curiosity of the Limping Doctor proves enough to bring him to us tomorrow morning."

"The Limping Doctor?"

My friend snorted. "That is what I have been calling him. It was obvious, from footprints and much else besides when we saw the prince's body, that two men had been in that room that night: a tall man, who, unless I miss my guess, we have just encountered, and a smaller man with a limp, who eviscerated the prince with a professional skill that betrays the medical man."

"A doctor?"

"Indeed. I hate to say this, but it is my experience that when a doctor goes to the bad, he is a fouler and darker creature than the worst cutthroat. There was Huston, the acid-bath man, and Campbell, who brought the Procrustean bed to Ealing..." and he carried on in a similar vein for the rest of our journey.

The cab pulled up beside the kerb. "That'll be one and ten-pence," said the cabbie. My friend tossed him a florin, which he caught and tipped to his ragged tall hat. "Much obliged to you both," he called out as the horse clopped out into the fog.

We walked to our front door. As I unlocked the door, my friend said, "Odd. Our cabbie just ignored that fellow on the corner."

"They do that at the end of a shift," I pointed out.

"Indeed they do," said my friend.

I dreamed of shadows that night, vast shadows that blotted out the sun, and I called out to them in my desperation, but they did not listen.

5. THE SKIN AND THE PIT

This year, step into the Spring—with a spring in your step! JACK'S.
Boots, Shoes, and Brogues. Save your soles! Heels our speciality.
JACK'S. *And do not forget to visit our new clothes and fittings em-*
porium in the East End—featuring evening wear of all kinds, hats,
novelties, canes, swordsticks &c. JACK'S OF PICCADILLY. *It's all*
in the Spring!

Inspector Lestrade was the first to arrive.

"You have posted your men in the street?" asked my friend.

"I have," said Lestrade. "With strict orders to let anyone in who comes, but to arrest anyone trying to leave."

"And you have handcuffs with you?"

In reply, Lestrade put his hand in his pocket and jangled two pairs of cuffs grimly.

"Now, sir," he said. "While we wait, why do you not tell me what we are waiting for?"

My friend pulled his pipe out of his pocket. He did not put it in his mouth, but placed it on the table in front of him. Then he took the tin from the night before, and a glass vial I recognised as the one he had had in the room in Shoreditch.

"There," he said. "The coffin nail, as I trust it shall prove, for our Mr. Vernet." He paused. Then he took out his pocket watch, laid it carefully on the table. "We have several minutes before they arrive." He turned to me. "What do you know of the Restorationists?"

"Not a blessed thing," I told him.

Lestrade coughed. "If you're talking about what I think you're talking about," he said, "perhaps we should leave it there. Enough's enough."

"Too late for that," said my friend. "For there are those who do not believe that the coming of the Old Ones was the fine thing we all know it to be. Anarchists to a man, they would see the old ways restored—mankind in control of its own destiny, if you will."

"I will not hear this sedition spoken," said Lestrade. "I must warn you—"

"I must warn you not to be such a fathead," said my friend. "Because it was the Restorationists who killed Prince Franz Drago. They murder, they kill, in a vain effort to force our masters to leave us alone in the darkness. The prince was killed by a *rache*—it's an old term for a hunting dog, Inspector, as you would know if you had looked in a dictionary. It also means 'revenge.' And the hunter left his signature on the wallpaper in the murder room, just as an artist might sign a canvas. But he was not the one who killed the prince."

"The Limping Doctor!" I exclaimed.

"Very good. There was a tall man there that night—I could tell his height, for the word was written at eye level. He smoked a pipe—the ash and dottle sat unburned in the fireplace, and he had tapped out his pipe with ease on the mantel, something a smaller man would not have done. The tobacco was an unusual blend of shag. The footprints in the room had for the most part been almost obliterated by your men, but there were several clear prints behind the door and by the window. Someone had waited there: a smaller man from his stride, who put his weight on his right leg. On the path outside I had seen several clear prints, and the different colours of clay on the boot scraper gave me more information: a tall man, who had accompanied the prince into those rooms and had later walked out. Waiting for them to arrive was the man who had sliced up the prince so impressively..."

Lestrade made an uncomfortable noise that did not quite become a word.

"I have spent many days retracing the movements of His Highness. I went from gambling hell to brothel to dining den to madhouse looking for our pipe-smoking man and his friend. I made no progress until I thought to check the newspapers of Bohemia, searching for a clue to the prince's recent activities there, and in them I learned that an English theatrical troupe had been in Prague last month, and had performed before Prince Franz Drago."

"Good Lord," I said. "So that Sherry Vernet fellow..."

"Is a Restorationist. Exactly."

I was shaking my head in wonder at my friend's intelligence and skills of observation when there was a knock on the door.

"This will be our quarry!" said my friend. "Careful now!"

Lestrade put his hand deep into his pocket, where I had no doubt he kept a pistol. He swallowed nervously.

My friend called out, "Please, come in!"

The door opened.

It was not Vernet, nor was it a Limping Doctor. It was one of the young street Arabs who earn a crust running errands—"in the employ of Messieurs Street and Walker," as we used to say when I was young. "Please, sirs," he said. "Is there a Mr. Henry Camberley here? I was asked by a gentleman to deliver a note."

"I'm he," said my friend. "And for a sixpence, what can you tell me about the gentleman who gave you the note?"

The young lad, who volunteered that his name was Wiggins, bit the sixpence before making it vanish, and then told us that the cheery cove who gave him the note was on the tall side, with dark hair, and, he added, had been smoking a pipe.

I have the note here, and take the liberty of transcribing it.

> My Dear Sir,
>
> I do not address you as Henry Camberley, for it is a name to which you have no claim. I am surprised that you did not announce yourself under your own name, for it is a fine one, and one that does you credit. I have read a number of your papers, when I have been able to obtain them. Indeed, I corresponded with you quite profitably two years ago about certain theoretical anomalies in your paper on the Dynamics of an Asteroid.
>
> I was amused to meet you yesterday evening. A few tips which

might save you bother in times to come, in the profession you currently follow. Firstly, a pipe-smoking man might possibly have a brand-new, unused pipe in his pocket, and no tobacco, but it is exceedingly unlikely—at least as unlikely as a theatrical promoter with no idea of the usual customs of recompense on a tour, who is accompanied by a taciturn ex-army officer (Afghanistan, unless I miss my guess). Incidentally, while you are correct that the streets of London have ears, it might also behoove you in the future not to take the first cab that comes along. Cabdrivers have ears, too, if they choose to use them.

You are certainly correct in one of your suppositions: it was indeed I who lured the half-blood creature back to the room in Shoreditch. If it is any comfort to you, having learned a little of his recreational predilections, I had told him I had procured for him a girl, abducted from a convent in Cornwall where she had never seen a man, and that it would only take his touch, and the sight of his face, to tip her over into a perfect madness.

Had she existed, he would have feasted on her madness while he took her, like a man sucking the flesh from a ripe peach, leaving nothing behind but the skin and the pit. I have seen them do this. I have seen them do far worse. It is the price we pay for peace and prosperity.

It is too great a price for that.

The good doctor—who believes as I do, and who did indeed write our little performance, for he has some crowd-pleasing skills—was waiting for us, with his knives.

I send this note, not as a catch-me-if-you-can taunt, for we are gone, the estimable doctor and I, and you shall not find us, but to tell you that it was good to feel that, if only for a moment, I had a worthy adversary. Worthier by far than inhuman creatures from beyond the Pit.

I fear the Strand Players will need to find themselves a new leading man.

I will not sign myself Vernet, and until the hunt is done and the world restored, I beg you to think of me simply as,

Rache

Inspector Lestrade ran from the room, calling to his men. They made young Wiggins take them to the place where the man had given him the note, for all the world as if Vernet the actor would be waiting there for them, a-smoking of his pipe. From the window we watched them run, my friend and I, and we shook our heads.

"They will stop and search all the trains leaving London, all the ships leaving Albion for Europe or the New World," said my friend, "looking for a tall man and his companion, a smaller, thickset medical man, with a slight limp. They will close the ports. Every way out of the country will be blocked."

"Do you think they will catch him, then?"

My friend shook his head. "I may be wrong," he said, "but I would wager that he and his friend are even now only a mile or so away, in the Rookery of St. Giles, where the police will not go except by the dozen. They will hide up there until the hue and cry have died away. And then they will be about their business."

"What makes you say that?"

"Because," said my friend, "if our positions were reversed, it is what I would do. You should burn the note, by the way."

I frowned. "But surely it's evidence," I said.

"It's seditionary nonsense," said my friend.

And I should have burned it. Indeed, I told Lestrade I *had* burned it, when he returned, and he congratulated me on my good sense. Lestrade kept his job, and Prince Albert wrote a note to my friend congratulating him on his deductions while regretting that the perpetrator was still at large.

They have not yet caught Sherry Vernet, or whatever his name really is, nor was any trace found of his murderous accomplice, tentatively identified as a former military surgeon named John (or perhaps James) Watson. Curiously, it was revealed that he had also been in Afghanistan. I wonder if we ever met.

My shoulder, touched by the Queen, continues to improve; the flesh fills and it heals. Soon I shall be a dead shot once more.

One night when we were alone, several months ago, I asked my friend if he remembered the correspondence referred to in the letter from the man who signed himself *Rache*. My friend said that he remembered it well, and that "Sigerson" (for so the actor had called himself then, claiming to be an Icelander) had been inspired by an equation of my friend's to suggest some wild theories furthering the relationship between mass, energy, and the hypothetical speed of light. "Nonsense, of course," said my friend, without smiling. "But inspired and dangerous nonsense nonetheless."

The palace eventually sent word that the Queen was pleased with my friend's accomplishments in the case, and there the matter has rested.

I doubt my friend will leave it alone, though; it will not be over until one of them has killed the other.

I kept the note. I have said things in this retelling of events that are not to be said. If I were a sensible man I would burn all these pages, but then, as my friend taught me, even ashes can give up their secrets. Instead, I shall place these papers in a strongbox at my bank with instructions that the box may not be opened until long after anyone now living is dead. Although, in the light of the recent events in Russia, I fear that day may be closer than any of us would care to think.

S—— M—— Major (Ret'd)
Baker Street,
London, New Albion, 1881

YOU SEE BUT YOU DO NOT OBSERVE

by Robert J. Sawyer

Robert J. Sawyer is the author of twenty novels, including *Hominids*, which won the Hugo Award, *The Terminal Experiment*, which won the Nebula Award, and *Mindscan*, which won the John W. Campbell Memorial Award. Sawyer's novel *Flashforward* is currently being adapted for television and is scheduled to air on ABC this fall. His latest novel project is the WWW trilogy, consisting of *Wake*, *Watch*, and *Wonder*. The first volume, *Wake*, was recently serialized in the pages of *Analog* and was released in hardcover in April.

"Where is everybody?" These words, exclaimed by Los Alamos physicist Enrico Fermi in 1950, led to his formulation of what's known as the Fermi paradox: Why haven't we found any evidence of extraterrestrial life, given the seemingly high probability that such life exists? Even if intelligent life evolves only rarely, the sheer scale of the universe would mean that advanced civilizations should be commonplace. (The Drake equation is a well-known model for organizing this line of reasoning.) There ought to be civilizations billions of years older than ours, in which case they should have colonized Earth long ago, or at least built large engineering projects such as Dyson spheres that we could detect with our instruments. But so far, nothing. Many explanations have been proposed, including that intelligence is much rarer than we think, that advanced civilizations tend to destroy themselves or each other, or that advanced civilizations have chosen not to talk to us, perhaps because they don't want to meddle with our development or because we're just too primitive to bother with. Our final tale presents a solution to the Fermi paradox that we can virtually guarantee you've never considered before.

I had been pulled into the future first, ahead of my companion. There was no sensation associated with the chronotransference, except for a popping of my ears which I was later told had to do with a change in air pressure. Once in the twenty-first century, my brain was scanned in order to produce from my memories a perfect reconstruction of our rooms at 221B Baker Street. Details that I could

437

not consciously remember or articulate were nonetheless reproduced exactly: the flock-papered walls, the bearskin hearthrug, the basket chair and the armchair, the coal-scuttle, even the view through the window—all were correct to the smallest detail.

I was met in the future by a man who called himself Mycroft Holmes. He claimed, however, to be no relation to my companion, and protested that his name was mere coincidence, although he allowed that the fact of it was likely what had made a study of my partner's methods his chief avocation. I asked him if he had a brother called Sherlock, but his reply made little sense to me: "My parents weren't *that* cruel."

In any event, this Mycroft Holmes—who was a small man with reddish hair, quite unlike the stout and dark ale of a fellow with the same name I had known two hundred years before—wanted all details to be correct before he whisked Holmes here from the past. Genius, he said, was but a step from madness, and although I had taken to the future well, my companion might be quite rocked by the experience.

When Mycroft did bring Holmes forth, he did so with great stealth, transferring him precisely as he stepped through the front exterior door of the real 221 Baker Street and into the simulation that had been created here. I heard my good friend's voice down the stairs, giving his usual glad tidings to a simulation of Mrs. Hudson. His long legs, as they always did, brought him up to our humble quarters at a rapid pace.

I had expected a hearty greeting, consisting perhaps of an ebullient cry of "My Dear Watson," and possibly even a firm clasping of hands or some other display of bonhomie. But there was none of that, of course. This was not like the time Holmes had returned after an absence of three years during which I had believed him to be dead. No, my companion, whose exploits it has been my honor to chronicle over the years, was unaware of just how long we had been separated, and so my reward for my vigil was nothing more than a distracted nodding of his drawn-out face. He took a seat and settled in with the evening paper, but after a few moments, he slapped the newsprint sheets down. "Confound it, Watson! I have already read this edition. Have we not *today's* paper?"

And, at that turn, there was nothing for it but for me to adopt the unfamiliar role that queer fate had dictated I must now take: our traditional positions were now reversed, and I would have to explain the truth to Holmes.

"Holmes, my good fellow, I am afraid they do not publish newspapers anymore."

He pinched his long face into a scowl, and his clear, gray eyes glimmered. "I would have thought that any man who had spent as much time in Afghanistan as you had, Watson, would be immune to the ravages of the sun. I grant that today was unbearably hot, but surely your brain should not have addled so easily."

"Not a bit of it, Holmes, I assure you," said I. "What I say is true, although I confess my reaction was the same as yours when I was first told. There have not been any newspapers for seventy-five years now."

"Seventy-five years? Watson, this copy of *The Times* is dated August the fourteenth, 1899—yesterday."

"I am afraid that is not true, Holmes. Today is June the fifth, *anno Domini* two thousand and ninety-six."

"Two thou—"

"It sounds preposterous, I know—"

"It *is* preposterous, Watson. I call you 'old man' now and again out of affection, but you are in fact nowhere near two hundred and fifty years of age."

"Perhaps I am not the best man to explain all this," I said.

"No," said a voice from the doorway. "Allow me."

Holmes surged to his feet. "And who are you?"

"My name is Mycroft Holmes."

"Impostor!" declared my companion.

"I assure you that that is not the case," said Mycroft. "I grant I'm not your brother, nor a habitué of the Diogenes Club, but I do share his name. I am a scientist—and I have used certain scientific principles to pluck you from your past and bring you into my present."

For the first time in all the years I had known him, I saw befuddlement on my companion's face. "It is quite true," I said to him.

"But why?" said Holmes, spreading his long arms. "Assuming this mad fantasy is true—and I do not grant for an instant that it is—why would you thus kidnap myself and my good friend, Dr. Watson?"

"Because, Holmes, the game, as you used to be so fond of saying, is afoot."

"Murder, is it?" asked I, grateful at last to get to the reason for which we had been brought forward.

"More than simple murder," said Mycroft. "Much more. Indeed, the biggest puzzle to have ever faced the human race. Not just one body is missing. Trillions are. *Trillions.*"

"Watson," said Holmes, "surely you recognize the signs of madness in the man? Have you nothing in your bag that can help him? The whole population of the Earth is less than two thousand millions."

"In your time, yes," said Mycroft. "Today, it's about eight thousand million. But I say again, there are trillions more who are missing."

"Ah, I perceive at last," said Holmes, a twinkle in his eye as he came to believe that reason was once again holding sway. "I have read in *The Illustrated London News* of these *dinosauria*, as Professor Owen called them—great creatures from the past, all now deceased. It is their demise you wish me to unravel."

Mycroft shook his head. "You should have read Professor Moriarty's monograph called *The Dynamics of an Asteroid*," he said.

"I keep my mind clear of useless knowledge," replied Holmes curtly.

Mycroft shrugged. "Well, in that paper Moriarty quite cleverly guessed the cause of the demise of the dinosaurs: an asteroid crashing into earth kicked up enough dust to block the sun for months on end. Close to a century after he had reasoned out this hypothesis, solid evidence for its truth was found in a layer of clay. No, that mystery is long since solved. This one is much greater."

"And what, pray, is it?" said Holmes, irritation in his voice.

Mycroft motioned for Holmes to have a seat, and, after a moment's defiance, my friend did just that. "It is called the Fermi paradox," said Mycroft, "after Enrico Fermi, an Italian physicist who lived in the twentieth century. You see, we know now that this universe of ours should have given rise to countless planets, and that many of those planets should have produced intelligent civilizations. We can demonstrate the likelihood of this mathematically, using something called the Drake equation. For a century and a half now, we have been using radio—wireless, that is—to look for signs of these other intelligences. And we have found nothing—*nothing!* Hence the paradox Fermi posed: if the universe is supposed to be full of life, then where are the aliens?"

"Aliens?" said I. "Surely they are mostly still in their respective foreign countries."

Mycroft smiled. "The word has gathered additional uses since your day, good doctor. By aliens, I mean extraterrestrials—creatures who live on other worlds."

"Like in the stories of Verne and Wells?" asked I, quite sure that my expression was agog.

"And even in worlds beyond the family of our sun," said Mycroft.

Holmes rose to his feet. "I know nothing of universes and other worlds," he said angrily. "Such knowledge could be of no practical use in my profession."

I nodded. "When I first met Holmes, he had no idea that the Earth revolved around the sun." I treated myself to a slight chuckle. "He thought the reverse to be true."

Mycroft smiled. "I know of your current limitations, Sherlock." My friend cringed slightly at the overly familiar address. "But these are mere gaps in knowledge; we can rectify that easily enough."

"I will not crowd my brain with useless irrelevancies," said Holmes. "I carry only information that can be of help in my work. For instance, I can identify one hundred and forty different varieties of tobacco ash—"

"Ah, well, you can let that information go, Holmes," said Mycroft. "No one smokes anymore. It's been proven ruinous to one's health." I shot a look at Holmes, whom I had always warned of being a self-poisoner. "Besides, we've also learned much about the structure of the brain in the intervening years. Your fear that memorizing information related to fields such as literature, astronomy, and philosophy would force out other, more relevant data, is unfounded. The capacity for the human brain to store and retrieve information is almost infinite."

"It is?" said Holmes, clearly shocked.

"It is."

"And so you wish me to immerse myself in physics and astronomy and such all?"

"Yes," said Mycroft.

"To solve this paradox of Fermi?"

"Precisely!"

"But why me?"

"Because it is a *puzzle*, and you, my good fellow, are the greatest solver of puzzles this world has ever seen. It is now two hundred years after your time, and no one with a facility to rival yours has yet appeared."

Mycroft probably could not see it, but the tiny hint of pride on my longtime companion's face was plain to me. But then Holmes frowned. "It would take years to amass the knowledge I would need to address this problem."

"No, it will not." Mycroft waved his hand, and amidst the homely untidiness of Holmes's desk appeared a small sheet of glass standing vertically. Next to it lay a strange metal bowl. "We have made great strides in the technology of learning since your day. We can directly program new information into your brain." Mycroft walked over to the desk. "This glass panel is what we call a *monitor*. It is activated by the sound of your voice. Simply ask it questions, and it will display information on any topic you wish. If you find a topic that you think will be useful in your studies, simply place this helmet on your head" (he indicated the metal bowl), "say the words 'load topic,' and the information will be seamlessly integrated into the neural nets of your very own brain. It will at once seem as if you know, and have always known, all the details of that field of endeavor."

"Incredible!" said Holmes. "And from there?"

"From there, my dear Holmes, I hope that your powers of deduction will lead you to resolve the paradox—and reveal at last what has happened to the aliens!"

"Watson! Watson!"

I awoke with a start. Holmes had found this new ability to effortlessly absorb information irresistible and he had pressed on long into the night, but I had evidently fallen asleep in a chair. I perceived that Holmes had at last found a substitute for the sleeping fiend of his cocaine mania: with all of creation at his fingertips, he would never again feel that emptiness that so destroyed him between assignments.

"Eh?" I said. My throat was dry. I had evidently been sleeping with my mouth open. "What is it?"

"Watson, this physics is more fascinating than I had ever imagined. Listen to this, and see if you do not find it as compelling as any of the cases we have faced to date."

I rose from my chair and poured myself a little sherry—it was, after all, still night and not yet morning. "I am listening."

"Remember the locked and sealed room that figured so significantly in that terrible case of the Giant Rat of Sumatra?"

"How could I forget?" said I, a shiver traversing my spine. "If not for your keen shooting, my left leg would have ended up as gamy as my right."

"Quite," said Holmes. "Well, consider a different type of locked-room mystery, this one devised by an Austrian physicist named Erwin Schrödinger. Imagine a cat sealed in a box. The box is of such opaque material, and its walls are so well insulated, and the seal is so profound, that there is no way anyone can observe the cat once the box is closed."

"Hardly seems cricket," I said, "locking a poor cat in a box."

"Watson, your delicate sensibilities are laudable, but please, man, attend to my point. Imagine further that inside this box is a triggering device that has exactly a fifty-fifty chance of being set off, and that this aforementioned trigger is rigged up to a cylinder of poison gas. If the trigger is tripped, the gas is released, and the cat dies."

"Goodness!" said I. "How nefarious."

"Now, Watson, tell me this: without opening the box, can you say whether the cat is alive or dead?"

"Well, if I understand you correctly, it depends on whether the trigger was tripped."

"Precisely!"

"And so the cat is perhaps alive, and, yet again, perhaps it is dead."

"Ah, my friend, I knew you would not fail me: the blindingly obvious interpretation. But it is wrong, dear Watson, totally wrong."

"How do you mean?"

"I mean the cat is neither alive nor is it dead. It is a *potential* cat, an unresolved cat, a cat whose existence is nothing but a question of possibilities. It is neither alive nor dead, Watson—neither! Until some intelligent person opens the box and looks, the cat is unresolved. Only the act of looking forces a resolution of the possibilities. Once you crack the seal and peer within, the potential cat collapses into an actual cat. Its reality is *a result of* having been observed."

"That is worse gibberish than anything this namesake of your brother has spouted."

"No, it is not," said Holmes. "It is the way the world works. They have learned so much since our time, Watson—so very much! But as Alphonse Karr has observed, *Plus ça change, plus c'est la même chose.* Even in this esoteric field of advanced physics, it is the power of the qualified observer that is most important of all!"

I awoke again hearing Holmes crying out, "Mycroft! Mycroft!"

I had occasionally heard such shouts from him in the past, either when his iron constitution had failed him and he was feverish, or when under the influence of his accursed needle. But after a moment I realized he was not calling for his real brother but rather was shouting into the air to summon the Mycroft Holmes who was the twenty-first-century savant. Moments later, he was rewarded: the door to our rooms opened and in came the red-haired fellow.

"Hello, Sherlock," said Mycroft. "You wanted me?"

"Indeed I do," said Holmes. "I have absorbed much now on not just physics but also the technology by which you have re-created these rooms for me and the good Dr. Watson."

Mycroft nodded. "I've been keeping track of what you've been accessing. Surprising choices, I must say."

"So they might seem," said Holmes, "but my method is based on the pursuit of trifles. Tell me if I understand correctly that you reconstructed these rooms by scanning Watson's memories, then using, if I understand the terms, holography and micro-manipulated force fields to simulate the appearance and form of what he had seen."

"That's right."

"So your ability to reconstruct is not just limited to rebuilding these rooms of ours, but, rather, you could simulate anything either of us had ever seen."

"That's correct. In fact, I could even put you into a simulation of someone else's memories. Indeed, I thought perhaps you might like to see the Very Large Array of radio telescopes, where most of our listening for alien messages—"

"Yes, yes, I'm sure that's fascinating," said Holmes, dismissively. "But can you reconstruct the venue of what Watson so appropriately dubbed 'The Final Problem'?"

"You mean the Falls of Reichenbach?" Mycroft looked shocked. "My God, yes, but I should think that's the last thing you'd want to relive."

"Aptly said!" declared Holmes. "Can you do it?"

"Of course."

"Then do so!"

And so Holmes and my brains were scanned and in short order we found ourselves inside a superlative re-creation of the Switzerland of May 1891, to which we had originally fled to escape Professor Moriarty's assassins. Our re-enactment of events began at the charming Englischer Hof in the village of Meiringen. Just as the original innkeeper had done all those years ago, the reconstruction of him exacted a promise from us that we would not miss the spectacle of the Falls of Reichenbach. Holmes and I set out for the Falls, him walking with the aid of an alpenstock. Mycroft, I was given to understand, was somehow observing all this from afar.

"I do not like this," I said to my companion. "'Twas bad enough to live through this horrible day once, but I had hoped I would never have to relive it again except in nightmares."

"Watson, recall that I have fonder memories of all this. Vanquishing Moriarty was the high point of my career. I said to you then, and say again now, that putting an end to the very Napoleon of crime would easily be worth the price of my own life."

There was a little dirt path cut out of the vegetation running halfway round the falls so as to afford a complete view of the spectacle. The icy green water, fed by the melting snows, flowed with phenomenal rapidity and violence, then plunged into a great, bottomless chasm of rock black as the darkest night. Spray shot up in vast gouts, and the shriek made by the plunging water was almost like a human cry.

We stood for a moment looking down at the waterfall, Holmes's face in its most contemplative repose. He then pointed further ahead along the dirt path. "Note, dear Watson," he said, shouting to be heard above the torrent, "that the dirt path comes to an end against a rock wall there." I nodded. He turned in the other direction. "And see that backtracking out the way we came is the only way to leave alive:

there is but one exit, and it is coincident with the single entrance."

Again I nodded. But, just as had happened the first time we had been at this fateful spot, a Swiss boy came running along the path, carrying in his hand a letter addressed to me which bore the mark of the Englischer Hof. I knew what the note said, of course: that an Englishwoman, staying at that inn, had been overtaken by a hemorrhage. She had but a few hours to live, but doubtless would take great comfort in being ministered to by an English doctor, and would I come at once?

"But the note is a pretext," said I, turning to Holmes. "Granted, I was fooled originally by it, but, as you later admitted in that letter you left for me, you had suspected all along that it was a sham on the part of Moriarty." Throughout this commentary, the Swiss boy stood frozen, immobile, as if somehow Mycroft, overseeing all this, had locked the boy in time so that Holmes and I might consult. "I will not leave you again, Holmes, to plunge to your death."

Holmes raised a hand. "Watson, as always, your sentiments are laudable, but recall that this is a mere simulation. You will be of material assistance to me if you do exactly as you did before. There is no need, though, for you to undertake the entire arduous hike to the Englischer Hof and back. Instead, simply head back to the point at which you pass the figure in black, wait an additional quarter of an hour, then return to here."

"Thank you for simplifying it," said I. "I am eight years older than I was then; a three-hour round trip would take a goodly bit out of me today."

"Indeed," said Holmes. "All of us may have outlived our most useful days. Now, please, do as I ask."

"I will, of course," said I, "but I freely confess that I do not understand what this is all about. You were engaged by this twenty-first-century Mycroft to explore a problem in natural philosophy—the missing aliens. Why are we even here?"

"We are here," said Holmes, "because I have solved that problem! Trust me, Watson. Trust me, and play out the scenario again of that portentous day of May 4th, 1891."

And so I left my companion, not knowing what he had in mind. As I made my way back to the Englischer Hof, I passed a man going hurriedly the other way. The first time I had lived through these terrible events I did not know him, but this time I recognized him for Professor Moriarty: tall, clad all in black, his forehead bulging out, his lean form outlined sharply against the green backdrop of the vegetation. I let the simulation pass, waited fifteen minutes as Holmes had asked, then returned to the falls.

Upon my arrival, I saw Holmes's alpenstock leaning against a rock. The black soil of the path to the torrent was constantly re-moistened by the spray from the roiling falls. In the soil I could see two sets of footprints leading down the path to the cascade, and none returning. It was precisely the same terrible sight that greeted me all those years ago.

"Welcome back, Watson!"

I wheeled around. Holmes stood leaning against a tree, grinning widely.

"Holmes!" I exclaimed. "How did you manage to get away from the falls without leaving footprints?"

"Recall, my dear Watson, that except for the flesh-and-blood you and me, all this is but a simulation. I simply asked Mycroft to prevent my feet from leaving tracks." He demonstrated this by walking back and forth. No impression was left by his shoes, and no vegetation was trampled down by his passage. "And, of course, I asked him to freeze Moriarty, as earlier he had frozen the Swiss lad, before he and I could become locked in mortal combat."

"Fascinating," said I.

"Indeed. Now, consider the spectacle before you. What do you see?"

"Just what I saw that horrid day on which I had thought you had died: two sets of tracks leading to the falls, and none returning."

Holmes's crow of "Precisely!" rivaled the roar of the falls. "One set of tracks you knew to be my own, and the others you took to be that of the black-clad Englishman—the very Napoleon of crime!"

"Yes."

"Having seen these two sets approaching the falls, and none returning, you then rushed to the very brink of the falls and found—what?"

"Signs of a struggle at the lip of the precipice leading to the great torrent itself."

"And what did you conclude from this?"

"That you and Moriarty had plunged to your deaths, locked in mortal combat."

"Exactly so, Watson! The very same conclusion I myself would have drawn based on those observations!"

"Thankfully, though, I turned out to be incorrect."

"Did you, now?"

"Why, yes. Your presence here attests to that."

"Perhaps," said Holmes. "But I think otherwise. Consider, Watson! You were on the scene, you saw what happened, and for three years—three years, man!—you believed me to be dead. We had been friends and colleagues for a decade at that point. Would the Holmes you knew have let you mourn him for so long without getting word to you? Surely you must know that I trust you at least as much as I do my brother Mycroft, whom I later told you was the only one I had made privy to the secret that I still lived."

"Well," I said, "since you bring it up, I *was* slightly hurt by that. But you explained your reasons to me when you returned."

"It is a comfort to me, Watson, that your ill-feelings were assuaged. But I wonder, perchance, if it was more you than I who assuaged them."

"Eh?"

"You had seen clear evidence of my death, and had faithfully if floridly recorded the same in the chronicle you so appropriately dubbed 'The Final Problem.'"

"Yes, indeed. Those were the hardest words I had ever written."

"And what was the reaction of your readers once this account was published in the *Strand*?"

I shook my head, recalling. "It was completely unexpected," said I. "I had antici-pated a few polite notes from strangers mourning your passing, since the stories of your exploits had been so warmly received in the past. But what I got instead was mostly anger and outrage—people demanding to hear further adventures of yours."

"Which of course you believed to be impossible, seeing as how I was dead."

"Exactly. The whole thing left a rather bad taste, I must say. Seemed very peculiar behavior."

"But doubtless it died down quickly," said Holmes.

"You know full well it did not. I have told you before that the onslaught of letters, as well as personal exhortations wherever I would travel, continued unabated for years. In fact, I was virtually at the point of going back and writing up one of your lesser cases I had previously ignored as being of no general interest simply to get the demands to cease, when, much to my surprise and delight—"

"Much to your surprise and delight, after an absence of three years less a month, I turned up in your consulting rooms, disguised, if I recall correctly, as a shabby book collector. And soon you had fresh adventures to chronicle, beginning with that case of the infamous Colonel Sebastian Moran and his victim, the Honorable Ronald Adair."

"Yes," said I. "Wondrous it was."

"But Watson, let us consider the facts surrounding my apparent death at the falls of Reichenbach on May 4th, 1891. You, the observer on the scene, saw the evidence, and, as you wrote in 'The Final Problem,' many experts scoured the lip of the falls and came to precisely the same conclusion you had—that Moriarty and I had plunged to our deaths."

"But that conclusion turned out to be wrong."

Holmes beamed intently. "No, my Good Watson, it turned out to be *unaccept-able*—unacceptable to your faithful readers. And that is where all the problems stem from. Remember Schrödinger's cat in the sealed box? Moriarty and I at the falls present a very similar scenario: he and I went down the path into the cul-de-sac, our footprints leaving impressions in the soft earth. There were only two possible outcomes at that point: either I would exit alive, or I would not. There was no way out, except to take that same path back away from the falls. Until someone came and looked to see whether I had re-emerged from the path, the outcome was unresolved. I was both alive and dead—a collection of possibilities. But when you arrived, those possibilities had to collapse into a single reality. You saw that there were no footprints returning from the falls—meaning that Moriarty and I had struggled until at last we had both plunged over the edge into the icy torrent. It was your act of seeing the results that forced the possibilities to be resolved. In a very real sense, my good, dear friend, you killed me."

My heart was pounding in my chest. "I tell you, Holmes, nothing would have made me more happy than to have seen you alive!"

"I do not doubt that, Watson—but you had to see one thing or the other. You could not see both. And, having seen what you saw, you reported your findings: first to the Swiss police, and then to the reporter for the *Journal de Genève*, and lastly in your full account in the pages of the *Strand*."

I nodded.

"But here is the part that was not considered by Schrödinger when he devised the thought experiment of the cat in the box. Suppose you open the box and find the cat dead, and later you tell your neighbor about the dead cat—and your neighbor refuses to believe you when you say that the cat is dead. What happens if you go and look in the box a second time?"

"Well, the cat is surely still dead."

"Perhaps. But what if thousands—nay, millions!—refuse to believe the account of the original observer? What if they deny the evidence? What then, Watson?"

"I—I do not know."

"Through the sheer stubbornness of their will, they reshape reality, Watson! Truth is replaced with fiction! They will the cat back to life. More than that, they attempt to believe that the cat never died in the first place!"

"And so?"

"And so the world, which should have one concrete reality, is rendered unresolved, uncertain, adrift. As the first observer on the scene at Reichenbach, your interpretation should take precedence. But the stubbornness of the human race is legendary, Watson, and through that sheer cussedness, that refusal to believe what they have been plainly told, the world gets plunged back into being a wave front of unresolved possibilities. We exist in flux—to this day, the whole world exists in flux—because of the conflict between the observation you really made at Reichenbach, and the observation the world *wishes* you had made."

"But this is all too fantastic, Holmes!"

"Eliminate the impossible, Watson, and whatever remains, however improbable, must be the truth. Which brings me now to the question we were engaged by this avatar of Mycroft to solve: this paradox of Fermi. Where are the alien beings?"

"And you say you have solved that?"

"Indeed I have. Consider the method by which mankind has been searching for these aliens."

"By wireless, I gather—trying to overhear their chatter on the ether."

"Precisely! And when did I return from the dead, Watson?"

"April of 1894."

"And when did that gifted Italian, Guglielmo Marconi, invent the wireless?"

"I have no idea."

"In eighteen hundred and ninety-*five*, my good Watson. The following year! In all the time that mankind has used radio, our entire world has been an unresolved quandary! An uncollapsed wave front of possibilities!"

"Meaning?"

"Meaning the aliens are there, Watson—it is not they who are missing, it is us! Our world is out of synch with the rest of the universe. Through our failure to accept the unpleasant truth, we have rendered ourselves *potential* rather than *actual*."

I had always thought my companion a man with a generous regard for his own stature, but surely this was too much. "You are suggesting, Holmes, that the current unresolved state of the world hinges on the fate of you yourself?"

"Indeed! Your readers would not allow me to fall to my death, even if it meant attaining the very thing I desired most, namely the elimination of Moriarty. In this mad world, the observer has lost control of his observations! If there is one thing my life stood for—my life prior to that ridiculous resurrection of me you recounted in your chronicle of 'The Empty House'—it was reason! Logic! A devotion to observable fact! But humanity has abjured that. This whole world is out of whack, Watson—so out of whack that we are cut off from the civilizations that exist elsewhere. You tell me you were barraged with demands for my return, but if people had really understood me, understood what my life represented, they would have known that the only real tribute to me possible would have been to accept the facts! The only real answer would have been to leave me dead!"

Mycroft sent us back in time, but rather than returning us to 1899, whence he had plucked us, at Holmes's request he put us back eight years earlier in May of 1891. Of course, there were younger versions of ourselves already living then, but Mycroft swapped us for them, bringing the young ones to the future, where they could live out the rest of their lives in simulated scenarios taken from Holmes's and my minds. Granted, we were each eight years older than we had been when we had fled Moriarty the first time, but no one in Switzerland knew us and so the aging of our faces went unnoticed.

I found myself for a third time living that fateful day at the Falls of Reichenbach, but this time, like the first and unlike the second, it was real.

I saw the page boy coming, and my heart raced. I turned to Holmes, and said, "I can't possibly leave you."

"Yes, you can, Watson. And you will, for you have never failed to play the game. I am sure you will play it to the end." He paused for a moment, then said, perhaps just a wee bit sadly, "I can discover facts, Watson, but I cannot change them." And then, quite solemnly, he extended his hand. I clasped it firmly in both of mine. And then the boy, who was in Moriarty's employ, was upon us. I allowed myself to be duped, leaving Holmes alone at the Falls, fighting with all my might to keep from looking back as I hiked onward to treat the nonexistent patient at the Englischer Hof. On my way, I passed Moriarty going in the other direction. It was all I could do to keep from drawing my pistol and putting an end to the blackguard, but I knew Holmes would consider robbing him of his own chance at Moriarty an unforgivable betrayal.

It was an hour's hike down to the Englischer Hof. There I played out the scene in which I inquired about the ailing Englishwoman, and Steiler the Elder, the innkeeper, reacted, as I knew he must, with surprise. My performance was probably half-hearted, having played the role once before, but soon I was on my way back. The uphill hike took over two hours, and I confess plainly to being exhausted upon my arrival, although I could barely hear my own panting over the roar of the torrent.

Once again, I found two sets of footprints leading to the precipice, and none returning. I also found Holmes's alpenstock, and, just as I had the first time, a note from him to me that he had left with it. The note read just as the original had, explaining that he and Moriarty were about to have their final confrontation, but that Moriarty had allowed him to leave a few last words behind. But it ended with a postscript that had not been in the original:

> My dear Watson [it said], you will honour my passing most of
> all if you stick fast to the powers of observation. No matter what
> the world wants, leave me dead.

I returned to London, and was able to briefly counterbalance my loss of Holmes by reliving the joy and sorrow of the last few months of my wife Mary's life, explaining my somewhat older face to her and others as the result of shock at the death of Holmes. The next year, right on schedule, Marconi did indeed invent the wireless. Exhortations for more Holmes adventures continued to pour in, but I ignored them all, although the lack of him in my life was so profound that I was sorely tempted to relent, recanting my observations made at Reichenbach. Nothing would have pleased me more than to hear again the voice of the best and wisest man I had ever known.

In late June of 1907, I read in *The Times* about the detection of intelligent wireless signals coming from the direction of the star Altair. On that day, the rest of the world celebrated, but I do confess I shed a tear and drank a special toast to my good friend, the late Mr. Sherlock Holmes.

ACKNOWLEDGMENTS

Many thanks to the following:

Jeremy Lassen and Jason Williams at Night Shade Books, for letting me edit all these anthologies and for doing such a kick-ass job publishing them. Also, to Ross Lockhart at Night Shade for all that he does behind-the-scenes, and to Marty Halpern for catching all my tyops.

David Palumbo, for the Holmesarific cover.

Gordon Van Gelder, the Dr. Joseph Bell to my Sherlock Holmes (i.e., the model upon which my career is based). Of course, unlike Holmes, I am not a fictional character, or so the voices tell me.

My agent Jenny Rappaport, the Mrs. Hudson of my literary estate.

David Barr Kirtley for serving as my Watson during the assembly of this volume. All the clever things in the header notes are his work. Anything lame you came across is mine.

Rebecca McNulty, for her various and valuable interning assistance—reading, scanning, transcribing, proofing, doing most of the work but getting none of the credit as all good interns do.

My mom, for the usual reasons.

All of the other kindly folks who assisted me in some way during the editorial process: Charles Ardai, Jack Byrne, Frances Collin, Andy Cox, Ellen Datlow, Jake Elwell, Jennifer Escott, Emily Giglierano, Lina M. Granada, Merrilee Heifetz, Patricia Hoch, Mary Robinette Kowal, Dorothy Lumley, Donald Maass, Andrew Marszal, Linda Moorcock, Barbara and Christopher Roden, Betty Russo, Charles Schlessiger, Steven Silver, J. L. Stermer, Craig Tenney, everyone who dropped suggestions into my Holmes fiction database, and to everyone else who helped out in some way that I neglected to mention (and to you folks, I apologize!).

The NYC Geek Posse—consisting of Robert Bland, Christopher M. Cevasco, Douglas E. Cohen, Jordan Hamessley, Andrea Kail, and Matt London (plus Dave Kirtley, who I mentioned above, and the NYCGP Auxiliary)—for giving me an excuse to come out of my editorial cave once in a while.

The readers and reviewers who loved my other anthologies, making it possible for me to do more.

And last, but certainly not least: a big thanks to all of the authors who appear in this anthology.

451

ACKNOWLEDGMENT IS MADE FOR PERMISSION TO
PRINT THE FOLLOWING MATERIAL:

"The Adventure of the Inertial Adjustor" by Stephen Baxter. © 1997 Stephen Baxter. Originally published in *The Mammoth Book of New Sherlock Holmes Adventures*. Reprinted by permission of the author.

"Murder to Music" by Anthony Burgess. © 1989 Anthony Burgess. Originally published in *The Devil's Mode*. Reprinted by permission of the Estate of Anthony Burgess.

"A Study in Emerald" by Neil Gaiman. © 2003 Neil Gaiman. Originally published in *Shadows Over Baker Street: New Tales of Terror*. Reprinted by permission of the author.

"The Adventure of the Lost World" by Dominic Green. © 2004 Dominic Green. Originally published online in *BBCi Cult Sherlock Holmes Magazine*. Reprinted by permission of the author.

"The Adventure of the Antiquarian's Niece" by Barbara Hambly. © 2003 Barbara Hambly. Originally published in *Shadows Over Baker Street: New Tales of Terror*. Reprinted by permission of the author.

"A Scandal in Montreal" by Edward D. Hoch. © 2008 Edward D. Hoch. Originally published in *Ellery Queen's Mystery Magazine*. Reprinted by permission of the Estate of Edward D. Hoch.

"The Adventure of the Mummy's Curse" by H. Paul Jeffers. © 2006 H. Paul Jeffers. Originally published in *Ghosts in Baker Street* (as "Sherlock Holmes and the Mummy's Curse"). Reprinted by permission of the author.

"Mrs Hudson's Case" by Laurie R. King. © 1997 Laurie R. King. Originally published in *Crime Through Time*. Reprinted by permission of the author.

Night Shade Books Is an Independent Publisher of Quality SF, Fantasy and Horror

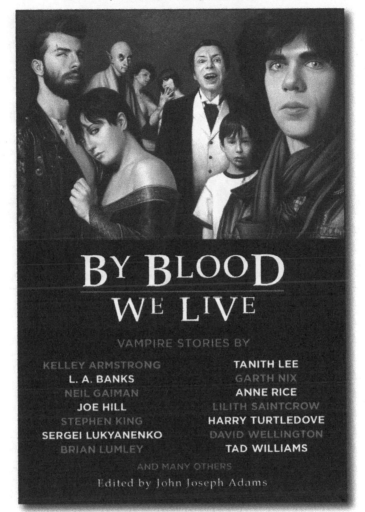

ISBN 978-1-59780-156-0, Trade Paperback; $15.95

From Dracula to Buffy the Vampire Slayer; from Castlevania to Tru Blood, the romance between popular culture and vampires hearkens back to humanity's darkest, deepest fears, flowing through our very blood, fears of death, and life, and insatiable hunger. And yet, there is an attraction, undeniable, to the vampire archetype, whether the pale, wan European count, impeccably dressed and coldly masculine, yet strangely ambiguous, ready to sink his sharp teeth deep into his victims' necks, draining or converting them, or the vamp, the count's feminine counterpart, villain and victim in one, using her wiles and icy sexuality to corrupt man and woman alike...

Gathering together the best vampire literature of the last three decades from many of today's most renowned authors of fantasy, speculative fiction, and horror. By Blood We Live will satisfy your darkest cravings...

Night Shade Books Is an Independent Publisher of Quality SF, Fantasy and Horror

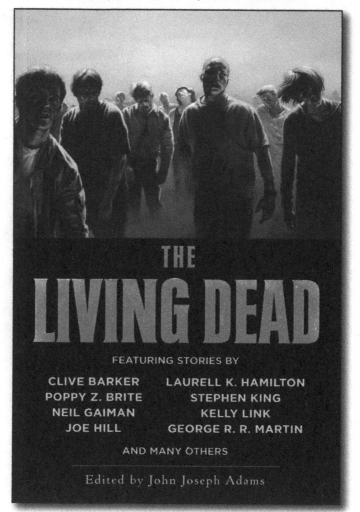

THE

LIVING DEAD

FEATURING STORIES BY

CLIVE BARKER	LAURELL K. HAMILTON
POPPY Z. BRITE	STEPHEN KING
NEIL GAIMAN	KELLY LINK
JOE HILL	GEORGE R. R. MARTIN

AND MANY OTHERS

Edited by John Joseph Adams

ISBN 978-1-59780-143-0, Trade Paperback; $15.95

From *White Zombie* to *Dawn of the Dead*; from *Resident Evil* to *World War Z*, zombies have invaded popular culture, becoming the monsters that best express the fears and anxieties of the modern west.

Gathering together the best zombie literature of the last three decades from many of today's most renowned authors of fantasy, speculative fiction, and horror, *The Living Dead* covers the broad spectrum of zombie fiction; from Romero-style zombies to reanimated corpses to voodoo zombies and beyond.

"When there's no more room in hell, the dead will walk the earth."

Night Shade Books Is an Independent Publisher of Quality SF, Fantasy and Horror

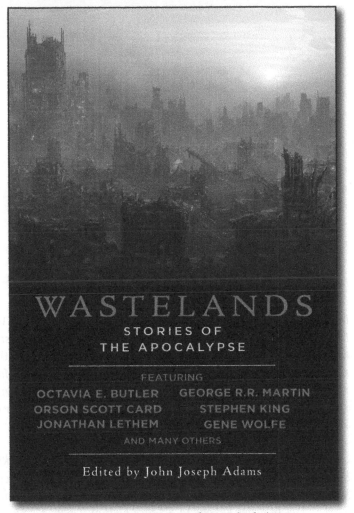

ISBN 978-1-59780-105-8, Trade Paperback; $15.95

Famine, Death, War, and Pestilence: The Four Horsemen of the Apocalypse, the harbingers of Armageddon - these are our guides through the Wastelands.

Gathering together the best post-apocalyptic literature of the last two decades from many of today's most renowned authors of speculative fiction, including George R.R. Martin, Gene Wolfe, Orson Scott Card, Carol Emshwiller, Jonathan Lethem, Octavia E. Butler, and Stephen King, Wastelands explores the scientific, psychological, and philosophical questions of what it means to remain human in the wake of Armageddon. Whether the end of the world comes through nuclear war, ecological disaster, or cosmological cataclysm, these are tales of survivors, in some cases struggling to rebuild the society that was, in others, merely surviving, scrounging for food in depopulated ruins and defending themselves against monsters, mutants, and marauders.

John Joseph Adams is the editor of the anthologies *By Blood We Live, Federations, The Living Dead, Seeds of Change,* and *Wastelands: Stories of the Apocalypse.* Forthcoming work includes the anthologies *Brave New Worlds, The Living Dead 2, The Mad Scientist's Guide to World Domination,* and *The Way of the Wizard.* He is also the assistant editor at *The Magazine of Fantasy & Science Fiction.*

He is a columnist for *Tor.com* and has written reviews for *Kirkus Reviews, Publishers Weekly,* and *Orson Scott Card's Intergalactic Medicine Show.* His non-fiction has also appeared in: *Amazing Stories, The Internet Review of Science Fiction, Locus Magazine, Novel & Short Story Writers Market, Science Fiction Weekly, SCI FI Wire, Shimmer, Strange Horizons, Subterranean Magazine,* and *Writer's Digest.*

He received his Bachelor of Arts degree in English from the University of Central Florida in December 2000. He currently lives in New Jersey. For more information, visit his website at www.johnjosephadams.com.